ISBN 978-0-276-44445-6

**www.readersdigest.co.uk**

The Reader's Digest Association Limited, 11 Westferry Circus, Canary Wharf, London E14 4HE

and in Canada
**www.rd.ca**

The Reader's Digest Association (Canada) ULC, 1100 René-Lévesque Blvd. West, Montréal,
Québec, H3B 5H5 Canada

# of love & life

Three novels selected and condensed
by Reader's Digest

Reader's
Digest

The Reader's Digest Association Limited, London, Montreal

# CONTENTS

# The
# Horse Dancer
## Jojo Moyes

*In 2007 I read a piece about a gifted fourteen-year-old girl called Mecca Harris. She had been taught a love of horses and skill at riding by the Philadelphia Black Cowboys, which is an institution that offers children in the city's toughest neighbourhoods a chance, through horses, to seek a different way of life. Tragically, Mecca never got to fulfil her dreams, because in 2003 she was murdered.*

*This story stuck in my mind because, while my life was never underprivileged as Mecca's was, my teenage years were spent at urban stables in London's backstreets. Horses kept me out of trouble and gave me a passion that has lasted thirty years.*

*I now live on a farm and keep a horse in green fields. Mecca Harris should have had her green fields. This book is dedicated to her, and children like her, for whom horses can be a way out.*

# PROLOGUE

HE SAW HER YELLOW DRESS before he saw her, glowing in the fading light, a beacon at the far end of the stables. He stopped for a moment, unsure that he could trust his eyes. Then her pale arm reached up, Gerontius's elegant head dipping over the door to take whatever treat she offered, and he was walking briskly, half running, the metal tips of his boots clicking on the wet cobbles.

'You are here!'

'Henri!'

His arms were round her as she turned; he kissed her, inhaling the glorious scent of her hair.

'We got here this afternoon,' she said, into his shoulder. 'I've barely had time to change. I must look awful . . . but I had to come to wish you luck.' She took a step back, allowing her gaze to travel from his black peaked cap all the way down his immaculate uniform. 'And you look wonderful.' She reached up to brush an imaginary fleck from one of his gold epaulettes. He noted, with gratitude, the reluctance with which she withdrew her fingers. There was no awkwardness, he marvelled, even after so many months. She was utterly guileless.

'I . . . cannot stay,' he said. 'We ride in ten minutes.'

'I know . . . Le Carrousel is so exciting. We've been watching the motorcyclists, and the parade of tanks,' she said. 'But you, Henri, you and the horses are definitely the big draw.' She glanced behind her towards the arena. 'Edith, her mother and I are in the front row. They simply can't wait to see you ride. We're staying at the Château de Verrières.' Her voice dropped to a whisper, even though no one was near. 'It's very grand. The Wilkinsons have an *awful* lot of money. Much more than we have. It was very kind of them to bring me.'

He watched her talk—distracted by the Cupid's bow of her upper lip. His hands, in their white kid gloves, cradled her face. 'Florence . . .' he breathed, kissing her again. 'Every day I miss you.'

'Henri . . .' She stroked his cheek, her body against his.

'Lachapelle!'

He whipped round. Didier Picart stood at the head of his horse, a groom at his side preparing his saddle. 'Perhaps if you think about your riding as much as your English whore we can achieve something, eh?'

Florence did not know enough French to understand, but she caught the look that flickered across Picart's face, and Henri saw she had guessed that what the Frenchman had said was not complimentary.

The familiar anger rose and he set his jaw against it. Picart had been like this—insulting, provocative—since the trip to England when Florence and Henri had met. English girls had no class, Picart had proclaimed in the mess. They did not know how to dress. They would lie down with anyone for the equivalent of a pint of foul beer.

Henri knew that it had been aimed at him. And it had taken him weeks to work out that Picart's bile had little to do with Florence and everything to do with his fury at having been usurped within Le Cadre Noir, jostled aside by the son of a farmer.

Picart's voice echoed down the yard, 'I hear there are rooms near the quai Lucien Gautier. A little more fitting than a stable yard, *n'est-ce pas?* Don't you know, farmer boy, that any whore will have you if the price is right?' He placed a boot in his stirrup and vaulted onto his horse.

Henri made to step forward, but Florence stopped him. 'Look, I'd better get to my seat,' she said. 'You need to prepare.' She hesitated, then reached up and kissed him again. He knew she was trying to tug his thoughts from Picart's poison. *'Bonne chance, écuyer.'*

*'Ecuyer!'* he repeated, momentarily diverted, touched that in his absence she had discovered the correct word for 'horseman'.

'I'm learning!' She blew a kiss, her eyes filled with mischief, with promise, and then she was gone.

**L**e Carrousel, the annual military festival, traditionally marked the end of a year of training for the young cavalry officers of Saumur. As usual, the July weekend was thick with visitors to the medieval town.

It was 1960 and the old guard was teetering in the face of an onslaught of popular culture and shifting attitudes, but in Saumur there was little appetite for change. The annual performance of the twenty-two elite French horsemen, some military, some civilian, who comprised Le Cadre Noir, the highlight of Le Carrousel weekend, was always enough to guarantee that the tickets were sold out.

Le Cadre Noir had been founded after the decimation of the French Cavalry in the Napoleonic Wars. In an attempt to rebuild what had once been considered a crack band of horsemen, a school was created in Saumur, a town that had housed an equestrian academy since the sixteenth century. Here, a corps of instructors had been gathered from the finest riding schools in France, to pass on the high traditions of academic riding to a new generation of officers, and they had continued to do so ever since.

This was the Le Cadre Noir in which Henri Lachapelle now found himself, and that night's performance was the most important of the year. In the heart of the elegant, honeyed buildings of the Ecole de Cavalerie, the crowds were already swelling. A low hum of excitement emanated from the crowd round Le Grand Manège, the vast sand arena.

'Attends!'

Henri, hearing the cry to attention, rubbed the nose of Gerontius, his horse, muttering words of praise and encouragement into his elegantly trimmed ears. Gerontius was seventeen and would soon be retired. He had been Henri's horse since he had arrived at Le Cadre Noir three years previously, and an instant bond had formed between them.

'Vous êtes prêt?' Le Grand Dieu, the master horseman, was striding down the centre of the preparatory arena, his gilded uniform and three-cornered cap marking him out. He stood in front of the young horsemen and their horses. 'This, as you know, is the highlight of our year. The ceremony dates back more than a hundred and thirty years, and the traditions of our school to the age of Xenophon and the Greeks.

'So much in our world today seems to be about the pursuit of what is free or easy. Le Cadre Noir still believes in the pursuit of excellence. Tonight you are ambassadors, showing that true grace, true beauty, comes as a result of discipline, patience, sympathy and self-denial.'

There was a murmur of approval; then the men began to mount their horses, trying to dispel the anxiety that was creeping in.

'You're ready, Lachapelle? Not too nervous?'

'No, sir.' Henri stood straight, feeling the older man's eyes travel over his uniform. He was conscious of the sweat trickling from his temples.

'It's no shame to feel a little adrenaline at one's first Carrousel,' Le Grand Dieu said, stroking Gerontius. 'This old hand will see you through.'

'Yes, sir.'

He knew the maîtres écuyers had been split over whether he should be granted such a visible role in the annual performance, given his history of arguments, his perceived lack of discipline. His groom had passed on to him the talk in the tack room: that his rebelliousness had nearly cost him his place in Le Cadre Noir altogether.

Henri Lachapelle's childhood had been a world of chaos, dominated by his father. Joining the cavalry had provided him with a lifeline, and his progression through the ranks until he was recommended for a position at Le Cadre Noir had been the summit of his expectations.

At twenty-five he was prodigiously talented. He had an aptitude for dealing with difficult horses. There was talk that he might eventually prove a *maître écuyer*—even, in more fanciful moments, another Grand Dieu. He had been sure that the rigour, the discipline, the sheer plea-sure and reward of learning would be enough for the rest of his days.

And then Florence Jacobs from Clerkenwell, who had taken up a free ticket to the French riding-school performance in England, had destroyed it all—his peace of mind, his resolve, his patience. From the moment Henri had noticed the dark-haired girl who had watched, wide-eyed, from the side of the arena for three nights running, she was all he could think about. He had introduced himself after his perfor-mance and his concentration disappeared almost overnight.

On his return to France, when he had missed the third training ses-sion in a row, and his groom had warned him there was talk of letting him go, he realised he had to get a grip on himself. 'There are two paths you can choose to travel,' the Grand Dieu had counselled. 'Which one you follow is up to you.' He bent himself to his travails and kept his nose clean. He had felt reassured by Florence's frequent letters, her promise that she would be over to see him that summer. And a few months on, perhaps as a reward, he had been given the key role in Le Carrousel: La Croupade—one of the most challenging movements a rider could attempt—displacing Picart.

Le Grand Dieu mounted his horse and took two steps closer to him. 'Don't let me down, Lachapelle. Let us treat this evening as a new start.'

Henri nodded. He mounted and gathered his reins. He could hear the murmur of the crowd, the expectant hush as the orchestra began to play. And then he was guiding Gerontius into his place, halfway along the militarily exact line of gleaming, beribboned horses, as the heavy red curtain was pulled back, beckoning them into the floodlit arena.

**D**espite the calm, orderly appearance of its twenty-two horsemen, the graceful nature of their public performances, life at Le Cadre Noir was physically and intellectually testing. Day after day Henri Lachapelle had found himself almost reduced to tears of frustration by the endless corrections of the *maîtres écuyers*, and his apparent inability to persuade the huge, highly strung horses to perform the 'airs above the ground' to their exacting standards. And he had felt a prejudice against those who had entered the elite school from the military, as he had, rather than as a member of upper-class French society, where individuals had the twin luxuries of fine horses and time with which to build their skills.

Yet slowly, steadily, working from six in the morning until late into the evening, the farm hand from Tours had built a reputation for hard work and a skill in communicating with the most difficult horses. It was the reason why, alongside his beloved Gerontius, he had been allocated Phantasme, an explosive, young, iron-grey gelding.

Now, with the eyes of the crowd upon him, the musical beauty of the strings filling his ears and the even tempo of Gerontius's paces beneath him, he cantered in formation, lost in the moment.

'Sit straight, Lachapelle. Why do you fidget so? Did your whore give you the itch?' Picart hissed, as he rode up alongside him.

Henri bit the inside of his lip, forcing himself not to let his anger travel down the reins to infect his sweet-natured horse, as Le Grand Dieu shouted, '*Levade!*' and, in a row, the riders raised their horses onto their back legs. He could hear the announcer explaining the technicalities of the riders' movements, and tried to corral his thoughts. He would not let Picart destroy this night.

'And now, you will see Gerontius, one of our older horses, performing *capriole*. The horse leaps into the air, kicking out behind him while all four feet are off the ground.'

Henri slowed Gerontius and felt the horse begin to rock with a stationary rocking-horse motion, building power beneath him. And then with a shout of '*Derrière!*' he brought his whip hand towards the horse's rear, his spurs to the horse's belly, and Gerontius was leaping upwards, into the air, his back legs shooting out horizontally behind him. Henri was aware of a sudden blinding bank of camera flashes, a great *whooo* of delight, applause, and then he was cantering towards the red curtain.

'*Bon! C'était bon!*' He was already sliding off Gerontius, his hand rubbing the horse's shoulder, the *dresseur* leading him away.

'Phantasme is very nervous.' His groom had appeared beside him, his brows knotted with concern. 'Watch him, Henri.'

'He will be fine,' Henri said absently. He watched the gunmetal-grey horse prance into the arena, led by a man at each shoulder.

'Go. Now. Go.' Three *écuyers* were now surrounding Phantasme, one at each side of his head, another at the rear. Henri strode out under the lights, wishing that, like them, he had the anchoring presence of a horse to hold on to.

'*Mesdames et messieurs, voilà La Croupade.* Monsieur Lachapelle will be riding Phantasme without reins or stirrups. This exercise, which dates back to Greek times, is a more elegant version of the rodeo, if you like.'

There was a ripple of laughter. Henri glanced at Phantasme, whose whitened eyes were rolling.

Henri touched the horse's tense shoulder. 'Sssh,' he murmured. 'It's OK. It's OK.' He glimpsed the quick smiles of Duchamp and Varjus, the two men at Phantasme's head.

'Sit deep, eh?' Varjus said, grinning, as he gave him a leg up.

It was then, as he folded his hands at the small of his back in the traditional passive position, that Henri looked down to the near side and realised who had been stationed at Phantasme's rear.

'Shall we see what kind of rider you really are, Lachapelle?' Picart said.

He had no time to respond. He lengthened his legs as far as possible.

'*Attends.*' Varjus glanced behind him. '*Un, deux, derrière!*'

Henri felt the horse building in impulsion, heard the sudden *thwack* as Picart's whip met his quarters. Phantasme bucked, rear end shooting up, and Henri was pitched forward, whiplashed so that he only just managed to maintain the clasp of his hands behind him. The horse steadied and there was a burst of applause.

'Not bad, Lachapelle,' he heard Varjus mutter, braced against Phantasme's chest.

And then, suddenly, there was another cry of '*Derrière!*' Phantasme's back legs were shooting him up and forward so that this time Henri's arms flew out to the sides as he tried to maintain his balance.

'Not so soon, Picart. You're unseating him.'

Disorientated, Henri heard Varjus's irritated voice, the horse's barely contained squeal as his back braced beneath him. 'Two seconds. Give me two seconds,' he muttered, trying to right himself. But before he could do so, there was another loud smack behind him and Phantasme, infuriated by this use of the whip, leaped forward and sideways and Henri was upside-down, reaching for Phantasme's neck as the horse bucked again, before—with an audible *ouf*—he hit the floor.

As he lifted his head from the sand, he could just make out the words, 'You see, *mesdames et messieurs*, sometimes it takes many years of practice to reach the very high standards of the *maîtres écuyers*.'

Varjus was at his side, hissing at him, 'Remount, remount.' Henri glanced down, realising that his immaculate black uniform was covered with sand. Then he was up on the horse, hands at his legs, his feet, and they were walking out of the arena to sympathetic applause. It was the most painful sound he had ever heard.

Ahead, he was aware of a low argument between Varjus and Picart.

'What was that?' Varjus was shaking his head. 'Nobody has ever fallen off during La Croupade. You made us look stupid.' It was a moment before Henri grasped that Varjus was addressing Picart.

'It's not my fault if the only thing Lachapelle can ride is an English whore.'

Henri slid off the horse and walked up to Picart. He was not even aware of the first punch, just of the loud crack as his knuckles met the man's teeth. Horses shrieked and leaped apart. Men shouted. Picart was splayed on the sand, his hand pressed to his face. Within seconds, Henri was atop Picart, his fists flying into face, cheeks and chest. And then hands were dragging him off, voices raised in disbelief.

'Picart! Lachapelle!'

As his vision blurred and righted, he saw Le Grand Dieu standing in front of him, his face bright with rage. 'Where is your self-control?' he hissed. 'You two have brought shame on us. Get back to the stables.'

He mounted his horse as Picart staggered past. Henri watched him go. Slowly it dawned on him that the arena beyond the curtain was strangely quiet. They had seen, he realised with horror. They knew.

'Two paths.' Le Grand Dieu looked down at him from the Portuguese stallion. 'Two paths, Lachapelle. I told you last time. It was your choice.'

'I cannot—' he began.

But Le Grand Dieu had already ridden out into the floodlights.

# ONE

THE 6.47 TO LIVERPOOL STREET was heaving. Natasha Macauley sat down, muttering an apology to a woman who had to move her jacket out of the way. The besuited man who had got on behind her forced himself into a seat opposite and promptly unfolded his newspaper.

It was an unusual route for her to take to work: she had spent the night at a hotel in Cambridge after a legal seminar. A satisfying number of business cards from solicitors and barristers lay in her jacket pocket.

Natasha glanced down at her diary.

* *9 a.m. LA vs Santos, Court 7*
* *Persey divorce. Child psych evaluation?*
* *Fees! Check with Linda re legal-aid situation*
* *Fielding—where is witness statement?* MUST FAX TODAY

Every page, for at least a fortnight ahead, was an endlessly reworked series of lists. Her colleagues at Davison Briscoe had largely switched to electronic devices with which to navigate their lives, but she preferred pen and paper. She noticed the date, winced and added:

* *Flowers/apols re Mum's birthday*

The train rumbled towards London, the flatlands of Cambridgeshire seguing into the grey, industrial outskirts of the city. It was going to be an unforgivingly hot day. She closed her eyes, then opened them at the sound of her mobile phone. She rummaged in her bag, locating it between her make-up and her wallet. A text message flashed up: Local authority in Watson case rolled over. Not needed in court 9 a.m. Ben

For the past four years Natasha had been Davison Briscoe's sole solicitor advocate, a solicitor-barrister hybrid that had proved useful when it came to her speciality: representing children. They were less fazed to appear in court beside the woman in whose office they had already explained themselves. Thanks. Will be in office in half an hour Natasha texted back. She was about to put her phone away when it rang again.

It was Ben, her trainee. 'Just wanted to remind you that we . . . ah . . . rescheduled that Pakistani girl for ten thirty.'

'The one whose parents are fighting care proceedings?' Beside her, a woman coughed pointedly. Natasha glanced up and saw NO MOBILE TELEPHONES etched on the window. She dipped her head and rifled through her diary. 'We've also got the parents from the child-abduction case in at two. Can you dig out the paperwork?' she murmured.

'Done it. And I got some croissants,' Ben added. 'I'm assuming you won't have had anything for breakfast. They're almond. Your favourite.'

'Slavish crawling, Ben, will get you a long way.'

Natasha closed the phone and put her diary away. She had just pulled the girl's paperwork from her briefcase when her phone rang again. This time there was audible tutting. She mumbled an apology, without looking anyone in the eye. 'Natasha Macauley.'

'Linda here. Just had a call from Michael Harrington. He's agreed to act for you in the Persey divorce. He wants to discuss a few matters. Are you free at two?'

'Great. I'm pretty sure that's OK.' She remembered her diary was back in her briefcase. She stuck the phone between ear and shoulder as she struggled to find it. 'Oh. No. I've got someone in. Linda, can we switch this afternoon around? I must have a gap somewhere.'

Her secretary's cackle rang in her ears after she had snapped shut her phone. She was about to put her diary back in her briefcase when something in the newspaper headline opposite caught her eye.

She leaned further forward, checking that she had read the name in the first paragraph correctly. The man holding the newspaper lowered it and frowned. 'I'm sorry,' she said. 'May I have a very quick look?'

He was too taken aback to refuse. She took the newspaper, flipped it over and read the story twice, the colour draining from her face, then handed it back.

'Thank you,' she said weakly.

**S**arah cut the second square of sandwiches twice diagonally, then wrapped both sets carefully in grease-proof paper. One she placed in the fridge, the other she tucked into her bag with two apples. She wiped the work surface with a damp cloth. Papa hated crumbs.

She checked her watch, then the filter paper in the coffee cup to see whether the brown liquid had drained through. She told Papa every week that real coffee cost loads more than instant, but he just said that some savings were a false economy. She wiped the bottom of the mug, then walked into the narrow hallway and stood outside his room.

'Papa?' He had long since stopped being Grandpapa.

She pushed the door with her shoulder. The room was glowing with the morning sunlight and for a minute you could pretend that outside was somewhere lovely—a beach or a country garden—instead of a tired 1960s estate in East London. On the far side of Papa's bed a small bureau gleamed, his hair and clothes brushes lined up beneath the photograph of Nana. He had not had a double bed since she'd died; there was more space in the room with a single, he said. She knew he couldn't face the emptiness of a large bed without her grandmother.

'Coffee.'

The old man pushed himself up from the pillow and scrabbled on the bedside table for his glasses. 'You're going now? What's the time?'

'Just after six.'

He squinted at his watch. 'Will you catch the ten past?'

'If I run. Your sandwiches are in the fridge.'

'Tell the mad cowboy I will pay him this afternoon. And get him to put some eggs by. We'll have them tomorrow.'

She made the bus, but only because it was a minute late. Puffing, she hurled herself on board, her bag swinging wildly behind her. The route to Cowboy John's took seventeen minutes at this time of the morning; an hour later, when the roads to the east of the City were clogged with traffic, it would take almost three times as long. She was the only person to whom John had given a spare set of keys. Most days, she would be letting out the hens by the time he came walking, stiff-legged, up the road.

Sheba, the Alsatian, barked as Sarah fiddled with the padlock on the wire gate, then, realising who it was, sat and waited, her tail beating an expectant tattoo. Sarah threw her a treat from her pocket and walked into the yard, closing the gates with a muted crash behind her.

Once, this part of London had been dotted with stable yards, tucked at the end of narrow, cobbled streets, behind barn doors, under arches. Horses had pulled the brewery drays, the coal and rag-and-bone carts, and it had not been unusual to see a family cob or a couple of fine trotters out for a circuit of the park on a Saturday. Cowboy John's was one of the few yards that remained, taking up some four railway arches, with three or four stables and lockups built into each, at the far end of a lane that ended on the high street. There was a walled, cobbled yard in front of the arches, where pallets, chicken coops, bins and an old rusting car that Cowboy John was selling, plus a brazier that never went out, filled the space. Every twenty minutes a commuter train would rumble overhead, but neither humans nor animals took any notice.

Twelve horses were resident, including twin Clydesdales owned by Tony, the retired drayman, the fine-necked, wild-eyed trotters of Maltese Sal and his betting cohorts, and an assortment of scruffy ponies kept by local children. Sarah was never sure how many people knew they were there—the park keeper, who regularly chased them off the common, did and occasionally they received letters addressed to 'The Horse Owners, Sparepenny Lane Arches', threatening court action if they continued to trespass. Cowboy John would laugh and throw them into the brazier. 'Far as I know, horses was here first,' he would drawl.

He claimed to be an original member of the Philadelphia Black Cowboys. They weren't real cowboys—not the cattle-ranching kind, at least. In America, he said, there were city yards like his, bigger ones, where men could keep and race their animals, and young kids came to learn and escape lives that were otherwise ghetto-bound. He had arrived in London in the 1960s, following a woman who had turned out to be 'way, way too much trouble'. He had liked the city, but missed his horses, so he'd bought a broken-kneed thoroughbred from Southall Market and some near-derelict Victorian stables from the council.

Cowboy John's was an institution now, or a nuisance, depending on where you stood. Town Hall officials were forever issuing warnings about environmental health and pest control, but the neighbours stopped by daily to chat or buy whatever fresh produce Cowboy John had on offer. Sarah was there whenever she didn't have to be at school.

She was throwing hay to the ponies when Cowboy John arrived. He was wearing his Stetson and his hollow cheeks were burnished with the effort of walking and smoking in the already-warm sun.

Sarah couldn't remember a time when she hadn't spent part of every day at Sparepenny Lane. When she was tiny, Papa would sit her on Cowboy John's shaggy Shetland ponies, and when her mother had first left home, Papa had brought her here so that she couldn't hear Nana crying.

It was here that Papa had taught her to ride, running up and down the backstreets until she had mastered the rising trot. And then, after Nana died, Baucher, who they called Boo, had arrived.

Papa, who saw dangers for a wide-eyed girl just into her teens, had decided she needed a route out. He began to train the copper-coloured colt and his granddaughter. He trained her far beyond what the local kids called riding: the vaulting onto a pony's back and haring down the streets until you reached the marshes, the scraping over park benches, fruit crates, any obstacles that offered a thrill. Papa would drill her relentlessly about the correct angle of her lower leg, the perfect stillness of her hands—until she wept. He told her that he wanted to protect Boo's legs from the tarmac roads, and that the only way to achieve something magical in life was through work and discipline.

He still talked like that, Papa. That was why Cowboy John and the others called him the Captain.

'You want tea?' Cowboy John gestured at his kettle.

'No. I've only got half an hour to ride. I have to be at school early.'

'You still working on your tricks?'

'Actually,' she said, with exaggerated politeness, 'this morning we will be working on our half-pass with a flying change of legs and some *piaffe*. Under the orders of the Captain.' She stroked the horse's neck.

Cowboy John snorted. 'I got to give it to the old man. Next time the circus comes by they'll be biting his arm off.'

In Natasha's line of work it was hardly unusual to find, within weeks, the child one had just represented up before the court again, recipient of a new ASBO or youth-custody order. But this one surprised her, not just for the severity of his crime but because of who he was. After ten years she had heard so many stories of despair, abuse and neglect from children that, just like the others, Ali Ahmadi should have faded from memory, processed by her staff, another name on the court roster.

He had come into her office two months earlier, with the hollow-eyed look of distrust and despair that so many wore. He was in need of an emergency injunction to prevent him being sent back to the country he claimed had nearly destroyed him.

'I don't really do immigration,' she had explained, but Ravi, who handled those cases, was off and they were desperate.

'Please, Natasha,' the foster-mother said. 'I know you can do this for us.' Two years earlier Natasha had represented another of her children.

As she had speed-read the notes, Ali had started to speak, growing more urgent as the woman translated. His family had been targeted as political dissidents. His father had disappeared on the way home from work; his mother had been beaten in the street, then had disappeared with his sister. Ali had walked to the border in thirteen days. He began to cry as he spoke, blinking away the tears with embarrassment. He would be killed if he returned home. He was fifteen.

Linda had been hovering by the door. 'Can you ring the judge's clerk for me? See if we can get Court Four?'

As they left she put her hand on the boy's shoulder. 'I'll do my best,' she said, 'but I still think you'd be better off with someone else.'

She won him the injunction, and would have thought no more of him, but, as she passed him in the courtroom, he had pulled a chain from his neck and pressed it into her hands. He wouldn't look at her; he just stood there, head down, his palms pressed to hers.

The same hands had, two nights ago, apparently perpetrated a 'prolonged and vicious attack' on an as-yet-unnamed sales assistant.

Her phone sounded again. More tutting, unrestrained this time. With another apology, Natasha stood, gathered her belongings and made her way through the crowded carriage. She lurched towards the standing area and found herself a small space by the window. She dropped her bags as the caller disconnected. Natasha swore. She had relinquished her seat for nothing. Then she saw the text message: Hi. Need to pick up some stuff. Any time next week good for you? Mac

Mac. She had no choice. No problem she typed, and shut her phone.

Natasha's cramped, book-stuffed room in the rickety Georgian building that housed her and five other lawyers bore more of a resemblance to an academic's tutoring room than a commercial enterprise.

'Here's the paperwork you asked for.' Ben, a gangly, studious young man whose fair, determinedly smooth cheeks belied his twenty-five years, placed the pink-ribboned file in front of her. 'You haven't touched your croissants,' he pointed out.

'Sorry.' She flicked through the files on her desk. 'Lost my appetite. Ben, do me a favour. Dig out the file for Ali Ahmadi, will you? Emergency judicial review from about two months ago.'

The door opened and Conor entered. He was wearing the blue striped shirt she had bought him for his birthday. 'Morning, Hotshot.' He leaned across the desk and kissed her. 'How'd it go last night?'

'Good,' she said. 'Really good. You were missed.'

'My night for having the boys. Sorry, but you know how it is. Until I get more access I daren't miss an evening.'

'Did you have a nice time?'

'It was wild. Harry Potter DVD, beans on toast.'

Ben came in again and, with a nod to Conor, laid a file on her desk. 'Mr Ahmadi,' he said.

Conor peered at it. 'Wasn't that your deportation case from a couple of months ago? Why are you digging him out?'

'Ben, go and get me a fresh coffee, will you?'

Noting that she was waiting for Ben to leave, Conor tossed a banknote at him. 'And me. Double-shot espresso.' He turned back to Natasha. 'What's up?'

'This.' She handed him the newspaper she had bought on her way from the station, pointing at the story.

He read it quickly. 'Ah. Your man there,' he said.

'Oh, yes.' She stretched out her arms, letting her face fall briefly onto the desk. Then she reached over and picked at an almond croissant. 'My man there. I'm wondering if I should tell Richard.'

'Our senior partner? Oh, nonononono! No need for a hair shirt.'

'It's a pretty serious crime.'

'And one you could not have predicted. Let it go, Natasha.'

'He just didn't seem the type and I put up a good case for him to stay in the country. I can't help feeling I'm responsible for him being here.'

'Get over yourself, Natasha.' Conor tapped the file. 'If Ravi had been here it would have been him. I'll see you for a quick drink tonight.'

But later Natasha found herself opening Ali Ahmadi's file for a second time, searching for some reason why this boy, who had cried, who had held her hands so gently, had been capable of such a random act of violence.

'Ben? I need you to find me an atlas.' Almost on a whim, she'd decided to look up where the boy had come from.

It was then, as she traced the place names with a finger, that she realised none of the care workers, the legal team or his foster-mother had asked Ali Ahmadi the obvious question. But there it was, staring up at her. How could anyone walk nine hundred miles in thirteen days?

That evening Natasha sat in the bar and cursed herself for not being thorough. If she had checked Ali Ahmadi's story, she might have guessed that he was lying. She told Conor the situation.

He shrugged. 'You know these kids are desperate,' he said. 'They tell you what they think you want to hear. Are you sure he couldn't have walked that far?'

'In less than two weeks?' Her voice was sarcastic. She couldn't help it. 'Seventy miles a day. I calculated it.'

'I don't know why you're so upset. You knew nothing of this while you were representing him, so what does it matter?' He drank the last of his wine. 'Ah, move on, Natasha. Some desperate kid managed to avoid being sent back to a plague-infested hellhole. So what?' He patted his pockets. 'Will you get me another? I've got to nip to the cashpoint.'

She checked in her bag for her wallet and found her fingers entangled in something. She pulled it out. It was the little silver horse that Ali Ahmadi had given her on the morning she had won his case. She had resolved to send it to his home, but had forgotten. Suddenly she recalled the unearthly apparition she had seen earlier.

'Conor—I saw the strangest thing this morning.'

The train had stopped for fifteen minutes in a tunnel outside Liverpool Street Station, she told him. When, finally, it had edged forward into the daylight, she'd seen a young girl standing in a quiet cobbled street, her arm raised, a long stick in her hand—not in threat but instruction. Above her, in the middle of the road, perfectly balanced on glossy, muscular haunches, a huge horse had reared.

Natasha dropped the silver pendant into her bag, barely suppressing a shiver. 'Did you hear what I just said?'

'Mm?' Connor was reading the newspaper.

She stared at him.

'Nothing,' she said. 'I'll go and get the drinks.'

# TWO

BOO WAS NOT A HORSE you might usually find in the backstreet yards of East London. He was a Selle Français: a large-boned thoroughbred, athletic but sure-footed. His short-coupled back made him good at jumping and his sweet, almost doglike nature made him tolerant and friendly. He was unfazed by the heaviest traffic and a fool for company.

When Sarah put on the saddle and breathed in the scent of warm horse and clean leather, she forgot that she was the skinniest girl in her class and didn't have a mobile phone or a computer. When she was riding Boo, she forgot that it was just her and Papa. Boo was hers, and he was special.

Papa told people who didn't know about horses that Boo was like a Rolls-Royce: everything was finely tuned, responsive, elegant. His only limits, said Papa, were Sarah's limits. Boo had the biggest heart of any horse he had ever known.

It hadn't always been like that. When they had broken him there had been days when he would snap off the lunge rein and go tearing across the park. Papa told Sarah every time that it was her fault, to the point at which she wanted to scream at him, but now she knew a little more and understood that he had been right. Papa never shouted at Boo. He never lost his temper, or got frustrated, even when it was clear that the colt was being as mischievous or unruly as any teenager.

And now Boo was eight years old, grown. He was educated enough to have manners, clever enough that his paces floated, elegant enough, if Papa had judged this as correctly as he seemed to judge everything else, to carry Sarah away from this chaotic city and on to her future.

Cowboy John leaned on his broom and looked through the gates at the park where the girl was making the horse canter in small, steady circles in the corner by the trees, slowing occasionally to praise him or let him stretch out. She was a good kid, not like a lot who came to the yard. They would race their horses on empty streets till their hoofs cracked, slinging them back in their stables, sweaty and overwrought.

He removed his hat and wiped his forehead, already feeling the heat of the day. Maltese Sal had assured him that if he took over the lease, the Captain's horse would be safe here, as would that of anyone else who was not in arrears. The place would remain as a stables.

'I need a base,' he kept saying to John. 'This is near my home. My horses are comfortable here.' He spoke as if it was already decided. *And this ramshackle yard would be a useful front for whatever you buy and sell*, John wanted to answer him, but you didn't say that to a man like Sal. Especially when he was offering the kind of money he was suggesting.

Truth was, Cowboy John was tired. He quite fancied the idea of retiring to the country, swapping his house for a little cottage with a plot of land his horses could graze on. City life was getting uglier and he was getting older, tired of fighting the council, tired of picking up the broken bottles that the drunks threw over the gates, tired of arguing with kids who didn't want to pay what they owed.

Sal was talking a good sum of money, money enough for John to make his dream reality. But still . . . part of him was reluctant to let it go to that man. He had a sneaking feeling that Sal's promises carried all the weight of diddly-squat.

'**B**on *anniversaire!*'

Sarah, fiddling to get the key out of the lock, stepped into their flat and heard her grandfather's voice before she saw him. She smiled. '*Merci!*'

She had thought he might have laid the table with a birthday cake, as he had the previous year, but instead she walked into the kitchen to find him standing in front of the television.

'*Voilà*. Sit, sit,' he instructed, kissing her on both cheeks.

She peered at the little kitchen table. 'We're not having tea?'

'Pizza. Afterwards. You choose,' he said, pointing to a menu. Takeaway was a rare treat.

'After what?' She put down her bag and sat on the sofa, feeling a jolt of excitement. Papa seemed so pleased, a smile twitching at the corners of his mouth. She couldn't remember the last time he had looked like this. Since Nana had died four years ago, he had retreated into himself, emerging only when Boo arrived. She knew he loved her, but he didn't tell her this, didn't ask what was on her mind. He made sure she was fed, washed and up-to-date with her homework. He taught her practical stuff, about money, mending things and horsemanship. Between them they had long since mastered the washing machine and the cheapest way to do a weekly shop. If she was sad, he would lay a hand on her shoulder; if she did wrong, he made his displeasure known with a certain curtness, a disapproving glance.

'First,' he said, 'we are going to watch something.'

She followed his gaze, seeing now the DVD player that had not been there when she had left that morning. 'You bought me a DVD player?'

'It's not new,' he said apologetically, 'but it is *parfait*. We are going to see *un spectacle*. But first . . .' He reached behind him to a bottle of wine, opened it with a flourish and poured. 'Fourteen, eh? Old enough for some wine.' He nodded as he handed the glass to her.

She took a sip, trying not to look as unimpressed as she felt by the sour taste. She would have preferred Diet Coke.

Apparently satisfied, he peered at the remote control and, with a hint of flamboyance, pressed a button. The television screen flickered into life and he settled into the sofa beside her. He took a sip of his wine. She glimpsed his look of pleasure and leaned against him. The music began, classical music, and a white horse pranced across the screen.

'Le Cadre Noir,' he said. 'Now you will see what we are aiming for.'

Sarah watched the forty-minute display in silence. She was mesmerised. She wanted to go to Boo and copy what she had seen. He could do this, she knew it. He was finer, stronger, than some of the horses she had seen on the screen, but he had the same beauty, power and agility. As she watched, her hands and feet twitched, riding the screen horses, encouraging them into the outlines, the movements that had been performed since ancient Greek times.

Her personal arena might be a bare-patched, litter-strewn park rather than the vast palace of an historic French town, her outfit a T-shirt and jeans instead of a formal black jacket, gold braid and a peaked cap, but she knew how those riders felt. When the camera had lingered on their faces, taut with effort and sympathy, with wanting, she had felt kinship. All the things Papa had been teaching her began to slot into place. Now she saw what he was aiming for—the great goal: Le Capriole. The most complex, demanding and beautiful movement a horse could make, taking all four hoofs off the ground into a balletic leap, kicking out behind in midair as if it scorned the laws of gravity.

Sarah had never been able to say what she felt when Papa went on and on about the French school. She had never been able to translate their training sessions in the park into the future he had mapped out. Now, as she watched the credits, she realised the DVD had had the opposite effect to the one he had wanted.

It didn't matter how good her horse was. How could anyone make the most gravity-defying leap of all, from the backstreets of London to the polished glory of Le Cadre Noir?

She felt guilty as soon as she had thought it. Her eyes went to him, and she wondered if her thoughts were transparent. It was then that she saw the tear running down his cheek.

'Papa?' she said.

His jaw tightened and then he said quietly, 'Sarah, this is how you escape. This is what I want for you.'

She swallowed. Escape what? She had never felt that her life was quite as bad as Papa seemed to think it was.

He held up the DVD case. 'I have a letter from Jacques Varjus, my old friend at Saumur. He tells me they have accepted two women now. For hundreds of years the academy will not take a woman and now they do it. You don't have to be military. This is a chance, Sarah.'

She was a little unnerved by his intensity.

'You have this ability. You need only the discipline. I don't want you wasting your life, ending up pushing a pram around this place.' He gestured out of the window.

'But I—'

He held up a hand. 'I have nothing to give you except this. My knowledge. My efforts.' He smiled, tried to soften his tone. 'My girl in black, eh? *La fille du Cadre Noir.*'

She nodded mutely. Her grandfather was never emotional and she was a little frightened. It was the wine, she told herself—he rarely drank. She tried not to look at his face. 'It was a nice present.'

He dragged himself back to her. '*Non! Un demi-cadeau,*' he said. 'You want to know the second part?'

He handed an envelope to her.

She opened it and pulled out four tickets. Two for a coach-and-ferry journey. Two for a performance of Le Cadre Noir. They had never been abroad, not even when Nana was alive. 'We're going to France?'

'It's time. Time for you to see, for me to return. My friend Varjus is now Le Grand Dieu. You know what that is? The most important, the most experienced horseman in Le Cadre Noir. *Non*—in France. I have filled in the passport forms. All I need is your photograph.'

'But how did you afford it?'

'I sold a few things. *Pas du tout.* You are happy? A good birthday?'

It was then she noticed he wasn't wearing his watch. The Longines had been his wedding present from Nana. So precious that as a child she had not been allowed to touch it.

'Sarah?'

She stepped into his embrace, unable to murmur her thanks into his soft, worn jumper because the words wouldn't come.

In the days when she could think about it rationally, Natasha would observe, with a kind of dark humour, that her marriage had begun with her left hand and ended with the right. Odd that her fingers could precipitate such a disaster.

The irony was that she and Conor had not even kissed when Mac left. Which was not to say they'd lacked opportunity. As her marriage had begun to deteriorate, and Conor's joking, attentive lunches had provided welcome relief, he had made it clear how he felt about her. 'You look hollowed out,' he would say. He would lay a hand on hers, and she would invariably remove it. 'You need to sort your life out.'

'And end up like you?' The viciousness of his divorce had become legendary in the office.

'Ah. It's only intense, debilitating pain. You get used to it.' But his situation meant he understood a little of what she was going through. Which was more than anyone else did.

In her parents' world, marriages ended through catastrophe, because of death, disaster or repeated blatant infidelity. They didn't die like Natasha's marriage, slowly, from neglect. Mac was hardly ever there, both emotionally and physically, since he disappeared on increasingly regular foreign assignments. When he was at home their most innocuous communications dissolved into bitter, vengeful exchanges.

'There's a gas bill here wants paying,' he would say.

'Are you asking me to do it or telling me that you're going to?'

'I just thought you'd want to take a look.'

'Why? Because you're not really living here? Do you want a discount?'

'Don't be bloody ridiculous.'

'Well, just pay it, then, rather than acting like it's somehow down to me. Oh, and by the way, Katrina rang again. You know, twenty-one-year-old Katrina with the fake boobs? The one who calls you "Mackie"?' Her voice trembled in a breathy impersonation of the model's.

At this he would invariably slam the door and disappear to a different part of the house.

They had met seven years earlier, on a flight to Barcelona. She had been with friends from law school; he had been returning after a brief holiday, having accidentally left his camera in his friend's apartment. She should have seen that as a warning, she realised afterwards, emblematic of the chaotic nature of his life. Hadn't he heard of DHL? But at the time, she could think only of her good luck in sitting next to the charming, crop-haired man, who not only laughed at her jokes but seemed interested, really interested, in what she did.

A petulant girlfriend had met him at Barcelona Airport, shooting dark looks as Natasha bade him a polite goodbye. Within six hours he had rung her mobile, having ditched the girlfriend, to ask if he could take her out in London. She shouldn't feel guilty about the girlfriend, he added cheerfully. It wasn't serious. Nothing in Mac's life ever was.

Their wedding had been her responsibility: he would have cohabited indefinitely. She had found, to her slight surprise, that she wanted marriage. 'If it means so much to you I'll do it,' he said, in bed one afternoon, his legs entwined with hers. 'But you'll have to organise it.' Participant, yet not quite—the story of their married life.

At first she hadn't minded. She understood that she had control-freak tendencies, as Mac jokingly called them. She and Mac understood each other's weaknesses, teased each other about them. But then the baby neither had known they wanted created a division between them that became a chasm.

By the time she miscarried, Natasha had known for only a week that she was pregnant. At first Mac had been shocked, and she couldn't be angry with him because she had felt the same. 'What shall we do?' she said to him, praying she wouldn't hate him for his answer.

'Dunno, Tash,' he said. 'I'll go along with whatever you want.' And then, before they'd had a chance to think about what that was, the little bunch of cells, the baby-in-waiting, had made its own decision and was gone. The grief she felt had shocked her. The relief she had expected failed to materialise.

'Next year,' they agreed, after she had admitted this to him. 'We'll take a couple of good holidays this year. After that we'll try properly.'

Then she was offered the position at Davison Briscoe, and they had agreed it would be best to wait another year. And then another, after they had bought the house in Islington and Mac had begun to renovate it. That year two things happened: Mac's career took a downturn, and her own went into the stratosphere. For months they barely saw each other. When they did she had to tread carefully, trying not to let her success amplify the lack of his.

And then—she was pregnant again.

Three would-be babies in four years, none of whom had lived much past the tadpole stage.

The doctor had told her she 'qualified' for further investigation, as if she had achieved something. But she hadn't wanted it. Didn't want evidence of what she suspected. And Mac, whom she'd hoped would hold her, reassure her, simply retreated.

By the time she had hauled herself together she felt betrayed. He had not been there when she needed him. It did not occur to her that he, too, might have been suffering. She could see only that he chose to travel to yet another assignment. Their sex life grew non-existent. She became super-efficient, handling everything with icy resolve and feeling furious with him when he couldn't

And all the while the girls kept ringing. 'They're just work,' he would insist. 'Those portfolios are my bread and butter. You know I don't even like doing them.'

Given the lack of intimacy between them, she wasn't sure what to believe. And all the while there was Conor—Conor who understood disastrous marriages because of the spectacular collapse of his own.

They had begun to have lunch together; then it was the odd drink after work. What was the harm, when Mac was never around? But when Conor leaned across the pub table one night and lightly placed his lips on hers, she withdrew. 'I'm still married, Conor,' she said, wishing she hadn't wanted so badly to return the kiss.

Their party, long planned, had originally been meant to celebrate Mac finishing the house, but by then she hadn't wanted to throw a party— she felt they had little to celebrate. But to cancel it seemed to make such a definitive statement that she didn't feel she could.

There were caterers and a four-piece band in the garden. To an outsider it might have seemed she and Mac were a dream couple, with Mac's set—photographers with gazelle-like models—and her legal friends mingling. The champagne flowed, the music played, the London sun filtered into the small marquee at the end of the garden. It was a golden scene. And she was utterly miserable.

All the women he had invited seemed to be six foot tall, she observed bitterly, as she stood at the top of the steps, watching him. They wore interesting clothes that made them look sophisticated and sexy.

'C'mon,' a voice said beside her. 'You're too transparent. Let's go and get a drink.'

Conor. She let him lead her down the garden, nudging through the groups of people, a smile now fixed on her face.

'You OK?' he said, when they were in the corner of the marquee.

She shook her head mutely.

Conor's eyes lingered on hers. He did not make a joke. 'Margarita,' he said. 'Cure for all known ills.' He got the bartender to make four and, ignoring her protests, forced her to drink two in quick succession.

'Oh, wow,' she said, some minutes later, hanging on to his arm. 'What on earth have you done? I feel about seventy per cent proof.'

'Loosened you up a little,' he said. 'You didn't want everyone whispering, "What on earth's wrong with her?" Come on, let's circulate.'

Natasha felt her heels sink into the grass and wasn't sure she had the balance to pull them out.

Conor, seeing her predicament, held out an arm. 'Better now?'

'Just don't move away from me. I may have to lean on you.'

'Any time, darling.' With a cheery greeting, Conor thrust them into a group of lawyers from a chambers they often used.

Natasha was only dimly aware of the people around her. The effects of the margarita seemed to be amplifying as the alcohol flushed through her. Her heels sank again and, feeling giddy, she rested against Conor for support. When she felt Conor's hand reach behind her back for hers, she took his little finger and held it, trying to convey to him her thanks. He had stopped her making a fool of herself.

She tuned out of the conversation and turned her head, just far enough that she could see Mac standing some twenty feet away. He was staring at her hand. Unbalanced, flushed, she dropped Conor's finger. Afterwards she realised that this was the worst thing she could have done, with its implication of guilt. But the damage had been done.

**Y**ou really should get a proper haircut one of these days,' Linda said, behind her. The office tea towel was slung over Natasha's shoulders, catching little feathers of dark blonde hair.

'No time.' Natasha went back to the file in front of her. 'Got to read through these files. I'm due back in court at two.'

'But your highlights need touching up.' Linda picked up a lock of hair and let it fall. 'You should go to a celebrity hairdresser.'

Natasha snorted. 'My worst nightmare.' She speed-read the last page of her notes, then closed the file. Her phone beeped. Mac had texted her twice that morning, asking when he could come to the house. She had put him off for almost ten days now. She didn't want to face him. He had stayed away for a year; another day or two wouldn't hurt him.

But today Mac appeared to have lost patience: I need my stuff. Next Friday latest. I can pick it up without you being there. Pls advise if locks changed.

She flipped her phone shut, regrouped her thoughts. 'Anyway, Lin,' she said, 'why should I go to a hairdresser? Your haircuts are fine.'

'Steady on the praise now, Mrs Macauley.'

Ben came in and put another file on the desk. Natasha leaned forward to pick it up, prompting a curse from behind her.

'Come on, Linda, you must have finished. I'm due in court in twenty minutes and I haven't had a sandwich yet.'

'**H**ow'd you go?'

Conor was waiting for her outside court. She leaned forward and kissed him, no longer concerned about the glances of other lawyers. They were an established couple now—two separated, older, wiser people. 'Got them. Pennington was woefully underbriefed.'

'That's my girl. Nice hair. Dinner?'

'I'd love to, but I've got to sort out a ton of paperwork for tomorrow.' She saw his face cloud and reached for his arm. 'A drink would be good, though. I've hardly seen you all week.'

They walked briskly through the relative peace of Lincoln's Inn and out into the crowded, bustling street. The sun bounced off the pavement as they crossed to the pub.

'I can't make this weekend,' Conor said pre-emptively, as they stood at the bar. 'I've got the boys. I thought I should let you know early.'

Conor's two sons were five and seven, apparently far too damaged to be alerted to the existence of Daddy's girlfriend, even though he had been divorced from their mother for more than a year. Natasha tried not to look disappointed. 'Shame,' she said lightly. 'I'd booked the Wolseley.'

'You're kidding.'

She tried to smile. 'Nope. It's our six-month anniversary, in case you hadn't noticed.'

'And there was me thinking you were a hard-headed unromantic.'

'You don't have the monopoly on nice gestures, you know,' she said coquettishly. 'I guess I'll have to find someone else to take.'

This possibility didn't seem to trouble him. He ordered their drinks, then turned back to her. 'She's going to Dublin for the weekend'—his ex-wife was always 'she'—'so I've got them from Friday till Monday. What about Monday night? I could come straight to yours.'

Why wouldn't he introduce her to his sons? Did she give off an unmaternal air? 'Monday, then,' she said, smiling.

They finished their wine and parted at the pub door. Natasha returned to her office for another hour. At nine she locked up, walked out into the late-summer evening and hailed a taxi home.

She watched the London streets fly by, couples strolling lazily along together. The world was full of couples when you were alone. Perhaps she should have gone out with Conor, but her work was the only constant in her life. Suddenly she felt overwhelmingly sad and fished in her bag for a tissue. C'mon, Natasha, get a grip, she willed herself, wondering why she felt so unbalanced. The answer wasn't hard to find.

She studied the text messages that had just arrived, took a deep breath and typed: Locks unchanged. Come when you like.

# THREE

WHEN SHE ARRIVED, Ralph was at the gates. Twelve years old, he rarely got up before midday. School, Ralph claimed, was an optional extra. He kept largely nocturnal hours. 'Maltese Sal's having a rumble,' he said, gesturing at the truck across the road. Sal was shrugging on his jacket, checking his mobile phone. 'You coming?'

'Where?'

'On the flyover by the football pitches. It's only going to take twenty minutes. Vicente says we can get a lift on the back of his pick-up.'

He looked at her expectantly, a lit cigarette wedged in the corner of his mouth. 'I helped Sal get the mare ready. She's busting out of her skin.'

She understood now why there were twice as many vehicles as usual on Sparepenny Lane. Men were climbing in, slamming doors, their voices low in the still morning. Sarah glanced again at her watch, unsure.

'Cowboy John's already there,' Ralph said. 'Come on. It'll probably be the last one of the summer.'

She should have been schooling her horse, but she had never seen a race. She hesitated, then ran after him towards the red pick-up truck. She hurled her bag into the back, took Ralph's hand and hauled herself up onto the pile of ropes and tarpaulins. Vicente told them to hold on, then pulled out behind four other vehicles, each full of dark-haired men, cigarette smoke trailing out of partially open windows.

'Sal's got a big bet against the travellers at Picketts Lock,' Ralph shouted, over the noise of the engine. 'He's racing the grey. He's got money riding on this, I tell you. *Big* money.'

'Don't tell Papa I came,' she yelled.

Unlike greyhound racing, sulky racing was an intermittent and unheralded fixture in sporting annals east of the City. There was no stadium, no floodlit track on which the best horses could compete, no regulated bookmaker to offer short odds or shout for punters. Instead, several times a year, the competitors would arrange to meet at some desolate location with a pre-agreed length of smooth tarmac.

The fact that this 'track' was a public road was no obstacle. Pick-up trucks from each side would simply head out after dawn when the traffic was quiet. They would manoeuvre alongside each other until they occupied both lanes of the dual carriageway, and then, at agreed points, slow to a halt, hazard lights flashing, so that any other vehicles were forced to stop behind them. Before the other drivers even worked out what was happening, the rival horses would be on the road, their lightweight two-wheeled sulkies behind them. The race would be run down a mile stretch, the drivers craning forward as they urged their horses flat out towards some agreed finishing line. The race decided, the participants would vanish into side streets to congratulate, argue or hand over winnings. By the time the police arrived there would be little evidence to suggest anything had happened there at all.

This, Ralph told her, was Maltese Sal's favoured racetrack. 'New tarmac, innit?' He slid an appreciative boot over the smooth surface.

They had jumped from the back of the van and now stood below the flyover that led out to an industrial park, watching as money changed hands a few yards away. Tattooed men from mobile homes, just visible beneath the pylons, peeled notes from huge wads of cash, spitting into their palms as they shook hands. The Maltese men, in scruffier vehicles but wearing immaculate clothes, were on one side of the road, the travellers on the other. Cowboy John leaned against a van, pointing at the horses and chatting to someone in the passenger seat.

A short distance away, Maltese Sal checked the buckles on his horse's harness, chiding the horse when it fidgeted, a broad smile revealing one gold tooth. He was laughing, berating his opponent's horse.

'They hate him,' Ralph observed. 'He got caught with someone's missus last year. If he loses, he has to give up the mare.'

'Won't that make him mad?' Sarah shivered.

'Nah.' Ralph spat on the ground. 'But I reckon we'll stay in Vicente's truck—case we need to get away in a hurry.' He laughed, relishing the prospect of trouble.

Above them, supported by giant, rough-cast concrete pillars, early-morning traffic thundered by on the flyover. Someone whistled, then Ralph was pulling her to the slip road. Three trucks reversed, headed back the way they had come, in a pre-agreed formation. They disappeared, ready to join the traffic on the flyover, and then it was just the men standing on the slip road, and the horses, steam blowing through their nostrils, held at the head by their handlers. Behind the grey mare, Sal crouched in his bright red sulky, legs braced, reins held loosely in one hand, glancing behind him repeatedly, waiting for the signal.

All eyes were on the traffic on the flyover now. The men muttered to each other as still it came. And then there was a shout, and above them, just visible, one of the travellers' pick-ups, its hazard lights flashing. 'Go!' someone shouted. 'Go!' And the two horses were on the slip road, sulky wheels almost touching, their drivers hunched forward, whips held high, as they urged the horses along the emptied road.

'Go, Sal!' Ralph was yelling. 'Go!'

Sarah felt him grab her sleeve, pulling her towards Vicente's pick-up, which was already revving, preparing to follow the racing horses, already almost out of sight. He shoved her aboard.

'He's doing it!' Ralph was yelling! 'He's ahead!'

And Sarah saw the grey mare, her unnatural trot too fast, an unearthly pace. She could see the grimace of the traveller, his whip hand raised as he pushed his own horse faster, his expletive as it broke, briefly, into a canter, incurring a roar of protest from the Maltese.

'Go on, Sal! *Muller* him!'

Her heart was in her mouth, her eyes on the brave little mare whose every sinew strained with the effort of maintaining such a speed at the trot, her little hoofs barely touching the road. *Go on*, she willed her, afraid that she would lose and be handed over to the travellers. *Go on*.

And then, with a shout of victory, it was over, the horses off the fly-over as swiftly as they had claimed it, and Vicente's truck was swerving left off the slip road, Sarah's knees and arms bumping painfully against the truck's sides as they hit a pothole, her schoolbag open and her books flying. She lifted her head and saw Sal, leaping from the sulky, his hand high in triumph. She and Ralph were laughing, clutching each other, infected by the madness and by Sal's victory.

The grey mare would be safe at Cowboy John's for a few weeks more.

The sun was sinking, the rush hour was under way, and around the park queues of traffic waited. Sarah didn't notice them. Papa stood beside her, his arms outstretched, helping to build the contained energy that would propel Boo upwards. 'Sit up straight,' he murmured.

She was sweating with the effort. She could feel the power building beneath her, but she sat as still as she could, her legs resting lightly against his sides, eyes looking straight through Boo's pointed ears. '*Non*,' Papa said again. 'Forward. Let him go forward. Now try again.'

They had been working on *piaffe* for almost forty minutes. Forward at a trot, then halt, then trot again, trying to build up the energy so that Boo would trot on the spot, the rhythmic gait that would be the starting point for the more elaborate moves. Some months ago, Papa had shown her from the ground how Boo could be persuaded to *levade*, balancing on his hind legs, as if rearing, and she was desperate to try the movements that would bring him off the ground.

But Papa would not let her. Certainly no *levade* in a public park with people watching. What was she trying to do? Tell Boo he was a circus horse? She knew he was right but sometimes it became so boring.

'Can we break for a bit? I'm so hot.'

'How are you going to achieve if you don't practise? No. *Continue.*'

She thrust her lower lip forward in mute protest. There was no point in arguing. She allowed the horse to move forward, then half halted again, attempting to bring him back with a shifting of weight.

'*Non!* You are tipping forward again.'

She collapsed onto the horse's neck, letting out a wail. 'I'm not!'

'You are sending him conflicting signals,' said Papa, his face creased with frustration. 'Concentrate.'

'I *am* concentrating. He's not listening to me any more.'

'He knows you don't listen to me. That is why he doesn't listen to you.'

It was always her. Never the horse. Why are we doing this? she wanted to shout. I'm never going to be good enough for what you want.

'You sit there *comme ça*. You are teaching him not to listen.'

She was too hot. 'Fine,' she said, throwing her reins into one hand, and sliding off. 'If I'm so useless, you do it.'

He glared at her, his eyes burning so that, like a disgraced dog, she found hers dropping to her feet.

'*Je m'excuse,*' he said abruptly. He walked briskly to Boo's side and, with a slight grunt of effort, placed his left foot in the stirrup and sprang upwards, lowering himself gently onto the horse's back. Boo's ears flickered backwards; he was startled by the unfamiliar weight. Papa said nothing to her. He crossed his stirrups over the front of the saddle, so that his legs hung long and loose. Then, his back impossibly straight, his hands apparently doing nothing, he walked Boo once in a large circle, then prompted the horse into action.

Sarah, her hand shielding her eyes from the sun, watched as her grandfather, a man she had never seen on a horse, asked, with almost imperceptible movements, for something the horse did not know how to give, and Boo, his mouth white with foam, lifted his legs higher and higher while he moved nowhere. Sarah's breath stilled. Papa was like the men on the DVD.

Boo was concentrating so hard now that sweat ran in glossy rivulets down his muscled neck. Still her grandfather appeared to do nothing, while Boo's hoofs beat a rhythmic tattoo on the cracked brown earth. Suddenly he switched to the rocking motion, and, finally, out of nowhere, she heard a 'Hup!' and, as she stepped back, Boo rose on his back legs, the front pair folded neatly under him, the muscles of his hindquarters quivering as he struggled to maintain his balance. *Levade.*

And then he was down. And Papa was swinging his leg over the saddle. He murmured something to the horse, running a hand slowly down his neck, thanking him, then handed her the reins. Sarah was stunned, but he spoke before she could work out what to say.

'He's trying too hard,' he said dismissively. 'He's too tense. We must take him back a stage so that he worries less about his balance.'

'Do you want me to keep trying?' she asked.

Papa ran his hand down Boo's neck. 'No,' he said quietly. Then he rubbed his own face, his hand coming away slick with sweat. 'No. He's tired. Mount up and we'll walk home.'

She let out the reins and Boo stretched his neck gratefully.

'Don't feel too bad,' Papa said, as he walked. 'Sometimes . . . some-times I ask too much. He is young . . . you are young . . .' He touched her hand, and Sarah realised that that was as close an admission as she would get that he had been wrong.

They walked once round the perimeter of the park to allow Boo's muscles to stretch and relax, then headed down the footpath to the park gates. With a nod and a wave to the gateman, who never minded them, they walked up the road, Boo's hoofs clattering on the tarmac.

Finally, as they crossed the main road towards the stables, Papa broke the silence. 'John told me he is thinking of selling up. He says we don't have to move Boo. The yard is to be sold as a going concern. He says someone close by is interested. I don't like it.' He paused to wipe his face, seeming distracted. His collar was dark with sweat.

When she thought back, she decided she should have noticed then how he failed to correct Boo when he wouldn't stand quietly at the kerb before crossing the main road.

In the street near the stable yard, Papa rubbed his face again, then his arm. Then he let go of the rein he had been holding. 'You take . . .' he said. 'Time to sit . . .'

'Papa?' They were in the middle of the road.

Boo was fussing, his hoofs kicking up sparks, his head jerking back as Sarah's grandfather began to sit down, his body angled slightly to one side. Everything slowed down around Sarah. She threw herself off the horse, landing lightly on her feet. 'Papa!' she yelled, pulling at his arm as she hung onto the reins. A car had stopped behind them and the driver sounded his horn impatiently.

Her grandfather's eyes were closed and his face had sagged to one side.

'Papa! Get up!' The shouting made Boo dance and pull against her.

Then, as the man climbed out of the car and walked briskly to her grandfather's side, she shrieked, 'John! John! Help me!'

The last thing she remembered was Cowboy John shouting something she couldn't hear as he ran stiffly down the road towards her.

The cleaner moved slowly up the linoleum, the twin brushes of his polisher humming efficiently. Cowboy John sat on the hard plastic seat beside Sarah and checked his watch for the forty-seventh time. Almost four hours, they had sat here. He should be back at the yard, but he couldn't leave her. She was just a kid.

'You OK there?' he asked. 'You want me to get you a coffee?'

The cleaner passed them slowly, then headed for the cardiac ward.

'Nope,' she said, then added quietly, 'thank you.'

'He'll be OK,' he said, for the tenth time. 'Your grandpa's tough as old boots. I bet you someone'll come out any minute now to tell us.'

A slight hesitation. Then she nodded.

'Miss Lachapelle?'

Sarah jolted when the doctor spoke. 'Yes,' she said. 'Is he OK?'

'Are you . . . family?' The doctor's eyes were on John now.

'As good as,' he said, standing.

The doctor glanced back towards the ward. 'Strictly speaking, I can't discuss this with anybody but—'

'I'm as good as you'll get,' John said slowly. 'The Captain has no other living family, just Sarah here. And I am his oldest friend.'

The doctor sat on a seat beside them. He addressed his words to Sarah. 'Your grandfather has suffered a cerebral haemorrhage. A stroke. Do you know what that is?'

She nodded. 'Sort of.'

'He's stable, but he can't talk or do anything for himself. The next twenty-four hours are pretty important.'

'Can I see him?'

'He's hooked up to a lot of machinery. You may get a bit of a shock.'

'She's tough,' Cowboy John said. 'Like her grandpa.'

The doctor checked his watch. 'OK. Come with me.'

The old man seemed suddenly thirty years older than he was, tubes up his nose and taped to his skin, his face grey and sagging. Around him machines drew neon lines, calling to each other with soft, irregular beeps.

'What are the machines doing?' she asked.

'Just monitoring his heart rate, blood pressure, that kind of thing,' the doctor said. 'As I said, the next twenty-four hours are crucial.'

The two men stood in silence as Sarah moved to the edge of the bed and sat on the chair beside it.

'You can talk to him if you want, Sarah,' the doctor said softly. 'Let him know you're here.'

She never cried. Not one tear. Her slim hand reached out to touch his, and held it for a moment. But her jaw was tight.

'He knows she's here,' John said, and stepped outside the curtain to give her some privacy.

It was dark when they left the hospital. John had been outside for a while, pacing the ambulance drop-off point, smoking. Seeing the Captain lying helpless in that bed—well, it made him shudder.

Then he saw her standing by the sliding doors with her hands thrust deep into her pockets, shoulders hunched.

'Here,' he said, realising she had brought no coat with her. 'Take my jacket. You're cold.'

She shook her head, locked in private misery.

'You'll be no good to the Captain with a chill,' he said.

She looked up at him. 'John, did you know my grandfather could ride—I mean, really ride?'

John was briefly unbalanced. 'Ride? Of course I did. Can't say I agree with all that prancing around, but, hell, your granddaddy's a horseman.'

She tried to smile, but he could see it was an effort. She accepted the old denim jacket he thrust over her shoulders, and they walked like that, the old black cowboy and the girl, all the way to the bus-stop.

The lights were on in the house. Natasha stared as she killed the ignition, trying to remember if she'd left them on that morning. She never left the curtains open: it advertised that no one was in. Except someone was.

'Oh,' she said, as she opened the front door. 'You were supposed to come weeks ago.'

Mac was standing in the hallway, holding an armful of photographic paper. 'Sorry. I did leave a message on your phone to say I'd be over.'

She rummaged for it in her bag. 'Oh,' she said. 'I didn't get it.'

They stood facing each other. Mac, there, in her house, their house. His hair was slightly different. He looked better, she saw, with a pang—better for having spent the best part of a year without her.

'I needed some of my equipment,' he said, gesturing behind him, 'except it isn't where I thought it was.'

'I moved it,' she said. 'It's upstairs, in the study.'

'Ah. That'd be why I couldn't find it.' He tried to smile.

'I needed to have some of my files down here . . . and . . .' She tailed off. *And it was too painful having all your stuff around.* She wished she had been prepared for him. Her make-up had long since rubbed off her face. She suspected she looked pale, worn.

'I'll nip upstairs, then,' he said. 'I won't keep you.'

'No—no! Don't rush. I've got to . . . I need to get some milk anyway.'

*'I'm sorry,' she had said. 'Mac, I'm so sorry.'*

*'For what?' His voice had been so calm, so reasonable. 'You just told me nothing happened.' He had looked at her in incomprehension. 'You really think I'm leaving because of him, don't you?'*

She was out of the house before she heard his protest. He probably imagined she was late home because she had been with Conor. Although he wouldn't say as much. That had never been Mac's style.

She didn't often use this supermarket, which was at the rougher end of the neighbourhood. She was standing in the dairy aisle, trying to avoid a mumbling vagrant. She had forgotten why she was there.

Because Mac was back in their home.

She had refused to think about him for so long and he had made it easy. Sometimes it was as if he had dropped off the face of the earth. *Take your stuff and go*, she willed him now. *Then just leave me in peace.*

She picked up a carton of milk and was dragged from her thoughts by a commotion at the check-out. An overweight man had hold of a teenage girl.

'Is everything all right?' Natasha asked. 'I'm a lawyer,' she explained to the girl. It was then that she spotted the man's security badge.

'There you go. You'll need one of them down the nick,' the check-out woman said. 'It'll save you a phone call.'

'I wasn't stealing.' The girl's face was pale under the neon lighting.

'Hmph. So the fish fingers just leaped out of the freezer and landed in your jacket?'

'I just put them there while I went to get some other stuff. Look, please, let me go. I wasn't stealing.' She was close to tears.

'Walked straight past me, she did,' said the check-out woman.

'Perhaps she could just pay for them now,' Natasha suggested.

'Her?' The big man shrugged. 'She ain't got no money.'

'I must have dropped it.' The girl was peering at the floor.

'How much are the fish fingers?' Natasha said, reaching for her purse. 'Let's assume this is an honest mistake. I'll pay for them.' She put the milk down and held out a five-pound note.

After a pause, the woman rang up the fish fingers and the milk, then handed her the change. 'I don't want to see your thieving face in here again,' she said, jabbing a nicotine-stained finger at the girl. 'Got it?'

The girl didn't answer. She shrugged off the security guard and hurried for the door, fish fingers in hand.

'Look at that.' The security guard's skin shone under the lights. 'Never even said thank you. She *was* thieving, you know. We had her in here last week. Except that time we couldn't prove it.'

'If it makes you feel any better, that's probably the best meal she'll have this week,' Natasha said. She went out into the night street.

She had walked only a few paces when the girl popped up beside her. 'I found some of it,' she said. 'I think it fell out of my pocket.' On her palm Natasha could just make out fifty pence and some pennies.

'Keep your money,' she said, continuing to walk. She reached the car and opened the door. 'It's fine.'

'I wasn't stealing,' the girl insisted.

Natasha turned. 'You always buy your supper at eleven at night?'

The girl shrugged. 'I had to visit someone in hospital.'

'Where do you live?' The girl was younger than Natasha had originally thought. Perhaps no more than thirteen or fourteen.

'Sandown.'

Natasha glanced at the tower blocks of the sprawling estate, visible even from this street. It had a reputation throughout the borough. She didn't know why she said what she said next. Perhaps she just hated the look of that place in the dark. Perhaps she wasn't ready to go home.

'You shouldn't be out by yourself this late at night. Come on. I'll drop you home.' She got into the old Volvo and opened the passenger door.

'You never told me your name,' Natasha said, pulling into the car park where groups of youths hung around hurling insults at one another, some breaking away to do wheelies on bikes. She found a space and backed the car into it.

The girl hesitated. 'Jane.'

'Have you lived here long?'

Jane nodded. 'It's all right,' she said, and made to open the door.

Natasha wanted to go home then, to her secure, friendly living room. Her own world. Experience told her she should start the car again and drive away. But then she looked at the pale, thin girl beside her. What kind of person would turf her out without seeing her safely to her door?

She tucked her wedding ring into her back pocket, her credit cards with it. If her purse was snatched all they would get was some cash.

'It's OK,' Jane said, watching her. 'I know them.'

'I'll see you in,' Natasha said. Then, when the girl didn't look over-joyed, 'It's fine. I won't say anything about what happened.'

'Just to the door, then,' Jane said.

They climbed out of the car and walked towards the entrance, Natasha's heels clacking officiously on the gum-pocked walkways.

As they approached the stairwell, a boy rode past. 'That your grand-dad's new bird, is it, Sarah?' He wheeled away, laughing.

'Sarah?'

The lifts were out of order so they walked up three graffiti-ridden, urine-scented flights of stairs, strewn with abandoned takeaway boxes.

'I'm just here,' Sarah said, pointing. 'Thanks for the lift.'

Natasha wasn't sure why she didn't just leave. Perhaps it was the fake name. Perhaps the girl was a little too keen to get rid of her. But she kept going, following Sarah, who hurried in front. And then they reached the door and she stopped. It was the stunned quality of her stance that made Natasha realise that the door was not open to wel-come the girl home. It had been crowbarred.

They stood motionless for a moment. Then Natasha stepped forward and pushed the door wide. Whoever had been in had long gone. The lights were blazing and Natasha saw that the hallway led to a kitchen/living room immaculate enough to throw any discrepancy into sharp relief. There was a gaping absence on a television stand, drawers pulled from a little bureau, a frame smashed on the floor. Suddenly Sarah seemed very young and small.

'I'll ring the police,' Natasha said, pulling her phone from her bag and switching it on. Mac, she saw guiltily, had tried to call.

'There's no point,' Sarah said wearily. 'They never care about any-thing that happens up here.' She was picking her way round the flat.

'What's missing?' Natasha asked, following the girl in and out of the rooms. This was not the chaotic home she had perhaps expected.

'The telly,' Sarah said, her bottom lip trembling. 'My DVD. The money for our holiday.' She appeared suddenly to remember something and bolted for one of the rooms. Natasha heard a door being opened, the sound of rummaging. Sarah emerged. 'They didn't get it,' she said, and for a moment there was a tiny smile. 'My papa's pension book.'

'Where *are* your parents, Sarah?'

'My mum doesn't live here. It's just me and my papa—my granddad.'

'Where is he?'

She hesitated. 'In hospital.'

'How long have you been on your own?'

'A couple of weeks.'

Natasha groaned inwardly. There was so much going on in her life, so many things she had to juggle. She should have walked out of the supermarket with the pint of milk she hadn't even needed.

She called Mac.

'Tash, where the bloody hell are you?' he exploded. 'How long does it take to buy a pint of milk?'

'Mac,' she said carefully, 'I need you to meet me. Bring your tools. And my briefcase—I need my contacts book.'

**M**ac had brought an old lock with him and it had taken less than forty minutes to fit it into place.

Natasha punched a number into her mobile phone. 'Crista? It's Natasha Macauley . . . Hi. Look, I've got a bit of an odd situation. I need to find an emergency placement for a teenage girl.' She outlined the facts.

'We've got nothing,' Crista said. 'We had fourteen unaccompanied asylum-seeking children arrive in the borough yesterday morning and all our foster placements are full. The only place I'll be able to put her for the best part of tonight is the local police station.'

When she went back into the living room, Mac had finished. He had brought an iron strip with him and had screwed it to the door frame. 'Stop anyone getting in again,' he said, as he packed away his tools.

Natasha smiled at him awkwardly, grateful for his practicality, for the fact that he had not issued one resentful word at being dragged out in the middle of the night. Now he sat a few feet from Sarah on the sofa. He was examining her framed photographs—the first point of reference for Mac in anybody's home. 'So,' he was saying, 'this is your grandfather?'

'He used to be a captain,' she said. She had a balled-up tissue in her hand and her voice was low.

'That's a fantastic picture,' he said. 'Don't you think, Tash? Look at the muscles on that horse.'

Natasha tried to look impressed, but all she could think about was that she had to tell Sarah that her next bed would be in a police cell. 'Did you get a bag together?' she asked the girl. 'School uniform?'

Sarah patted the holdall beside her. She seemed uneasy.

'Where are we taking you, then, young lady?' Mac asked, but addressed the question to Natasha.

'I've been on to the people I know and I'm afraid that we'll have to take you to the police station until they can find you something more suitable. Nothing to do with earlier,' Natasha assured her, as she saw Sarah's face blanch. 'It's just that there are no foster-carers available.

Or hostel beds. It's unlikely to be for more than a few hours.'

'The police station?' said Mac, disbelievingly. 'But you must have contacts. You spend your life forcing authorities to put children up.'

Sarah shook her head. 'I'm not staying in a police cell. I'll be fine here.'

Natasha sat down, trying to think. 'Are there any schoolfriends you can stay with? Other relatives?'

'No.'

'Don't you have a number for your mum?'

Sarah's face closed. 'She's dead. It's just me and Papa.'

Natasha turned to Mac, hoping he might understand. 'Mac, we can't leave her here.'

'Then she can come back to ours.'

She was as nonplussed by his use of the possessive as by the idea.

'I'm not going to dump a fourteen-year-old girl who's just been burgled in a police cell with God knows who,' he added.

'I can't take her home. It's against every kind of procedure—'

'If procedure says it's right to stick a young girl in a police cell rather than in someone's warm, safe home for a night,' he interrupted, 'then your procedure is worthless.'

'Mac, we're not cleared as foster-carers. She'll be deemed vulnerable.'

'I'm CRB-checked. I had all that stuff done when I started teaching.'

*Teaching?*

He turned to Sarah. 'Would you be happier at . . . ours? We can ring your grandpa and let him know.'

She looked at Natasha, then back at him. 'I guess so.'

If it got round chambers that I was taking in waifs and strays, my professional judgment would be called into question, Natasha wanted to say. And I don't know this girl. I found her shoplifting . . . She stared at Sarah, trying not to think about Ali Ahmadi, another young person who had seemed desperate, prompting her to go out on a limb.

'Give me five minutes,' she said, then walked into Sarah's bedroom and phoned Crista. 'The girl's refusing to go to a police station, Crista. My . . . husband doesn't like the idea either. He—he's CRB-checked and thinks she should stay at ours instead.'

'You know her at all?'

'Met her tonight.'

'And you're . . . happy with this?'

'She seems'—Natasha paused—'a nice kid. She's got no one at home and the flat's been burgled. It's . . . difficult.'

'I tell you what,' Crista said. 'We never had this conversation. If you think the girl's OK, and you think she'll be safer with you guys, then

I don't need to know she exists until tomorrow. Call me then.'

Natasha flipped the phone shut. Sarah's room was neat and orderly. There were large, free-with-this-magazine pictures of galloping horses in full colour everywhere, and small photographs of a girl, who might have been her, with a brown horse.

She walked out into the living room. Mac and Sarah looked at her. Sarah's eyes, Natasha noticed, were shadowed blue with exhaustion.

'You're coming to ours for one night,' she said, forcing a smile, 'and tomorrow morning we'll get you sorted out with a social worker.'

**S**arah had been silent during the journey, as if the precariousness of her position had dawned on her, and Mac, perhaps guessing this, had gone to some lengths to reassure her. He was sweet, considerate, gently spoken. It was painful to see the best of him directed at someone else.

'Is the spare room made up?' Mac asked, as Natasha let them in.

'There are some boxes on the bed.' His books. Things she had sorted out on the days when she could face such a task.

'I'll move them.' He gestured to Sarah. 'Why don't you find out if she'd like a drink?'

'Hot chocolate?' Natasha asked. 'Something to eat?'

Sarah shook her head. She glanced through the open door at the living room. 'You have a nice house.'

Natasha saw it suddenly through the eyes of a stranger: large, plush, tastefully furnished. 'I'll show you upstairs, then,' Natasha said.

'**I** hope you don't mind,' Mac said, as she came slowly down the stairs, 'but I made up the sofa bed in the study.'

She had half expected it; she could hardly turf him out at this hour of the morning, not after everything he'd done. The girl had gone to sleep without a murmur. 'Glass of wine?' she said. 'I know I need one.'

He let out a long sigh. 'Oh, yes.'

She poured two glasses and handed him one. He sat on the sofa and she kicked off her shoes, then folded her legs under her on the armchair. It was a quarter to two. 'You'll have to sort everything out tomorrow, Mac,' she said. 'I've got court first thing.'

'Just tell me what to do.'

She observed absently that he couldn't have any work or he wouldn't have offered.

'Write down who I should call, or where I should drop her. I might let her sleep a bit—she's had quite a night. Nasty shock for her. It was the right thing to do,' he said, waving at the stairs.

'Yes.'

They sipped silently.

'So, what are you working on?' she asked eventually.

'I'm doing three days' teaching a week, and commercial stuff the rest of the time. Portraiture. A bit of travel stuff. Not much, to be honest.'

'Teaching?' She struggled to keep the incredulity from her voice. 'I thought I'd misheard you.'

'I don't mind it. It pays the bills.'

Natasha digested this. When the advertising work had dried up, he had scorned her idea that he teach. He hadn't wanted to be tied down, committed in a way that might stop him doing something more interesting at short notice. Even though it meant that his side of their finances was distinctly feast or famine, usually the latter.

Now he was Mac the Mature, Mac the Motivated. She felt cheated.

'Yup. I got a bit disillusioned with the whole commercial scene. Teaching's not as bad as I thought it would be. I'll keep doing it till I work out where I'm going. It doesn't pay brilliantly.'

She stiffened, braced herself as if for impact. 'And . . .'

'And at some point, Tash, we need to sort out the house. I can't live out of a suitcase for ever. It's been almost a year.'

She stared into her glass. She knew what he was saying: Permanent Financial Settlements. But when she looked up at him she made sure her face was blank. 'I can't think about this now. I'm too tired.'

'Sure. Tomorrow, perhaps?'

'I'm in court first thing. I told you. I've got a big day ahead so, if it's OK by you, I'd like to divide up the marital assets some other time.'

'OK. But I may as well tell you that I need to be in London from now on, with somewhere to stay. And unless you have a really good reason, I'd like to use the spare room until we've sorted things out.'

Natasha sat very still. 'Stay *here*? You are kidding?'

He raised a small smile. 'Living with me was that bad, huh?'

'But we're not together any more.'

'Nope. But I own half of this property and I need a roof over my head. It's only for a few weeks, Tash. I'm sorry if you don't like it, but as far as I'm concerned, I've given you the best part of a year with sole occupancy. Now I'm entitled to something.' He shrugged. 'Come on. It's a big house. It'll only be a nightmare if we make it that way.'

He was disconcertingly relaxed. Happy, almost. She wanted to throw something at his head. But there was a fourteen-year-old stranger in her home for whom she had just agreed to take joint responsibility. She stalked out and upstairs to the bedroom that no longer felt like hers.

# FOUR

THE GIRL IN THE PHOTOGRAPH was beaming up at her parents, who each held one of her hands as though they were about to lift her off the floor. *Fostering*, the poster read. *Make All the Difference*. Not her parents, then.

Suddenly irritated by the child's smile, Sarah shifted on her seat in the social worker's office. She needed to get over to Sparepenny Lane. She knew Cowboy John would take care of Boo if she didn't turn up, but her horse needed to go out, to keep up with his training.

The woman had finished scribbling. 'So, Sarah, we're going to take your details now and we'll set out a care plan for you. We're going to try to find you a temporary home until your grandfather is better.'

The woman talked to her as if she was the same age as the child in the poster. Tears prickled behind her eyes and she clenched her jaw.

The woman looked at a file. 'I see your grandparents have a residency order for you. Do you know where your mother is, Sarah?'

She shook her head.

'Can I ask when you last saw her?'

Sarah glanced sideways at Mac. 'She died a few years ago.' She felt quietly furious that she had to give out this information.

She saw the sympathy on their faces, but she had never even missed her mother, not like she did Nana. Her mother had been a chaotic, unpredictable shadow over her early years. Sarah remembered her as a series of images, of being dragged into different people's houses, left to sleep on sofas, the hum of distant loud music and arguments. Then, when she had gone to live with Nana and Papa, order, routine. Love.

The woman was scribbling. 'Are you sure there are no friends you can stay with? Any other family?' She sounded hopeful, but Sarah had to admit that she was not popular. Her few friends lived in flats as small as hers; she knew no one well enough to ask, even if she had wanted to.

'I need to go,' she said to Mac quietly.

'I know,' he said. 'Don't worry, the school knows you'll be late.'

'And where did you say your grandfather is now?' The woman smiled at her.

'He's in St Theresa's. Will I be able to see him every day?'

'I'm not sure. It'll depend on where we can place you.'

'Won't it be somewhere close to her home?' asked Mac.

The woman sighed. 'I'm afraid we can't guarantee that clients will be close to their home. But we'll make every effort to ensure that Sarah sees her grandfather regularly until he can come home.'

Sarah had visions of herself being placed with some smiling family miles from Papa. From Boo. This wasn't going to work.

'You know what?' she said, glancing at Mac. 'I can look after myself. If someone could just help me a bit, I'll be fine at home.'

'We're not allowed to leave you by yourself, Sarah,' the woman said.

'But I can cope. It was getting burgled that was the problem. I need to be near my home.'

'And we'll make every effort to ensure that that happens,' the woman said. 'And now we'd better get you to school. Your social worker will meet you afterwards and, hopefully, take you to your placement.'

'I can't,' Sarah said abruptly. 'I need to be somewhere after school.'

'If it's an after-school club, we can set that straight with the school.'

Sarah tried to work out how much to tell them. What would they do if she told them about Boo?

'Right, Sarah. If we can move on to religion, I won't keep you much longer. Can you tell me which of these categories you fall into?'

The woman's voice receded and Sarah looked at Mac. He kept fidgeting as if he would rather have been anywhere else. Well, now he knew how she felt. She hated him and his wife for putting her in this mess.

'Sarah? Church of England? Catholic? Hindu? Muslim? Other?'

'Hindu,' she said mutinously, and then, when they looked at her disbelieving, she said again, 'Hindu.'

'Ooohh-kaaaay.' The woman carried on writing. 'Nearly done. Mr Macauley, if you need to go now I can take it from here.'

Mac was scribbling. 'You all right?' he asked Sarah quietly.

'Just great,' she said.

He looked troubled. He knew he had ruined her life, she thought. He handed Sarah a piece of paper. 'My numbers,' he said. 'Any problems, give me a call.' He stood up to leave. 'I hope you get home soon.'

Sarah kicked at the leg of her chair and said nothing.

'**S**orry. Got caught up.' Mac dumped his camera bags on the floor. He kissed Louisa, the art director, then turned to the girl who was sitting at the mirror, texting furiously, oblivious to the attentions of the make-up artist behind her. 'Hi, I'm Mac,' he said, holding out a hand.

'Oh. Hi,' she said. 'Serena.'

'You should have been here an hour ago.' Maria, the make-up artist, tapped her watch. Her jeans were positioned so low on her hips that they were almost indecent.

'Just thought I'd give you extra time to work your magic, sweetheart.' He kissed her cheek. 'Louisa, do you want to talk me through the brief?'

Louisa outlined the look they wanted for the shot of the young actress. Mac nodded, appearing to give her his full attention, but his mind was in that children's welfare department. He had left the building forty minutes earlier, feeling less relieved than he had expected.

'. . . lots of red. She's not just another young starlet, Mac, but a serious actress of tomorrow, a young Judi Dench or Vanessa Redgrave.'

Mac eyed Serena and stifled an internal sigh. He had lost count of the exceptional young starlets he had shot over the past ten years. Barely two had survived the initial burst of publicity.

'OK. She is ready for you.' Maria appeared in the doorway.

'We'll be ten minutes. I'm just going to check the backdrop.' Louisa left them.

Maria walked up to him. 'I was going to ask why you so late,' she said, in her heavy Slavic accent, 'but then I realised I didn't care.'

He hooked a finger in her belt loop and pulled her close to him. Her skin smelled of make-up and hairspray, the layered unguents of her trade. 'If I told you, you wouldn't believe me.'

'You were out picking up women,' she said.

'Fourteen-year-old girls, actually.'

Her mouth was so close now that he could see the freckle to the side of her upper lip. 'This does not surprise me. You are disgusting man.' She kissed him, then pulled away. 'You want to meet up later?'

'If we can go to yours.'

'You are at your ex-wife's house?'

'It's my house too. I told you.'

She narrowed her eyes. 'I don't trust her. What woman with any self-respect would take back her ex-husband like this? When my ex-boyfriend in Krakow tried to return to my house I turned my father's gun on him.' She headed for the door. 'Is just as well I missed.'

The darned gates were jamming again. Cowboy John was hauling at them, trying to make them line up as he wrestled with the padlock, when he saw a familiar figure running towards him.

'I was just about to close up,' he said, unhooking the padlock. 'I was waiting for you all yesterday. I thought something had happened to you. Where have you been, girl?' He coughed, a hoarse, rasping sound.

'They've put me in Holloway.' She dropped her schoolbag on the cobbles and ran past him to Boo's stable.

He pulled the gates shut and followed her. 'You went to prison?'

'Not the prison,' she said, wrestling with the bolt on the stable door. 'Social Services. They said I can't stay at home with Papa not being there and they made me go to this stupid family in Holloway. They think I'm with Papa now—it's the only way I could get here.' She threw herself against the horse's neck and he saw a long shudder escape her.

'Hold on.' He flicked on the lights. 'What the Sam Hill is going on?'

She faced him, eyes glittering. 'Our flat got broken into on Tuesday. And this woman who gave me a lift home, this lawyer or something, she made me stay with her because she said it wasn't safe where I was. And then they took me to Social Services and the next thing I'm living in Holloway. It took me an hour and a quarter on the bus to get here.'

'What they want to make themselves busy for?'

'I was fine,' she said, 'until the break-in.'

'Your grandpa know about this?'

'I don't know. I can't get to the hospital till tomorrow. And I can't tell them about Boo or they might put him somewhere too. But I haven't got the stables money for you. They took Papa's pension books so I've got nothing except my bus and lunch money.'

'Don't you fret. Your horse ain't going nowhere. I'll sort out the rent with your papa when he's up and about. You got money for horse feed?'

She thrust her hand into her pocket, counted out the cash and handed it over. 'I've got enough for four bales of hay and a couple of sacks of food. But I need you to feed him for me. I don't even know if I can get here to muck him out.'

'OK, OK. I'll clean his stable for you, or get one of the boys to do it.'

She seemed to relax a little. She took up a brush and started to groom the horse, sweeping her arm down his flank methodically.

He stood there for a minute. 'I tell you what. You want me to go visit with your grandpa for you tomorrow so that you can come here?'

She turned. 'Would you? I don't like to leave him alone for two days.'

'No problem. He'd want to know Boo here was still doing his circus thing. But I got to tell him something. And, sweetheart, I have to talk to you about it too. I'm thinking of selling up to Maltese Sal. Like I'll tell your grandpa, nothing's going to change. I'm going to hang on here anyway till my house is sold.'

'Where are you going?' She had put her arms round the horse's neck and was hanging on as if he, too, might be spirited off somewhere.

'I'm moving out to the country. Somewhere with a bit of green.

I figure my boys deserve it.' He nodded at his horses. 'Maltese Sal knows about the Captain, knows it ain't easy for you right now. He says he'll keep things just as they are.'

She didn't have to say anything. He could see it in her face. Given where she had ended up right now, how the hell could she believe that?

Natasha jumped when she heard the front door open. There was a pause, then she heard him offer, tentatively, 'Hi,' from the hallway.

She waited a moment, then shouted, 'I'm upstairs,' making sure it didn't sound like an invitation. Maddeningly, he came up anyway.

'I'm thinking of getting a takeaway. Would you like one?'

'No,' she said. 'I—I'm going out.'

'Going away,' he corrected, noting the suitcase on the bed.

'Just for the weekend.'

'Anywhere nice?'

'Kent.' She had wondered whether to tell him about the cottage she had rented since he had gone. But Conor had warned her not to reveal anything to Mac, no matter how nice he seemed. She went into the en suite to gather up her moisturiser and make-up.

Mac had thrust his hands into his jeans and was looking around. 'So,' he said, 'all-night party for me, then.'

She whirled round.

'I'm joking.' He rubbed a hand over the back of his head. 'I take it you're going with Conor?'

She kept her back to him now, putting things into the case. 'Yes.'

'If you're going because I'm here, you just say the word and I can go out for the evening,' he said. 'Don't feel you have to go.'

'I don't,' she lied. 'We go away most weekends.' She continued to pack, his presence making her feel increasingly self-conscious.

'Where in Kent are you going?' he asked.

'What is this? *Twenty Questions*?' It flashed out before she could censor it.

'I'm just being polite, Tash. We're skirting round each other every day. I'm trying to act as if we can at least have a civil conversation.'

She wanted to tell him she was finding this far more difficult than she had anticipated, but even that small admission felt like giving too much away. 'Just a village near the Sussex border.'

He frowned, shifted his feet. 'Well, I shouldn't be around much longer. The agents rang. The house goes on the market tomorrow.'

That feeling of being winded again. She stood in the middle of the room, a pair of boots dangling from one hand.

'We did agree, Tash,' he said, catching her expression.

'Don't keep calling me that,' she said irritably. 'I'm Natasha.'

'I'm sorry,' he said. 'If I had enough money, I wouldn't be doing this.'

'Well, if it's got to be done, then let's get it over with.' Natasha zipped the case shut, walked by her soon-to-be-ex-husband and down the stairs.

They had moved him again, and it took Sarah twenty minutes to locate him. He was in the stroke ward, where he had been until last week, when pneumonia had sent him back to intensive care.

'We hoped he'd be a bit further along by now,' said the nurse, as she showed Sarah to his curtained area. 'Poor old boy, he's struggling a bit.'

'He's not a boy,' Sarah said curtly. 'He's seventy-four.'

Inside the room, Sarah drew a chair close to the bed. The back had been raised so that her grandfather sat half upright. Sarah ached at the sight of his greyed chin, resting loosely on his chest. She had never seen him with more than overnight stubble. She opened the bedside cabinet and took out the picture of him and Nana, which she put on top of the cabinet. If she positioned it carefully he could look at her all day.

She glanced at her watch, trying to work out how much time she had. The Hewitts wanted her at their house by four o'clock, even though she had told them where she was going. It was almost two now, and impossible for her to get to Sparepenny Lane to take Boo out.

She touched her grandfather's hand. His skin, dry and papery, made something inside her contract. Four weeks in hospital seemed to have sucked the essence out of him, shorn him of his robustness. It was hard to see him as someone who had ridden a rearing horse just weeks ago.

'Papa?'

He opened an eye and peered vacantly. 'I brought you some yoghurt.' His eyes softened and she could see that he knew her now. She laid her hand on his. 'The black cherry. The one you like.' His hand clenched under hers. 'Just thought I'd tell you, Boo's getting his winter coat already, but he's really well. We did lots of walk to canter yesterday, and he didn't hot up. I've upped his food, as it's October now and the nights are colder. I'm giving him an extra scoop of sugar beet—is that OK?'

It was the slightest nod, but it was enough. Things were as they should be now: her seeking his approval. She kept talking, as if mundane chat could persuade some normality back into their lives.

Since Natasha had rented the cottage in Kent, Conor had come down with her most weekends when he didn't have his boys. He wasn't practical, as Mac had been, but he was happy to keep her company. Most of the time, if the weather was good, he sat outside and enjoyed a beer while she clipped and pruned the garden into shape.

Conor was not the possessive type, so Natasha had little reason to believe that her new domestic arrangements might be a problem. Until, as they unpacked his car, she told him.

'Mac's been there all week?' Conor put down his case.

'Since Tuesday.'

'And you never thought to tell me?'

'I've hardly seen you this week. And I'm not going to rush past you outside court whispering, "Darling, my ex-husband's moved back in."'

'You could have rung.'

'Yes. But I didn't want to. It felt awkward.'

'I imagine it would.' He picked up his case and a bag of shopping, then walked into the house, his back bristling.

She followed him into the kitchen. 'He's got nowhere to stay and he does own half the house.'

He turned to face her. 'I could be terminally ill, bankrupt and lobotomised and you wouldn't get me within fifty feet of my ex and her house.'

'Well, we haven't been through the whole process you have.'

'You mean you haven't got divorced. Am I missing something here?'

'You know we're going to, Conor. It's just early days.'

'Early days? Or not quite definite?'

He had begun unpacking the shopping with unnecessary vigour.

'Are you serious?'

'You've just told me your not-quite-ex-husband has moved back in with you. How can I not be serious?'

Natasha stalked past him. 'You're the last person I'd expect to be playing Mr Possessive, Conor.'

'What's that supposed to mean?'

'You won't commit to a holiday and you won't even introduce me to your kids.'

He threw up his hands. 'I knew you'd bring them into it. Their lives have been in turmoil. Their mother and I can hardly speak to each other. Introducing them to mummy number two is hardly going to help matters, is it?'

'Why do I have to be mummy number two? Can't I just be your friend?' She was shouting now. 'If we're together, I'm going to be a fixture in their lives someday. Or am I the one who's missing something?'

'Of course you're not. And, yes, we're together. But what's the hurry?' Then his voice softened. 'You don't understand kids, Natasha. You can't until you've had some. They have to come first. I have to protect them.'

She stared at him. 'And I couldn't possibly understand that, could I, Conor. What with being *barren* and all . . .' She ran upstairs two at a time and shut herself in the bathroom.

Sarah ducked in past Maltese Sal and closed the gates behind her. Cowboy John was elsewhere, and she always felt self-conscious around Sal and his men. She was conscious of their stares as she made her way up to Boo's stable. The horse whickered softly as she approached, his head already reaching over the stable door. She gave him a mint and held his neck, letting him nose her pockets for more treats, then set about refreshing his water and tidying the bedding.

Despite Cowboy John's help, caring for Boo was becoming increasingly difficult. The Hewitts had become frustrated by her apparent failure to arrive home when they expected her. She had no excuses left to give them. School did not seem to have registered her absences yet, but she knew she was on borrowed time.

She walked Boo on a long lead rope up and down Sparepenny Lane, keeping to the kerb to avoid the passing cars and talking softly to him when pent-up energy caused him to skitter sideways. It was only to be expected: he was a horse who needed not just the physical challenge but the mental exercise. He tossed his head, his pricked ears and easy jog a mute request to go faster, farther. When she turned back to the gates, his head dropped, as if in disappointment.

It was as she opened her lockup, where she stored her feed, that her heart sank. There were four flaps of hay—less than half a bale. She had forgotten to ask Cowboy John for more.

Sal was whistling as he opened his lockup. Through the doorway, she saw the stacked bales, the bags of expensive horse feed. As she stared, he turned abruptly and she blushed to be caught looking.

He peered past her into her lockup. 'You short, huh?'

She didn't answer him, but busied herself opening a haynet.

Maltese Sal let the door close behind him and took a step towards her. His gold tooth glinted when he opened his mouth. 'You got enough hay?'

She met his eyes, then looked away. 'John was going to lend me some.'

'John isn't back till tomorrow. So, you got a problem.'

'I've got enough.' She made to move past him, but he stood in her way.

'You got a nice horse. You can't feed a horse like that shit off the floor.' He took the cigarette from his mouth and pulled a piece of hay from the bundle she was carrying, put the glowing end against it. 'Good for burning. Nothing else. Your grandfather's still sick, huh?'

She nodded.

'I don't want you to feed your horse that shit. Here, put it down.' He stuck his cigarette back in his mouth, walked into his lockup and brought out a bale of hay. It was still slightly green and gave off a soft, meadowy scent. He carried it, effortlessly, swinging it by its twine, into her lockup and put it in the corner. As she stood against the wall, he went back and got a second. Then he picked up a large bag of premium horse feed and, with a grunt, swung it through her doorway. 'There,' he said. 'That'll keep you going.'

'I can't,' she whispered. 'I haven't got any money.'

'You take it from John, yes?' He seemed to see right through her. She nodded reluctantly. 'So you take it from me. Pay me when you got the money, OK? If I'm going to run this place I don't want to see a good horse going down because of a bad diet. Now, I need to get on.'

He walked away into the yard, a slight swagger in the way he moved.

The silence of a London house had a curious poignancy to it, Natasha observed as she closed the door behind her, her call echoing into nothing. She stepped over the now omnipresent camera bags and went into the living room. The steady red light on the answering machine told her there were no messages.

She walked back into the hallway, picked up her bag and went upstairs, the sound of her footfall echoing in a way that made her feel self-conscious, a stranger in her own home.

She and Conor had recovered the weekend after its acrimonious start, but she knew they had been shocked by the ferocity of their argument. 'You will meet the kids, Hotshot,' he'd said, as he had dropped her off. 'Just give me some more time, yes?'

She dropped her bag on her bed and undid the catch. Then she straightened and, almost without knowing what she was doing, went across the landing to the spare room. She called again, then pushed tentatively at the door, registering Mac's rumpled bed, the pile of unwashed clothes in the corner. She hovered in the doorway, then found herself treading quietly through the room and into the en-suite bathroom. His razor stood in a glass, with toothpaste and a brush. The bath mat lay skewed on the tiled floor. The mess was perversely reassuring: an echo of the man he knew he was. Chaotic. Imperfect. This is why we're divorcing, she reminded herself.

It was as she made to walk out again that she caught sight of the pot on the glass shelf at the end of the bath, packaged in an expensive cream and gold box: a woman's moisturiser. Beside it lay a packet of make-up remover pads.

# FIVE

'IT'S THE FOURTH TIME you've missed double English in this half of the term, Sarah. It used to be one of your better subjects.' The headmaster, Mr Phipps, examined the papers in front of him.

Sarah twisted her hands.

'I know things are difficult for you, but your attendance record was always good. Are you having problems getting to school? Are your foster-family not helping?'

She couldn't tell him the truth—that she had told the Hewitts she had lost her bus pass, and the money they had given her for fares had gone towards Boo's bedding.

'I . . . get confused about the different bus routes. I missed the bus.'

Boo was beginning to react to the loss of his routine. When she had got him to the park that morning, he had bucked, setting his mouth against the bit. She had been angry and frustrated with him.

'The local authority will pay for a minicab, Sarah, if transport really is the problem.' He placed the tips of his fingers together. 'But I don't think that's the whole story. It says here that you've missed geography twice on Thursday afternoons, and PE three times on Friday afternoons. Do you want to tell me how that came about?'

She stared at her feet. 'I went to see my granddad,' she muttered.

'Is his health improving?' The headmaster's expression had softened.

'A bit,' she said.

'It's an unsettling time for you. I do understand that. But what you can't do is take time off to see your grandfather whenever you want to. I want to see an improvement, Sarah. A real improvement.'

Cowboy John had been at the yard the last time she was there. He had been to see Papa and the first thing he had said when she stepped through the gates was that he was letting her off the back rent. He would tell Maltese Sal and she would be square. She could tell from his face that he had thought she'd be relieved. But she had felt the blood drain from her face. She knew this meant that he no longer believed Papa would be able to pay him back. He no longer believed Papa would come home.

'No more skipping class, Sarah. Right?'

She raised her face. 'Right,' she said, and wondered if Mr Phipps could see straight through her.

Natasha jumped when she found him in the kitchen. It was a quarter to seven. When they had lived together he had barely stirred until ten.

'Got a job up in Hertfordshire. Publicity shot. Make-up, hair, the full works. It's going to take me a good hour and a half to get there.' Mac gave off a faint aroma of shampoo and shaving cream, as if he had already showered. 'Hope you don't mind. I used the last tea bag.' He lifted a hand, waving a piece of toast. He was reading her newspaper. 'I'll get some more while I'm out. You still drink coffee, right?'

She closed the cupboard door. 'I guess I'll have to,' she said. He had spilled some milk on the worktop.

'You want this?' He motioned towards the newspaper.

She shook her head. She tried to work out where to sit. Opposite him and they risked touching feet. On the adjoining side of the table, she might seem to be cosying up to him. Paralysed by these two choices, Natasha remained by the kitchen units with her bowl of cereal.

'There are two couples coming round at the weekend,' she said. 'The agent has keys so you won't have to be here.'

He adjusted his chair so he could see her better. 'I don't have to be here? You're away again? Where are you going this time?'

'Does it matter?'

He held up both palms. 'Just making polite conversation, Tash.'

'I'm going back to Kent.'

'Nice. You must like it. Conor got a place there, has he?'

'Something like that.'

'Doesn't come here much, does he?'

'I wonder why.' She focused on the cereal.

'I told you that if he wants to come here I can make myself scarce. We can have set nights, if you like. I'll stay away Tuesdays, you stay away Wednesdays, that kind of thing.' He studied something in the newspaper with great concentration, adding, 'We can be modern.'

She reached across for her coffee. 'I assume this will all be sorted out long before we start regularising "date nights".'

Date nights. She felt the existence of the invisible woman keenly— she knew that at the weekends when she was not there, the woman was, even if Natasha no longer crept into the spare bathroom to confirm it. Sometimes she suspected she could detect her scent. At other times it was just Mac's demeanour. He was loose, relaxed—like he used to be after they had spent much of the day in bed. You've been having sex all weekend *in our house*, she would think, then curse herself for it.

The cereal had turned claggy in her mouth. She finished her mouthful and pushed the bowl towards the dishwasher.

'You OK?'

'Fine.'

'Fine again. Not finding this too hard?'

Sometimes she felt he was testing her. As if he wanted her to say she couldn't bear it, and leave. Don't leave, Conor had warned, despite his feelings. The moment she left the house she would lose the moral and legal advantage. If Mac had invested a lot of time and effort in the house, he might not want to leave as much as he told her he did.

'He's the one who wants to sell it,' she had protested.

'That's what he wants you to think,' Conor had replied. He could see subversive possibilities in almost any kind of behaviour.

'Not finding it hard at all,' she said brightly.

'Great.' His voice softened. 'I did worry about how it would work out.'

'Well, don't worry on my account.'

He was staring at her. 'Nothing changes, does it, Tash? You still don't give anything away.'

Their eyes locked. He looked away first and gulped his tea.

'Oh, by the way, I bunged a load of washing in last night and there was some stuff of yours in the basket so I put that in too.'

'What stuff?'

'Ah . . . blue T-shirt. And underwear, mostly.' He finished the tea. 'Lingerie, I should say.' He flicked a page in the newspaper. 'Gone up a notch since we split, I noticed . . .'

Heat flooded Natasha's face.

'It's OK. I put it on a low temperature. I know about these things. I may even have put it on the hand-wash setting.'

'Don't,' she said. 'Don't.' She felt horribly exposed. The thought of it.

'Just being helpful.'

'No. No, you're not. You—you're—' She picked up her briefcase and pushed past him towards the door, then spun round. 'Don't touch my underwear, OK? Don't touch my clothes. Don't touch my stuff. It's bad enough you're staying here without rifling through my pants as well.'

'You really think the biggest thrill I could get is going through your pants?' He slammed the paper down. 'Don't worry. I won't go anywhere near them in future. Hardly ever did anyway, if I remember.'

'Oh, that's nice,' she said. 'That's really, really nice.'

'Sorry. I just . . .' He let out a long breath.

They stared at the floor, before their eyes lifted, met and locked. He raised his eyebrows. 'I'll do my washing separately in future. OK?'

'Fine,' she said, and shut the door firmly behind her.

Sarah was bent low over her horse's neck, her toes jammed in the stirrups, the wind whipping tears that tracked horizontally from the corners of her eyes. Her breath came in gasps, her arms pressed against his neck as he flew, the thunder of his hoofbeats filling her ears. He had needed this for weeks, and here the marshes were wide and flat enough for her to let him go until he was tired.

'Go,' she whispered to him. 'Go on.' The words flew backwards into her throat. Boo would not have heard her even if she had shouted; he was lost in some purely physical world of his own, instinct telling him to relish this freedom, to allow his tight muscles to stretch, his legs to fly across the rough ground, his lungs to tighten with the sheer effort of maintaining such a speed. She understood it. She needed it too.

She had never gone so far with him before, never let him run so fast, and she wondered whether she would be able to stop. She lifted her head, trying to gauge how much distance she had left, then pulled slightly on the reins, recognising that she had little strength left to pull him back, should he fight her.

How much easier it would be for them to keep going. To race up that grassy bank, straight across the motorway, skidding through the cars, his shoes sending up sparks. They would jump the cars, the fences. They would fly under the pylons, past the warehouses and car parks, and keep going until they hit the countryside. Just her and her horse, galloping through the long grass into some uncomplicated future.

But some part of Boo was still owned by Papa. Feeling the increasing tension in the reins, he slowed obediently, his ears flicking back and forth, as if he was trying to check that he had read her message correctly. Sarah allowed herself to sink back into the saddle, her body becoming upright, reinforcing what she was telling him: to slow down. To do as she asked. To return to their world.

Some fifty feet from the dual carriageway, Boo slowed to a walk, his frothing sides heaving with the effort of what he had just done. Sarah sat very still, squinting back at the distance she had covered. She was no longer in the wind, but the tears in her eyes kept coming.

Ruth, the social worker, was at the school gates, her neat little red car parked across the road, as if she did not want to be obtrusive.

'Sarah?'

Her heart lurched as she grasped the possible significance of the woman's presence. Ruth must have registered it because, as Sarah hurried towards her, she said, 'No need to worry. There's nothing wrong with your grandfather.'

Her chest deflating with relief, Sarah followed the social worker reluctantly to the car. She had planned to see Papa tonight; perhaps she could persuade Ruth to give her a lift. As she got in, she noticed two black bags on the back seat. At the mouth of one she could see her track-suit bottoms. Five weeks and two moves had told her what those bags meant.

'Am I going somewhere?'

'Sarah, I'm afraid the Hewitts have had enough.' Ruth started the car. 'Taking responsibility for someone who keeps disappearing is too much for them. They're frightened something will happen to you. And the school tells me you've been skipping classes. Do you want to tell me what's going on?'

'Nothing's going to happen to me. Nothing's going on.'

'Is there some boy involved? Some man?'

'No. There's no boy. No man.'

'So what is it?'

Sarah wished Ruth would drive somewhere instead of sitting outside the school gates so everyone could stare into the car as they filed past. But she was waiting for her to answer. 'I wanted to see my granddad.'

'But it's not just that, is it? I went to the hospital on Tuesday when the school last rang to tell me you'd disappeared. I went to pick you up but you hadn't been there that day. Where were you?'

Sarah stared at her hands. They were going to find out. She knew it. She thought of Boo, of the feeling of him beneath her, the fleeting sense of freedom as they ran towards a different future.

'You've got to help me, Sarah. I'm running out of options for you. The Hewitts are good people, nice people. Do you want to end up being placed in care?'

Sarah reached into her bag and pulled out the piece of paper. *Any problems, give me a call.* 'Mac,' she said, lifting her eyes to Ruth's. 'I want to go back to Mac's house.'

Ten people. Six lots of viewings. And not a single offer. The estate agent had been apologetic. 'It's interest rates,' he had said. 'It makes people nervous. Takes them twice as long to make an offer.'

'But we need to sell this house.' Natasha had surprised herself. She had not wanted to leave, but that was before Mac had returned.

'Then I can only suggest a price reduction. Everything sells if it's cheap enough.'

Natasha lay in the bath, wondering how much they should drop to achieve a sale. It was a beautiful house in a nice street. And she needed enough to buy a flat somewhere else.

'Natasha?'

She sat up and checked that she had locked the door. 'I'm in the bath,' she called. *Please don't let him have brought anyone home.*

She heard the dull thud of things being dropped on the floor, his footsteps on the stairs.

'I'm in the bath,' she called again. She heard him stop outside the door and felt oddly self-conscious.

'I've been to the supermarket,' he said. 'Bought a load of stuff. It's in the kitchen. Tea bags and all.'

Great, she thought. You want a medal?

'And I called the estate agent. They said those last people still might offer. It's only two days since they viewed.'

'They won't, Mac. You like somewhere, you offer straight away.'

She could hear him receiving a text message. She sank down into the bath again, letting the bubbles rise to her chin.

'Anyway, there's someone coming next Wednesday. So you never know. And I had another call.' He was tentative. 'From Social Services.'

Natasha wiped her eyes. 'What?' She pushed herself upright.

'They asked if we'd consider fostering that girl who spent the night with us. Her current placement isn't working.' He paused. 'Just for a few weeks. She asked to come to us.'

Natasha thought back to the girl's wary eyes gazing at her breakfast plate, her shocked face confronting the devastation of her front room.

'She's told them we're friends of her family. I didn't like to contradict her. But I said I didn't think it would be possible.'

Natasha climbed out of the bath. 'Why?'

He didn't answer immediately. 'You just seemed . . . reluctant before. I told them you might have too much work on.'

She wrapped herself in a soft white towel and sat on the side of the bath. 'What do you think?' She was facing the door.

'I wouldn't mind, if it helped her out for a few weeks. Just till we sell the house. She seemed an OK kid.'

She could hear it in his voice. He would be as relieved as she would. A different focus. An enforced break in the tension.

She thought back to a stolen packet of fish fingers. The girl had sworn she would have paid for them. She might just need a chance.

'Tash?'

*It might be the closest to parenting she was ever going to get.*

'I don't see why a couple of weeks would hurt,' she said, 'but you'd have to fit your work around her. I've got a big case coming up and I won't be able to take time off.'

'I can manage that. I'll ring them and find out what we do next.'

She heard Sarah coming downstairs before she saw her. Her footfall was deceptively light, almost as if she wanted not to be heard, but for Natasha, still acutely aware of the presence of other people in her house, it was enough to make her break off from her files. She had been working at the kitchen table and now leaned back in her chair to see through the doorway. 'Are you going out?'

Sarah whipped round in the hallway. She was wearing a puffy jacket and a striped woollen scarf. 'I won't be long,' she said.

'Where are you off to?' Natasha tried to make her question casual.

'To see a friend.'

Natasha stood. 'Would you like a lift?'

'No . . . thank you. I can get the bus.' And before Natasha could say anything else, she was gone.

Sarah had been with them for ten days and, after the initial strangeness of the first two days, the three had fallen into something like a routine. Natasha would make breakfast and Mac would drop Sarah at school, on the advice of the social worker. He was in charge for the first couple of hours after school, and then, depending on how late Natasha stayed at work, either Sarah and Mac, or the three of them, would eat together in some facsimile of family life. Conversation was awkward, at first, but Mac chatted to Sarah, and if she didn't say much in return, they had at least settled into something that felt, on occasion, companionable.

Twice, the school had rung to say she had missed lessons. They had been warned by Ruth that the girl did not always follow the routines set for her. 'We've had some issues about her not being where she should be,' the social worker had said.

'Surely that's the whole point of being a teenager?' Mac had said cheerfully. 'I was never where I was meant to be.'

'I just don't think you should give her too much freedom.' Ruth directed her comments at Natasha. 'By all accounts her grandfather was quite strict, and she seems to be responding to the lack of that stability by going a bit off the rails. And she seems unwilling to talk about what she's doing. I'm not suggesting she'll be a problem for you,' she added quickly. 'But if you can negotiate some boundaries with her about when and where she goes out, I think it will work better for everyone.'

They had the advantage, Ruth had said, smiling, that Sarah had asked to be with them. 'We find that young people do much better in their chosen environment. I'm sure that will be the case here.'

Natasha had not had time to feel flattered by this. Sarah seemed to want to spend as little time with her as possible. She escaped to her room most of the time she was at home, and was out so often that sometimes it felt as if they were not housing another person at all.

Natasha had thought having her here was simply Mac's smoke screen for their discomfort with each other. But he was throwing himself into Sarah's care. He had even scanned the cookery books so that he could cook when Natasha was not at home. He seemed to know instinctively how to talk to Sarah, whereas Natasha struggled to find the right tone—she sounded frequently, even to her own ears, as if she was addressing a client. 'Do you need anything? What kind of things do you generally have for a school lunch?' It sounded awkward, interrogative.

She had snuck into the girl's bedroom one afternoon when she was at school, trying to get a grip on who she was, what she might need, but her few belongings had offered few clues: some chain-store clothes, a photograph of her with two old people, probably her grandparents. Some books on horses and her school uniform. Oddly, despite her neatness, her shoes were often filthy and her jeans bore a pungent smell that Natasha couldn't identify. When she tried to bring this up one evening, Sarah had said she and a friend had been walking a dog.

'It's OK. She'll open up, given time,' Mac said, after Sarah had disappeared to her room again. 'Think how strange it is for her. Her whole life has been turned upside-down in the past couple of months.'

Hers isn't the only one, Natasha wanted to say. She was feeling, increasingly, like an intruder in her own home.

Conor seemed unable to believe what he was hearing. 'You and Mac are fostering a kid?' he repeated. 'Am I missing something here, Hotshot?' he had said. 'First he moves back in with you. Now you're fostering a kid together. And you can't come away with me to the cottage this weekend because you're playing happy families.'

She had stayed very calm. 'It's her first weekend and the social worker is visiting on Friday evening to make sure she's settled in OK.'

'So you're playing happy families?'

'Conor, it was impossible as things were. Having a third person in the house means Mac and I don't have to deal with each other.'

'It's all very neat, but when you have children you—'

'It's not *having* children. This is a girl with her own life, her own interests. She's hardly even there half the time.'

'So what's the point if she's hardly there? You said her being there meant you didn't have to deal with each other.'

God, she hated arguing with a lawyer. 'Don't twist my words. She asked to stay, and both Mac and I saw it as a way of making a difficult domestic situation less difficult. And a way of helping a young person.'

'How altruistic of you.'

She walked round her desk to where he was sitting and perched beside him. 'By the time we've sold the house, she'll be back home and all three of us can go our separate ways. It works for everyone.'

She reached out to take his hand, but he withdrew it, cocked his head to one side. 'Just explain one thing to me.' He leaned forward. 'How did you describe your set-up to the authorities? Two people who've barely seen each other in a year, who don't even like each other by all accounts, suddenly offering to take on a troubled soul . . .'

She took a deep breath.

'Oh. You didn't tell them, did you? They think you're still together. To all intents and purposes, you're just another married couple.' His voice was scathing.

He'll come round, Natasha told herself. She stared at her mobile phone, which showed, for the fourteenth time that day, that no one except her office had rung. Work, she told herself. Focus on your work.

**I**t had happened again. Three fresh bales of hay sat against the wall of her lockup, giving off a sweet scent. Against them rested an unopened bag of feed. Sarah had paid for none of it. She held the cold padlock, staring at the sight that had greeted her twice in the past couple of weeks, and felt an uneasy mixture of gratitude and concern.

Sarah peered out of the lockup at the brazier, into which Cowboy John was feeding manila envelopes. He had been clearing out the brick shed he called his office. She had asked him for hay, but he had told her, apologetically, that he had sold all but what he needed to Sal.

She filled a haynet, then trudged up the yard to Boo's stable, where she topped up his water buckets and cleared his bedding. She had thought staying with the Macauleys would make things easier, and to some extent they were. The house was nice. It was closer to school, and to the stables. But money was a problem. They gave her pocket money every weekend, but it still didn't cover what Boo cost.

She didn't like to think how much she owed. Even without the hay. She thought of the jar she had seen in Natasha's room. The woman couldn't have the faintest idea how many pound coins it contained. Passing the doorway, Sarah had been transfixed by it, calculating that there were probably hundreds, all mixed in with silver coins.

Sarah knew what Papa would say about girls who took money that didn't belong to them. But increasingly she found herself answering: *How else am I supposed to keep our horse until you come home?*

'Sarah.'

She jumped. Cowboy John had disappeared, and Sheba hadn't barked as she normally would. 'You gave me a fright.' She stepped back against the door to her lockup, the padlock still in her hand.

Maltese Sal stood behind her, his face indistinct in the evening gloom. 'I was passing and saw the gates open,' he said. 'Just wanted to make sure everything was OK.'

'Everything's fine,' she said. 'I was about to go home.'

'You locking up for John?'

'I've always had a set of keys,' she said. 'I help him out if he needs to go early. I . . . I don't mind carrying on when you take over.'

'When I take over?' The gold tooth glinted. 'Sweetheart, I own this place now. Have done for over a week.' He leaned against the door frame. 'But, sure, you can keep your keys. It might be useful.'

Sarah scrabbled on the floor for her schoolbag.

'Where you going?'

'Home,' she said.

'Your granddaddy's back?'

'No,' she said. 'I'm—I'm staying with someone.'

'You want a lift? I got plenty of time.' He smelled of tobacco.

'I'd better not.' She made to move past him, but he stood there. She suspected it was a game for him, making people uncomfortable.

'You got the hay OK?'

'Thank you. Sorry. I meant to say.' She reached into her pocket and pulled out the money she had counted that morning. 'This is for the last two lots.' She handed it to him, flinching as her fingers met his hand.

He held it up, scrutinising it under the light. Then he laughed. 'Sweetheart, what's this for?'

'The hay. And the feed. For two weeks.'

'This wouldn't cover two of those bales. That's good stuff in there.'

'Two pounds a bale. That's what I pay John.'

'This is way better than his. Five pounds each, those bales. I told you I'd only feed your horse the best. You owe me three times that amount.'

She stared at him. He did not appear to be joking. 'I haven't got that much,' she whispered. Sheba was whining at her legs.

'That's a problem.' He nodded, as if to himself. 'That *is* a problem. Because there's the back rental as well. According to Cowboy John's books you haven't paid for six weeks.'

'But John said he was letting us off the back rent. Because of my granddad.'

Maltese Sal lit a cigarette. 'His promise, sweetheart. Not mine. It's me you owe the money to.'

Sarah began to calculate six weeks' rent, adding it to the money he said she owed for the food. The figure made her head swim. 'I . . . can't find that sort of money, not straight away.'

'Well . . .' Sal stepped back so that she could pass. 'That's OK for now. I'm not going anywhere, Sarah. You sort it out and see me later.'

# SIX

SHE WAS COMING OUT of court when Linda came hurrying up the stone steps and thrust a piece of paper into her hand. 'You need to ring this woman,' she said. 'She says some girl called Sarah didn't turn up at school again. She said you'd know what this meant. Is she a client?'

Natasha glanced at her watch. It was a quarter to twelve. 'Did you ring Mac?'

'Mac?' said Linda. 'Your ex, Mac? Why would I ring him?'

Natasha began to search for her mobile phone. 'Don't worry. I'll explain another time.' Finding the phone, she strode down the corridor until she reached a quiet corner.

'Natasha?' Mac sounded surprised to hear from her. In the background she could hear laughter and music.

'The school rang. Sarah's not there again. Did you see her go through the school gates after you dropped her off?'

A pause. 'Now you mention it, no. She waved me off.'

'They've rung me twice. You'll have to sort this, Mac. I've got less than an hour, then I'm stuck in court all afternoon.'

'Damn. I'm in the middle of a shoot.' She could picture him thinking. 'OK. You ring the school, check she hasn't arrived, and I'll go home, make sure she's not there, and ring you back.'

Sarah wasn't at home or at school, and she wasn't at the hospital either. Mac called as Natasha paced her office, bolting a sandwich, and told her not to ring the social worker until the evening.

'What if something's happened to her? Last time it was just a lesson. This is the best part of a day. Mac—we need to ring her social worker.'

'She's fourteen. She's just kicking up her heels. She'll be back.'

Natasha couldn't share his certainty. That afternoon she struggled to keep her mind on the hearing. Something was going on with Sarah that they didn't know about and it made Natasha nervous. She felt her normal focus dissolving.

'Mrs Macauley, have you anything to add?' the judge asked now.

She wasn't on top of this. 'No, Your Honour. That's all.'

'I thought you were going to bring up the psychiatrist's report,' Ben whispered.

*Damn.* She stood up. 'Actually, with apologies, Your Honour, there is one further item I would like to draw to your attention . . .'

Mac was at the kitchen table when Natasha arrived home. She threw her case down and unwound her scarf from her neck. 'Still nothing?'

'Not since you left work, no.'

'It's getting dark. How long do you think we should leave it before we ring someone?'

'We'll give her another half an hour,' Mac said. 'That takes it to six o'clock. By then we'll have given her enough chances.'

She sat down opposite him and accepted the glass of wine he had poured for her. His relaxed air of earlier had disappeared. 'Did you manage to get through your shoot?'

He shook his head. 'I thought I should go to the school gates for chucking-out time. Just in case she turned up.' He sighed and sipped his wine. 'They let me reschedule for tomorrow.'

Their eyes met briefly. *As long as she's here by tomorrow.*

'I was useless in court,' she offered. 'Couldn't keep my mind on the job at all.' She had lost the case. Ben's expression as she left the High Court had told her she was the reason why.

'Kids, eh?' Mac said mirthlessly.

The doorbell rang and they jumped. 'I'll go,' he said, pushing himself back from the table. She sat there, listening to him open the front door. He muttered something, then his footsteps were returning down the hallway. Behind him, her face half obscured by her scarf, stood Sarah.

'Welcome back,' Mac said, turning to her. 'We weren't sure whether you'd booked into another hotel.'

Her eyes were just visible and darted between them.

'Care to tell us where you've been?' Mac's voice was light, but Natasha could detect frustration in it.

Sarah pulled down the scarf a fraction. 'Went out with a friend.'

'Not just this evening,' Mac said. 'I meant all day. When you were supposed to be at school.'

She kicked at something invisible on the floor. 'I wasn't feeling well. I went for a walk. To clear my head.'

Natasha could bear it no longer. 'For nine hours? You went for a nine-hour walk to clear your head? Do you have the slightest idea how much trouble you've caused?'

'Natasha—'

'No!' She brushed aside Mac's warning. 'I lost a case today because I was so busy worrying about where you were. The school has been on at us every hour. Mac had to reschedule an important job. The least you can do is tell us where you've been. We're legally responsible for you, Sarah. We have to make sure you get to school and that you come home again. As a matter of law. Do you understand?'

She nodded.

'So, where were you?'

There was a long, uncomfortable silence. Finally the girl shrugged.

'Do you want to end up in secure accommodation? Because this is the fourth time you've disappeared in ten days. If you do this again, and the school notifies your social worker first, instead of us, you will end up in secure accommodation. Do you know what that is?' Natasha's voice had lifted now. 'It means you'll be locked up.'

'Tash—'

'It won't be up to us, Mac. They'll just decide we're incapable of taking care of her and apply for court proceedings to put her in secure.'

The girl's eyes were wide over the scarf.

'Is that what you want?'

Sarah shook her head slowly.

'Come on,' said Mac. 'Let's calm down. Sarah, we just want you to stick to the rules, OK? We need to know where you are.'

'I'm sorry,' she said.

She didn't look sorry, Natasha thought. 'Tomorrow,' she said, 'Mac will be taking you in before registration and handing you over to your teacher. And one of us will be at the school gates when you come out. Until you prove to us that we can trust you to be where you say you are.'

Mac stood up, went to the cupboard and pulled out a bag of dried pasta. 'OK, we'll leave it there and trust that this won't happen again. Take your coat off and sit down. You must be hungry. I'll make us some food.'

But Sarah turned on her heel and walked out of the kitchen. They heard her tread heavily up the stairs and the door of her bedroom close.

'That went well.'

Mac sighed. 'Give her a chance. She's having a tough time.'

Natasha swallowed some wine and let out a long breath. 'Does that mean it isn't the time to tell you that money has been disappearing from the jar in my room?' She wasn't sure he'd heard her. 'Quite a lot. I just noticed that the level has dipped. And I remember tipping four pound coins into the top of it the other night. Yesterday they were gone.'

He carried on pouring pasta onto the scales. 'I didn't want to say anything,' he said, 'but I remember dropping a fiver out of my jeans pockets onto the coffee table the other night, and when I came down in the morning it was gone.' He went to the kitchen door and shut it silently. 'You think it's drugs?' he asked.

'I don't know. I've never suspected her of being high.'

'No . . . she doesn't seem . . .'

'It's not clothes,' she said. It was one of the things Natasha had found almost endearing. Sarah seemed uninterested in fashion. 'She doesn't have a phone, to my knowledge. And she doesn't smell of cigarettes.'

'Something's up.'

Natasha stared at her wineglass.

'Mac,' she said, 'I have to tell you something. When I first met her, she was being held for shoplifting.'

He stopped what he was doing.

'It was a packet of fish fingers. I bumped into her in a supermarket. She swore she was going to pay for it.' *I've been fooled again. I thought I was doing a good thing.* 'I'm sorry,' she said. 'I should have told you.'

He shook his head. She realised, with gratitude, that he wasn't going to make a big deal of it. 'I can't do it tomorrow,' he said, finally tipping the pasta into the boiling water. 'But give me a day or two and I'll follow her. See what she's up to. We'll get to the bottom of this.'

For two days Sarah was a model of obedience. She allowed Mac to accompany her to the classroom, albeit bristling with resentment, and was there at the school gates when he arrived to pick her up.

On day three, as he dropped her at school, he told her he didn't have time to run inside with her, and would she be OK going in by herself? He saw the brief glint in her eye, quickly suppressed, then he waved, accelerated away as if he was in a hurry and drove round the block. He pulled up by some garages, counted to twenty, then drove back onto the high street past the school. Sure enough, there was Sarah, half walking, half running up the road towards the bus-stop.

Damn it, Sarah, Mac told her silently. Why are you so determined to sabotage your own future? He watched as she leaped onto a bus, registering the number and its destination. The wrong direction for the hospital, he noted. The social worker had given him the address and he had promised to take Sarah at the weekend. So where was she headed?

He sat in his car behind the bus, no longer able to see her, but trusting he would catch sight of her when she jumped off again. He allowed two cars to cut in front of him, to make himself less conspicuous. Finally, where the glass towers of the financial district began to morph into grimy residential blocks of flats, he caught sight of her. She skipped off the bus, ran round the rear of it and leaped onto the island in the middle of the road. Mac held his breath, knowing that if she glanced to the right she would see his car. But her attention was on the traffic going the other way. Before Mac realised he was now facing the wrong way, she had run across the road and was off down a side street.

'Shit,' he said aloud. It started to rain as he accelerated towards the next roundabout, skidded round it and took the main road in the opposite direction. He soon saw the side street she had run into and turned into it, but at the end there was nothing but a row of Victorian buildings. On impulse, he turned right, driving now on cobbles, searching for a girl in school uniform. But it was as if she had disappeared into thin air.

Mac pulled into a parking space. He sat there for a moment, cursing himself. Cursing her. *What the hell am I doing? I'm chasing a schoolgirl I hardly know across London, and for what?* In a few weeks she would be gone anyway. If she wanted to wreck her life with stupid boyfriends or drugs, was that really his problem?

His phone was ringing. He picked it up from the floorwell.

'Hey, Maria,' he said.

'Don't say it, you wanted to ring me but you're trapped under large piece of furniture.' Her voice was bruised with hurt. 'You were going to ring me about lunch.'

'Sorry, sweetheart. I've got caught up. I'm not going to make it.'

'Is job?'

'Not exactly.' He leaned back in his seat. He'd have to ring Tash and tell her he'd lost her. They'd decide whether to call the social worker.

'Are you becoming homosexual?'

'Not today, no, but I'll give it some thought . . .'

He had stopped listening. A large brown horse was emerging through a pair of wire mesh gates farther up the road. It skittered sideways as it came down the cobbled road towards him, its hoofs clattering on the hard surface. He squinted as it got closer. There was no doubt about the identity of the rider.

'Maria, got to go. Ring me and we'll sort something out.' He shoved the phone into his pocket, and then, as the horse was a good twenty feet away, opened his door quietly and climbed out. Sarah's hair was tied back, her slender frame perched lightly on the huge animal.

Mac shut his door, moved swiftly to the boot and pulled out his Leica, his eyes barely leaving the girl on the horse. He locked the car, and began to walk down the road behind her. As horse and rider turned the corner, he saw they were heading for a park.

He thought for a moment, then reached for his phone and dialled the number, stepping into a doorway so that his voice did not carry. 'Is that the school office? It's the guardian of Sarah Lachapelle here. I'm ringing to say she's got a doctor's appointment this morning and won't be in. Yes, I'm sorry . . . Yes, I know I should have called earlier . . .'

**A**s they entered the park, she felt Boo's energy build beneath her. The rain would empty the place, allowing her room to work without interruption. But the horse was excited. Sarah had been forced to stay away for two days and, after his confinement, Boo's hoofs would react to that springy surface as if to an electrical charge.

*Listen to me*, she told him, with her seat, her legs, her hands. But there was something exhilarating about knowing such power was just waiting to be unleashed.

*Levade*, a little voice said, inside her head.

Papa had told her she was not to try it, that it was too ambitious a movement. *Levade* asked the horse to shift its weight onto its back legs, keeping at an angle of thirty-five degrees. It was a test of strength and balance, a transition to the greater challenges of classical dressage.

But Papa had done it. She knew Boo was capable of it.

Sarah breathed in the damp air, wiping the moisture from her face. She trotted Boo in small circles, halting, then moving forward, forcing him to concentrate on her. When she was sure he was warmed up, she began to canter, first on one rein, then on the other, trying to hear her grandfather's instruction, and within minutes it was just her and Boo locked into their paces, working until they steamed under the fine mist of rain. She brought him back to walk, and loosened the reins, allowing him to stretch out. Hard work had relaxed him, grounded him. Papa would be pleased, she thought, running her hand along his wet neck.

*Levade*. Would it really be such a sin to test him a little? Would Papa ever have to know? She took a deep breath and gathered up the reins again, urging him into a slow trot, which she gradually restricted until he was in *piaffe*, lifting his hoofs rhythmically on the spot. She straightened her back. The hind feet must come under the horse's centre of gravity, the hocks almost sinking to the ground.

She leaned back a little, her legs encouraging him, telling him that his energy must go somewhere, holding him back with the faintest pressure on her reins. She clicked her tongue, a series of instructions, and he tensed, listening to her, his ears flicking. Then she felt his rear sink beneath her, and suddenly his front end was rising in front of her and she leaned forward to help him, feeling him quiver as he tried to maintain it. They teetered there, defying gravity, and then he was down. Caught off-guard, she collapsed onto his neck and he shot forward, bucking once, twice with exuberance so that she struggled to stay on.

Sarah pushed herself upright and laughed. She felt a bubble of elation rise inside her and she clapped the horse on the neck.

'Impressive,' said a voice behind her. Sarah twisted in the saddle.

Mac's jacket was dark with moisture. 'May I?' he said, then strolled forward and stroked Boo's neck. 'He's hot,' he observed.

She couldn't speak. Her thoughts dissolved and dread flooded her.

'Have you finished? Shall we head back?' Mac gestured towards Sparepenny Lane.

She nodded, her fingers tightening on the reins. Her mind raced. She could go now. She could urge Boo on and the two of them could fly across the park to the marshes. But she had nothing. Nowhere to go.

She walked slowly back to the yard, Boo stretching his neck down, her own posture now defeated. She halted in front of the gates. Cowboy John appeared from his shed and opened them.

'Taken a shower, Circus Girl? You're drenched.' He patted the horse as he passed, then caught sight of Mac, hovering beside her. 'Can I help you, young man? You interested in some eggs? Fruit? I got some fine avocados. I can do you a tray for just three of your English pounds.'

'Avocados?' said Mac. 'Sounds good.'

Sarah led Boo to his stable. She removed the saddle and bridle, wiped off the raindrops, and put them carefully into her lockup, then began to muck out. She could see Cowboy John talking to Mac. Eventually, as Sarah filled Boo's bucket with clean water, the two men strolled up to the stable. It was raining even harder now.

'You done there, Circus Girl?'

She nodded, standing close by the horse.

'I never seen you for two days. You been having trouble getting here? Old Boo was threatening to bust out again this morning.'

She glanced at Mac. 'Something like that,' she said.

'You seen your grandpa?'

She shook her head. She thought, to her horror, that she might cry.

'We're going over there now,' said Mac.

Her head shot up.

'You want to?' he asked.

'You know this girl?' Cowboy John stepped back theatrically, then gestured towards Mac's tray of avocados. 'You know Sarah? Man, you should have said something. I'd never have sold you that crap if I'd known you was a friend of *Sarah's*.'

**H**er clothes were still wet when she climbed into the car.

'You need something dry to wear?' he said. 'There's a spare jumper in the back. Put it on over your uniform.'

She did as he asked. He pulled out into the road and began to drive. When they stopped at traffic lights, he said, 'So that's what it's all about. The absences. The disappearing.' He didn't mention the money.

She gave the smallest nod.

He indicated and turned left. 'Well . . . you're full of surprises.' He felt reassured. She was just a kid with a pony. If a slightly oversized one.

'What was the whole jumping-up-in-the-air thing?'

She muttered something he couldn't hear. '*Levade*,' she repeated, louder. 'A movement from *haute école*. It's like dressage.'

'Dressage? Is that the thing where they go round in circles?'

She smiled reluctantly. 'Something like that.'

'I don't know anything about horses, but he looks amazing. How'd you end up with a horse like that?'

She observed him, as if calculating how much information he could be trusted with. 'Papa bought him from France. He's a Selle Français. They use them in the French riding academy Papa trained at.' She paused. 'Papa knows everything there is to know about riding.'

'Everything there is to know . . .' Mac murmured. 'Have you been doing that for long?'

'Long as I can remember,' she said. She had brought the sleeves of his jumper over her hands and brought her knees up under it. 'We were meant to be going back. To see them. In France. Before he got ill.'

'Well'—Mac glanced in his rearview mirror—'a lot of people postpone their holidays when someone's ill. I'm sure if you explain what happened the travel agent will let you go when your grandfather's better.' He watched her bite her nails. 'I'll call them later, if you like.'

She smiled at him again, cautiously. Twice in one day, he thought. Perhaps we can do some good here, after all.

Mac knew little about medical matters, but it was clear to him that, whatever Sarah chose to believe, Mr Lachapelle was not going on holiday—or coming home—anytime soon. He lay propped up by pillows, his skin the liverish tone of the properly ill, and did not wake when they entered his room. Finally, when Sarah took his hand, he opened his eyes. Mac stood awkwardly near the door, feeling like an intruder.

'Papa,' Sarah said softly.

The old man's eyes were immediately fixed on her, a veil lifting as he registered who was before him. He smiled lopsidedly.

'Sorry I couldn't come the last two days. It was difficult.'

The old man squeezed her hand. She saw his gaze slide over to Mac. 'This is Mac. He's one of the people looking after me.'

Mac felt himself being scrutinised.

'He's . . . very kind, Papa. Him and his wife,' she said.

'Pleased to meet you, Mr Lachapelle.' Mac stepped forward and took the old man's hand. '*Enchanté*.'

Another small smile. A broader one from Sarah. 'You never said you knew French.'

'I'm not sure your grandfather will agree that I do,' he said. He took the chair on the other side of the bed. 'I've been watching your granddaughter ride. She's amazingly talented.'

The old man's eyes slid back to Sarah.

'I rode out this morning.'

'Good,' he said slowly, his voice creaking like an underused hinge.

Sarah's smile this time was instantaneous. 'Good!' she repeated. 'He tried really hard, Papa. It was raining and yet he managed to stay focused. He was listening, really listening.' Sarah was riding now, her back straight, her hands in front of her and the old man was drinking in everything she said. 'You would have been pleased. Really.'

'I never saw anything like it,' Mac interjected. 'When I saw him doing all that leaping around on his back legs, it took my breath away.'

There was a sudden silence; then the old man turned his eyes to his granddaughter. He was no longer smiling. Sarah, he saw, had blushed to the roots of her hair. The old man kept his eyes on her.

'*Levade*,' she whispered, her voice heavy with guilt. 'Sorry.' The old man moved his head from side to side. 'He was just so full of energy. And I needed to give him something new to keep his attention . . .'

The more she protested, Mac saw, the more the old man shook his head in mute fury. Mac felt mortified. Then he lifted his camera, still hanging round his neck, and held it up. 'Mr Lachapelle? I took some pictures of Sarah trotting and stuff. I was wondering, would you like to see?' He flicked through the digital images. Finally alighting on one that was unlikely to raise the old man's ire, he enlarged it.

Sarah placed her grandfather's glasses on his face. The old man studied the picture, then nodded, apparently satisfied, and Mac felt a slow breath easing out of his own chest. He handed the camera to Sarah. 'I have to make a couple of calls,' he said. 'I'll leave you two alone. You can sort through the images like this . . . and enlarge them with this button. I'll meet you downstairs in half an hour.' He lifted the old man's hand. 'Mr Lachapelle, it was a pleasure.'

'Captain,' said Sarah. 'Everyone calls him Captain.'

'Captain,' said Mac. 'I hope to see you again soon.'

Natasha took off her glasses and looked at him. 'A *horse*?' She handed back the prints. 'What the hell are we supposed to do with a horse?'

'We don't have to do anything. She owns it. She looks after it. I haven't confronted her about the money, but I think we can assume that's where it's going.'

'But how does a kid like that end up with a horse?'

'She keeps it under a railway arch,' Mac continued. His brain was still spinning with the images of the inner-city yard. 'Turns out it's something to do with the granddad. He's some kind of horse master. She does dressage stuff with it. Leaping around in the air.'

'Oh God.' Natasha looked into the distance. 'What if it injures her? The social worker didn't say anything about a horse.'

'The social worker doesn't know about it. Sarah thinks if the authorities find out about the horse it will be taken away from her. She made me promise,' Mac continued, 'that we wouldn't say anything.'

Natasha was incredulous. 'We can't promise that!'

'Well, I did. And she's promised she won't miss any more school.'

He had dropped Sarah at school at lunch time, having hastily scribbled a note for her. She had seemed unable to believe he was colluding with her. 'This is the only time,' he had warned, aware that he had already been too soft. 'We'll sort it out when you get home. OK?'

Natasha sat down heavily.

'Look, this is good news, Tash,' Mac said. 'It means she's not on drugs. It's not some dodgy bloke. She's just a teenage girl obsessed with horses. We can handle that.'

That evening, when Natasha got home, there was a message from the estate agent on her answering machine. Mr and Mrs Freeman, the last couple to view the house, had put in an offer. It was, the agent advised, a 'sensible' offer, only a couple of thousand below their asking price. The buyers were chain-free and in a position to move quickly. 'I'd recommend your acceptance, given the state of the market,' he said.

An hour later, Mac staggered through the front door carrying a large quantity of photographic equipment. He dropped it in the hallway.

'We've had an offer on the house,' Natasha said. 'Two thousand less than we were asking, but the buyers are chain-free. The agents think we should go ahead.'

He held her eye a fraction longer than was necessary. 'Sounds good to me. If you're happy.'

'We'll have to tell Sarah,' Natasha told him, 'in case . . . in case things move quickly and we have to find her somewhere else to stay.'

'Let's cross that bridge when we come to it.' Mac turned away.

'I'll ring them tomorrow morning, then,' she said, and walked into the kitchen.

After supper, Sarah disappeared for a bath, then emerged to say that if it was OK by them she'd go to bed. She was clutching a battered paperback under her arm.

'It's only nine thirty!' Mac exclaimed. His feet were resting on the log basket. 'What's the book?'

Sarah pulled it out from under her arm. It was covered in red paper, held together with sticky tape. 'It's my granddad's,' she said, and then, when they looked expectant, 'It's Xenophon.'

'You read classics?' Natasha couldn't hide her surprise.

'It's about horsemanship. Papa used to read it.'

'The Greeks can teach you about riding?'

She handed it to Mac. 'Nothing very much changes,' she said. 'You know the white horses of Vienna?'

Even Natasha knew of the gleaming white stallions.

'Their riders still work from the Treatise of La Guérinière and that was written in the 1730s. The airs, the movements, that is, haven't changed since they were performed in front of the Sun King.'

'A lot of the principles of law date back that far,' said Natasha. 'I'm impressed that you're interested in classical texts.'

But Sarah was shaking her head. 'It's just about teaching Boo. While Papa isn't here.'

'Tell me something, Sarah.' Mac handed the book back to her.

'What's this fine-tuning stuff all about? Making sure your feet are in exactly the right place and that your horse moves his legs exactly this way or that. I watched you in the park, going over the same things, again and again. It looks lovely, but I don't get what you're pursuing.'

She looked at him steadily. 'Why do you keep taking pictures?'

He grinned, enjoying this. 'Because there's always a better one to take.'

She shrugged. 'And I could always do it better. *We* could always do it better. It's not just technical—it's about two minds, two hearts . . . When we get it right together, there's just no feeling like it.' Her hands closed unconsciously on imaginary reins. 'A horse can do beautiful things, incredible things, if you can work out how to ask him properly. It's about trying to unlock his ability and then getting him to do it because *he* wants to. Because doing it makes him the best he can be.'

There was a short silence. She was a little awkward now, as if she had revealed too much.

'Anyway,' she said, 'I'm going upstairs.' She made as if to leave the room, then turned back. 'Are you selling your house?' she said, from the doorway. 'I heard you talking earlier.'

Natasha looked at Mac, who blew out a long breath. 'Yes,' he said. 'Yes, we are.'

'Where are you moving to?'

'Well, I'm probably moving to somewhere else in Islington, and I'm not sure where Natasha's going, but you needn't worry. It isn't going to happen till long after you're back with your grandfather.'

She dawdled in the doorway. 'You're not together any more, are you?' It was an observation more than a question.

'Nope,' said Mac. 'But we're good friends, and we're happy to stay together until everything's sorted out. Aren't we, Tash?'

'Yes.' It came out as a croak. Sarah was watching her and she felt that the girl could see through her.

'I'll sort out my own breakfast,' Sarah said, tucking the book under her arm. 'I'd like to go to the yard really early, if that's OK.' And then she was gone.

**T**he first night Mac and Natasha had spent in the house they had slept on a mattress on a dusty floor. She remembered it now, lying in his arms beneath the bare windows, a distant plane crossing the night sky. The strange feeling of sleeping in a house that they owned but which was not yet theirs.

She had lain there, relishing one small, perfect moment, a convergence of happiness and possibility, as if this was simply the starting point for something as endless as that sky. And she had turned to gaze at him, this beautiful, besotted man, running her fingers lightly over his sleeping face, dropping kisses on his skin until he woke and, with a sleepy murmur of surprise and pleasure, pulled her against him.

Natasha poured herself a large glass of wine. She stared at the television, unsure what she was watching. She realised, with horror, that her eyes were pricking with tears. She turned a little away from Mac, blinking furiously, and took a long swig from her glass.

'Hey,' said Mac, softly.

She couldn't turn round. She'd never been able to weep discreetly. By now her nose would be glowing like a beacon. She heard him get up and walk across the room to close the door. Then he sat down and turned off the television. She cursed him silently.

'You OK?'

'Fine,' she said briskly.

'You don't look it.'

'Well, I am.' She lifted her glass again.

'Is it . . . the house?'

'All those years of planning and decorating and imagining,' she said. 'It's just hard, knowing it's all going to disappear. I was thinking about what it was like when we first got here.'

'I've still got the pictures,' he admitted. 'A print of you knocking through the back wall with your sledgehammer.'

'It just seems weird, the idea of someone else being here.' She was aware that the wine was prompting her to say too much. 'It feels . . . like leaving a piece of yourself behind.'

He met her eyes and she had to look away.

'I don't think,' she said, almost to herself, 'that I could put that much work in somewhere else.'

Upstairs she heard Sarah opening and closing a drawer.

'I'm sorry, Tash.' He hesitated, then reached across and took her hand. She stared at their fingers, intertwined. The strange, yet familiar feel of his skin on hers knocked her breath from her chest.

She pulled away, her cheeks colouring. 'This is why I don't drink very often,' she said, and stood up. 'It's been a long day. And it's just a house, right?'

Mac's face revealed nothing.

'Sure,' he said. 'It's just a house.'

# SEVEN

SARAH SAT on the top deck of the bus and counted out the money in her pocket for the fourth time. Enough for two weeks' rent, five bales of hay and one bag of feed—enough to fill her lockup for another fortnight. Not nearly enough to stave off Maltese Sal. It was a quarter past three. He rarely got to the yard before four thirty. She would leave what she had with Cowboy John, or under the office door with a note.

The previous evening Mac had called her into the kitchen (Natasha was at work) and had handed her an envelope. 'John told me how much you need,' he had said, handing it over. 'We'll pay for Boo's keep for now, but if we find you've missed any school, or not been where you should be, we'll send him somewhere else. Is that a fair deal?'

She had nodded, feeling the notes through the thin white envelope. It was all she could do not to snatch it. When she looked up, he was watching her. 'So . . . do you think this might stop some of the loose change in the house going missing?'

She had blushed then. 'I guess so,' she mumbled.

She couldn't tell him about all the money she owed Sal, not now that he had virtually accused her of stealing.

She tried to look on the bright side. Things weren't so bad. She had Boo and she was in a routine of sorts. She got up early and did the stables before school. Life was as it should be. Or as close as it could get to it, without Papa being home.

'So, how's it going?' Ruth Taylor accepted the mug of tea, leaning back a little in the plush beige sofa. It was not the kind of living room she tended to see in her everyday work, she thought, noting the artwork on the walls. She pulled Sarah Lachapelle's file from her bag.

The couple looked at each other. A definite unspoken something passed between them before the man spoke. 'Fine,' he said. 'All fine.'

'She's settled in OK? It's been—what—four weeks now?'

'Four weeks three days,' said the woman. Mrs Macauley had arrived just after Ruth and was perching on her chair, her briefcase by her feet.

'And school? Any problems with attendance?'

Another exchange of a glance. 'We had a few problems at the start,' Mr Macauley said, 'but I think we all understand each other a little better now. She's in good health,' he continued. 'Eats well. Does her homework. She has . . . her own interests.' He turned to his wife. 'Don't know what else to say, really.'

'Sarah's doing fine,' she said crisply.

'Don't worry. I'm not here to judge you, or mark you on your parenting skills.' She smiled at them. 'I've already spoken to Sarah, who says she's happy here. But I just thought that, given her recent history, it would be a good idea for me to stop by to check how it was going.' She glanced down at her file. 'I'm told her grandfather's not recovering quite as fast as they'd like. Are you happy with Sarah continuing to stay? I know we originally thought this would only be a couple of weeks . . .'

'There is one possible complication,' Mrs Macauley said. 'We'll be selling this house fairly soon. In fact, we've accepted an offer on it.'

'And will there be room for Sarah in your new home?'

They didn't look at each other this time. The man answered. 'I'm not sure yet. We're trying to work it out. It's just we haven't yet decided where we're—ah—going, have we, Tash? But she's definitely OK here for the next few weeks.'

A few weeks. Anything could happen in a few weeks. Ruth relaxed a little. 'Well, let's hope she's back with her grandfather before long.'

**T**here was a message under her lockup door. She picked up the piece of paper and opened it, noting an unfamiliar scrawl.

*Howdy, Circus Girl,*

*Sorry I couldn't tell you in person but I got to go back to the States. My sister Arlene got sick, and being as how there's no one else in our family (fool woman done frightened off three husbands), I got to see she's OK. Maltese Sal has keys and he's gonna feed my animals.*

*Tell the Captain I'll be back in a week or two. Gonna bring him some Jimmy Beam too, if I can get it past those Nazi nurses.*

*CJ*

She folded the note neatly and put it into her pocket, feeling oddly shaken by the prospect of Cowboy John's absence. The few times he had disappeared to see his sister in America, Papa had always been left in charge.

She put her coat on the peg and changed into Papa's old overcoat. Knowing, instinctively, that activity would ease her anxiety, she checked Sheba's water bowl, mucked out Boo, replaced his hay and water, then set about the horses, straightening skewed rugs, making sure the stable doors were firmly shut. Finally she returned to the lockup to change.

It was as she was about to close her padlock that she remembered the money in the envelope. She reached into her pocket—and jumped as a hand landed softly on the back of her neck. She spun round.

'What's the matter? You think I'm a crazy man come to get you?' Maltese Sal was highly amused, the gold tooth in his mouth just visible in the gloom of the lockup as he wagged a finger in front of her.

She shivered, her hand creeping to her neck.

'You leaving me a love letter, Circus Girl?' He took the envelope from her, his other hand holding a lit cigarette. The scent of aftershave and tobacco smoke now overshadowed the subtle sweet scents of hay and forage. 'You know you can always tell me in person.'

'Money,' she said, her voice cracking as she spoke. 'It's your money.'

'Ah . . .' He took it from her, his fingers brushing against hers.

'I've got to go,' she said, picking up her bag, but he held up his palm. He peeled open the envelope and peered inside, frowning. 'And this is?'

'My rent money. Two weeks. And for the hay and feed.'

Outside it was raining harder. Sheba slunk in behind them.

'And the arrears?'

She swallowed. 'I haven't got the money. Not yet. But I always pay my debts. Papa always pays his debts. John knows that.'

'But John ain't here. Your papa ain't here. And this is my yard now.' Sal took another step towards her. 'Your papa's real sick, Sarah, from what John says. So how are you going to pay me what you owe me?'

She tried to keep her eyes down. She had heard dark rumours about Maltese Sal. He had spent time in prison, had bad friends.

'I told you—'

'You told me nothing. We got to work out some way of you returning my investment.'

Don't you understand, she wanted to say to him, that that's all I want too? This debt hung over her, twisted her gut into a knot of anxiety whenever she totted it up. 'I could muck out for you,' she blurted.

'I got boys to do that, Sarah.'

He glanced behind him, then turned back to her and took another step forward so that she was backed against her door. He smiled, a long, slow smile, then, as she tried to smile back, he placed a hand on her right breast, running his thumb across the nipple. This was done so lightly that it took her two seconds to register what he was doing.

'Doesn't have to be about money, Sarah,' he said softly. Then he removed his hand before she had a chance to lift her own in protest.

'You're growing up fast, sweetheart,' he said, pocketing the envelope and shaking his fingers, as if he'd just touched something hot. 'Always a way through for a pretty girl. You just let Sal know.'

'I'm out this evening,' Natasha told him.

'OK. I promised I'd take Sarah to the hospital after school anyway. But I'll be out tomorrow, if that's OK?' He didn't volunteer where.

'OK.' Natasha stepped forward, but he didn't move out of the way. 'I've got a meeting, Mac, and I'm late already,' she said. He was wearing the jeans she had once loved, she noticed, a deep indigo, soft and buttery.

'We haven't really talked about this, Tash, but what do we do if the old boy doesn't get better? He's not good, you know. I can't see him bouncing back quickly.'

Natasha took a deep breath. 'Then she has to become someone else's problem.'

'Someone else's *problem*?'

'OK. Someone else's responsibility.'

'But what do we do about the horse?'

'Mac, the day we leave here we stop being a family. We stop being able to offer her a home, horse or not.'

She rifled through her bag to hide the colour that had begun to rise in her cheeks.

'You don't seem to like her.'

'Of course I like her. What am I supposed to do? Don't make me out to be the bad guy here, Mac.'

'That's not what I'm saying.'

'Then what *are* you saying? That we should be bonding over make-up tips? Going out to supper together? I've tried, OK? Have you ever considered the possibility that she just doesn't like me?'

'She's a *kid*.'

'What? So she's incapable of disliking someone?'

'No. I just mean it's an adult's job to overcome it.'

'Oh. So now you're the expert on child rearing.'

'No. Just someone with a bit of humanity.'

Natasha's cheeks were scarlet. 'It must be nice being you, Mac. Everyone loves you. And, for whatever reason, you seem to have had the same effect on Sarah. And that's great for both of you. But don't attack me for falling short, OK? I'm just doing my bloody best.'

'Tash—'

'And STOP calling me TASH.'

She pushed past him and wrenched open the front door.

The old man took the white plastic fork from Sarah with his better hand and put the slice of mango into his mouth with silent, intense satisfaction. Mac had bought a ready-prepared pack from the supermarket on the way over and Sarah was spearing each piece, then handing her grandfather the fork, allowing him the dignity of feeding himself.

Mac waited until they had finished before he pulled out the folder. 'I've got something for you, Captain,' he said. He pulled a chair to the other side of the bed and opened the folder so that the contents were visible. 'We've decided to decorate your room.'

He pulled out the first print, a black-and-white blowup of Sarah and her horse performing the stationary trot she called *piaffe* at the park. The old man peered at it, then turned towards his granddaughter.

'He did well that day,' she said. 'He was really listening to me. Really trying. Every movement . . .'

'Little act of beautiful,' he said carefully. Apparently overcome by this sudden rush of language, she crept onto the bed and slid over beside him. Her head lay against his pyjama-clad shoulder.

Mac took out another print. 'I think this one was . . .'

'Shoulder-in,' she said.

The Captain nodded his approval.

'These are all for your room,' Mac said, and reached into his pocket for the Blu-Tack. He began to stick the pictures carefully around the bed, slowly obscuring the blank, pale green walls. The old man gazed at each one in turn, as if he was drinking in every last detail.

'And I've saved the best till last.' Mac unwrapped the one he'd had framed. It was a picture of Sarah, her cheek pressed to that of her horse, bright and defined enough for the old man to make out every detail.

'Baucher,' the Captain said, staring at the picture. 'Sarah.'

'I love that one,' Mac said. 'It was just before we left the yard one morning last week. She didn't even know I was taking it.'

There was a long silence. Then the old man beckoned him closer. As Mac stooped, he took Mac's hand between his own and pressed it. His eyes were moist. '*Merci*,' he whispered huskily. '*Merci*, monsieur.'

Mac swallowed hard. 'It's nothing,' he said, forcing a casual smile.

It was only then that he noticed Sarah. She was still leaning against her grandfather, her hand wrapped tightly round his arm. Her eyes were shut and a solitary tear trickled down her cheek.

NATASHA DROVE into the Sandown estate, past the burnt-out cars and flickering streetlights. Sarah sat in silence beside her, clutching her keys. She had not spoken since they left her grandfather's ward, and

Natasha, still shocked by what she had seen, had not attempted to make her. Nothing had confirmed the magnitude, the foolhardiness of what they had taken on, more than the sight of the frail old man.

Natasha had seen Henri briefly as she'd dropped Sarah off. Then, outside in the corridor, she had quizzed a nurse as to how long he'd have to remain in hospital. The nurse wasn't hopeful that he'd be released anytime soon.

She drove to the Sandown estate car park and stopped the car. It had started to rain and a few youths were sheltering under hoodies. They watched Natasha and Sarah get out of the Volvo.

'What is it you wanted to pick up again?' Natasha walked behind Sarah up the dank stairwell.

'Just a few books,' she said, and added something else that Natasha could not hear.

They walked along the balcony, unlocked the door and closed it swiftly behind them. Inside, the flat was cold. Sarah disappeared into her bedroom, while Natasha waited in the front room. She heard the sound of drawers being opened and closed, and the zip of a holdall. Sarah would not be returning to this home, she felt sure. The thought hung heavily on her. What did Sarah think would happen to her?

'I tell you what, why don't we go out for a pizza?' Natasha said, as they climbed back into the car, brushing raindrops from their sleeves.

Sarah looked sideways at her and Natasha realised, with shame, that she was surprised by this casual invitation. She had seemed withdrawn the past few days, even by her self-contained standards.

Natasha had thought about what Mac had said. It *was* her responsibility to do something, or at least to try. 'Go on. I don't fancy cooking, and it's been a long evening. I know a nice place at the far end of the high street.' She tried to sound cheerful, relaxed. God, it would have been so nice if Sarah could show some enthusiasm, even pleasure. 'The pizzas are pretty good,' she said.

Sarah clutched her holdall on her lap. 'OK,' she said.

The restaurant was only half full, and they were shown to a table near the window. Natasha ordered garlic bread and two colas, while Sarah tucked the holdall neatly under her chair, then gazed out at the busy, darkened street. She chose a ham and pineapple pizza from the menu, then barely touched it.

'So,' Natasha said, when the silence between them became uncomfortable, 'which part of France did your grandfather come from?'

'Toulon, originally, and then he lived at Saumur. At the academy.'

Natasha persisted, 'How did he end up living here?'

'He fell in love with my grandmother. She was English. That was why he stopped riding.'

'Wow.' Natasha pictured the French countryside, the move to an estate like Sandown. 'And what did he do when he got here?'

'He worked on the railways.'

'That must have been hard for him. To leave the horses. France.'

'He loved her.'

To Natasha's ears, that had sounded almost like a rebuke. Were things really so simple? It was clear that horses were the old man's passion. How had he come to terms with what he had lost?

'How did you meet Mac?'

Natasha put her fork down on her plate. 'It was on an aeroplane.'

'Did you like him straight away?'

Natasha thought for a moment. 'Yes. He . . . he's an easy person to like.'

'Did you leave him, or did he leave you?'

Natasha took a sip of her cola. 'If you're asking me who left the house, Mac did. But we both agreed we needed a breather from each other.'

'Do you want to get back together?'

Natasha felt colour rise to her cheeks. 'It's not really an issue.'

Sarah pulled a tiny piece of crust from her pizza and placed it in her mouth. She chewed, swallowed, then said, 'My nana once told me she hoped Papa would die first. Not because she didn't love him but because she was worried about how he'd cope without her.'

'But you and he have coped together.'

'He's not as happy as he was when she was alive. My nana could always make him laugh.' She thought about it. 'Do you think he'll be home in time for Christmas?' she asked.

Natasha lifted her napkin, stalling for time. 'It's impossible to say.'

Sarah chewed her lip, fixed her eyes on something in the street.

'I'm sorry, Sarah,' Natasha said. She wondered whether to reach out a hand. 'I know this must be very hard for you.'

'I need some money. I need to buy Papa some Christmas presents. New pyjamas and stuff,' Sarah said matter-of-factly.

Knocked off beam by the change of subject, Natasha put another piece of pizza into her mouth. 'What does he need?' she asked, when she'd swallowed. 'I can pop into the shops tomorrow on my way to work.'

'I can do it, if you give me the money. I can go out at lunch time.'

'You're not meant to leave the school grounds then.'

'This is because I took the change from your bottle, isn't it? I'm sorry, OK? It was when I couldn't tell you about Boo. I'll pay it back.'

'That's really not necessary.'

'Then let me buy some things for Papa. I know what he likes.' Her voice rose. 'I wouldn't ask unless I really had to.'

Natasha wiped her mouth with the napkin. 'Then let's go together on Saturday morning. We'll get whatever you think he needs and I'll drop you at the stables afterwards.'

Sarah's eyes betrayed her feelings about this idea.

Why did she want to go by herself? Natasha wondered. Was it that the money was for something else? Sarah was staring out of the window, as unknowable and unreachable as she had been at the start.

'Do you want some ice cream?'

Sarah shook her head. She didn't even look at her.

'I'll settle the bill,' Natasha said wearily, 'and then we'd better go. I didn't tell Mac we were going out.'

She didn't trust her. Sarah cursed herself for having taken the money from Natasha's change jar. If she'd left it alone, she could have helped herself to some now when it really mattered.

She placed her foot on her holdall, reassuring herself that it was still there. Social Services had taken Papa's pension and savings books, to ensure the rent got paid, but they hadn't known about his Premium Bonds. If she could cash them in, and avoid Maltese Sal for a bit longer, she might still be able to pay him off.

She needed that money. She thought of the other things she had picked up: an old glass ornament, which she had wrapped in a jumper, and which she thought she might be able to sell to the man in the house-clearance shop. Her CDs, which someone might buy at school.

'Goodness,' Natasha said. 'It's a quarter past ten. I had no idea it was so late.' She pulled out her wallet to pay the bill. She put a card into the hand-held machine and chatted to the waiter as she punched in the number.

2-3-4-0.

Easy to remember.

Sarah closed her eyes, wincing at what Papa would say if he knew her thoughts. Nothing could excuse stealing, he would tell her. But as she walked back to the car with Natasha, those four digits beat a rhythmic tattoo, imprinting themselves on a dark corner of her mind.

He had promised to drop her home, and now asked her to wait on the steps for two minutes while he ran in and picked up his car keys. Sarah's light was on, he noted. Natasha's car was absent. She had said she might be working late, but he was surprised that she had left Sarah alone for so long. As he stood on the step, fumbling for his door key, Maria was suddenly behind him. She pressed against him. 'Let's go in.'

'No, sweetheart.'

'You bring me here at weekends, why not now?'

He glanced down the road. 'Because my ex will be back soon and it's not fair.'

She pulled away from him. 'It's not fair on me. Why you letting your life be dictated by this miserable woman? She has boyfriend, yes?'

'Yes.'

'She has sex with him?'

'I don't know,' he muttered uncomfortably. 'I guess so.'

'Of course she does.' She laid a hand on his chest. 'How you know she not with him now? Come. You sneak me into your room. We have quickie and then I go.' She wrapped her arms round his waist, fed her hands into his back pockets, pulling him to her.

He glanced at his watch. He couldn't guarantee that Sarah would be asleep. 'Tell you what, let's go to yours.'

'My two cousins are staying at my flat. And my uncle Luca.' Her voice dropped to a husky murmur. 'Mac . . . I like your house.' She twirled her fingers in his hair. 'I like your room. I like your bed . . .'

Sarah would probably be asleep and Natasha was almost certainly at Conor's, he rationalised, as he propelled Maria, giggling, through the door.

'The lights are on. Mac must be home already,' Natasha said. Her mouth had compressed into a thin line, Sarah saw. She pulled her key from the ignition. 'Do you need a hand with that bag?'

As if she were a child. 'No,' said Sarah. 'Thank you.' She couldn't let go of the holdall.

'You'll have to get the bus in tomorrow,' Natasha continued, as she locked the car behind them. 'Mac texted me earlier to say he's got some job on early, and I have to be in a meeting. OK?'

'Yes.'

'And we'll make sure your grandfather gets some nice new things.' She opened the front door and turned to face Sarah as she closed it behind them. 'It's not a matter of trust, Sarah. Really. If I didn't trust you I wouldn't have you in my home. I'll get my paperwork done on Saturday morning and I'll pick you up from the stables in the after-noon. We could go to Selfridges, if you like. How does that sound?'

Sarah shrugged. She could tell Natasha was exasperated.

'Look, it's late. You'd better go up. We'll talk again in the morning.'

They turned when they heard clattering in the kitchen. Natasha headed towards the door. 'Mac? I was just telling Sarah about—'

She stopped dead as a tall, blonde woman, dressed only in a man's T-shirt and knickers, stepped into the hallway, carrying two glasses of wine. She had the kind of hair you see in shampoo adverts and endless, lightly tanned legs. 'You must be Natasha.' She smiled, balanced the glasses clumsily in one hand, and held out the other. 'I am Maria.' The smile was wide but not friendly. Sarah stood behind Natasha, fascinated, as the hand dangled, outstretched, in the air.

Natasha seemed to have lost the ability to speak.

'Mac has told me so much about you,' the tall woman said, taking back her hand with no apparent offence. 'I was going to make tea, but you don't have any soya milk, do you? Dairy is so bad for the skin.' Her eyes lingered on Natasha's complexion a moment too long. 'Do excuse me. I must get back upstairs.' She moved past Natasha, her braless breasts buoyant under the T-shirt.

Sarah saw that Natasha was quite pale. She took a tentative step forward. 'Do you want me to make a cup of tea?'

Natasha forced her face into a smile. 'That's . . . very sweet. But no thank you.' She raised a hand to her cheek. 'You know . . . I think I might . . .'

They heard a door open and laughter, then Mac was scrambling down the stairs. He was wearing jeans and his top half was bare. 'Tash.' He halted halfway down. 'I'm sorry. I thought you were . . . Sarah was . . .'

Natasha stared at him. 'Classy, Mac,' she said, in a small voice. Then she turned on her heel, opened the door and walked out of the house.

Sarah lay in her bed, her knees pulled up to her chest and her arms wrapped round them. The goosedown duvet rested lightly on her curled form, creating a soft nest, a cocoon she pretended she need never leave. She stared at the wall, concentrating on her breathing. If you didn't think about it, your breath just travelled in and out of your body regardless. Didn't matter what you did, running, riding, sleeping; it just went in and out, doing its job, keeping you alive.

There was no avoiding him now. He would be there on Friday and at the weekend. He would not be fobbed off with what she had scraped together. Sarah hugged her knees tighter, a shudder escaping her.

Two miles away, Natasha woke to the sound of her neighbour's bath running and mused sleepily on the selfishness of people who thought it acceptable to turn their television up to full volume. Why did anyone need to listen to the television while they were in the bath?

A news break. Half past six. She could even make out the time through the paper-thin walls. She pushed herself upright, felt the first warning shots of a weighty headache and, for a moment, struggled to work out where she was: an unfamiliar bed cover; a patterned beige carpet; an empty bottle of red wine . . . the previous night flooded back to her and she collapsed on the hotel pillows, closing her eyes again.

The way that woman had looked at her—as if she was an irrelevance. The laughter in her eyes that hinted at secrets exposed . . . How could Mac have done that? Then again, why would he not?

So many images: Mac, when they had been together, surrounded by women who seemed to regard her as something less than an obstacle. The look of him: a man who turned women's heads, always one step higher than her on the ladder of human attraction, and the women knew it. At first it hadn't mattered, when he had shone the full beam of that charm only on her, when she had felt adored, needed, wanted. And then, with each miscarriage, her confidence in her own femininity had shrunk. She would find herself silently assessing other women's fertility, comparing herself unfavourably. She had begun to feel old, dried up inside. And there he stood, charming them, perhaps already planning some new relationship with a younger, more beautiful partner. One who was fecund and ripe and would give him children.

Natasha got heavily out of bed, walked into the bathroom and turned on the taps. Then she went into the bedroom and turned on the television. Very loudly.

Normally the faint creaking of a teenage girl making her way downstairs would not have roused him. But Mac had been awake for hours.

The previous evening Maria had left shortly before eleven, a good half an hour after Natasha had driven off. There had been little point in him following Natasha: he had had no idea where she was going or what he would say to her if he found her.

Maria had snorted scornfully when he came back upstairs, sat heavily on the bed and declined the wineglass she held out to him.

'I think you'd better go,' he had said.

'Why you care anyway?' she'd exclaimed, pulling on her jeans. 'You getting divorced in weeks. You told me this.'

He hadn't been able to answer her. Because he didn't want to hurt Natasha's feelings? Because when he had first moved back in he had thought that once they had made their way past the trauma of divorce, this funny, sarcastic, brilliant woman might still be in his life? Or because her pale face and the reproach behind the glittering fury in her eyes would haunt him through the small hours?

He rose, splashed his face with cold water, pulled on his jeans and padded downstairs. Sarah was in the kitchen, making a sandwich.

'You off to the stables?' He glanced at the clock. 'You'll be cutting it fine. I'd give you a lift but I've got—'

'I don't need a lift,' she interrupted.

'You want an apple for Boo?' He reached into the fruit bowl and threw one at her, expecting her hand to shoot out and catch it, but she stepped aside, letting it thump onto the limestone floor.

He picked it up and studied the stiff back. 'Are you angry with me?'

'Not my business,' she said, packing the sandwiches into her bag.

Mac picked up the kettle and filled it. 'I'm sorry about last night.'

'I don't think it's me you should say sorry to.' She was pulling on her coat.

'I didn't know she was coming back,' he said.

'Whatever.' She shrugged. 'Like I said. It's not my business.'

He made himself a coffee, astonished at how bad a fourteen-year-old girl could make a grown man feel.

'Can I have some money?' She was standing behind him.

'Sure,' he said, glad to do something, anything, that might lift the atmosphere of opprobrium. 'How much do you need?'

'Fifty?' she ventured.

He put a hand in his pocket. 'Here,' he said, holding out a silver coin.

'Fifty pence?'

'You wanted fifty pounds? Very funny. You can have a tenner. Treat yourself. Go for a burger with your mates later.'

She didn't seem as pleased as he had hoped she might. But it would be better if he didn't have to worry about what he was going to do for supper this evening and if Sarah was safely out of the way.

**N**atasha sat opposite Michael Harrington, QC. They had met at his office to discuss the Persey divorce case, which was about to begin. 'You look tired, Natasha,' he said, and called for his pupil. 'I hope the details of this brief aren't keeping you awake?'

'Not at all.'

'I think we should have a meeting with Mrs Persey tomorrow morning. I see we're also awaiting statements from the forensic accountants. Can you bring them with you?'

He was staring at her, and she wasn't sure how long she had been peering down at the papers.

'Natasha? Are you OK? Can you be there?'

She glanced at her diary. 'I'll make time.'

'Good. Right. That's probably it for today.' He stood, and she gathered her things together. 'No, no. I didn't mean you to go immediately. Do you have a few minutes? Time for a quick drink?'

'Tea will do me,' she said, and sat down again. 'Thank you.'

'Good.'

His pupil had stuck her head round the door.

'Beth, can you make us two cups of tea, please? Sugar? No sugar in either. Thank you.' When she had left, he turned back to Natasha. 'Actually, I've been meaning to talk to you for a while. We've been attempting to restructure things here, change the balance of our chambers. I've been watching your career with interest, Natasha. If a vacancy were to arise here, might you be interested?'

Natasha was taken aback. Harrington Levinson was a modern, progressive chambers with a fearsome reputation. Now Michael Harrington, the founder, was actively seeking her out. 'I'm very flattered,' she said. His pupil came in with the tea. They waited until she had closed the door behind her. 'I should tell you that there is a possibility I'll be made a partner at my current firm.'

'I'm not sure that's your best move. You know that many solicitor advocates are now choosing to move into full-time advocacy?' he said. 'The steppingstones are in place. And we would be happy to have you as a probationary tenant. You could be at the bar in less than two years.'

She tried to digest what he was saying, its implications. She would leave the day-to-day chaos of her solicitor's job behind, and adopt the more distant stance of a barrister. 'Michael, this is a big move,' she said, thinking of Conor. 'I'll need to consider it carefully.'

He scribbled on a piece of paper and handed it to her. 'My numbers. Don't try to reach me through the clerks, but do speak to me about any questions you may have about our set-up.'

Natasha put her cup and saucer on the desk. 'I will ring you, Michael. Thank you. I'll consider your offer very carefully.'

Jessica Arnold had had twenty-three boyfriends: fourteen from her year, four from the year above, and the rest out of school, from the Sandown and surrounding estates. Her current boyfriends were older men, who waited outside the school gates in low, souped-up cars that roared off down the road, pulsing with loud music, the instant she climbed in. She had slept with most of them.

If Jessica was at one end of the spectrum of year ten's sexual activity, Sarah was lurking at the other. She never spoke to boys, let alone kissed them. It wasn't that Sarah was ugly, she was just not interested in them.

The boys she knew would not want to hear about Boo and come to the yard with her. They would shout and worry the horses, and smoke near the straw. They wouldn't understand her life.

She had never told Papa, but sometimes she pictured herself at Le Cadre Noir. She would be the finest rider they had ever seen. There would be a handsome young captain in his black uniform with the gold epaulettes. He would be a brilliant horseman, and would understand everything she wanted. It was a chaste, horse-driven romance.

But she had only seven pounds fifteen pence from the sale of her CDs and ornaments, Mac's ten pounds and a Premium Bond certificate that would take at least three weeks to redeem, and only then with her grandfather's signature. That knowledge gap looked as if it would close sooner than she had thought.

'I need to talk to you.'

'So talk.' Maltese Sal was packing away his grooming brushes.

She nodded across the yard to where his men were standing. 'Not with them here.'

'What do you want, Circus Girl?'

She lowered her voice, twisted the strap of her schoolbag round her left wrist. 'I wanted to know,' she said, quietly, 'how much . . . how much money you would let me off . . . if . . .'

He nodded a little, as if confirming something to himself, then looked at her and turned on his heel. He walked over to his men, who were standing around the brazier, the cold air clouding their breath.

She went to Boo's stable and let herself in, fiddling with his rug, laying her head against his warm skin to glean some comfort from it. His great head swung round and she stroked his face.

She could see Sal through the doorway. He saluted, shouted something in Maltese as the men disappeared through the gates. Then as the last car pulled away, he wedged them shut, pulling the heavy chain through in a loop. And then he was walking up to Boo's stable, a cigarette held lightly between thumb and finger.

'So,' she said, trying to sound tough, when he stood at the door. She tried to mimic the girls from Sandown. Hard. Nonchalant. As if nothing could hurt them. 'How would this work?'

He took a deep drag of his cigarette, then walked into the stable and shut the door. Boo had gone back to his hay, chewing steadily behind her. Only the sodium light from outside the yard crept in now.

'Take off your top.'

He said it so casually, as if he'd asked her to lock the gates.

'What?'

'Take off your top. I want to have a look at you.' He took another drag of his cigarette, his eyes not leaving hers.

She stared at him. 'But—'

'If you don't want to sort this out . . .' He made as if to turn away, his face closing. 'You let me think I could take you seriously.'

He took his cigarette from his lips and flicked it out onto the concrete. It glowed briefly before it was extinguished by the wet. Almost before she knew what she was doing, she pulled her top over her head. She had been wearing a sweatshirt. Without its fleecy lining she felt the draught through the door penetrating with icy fingers.

He turned. She couldn't see his eyes, but she felt them on her, extracting every last bit of what he would decide was her value. It will soon be over, she told herself, forcing herself to stand straight. And then I will owe him nothing.

'And your brassiere.'

She was shivering, goose bumps rising on her arms. 'But what do you want—?' she protested. 'You haven't said—'

'You're telling me what to do now? Dictating terms?' His voice hardened. 'Take it off.'

She swallowed hard, then reached behind her, her jaw clenched to stop her teeth chattering, out of fear or cold, she wasn't sure. Without opening her eyes, she removed her bra. He took it from her now, dropped it to the ground at one side of her. She felt the cold air on her skin, her nipples tightening in protest. She heard his sharp intake of breath, the footsteps bringing him closer.

She couldn't open her eyes, couldn't breathe. This was not her, standing bare in the stable with this man's hot, dry hand now sliding across her cold skin, his warm breath near her face, his foul, alien words murmured into her ear. His sharp belt pressed painfully against her hip as he pushed her back against the chilled stone wall. The real world receded until it was just him and those words and his insistent, relentless touch that was not hers to stop. What had happened to Sarah anyway? This was no longer her life, her family, her future. She had no say in any of it. So what difference did it make to have this man now claiming possession of her, inch by kneading, hot-breathed inch?

She was absent, a nothing. It was not her, after all, whose hand he now pulled from her trembling side towards him. She heard a zipping sound, his laboured breathing growing in intensity. She felt rough denim against her fingertips, then something soft and warm, yet unyielding. Something that instinct told her she should not be touching.

And she could not help herself. She snatched back her hand and she was pushing him, hitting him, yelling at him—'*Get off! Get off me!*' as Boo flinched and jumped sideways, his hoofs crashing against the stable wall. And then, snatching up her sweatshirt and her bag, she was out of his grasp and away, out of the lockup, running for the gates. Wrenching them open, she ran towards the bright lights of the rush-hour high street, even as she pulled her sweatshirt on over her head.

'**I** wondered if you'd be here.' Conor was standing in front of her, holding a pint. 'Linda's worried about you.'

She leaned back in the booth. 'Linda is far too interested in everybody's lives. You can see for yourself—I'm fine.'

Conor's eyes travelled across the empty glasses in front of her. He slid into the booth opposite her and took a sip of his beer. 'What's going on, Natasha? You're not . . . you're not behaving rationally.'

'Ah. That will be because I'm drunk.'

'OK. I'll put you in a cab home. Come on, Hotshot.' He took her hand, but she pulled it away.

'I'm not going home.'

'Why?'

'Because I'm staying in a hotel.'

He regarded her as one might an unexploded bomb. 'You're staying in a hotel? May I ask why?'

No, she wanted to yell. No, because you bailed out of my life at the first sign of trouble. No, because you've ignored me and behaved like my happiness was none of your concern. 'It was simpler.'

She heard the question in his silence. She could just make him out on the other side of her table. Why didn't he go?

'It was easier, OK? You were right. It got too complicated at home. I made a mistake even thinking I could cope with it. Happy now?'

He said nothing. She swallowed hard and tried to concentrate on the glasses in front of her, but they kept swimming up to meet her. Finally she gave up and looked at him. His expression was sorrowful.

'Oh, Hotshot. I'm sorry.' He got up and came round to her side of the table, then sat down beside her and put his arm round her shoulders. She leaned against him a little reluctantly. 'I'm sorry,' he murmured into her hair. 'I'm a jealous fool. I never wanted . . . this.' He held her face and tilted it towards his. 'Come to mine.'

She shifted out of his embrace. 'Conor,' she said, 'I don't know. My life is a mess. I've got myself into a complete hole and I don't know how I'm going to dig my way out of it.'

'I know how.' He pushed her hair out of her eyes. 'Come to mine. To stay.' He paused. 'To live, if you like.'

She didn't move, unsure she had heard him correctly.

'Let Mac clear the whole thing up,' he continued. 'He's got you into this mess. And you can . . . come and live with me.'

'You don't have to do this.'

'I know I don't. But, believe me, I've thought of nothing else this past couple of weeks. Imagining the two of you eating dinner together, doing'—he rubbed his face—'God knows what. Don't tell me if you have, by the way, because I don't want to know. But it got me thinking. Let's just get on with it.'

'"Get on with it",' she repeated. 'You old romantic.'

He had said it. He had offered her the thing she had wanted for months, even if she hadn't been able to admit it to herself. Perhaps it was the shock of the previous evening, or the past weeks, but she didn't know how to respond.

'It's a big move, Conor. We're both . . .'

'. . . a mess. Matching messes.'

'You make it sound so inviting.'

'I mean it, Natasha.' He hesitated. 'I love you.'

She felt a sudden tenderness and reached for his hand. 'I'll come tonight,' she said. She leaned against him and closed her eyes, letting herself be enfolded. 'But let's just take things one step at a time.'

# EIGHT

FIFTEEN TIMES HE'D TRIED to call her between Monday night and this morning, and every time he had gone straight to the answering service. Her office claimed she was 'in court'. He suspected she had briefed them not to put him through.

Upstairs, Sarah was asleep. She had gone straight to her room when she came in on Monday evening, refused food and drink and didn't want to talk. She had been so evasive, avoiding eye contact, hiding in her room, that he had suspected he was still being punished. Odd, really, that she was suddenly so loyal to Natasha.

Yesterday she had pleaded illness, had spent the day locked in her room. She was peaky, a translucent pallor to her skin. She hadn't had to try very hard to persuade him to let her have the day off.

At 6.20 a.m., some thirty-six hours after Natasha had left, Mac heard a key in the front door. She shut it quietly, slipped her shoes off on the doormat and walked down the hall in her stockinged feet. She was wearing the suit she had disappeared in, but with a T-shirt underneath. Conor's T-shirt, probably, Mac thought.

They stared at each other.

'I've got a big case on,' she said. 'I've just come to change my clothes and pick up my phone charger.' She looked exhausted.

'I tried to ring you. Loads of times.'

She waved her phone. 'Dead. As I said, I need my charger.' She started up the stairs.

'Natasha, please, we really need to talk.'

'I haven't time today. I've got to be in my office within the hour.'

'But we do need to talk. Are you still angry with me? About Maria?'

She shook her head unconvincingly.

He took the stairs two at a time, pushing past her so that he stood above her, looking down. 'Oh, come on,' he said. 'It's not like you haven't got a boyfriend.'

'It's not like I ever invited him here to humiliate you,' she shot back.

'How did Maria being here humiliate you? All that happened was you met her. Look, it was a genuine mistake. I thought you were out.'

She didn't seem to want to look at him. When she finally did, her eyes were cold. She seemed oddly defeated. 'I can't do this, Mac. OK? You win. Have the house until it's sold. Have whoever you want here.'

Mac spread his arms across the stairs so that she couldn't pass him. 'Whoa, whoa. What? You're just leaving? What are we doing about Sarah? You know I can't take care of her by myself.'

'I'm going as soon as we can sort out her next placement. You know as well as I do that her grandfather isn't getting better. She needs to go to a stable family who can look after her properly.' She spoke the words as if she had rehearsed them. 'Somewhere she's not being used as some kind of buffer between two grown people who are apparently incapable of dealing with each other in an adult manner.'

'That's how you see this?'

'Are you going to tell me it was any different?' She forced her way up another step so that he had to move back.

'And the horse?'

'Believe it or not, Mac, the horse is not top of my list of priorities.'

'So you can just walk away from Sarah?'

'Don't you dare use her,' Natasha said. 'This is about you and me. This was never going to end in happy families, Mac.' Her knuckles were white where she gripped the banister. 'We should never have offered her a home when it wasn't a proper home in the first place. We've been unfair to her to pretend otherwise. Now, I really need to get changed.' She pushed past him and made her way up the rest of the stairs.

'Tash.'

She ignored him.

'*Tash*—don't end it like this.' He reached out to her. 'Come on, I made a mistake.'

She turned to him. 'How are we meant to end it, then? Did you think we were going to wave goodbye to each other fondly and sail off into the sunset? Divorce is never tidy, Mac.' She let out a long, shuddering sigh. 'And I—I can't be around you any more.'

They stood inches apart now, neither able to move. Mac knew he should walk down, but he couldn't lift his feet. He could see her hand, still clutching the banister for support she couldn't do without.

'You know what's the worst thing about all this?' He waited for the next verbal blow. 'You know what I really can't stand.'

He couldn't speak.

'It feels like it did before you went in the first place.' Her voice cracked. Then she walked heavily to her room.

Upstairs, Sarah shrank from the banister and tiptoed back into her room. Her ears rang with Natasha's words. It was all falling apart. Natasha was going and she would have to leave too. *We should never have offered her a home.* She hadn't been able to make out everything they were saying, but she had heard that much.

She sat on the floor by the bed and rammed her fists into her eyes to stop herself crying. All the previous day and last night she had felt Sal's hands on her skin, heard his disgusting words in her ears. She had scrubbed herself with Natasha's expensive creams and potions, trying to obliterate his smell and the invisible trail left by his mouth. She had shuddered at the thought of who might come across her bra, still in Boo's stable. For some reason the thought of it lying in the straw upset her more than anything else.

In the next room she could hear Natasha opening and closing drawers, the soft click of her built-in wardrobes.

She would have to tell Papa. She would miss school this morning and, after she had been to the yard, she would tell him that he *had* to come home. She would look after him, no matter what they said. It was the only way. If Sal knew Papa was back, he would leave her alone.

Sal's four-wheel drive sat outside the yard, a gleaming, squat affront, a sight to make her stomach clench and her arms cross defensively in front of her. She pulled her coat tightly round her neck, then let herself in through the wire gates.

He was at the far end of the yard, talking to Ralph and a couple of his cronies. Ralph caught sight of her and busied himself stroking one of Sal's horses. She hoped this didn't mean he hadn't fed Boo for her yesterday. She hadn't turned up, reasoning that it might be better to let Sal cool down for twenty-four hours.

Perhaps she needn't have worried; Sal didn't look up at her, although he must have heard her push back the gates. She prayed he had either failed to notice it was her or perhaps decided it would be better for them to pretend that the other evening hadn't happened.

She let herself into her lockup and swapped her school shoes for her riding boots, then fumbled with the buttons of her coat to change and be out of there before he could enter. She made up Boo's morning feed in a bucket, filled a haynet and, hoisting it over her shoulder, walked briskly to the stable, head down, determined not to meet anyone's eye.

It took her a moment to realise that Boo was not there. His stable door swung open, his straw bedding still scattered with droppings. She glanced down the yard. Why had he been moved to another stable?

She dropped the haynet and walked down, checking the others. Various heads poked out, skewbald, piebald, chestnut. No Boo. Panic rose in her chest. She half walked, half ran to where the men were standing, anxiety overriding any feelings she had about speaking to Sal. 'Where's Boo?' She tried to keep her voice calm.

'Boo who?' Sal didn't even turn round.

'Boohoo,' muttered one of his men, and laughed unpleasantly.

'Where is he? Have you moved him?'

'Is there a cat trapped somewhere? I can hear a bad noise.' Sal cupped his ear. 'Like a mewing sound.'

She walked round the men so that he was forced to look at her. 'Where is he? Where have you put him? Sal, this isn't funny.'

'Do you see me laughing?'

She grasped his coat sleeve. 'Where is my horse?' she demanded.

He shook her off. '*Your* horse?'

'Yes, my horse.'

'I sold *my* horse, if that's what you mean.' He reached into his pocket, pulled out a little leatherbound book, opened it and held out the pages for her to see. 'Eight weeks' rent, you owed me. Eight weeks. Plus hay and feed. The terms of your contract say that if you don't pay for eight weeks your horse becomes mine. You don't have a horse. I sold him to pay your bill.'

The sounds of the street outside were replaced by the ringing in her ears. The ground dipped dangerously in front of her, a deck in high seas. 'You—you had no right! What contract?'

He cocked his head to one side. 'Everyone has a copy of the terms and conditions. Yours are in your lockup. Perhaps you didn't notice them. I'm acting within my legal rights as the owner of the yard.' His eyes were the cold black of fetid, brackish water. She glanced at Ralph, who was kicking a loose cobble. It was the truth. She could see it in the discomfort on his face.

She turned back to Sal, her mind racing. 'Look,' she said, 'I'm sorry about the money. I'm sorry about everything. Just let me have him back. I'll do . . . I'll do anything.'

She didn't care now. She would do what Sal wanted. She would steal from the Macauleys. Anything.

'Do you not understand?' Sal's tone had become rough, unpleasant. 'I sold him, Sarah. Even if I was inclined to get him back, I couldn't.'

'Who? Who did you sell him to? Where is he?' She had both hands on him now, gripping him tightly.

He wrested her away from him. 'Not my problem. I suggest you meet your financial commitments next time.' He reached into his jacket. 'Oh, yes. He didn't make such a good price. Bad temperament. Like his owner.' He turned to his men, waiting for the inevitable laugh. 'Here's what you made once your debt was paid.' As she stood there, disbelieving, he peeled off five twenty-pound notes and handed them to her. 'So now we're square, Circus Girl. Find yourself another trick pony.'

She could see from the faint smiles on the men's faces that they knew what she knew: that he would never tell her to whom he had sold Boo. She had crossed him and he had exacted his revenge.

She stumbled back into the lockup, and sat down on a bale of hay. In the corner of the lockup, behind the door, a white sheet of type-written paper, with the supposed terms and conditions, glowed ominously in the dim light. He would have put it there yesterday.

She dropped her head onto her knees and hugged them, imagining her horse, eyes wide, frightened, loaded into a lorry, a million miles away already. Her teeth were chattering. She lifted her head, and through the gap in the door saw the men talking, breaking off to laugh at something. 'Boohoo,' one wailed mockingly. Ralph's gaze flickered towards the lockup, then he, too, turned away.

'Nice work,' Harrington said, as they left Court Four. 'You did a great job taking that witness apart. A light touch. We've made a good start.'

Natasha handed her papers to Ben and removed her wig. 'Tomorrow won't be so straightforward,' she said.

Conor appeared in the corridor. He winked at her, and she waited until Ben was deep in conversation with Harrington before she went to meet him. 'How'd it go?' he said, kissing her cheek.

'Oh, not bad. Harrington pretty much decimated their financial claims.'

'That's what he's paid for.' He took her arm, an unusually possessive gesture. 'You still good for this evening?'

'I can't stay,' she said. She shrugged on her coat. 'I need to talk to Sarah about her future. But a long soak in your bath and a glass of wine before I have to do it will suit me just fine.'

She couldn't see the words on the front of the bus. She had sat in the shelter for almost an hour now, staring as red buses trundled along, disgorging one load of passengers onto the pavement and swallowing the next. She felt paralysed, her eyes blurred with tears, her fingers and toes numb with cold.

'Sarah?' He said her name twice before she heard it. Ralph was standing in front of her, a cigarette in the corner of his mouth. 'You all right?'

She couldn't speak. She wondered that he would even ask.

He huddled into a corner. 'I'm sorry, right? It weren't nothing to do with me. He said you owed him a load of money. I did try, but whatever you done you wound him up something major.'

They shipped horses abroad, she had heard, crammed into lorries, deprived of food and water. A solitary tear slid down her cheek.

'Anyway.' He spat noisily on the pavement. 'If I tell you something you mustn't tell him I told you, all right?'

She looked up slowly.

'"Cos if you knew anything, he'd know it come from me, right?'

She nodded. Something was igniting inside her.

He glanced behind him. 'He's down at Stepney. Behind the car site. The pikeys have got him. Sal's going to race the grey mare against him the day after tomorrow, him and the bay trotter.'

'But Boo can't pull a sulky. He's never been driven in his life.'

Ralph looked awkward. 'He has now. Sal put him in his two-wheeler and drove him down there before breakfast.' He shrugged. 'He were quite good. Not fast, like the grey mare, but he never kicked it out.'

All that long-reining, Sarah thought absently. He would have obeyed everything Sal told him. 'Where are they racing?'

'Usual place. The flyover. Be about six thirty.'

'What can I do?' she asked. 'How can I get him back?'

'Nothing to do with me. I've said too much already.'

He made to leave, but she grabbed his wrist. 'Ralph. Please. Help me.' Her mind was racing. 'Please. I can't do this by myself,' she said.

He shook his head. 'I've got to go, mate,' he said. 'Places to be.'

'Meet me. Not near the race—nowhere Sal could see you. Meet me at the back of the furniture factory. With Boo's saddle and bridle.' She reached into her pocket, pulled out the yard keys and pressed them on him. 'Here. You can get them long before Sal's there.'

'What? You're just going to go along and tack him up, are you? Ride away? Please, mister, can I have my horsy back?'

'Just meet me, Ralph.'

'Nah. What's in it for me?'

She didn't let go of his wrist, but dropped her voice. 'A gold credit card. And the pin number. I promise you, Ralph, I can get it for you.'

He scanned her face, then removed his arm from her grip. 'You'd better not be mucking me about.'

'You have to promise me you'll be there,' she said. 'No tack, no deal.'

He glanced behind him again, then spat on his palm and held it towards her. 'Friday morning by the furniture factory. If you're not there by seven I'm outers.'

For a long time before he had become a photographer, Mac had used a strategy in life that, if it didn't presage his career, perhaps suggested some aptitude for it. When situations became uncomfortable or overly emotional, when he didn't want to have to deal with what was happening in front of him, he would turn down the sound in his mind and view the tableau from a distance, as if he were posing a picture.

He did it now, watching the two females seated in front of him, the older perched neatly on the sofa in her work suit explaining to the younger why she herself would be leaving the house tomorrow morning and would not return, and why the girl would ultimately move to another, more appropriate home.

Sarah did not shout, beg or plead, as he had dreaded. She just watched Natasha talk and nodded, asking no questions. Perhaps she had anticipated this from the moment she had arrived. Perhaps he had been fooling himself with hopes of how they could make it work.

But it was Natasha who drew his eye. Now, against the pale sofa cushions, her back straight and poised, it was as if a storm had passed over her. She's let go, he observed. Whatever I did the other night, I set her free. This thought came with unexpected pain, and he realised that he, standing back, was the most emotional of the three: only he was blinking back tears. 'I'll pay your horse's rent, Sarah,' he found himself saying, as the room became silent. 'We won't just let you fall.'

Finally Natasha rose. 'Right,' she said. 'Everyone knows what's going on. Are you two OK if I go and pack?'

Mac watched her go upstairs. Sarah fixed her gaze diplomatically on Natasha's handbag.

'You all right?' he said to her. Upstairs they could hear Natasha's heels as she went to and from the cupboards.

'Fine,' Sarah said calmly. 'Actually, I'm a bit hungry.'

He smacked the side of his head, forcing a smile. 'Supper. I knew I'd forgotten something. I'll go and make it. You coming through?'

'I'll be along in a minute,' she said.

It was as if she had guessed he needed a moment alone. Or, at least, that was what he thought at the time. Later he discovered it had been something quite different.

Sarah stood behind the parked white Transit van, a hundred yards from the intersection of the two flyovers. She had been there for the past half an hour, long enough for her toes to lose all feeling in the chilly morning and her jacket to dampen under the persistent drizzle.

She had almost lost hope, but then the first trucks had started to arrive. Now she shifted, trying to ease the weight of her rucksack on her shoulders, her eyes never straying from them as they disgorged their passengers onto the slip road. Even from here she could see Maltese Sal's men, clapping their hands in the cold, laughing and exchanging cigarettes. The side road under the flyover was filling quickly with a line of vehicles, a small crowd spilling out, the atmosphere upbeat, expectant, despite the early hour. The end of the race was here, at the beginning of her own. She reached down, placing her fingers around the reassuring edges of the plastic card in her pocket.

It was 6.35.

She had asked Ralph three times if he knew for sure, and each time he had sworn he did. But could she trust him? Could his friendship with her override his worship of Maltese Sal? Was this a trap? Ralph lived by his own rules: singular, self-serving. But she had to trust him: she had no other option.

She couldn't think what she would do if Boo didn't come; she had no back-up plan. She thought of Mac and Natasha. How soon before they would guess what she had done?

She heard a familiar voice, carrying towards her on the wind. 'Those marshes over there got more green than you boys got. Put yo' money where yo' mouth is.' Cowboy John was sauntering down the centre of the line of vans, his hand outstretched as he greeted the others.

'You come here straight from the airport? Jet lag's affected your judgment, Cowboy.'

'You fo'get worrying about my judgment. Worry about that horse's legs. I seen three-legged dogs with a better turn of speed than yo' horse.' There was laughter. 'They started yet? Sal texted me. Told me you guys were starting six thirty. I should be in bed but my system's all shook up from the time change.'

'Started back by the Old Axe. They should be along anytime now.'

It was 6.41.

Her head jolted upwards at the honk of a horn, a yelled exclamation. As if on cue there was a silencing of traffic overhead. The men jogged up the slip road for a better view. And first a small dot, then a distinct outline—there he was, trotting flat out down the flyover above them, pinned between the poles of a blue sulky, his head lifted with anxiety as a grey-haired, thick-necked man pulled hard on the reins from the seat of the sulky behind him. Maltese Sal's grey mare, a short distance away, trotted alongside as Sal leaned across to shout an insult as he passed.

She couldn't take her eyes off her horse, his feet a blur on the road as he went by her. He was wearing blinkers, which made him seem blind, vulnerable. They were off the dual carriageway on the exit slip, briefly obscured by the intersection, then coming back round in a loop towards the crowd, as the flyover traffic surged forward above them.

Sarah stepped back behind the white van as the men on the ground walked down the slip road. She watched the two horses coming along the side road, then pulling up beneath the huge concrete pillars. There were cheers, exclamations, the sound of slamming car doors. Boo wheeled, unsure whether he should be stopping, and his head was pulled back roughly, causing him almost to drop onto his haunches.

She heard Cowboy John's voice. 'What the Sam Hill is *he* doin' here?'

What if she failed? What if this all went wrong? She felt her breath rise up to her throat and stall, then leave her lungs in a long shudder. *Think. Assess.* She had spent her sleepless hours reading Xenophon's advice to cavalrymen, and a sentence floated back to her now: *To be appraised of the enemy's position in advance, and at as great a distance off as possible, cannot fail to be useful.*

She shifted her position behind the white van, her eyes fixed upon her horse. I'm here, Boo, she told him, and readied herself for action.

**M**ac heard Natasha's shower kick in, glanced at the clock and winced at its confirmation of this unearthly hour. Then the significance of the morning bumped its way into his consciousness. She was leaving.

'I'll come and sort out the house in time for the move,' she had told him, after Sarah had gone to bed the previous evening. 'And I can talk to the social worker, if you'd prefer not to do it yourself. But I won't be staying here from now on.' She had barely looked at him as she spoke.

'You don't have to do this, Tash,' he had said quietly.

But she had brushed aside his words. 'I've got a big case, Mac. Biggest of my career so far. I need to focus.' There had been no rancour, no anger. It was the Natasha he had hated: closed-off, unreachable.

He heard the doorbell, shrill and invasive. Postman? At this hour? Sighing, he pulled on a T-shirt and headed down the stairs.

Conor was on the front step. Mac took in the smart suit, the neatly shaven chin, and recognised how much he disliked the man.

'Mac,' Conor said evenly.

'Conor.' He wasn't going to make this easy. He stood, waiting.

'I've come to collect Natasha.'

To collect her. As if she was something he had loaned. Mac hesitated, then stood back to allow him into the hall. Conor walked in, turned left into the living room and sat on the sofa with the relaxed confidence borne of familiarity, then flicked open his newspaper.

Mac bit his lip. 'Excuse me if I don't stay and chat,' he said. 'I'll just tell my wife you're here.' He walked up the stairs, feeling a burning anger. The shower had stopped. He knocked on the bedroom door and waited. When there was no response, he knocked again, then opened it tentatively. 'Tash?'

He saw her reflection before he saw her. She was standing in front of the mirror, a towel wrapped round her middle, water still running in droplets over her bare shoulders from her wet hair. She flinched as he entered, and her hand shot unconsciously to her throat.

'I did knock.'

There were half-packed bags all round the room.

'Sorry. In my own world.'

'Conor's here.'

Her eyes widened. 'I wasn't expecting him.'

'Well, he's downstairs, waiting to collect you.'

'Oh,' she said. She took her dressing gown off the bed and pulled it round her. Bending, she started to towel her hair. 'Tell him . . .' she began. 'Actually, don't worry.'

He ran his hand along the rim of an open suitcase. 'So this is it,' he said. 'You just go.'

'Yup. Like you did,' she said briskly. 'Is Sarah up?'

'Haven't checked.'

'With everything that went on last night, I forgot to mention she had a form that needed signing. For some school trip.'

'I'll do it.'

She laid her suit on the bed and held first one shirt, then another against the dark blue jacket. 'What do you want to do about the social workers? Do you want me to ring them when I'm out of court?'

'No,' he said. 'I'll talk to Sarah first. Work out when would be . . .' He could not say 'best'. Nothing was going to be best for her. 'Tash . . .'

She had her back to him. 'What?'

'I hate this,' he said. 'I don't see why it all has to end this way.'

'We've had this conversation, Mac.'

'No, we haven't. We've lived here together for the best part of two months and we haven't had any real conversation at all. We haven't—'

He turned abruptly. Conor was in the doorway. 'I thought you might need a hand with your bags. Is it this lot on the bed here, Natasha?'

She was about to answer, but Mac interrupted. 'If you don't mind,' he said, stepping in front of Conor, 'I'd prefer you to wait downstairs. You're walking into my bedroom.'

'I don't think, strictly speaking—'

Mac turned on him. 'Listen, mate,' he said, hearing the barely controlled antagonism in his voice, 'I own this house, half of it. I'm asking you nicely to get out of my bedroom—our bedroom—and wait downstairs so I can finish having a conversation with the woman who, theoretically at least, still happens to be my wife. *If* that's all right with you?'

Natasha had stopped brushing her hair. She glanced between the two men, then nodded at Conor.

'I'll put the seats down in the car,' Conor said, and walked out, his car keys jangling ostentatiously in his hand.

Mac felt his heart rate gradually subside. 'Well, that's it, then.'

Her expression was unreadable. 'Yes,' she said. She began to busy herself again. 'I've got to get on, Mac. Ring me tonight when you and Sarah have worked out the time frame for everything.'

There had been two trotters in this race, Sal's mare and Boo. Boo had not been expected to win, Ralph had told her; there was heavy money against him, despite his good looks, and sure enough he had come last.

From her vantage point behind the van, she watched the jockey leap down from the sulky, grab at a rein and kick Boo hard in the haunch. The horse skittered sideways, his head arched backwards in pain. A moan of protest escaped her. Boo was dancing now, unhappy at the weight of the sulky, afraid of another thumping boot, and the man tied him roughly to the wing mirror of his truck, growling at him, his hand raised as if in threat as he walked away. She fired invisible bullets into the back of that fat head. She had never been so filled with rage.

Forcing herself to breathe, she caught sight of Cowboy John, a short distance away, in urgent conversation with Sal. He was looking at Boo, his hat dripping with rain and shaking his head. Sal shrugged and lit another cigarette as he was called back to the ring of men where the money was being counted.

She was calm now. She watched with the forensic attention of a hunter, all the while edging forward, camouflaged by the parked cars, the vast, roughcast pillars of the intersecting flyovers. She was a matter of feet from Boo now, close enough to see the sweat on his neck.

'We got to get off now,' someone was shouting, in an Irish brogue. 'Get on home. The rozzers will be up here.'

She slipped to the far side of Boo and saw the horse craning his neck to gauge who this was, trapped by his harness and his blinkers. 'Ssssh,' she told him, running a hand down his heaving flank, and watched his ears flick back and forth in recognition. She slipped the poles through the harness, her fingers nimble on the buckles.

The voices were silenced briefly, and she ducked backwards, behind the pillar, heart beating erratically. Then they lifted again, this time in argument. She peeped out, saw money being divided, disputed, slapped into palms.

She had but seconds left. It was as she wrestled with the last strap that she heard it, the exclamation she had dreaded. 'Oi! You!' The big man, the one with the neck wider than his head, was walking towards her. He was bristling with menace. 'What do you think you're doing?'

Boo danced sideways now, infected by her anxiety, and she hissed at him to stand. 'Come on,' she muttered at the buckle, as the other men glanced behind them. Then she saw John's confusion, Sal's face, his sudden, shocked recognition. 'Come on.'

The man broke into a run. The last buckle would not give. She wrenched at it, her breath coming in short audible bursts. And then, as the man was just feet away, the poles of the sulky dropped with a clang to the ground. Boo was released. Grabbing a strand of his mane, she unclipped the rope from his bit and vaulted onto his back, fear lifting her feet. 'Go!' she yelled, clamping her legs to his sides, and the horse leaped forward along the side road, as if this was the moment he had waited for, his muscles gathering beneath her.

Chaos broke out. She heard shouts, the sound of revving engines as she dropped low on his neck, her voice lifting in panic. 'Go on!' she yelled, and pointed him towards the slipway up onto the flyover, and then in three, four strides she was on top, hearing the screech of tyres, the horns as she flew across two lanes of dual carriageway.

And she was galloping high above the city, racing between the cars, barely aware of the drivers who swerved to avoid her. She could see nothing but the distant marshes ahead, hear nothing but the rushing of her blood. She knew where to go: she had rehearsed this moment for much of the night, going over and over her escape route. And there it was, already coming up to meet her. She could see the exit left off the flyover, clogged with stationary vehicles, a few hundred yards in front of her. Knew that once she reached it and headed towards the industrial estate, they would not be able to reach her.

It was then that a blue hatchback pulled onto the hard shoulder, oblivious to the galloping horse behind him. She gasped, trying to check Boo's speed, seeing that, with the car there, the queues in the two lanes, she was blocked. She glanced under her arm, and behind her she saw Sal's red four-by-four, its horn blaring as it fought its way through the cars. If she stayed on the flyover he would catch her.

She eyed the blue car. She had little choice. Forgive me, Papa, she said silently and, grabbing a handful of his mane, pushed Boo on, aiming for the vehicle's bonnet. Boo hesitated, felt the answering squeeze of her legs, heard her words of encouragement, and suddenly he was in the air, his huge muscular back stretching beneath her as he leaped over the car. And she was Xenophon, hearing the sounds of battle below her, trusting to the courage of the animal beneath her. The world stilled, and then, with a grunt of impact, they were down, him stumbling on the slippery surface, and she half falling from his neck, grabbing frantically at reins, mane, anything, to stay on.

He was galloping along the road, his legs a pumping blur and, with a roar of effort, she reached up with her left arm, grabbed at the harness and hauled herself back across him. And they were away, finally swerving off down the side street that led to the canal, as the sound of the blocked traffic, the disbelieving horns, gradually faded behind them.

'**W**ho's your first witness?'

Natasha was queuing in a coffee shop with Conor. 'The child psychologist. One of ours. We're going to frighten the husband with the suggestion that we might be able to back up the abuse allegations, while Harrington and the solicitor work on Mrs P behind the scenes, trying to get her to agree to access in return for a better financial deal.'

'The wife will get what she wants,' Conor said bitterly, 'and a perfectly good father will get his name slung through the mud. I never thought you'd play dirty.'

She nudged him. 'It's the only way I'll be able to keep the child with its mother. Come on, Conor, you'd do exactly the same if you were me.'

She couldn't afford to get any of this wrong. It was vital not only to win the case but to use it as a showcase for Michael Harrington. His offer hung in her consciousness. She had not mentioned it to Conor.

He touched her foot with his. 'I haven't got much on this morning so after I've dropped you I'll take your stuff home for you.'

He had surprised her. 'Thanks, Conor.'

'No problem. As I said, I've nothing much on for an hour or so.'

'I meant for having me to stay.'

He looked at her a little strangely. 'You're not a guest. Are you telling me this is just a stopgap?'

'Don't be silly. But I just don't know if I should go straight—'

'—from the frying pan into the fire.'

'I didn't say that. But you did make the point that we were both a mess, as you so delightfully put it.'

'*Matching messes.* Counsel, please get your facts straight.'

Natasha realised she was at the head of the queue for coffee. 'Oh, sorry. Decaf skinny latte, please.'

'And I'll have a double-shot *macchiato*,' said Conor.

'Let me get this case out of the way, Conor. I can't think about anything else right now.'

She waited for him to say something, and when he didn't, she reached into her bag. 'I'll get these,' she said, determinedly cheerful. 'Least I can do, seeing as you missed breakfast for me. Do you fancy a muffin?'

Then she looked into her purse.

**S**he couldn't see him. She skidded into the yard of the furniture factory and round the corner to where the delivery vans shielded the car park from public view, her breath coming in short bursts, the rain running down her face. She slid off. Boo was sweating and shaken and she had to pull on the reins to get him to walk forward behind her.

'Ralph?' she called. Around her the blank windows of the office block looked down with disinterest. The shutters of the furniture factory were still down. There would be no one at work for another half an hour. She stepped forward. 'Ralph?'

Nothing.

She wiped the rain from her face, her confidence waning, the adrenaline of the past half-hour seeping away. She had been naive to think he would come. In fact, he might have told Sal where she was due to meet him. She forced down rising panic, tried to think strategically. Could she do this without a saddle? Could she do it in this stupid blinkered bridle? The answer was straightforward: she had little choice. She gathered her reins in her left hand, preparing to vault onto Boo's back.

'You don't have to shout, Circus Girl.' Ralph stepped out from a doorway and sauntered towards her, pulling his hood over his head. 'Bloody hell,' he observed, looking at the horse.

'Did you bring it?' she demanded.

He held out his hand. 'Plastic first.'

'I'm hardly going to stiff you, Ralph.' She reached into her pocket, pulled out a wad of notes.

'Where's the card?'

'Couldn't get it, but here's fifty pounds.'

'Get lost. You think I'm a mug? I could sell the saddle for more than that. One fifty.'

'A hundred. That's everything I've got.'

He held out his palm. She counted the money into it. Sal's money. She was glad to get rid of it.

'Where's the saddle?'

He pointed towards the doorway, busy recounting the notes. She asked him to hold Boo while she put it on, her breathing still rapid as she drew up the girth. Then she took off the blinkered bridle, hurled it over the wall into the wasteland beyond, and put on Boo's own.

'I tell you what, girl.' Ralph stuffed the cash into his jeans pocket. 'You've got some bollocks. Sal'll be after you, you know.'

She placed her foot in the stirrup and sprang onto her horse's back. 'Listen, Ralph, I need you to do one more thing for me. Go to St Theresa's. Tell my granddad that Boo and I have gone on our holidays. He'll know where I mean. Tell him I'll ring him. Please, Ralph.'

He patted his pocket and sauntered off. 'I might,' he said, his oversized trainers loose on his twelve-year-old feet, 'but I'm a busy man . . .'

'I can't talk now, Natasha. I'm about to leave the house.' Mac dropped his photographic bag on the hall floor.

'My credit card, Mac, is it on the coffee table where I left my bag last night?'

Mac bit back his response: she had left home and could hardly expect him to go chasing around after her loose bits of handbag stuffing. He peered round the doorway. 'Nope,' he said. 'Nothing there.'

There was a brief silence. He could hear chatter in the background, the clinking of cups. 'Bugger,' she said.

He lifted an eyebrow. Natasha rarely swore. 'What's the problem?'

'Is Sarah there?'

'No. I looked in. She must have left before us.'

'She's taken my credit card.'

'What?'

'You heard me.'

He lifted his eyes to the ceiling. 'You're on her case again. You've probably put it down somewhere.'

'No, Mac. I've just opened my purse to find one of my cards missing.'

'And you're sure it's her?'

'Well, it's hardly going to be you, is it?'

'But she won't know the pin number.'

She heard a muffled conversation, then Natasha returned to the phone. 'I've got to get to the court. I can't possibly be late. Mac, can—'

'I'll pick her up from school later. I'll talk to her.'

'I don't know whether to stop it.'

'Don't stop it now. Let me talk to her first. I'm sure there'll be an explanation. Didn't you say she wanted to buy stuff for the old man?'

'Yes, she did, but that doesn't make stealing acceptable.' She hung up.

Mac pocketed his phone and was about to pick up his camera bag when he remembered Sarah's odd composure the previous evening while he had gone off to make supper. He had believed she was being diplomatic. He still believed that. He stood for a moment more, then walked slowly back upstairs and opened the door to Sarah's room.

It was impossible to enter the room of a teenage girl without feeling like some kind of seedy interloper. He wasn't sure what he was looking for; he just knew he wanted reassurance that things were as they should be. He opened the wardrobe and sighed with relief. There were her clothes, her jeans, her shoes. Her bed was neatly made. He was about to leave the room when he turned back.

The framed picture of her grandfather was gone. As was the Greek book on horsemanship she had been reading. He stared at the empty spot on the bedside table where both had stood, then walked into the bathroom. No toothbrush. No hairbrush. No soap. And hanging over the back of the radiator was her school uniform. The only set she had.

Mac ran back downstairs and snatched up the phone. 'Tash?' he said, then swore under his breath. 'Yes, I know she's in court. Can you get hold of her for me? It's urgent. Tell her . . . tell her we've got a problem.'

# NINE

IT HAD STOPPED RAINING. Sarah trotted briskly along the endless grass verges towards the Royal Docks, towards City Airport. Boo had calmed down, reassured by the familiar feel of her on his back, her voice. But Sarah's heart still thumped and her neck ached from glancing behind her.

She had headed east, out through the endless, Soviet-style estates of Newham and Beckton, crossing into the flatlands of north Woolwich, letting the shining towers of Canary Wharf recede behind her. The spaces were greater here, the grey sky unbroken by looming buildings.

She and Boo could move fast, but they were exposed. She checked for traffic, then crossed a tarmac road. When she hit the grass she began to canter again, leaping the drainage ditches. In front of her, she could see the airport. With its warehouses and blocks of cheap hotels, marooned between surging carriageways, this was not an area where one would stop unless it was necessary. She had her windcheater on, the hood up so that her face was obscured.

Boo was tiring and Sarah slowed to a walk. A grimy pub stood solitarily in a wasteland with a few tired houses nearby. Beyond them stood banks of newly built apartments close by the dull sheen of the Thames. And then, flanked by concrete buildings, the ferry terminal. She glanced behind her once more, then pointed her horse towards it.

As they stood on the quay, Sarah could see that the approaching ferry was empty. A line of benches stood forlorn and empty, their besuited occupants having departed some minutes earlier on the other side of the river, hurrying on to the Docklands Light Railway.

As the *Ernest Bevin* docked, Sarah hesitated, then led Boo down the long ramp and onto the traffic deck, positioning him well away from the cockpit. Boo gazed around him and shifted a little on the oily surface as the engines began to vibrate, but was apparently unperturbed by this strange transport. There were no lorries, no cars aboard, just her, Boo and this empty deck. She glanced behind her again, willing the ferry to move off, praying she wouldn't catch sight of Sal's pick-up truck. She knew, rationally, that there was little chance they could have followed her, but fear had embedded itself in her very bones.

The conductor, a tall, slightly stooping man with a salt-and-pepper beard, emerged from the cockpit and stood very still for a moment, as if to confirm what he was seeing, then walked slowly towards her. Sarah's grip on Boo's reins tightened, and she braced herself for an argument. But as he drew closer the man was smiling. 'That's got to be the first horse I've seen on here in thirty years,' he said. He stood still, a few feet from Boo, shaking his head. 'My dad worked on the ferry back in the thirties and forties. He can still remember when nearly all the traffic on here was horse-drawn. Lovely boy, ain't he?' The man drew his hand along Boo's neck. 'Beautiful animal. Horses up the top, men down the front there, it used to be.' He pointed. 'He all right, is he? Well behaved?'

'Yes,' Sarah muttered. 'He is.'

'What's his name?'

She hesitated. 'Baucher,' she said, and added, not quite sure why she did so, 'He's named after a famous French rider.'

'Grand name, eh?' The man rubbed Boo's forehead.

'How much?' she blurted. 'How much do we have to pay?'

'You don't need to pay nothing on here, sweetheart. Oh, no. Ain't no one paid to cross on this ferry since 1889.' He chuckled. 'About back when I started.' He walked stiffly back to his cockpit and disappeared.

The ferry vibrated, then moved off from the north side of the Thames and out into the murky, swirling water. She gazed down the desolate stretch of river at the hovering cranes, the gleaming hoods of the Thames Barrier and the blue and silver sheds of the Tate sugar refinery.

She was hungry. It occurred to her now that for the past twelve hours her stomach had felt nothing but knotted anxiety. She pulled her rucksack from her back, opened it and found a biscuit. She broke off a little and gave it to Boo, whose velvety lips pushed at her coat until she gave in and handed him more.

As the distance from the shore grew, she began to feel as if she was emerging from some great shadow. The pick-up truck was on the north shore, together with all the mess and anxiety and fear that had suffocated her for months. She found she was smiling.

'Here,' she said, granting Boo another piece of biscuit. 'Time to go.'

**B**en thrust a second note over the bench and into Natasha's hand. The first one still lay beside her papers. *Call Mac urgent*, it read. 'He's rung Linda four times,' he whispered.

Natasha glanced at the paper in her hand.

'Call him back,' she whispered, handing him her switched-off mobile phone. 'His number's in the directory. Tell him I can't talk to him until we're in recess.'

'She said he sounded frantic. Something to do with . . . Sarah going.'

Across the room, Simpson, Mr Persey's barrister, was attempting to pick apart the testimony of her expert witness.

'Tell him we'll sort out her leaving date after he's spoken to her about my card,' she whispered to Ben. 'And tell him I can't answer any more calls so there's no point in ringing me again.'

She began taking notes, trying to collect her thoughts.

Within minutes Ben was back. *Not going, gone* the note said. *Disappeared.*

*??? Where?* Natasha scribbled.

*He doesn't know. Is this someone in your family?*

Natasha's head sank into her hands.

'Mrs Macauley,' came the judge's voice, 'are you all right? Do you need to take a short recess?'

She thought quickly.

'If Your Honour would allow it. A pressing matter has come up unexpectedly that I should deal with.'

'Very well. We will adjourn for ten minutes.'

**M**ac picked up the phone before it had even had time to ring. 'She's gone,' he said. 'Cleared out. Photos, toothbrush, the lot.'

'Have you rung the school?'

'I rang in saying she was sick.'

'She's probably at the stables. Or with her grandfather.'

'I rang the hospital. He's had no visitors today. I'm on my way to the stables now.'

'She won't leave the horse, Mac,' she said confidently. 'She wouldn't leave the horse and she wouldn't go far from her grandfather.'

'I hope you're right. I don't like this.' Mac sounded jumpy.

She thought suddenly of Sarah, silent and strangely accepting, the previous evening. She'd felt something was not right. 'I've got to go back into court. Ring me when you get to the stables. She's got my card, remember? Like you said, she's probably gone to buy her grandfather some new pyjamas.'

**M**ac wrestled with the gate, trying to ignore the warning growl of the Alsatian. The cowboy was leaning against the rusting car, talking to one of the young boys.

'Ah . . . Mr . . . ah . . . John? Mac—you remember me? Sarah's friend.'

The cowboy stuck his roll-up into his mouth and shook Mac's hand. He pursed his lips. 'Oh, I remember you, all right,' he said.

'I'm looking for Sarah.'

'You and everyone else,' the old man said. 'I'm damned if I know what the hell's been going on here while I been gone.'

The boy glanced from John to Mac and back again. 'Like I said, John, I've hardly been here. I don't get involved with nothing.'

'Has she been here?' Mac said.

'I only seen her for a split second. She never even told me what was going on. It's a mess for sure.' Cowboy John shook his head mournfully.

'Hold on—you *have* seen her? Today?'

'Oh, I seen her. I seen her seven o'clock this morning. Last I seen her she was taking off over the flyover like that circus horse had wings. How she never got herself killed is between her and the Almighty.'

'She's been out riding?'

'Riding?' Cowboy John regarded him as if he was stupid. 'She's gone. She's took that horse before anyone worked out what she was doin'.'

The boy lit a cigarette, his face bent low over the flame of his lighter.

Mac went to Sarah's lockup. 'You got a key for this?'

'I don't own this place no more. I gave—'

'I got one,' the boy said. 'She gave it to me so I could feed her horse when she weren't here,' he explained.

'And you are?'

'Dean.'

'Ralph,' said Cowboy John, shoving the boy. 'His name is Ralph.'

The boy fiddled in his pocket, withdrawing a bunch of keys and pulling out one that he used on the padlock. Mac pushed open the door. The lockup was deserted. There was no saddle on the rack, no bridle, only a webbing headcollar and some brushes in a box. 'John? Are you saying you think she's taken off with the horse?'

Cowboy John raised his eyes to heaven and nudged Ralph beside him. 'Quick, ain't he?' he said. 'Yes, she's taken the darn horse, and she's left me a big ole pile of doo-doo in its place. For starters, I got to work out how to tell Le Capitaine in the hospital there I ain't got the slightest idea where his precious little girl is.'

Mac closed his eyes and let out a sigh. 'That makes two of us,' he said.

The sun was at its highest point, which, given the time of year, wasn't very high at all. It had travelled round so that it faced her, causing her to squint, and she made a few calculations, trying to work out how far she could get before dark . . . before Boo became too tired to go on.

Sarah talked to him now as they headed through the suburbs at a brisk trot, following the signs for Dartford. She could feel the spring in his paces slackening, read the hope in his ears, his steadied gait, that she might ask him to slow. Not yet, she told him silently, with a faint squeeze of her legs, a gentle urging of her seat. Not yet.

It was busier here, and the sight of a girl on a horse drew curious glances, but she kept her head down. She found a cash machine in a quiet street and dismounted, then pulled Natasha's card out of her pocket and typed in the number she knew by heart. The machine hummed and considered her request for what seemed an interminable time. Her heart began to thump, then, finally, the message flashed up on the screen: £10, £20, £50, £100, £250? How much money would she like? The figures were dizzying. She didn't want to steal, yet she knew that, once the Macauleys had worked out that she had taken it, the card would be stopped. This might be her only chance.

Sarah took a deep breath and placed her fingers on the keypad.

He was waiting outside the courtroom when Natasha emerged at midday. He had his back to her and spun round when he heard her voice. 'Any news?'

'She's taken the horse.'

He watched Natasha register this: first, a kind of blank inability to digest what he had said, then the same disbelief he himself had felt.

'What do you mean she's taken the horse?'

'I mean she's run away with the horse.'

'But where could she go with a *horse*?'

Her eyes left his face and focused behind him on Cowboy John, sauntering along the corridor, humming as he came. It had taken him a while to get up the stairs. 'I don't know why you couldn't have used a phone,' he wheezed, clamping a hand on Mac's shoulder.

Mac stepped back, propelling the old man forward. 'Natasha, this is Cowboy John. He runs the stables where Sarah keeps her horse.'

'Used to run. Hell! If I'd kept a hold of things we'd never've been in this mess.' Cowboy John took her hand briefly. 'I say we split up and start askin' around. Girl on a horse like that gotta attract attention.'

'John saw her this morning near the marshes,' Mac explained.

John touched the brim of his hat. 'She knew where she was headed.

Had a rucksack on her back, and she was hitting some speed.'

'She'd planned it. We should call the police, Tash.'

John shook his head. 'You don't want to go involvin' busybodies. She made a mess, yes, but that girl ain't done nothin' wrong.'

Mac caught Natasha's eye. Neither of them spoke. He waited, wrong-footed by her reticence; then he reminded her, 'You were the one who said we had a legal duty to report her missing.'

Natasha peered down the corridor and blinked hard. 'Look, I don't want to report her yet. She turned up last time, didn't she?' She turned back to John. 'Where might she have gone?'

'Only place that girl would ever go is to see her grandpa.'

'Then let's go to the hospital,' Mac said. 'We'll talk to the old man.'

'I can't leave this case, Mac. This is the biggest case of my career.'

His stomach constricted with anger. 'Tash, Sarah is *missing*.'

'I am well aware of that. But she's done this before. I can't just drop everything, Mac.'

'Then I'm sorry to have troubled you,' he said tightly. 'I'll ring you at Conor's when she turns up, shall I?' He turned away. Somehow nothing she had done had disappointed him as much as this.

They had rested a little way outside Sittingbourne, Sarah allowing Boo to graze the lush edges of the fields on a long rein, finally hungry enough herself to eat one of the rolls she had packed. She had ridden fast in open country, galloping down the edges of ploughed fields, following bridle paths when she could, staying on verges to protect Boo's legs. All the while she kept the motorway on her right, the distant hum of its traffic within earshot, knowing she could not get lost while it was close. Boo had been energised by the green. He had bucked several times when she first let him go down a long, flat stretch, his great head tossing with excitement, his tail lifting. She had found herself laughing, urging him on, even as she knew she should be conserving his energy.

When had he ever been free like this? When had his eyes been filled only with distant green horizons, his hoofs cushioned by soft ground? When had she been free? For a few glorious miles she allowed herself to forget what she was leaving and focus only on the sheer pleasure of being welded to this magnificent animal, sharing in his pleasure at his surroundings. They flew down the edges of the fields, leaping small hedges and ditches filled with brackish water.

She urged him to go faster, gulping, laughing, tears gathering at the corners of her eyes and streaming, horizontally, along her face. He took the bit, stretched out and ran, as horses have run since the beginning of time, for fear, for pleasure, for the glory of doing what they did. This was what Papa had meant. 'This is how you escape,' he had told her.

*This is how you escape.*

'Second visitor this afternoon. He *will* be pleased.' The nurse had just closed the door behind her as they arrived at the Captain's room. She hesitated. 'I have to tell you, we suspect he's suffered another stroke. You may find him a little hard to understand.'

Mac saw the dismay on John's face. He had already insisted on a lengthy cigarette break outside so that he could face the ordeal ahead.

'Second visitor?' Mac said. 'Has his granddaughter been in?'

'Granddaughter?' she said brightly. 'No . . . a boy. Nice kid.'

Cowboy John seemed hardly to register this. He gave a little shake of his head, as if pulling himself together, and they entered the room.

The Captain's head lolled back on the pillow, his mouth slightly open. They placed themselves on either side of him, lowering themselves carefully onto chairs so that they wouldn't wake him. John glanced at the old man, then stared at the pictures of Sarah and Boo. 'I like them pictures,' he said. 'They're good for him to see.'

They sat there for some time, neither willing to wake the old man and impart the catastrophic news that they had both failed him.

Mac broke the silence. 'We can't tell him, John,' he whispered.

'It ain't your right *not* to tell him. She's the man's closest kin. She gone missin', he got a right to help us find her.'

How would he be able to do that? Mac wanted to ask. How can this knowledge do anything other than destroy him? He rested his elbows on his knees and dropped his head.

'Hey . . . hey, Capitaine . . . How you doin', you lazy son of a gun?'

Mac looked up. Cowboy John was smiling. The Captain had moved his head towards him.

'You want anything?' John leaned forward. 'A drink of water? Somethin' stronger? I got some Jimmy Beam in my pocket.' He grinned.

The Captain blinked. He might have been signalling amusement. Or he might just have been blinking.

'Capitaine, I—I got somethin' to tell you.' He swallowed. 'I got to tell you that your Sarah has done somethin' a little crazy. She's took off with that horse of yours.'

'We didn't want to worry you,' Mac began. 'And I have to tell you she's been fine with us. Really. She's been happy—as happy as she could be without you—but this morning I went into her room and that book of yours is gone and a rucksack, and when I looked in the bathroom—'

'Mac—' John interrupted. 'Mac, shut the hell up.' He nodded towards the old man. 'He's tryin' to speak,' he said, and bent low, closer, removing his hat so that he could get his ear close to the old man's mouth. His eyes met Mac's. 'No?' he said, puzzled.

Mac leaned forward, straining to hear the breathy whisper. Then he sat up. '"I know,"' he repeated. His eyes met John's. 'He says he *knows*.'

The rain had set in around midafternoon. At first it was just a few, tentative drops, but their weight—and the fast-approaching slice of black sky that scudded towards her—warned of what they heralded. It was light one moment and then, minutes later, black, with heavy, drenching rain.

The driver swerved to a halt in front of her. She pulled Boo back, but the man stuck his head out of the window. 'You idiot! You should be wearing a reflective strip,' he yelled. 'I could have hit you both. Get onto the main road where you can bloody well be seen.'

The rain came down for an hour and it was dark by the time she reached the dual carriageway. She kept to the verge, ignoring the mind-numbing roar, picking her way past the lorries that lined up on the specially widened hard shoulder, all stationary along the last part of the fast road. She passed cabs where pulled curtains hinted at sleeping drivers; others in which small televisions cast moving shadows.

Boo had started to feel uneven, his legs struggling under the distance. And then, as they came over the brow of the hill, she saw the ferries, their windows glowing, sitting in the harbour. She felt a germ of something like excitement inside her.

Two more miles. She ran her hand down her exhausted horse's neck, pleading with him to go a little farther. 'You can do this,' she murmured. 'Just get us there. And I promise I'll never leave you again.'

'You want a what?'

She stood at the foot-passenger ticket office, her jacket dripping onto the floor of the oversized Portakabin. She had removed her hat, but the sight of a girl in boots and wet jeans still drew attention. She could feel the eyes of the other foot passengers burning into her. 'A ticket,' she said quietly. 'For a person and a horse.'

'Are you having a laugh?' The fat man looked past her at the people in the queue, searching for affirmation.

'I know you take horses. They cross the Channel all the time.' She held up Boo's passport. 'My horse even comes from France.'

'And how do you think he got here?'

'On a boat.'

'Did he row it?'

There was a smattering of laughter behind her.

'A ferry. I know they cross all the time. Look, I've got the money. And we both have passports. I just need to . . .'

He was gesturing to someone seated a short distance away behind the big sheet of glass. A colleague, in the same liveried blazer, got up and approached the window. 'You can't take a horse on with the foot passengers,' the woman said, when the man had explained.

'I know that.' Anxiety hardened Sarah's voice. 'I just want to know how I can get a passage for him.'

'He has to be on a transporter. You need to go via a specialist company. He's got to have veterinary papers. There are strict controls about how animals cross the Channel.'

'Can you tell me where I can find a company like that?'

The damp, brightly lit room was closing in on her. She had tied Boo to the white railing outside and, through the window, she could see him standing obediently, even as a small group gathered around him.

'I need to cross tonight,' she said, and her voice broke.

'There's no way you'll be doing that, not without papers.'

She felt suddenly exhausted, tears of frustration pricking her eyes. She turned wordlessly and walked to the door. Outside, she untied Boo. A transporter? Papers? She gazed across at the ferry and a great suppressed sob worked its way up through her chest.

A man approached her. He looked Boo up and down with the kind of benign assessing gaze that spoke of someone who knew horses. 'Are you on some kind of sponsored ride?' he said.

'No. Yes,' she said, wiping her eyes. 'Yes. I'm on a sponsored ride.'

'I heard what you said in there. You'll be wanting lairage,' he said. 'It's like a hotel for horses. There's a place about four miles down the road. They'll be able to sort you out. Here.' He scribbled a name on a business card and handed it to her. 'Go back to the roundabout, take the third exit and you'll find it three or four miles down.'

She stared at the card. *Willett's Farm*, he had written. 'Thank you,' she called. But he had already gone.

**N**atasha sat back in her chair, passing the silver horse from hand to hand. It had tarnished a little, and she rubbed it, watching the smudge of grey discolour her fingers.

Richard, the senior partner, was in conversation with a client. His booming voice and the ramshackle acoustics of the old building meant the sound carried up the corridor. He was laughing now, a hearty, explosive sound.

It was a quarter to four.

The files in front of her were stacked and labelled. She placed the little horse carefully on top. Sarah, in her way, was no different from Ali Ahmadi. She had seen an opportunity and taken it; the route of all children whose early years had forced them to rely only upon themselves. Although Natasha was angry, she knew she couldn't blame the girl.

It had taken her almost forty minutes to persuade Mrs Persey that Richard was the right person to take over her case.

'But I want you,' she had protested. 'You said you'd be there.'

'We instructed Michael Harrington for a reason. He's the finest, toughest advocate in this field. Believe me, Mrs Persey, my absence won't disadvantage you. With luck, I'll be back within a day or two, and in the meantime Richard is fully briefed and ready for you.'

She had been forced to offer a concession in payment, for the 'inconvenience'. It would, Richard said tersely, have to come from her own fee.

'Natasha? Is this some sort of joke?' Conor entered her room without knocking. She had half expected him.

'No, it's not,' she said, standing and ferreting in a drawer for her keys. 'Yes, I'm handing over the Persey case and, yes, everyone can manage quite well without me for a couple of days.'

'You can't just drop the bloody case. This is a huge deal, Natasha.' Conor stood at the other side of her desk, his hands resting on it. 'Mrs Persey wants *you*. You can't leave her bang in the middle of it.'

'I've already discussed it with her. I'm not down to take any more witnesses. I can leave the rest to Harrington.'

Conor shook his head. 'Where are you going?'

'I'm not sure.'

'You're not *sure*?'

Linda had walked in with a mug of tea, Ben tailing her.

'Family emergency,' Natasha said, closing her briefcase.

Conor stared at her. 'The girl. I thought you were putting her back in the care of Social Services. She was meant to be someone else's job now. Let Mac deal with it.'

Her eyes told him to be quiet. She could see Ben and Linda's curiosity. 'I can't.'

'Mac?' Linda repeated, no longer even pretending not to listen. 'Your ex, Mac? What's he got to do with anything?'

Natasha stood up and went to the window. 'Lin, Ben, can we have a minute, please?' She waited until they had gone.

'Conor, I—'

'Didn't you catch her stealing? Is a little thief worth ruining your career for? Jesus, Natasha, just a few weeks ago you were worried that that kid with the mileage problem was going to ruin your career. Now you're about to throw it away for a scumbag you're not even representing.'

She heard his words as one of those children might hear them. *Thief*, *scumbag*, writing them off. She reached for her coat.

'Look,' he said, 'I'm sorry. I didn't mean that. I'm just trying to protect you, Natasha. If you walk out on this case at this point, you're committing career suicide as far as this firm goes. It's the *Persey divorce*. You have instructed Michael Harrington. If you disappear halfway through this case, we don't just lose money, our reputation takes a massive kicking. How hard do you think it'll be for us to pick up a decent silk for the next big case if they think they're going to be left in the lurch?'

'Who needs to know? I'll explain it to Harrington. He'll understand.'

'Well, it's more than I bloody can. You're going to throw away *every-thing*'—there was a horrible emphasis on the word—'on a kid you don't even like and an ex-husband who made your life a misery. Well, good luck,' he said. His voice was icy. 'I hope it will all be worth it.'

**B**oo heard the sound before she did. He had been so tired over the last half-mile that she had almost wept with guilt at every step. He dragged each hoof, his head hanging low, begging her with every reluctant muscle to let him stop. But she had had no choice: aching, her bones deadened by tiredness, she had urged him onwards. Finally, when she had seen the sign that told her Willett's Farm was half a mile up on the right, she had dismounted and walked.

And then they had heard it, carried towards them on the blustery wind: a distant crash, a grunt and a squeal, men's voices raised, then gone as the gust briefly changed direction.

The effect on Boo was electric. His head shot up, his exhaustion forgotten, and he had stopped, his whole body tuning to this unexpected sound. He began to quiver and, as she strained to hear what he was hearing, she had to suppress a shiver. The sound, faint as it was, told of something terrible ahead.

They walked forward, Boo with the delicate, trippy gait of a creature half afraid to see what was there. Then they were in the gateway, staring at the scene in front of them. A huge HGV lorry was parked in the centre of the yard, its brightly lit rear revealed to them. A woman in a quilted jacket hovered at the edge of the ramp, her hands raised to her face, while inside two men struggled to hold on to a horse that appeared strangely buckled, its rear end forced down, its front not visible. A partition appeared to have partly collapsed across it, and the two men, shouting and gesturing to each other, were trying to untangle it.

Blood was everywhere. Boo snorted and backed away in fear.

'I can't stop the bleeding. I need another bandage, Bob.' One of the men was kneeling on the horse's neck, injecting it with something. The horse's legs thrashed convulsively.

'The vet's coming,' the woman shouted, 'but it'll take him a few minutes. He's up at Jake's.'

'We don't have a few minutes,' the older of the two men grunted.

'Can I do anything?'

The woman turned, took in Boo, Sarah's riding hat—shorthand symbols that said she might be of some use. She jerked her head towards a stable. 'Bung him in there, sweetheart, and help me lift this.'

Sarah shoved Boo into the stable and ran back to the lorry.

'There's a cabinet in the office there,' the woman barked at her. 'It's open. Find a bottle marked—ah, hell, what is it—Romifidine and a syringe and bring them out, would you?'

She flew, energised by the terrible atmosphere, the desperate banging and crashing that was still coming from the lorry. She scrabbled in the cabinet until she located a small clear bottle and a plastic-wrapped needle. As she got back, the woman's hand was thrust out for them.

'Ah, Jesus, Jackie, I think he's snapped it.' She heard a despairing Irish voice in the lorry.

'Give him the sedative anyway, Thom. If he's borderline it might just keep him still long enough. Here.' Jackie gestured to Sarah. 'Try to hold that up.'

Sarah climbed up onto the back and grabbed the bottom of the partition, which was badly buckled. She stared out at the yard, trying not to look at the horse alongside her.

Jackie was ripping at the needle's plastic covering with her teeth. She unscrewed the bottle top, thrust the point into the neck and pulled the plunger, then handed it farther back inside the lorry. Sarah jumped as a rear leg kicked towards her.

'You OK there, sweetheart?'

She nodded mutely. The two men were soaked in blood and Sarah saw that her jeans, her jacket, were already smeared with it.

'Easy, fella, easy there now.' The Irishman was soothing the horse. 'There. His eyes are closing, Jackie. I think that one's done it. But I can't get to the leg until we've got the partition out.'

Sarah glanced up as headlights swung into the yard, blinding her;

then she heard a car door slam, wet footsteps. A red-headed man was running up the ramp, his case already open. 'Ah, hell, this doesn't look too pretty. How long's he been bleeding like this?'

'Minutes. I've tourniqueted the off fore, Tim, but it took a hell of a crack when he went down. He panicked when we unloaded the year-ling, went up and somehow got his front leg over the top. When he pulled backwards he dragged the whole lot down on himself.'

'Never ceases to amaze me the trouble horses can bring on themselves,' the vet said. 'Come on, let's get this partition out so I can take a better look at him. You girls take the back end, and we'll pull him towards us and free the front.'

Sarah braced herself, sweating now, conscious of the curly-haired woman beside her who was puce with effort. At last the central partition was released. They angled it, removing it carefully from the lorry.

Jackie wiped her hands on her jeans. 'You want a cup of tea?'

The thought of hot tea was so tempting that Sarah followed Jackie into a little office and sat where she was told. The grey plastic chair was streaked immediately with the blood from her clothes.

'Rotten ruddy business,' Jackie was saying, as she filled the kettle. 'We only lose a couple a year, but it gets me every time. It's not Thom's fault. He's one of the careful ones.' She glanced behind her. 'Sugar?'

'Yes, please.' Sarah was shaking. She had caught a glimpse of the horse when the partition had gone; he had looked like Boo.

'I'll give you two. I'm having two. Bloody horse.'

A large whiteboard hung on one wall with some fourteen horses' names entered on it. Documentation, Defra guidelines and a list of emergency numbers were pinned beside it.

'Here.'

She accepted the tea from Jackie, grateful for the warmth of the hot mug in her chilled hands.

'I'll wait until they come out before I do theirs. If he's saved, they'll be a while yet.'

'Do you think he'll live?'

Jackie shook her head. 'I doubt it. Never seen a horse get itself in such a tangle. He must have bashed his leg hard to buckle the partition like that. And those thoroughbreds have such weedy legs . . .' She sat down heavily behind the desk and glanced up at the clock. Then she looked at Sarah, as if seeing her for the first time. 'You're late to be riding. Not from round here, are you?'

'I—I was told to come to you. I need a stable for the night.'

Jackie scrutinised her. 'You off somewhere?'

Sarah took a sip of her tea. She nodded. If these last months had taught her anything it was to say as little as possible.

'You look very young.'

Sarah met her eye. 'Everyone says that.' She forced a smile.

Jackie opened a big book in front of her. 'Well, we can certainly do you a stable. Looks like we'll have one spare, after all. What's your horse's name?'

'Baucher,' Sarah said.

'Passport?'

Sarah reached into her rucksack and handed it over. 'All his vaccinations are up to date,' she said.

Jackie flicked through it, scribbled a number and handed it back to her. 'We're twenty-five a night, hay and food inclusive.'

'Could we stay a couple of days? I need to sort out the next part of my journey.'

Jackie fiddled with her ball-point pen. 'Stay as long as you like, sweetheart, long as you're paying. Just leave me a contact number.'

'Can't I stay here? I thought this place was for people too.'

'We don't do humans, sweetheart. But I can give you a number if you like. Here.' She pointed at a list on the wall. 'The Crown can usually do you at short notice. Forty pound a night with an en suite. Kath'll look after you. She's quiet this time of year. I'll give her a ring.'

'Is it far?'

'About four miles up the road.'

Sarah's shoulders slumped. She was silent while she fought to get her voice under control. 'I rode here,' she said finally, her voice muffled by her collar. 'I haven't got any way of getting there.'

A muffled shot rang out.

They looked up. Jackie pulled a packet of cigarettes from a drawer in front of her, removed one with a flick of her wrist and tamped it on the desk. 'Did you just say you rode here? From where?'

Sarah's pulse was still reverberating with that shot. 'It's complicated.'

Jackie lit the cigarette, leaned back in her seat and took a deep drag. 'You in trouble?' Her voice had hardened.

'No.'

'That horse yours?'

'You saw his passport.'

The woman was staring at her.

'My name's on it. Look, he knows me. I'll make him call to me if it helps. I've had him since he was four.'

The vet was emerging from the lorry, his case closed.

'We've got a spare room at the back. Twenty-five quid and I'll throw in a bit of dinner, seeing as you got stuck in with us. Another at the table won't make much difference. But,' she leaned forward, 'I'm keeping you off the books. There's something not quite right here. I'll put you up, but I don't want to get involved.'

They were interrupted as the door opened. Bob and Thom walked in, filling the little room. The Irishman shook his head.

'Ah, shame,' Jackie muttered. 'Here, sit down, Thom. I'll do you a tea. And you, Bob. Sit next to . . .'

'Sarah,' she said. She kept her hand round her mug, fearful that if she said or did too much she might lose the chance to stay.

# TEN

DESPITE THE RAIN, she was already outside the office, pacing the pavement with small, impatient steps. As soon as she saw his car, she ran to it, briefcase and handbag thrust under her arm. He smiled as he leaned over to open the passenger door, and she climbed in, disregarding the horns sounding from the traffic behind them. 'I thought you—'

'Don't say anything,' she interrupted, jaw set, hair slick with rain. 'And as soon as we've found her, you and I don't have to deal with each other again. OK?'

Mac's smile died on his lips. He had been about to pull into the stream of traffic, but he paused. 'You know what?' Mac's patience was already at a low ebb. 'This is hard enough as it is without dealing with your crap. If you're going to be like this, I'll drop you at the house now. We'll go in separate cars.'

'Dealing with my crap? Have you any idea what I've had to drop to come and look for her? Or what this has just done to my reputation?'

'Nice to see you again.' Cowboy John thrust his head through the gap between the front seats. 'Just thought I'd remind you folks that you have an audience.'

Natasha turned to Mac, open-mouthed.

'John knows about horses,' he explained, 'and he's known Sarah since she was a kid.' When Natasha said nothing, he added, 'Are you going to sort the horse out once we find them, Tash?'

She rummaged in her handbag. 'So, where is she? Have you heard anything? I've got to be back at work as soon as possible.'

'Yeah,' Mac muttered, at last swinging the car out into the traffic. 'Because you're the only one with a real job, after all. All you've done is go on about how difficult this is for you. How it's disrupting your life. How *I* have disrupted your life. Have you considered the possibility that any of this might be down to you?'

Cowboy John sat back and tilted his hat over his face. 'Oh Lordy.'

'*Me?*'

The traffic was terrible. Mac stuck his right arm out of the window, forcing his way into another, equally sluggish queue. 'Yes. You,' he said. 'You were the one who signed up to look after her, then decided it was all too difficult. You were the one who walked out, Natasha. ' He sensed the outrage in her silence, but he didn't care. 'You think you're the only one who's been inconvenienced here? I've had to cancel jobs, and John here has better things to do.' He wrenched the wheel and whizzed up the inside lane. 'Maybe if you'd stuck around, put Sarah before your own hurt pride, we wouldn't be in this mess.'

'You're blaming *me* for this?'

'I'm just saying you played a part.'

She was shouting at him now. 'Well, who brought his girlfriend home and paraded her around in front of Sarah in her underwear?'

'I didn't parade her around!'

'She had almost nothing on. You think that was nice for Sarah to see? When we'd been playing happy families around her?'

'Oh, don't pretend *that* had anything to do with Sarah going.'

'Well, it hardly made for a harmonious atmosphere, did it?'

'I said I was sorry.' Mac thumped the steering wheel. 'I told you it wouldn't happen again. But, come on, it's not as if you didn't have your boyfriend in our house, right? In my bedroom.'

'It's not *your* bedroom.'

'What was *our* bedroom.'

'Better and better,' said John, lighting a cigarette.

'He didn't stay *once* while you were living there. So don't you—'

'Only because you had somewhere else to go.'

'Oh.' She sat back in her seat, arms folded. 'I wondered how long it would be before you brought that up.'

'Brought what up?'

'My second home. I was warned about this.' She shook her head.

He glanced at her. 'What the hell is that supposed to mean?'

'That you'd use it against me when it came to negotiating a settlement.'

'Oh, for Chrissake. You think I give a stuff about your rented cottage? I couldn't care if you had the bloody *QE2* to spend your weekends on.'

'I hate to interrupt here.' John leaned forward again, letting out a long plume of smoke. 'And, believe me, I could listen to you two for *hours*. But can you lovely people call a truce? Just till we find Sarah?'

'Fine by me.' Natasha's voice was small. She reached for the battered *A–Z*. 'Where are we headed, anyway?'

'She's going to love this.' John chuckled.

Mac kept his gaze firmly to the front. 'France,' he said, chucking her passport into her lap. 'She's headed for France.'

It took the entire clogged length of the Blackwall Tunnel to explain what had happened at the hospital. She had questioned them several times as to whether they had heard him correctly, whether the old man was even in his right mind, until Cowboy John had become irritable. 'He's sick, but he's just as sharp as you, lady,' he grumbled.

'Even if you heard right, I find it very hard to believe that even Sarah thinks she has a realistic chance of riding all the way to . . . Where is it?'

'Look at the map.' Mac gestured with a finger. 'Halfway down France.'

Natasha squinted. 'But she won't get there, will she?'

'She ain't goin' to make it past the coast. Unless that horse can swim the Channel.'

'John and I think she won't even get to Dover.'

They emerged into the darkening evening sky and Mac's heart sank when he saw that the traffic was just as dense and slow on the other side. He indicated right, pulling onto the dual carriageway. Just to add to the tension, it had begun to rain heavily, and in no time at all Mac's car was sitting in a long queue on the A2, the stream of red brake lights like the tail of some great red dragon.

Natasha remained silent, sending messages on her phone, flicking through paperwork and making notes. She had a whispered conversation with someone he suspected was Conor. When she slammed the phone shut he felt slyly gratified. He fiddled with the radio, trying to find the latest traffic report.

'I don't know why you keep doing that,' she snapped. 'It's obvious we're stuck in traffic.'

Mac let it slide. He could see that her communications had wound her up. To explain that he was listening for news of horse-related accidents would not improve matters.

'My feeling is she's got to be out of London by now,' he said, tapping his fingers on the steering wheel. 'I say we come off the A2 at the next junction, maybe follow a B road. She would probably have cut off a long time before this. If we're lucky, we might even overtake her.' He stuck a hand out of the window at someone who allowed him into the adjoining queue of traffic. 'I suggest we go as far as we think she could go and if we haven't found her by eight o'clock we ring the police.'

In the back seat, all that was visible of John was his hat. It nodded. 'Sounds like a plan,' the hat said. 'Though I still ain't too happy about the police.'

Mac glanced at Natasha. 'I've been thinking about something else. If we cancel your credit card, she won't have any money. She'll have to turn round and come back.'

Natasha considered this. 'But if we leave her with no money, she'll be at greater risk.'

Cowboy John's voice cut in. 'I don't think havin' no money's goin' to stop her. She's pretty determined.'

'It depends how much she's taken out already,' said Mac. 'But if she's allowed to keep on using it, there's no telling where she could go. We're almost facilitating her running away.'

'You absolutely sure she's taken your card?' John said. 'I tell you, I've known that girl a long time and she ain't the type to steal.'

Mac waited for Natasha to speak up, perhaps to mention fish fingers in a supermarket, money missing from their home. But she sat silently beside him, apparently deep in thought. 'Tash?'

'If she keeps using it,' she said, thinking aloud, 'it'll tell us where she's been. It has a facility you can ring up to find out the details of your last transaction.' She turned to him, and for once she didn't look as if she was accusing him of something. 'It's our best chance of tailing her without the police getting involved. And if she's booked into a hotel, well, great. We could go straight there.' She allowed herself a small smile. 'It's possible we might even find her tonight.'

Cowboy John let out a long puff of smoke. 'She ain't as silly as she looks, your missus.'

'I'm not his missus,' Natasha said briskly, and dialled again. 'Open your window, Cowboy. This car stinks.

'Dartford,' she said triumphantly, fifteen minutes later. 'She withdrew a hundred pounds at Dartford before midday. We're on the right track.'

**B**y the time they reached Canterbury, Natasha was convinced that they had gone too far. She would never have reached this point, she told the men. 'Look at the weather. I think we should turn back,' she said.

But Mac insisted they should keep going. 'Sarah left town at seven o'clock this morning,' he pointed out. 'She could have got a hell of a way by now.' He was hunched over the wheel, his eyes scanning the dark horizons.

By seven o'clock the traffic had thinned a little, the signs for Dover becoming more frequent. They had stopped four times, when hotels and B&Bs were signposted. But when Natasha asked inside each one if a girl and a horse had checked in, the receptionists, without exception, looked at her as if she was insane.

Sometime in the last half an hour they had lost confidence. Mac kept up a running mathematical equation, trying to calculate how far a girl and a horse travelling at a nominal fifteen miles an hour might get, given that they were in adverse weather conditions and without food.

'They gonna be awful wet,' John said mournfully, wiping his window with his sleeve.

'We're going to need fuel,' Mac said. 'I vote we head to Dover. If that's where she's going, it doesn't matter if we've passed her. We could drive around in the dark all night achieving nothing. Let's do as you suggested, Tash, set up somewhere with a land line. We can ring round and get ourselves something to eat while we're at it. We're all exhausted.'

'And then what?' Natasha placed Mac's phone on the dashboard.

'Well . . . pray we can find out where she's staying from your credit card, I guess. After that I have no bloody idea.'

The hotel was one of an anonymous midrange multinational chain, two squat maroon-brick blocks linked by a glass walkway. Natasha stood in the oversized reception area. Mac, in front of her, was chatting to the receptionist; Cowboy John was in an easy chair by the wall.

'OK,' said Mac, shoving his wallet back in his pocket. 'We've got one double and one twin.'

'But we need three rooms.'

'That's all they've got left. If you want to try somewhere down the road then go for it, but I'm shattered. This'll do me fine.'

In the lift, it was John who settled the matter. 'I'm goin' to have a bath and somethin' to eat,' he said, taking a key from Mac as the doors opened at the second floor. 'You guys call me when you know what we're doin' next.' He strolled out into the corridor and then she and Mac were alone, suddenly self-conscious.

The room, as with every hotel room Natasha thought she had ever slept in, was at the far end of the building. They walked down the carpeted corridor in silence. When they reached the door, she was about to speak, but Mac handed her the key. 'You hit the phones. I'm going down to the ferry terminal to make sure she's not there.'

'Aren't you going to eat?'

'I'll get something while I'm out.'

She watched his back disappear down the corridor, the unexpected stoop to his shoulders, and grasped the full weight of the responsibility he felt for Sarah.

**I**t was almost half past ten when Mac returned. She had borrowed a telephone directory from Reception, had called not just all the hotels in the Dover area but all the hotels and B&Bs within ten miles. Nobody had heard of Sarah Lachapelle or seen a girl with a horse.

Cowboy John had called from his room half an hour previously, and announced that if nothing else was going on he'd get a few hours' shut-eye. Stiff-necked and exhausted, she ordered food from Room Service and a bottle of wine. It had just arrived when she heard another knock.

Mac stood in the corridor. He said nothing as he walked past her and sat heavily on one of the twin beds. He let himself fall backwards, one arm shielding his eyes against the light of the room.

'Nothing,' he said. 'It's like they've vanished into thin air.'

Natasha poured him a glass of wine and held it out. He raised himself wearily and took it from her. 'I've been all over Dover. I've even walked the beaches in case she was down there.'

'Did you go to the ferry offices?'

'I asked the guys who load the vehicles. I figured they'd see if anyone came by. They told me that all animals were transported there on lorries. She can't get further than here, Tash. It's not possible.'

They sat in silence, drinking their wine.

'We're out of our depth,' Mac said. 'I think we should call the police.'

'You're underestimating her. She planned this, Mac. She's got my credit card. She'll be safe somewhere. Maybe she's staying on a farm. Or at a riding stables. There are a million places she could be.'

'Which is why we should call the police.'

Natasha sat at the end of the other bed and let out a growl of frustration. 'Oh Jesus, Sarah. What the hell do you think you're playing at?'

'I don't think she's playing, Tash.'

'You think she stole my card by accident?'

'I think she was desperate.'

'For what? We gave her everything she asked for. We took care of her horse. I was about to take her shopping to buy her grandfather whatever she wanted for him.' She shook her head. 'No,' she said. Fear and exhaustion made her severe. 'I think it was all too much like hard work. She didn't like our rules. She didn't like the fact that she couldn't go and see her horse when she wanted to. This is her way of repaying us.'

'Repaying us? Jesus. You've become hard.' Mac was staring at her.

It was like a blow. 'I've become hard,' she repeated slowly. 'OK, Mac. Why do you always assume that Sarah's the victim in all this?'

'Because she's fourteen? Because she's got nobody?'

An image of Ali Ahmadi rose in front of her. 'That doesn't make her an angel. She's stolen from us, taken my card. And now she's run away.'

'You've always seen the worst in her.'

'No, I just see her without your rose-tinted spectacles. Seeing her as she is doesn't stop me being concerned for her welfare.'

'Is this really about her welfare? Doesn't look too good for you, does it? The legal champion of lost children unable to look after the one girl she took on. I think that's why you don't want us to call the police.'

'How dare you?' She fought the urge to hurl the wine in his face. 'I see kids like her every day. I see them helpless and pathetic on the benches, then have to listen to them cheerfully swearing at me forty minutes later when I've got them off or found them somewhere else to live. I know that half the time they're going straight off to nick another car, or shoplift another bin bag of clothes. They're not stupid and they're not always helpless.' She took off her shoes, hurling them onto the carpet. 'Sarah is no better and no worse than any of them. And the fact that I can see that doesn't make me a bad person.'

She went into the bathroom, slammed the door, and sat on the toilet lid. She held up her hands in front of her, saw that they were trembling, then flung a bath mat and two towels at the door in an impotent expression of fury.

There was no sound from the bedroom.

The worst of it was that there was truth in what he had said. She didn't want the police involved. She didn't want to have to explain the circumstances under which she had taken Sarah in, her utter failure to look after her or even ensure her basic safety. If they could just find her, Sarah could go quietly to someone more capable.

She let out a shuddering breath. Oh, it was easy for Mac to be the nice one when it never came at any personal cost to him. It had been the story of their marriage. Natasha dropped her head into her hands and waited for her head to clear.

When she emerged, her expression composed, her mind humming with rehearsed argument, it was to a silent room. Mac was asleep on the bed, his arm still half covering his face. She walked silently to the other single bed and stared at him for a moment, this man, this almost-ex-husband, crushed by his proximity and by his dislike of her.

She did not approach her own bed, but turned off the light and then sat by the window, gazing out at the windswept car park, the distant inky blackness of the sea, still half expecting to see the shadowy figures of a girl and a horse making their way down the darkened street.

When she woke in the chair, her neck stiff, the room was illuminated by the watery blue light of daybreak and Mac was gone.

Sarah was just finishing the last of Jackie's stables and jumped at the sound of Thom's voice.

'I didn't mean to scare you,' he said, from the other side of the door.

'I—I just didn't hear you.' She spoke into her scarf, her hot breath bouncing back on her skin.

'I came to ask did you want some of the breakfast Jackie's making? She's pleased as punch that you've done all the horses for her.'

Sarah squinted into the low sun. 'I was up early. And she washed my jeans and stuff . . .'

'Ah, manners *and* a work ethic. Your parents did something right.' He grinned. He had spent the previous hour washing out the big lorry. She had been dimly aware of the high-pressure hose behind the stables, water spattering off metallic surfaces, his sporadic scrubbing.

She had woken shortly after six thirty, briefly bewildered by her surroundings. Then, almost reflexively as her memory returned, she had leaped from her bed, still in her T-shirt, and run from the house to find Boo. When he thrust his head over the stable door and whickered, her breath returned. She let herself into the stable, shivering in the morning air. He stood quietly in his borrowed rug, showing little sign of the journey he had endured the previous day. She had checked his legs, lifted his feet, then, reassured, pressed her face to his neck before returning to the house where, unable to sleep, she had dressed and gone outside again to clean out his stable.

'Yesterday . . . was tough for you to see,' Thom went on. 'I hope it didn't give you nightmares.' He had eyes that were either used to smiling or had spent too much time squinting into the sun. You would have known he was Irish even before he spoke.

She leaned on her fork, picturing the stricken horse. 'Do you think he suffered much?'

'No. They go into shock. Like humans. And then the vet put him out pretty swiftly.'

'Are you sad?'

He shrugged, seeming surprised. 'Oh . . . no. He wasn't mine. I don't own the horses. I just shift 'em around.'

'Will his owner be sad?'

'Don't take this to heart, kiddo, but probably not. He was just a failed point-to-pointer with dodgy legs. The owner sold him in a job lot to a French dealer. To be honest, when I rang this morning, he was more concerned about the insurance claim.'

Sarah dislodged some dried mud from the stable floor with the toe of her boot. 'What was his name?'

'The horse? Oh Lord, now you're asking . . .' He looked up towards the sky. 'Diablo Blue. That was it. Right. Shall I tell Jackie you'll be in soon? I've got to shoot into Dover to get the partition fixed.'

Something about Thom told her he was not a threat.

'Can I get a lift with you?' she said, putting on her coat. 'I need to get to a cashpoint.'

In theory, Thom Kenneally lived in Ireland, but he spent a good part of each week moving horses between England, Ireland and France. Not everyone could do it, he said. A lot of horses were reluctant to load, and it was not enough to have patience and a calm manner to get them on and off safely. Until the previous evening, he had only ever had one fatality in six years. But, no, it wouldn't put him off.

'The job suits me,' he said. They had left the partition with a welder, who had promised to have it back by midday. Thom would leave with his remaining cargo after lunch. 'I like the horses. Besides, my girlfriend's the independent sort. Needs her own space. Look, there's your cashpoint.'

He slowed the lorry and pulled up outside a convenience store. Sarah climbed down from the cab and ran across the road. She pulled the card out of her pocket, fed it into the machine and typed in the number, glancing behind her to see if Thom was watching, then held her breath.

Astonishingly, the machine was still obliging. She withdrew another hundred pounds and thrust it deep into her pocket, apologising silently to Papa, Mac and Natasha as she did so. It was as she was about to run back across the road that she noticed the old-fashioned phone box with a glass-paned door. Thom appeared to be reading the newspaper so she nipped inside it. It accepted the credit card and she dialled the number.

The phone rang steadily at a distance. Finally, when she was about to give up, she heard a click. 'Stroke Ward.'

'Can I speak to Mr Lachapelle?' She had to shout over the noise of a passing lorry. 'It's Sarah, his granddaughter. He's in room four.'

'Hold on.'

Sarah stood in the cubicle, gazing at the busy road. Thom, in the cab, saw where she was and nodded, as if to say she could take her time.

'Hello?' A different voice now.

'Oh. I want to speak to Mr Lachapelle. It's Sarah.'

'Hello, Sarah. It's Sister Dawson here. I'll just take the phone in. I have to tell you, though, if it's noisy at your end you might not be able to hear him too well. What time are you coming in?'

'I can't,' she said. 'I can't get to you today. Is he OK?'

There was the faintest hesitation, enough for Sarah's heart to sink.

'Well, his speech isn't so good. You'll have to speak up to make yourself clear. It's quite a bad line. I'll put you on to him.'

The sound of feet, a muffled voice. 'Mr Lachapelle, it's your granddaughter. I'm just going to put the phone to your ear. All right?'

Sarah held her breath. 'Papa?'

Nothing.

'Papa?'

A long silence. Perhaps a sound. It was hard to tell over the noise of the traffic. She clamped her hand over her other ear. The nurse cut back in. 'Sarah, he *can* hear you. It would be best if you just talked to him for now. Don't expect too much in response.'

Sarah swallowed. 'Papa?' she said again. 'It's Sarah. I . . . I can't come in today. Papa, I'm in Dover. I had to take Boo. Things got difficult for us. But I'm ringing to tell you . . .' Her voice was breaking. She screwed her eyes shut, willing herself to keep it together, not to let him hear how she was feeling in her voice. 'We're going to Saumur, me and Boo.'

She waited, trying to hear something, trying to gauge his reaction. The answering silence was painfully oppressive.

'I'm sorry, Papa,' she yelled into the receiver, 'but I couldn't tell you until we were away. I wouldn't have done this if I didn't have to.' She had begun to cry, great salty tears plopping onto the concrete slab at her feet. 'It was the only way to keep him safe. For me to be safe. Please don't be angry,' she whispered, knowing he would not hear.

Still he said nothing.

Sarah wept silently until the nurse came back on the line.

'Did you say everything you wanted to say?' she asked brightly.

Sarah wiped her nose on her sleeve. She could see him so clearly, lying there, his face a mask of anxiety, of barely compressed fury. Even confined to his bed all those miles away she could feel the chill of his disapproval. How could he understand?

'Sarah? Are you still there?'

She sniffed. 'Yes,' she said, her voice artificially high. 'Yes, I couldn't hear you. There was a lorry going past. I'm in a phone box.'

'Well, I don't know what you said but he wants me to say . . . "Good."'

A brief pause. 'What?'

'Yes. That's definitely it. He says, "Good." He's nodding at me. All right? We'll see you soon.'

When she climbed back into the lorry, she turned towards the passenger window to hide her reddened eyes. She sat, letting her hair fall across her face, waiting for the sound of the key in the ignition.

*Good.* Papa's silent word kept ringing in her ears.

Thom didn't start the engine. When, eventually, she looked at him, he was watching her.

'OK, kiddo. You want to tell me what's up?'

He wasn't buying the sponsored ride. Her voice steady now, she had told him the story, the one she had rehearsed in her head for much of the morning, eyes clear, expression neutral.

'To France,' he repeated. 'You're doing a sponsored ride to France. To raise money for stroke victims. And you don't have any papers.'

'I thought I'd get them in Dover. I was going to ask you how.'

They were seated in a roadside café. He had bought her a muffin with her cup of tea and it sat on the plate in front of her, damp and solid in its plastic wrapper.

'And you're travelling by yourself.'

'I'm very independent.'

'Evidently.'

'So will you show me how to get the right papers for Boo to travel?'

He made as if to speak, then stopped himself. Instead he stared out of the window to where cars headed in a line towards the ferry terminal. 'I have a stepdaughter who's a little like you,' he said quietly. 'When she was about your age she used to get herself into all sorts of trouble, mostly because she kept everything bottled up and thought she could sort it out. Eventually we were able to persuade her that nothing is so bad that you can't tell someone. You know that? Nothing.'

But he was wrong. Sarah knew that. If she hadn't told Natasha the truth about Papa that first evening . . .

'Sarah, are you in some kind of trouble?'

She had perfected an expression of almost total blankness. 'I told you,' she said evenly. 'I'm on a sponsored ride.'

He took a sip of his coffee.

'Jackie nearly didn't let you stay last night, you know. She's got a nose for trouble.'

'I paid her what she asked. I'm no different from anyone else.'

'Sure. Just your average teenage girl with no transport who's trying to get a horse across the water.'

'I told you. I can pay you too, if that's what you want.'

'I'm sure you can.'

'Well, then?'

She waited for him to look up from his coffee. He seemed to find it fascinating.

'You want to give me that card you used to get the money out?'

'I'll pay you cash.' She felt her stomach tighten.

'I'd rather take a credit card. Not a big deal, is it?' His eyes met hers. 'Unless, of course, your name isn't the name on the card . . .'

Sarah rose from her seat. 'You know what? I don't need you on my case just for a lift to the cashpoint. And I don't need you hassling me, OK? If you're not going to help me, just leave me alone.' With that, she was out of the door, striding across the car park to the main road.

'Hey,' he called, behind her. '*Hey.*'

When she didn't turn round, he yelled, 'You won't get papers without a vet. It'll take days, weeks even. And you need to be eighteen to sign them. I'm pretty sure you're not eighteen, Sarah. And I'm not sure how long Jackie's going to feel comfortable having you around, no matter how many stables you muck out. You need to think again.'

She stopped.

'I think, kiddo, you might want to think about going home.' His expression was kind. 'You and your horse.'

'But I *can't*. I just can't.' To her horror, tears had welled in her eyes and she blinked them away furiously. 'I haven't done anything wrong, OK? I'm not a bad person. But I can't go back.' She dropped her eyes, trying to evade Thom's gaze. 'Look, I really need to get there. I can't tell you anything else. But I have to get to France.'

Thom stared at her for a while longer, then turned away. Finally he turned back to her. 'So . . . if I don't help you, what will you do?'

'I'll find someone who will,' she said defiantly. 'I know I can get someone to help me.'

'That's what I'm worried about,' he muttered. He paused, considering. 'OK,' he said. 'I might be able to get you to France. Yes,' as she tried to interrupt, 'you and your horse. But I need you to talk. That's the deal, Sarah. I'm not helping you until you tell me what's going on.'

'**D**iablo Blue' was reluctant to walk up the ramp. He snorted, planted both front feet at its base, eyes flashing white. His arched, muscular neck tensed and his ears flicked back and forth, his legs tripping awkwardly at the unfamiliar feel of the protective padded bandages Thom had wrapped round his legs.

Thom was unfazed: he stood quietly beside him, talking to him gently when the horse refused to move, relaxing the tension on the long rope in the moments when the animal briefly stopped pulling backwards. 'When he pulls back, he feels pressure,' he explained to Sarah. 'Hey, it's OK. Don't look so worried. We'll take our time.'

Sarah did not share his ease. 'Jackie said she'd be back by one thirty.'

'Ah, we'll be gone long before then.' Thom sat on the ramp, a hand reaching up to stroke the horse's nose, his manner that of someone who had all the time in the world.

'You're too tense. In fact, you standing there isn't helping. Go and sit in the cab. It'll be quicker that way.'

His tone did not brook discussion. She climbed into the passenger seat, then reached into her pocket, feeling for the credit card. 'How much are you willing to pay for your passage?' Thom had said, and she had stepped back from him, fearful that she had read him wrongly. 'Let's go back in the café for a minute.'

She had despised him then, seeing in him just another conman, until he had taken the phone from his jacket.

'Clive? It's Thom Kenneally. About those horses.'

She had sat silently across from him at the Formica table as he explained to this unknown man—whom he knew well enough to ask after his children—that there was a problem with his lorry. 'I got to tell you, mate, I may have a few problems with the old insurance. The welders say there was a bolt gone in the partition, nothin' I could have seen but a bit of a loophole for them. Yes . . . Yes, it is, isn't it? Now. This Diablo Blue of yours, I see from the papers he wasn't in the Desert Orchid league, you know what I'm saying?' He laughed. 'He did, did he? Yes, well, I was wondering if you'd let me sort you out with a bit of cash compensation and keep it out of the books. Less hassle all round?'

When Thom finally rang off, it took the determined smile a few seconds to fade from his lips. 'OK, kiddo. You owe Mr Clive there three hundred and fifty smackers for his dead horse.'

'I don't understand . . .'

'That's the price of your horse's new papers,' he said. 'God help me for getting involved, but that's the price of your ticket.'

It had taken another ten drawn-out minutes before a dull thud of hoofs and a thump told her the ramp had finally gone up. Then there was the sound of bolts being drawn, safety catches being slid into place.

Thom climbed into the cab. 'Not so bad, was he, all things considered? The other two are great travellers. They'll help him.' He started the engine. The lorry vibrated, its huge engine growling into life. 'Did you leave Jackie the note?'

Sarah reached for her seat belt. 'And the cash. I told her I'd changed route and was going to Deal instead.'

'That's the girl. Ah, come on, kiddo. Don't look so tense. The horses get a better ride than we do. I'll bet you he'll be eating from his haynet before we've hit the end of the lane.'

She couldn't tell him that it wasn't Diablo Blue's demeanour that frightened her. It was the thought of Customs officials looking too hard at his description and working out that Diablo Blue had grown two inches in the three weeks since his travelling papers had been issued.

'You sure about this?' Thom asked. 'It's not too late to go back. I expect if I spoke to your foster-family we could work something out.'

*Good*, Papa had said. *Good*. The nurse had been certain of it.

'I just want to go. Now,' she added.

'OK.' Thom swung the huge wheel round and the lorry headed for the main road. 'It's the big *bateau* for you, me and Mr Diablo Blue, then.'

# ELEVEN

COWBOY JOHN SAT DOWN with his fourth plate of egg, bacon and fried bread and rubbed his hands. 'Not bad,' he said, tucking his napkin into his collar. 'Not bad at all for motorway food.'

Mac had another swig of his coffee. 'I don't know how anyone could eat four breakfasts,' he said, eyeing the depleted breakfast buffet.

'I paid for it,' John said. 'Might as well get my money's worth.'

Actually, *I* paid for it, Mac observed silently. But it was a relief to spend time with someone cheerful, so he said nothing. He had risen before dawn and, unable to sleep, had again walked along the deserted seafront, watching ferries come and go in the encroaching light, wondering, with a sick dread, where in the world Sarah might be.

He had returned shortly after eight o'clock, let himself into the room and found Natasha curled up on the other single bed. On the desk, even at this hour, her phone flashed with silenced messages. He considered checking them, in case Sarah had decided to call, but the thought of her waking and finding him violating her privacy stopped him. Instead he had showered, then made his way down to breakfast.

'So what's the plan today, chief?' John wiped up a pool of egg with the corner of fried bread.

'I haven't a clue.'

'Well . . . I been thinking and I'd lay money on it she's round here somewhere. The girl can't swim the darn horse to France. So, the way I see it, she'll either find somewhere to leave him and go to France on foot, in which case someone could hang out by the ticket office, or she'll stay around here while she thinks up what to do next.'

'I can't imagine her leaving the horse,' Mac said.

John grinned. 'My thoughts precisely, my man. So she's gotta get here and stay here likely as not. So let's not call the cops just yet. All we gotta do is make sure we got all the bases covered.'

Mac sank back in his chair. 'You make it sound simple.'

'Best plans usually are, and unless you got an alternative . . .'

Natasha appeared at the table. Her hair was damp and she seemed wary, as if she might be criticised for being the last one up.

'Here.' Mac pulled out a chair. 'You want some coffee?'

'I didn't mean to sleep late. You should have woken me.'

'I thought you could do with the rest.' He saw the faintest flash of something pass across her face, saw her try to hide it. How easily an innocent remark could be misconstrued when every conversation was loaded with history.

'Your phone,' she said, handing it to him. 'You left it in your room. Your girlfriend's been calling.'

'Probably about a job I'd lined up for this morning . . .' he began, but she had already left the table for the buffet.

John leaned forward. 'I been thinking something else. Sarah's old papa. He trained that horse pretty good, better than any horse I've ever seen, and I been around horses a long time. She's safe with him.'

'Safe with who?' Natasha sat down, a piece of toast clenched between her teeth.

'The horse. John thinks she's safe with him.'

Natasha put the toast on her plate. 'So it's like Champion the Wonder Horse? It'll fight off attacking snakes? Warn of approaching Injuns?'

Cowboy John tipped his hat back and glared at her. He turned point-edly towards Mac. 'I mean she can outrun things, situations she don't like. A lot of people are intimidated by horses, and people who might otherwise feel quite happy approachin' a little girl out by herself are going to leave her alone.' He swigged his coffee. 'In my eyes she's a damn sight safer on that horse than she would be without him.'

Natasha drank some juice. 'Or she could be thrown from it. Or fall under it. Or be attacked by someone who wants to steal it.'

John eyed her warily. 'Boy, you're a cheerful soul. I can see why you're a lawyer.'

A young waitress was lingering by their table, offering a top-up of coffee. Mac smiled and held up his mug. As she walked away, he caught Natasha's eye on him. It was not a friendly look.

'I think Mac would rather I'd been a waitress. He was one of those men who used to say how much he liked smart women. Until "smart" came to mean "complicated", at which point he decided he liked twenty-two-year-old waitresses and models instead.'

Mac took refuge in his coffee. 'Perhaps I just found it easier to be around people who weren't angry with me all the time.'

That got to her. He saw her colour and felt curiously ashamed.

John rose stiffly from the table. 'Well, you two lovebirds sure have reminded me why I stayed single. If you want to sort out a plan of action I'm going to brush my teeth. I'll be down and ready in five.'

They watched him saunter across the restaurant. Natasha chewed her toast. 'I'm sorry,' she said, into her plate. 'I shouldn't have—'

'Tash?'

She looked up at him.

'Can we call a truce? Just till we find her?'

'You're right,' she said. 'Like I said, I'm sorry.'

**N**atasha and Cowboy John sat on a bench outside the ticket office, their heads tucked low into their jackets in an attempt to shield themselves from the wind. They had spent the morning ringing round most of the hotels in southern England from two hotel rooms, and then, fidgety with cabin fever and unease, had come to meet Mac outdoors. Every hour with no sighting of Sarah added to a growing unease.

Periodically, Ben would call up with some query, often from Richard. In his last call he had told her that the morning in court had gone well. Richard had quizzed the family doctor, and Harrington had quizzed the forensic accountant, skewering Mr Persey's claims of financial loss. He had been so shaken, Ben said, that Harrington had claimed afterwards he would be surprised if they couldn't reach a deal the following day. Natasha tried to ignore the feeling of envy and loss it invoked in her.

Mac was coming towards them now, clapping his hands, the hair at the front of his head blown upright by the wind.

'No sign?'

Natasha shook her head. 'Nobody remembers seeing a horse. But they said it would have been different staff in the ticket office last night. And they wouldn't let us see the passenger lists—data-protection laws.'

Mac swore under his breath. 'Nothing from the credit-card company?'

'No, but sometimes it takes a few hours for data to be processed.'

They were running out of ideas. And, in the absence of any firm plan, the urgency of the previous day had seeped away, to be replaced by a strange melancholy

The day dragged on. They split up and took it in turns to drive or walk round Dover. Mac, increasingly frustrated, stopped people on the street, shop owners and ferry workers. Cowboy John retreated to his hotel room, ringing his way through the phone directory. Natasha fielded more calls from work, explained that, no, she was not going to be back by tonight, and walked the damp streets of Dover, fighting an encroaching sense of despair.

They agreed to meet at six in a pub on the seafront. Natasha waited until the men went to the bar before she dialled the number. She sat down, pressing her other hand to her ear to drown out the noise of the television that blared sports results above her.

It took him eight rings to answer. She wondered whether he had seen who was calling and had been unable to decide whether or not to pick up.

'Conor?'

'Yup.'

'I just wondered how you were.'

'Have you found her?'

'No. I'm in Dover. She's definitely come this way but we can't locate her.' She wished, as soon as she had said it, that she had omitted the 'we'.

There was a lengthy silence.

'Conor?'

'Yup.'

'I just wondered . . .' She ran her fingers through her hair. 'I just wanted to make sure we were OK. I hated leaving things like that.'

'You just don't get it, Hotshot, do you?'

'Get what?'

'Not once, when you were about to throw up your whole life for this thing, did you ask me to help you. What does that say about us?'

'I didn't think you'd—'

'No. You didn't think to ask. I don't know what's going on with you and Mac, but I don't want to be involved with someone who can't even be honest about her own feelings.'

'That's not fair. I—'

But he had already rung off.

Sarah was waving a piece of bread in the air, oblivious to the fact that her high English voice was attracting the attention of French diners at the surrounding tables. 'They're like this kind of brotherhood, you know. They have black caps and black uniforms—'

'Ah. I knew it would be about fashion,' Thom teased.

Sarah ignored him. '—and they can get their horses to do absolutely anything. They'll jump a chair about a foot wide. You know how hard it is to jump a chair?'

'I can imagine.'

'Papa always said that when he came to Le Cadre Noir it was the first time in his life he had felt understood. Like there were just a few other people in the world who spoke his language and all of them lived in that one place.'

'I know that feeling.'

She had insisted on paying. He hadn't felt entirely comfortable about his supper being financed by a stolen credit card, but she had assured him she would pay back every penny when Papa was better, and the thing about Sarah was that you couldn't help but believe her.

When they had arrived in France and made their way down the *autoroute* she had become so animated that it was hard to reconcile the chatty, confident girl with the silent, wary child of the previous evening.

'Papa's friend John always jokes that what we do are circus tricks, but there are no tricks. The horses do it because they love to. It's about training them to want to do it. They're brought on really slowly, bit by bit, so that they understand how to do their job without resisting it. That way, when they perform there's no strain, no tension.'

The door to the service-station café opened and closed, allowing in a French family. They watched, eating, as the mother spoke to the children, pointing out the things they were allowed to have from the buffet.

'So how long have you and your granddaddy been on your own?'

'Four years.'

'You never stayed in touch with your mum?'

'She died before Nana.'

'I'm sorry.'

'I'm not. I don't mean to sound horrible but . . . she was the kind of person who causes problems. I was really young when she left. Me, Nana and Papa were really happy. One day, I'm going to bring Papa back here.' She gestured at the French countryside. 'We were meant to visit in November, but then he had his stroke and everything got . . .' She fell silent, but then composed herself. 'When he hears I'm there, I think it will help him. He'll be happy. When he's fit he can come over.'

'You're pretty sure you can make all this happen.'

'My grandfather was one of the best riders in France. He could make a horse float in the air, do things it didn't know were possible.' She finished the last of the food. 'All I'm trying to do is ride a few miles.'

Tom looked at her, this child, her stowaway horse. She made it sound like perfect sense.

**N**atasha flipped her phone shut and swore. It was dark and the three of them had just returned from a cashpoint situated in a sleepy industrial area of Dover. This, according to the credit-card company, was the last place that money had been withdrawn. To be so close, and yet to have no sign of Sarah, was steadily ratcheting up the tension in the little car. No one mentioned the earlier promise to call the police: they knew she must be close by. That little piece of plastic proved it. But why would a girl on a horse end up in a place like this?

Natasha turned in her seat to face Cowboy John. 'Tell me something, John. How did Sarah's grandfather end up living where he did? It's not, well, the nicest place, is it?'

'You think he set out to live somewhere like that? You think that was what he wanted from his life? OK, I'll tell you about Henri Lachapelle. He came from farming people somewhere in the south of France. When he was young he joined the military and from there he ended up on horseback, mounted cavalry or some such. In the 1950s he worked his way up until he was accepted by Le Cadre Noir, when they were building up again after the war.' He eyed the two people in front of him. 'That ain't no small achievement, you know. It's an elite academy.'

'Then how the hell did he end up living at Sandown?'

'Women.' John scowled at Natasha. 'He fell in love.'

Le Cadre Noir had been in London on one of its first international tours in 1960 when Henri had noticed the small, dark-haired woman at the front of the audience. She was there for each of the three performances and had been transfixed by the young man in the stiff black collar who had made riding a horse look magical.

He had come out to see her after a performance one evening and, as he had described it to John years afterwards, it was as if everything in his life up to that point had been a rehearsal.

'I don't think he'd had too much in the way of love, and it hit him real hard,' John said, lighting a cigarette. 'They wrote and she made plans to visit him. Problem was,' he said, 'being apart from her made him cranky. He started off not paying attention; then his performances suffered. He began to question things they were telling him in the school. In the end they told him it was their way or the highway and so he went to England, married his girl and—'

'Lived happily ever after,' Natasha concluded, thinking back to that photograph. The woman who was well loved.

John's glare was withering. 'Are you kidding me?' he said. 'Who the hell gets to live happily ever after?'

Henri Lachapelle realised almost within the first year that he had made a terrible mistake. It wasn't Florence's fault: she loved him, kept herself pretty and tried to be a good wife. It wasn't her fault that her anxiety about his happiness made him feel little more than guilt or that this frequently manifested itself in a kind of irritation.

He had asked Florence to marry him the evening of Le Carrousel, breathless, bloodied and still covered with sand. The audience in the seats around her had stood and cheered. They had walked the streets of Saumur for hours, planning their future, giddy with dreams. The next morning he had not appeared for early training but had packed his few possessions in his kitbag, and asked to see Le Grand Dieu. He had informed him that he wished to be released from his position.

Le Grand Dieu had peered at Henri's black eye. 'You know why we take the hind shoes off our horses, Lachapelle?' he asked.

Henri blinked painfully. 'So they cannot hurt other horses?'

'And so that when they are learning to find their feet, when they flail and thrash and kick out, as they inevitably will, they do not accidentally hurt themselves.' He placed his hands on the table. 'Henri, if you do this, you will hurt yourself more deeply than you can know.'

'With respect, sir, I don't believe I can be happy here.'

'You think that me cutting you loose will give you happiness?'

'Yes, sir.'

'There is no happiness in this world other than what is achieved by love of one's work. This is your world, Henri. A fool could see it.'

'With respect, sir, I would like to be released.'

It had felt good to be so determined, to see his future so clearly. The only moment he had come close to changing his mind was when he walked down to see Gerontius for the last time. The great horse whinnied as he approached, then rested his head on Henri's shoulder as Henri tickled his nose. Henri blinked back tears. Until Florence, he had never loved anyone. Just this magnificent, gentle horse.

He closed his eyes, breathing in the familiar scent of the animal's warm skin. And then, hoisting his bag over his shoulder, Henri Lachapelle turned and walked towards the gates of the Ecole de Cavalerie.

The first months in England had been tolerable, their trials masked by the quiet satisfaction he felt as a newly married man. Florence glowed under his attention; a million times a day he saw in her little things that enabled him to justify his decision. Her family, while wary of the young Frenchman who had whisked their daughter off her feet, were polite. Cleverly, Florence had asked him to wear his uniform when he first met them; her parents' generation found it hard to see anything but good in a man in uniform. 'You're not thinking of settling in France, though?' her father had said. 'Florence wouldn't do well so far from home.'

'My home is here,' Henri said, believing it. And Florence, seated beside him, had flushed with pleasure.

He had taken lodgings and, just weeks after he arrived in England, they had married in Marylebone Register Office. Henri travelled across London and to the suburbs, trying to find employment as a riding instructor, but riding for pleasure was still very much the preserve of the wealthy, and on the few occasions he was taken on trial, his poor grasp of the language and formal opinions on riding won him few admirers.

He found England a disappointment. The food was worse than he had received in the cavalry. The people seemed happy to eat everything from tins. He felt stifled by the forbidding grey skyline, and would return to the narrow house in Clerkenwell to reveal that he had been 'let go' again, often without being paid what he was owed. Florence's father, Martin, would ask over tea whether he had found another job yet, and when the answer was no, whether he might think about improving his English a little so that he could get a 'proper' one. One that apparently involved sitting behind a desk.

At night he dreamed of Gerontius. He danced, pirouetted, rose up on his back in a perfect *levade*, and saw the world laid out beneath him. And then, inevitably, he woke in the cramped bedroom of Florence's childhood, where they now lived, with its drab brown furniture, view of the high street, and his wife, her hair in rollers, beside him.

A year on, he could no longer disguise the magnitude of his error. The English were worse than Parisians, suspicious when he opened his mouth, the older men muttering disparaging comments about the war that they thought he could not understand. Those who surrounded him seemed to care only about earning money that they would drink on a Friday night with a kind of grim determination. Or they would stay locked in their houses, hypnotised by their new television sets.

Florence detected his unhappiness and tried to compensate, praising him, assuring him that things would improve. He saw only the desperation in her eyes, and felt her adoration morph into clinginess.

Almost fifteen months after he had arrived, he plucked up the courage to write a brief letter to Varjus: *My dear friend, Would they take me back? It is too hard to live only with gravity.* He handed it over at the post office feeling terrible guilt but also hope. Florence would adapt to France eventually. And if not—here he would feel shame lodging deep within him—would it be so bad if he never returned?

He held the knowledge of that letter winging its way across the continent throughout another interminable supper. It was chicken. Mrs Jacobs had cooked it to a leathery texture.

'Florence has something to tell you, dear.' Mrs Jacobs was addressing her husband.

Florence wiped her mouth and put her napkin on her lap. 'I was going to keep it secret a bit longer, but I couldn't.' She blushed a little. 'I told Mother. We're going to have to set another place at our table.'

'Why?' said Mr Jacobs, tearing his attention from his newspaper. 'Who's coming?'

Florence and her mother burst out laughing. 'No one's coming, Father. I'm . . . I'm in the family way . . .' She took Henri's hand over the tablecloth. 'We're going to have a baby.'

**H**enri was leaving the flat when he met the postman on the landing. Varjus, true to his nature, had written back within a week. He ripped open the envelope and read the hastily written words, his face impassive: *Le Grand Dieu is a good man, an understanding man. I think if you approached him with humility, he might allow you this one mistake. Most of all, he knows you are a horseman! I look forward to your return, my friend.*

Henri screwed the note into a ball and thrust it deep into his pocket.

**H**e opened the front door to let himself into the narrow hallway. The smell of overcooked cabbage pervaded the air and he closed his eyes. Then a sound made him stop. In the living room, on the other side of the anaglypta wallpaper, he could hear noisy sobs.

The kitchen door opened and Florence appeared. She navigated herself along the passageway and reached up to kiss him.

'I've told them that after the baby is born we're going to France,' she said. Her voice was calm as she took his hands. 'I've been thinking about it for ages. You've given me everything—*everything*'—she glanced down at her belly—'but I know you're not happy here, Henri. So, I've told Mother and Father that after the birth, you'll provide for me there. As you can probably tell, Mother hasn't taken it too well.' She searched his face. 'Will Le Cadre Noir take you back, darling? I'm sure once I've got the hang of it I could keep a little house for you nearby. I'll learn French. Bring up the baby there. What do you think?'

This brave, beautiful Englishwoman. Henri was moved beyond words. He didn't deserve her. He stepped forward and buried his face in her hair. 'Thank you,' he whispered. 'You don't know what this means. I will make sure we have a better future . . . for us and our baby.'

'I know you will,' she said softly. 'I want you to fly again, Henri.'

**H**e heard the baby crying even before he reached the little house, a thin wail echoing over the quiet street. He knew what he would find.

She was bent over the crib, uttering soothing noises, her hand fluttering vainly over the child. At Henri's approach, she turned. She was pale and her eyes spoke of long anxious hours.

'How long has she been crying?'

'Not long. Really.' She straightened up. 'Just since Mother went out.'

'Then why . . .?'

'You know I'm afraid to carry her when you're not here. My hands aren't working again. I dropped a cup this afternoon and—'

He gritted his teeth. '*Chérie*, there is nothing wrong with your hands. The doctor said so. You just need confidence.'

He plucked Simone from her cot, holding the baby close to his chest, and she quietened immediately. Her little mouth opened and closed near his shirt, seeking milk. Florence sat on the chair in the corner, holding out her arms to receive her, closing them around her daughter only when she was sure she had been safely delivered into her embrace.

While she fed the baby, Henri removed his boots, placing them neatly by the door. He took off his jacket and put the kettle on the stove. He had finally found a job on the railways. It was not so bad. Nothing was so bad, now that he knew it would be temporary.

'Have you been out today?'

'I meant to . . . but I told you, I was afraid to carry her.'

'Nerves,' the doctor had called it when Florence had begun to complain that her body wasn't working as it should be. 'Mother and baby should stay with Granny for a while. Just until she has become a little more . . . comfortable with motherhood.'

What could Henri have said? He had nodded his acquiescence, marvelling that they could not see how every atom of him was straining towards the Channel. He thought of Gerontius, perhaps even now waiting for him, his head bowed over the stable door.

'I'm sorry. I know you thought France would be the answer for us,' she said quietly, teardrops falling on Simone's cotton gown.

And there it was. She could not cope alone, and he could not risk anything happening to the child. He could not return to Le Cadre Noir. He had no family he could place her with, no money to pay for a nurse. They would have to remain here, in reach of her parents.

He walked over to her chair. 'I will write to Varjus,' he said. 'We will stay in England a little longer.' He shrugged, his teeth gritted. 'It's fine.'

'It was about a year after that that I met him. He was working on the railway track above my yard.' Cowboy John tilted back his hat. 'I looked up one afternoon and saw him staring at my old mare. We were both new to the area then, both outsiders. I waved him down and he ate his sandwiches outside the stable.

'A lot of people found him a little stiff, but I liked him. For years he used to talk about the little farm he'd have in France one day, the riding school he was gonna set up.'

'Is that what Florence wanted?' Natasha asked. She had been so lost in the story that she had almost forgotten why they were all in the car.

'Oh, Florence would have gone along with pretty much anything that man asked her. I think she felt real guilty about what she'd saddled him with. She knew, like he did, that she wouldn't be able to cope in France, what with the illness.'

'I don't understand. Illness?'

John looked at them, frowning. 'Sarah didn't tell you? Her nan had multiple sclerosis. She was in a wheelchair for years. Sarah was helping her grandpa look after the old lady from the time she could walk.'

They had given up on Dover and decided to head down the coast road towards Deal. Natasha was still talking to John, her imagination captured by Henri Lachapelle's travails.

'The way Sarah talks about her grandparents, they sounded so close.'

John snorted. 'Sure they were close, but that man's whole life is one of regrets.'

'You mean Sarah's mother?'

'Oh, man, Simone was a mess. She was fiery, argumentative—the opposite of him. Everything he kept in, she let out. Florence couldn't manage her, didn't have the strength, and Henri tried to keep their daughter on a tight rein, like he does Sarah. He was an old-fashioned disciplinarian, and Simone wasn't having it. Oooh, no. The more he pulled her one way, she pulled straight back the other. By the time he worked out what he was doing wrong, she was on the drugs. Then there were about four, five years when she ran off to Paris and they never heard from her. Till ten, eleven years ago, Simone turns up on their doorstep one day with this little child, sayin' she can't cope. She'd had a baby in France. Never said nothing to them.

'And she starts leavin' the child with them. Each time it's for a bit longer and a bit longer. In the end they apply for custody and get it. Simone never even turned up for the hearin'. Henri was mad at first but, if truth be told, they was both real happy to have Sarah around.'

'Anyhow, then Florence passed away around four years past. After her funeral Henri got some kind of financial incentive to give up their ground-floor place—it was needed for other disabled people—so he took the money and moved them to that flat in Sandown. He spent the money on Baucher, that Rolls-Royce of a horse of theirs. Everything was about getting Sarah into a better place. She is the one thing that Henri ever felt he got right.'

The girl had fallen asleep. Thom drove on through the night, occasionally glancing at her, curled up on the front seat, her head resting against the window. And then, almost reflexively, at the CCTV monitor that showed her horse, partitioned between the other two, standing vigilantly as if he was bracing himself for the next stage of his journey.

Thom had not told his girlfriend what he was doing—he knew what she'd say. She'd accuse him of being irresponsible, of endangering the child's life. But how many people got the chance to chase a dream? How many people even knew what they wanted? When Sarah talked about her love for the horse and the uncomplicated life she pictured for herself, for her grandfather, he saw how easy it was to get buried in routine concerns.

None of it stopped him thinking several times that he should stop the truck on the side of the road and call the police. He glanced up again at the CCTV. The horse lifted its head a little and, for a moment, gazed directly at the camera.

'Look after her, old fella,' said Thom quietly. 'God knows she's going to need all the help she can get.'

**A**t a quarter past eight, they stopped at a fast-food restaurant. Cowboy John asked for a large, black coffee with two sugars and strode off to the payphone to call the hospital. Routine, he announced cheerfully. Henri would want to know what was happening.

'What are you going to tell him?' Natasha asked.

'The truth. We know she's close by, we just ain't worked out where.'

Natasha put the plastic tray with three coffees on the table in front of Mac, trying not to notice that he flipped his mobile phone shut. She held up the black coffee as John returned, but he shook his head.

'Guys, I'm gonna have to split. Henri ain't too clever. If Sarah ain't around . . . Well, someone should be with him.' He was shuffling for change in his pockets, checking what he had with him.

Natasha stood up and reached into her bag, the coffee forgotten. 'We'll take you to the station. Here'—she handed him some cash—'take that for the train.'

He looked down at the notes she was holding out, took them and tipped his hat to her. 'Well, thank you,' he said. 'I'll ring you when I know how he is.'

It was as they reached the station car park that her telephone rang. Natasha flipped it open. 'Yes, it is,' she said, glancing at John, who was letting himself out of the car. 'Yes . . . Thank you for letting me know.'

'Everything OK?' John was holding open the rear door.

She shut the phone. 'That was the credit-card company. You're not going to believe this. Sarah's in France.'

**S**arah woke to a blast of cold air and saw Thom peering through the driver's door. She pushed herself upright. The clock on the dashboard told her it was a quarter to eight.

'Morning.' He was dressed and clean-shaven.

'Where are we?'

A short distance away she could see a man was mucking out a stable, swinging forkfuls of straw into a wheelbarrow.

'Just outside Blois,' he said. 'You've had a good night's sleep.'

'Where's Boo?' That same reflexive panic.

'You mean Mr Diablo? In the yard.' He jerked his thumb towards the stables. 'He's in the third stable along from the left. He's fine.'

She blinked, just able to see Boo's nose reaching for a haynet.

'You can have that night on me. But I need to be headed back for Calais, Miss Sarah, so I'm afraid this is where you and I must part.'

Sarah tried to collect her thoughts as Thom helped her tack up, and handed her two croissants, which he'd begged from the owner of the lairage. He opened out a small map on which he had marked her route.

'It's sixty, seventy miles from here, headed southwest,' he said, point-ing her along a red road on the map. 'I'd drive you if I could, but I can't lose another four hours. It's beautiful riding weather, though, and these roads are pretty quiet. Just take your time, yes?'

She was close, she realised, with a sudden thrill. She could see the name on the map.

'There's another lairage just here.' He had circled a village with a ball-point. 'Here's the phone number, just in case. Now, I've rung ahead and they'll be expecting you. You should be able to get a meal there tonight. Don't forget they're expecting a horse by the name of . . .'

'Diablo Blue,' she said.

'Now, here's my number. Will you do me a favour and ring me if you get into trouble? Hell, ring me when you get where you're headed.' He placed the folded map in her hand. 'I'd be glad to know you're OK.'

She nodded, shoving the piece of paper deep in her pocket.

'You have the euros we changed up?'

She reached into her rucksack, feeling for the envelope.

Thom sighed. 'God help me. You're the strangest hitchhiker I've ever met.' He hesitated, as if unsure that he was doing the right thing.

'I'll be fine, Thom,' she insisted. 'Thanks, though.'

'It's been a pleasure travelling with you, young Sarah.' He waited for her to mount, then walked back towards his lorry.

**T**he fields in France were wider than those en route to Dover: flat, sprawling expanses with no boundaries in sight. The earth, however, looked as it had in England: a rich, claggy brown, turned in rough clods that resembled choppy seas. Boo, refreshed, strode out on the grass verges, his ears pricked forward, clearly glad to be on solid ground.

She passed through small villages, the streets quiet, civilised, the rows of small houses uniform, in grey stone, but for the odd carefully tended window box or brightly painted shutters. In one, she passed close by a man carrying two baguettes and a newspaper tucked under his arm. He nodded at her. '*Bonjour*,' he said.

'*Bonjour*,' she replied. It was the first French word she had uttered since she had been there. She stopped at an animal trough in the square, from which Boo took great draughts of water. She dismounted and rested there for half an hour, splashing her face with the cold water, eating her croissants. Then she remounted and they continued towards a signpost that pointed her to Tours.

Within minutes they were in open countryside again. Her senses felt sharper, as if she was absorbing this new landscape through every cell. It was just her and her horse, unobserved, free.

*I'm in France, Papa,* she told him, *and it's beautiful.* She pictured him in the bed, dreaming of the roads she was travelling now. And perhaps sensing his voice, his instruction, she straightened a little, corrected the precise angle of her lower legs, shortened her reins and began to canter, Boo's feet placing themselves elegantly along the verge.

Natasha's credit card had been used, the previous evening, at a French motorway service station. The difficulty, the credit-card operator had advised, was that the transaction said, 'La Bonne Route, Paris,' a description that encompassed seven such places across northern France.

'Well, I think we should head for the horse place,' Mac had said on the ferry the previous night. They had managed to get the car onto a late-evening crossing. Natasha sat in near-silence, staring out of the glazed window at the dark, churning waters below. How could Sarah have crossed the Channel with a horse?

'What if it's not her?' she said. 'What if she sold the card, or it was stolen from her? What if we're following the wrong person?'

'It's possible, but we don't have any other leads, do we?' Mac took the top off a bottle of water and drank. 'God, I'm thirsty.' He hadn't shaved and his chin bore a layer of stubble.

Natasha pointed at the map on the table between them. 'Look at the distances here, Mac. John said a horse could travel thirty or forty miles a day at a push. It would have been tough enough for her to make it to Dover in that time. How could she have got across the Channel with a horse and then have ridden halfway down France? And, look, Saumur's more than three hundred miles from Calais.'

'So what are you saying?'

She leaned back in her seat. 'We should turn round.' Her voice was uncertain. 'Or maybe call the police. We should have called them yesterday morning. You were right—I didn't want to get them involved because I didn't want all this out in the open. But it's gone beyond that now, Mac. I say when we get off the ferry we call the police.'

'No,' he said, adamant. 'The moment we call them, she loses everything. She's only lost in that *we* don't know where she is. *She* may know exactly where she's going. I think we should drive to Saumur and wait for her there. I'm prepared to trust her to be OK and I'll take responsibility if I'm wrong.'

He had never been so decisive when they were married. Hurt

made Natasha's voice harder than she had intended. 'And if you're wrong, if she's not safe, you'll be happy to live with that, will you?'

Since then they had barely spoken. Mac drove the car off the ferry at Calais and on through the night. He didn't take the *autoroute*, but the smaller roads, roads on which a horse might travel.

She dozed, and woke to the sound of his voice. He was speaking into his phone, low and insistent. 'It's not that,' he said, and, some time later, 'No, no, sweetheart. I don't think that's a good idea. I know. I know.' Natasha, uncomfortably awake, kept her face turned away, her eyes shut, until he rang off. She left it another ten minutes before she yawned ostentatiously. At that point he suggested they pull into a rest stop and grab forty winks. It was after one in the morning and there was little chance of them finding a hotel. 'We won't sleep long,' he said. 'A couple of hours at most. Then we'll drive on.'

After the silent tension of the past hour, Natasha was glad to accept. They pulled off the empty road into the car park of a service station and sat awkwardly beside each other as the engine ticked its way to silence. Mac offered her the back seat and she climbed into it, rolled her coat into a pillow and laid her head on it.

Mac fell asleep at once, with his seat tilted back and his arm across his forehead. Natasha did not sleep. She lay in a strange car in a foreign country, her mind racing like the speeding traffic in the distance, thinking about her lost career, a man in London who didn't love her any more, and a girl who was out there now, somewhere under the same sky, a web of unhappiness and loneliness, with herself at the centre.

'Linda. Natasha.'

'How's it going? Have you sorted out your . . . family problems?'

They knew. Conor would have told them everything. Natasha regarded her creased skirt, her now-laddered stockings, painfully visible in the harsh light of morning. 'No. Not yet.'

'Where are you? When are you back?'

Mac had woken shortly after dawn, and a silent, bleary couple of hours' driving later, they had stopped at a service station to freshen up.

'I'm not sure. It's taking longer than we thought. Can I speak to Ben?'

'He's out. With Richard.'

'Richard? Why is he out with Richard?'

'It's the Perseys. They've settled. Richard's out celebrating with Mrs Persey. He took Michael Harrington and Ben with him. They've gone to the Wolseley for a champagne breakfast.'

Richard hadn't bothered to call. Her gratitude that the case had been settled satisfactorily evaporated, tempered by the knowledge that she would receive no credit for it. She knew, in that moment, that she would not be made partner this year. Not, perhaps, for many years.

A dull ache penetrated her temple. She stood in the car park of a French service station, in two-day-old clothes, rubbing her forehead while she surveyed the vehicles that passed in a blur. How had she ended up here?

'So, how are you doing?'

'I'm fine,' she lied.

'No one here knows quite what to make of this,' Linda said carefully. 'You've held your cards close to your chest.'

'And now I'm paying for it, right?'

'There's a view that you could probably have handled things better.' Natasha closed her eyes. 'I've got to go, Lin,' she said. 'I'll ring later.' Mac was walking back across the car park.

'Oh! Natasha! I nearly forgot to tell you. We had a visitor here first thing. You'll never guess who.'

He had stopped to say something to two women who had just climbed out of a car. Whatever he said made them laugh, and she could see his broad smile.

'Mm?'

'Ali Ahmadi.'

Natasha tore her eyes from him. 'What did you just say?'

'Hah! I knew that would get you. Ali Ahmadi.'

'But that's not possible! He's on remand.'

Linda laughed. 'That kid we read about was a different Ali Ahmadi. Did you know Ahmadi is one of the most common names in Iran? Anyhow, the one you represented came in to tell you he's got a place at sixth-form college. He starts in September. Sweet kid. He brought you a bunch of flowers. I've put them in your office.'

Natasha pressed the phone against her ear. 'But . . .?'

'I know. We should have checked. Restores your faith in human nature. I could never quite see him as the violent type. Oh, and I gave him back that little horse pendant we meant to send him.'

'But—but he lied about the distance he'd walked. He still caused me to misrepresent his case.'

'That's exactly what I said to Ben. And because the interpreter was in we got the file out and asked her to have another look at the translation notes. Ali Ahmadi indeed said he'd *travelled* nine hundred miles in thirteen days, but not that he *walked* it. That was what we—the interpreter too—all assumed. Before he left, Ben asked him—oh, you wouldn't believe how well his English has come on—anyway, Ben asked him how he'd got so far. Ali explained that he'd walked some of the way, got a lift on a truck, and then he held up that little horse. Some of it he'd ridden. Mule or something. But that's the thing—he never lied to you.'

Natasha lost the thread of whatever else Linda was trying to tell her. She lowered her head and thought about a boy who had held her hands in a gesture of thanks. A boy who had only ever told the truth.

When she looked up, Mac was standing a few feet away, a poly-styrene cup in each hand. He glanced away abruptly, as if he might have been staring at her for some time. She shut her phone.

'OK,' she said, taking her coffee from him. 'You win. Head for Saumur.'

# TWELVE

SHE HAD TAKEN a wrong turning. She stared again at the little map, already worn soft from repeated foldings, which didn't explain why the route that should have taken her past Tours, and a few miles beyond to the lairage Thom had booked, had somehow led her into a never-ending industrial estate. For some miles she had been travelling roughly alongside a railway line, but as Thom's map didn't show the railway she had little idea if she was heading the right way or not. She had trusted that there would be a sign for Tours, but it hadn't come.

The sun had begun to dip in the sky, and she halted, stared again at the map. She appeared to be heading into a sidings: the track had split and become more tracks, each with lines of stationary carriages, a web of pylons and cables above her. Uneasy, Sarah decided to go back the way she had come. She gave a long, weary sigh and began to turn Boo.

'*Que fais-tu ici?*'

She spun round in the saddle to see five bikes, scramblers and mopeds, two with a passenger riding pillion. A couple wore helmets; the rest were bareheaded. Smoking, hard-eyed.

'*Eh? Que fais-tu ici?*'

She didn't want to speak. She knew her accent would mark her out as English. She turned away from them and walked on, steering Boo to the left. She knew these young men as she had known the boys on her estate. She hoped they would lose interest and go away.

'*Tu as perdu les vaches, cowboy.*'

Her legs closed involuntarily round Boo's sides. A well-trained horse will detect even the faintest tension in its rider, and this movement, with a slight increase in pressure on the reins, caught Boo's attention.

'*Hé!*'

One roared past. Her face impassive, she rode on.

'*Hé! J'ai parlé à toi!*'

'*Allez-vous en,*' she said, trying to sound more confident than she felt.

She could hear the others behind her, catcalling, laughing. '*Allez-vous en!*' One mimicked her voice.

Sarah began to trot. She sat very upright and heard the motorbikes skidding and revving behind her. She felt her horse tense and rested her hand on his neck. They'll go in a moment, she told him silently. But a bike came up beside her and then skidded in front of Boo. He stopped abruptly, his haunches dropping, his head shooting up into the air. Two more bikes swung round so that three were now facing her.

One of them threw a cigarette to the ground. '*Putain! Tu ne sais pas qu'il est impoli d'ignorer quelqu'un?*' The youth cocked his head at her.

'*Je dois aller à Tours,*' she said, trying to stop her voice quavering.

'*Tu veux aller à Tours . . .*' The laughter was unpleasant.

'*Il y a quoi dans ce sac?*'

'*Rien,*' she said. They were after her bag.

'*Il est trop plein pour rien.*' One of the boys, pale-skinned, his shaven head tucked under a baseball cap, had climbed off his motorbike. He walked towards her, then stopped a few feet away, eyeing her. Then, without warning, he leaped forward, yelling, '*Rah!*'

Boo snorted and jumped backwards. The boys laughed. 'Easy,' she murmured, closing her legs around him again. 'Easy.'

The boy with the hat moved forward again. They wouldn't stop now, she guessed. They had scented some new game. Discreetly she scanned the distance, trying to establish the best route past them, the way out.

'*Rah!*' This time, she was ready for him and Boo flinched but did not jump. She had him firmly between leg and hand, telling him silently not to move, refusing him the chance to feel fear. He was uncertain, though, and, as the bikes revved again, she knew what she had to do.

'*S'il vous plaît,*' she said, '*laissez-moi la paix.*'

'*Renvoies-moi et je te laisserai la paix.*' He gestured at her rucksack.

Sarah gathered Boo up, her legs signalling her instruction. He refused to hear her for a few seconds, transfixed by anxiety, then training took over, and he began to trot on the spot, his legs lifting carefully, rhythmically, two at a time in an exaggerated version of *piaffe*.

'*Regardez! Un cheval dansant!*' The boys began to catcall, the bikes revving, drawing closer, closer. Sarah tried to block out the noise, concentrating, building a core of energy at Boo's centre. His head dropped to his chest, his legs lifting higher. Her heart constricted at his trust in her, that he was prepared to do what she asked of him, despite his fear. She heard one of the boys yelling something else at her, but the noise was lost in the pounding of blood in her ears.

'*Alors, comme ça on se fait valser, hein?*' The boy on his feet had moved closer. His smile was hard, mocking.

'*Faites-la descendre!*' another boy yelled, gesturing to the others to get her off Boo. She felt a hand reach for her leg. It was all the prompt she needed. Her heels clamped to Boo's sides, her seat telling him to rise, rise, and then she yelled, 'Hup!' and he was leaping into the air, towering above them as, with a seismic bounce, his rear legs kicked out horizontally behind him. *Capriole!* The world stood still, and she saw what men in battle must have seen two thousand years ago—their opponents' faces filled with terror as the great beasts rose, defying gravity, into the air, their legs, their very selves transformed into airborne weapons.

Beneath her there was a shout of outrage. Two bikes fell over and the boy on his feet collapsed onto his rear. As Boo's front hoofs hit the ground, she threw herself forward. 'Go!' she yelled. 'Go!' And the great horse leaped past the motorbikes, skidded round the corner, and flew down the road, back the way they had come.

**I**n a darkened hospital room several hundred miles away, Henri Lachapelle, his head tilted to one side where it had been propped on pillows by the evening-shift nurses, woke and let his gaze settle on the blurred image of the horse beside him, waiting for it to clarify, solidify. It had somehow drawn closer while he slept, and now looked back at him, its iridescent eye gazing into his own with a gentle reassurance. Henri's own eyes, dry and sore, closed and opened several times amid a creeping confusion. Then: 'Gerontius!' he exclaimed, with gratitude. The horse blinked slowly, its nose dipping, as if in acknowledgment, and Henri tried to remember how they had ended up here.

He could feel the stiff leather of the boots around his calves, the soft black serge of his collar on his neck, and then he was astride, riding out through the red curtain, his gloved hands light on the leather reins, his eyes fixed calmly between the cocked ears of his horse. He felt Gerontius's long, strong legs move beneath him; those distinctive, elegant paces, as familiar to him as his own stride, and a deep joy, a kind of euphoria, crept through him. *This time he would be a man on wings.*

The horse arched his neck, his hoofs lifting beneath him, and then, with a *whoosh*, he was on his hind legs, his proud head fixed and steady, looking out at the audience. And Henri was there, tilted behind him, a gasp of exultation escaping him as he understood that this was it; they were airborne and he need never come down.

And it was then that he saw her: the girl in the yellow dress, standing in her seat before him. She was clapping, a smile breaking across her face.

'Florence!' he cried. 'Florence!' The applause that burst forth from the arena filled his ears, his heart, deafening him, the lights exploding in front of him, so that it became everything, bearing him ever higher, drowning out the distant shrill ringing of the machines, the urgent voices, the sudden bursting open of the ward door.

Mac was knocking at the door of her room. 'Are you ready? Madame said dinner at eight.' Natasha had put on the badly cut trousers and the thin red cotton shirt that had been the only items she could find to fit her at the local hypermarket, and said, wearily, 'Give me five minutes. I'll meet you down there.'

She heard his footsteps echoing along the corridor, bouncing off the wood panelling, and scrabbled in her bag for mascara, something that would enliven her pale, exhausted face.

They had arrived in the town shortly after five. Their first stop had been the Ecole Nationale d'Equitation, the home of Le Cadre Noir, but the gates had been closed. A voice had come over the intercom to explain that it was not open to the public until after Christmas. And, no, to Mac's next question, no English girl had arrived with a horse.

'She would never have beaten us here anyway,' Natasha pointed out. 'We're best finding a base and taking it from there.'

The Château de Verrières was in the centre of the town; it backed on to the Ecole de Cavalerie and was vast, ornate, a thing of beauty.

'I guess we may just as well stay in a nice place as a chain,' Mac said. He was trying to be cheerful, but she knew that since they had hit French soil his fears had escalated, as had hers.

She arrived downstairs to find Mac seated in front of a boisterous log fire, explaining the situation to the chateau's owner. 'You think the child has ridden here from Calais?' the Frenchwoman repeated. 'If a fourteen-year-old English child had turned up here unaccompanied on a horse, the whole of Saumur would know. Are you sure she has come this far?'

'We know she withdrew money outside Paris yesterday evening.'

'But it is over five hundred kilometres . . . if you like, I can call the gendarmes and ask if such a thing has been reported,' the woman said.

'That would be very helpful,' Mac said. 'Thank you.' Then, as the chatelaine disappeared to check their food, 'You OK?'

'Fine.' Natasha stared out of the window, willing the child to emerge from behind the trees at the far end of the bay hedge. She had begun to see Sarah everywhere: behind parked cars, at the end of narrow lanes.

Face to face with Mac over dinner, in such a romantic setting, she found she was not hungry and drank instead. Three, four glasses slipped down without her noticing.

When Mac refused dessert, saying he was going to take a long bath, she was filled with relief. 'I think I'll take a walk outside,' she said.

The cold air carried the faint tang of wood smoke and knocked the breath from Natasha's lungs. She walked towards a horse chestnut tree and, on reaching it, stopped to peer up through the elegant branches at the sky, a vast, inky expanse glittering with a million pinpricks of light.

She was not sure how long she had been standing there when she heard footsteps behind her. It was Mac.

'What is it? Is it the police?' she said, when she realised he was holding his phone. 'Did they find her?'

His hair was dry—he couldn't have had a bath. 'Cowboy John called.' His face was grave. 'Sarah's grandfather died this evening.'

She couldn't speak. Something was rising in her chest, a horrible unfamiliar choking sensation that filled her with panic. She brushed past him and walked, then ran, towards the house. She went through the hallway, up the mahogany stairs to her room. The tears came even before she had lain on the vast bed. Now, freed perhaps by alcohol, Natasha's sobs racked her frame, seeming to haul their way up from her very depths. She cried silently, not knowing how she would ever stop.

**S**he could hear the bikes behind her. She was galloping flat out now, breathing in short bursts, gripped by fear. Boo ran, his neck ramrod-straight, his hoofs sending up sparks beneath her in the darkening light. She wrenched his head to the right, flying towards what looked like a road, heard tyres squeal behind her, another threatening cry of 'Putain!' and found she was in a supermarket car park.

She galloped across the parking spaces, dimly aware of a driver, halted in mid-reverse. The motorbikes had spread out now; she could see them from the corners of her eyes.

She tried to pull Boo back, but his neck was rigid, impervious. Boo, terrified, was lost in a world of his own, the white markings blurring beneath him. 'Boo! Whoa!' she cried, but realised, with terror, that she was not going to be able to stop. Briefly recognising that she should just stay on, she jumped a small rail and saw that she had reached the edge of the estate, that the black nothing beyond a low wall was empty countryside. But she, like the horse, had not seen the drop on the other side of the wall, so that when he took off, still blind with fear, it was only as his front feet soared into midair that both horse and rider saw his mistake.

The sounds of the bikes disappeared. Sarah flew into the dark sky, dimly aware of a scream that might have been her own. And then Boo's head disappeared beneath her and Sarah was falling. She saw a brief flash of illuminated road surface, heard a terrible crunch, and everything went black.

When there was no response to his discreet knock, Mac turned the doorknob, afraid that it might prompt some new antagonism between them. But he couldn't return to his room: she had looked so lost.

'Tash?' he ventured softly. He said it again, then opened the door.

She was on the canopied bed, her arms crossed over her head. He thought that she was asleep. And then, as he was about to close the door, he caught the smothered hint of a sob. He stood very still, then walked tentatively across the floor.

She flinched when he placed a hand on her shoulder. 'Tash?'

When she lifted her face from the covers, it was pale and blotchy with tears. What remained of the mascara had run down her cheeks and he fought the urge to wipe it away.

'What if we don't find her?' Her eyes glittered.

The evident depth of her pain was shocking. 'We'll find her.' It was all he could say. 'I don't understand, Tash . . .'

She raised herself to a sitting position, drew her knees up under her chin and buried her face in them. It took two attempts before he could make out what she was saying.

'He trusted us. I let him down. I let her down.' Her voice was distorted by tears. 'I never looked after her like I should. But it was too . . .'

Mac sat on the bed beside her. 'You did fine. You did your best.'

He could see her thin arms in the red shirt, smeared with the inky marks of her tears. He wanted to reach out a hand to her, but he was afraid that if he did she might close herself off again.

'She showed me I would never have been any good at being a mother. Having Sarah there made me see . . . that perhaps there was a reason I never had children.' She swallowed hard. 'And what's happened to her since shows me I was right.'

Mac was stunned by her grief for their lost babies. 'No, Tash,' he said quietly, reaching for her hand now. 'That's not it.' Her fingers were wet with tears. 'Come on.' He pulled her close to him, put his arms round her, rocking her, hardly knowing what he was doing. 'Oh Christ. No . . . you would have been a great mother, I know you would.'

He rested his face on the top of her head, breathing in the familiar smell of her hair, and realised that the tear sliding down his cheek was his own. And he felt his wife's arms creep round him so that she clung to him, a silent message that perhaps he had been needed, wanted, that he had had something to offer her, after all. They sat in the dark, holding each other, grieving, too late, for the children they had lost, the life together they had relinquished.

Her sobs quieted, and in their place, unspoken, a question filled the air around them, became written in their skin where it touched. He lifted her face in his hands and kissed her bottom lip. For a moment, he felt her hesitate, but then her fingers were clamped round his own and Mac was pressing her down, a sigh of relief and desire escaping him.

'I want you.' He heard her voice in his ear as if it were a surprise to her. 'I want you,' she said again, and Mac, pulling his shirt over his head, understood that although it had not been a question there was only one possible answer.

**A** white bird was circling above her; it moved in huge, lazy circles, emitting a droning hum that grew louder and then, when the noise became unbearable, receded. Sarah blinked, unable to distinguish it against the bright light behind it, pleading with it silently to quieten.

She lay still as the noise grew in volume, and this time the ground vibrated beneath her so that she frowned, conscious of the pain in her head, in her right shoulder. Finally, as it became unbearable, the noise stopped. She felt a vague gratitude, before it was interrupted by a door slamming. An exclamation. She opened her eyes a fraction to see a dark shape looming above her.

'Ça va?'

She blinked, the pain forgotten as she made out the shape of a man staring down at her. She saw that she was lying in a drainage ditch and clawed herself upright.

*Men. Motorbikes. Terror.*

The farmer stood a few yards from her, his face concerned, his huge yellow agricultural machine a short distance away.

'Que faire?' he said.

Sarah's eyes refused to focus. She glanced around, beginning to make out the expanse of ploughed field, the distant sheds of the industrial estate. *The industrial estate. A leap into the dark.*

'My horse,' she said, struggling to her feet. 'Where is my horse?'

The farmer was backing away, gesturing at her to stay where she was. But she was already stumbling forward, towards the road, trying to clear her head, her vision. 'Boo!' she shouted. 'Boo!'

'*Tu as besoin de mon aide?*' the man asked cautiously.

She did not hear him.

'Boo?' she called. She clambered onto a concrete post, wincing as she tried to keep her balance. Her body ached; her vision refused to clear. But even she could see that the fields were empty.

She turned back to the farmer. '*Un cheval?*' she pleaded. '*Un cheval brun? Un Selle Français?*' She was trembling—a mixture of cold and fear. This couldn't be happening. Not now, not after all this. It was too terrible a prospect. He could not have gone.

The farmer was standing by the door of his machine now. '*Tu as besoin de mon aide?*' he said again.

In fact, Sarah, already limping down the road, not sure where she was going to look first, was too busy shouting her horse's name to hear him. The sheer blinding shock of Boo having gone overrode the pain she could feel in her shoulder, the repetitive hammering in her head.

She had walked almost the whole length of the ploughed field before she realised that her horse was not the only thing that was missing.

**A**lmost thirty miles away, Natasha also woke to an unexpected sense of absence. Even before she worked out that the sound she had heard was Mac disappearing into the bathroom, she had been aware of the loss of his body beside hers. She still felt the weight of his arm across her, his breath warm on her neck. Without him she was untethered. *Mac.*

She heard him lift the loo seat and allowed herself a small smile at this indication of domesticity. She burrowed deeper under the covers, lost in the fug that told of hours of pleasure, of desire met and reciprocated. She thought of him, of his lips on her, the intensity in the way his eyes had examined her, as if all the previous year had been made irrelevant by the strength of their feelings. She thought of her own actions, her lack of inhibition, the desire. She had surprised him, she knew, and she had surprised herself.

She slid over to his side of the bed, breathing in the imprint of his skin as she listened to the sound of running water in the bathroom. Would it be wrong to wrap herself round him again before they got up and restarted the search? Would it be wrong to use his lips, his hands, his skin, to fortify herself against the day ahead? I love him, she realised, and the knowledge came as a relief, as if to admit it meant she could stop struggling.

It was at that point that she heard the voice. At first she had thought it was someone out in the corridor, but as she lay, straining to hear, she realised Mac was talking. She climbed out of bed, wrapping the bedspread round her, and padded barefoot to the bathroom door, hesitated for a moment, then rested her ear against the old oak panel.

'Sweetheart, let's talk about this later. You—you're impossible.' He was laughing. 'No, I don't . . . Maria, I'm not going to have this discussion now. I told you, I'm still looking . . . Yes, I'll see you on the 15th . . . Me too.' He laughed again. 'I'll speak to you when I'm home.'

For years afterwards, Natasha would struggle to disassociate the smell of beeswax from a premonition of disaster. She backed away from the door, the smile gone, the glow transformed as if by alchemy into ice in her blood. She had just made it to the bed when he emerged from the bathroom. She slowed her breathing, unsure how to appear to him.

'You're awake,' he observed. She could feel his eyes on her.

'What's the time?' she asked.

'A quarter past eight.'

Her heart was beating uncomfortably inside her chest. 'We'd better get going,' she said, casting around on the floor for her clothes.

'You want to get up?' He sounded surprised.

'I think it would be a good idea. We have to speak to the police, remember. Madame . . . was going to ring them for us.' She could see her knickers under the great walnut chest of drawers. She flushed at the thought of how they had ended up there.

'Tash?'

'What?' She pulled them on, her back to him, the bedspread hiding her naked body from him.

'Are you OK?'

'I'm fine.' She wrestled the knickers over her hips and turned to him. She kept her gaze bright, neutral. Behind it she wished him a slow, painful death. 'I just think we should get on,' she continued. 'Remember what we're doing here.'

And before he could say anything, she had headed for the bathroom.

The gendarme had spoken to the administrative staff at Le Cadre Noir before he had come to the chateau.

'There have been no reports of such a girl here,' he said, as they sat in the drawing room over coffee provided by Madame, who had retired to a discreet distance, 'but they have assured me they will certainly let you know should she arrive. Will you be staying on?'

Natasha and Mac glanced at each other.

'I guess so,' said Mac. 'This is the only place Sarah's likely to come to.'

Their story had prompted the same response in the policeman as it had in Madame: faint disbelief, the query hanging in the air as to how would-be parents could tolerate the idea of a child travelling so far alone.

'May I ask why you think she would head for Le Cadre Noir? You are aware that it is an elite academy?'

'Her grandfather. He was a member, or whatever you call it, a long time ago. It was he who seemed to believe that she would come here.'

The inspector seemed satisfied with that response. He scribbled a few more notes in his pad.

'And she has been using my credit card,' Natasha added. 'The withdrawals indicate that she is headed this way.'

The policeman's expression revealed nothing. 'We will place the gendarmes within a fifty-kilometre radius on alert.' He shrugged. 'It will not be easy, though, to distinguish one young woman on a horse. You must understand that in Saumur we are surrounded by people on horseback.'

'We do understand,' said Natasha.

'We could drive around,' Mac said, after the gendarme had left. 'I guess it's better than sitting here all day. Madame could ring us if anything happened.' He made as if to touch her arm, but Natasha moved away, busying herself with her bag.

'I don't suppose it makes sense for both of us to travel,' she said. 'I'll have a walk around the academy. You go. We'll keep in touch.'

'That's ridiculous. Why would we split now?' Mac looked hurt and she wanted to punch him. 'Natasha, we'll go together.'

There was a brief pause; then she gathered up her things. 'OK,' she said finally, and left the room.

There were hoofprints at the far end of the ploughed field, but after a few muddy clods on the tarmac, Boo's trail had disappeared. Sarah walked for another hour, zigzagging across the fields, her voice hoarse from shouting, until she found herself in the next village. By then she was shaking, her body chilled and empty.

It was as she reached the village that she saw the little row of shops. The scent of bread from the *boulangerie* was rich and comforting, completely out of reach. She thrust a chilled hand into her pocket, and came up with three coins. Euros. She couldn't remember why they might be there: Thom had put her money in an envelope into her missing rucksack. Everything was gone: her passport, Boo's papers, her money, Natasha's credit card.

There was only one person who might be able to help her. She reached into her inside pocket for the photograph of Papa, then walked stiffly across the square, went into the *bar tabac*, and asked for a telephone. '*Tu es tombe?*' the woman behind the bar asked.

Sarah nodded, suddenly aware of her clothes, the mud. '*Pardonnez moi,*' she said, checking that she had not left a trail of footprints.

The woman was staring at her face, frowning in concern. '*Alors, assieds-toi, chérie. Tu voudrais une boisson?*'

Sarah shook her head. 'English,' she said, her voice barely rising above a whisper. 'I need to call home.'

The woman eyed the three coins in Sarah's hand. She reached out and touched the side of her face. '*Mais tu as mal à la tête, eh? Gérard!*'

A few seconds later a moustachioed man appeared behind the bar. The woman muttered to him, gesturing towards Sarah.

'Telephone,' he said. He lifted the bar and shepherded her through to a dark hallway. A telephone stood on a small chest of drawers. When she held out her coins, he shook his head. '*Ce n'est pas nécessaire.*'

Sarah tried to remember the code for England. Then she dialled.

'Stroke Ward.'

The English voice made her feel homesick. 'It's Sarah Lachapelle,' she said, her voice tight. 'I need to speak to my grandfather.'

There was a silence. 'Can you hold on a moment, Sarah?'

She heard murmuring, the kind that takes place when someone puts a hand over the receiver.

'Sarah?'

'John?' She was thrown by his voice, having expected a nurse.

'Where are you, girl?'

Sarah froze. She didn't know what to tell him. Would Papa think it was OK to tell John where she was?

'I need to speak to Papa,' she said. 'Can you put him on, please?'

'Sarah, tell me where you are. We got people looking for you.'

'No,' she said firmly. 'I want to talk to Papa.'

'Sarah—'

'It's really important, John. Please don't make it difficult.' She was close to tears. 'If you put the phone to his ear he can still hear what I—'

'Sarah, girl, I can't. Yo' grandpa's gone.'

She stared at the wall. Someone had turned on a television in the bar, and she could hear the distant roar and excited commentary of a football match. 'Gone where?'

A long pause. 'Sarah, baby, he's gone.'

A new cold crept over her, flooding her from the ground up. She shook her head. 'No,' she said. 'You're lying.' Her teeth were chattering.

'Sweetheart, I'm so sorry.'

She slammed down the phone. Her whole body was shaking and she sank, very quietly, to the linoleum floor and sat there, while the hallway travelled gently around her.

'*Alors!*' She was dimly aware of the woman shouting for her husband, and two pairs of hands hauling her to her feet. She was walked through to the main bar, sat gently on one of the red leatherette banquettes, and then the woman was placing a steaming mug of hot chocolate in front of her and unwrapping cubes of sugar, which she stirred into it.

She was aware of more sympathetic faces and voices. Someone removed her riding hat and she was ashamed of her dirty hair, the mud under her fingernails. The woman was rubbing her hand now, encouraging her to drink the hot chocolate. She sipped politely.

'*Tu as perdu ton cheval?*' someone was saying, and her brain felt so strange that it took her several attempts to nod.

'*De quelle couleur est il?*'

'*Brun,*' she said, hearing everything at a remove. She felt her eyelids droop, and then the woman was pushing the mug to her lips again.

'*Mademoiselle.*' A thin man with a cigarette was standing in front of her. '*Le cheval est brun? Il est de quelle taille? Comme ça?*' He held his hand high, close to his shoulder.

Suddenly she could focus. She nodded.

'Come, come,' he said. 'Please come.' She felt the woman's supporting arm under her own and was suddenly grateful for it. Her legs felt weak, like pipe cleaners that might bend under the least pressure. She blinked, the glare of the morning light too bright after the gloom of the bar. And then the woman was climbing into the back seat of a car with her, the thin man getting into the front. They could be taking me anywhere, Sarah thought absently. She was doing everything Papa had told her not to, but somehow she couldn't work up the energy to care.

A mile or two on they were pulling into a farmyard, down a driveway littered with rusting farm machinery. A goose hissed angrily as they got out and the thin man shooed him away.

Then, turning the corner of a shed, she saw him: he was standing in a cow byre, his saddle and bridle placed neatly at the far end of the gate. 'Boo?' she said disbelievingly, the pain in her shoulder forgotten.

'*Il est le tien?*' the man said.

Boo whickered, as if to answer conclusively.

'*Le fermier l'a trouvé ce matin, en haut par le verger. "En tremblant comme une feuille," il a dit.*'

She barely heard him. She wrenched herself from their grasp and propelled herself towards him. She clambered over the gate and half fell into the byre, her arms round his neck, her tear-stained face pressed against his skin.

Who would have thought a girl could cry so much for a horse? they said, in the *bar tabac*, sometime later, after Sarah had been sent on her way with another hot chocolate and half a baguette inside her. She had cried for thirty minutes, while she bandaged the horse's knees, while she stroked him and cooed to him, and refused to leave his side. It wasn't quite normal to see a girl so emotional about an animal.

**M**ac waited for Natasha to climb into the car before he fired the ignition. She had barely spoken to him all morning. She had wanted him last night—it wasn't as if he had forced himself on her. Why the hell was she treating him like this? It was hard to reconcile the passionate creature of last night with the cold, shuttered woman beside him.

*I want you.*

So, how to explain this change in her?

'Did you hear me on the phone this morning?' he asked suddenly.

Her cheeks flushed. 'No,' she said. She'd never been good at lying.

'Maria and I are not together, if that's what this is about. We're friends. We were meant to be doing a job together today. I had to cancel.'

She waved a hand. 'Look. Here we are.'

'She has a new boyfriend,' he said, but she was already out of the car.

They had pulled up at the Ecole Nationale d'Equitation, and now Mac followed her to the offices where a young woman apologised for the misunderstanding of the previous day: they had not understood the situation, she explained, or their connection to Le Cadre Noir.

'Here,' Mac said, pulling out a folder of photographs. 'This is Sarah and her horse. You can see her face a bit better in this one.'

The woman examined them, nodded. 'She rides very well.'

'Her grandfather's name is Lachapelle. That's him.' He pointed at the black roll of honour on the wall: all the *écuyers* of Le Cadre Noir since the 1800s, their names outlined in gilt. One jumped out at him: *Lachapelle, 1956–60.* He thought of the old man, who had probably never known that he had been honoured in this way.

'Is he with you?' the woman asked.

'He died last night,' Natasha said.

'Is this why his granddaughter has run away?'

'No,' Natasha said, glancing at Mac. 'We think she doesn't know yet.'

The woman handed Mac the photos. 'I'm sorry we cannot be of more help, but if we hear anything, madame, monsieur, we will of course let you know. Would you like to look around while you are here?'

A young man was appointed to give them a tour, and they walked out into the *Carrière d'Honneur*, a vast outdoor sand school where a man in a black cap was riding a sprightly chestnut. He cantered one way, then another, his mount snorting with the effort.

As they walked, the young man began to explain: this was where the show horses were kept, that way were the dressage horses, over here were the showjumpers.

'Why are we sightseeing?' Natasha grumbled. She flipped open her phone. 'I'm going to try the credit-card company again,' she said. 'It's been a couple of hours.'

'You are photographer?' their guide asked, as Natasha strode away. He pointed at Mac's bag.

'Yes. But I'm not here for work.'

'You should photograph Le Carrousel. This is the show that marks the end of the student year. All the *écuyers* perform.'

'Please excuse me a moment.' Mac's phone was ringing.

'What is it?' Natasha said, breaking off from her call.

He turned away from her, running his hand over his head as he listened. 'Oh Christ,' he said, closing his phone.

'She knows.' Natasha's hand flew to her mouth. 'She knows he's dead.'

Mac nodded. He wondered if the colour had drained from his face as well as hers. 'Put a block on the card, Tash,' he said finally. 'If she's decided she's not coming here, we have to stop her going elsewhere.'

'Monsieur?' The young guide was pressing his walkie-talkie to his ear. 'Monsieur? Madame? *Attendez, s'il vous plaît.*' He spoke in rapid French. Then, 'There is an English girl here. A girl with a horse. Mademoiselle Fournier says you should come with me.'

**I**t was not how she had imagined it, her triumphant arrival. For the first two days of her journey she had pictured it repeatedly, the elation as she reached the place that would surely feel like a second home.

She had almost let out a sob when she saw the signs for the Ecole de Cavalerie, then recognised on a residential street the Georgian façade of the horseshoe-shaped building. But the men who walked its courtyards wore not black but the camouflage of modern warfare. 'Le Cadre Noir?' she had asked one, as he crossed the place du Chardonnet.

'*Non. Le Cadre Noir n'a pas été ici depuis 1984. C'est à St Hilaire de*

*Fontaine.*' He pointed towards a roundabout. '*Cinq kilometres.*' She had braced herself and followed the soldier's instructions, and suddenly there it was, larger than she expected, more modern in aspect. She rode through the open gates, her eyes almost closing with exhaustion, until she saw the sign, GRAND MANÈGE D'ECUYERS, that told her her journey was at an end.

She walked Boo round the covered arena, past the front entrance, and round to the rear, where sawdust hoofprints and a concrete path from the stables told of an equine route in. From the other side of the huge wooden doors, she could hear a man's voice. She straightened a little, took a deep breath, then leaned across, wincing, and banged, several times, on the door. There was a brief silence inside, broken by someone instructing, '*Hup!*' Sarah banged again on the wooden panels.

She heard a bolt slide away from her and the door opened to reveal a cavernous interior: a modern cathedral floored with sand. Around its edges stood a number of horses, all mounted, their riders in the distinctive black and gold uniform she knew from her childhood.

The man who had opened the door stared at her, then castigated her in French. She was so tired she could barely make out what he was saying, but she cut across him. 'I need to speak to the Grand Dieu,' she said, her voice cracking with tiredness. '*Je dois parler au Grand Dieu.*'

There was a brief, stunned silence, and she took advantage of the man's momentary inaction to ride past him.

'*Que faire?*' An old man in a peaked cap came towards them. His face was scored with lines, his black uniform was immaculate.

'*Désolé*, monsieur.' The younger man had taken hold of Sarah's reins.

'*Non!*' Sarah pushed Boo forward, swatting at the man's hand. 'Let go of him. *Je dois parler au Grand Dieu.*'

The man strode up to her. '*Je suis Le Grand Dieu.*'

She sat a little more upright.

'Mademoiselle,' he said, his voice low and grave, '*vous ne pouvez pas entrer ici. C'est Le Cadre Noir. C'est pas pour—*'

'I have to ride for you,' she interrupted. She fumbled in her jacket and pulled out the photograph of Papa. 'Monsieur! *Regardez! C'est Henri Lachapelle.*' She held it in front of him, her arm straight, hand trembling. '*Mon grandpère.*' A lump had risen in her throat. 'He was here. He told me to come. Please let me ride for you.'

The old man's eyes were assessing her. 'You have . . . you have ridden here from England?' he said slowly.

She nodded, hardly daring to breathe.

He shook his head a little. 'Henri Lachapelle,' he murmured. He gazed at her and then he nodded. '*Commences.*'

Natasha hurried after Mac. 'It might not be her,' she had told him, trying to keep the excitement from her face.

He had raised an eyebrow. 'How many other English girls on horses do you think they see around here?'

Their guide beckoned to them. They were back in the front foyer beneath the photographs, the gilded roll of members past. Another door opened, and she saw that Mac, in front of her, had stopped in his tracks. No one spoke. The building was vast, a monument to the art of horsemanship, the echoing space inside dotted with black-clad men on horses. The guide gestured them to the audience seating below.

She felt Mac's hand tugging at her sleeve. 'Tash, look,' he said quietly.

Natasha followed his line of vision, walking down the steps after him until they reached the side of the arena.

Sarah was riding very slowly towards the centre. Her horse, the bois-terous, glossy animal that had been in such rude health in Kent, was scratched and muddy. Two makeshift bandages sat bulkily on his knees. His eyes were hollow with exhaustion. But it was Sarah she saw: the child was so pale that she seemed ghostly, ethereal. A huge bruise had half closed one eye; her back and right leg bore a continent of mud. To all this she seemed oblivious: she was lost in what she was doing.

A short distance away an old man was watching Sarah, as she asked Boo to trot, to canter, creating small, elegant circles round the men who sat on their own horses, watching impassively.

Sarah's face was a mask of concentration. Natasha watched the minuscule movements of her heels, the tiny messages she sent through the reins. She could see the horse listening, accepting, obeying even through its fatigue, and understood that while she knew nothing about horses, what she was watching was beautiful, something that could only be achieved through discipline and work. She glanced at Mac, beside her, and knew that he could see it too. He was leaning forward, his eyes locked on the girl as if willing her to succeed.

The horse's legs moved up and down, a rhythmic dance, his great head lowering in obedience to the task. Only the flecks of spittle that sprayed from his mouth betrayed the effort this movement cost him. And then he was dancing a circle round his own hindquarters, a con-trolled, flowing manoeuvre that made Natasha want to applaud for the elegance, the unlikeliness of it. Sarah murmured something to Boo, a small hand reaching out to thank him, a gesture that brought tears to Natasha's eyes. Then, as the horse rose onto his hind legs, teetering, absorbed in the effort of combatting gravity, she was crying as she watched the lost child and the broken horse giving their all.

She felt Mac's hand surround hers and squeezed it, grateful for its warmth, its strength. And then Sarah was cantering around the edge of the vast arena, a beautiful, slow, controlled pace, and Natasha saw that the men on the horses had removed their hats, were sliding them down their chests in a formal gesture, and one by one were striking off in the same direction, following her, their heads dipped, as if in salute.

Mac dropped her hand and reached for his camera, firing off shots as the horse slowed to a trot, then to a walk. As the girl walked up the centre of the arena, facing the old man, the men replaced their hats and peeled off to the sides to watch. Sarah, grey now with the effort of what she had achieved, stopped her horse squarely in front of him, all four feet lined up neatly beneath him.

'She's done it,' Mac was murmuring.

The girl, breathing hard, dropped her head, saluting the old man, a warrior, returning from battle. The old man removed his own hat, nodding in reply. Natasha discovered she was holding her breath and reached again for Mac's hand.

The Grand Dieu stepped forward, his face was sombre, his eyes kind.

'Non,' he said. 'I am sorry, young lady, but *non*.' He reached out a hand and stroked her horse's neck.

Sarah's eyes widened as if she couldn't quite believe what she was hearing. She clutched Boo's mane, then glanced towards the spectator area, perhaps seeing Natasha and Mac for the first time. Then, with an almost imperceptible breath, she slid off her horse in a dead faint.

# THIRTEEN

SHE WAS SILENT for the short journey back to the chateau, accepting without protest Natasha's hand round hers, perhaps there for reassurance, perhaps from fear that she might disappear. They didn't push her to speak; it was understood that this was not the time for questions.

When they arrived, Natasha took Sarah upstairs to her room, undressed her as if she were a much younger child, and laid her on the big bed. As she brought the covers over the thin shoulders, the girl closed her eyes and slept. Natasha sat beside her, one hand resting on the arc of her sleeping body, as if that small human contact might offer comfort. She was not sure she had ever seen anyone look so pale, so hollowed out. Now that she allowed herself to consider the scale of what Sarah had been through she was profoundly shaken.

For a few moments after the Grand Dieu had given his verdict, chaos had broken loose. As Sarah had hit the sand, Natasha and Mac had run, in tandem, into the arena, Mac scooping up the seemingly lifeless body as the Grand Dieu caught hold of the horse. Some minutes later, as Sarah gradually came round in an office close by, they had placed themselves on each side of her, Natasha cradling her head.

'It's all right, Sarah,' Natasha found herself saying, stroking her sweaty, matted hair. 'You're not alone. You're not alone now.' But the girl hadn't seemed to hear her.

The doctor, summoned from the other end of the Ecole Nationale, had diagnosed a fractured collarbone and severe bruising, but recommended that what the child needed more than anything was rest.

*C'est incroyable.* The tale had spread across the Ecole Nationale and groups of people emerged, some in jodhpurs and peaked caps, to glimpse the young English girl who had ridden halfway across France.

Boo was taken to the veterinary centre to have his injuries dressed and would spend the night in the stables. It was, the Grand Dieu remarked, the least they could do for such an animal. Mac said afterwards that the old man had stood in front of the stable for some time, gazing over the door at Boo. '*Alors,*' he had said, not looking at Mac. 'Every time I think I know everything about horses, there is something more to surprise me.'

'I feel the same way about humans,' Mac said.

The Grand Dieu placed a hand on his shoulder. 'We will talk tomorrow,' he said. 'Come to me at ten. She deserves an explanation.'

When Natasha emerged into the corridor, some time after eight, Mac was waiting. She closed the door quietly behind her. 'She's fine,' she said, 'but she's out cold. Do you want to see—'

He shook his head. Then he let out a long breath, attempting to smile. 'We found her,' he said.

'Yes.' She wondered why neither of them seemed to feel the elation they might have expected.

'I keep thinking—' He broke off. 'What could have happened . . .'

'I know.'

He took a step closer and nodded to his room. 'You want to crash in mine?' he said. 'I mean, if she's in your bed, you'll have nowhere . . .'

*There would always be another Maria.*

When she spoke, her voice was neutral, businesslike. 'I—I don't think she should be left alone,' she said. 'I'll sleep in the chair in there.'

'You're probably right.' He tried to smile.

'You need to rest too,' she said softly.

'I'm fine,' he said, not meeting her eye. 'You two sleep well. Call for me in the morning.'

'**I**f she doesn't want to talk, I don't think we should push her.' Natasha was standing in the great hallway while Mac settled the bill. She gazed down the steps to where Sarah waited in the back of the car.

'It's not just that she doesn't want to talk about her grandfather, Mac. She doesn't seem to want to talk at all.'

The police had found her passport, with the empty wallet and a few belongings, on the road to Blois. Even the handing over of the precious dogeared paperback of Xenophon did not stir her from inertia.

Mac took back his credit card and thanked Madame, who had insisted on making up a small package of food for the girl.

'She's been driven by this idea for the last however long it was, and she's just been told it's not going to happen,' Mac said. 'Her grandfather died. She's shocked, tired and disappointed. And she's a teenager.'

Natasha wrapped her arms around herself. 'I suppose you're right.'

The sun emerged sporadically on the short drive from the chateau to Le Cadre Noir, but none of them noticed. The gateman had obviously been warned to expect them; Natasha saw him peer curiously at the back seat as they passed through.

Mademoiselle Fournier was waiting for them outside the main stables. She greeted them both with kisses, then held Sarah's shoulders, beaming. 'How are you feeling today, Sarah?' she said.

'Fine,' she muttered.

'You want to see your horse while we are waiting for Monsieur Varjus? Baucher has had a comfortable night. He is just over here . . .'

She had begun to lead them towards the show block, when Sarah cut in. 'No,' she said. 'I don't want to. Not now.'

'I suspect Sarah is probably waiting to speak to the Grand Dieu.' Mac's apology was audible in his voice.

'Of course. I should have thought.' Mademoiselle Fournier's smile did not falter. 'If you would follow me?'

The Grand Dieu sat at his desk and considered Sarah for a moment, as if surprised again that a child of such a size could be responsible for what he had witnessed the day before. He explained in heavily accented English that Le Cadre Noir accepted no more than five new members each year, usually only one or two. There was an exam, overseen by some of the most senior horsemen in the country, for which the minimum age was eighteen. To join, she would not only need to succeed in this but would have to be a French national.

Sarah said nothing.

'All this aside, Mademoiselle, I would like to say that what you did was magnificent. You and your horse.' The old man leaned over the desk. 'If you can fulfil the requirements of our system there is no reason why, within a few years, you and your horse should not return here. To achieve what you have achieved at your age is'—he shook his head—'something I am still having difficulty in accepting.'

He looked down at his hands. 'I would also like to tell you that your grandfather was a fine horseman. I was always very sorry that he left. I believe he should have been a *maître écuyer*. He would be very proud of what you have achieved.'

'But you're not going to take me.'

'Mademoiselle, I cannot possibly take a fourteen-year-old girl here. You must understand this.'

Sarah looked up at the Grand Dieu. 'Will you take my horse?'

'*Pardon?*' The old man blinked.

'Will you take Baucher?'

Natasha glanced at Mac. 'Sarah, you don't want to give away Boo.'

'I'm not talking to you,' she said firmly. 'I'm talking to him. Do you think he's talented? *Est-ce que vous pensez qu'il est bon?*'

'*Mais oui. Il a courage aussi, c'est bien.*'

'Then I give him to you. I don't want him any more.'

The room fell silent. The man from the administrative section muttered something in the Grand Dieu's ear.

Natasha leaned towards them. 'Gentlemen, I think Sarah is very tired still—I don't think she means—'

'Stop telling me what I mean!' Her voice filled the little room. 'I'm telling you, I don't want him any more. Monsieur can have him. Will you take him?' Her voice was insistent, imperious.

The Grand Dieu looked carefully at Sarah, as if assessing how serious she was.

'You genuinely want to give him to Le Cadre Noir?'

'Yes.'

'Then, yes, I will gratefully accept, mademoiselle. It is obvious he is a very gifted horse.'

Something in Sarah seemed to relax. She straightened her shoulders and turned to Natasha. 'Right. Can we go now? *Now*,' she said, when nobody moved. 'Or I'll go by myself.'

It was all the prompt they needed. They rose as one, Mac shooting a bemused look at the old man as he followed Sarah into the sunshine.

'Madame,' Le Grand Dieu said, when they were out of Sarah's earshot. He took her hand in both his own. 'If she wants to visit him, or even if she changes her mind, it's fine. She is young. A lot has happened.'

'Thank you,' Natasha said. She would have said more, but something had lodged at the back of her throat.

The rain began to fall in unremitting sheets shortly after they left Saumur. They drove in silence, Mac's car forging through plumes of surface water, his attention on the road.

Sarah's face was impassive, but the air of misery that hung about her was so overwhelming that it had permeated the whole car. Give her time, Natasha kept telling herself. Put yourself in her shoes. She has lost her grandfather, her home. But she couldn't make sense of it. Why would a girl who had fought so hard to keep her horse, her link with the past and perhaps her future, let it go so casually?

She thought back to the last moments of their visit to Le Cadre Noir. The Grand Dieu had accompanied them to the stables. 'I would like you to see your horse before you leave, Sarah,' he said.

Natasha had guessed his motive: he believed that seeing Boo would change her mind. But Sarah had walked almost reluctantly towards the stable and had glanced only briefly at the vet's handiwork. Even when the horse had stuck his head over the door, she had not moved towards him. Her shoulders stiffened and then, with the slightest of nods towards the Grand Dieu, she had turned and walked towards the car.

It was not only Sarah and her losses that preoccupied Natasha. When they left this car in England it would all be over for her too. There would be a negotiated agreement over who occupied the house for its final weeks, some financial discussions, and then Mac would be gone to his new home, and she would be alone, picking up the pieces of what remained of her life. It was a terrible thing to discover you no longer wanted the life that stretched ahead of you.

Natasha closed her eyes. When she opened them, gazing out at the town below the motorway, she caught a glimpse of a girl riding a bicycle, stooped, moving through the empty street with a steady grace. And she recalled suddenly the train journey, months before, when she had seen a girl astride a rearing horse in a London backstreet.

'Mac, stop the car,' she said suddenly.

'What?' said Mac.

'Stop the car.' She knew only that she could not allow this journey to continue. Mac pulled up and, as he looked on, confused, she found herself clambering out, opening the rear door. 'Come on,' she said to Sarah. 'You and I need to talk.'

The girl shrank away from her.

'No,' Natasha said, not even sure where the words were coming from. 'We're not going any further, Sarah, until you and I talk.'

She took her hand, then pulled her out of the car and through the rain until they reached the awning of a café opposite. She heard Mac's protest, and her own determination, as she told him to leave them alone.

'Right.' Natasha pulled out a chair and sat down. There were no other customers.

Sarah flung her a look of deep distrust and sat down beside her.

'OK, Sarah. I'm a lawyer. I spend my life trying to anticipate the games people play, trying to out-think them. But I'm struggling here. I cannot work out why a girl who would lie, steal and cheat to keep a horse, a girl who had only one aim in life, which revolved round that horse, would give it all away.'

Sarah said nothing. She stared at the table.

'Is this some kind of temper tantrum? Are you thinking that if you throw it all up in the air, someone will step in and change the rules for you? Because if so, I can tell you they're not going to change anything.'

'I never asked them to change anything,' she snapped.

'OK, then. Is it about your grandpa? Are you afraid you can't look after the horse without his help? Because we can help you there, Sarah.'

Natasha was aware that she had sounded as if she was talking to a client. But she couldn't help it. That's the best I can do, she told herself.

Sarah just sat there. 'Can we go home now?' she said.

Natasha screwed her eyes shut. 'No, we can't. I know you're lying to me, so I'm not going to take you anywhere until you tell me what's going on.'

'You want the truth?'

'Yes.'

'Because you *always* tell the truth.' Her tone was mocking now.

'What do you mean by that?'

'Uh . . . like you're still in love with Mac, but you don't tell him?' She nodded towards the car where Mac, just visible through the rain-washed window, was poring over a road map. 'It's so obvious it's pathetic. Even in the car I see you sneaking little looks at him. But you won't tell him.'

Natasha swallowed. 'It's complicated.'

'Yes, it's complicated. Everything's complicated. Because you know like I do—' There was a break in her voice. 'You know like I do that sometimes telling the truth makes things worse, not better.'

Natasha stared across the road at Mac. 'You're right,' she said finally. 'OK? You're right. But whatever I feel about Mac, I can live with it. When I look at you, Sarah, I see someone who is throwing away a life-line. I see someone who is creating more pain.' She leaned forward. 'Why, Sarah? Why would you do this to yourself?'

'Because I had to.'

'No, you didn't. That man thought you might be good enough in a few years if you—'

'In a few years.'

'Yes. I know it seems like a long time when you're young, but—'

'Why can't you just leave it? Why can't you trust me to make the right decision? I had to let him go.'

'No, I'm telling you you didn't. Christ! What would your grandfather say if he knew what you'd done?'

Sarah's expression was ferocious. 'He'd understand!' she shouted. 'I *had* to let him go. It was the only way I could protect him!'

There was a sudden silence. Natasha sat very still.

'Protect him? When she spoke again, her voice was soft. 'Sarah, what happened?'

Suddenly, abruptly, the girl began to cry, a terrible, grief-stricken sound. Natasha hesitated, then pulled the girl to her, holding her tightly, murmuring words of comfort. 'It's OK, Sarah,' she said. 'It's OK.' But as the sobs subsided into hiccups and Sarah began to whisper a halting tale of loneliness, of secrets, debt, fear and a dark path so nearly taken, Natasha's own eyes filled with tears.

**T**hrough the blur of the windscreen, Mac watched Natasha holding Sarah so tightly that there was a kind of fierceness in it. She was talking now, nodding, and whatever she was saying, the girl was in agreement. He didn't want to interrupt if she was managing to elicit some explanation for the past three days. So he stayed in the car, watching, waiting.

A woman arrived at the table, the owner probably. Natasha was ordering something and, as he watched, she turned to him. Their eyes met, and then she was beckoning him to join them. He climbed out of the car, locked it behind him, and went to where they were sitting under the awning. They were both smiling, shy smiles. His wife, his almost-ex-wife, he thought, with an ache, looked beautiful.

'Mac,' she said, 'there's been a change of plan.'

He glanced at Sarah. 'Would this change of plan involve a horse?'

'It certainly would.'

'Thank God for that.' Mac pulled out a chair and sat down.

All the way back to England, Natasha sat with Sarah in the rear of the car, their voices a low murmur, occasionally lifting to include Mac in the conversation. They would not return to Saumur today; Sarah knew a man, she told them, the one man she would trust to bring Boo back for her. They had rung Le Cadre Noir, who, to Sarah's visible relief, seemed to have been expecting their call. The horse would be safe there until someone came to collect him.

Occasionally Mac would glance back at the two heads, organising, talking. Sarah would stay with Natasha. They were considering all the options: boarding schools—Natasha rang her sister, who said she had heard there was one that took horses—or livery yards far from the East End of London. There would be no more problems with Sal, Natasha told her. Without Sarah's signature on the terms and conditions, his claim on the horse was worthless, and she would send a legal letter telling him as much and warning him to keep away. They would find a different kind of life for Boo.

Natasha, Mac thought, was doing what she did best: organising. Occasionally, when Henri Lachapelle was mentioned, Sarah's face crumpled a little and Natasha's hand reached out to squeeze hers, or just to pat a shoulder. Little acts of kindness to tell her, again and again, that she was not alone.

Mac saw all this in the rearview mirror, his gratitude tempered by the odd sensation of exclusion. He knew Natasha was not deliberately leaving him out, that whatever had occurred between the two of them, he would keep Sarah in his life too. Perhaps this was Natasha's gentle way of telling him that their night together had been a mistake, that away from the intense atmosphere of the search she was seeking to return to a more stable existence with Conor.

When they reached Calais, Sarah finally telephoned the man she had said could transport her horse back to England. She took Natasha's phone and walked away across the tarmac for some time, as if she needed this conversation to be private.

'You're very quiet, Mac,' Natasha remarked, as Sarah talked some distance away, walking between the cars queuing for the ferry, her left hand pressed to her ear.

'I guess there's nothing I need to say,' he said. 'You two seem to have it all figured out.'

'Here,' said Sarah, returning before either of them could say anything else. 'Thom wants to talk to you.' She stood close to Natasha as she took the phone, as if the distance between them had been bridged. Mac turned away.

'No, that's really not . . . Are you sure?' Natasha said, and then, after a pause, 'Yes. Yes, I know.'

Mac turned back as she ended the call. Natasha was looking at Sarah. 'He won't accept any money,' she said. 'He says he's heading that way in the middle of the week and he'll bring Boo back then.'

Sarah's smile was brief and surprising, as if she was as taken aback as Natasha by this act of generosity.

'But there's a catch,' Natasha added. 'He said that in return you have to invite him to your first performance.'

The beauty of young people, Mac thought as he headed for the car, was that it took only a few words of faith to relight a spark of confidence that the future could be something wonderful, instead of a series of obstacles and disappointments. If only the same was true of adults.

Natasha fiddled with the key in the lock, and opened the front door onto a dark hallway, flicking on the lights. It was shortly after one in the morning, and Sarah, bleary with sleep, walked in and up the stairs on automatic pilot, as if she was at home. Natasha followed her, straightened her bed, handed her a fresh towel, and finally, when she was sure that the girl would sleep, came downstairs.

Mac was on the sofa in the living room, his long legs stretched out, feet on the linen-covered footstool, car keys still in his hand. His eyes were closed, and she allowed herself a lingering glance at him.

He yawned, pushed himself upright, and Natasha busied herself, afraid he would feel her scrutiny. The floor, she noticed, was carpeted with photographs lined up on the polished wood floor where he must have left them days ago, the morning he had discovered Sarah gone. It was as she let her gaze run over the series of black-and-white images, the horses in midmovement, the glowing tones of Cowboy John's shrewd old face, that her eyes fell on one in particular. The woman was on the telephone. She was smiling, oblivious to the camera's attentions.

She stared at it for several seconds before she realised the woman was herself. It looked like some idealised version of her, a person she had ceased to know. 'When did you take this?'

He opened his eyes to look. 'A few weeks ago. In Kent.'

'Mac?' she said. 'Is this how you see me?'

Eventually she dared to look at him. The man before her had lines of sadness on his face; his skin was grey with tiredness. He nodded.

Her heart had begun to thump. She thought of Henri, of Florence, of Sarah, bravely blurting out the truth into a rainy unknown. 'Mac,' she said, her eyes still on the photograph, 'I have to tell you something, even if it turns out to be the most humiliating thing I ever do.' She took a deep breath. 'I love you. I always have loved you, and even if it's too late for us I need you to know that I'm sorry. I need you to know that letting you go will always be the greatest mistake of my life.'

His usual relaxed charm had deserted him. 'What about Conor?' he said, almost snappy.

'It's over. It was never—'

'Fuck,' he said. Then he stood up. 'Fuck.'

'Why are you—' She stood up, shocked by his outburst, the uncharacteristic cursing. 'What do you—'

'Tash,' he said, striding across his photographs, which skidded across the polished floor. He was inches from her. He was so close she could feel the warmth of his skin. She held her breath. *Don't say no*, she willed him. *Don't find a diplomatic reason to leave. I can't do this a second time.* 'Tash.' He took her face in his hands. His voice was low. 'Wife.'

'Do you mean—'

'Don't shut me out again.' His words were almost angry. 'Don't shut me out.' She had begun to apologise, but the words were lost in their kisses, their tears. He picked her up and she wrapped herself round him, her legs, her skin against his skin, her face buried in his neck.

# EPILOGUE

MACAULEY AND PARTNERS had suffered a difficult birth, but almost eighteen months on, Natasha was beginning to feel that her choice to leave Davison Briscoe and set up on her own had been right. Thank God for Linda Blyth-Smith. Having her trusted secretary jump ship with her to run the office had kept her afloat.

She glanced out of the window and saw that the Gray's Inn Road below was already thickening with Friday-afternoon traffic. Then she spotted him, pulling in on the other side of the road.

'Have a good weekend, Lin.' She threw her coat over her arm, ready to run down the stairs.

'You too. Hope it all goes well.'

Downstairs on the pavement she glanced to either side of her, then ran across between the slowly moving vehicles.

'Dead on time,' said Mac, as she leaned across to kiss him.

'You're a marvel. And you,' she said, peering at the baby beaming at her from his car seat, 'have wiped banana all over your dad's jacket.'

'You're kidding,' said Mac, glancing behind him. 'How could you, mate?'

Natasha chuckled and did up her seat belt.

'So what's this we're going to again?' Mac asked.

'It's an end-of-year celebration for gifted and talented pupils.'

Everyone knew the refrain of working mothers about the impossibility of balancing childcare with work, Natasha thought, as they made their way across the city. In her own case, she had acquired two children and a horse within nine months. The great irony was that, after all the years of being told to reduce her stress levels, drink less and have carefully timed sex, she had conceived during the most fraught three days of her life. But that, they agreed, when they lay on either side of Henry, gazing at his fat limbs, his cheeks, his Mac-like thatch of hair, was the beauty of it. He had come because he was meant to.

The Kent house had long gone, replaced by a new rented cottage, the London house taken off the market. Mac, Natasha and the baby spent weekdays there, while Sarah was at a select boarding school in the country that didn't just accept horses but could offer tuition at the level Sarah needed. The cost was crippling, even with her scholarship. But they didn't begrudge the money because Sarah had flourished there.

At weekends, when they drove up to their cottage four miles from the school, and Sarah stayed with them, her conversations were dominated not just by Boo's behaviour in the arena, his many achievements or minor disappointments, but increasingly by the activities of her friends. They had come a long way. Each of them.

Sarah had seen them even before the steward had motioned Mac's car into a space. 'You made it,' she said, as Natasha climbed out.

'Wouldn't miss it,' said Mac, kissing her cheek. 'How are you?'

But Sarah was already wrenching open the car's rear door. 'Hello, Henry, my little soldier! Look at you!' She wrestled with his seat belt, and then she held him in front of her, grinning as he reached for her hair.

'You'll get banana all over that shirt.' Natasha kissed her. 'Hello, love. Are you all prepared, then?'

'Yup. Boo's going beautifully. Ooh, I missed you. Yes, I did. Yes, I did.' Sarah was hugging Henry, prompting the same delighted response she always elicited from him.

They began to walk to the arena, where the seats were already filling. A boy in uniform handed them a programme and Natasha noticed with pride that Sarah's interpretation of Le Carrousel got top billing.

'Do you want me to baby-sit this weekend?' Sarah asked them.

'I thought you were going to a party,' Natasha reminded her.

It was the smallest glance, but Mac caught it. 'Uh-oh. What's this about? What are you after, young lady?'

'Look, I've saved you really good seats. I didn't get one for Henry, but I thought you'd have him on your laps. You'll be able to see everything.'

Mac paused. 'Come on, you. What is it?' He'd always been better than Natasha at reading her.

She tried to look embarrassed, but she was beaming. 'I've been accepted for the summer training course at Saumur. Six weeks under Monsieur Varjus. I got a letter this morning.'

'Sarah, that's wonderful.' Natasha hugged her. 'What an achievement.'

'I know.' She hesitated. 'But it's very expensive.' She whispered the sum.

Mac whistled. 'That's a hell of a lot of baby-sitting.'

'But I've got to go. If I do well at this, it'll stand me in good stead when I make my application. Please! I'll do anything.'

Natasha pictured the estate car she and Mac had inspected in the showroom the previous week, and watched it disappear. 'We'll find it. Don't worry. There might be some of your papa's money left . . .'

Someone was calling her, their voice lifting over the crowd.

'You'd better go.'

The orchestra was tuning up. Sarah thrust Henry at Natasha and ran towards the stables. 'Thank you!' she yelled, waving over the heads of the spectators. 'Thank you so much! I'll pay you back some day. Really!'

Natasha held her son close to her. 'You already did,' she said quietly.

## Jojo Moyes

**In your introduction to *The Horse Dancer* on page 8, you say that you dedicated your book to a young girl called Mecca Harris. Can you tell us more about her?**
Alongside the newspaper article I talked about, there were compelling pictures of Mecca as a skinny little jockey with braids under her riding hat. It seems she had a natural ability and determination and, with the help of the Philadelphia Black Cowboys, she was chosen to play polo against Yale with the all-black Work to Ride team. In 2003 she received application forms from a prestigious polo school in California, but soon afterwards she, her mother and her mother's boyfried were found murdered in their home, victims of an alleged drug killing.

**So Mecca's life ended tragically, but the image of her riding struck a chord with your own inner-city childhood and also gave you the character of Sarah?**
Yes. Sarah is based on me, though I never had to deal with all the things that she does. But I was an only child, of divorced parents, and fairly solitary. Looking back, I think I probably didn't trust people enough, or tell them what was going on.

**How did you get introduced to riding in the East End of London?**
I lived in Hackney, and when I was seven or eight my parents took me to Lee Valley Riding School. I was plainly a little girl who was interested in being out of doors and doing country stuff and my parents tried hard to give me a rounded

experience in everything. Neither of them had the slightest interest in horses but I developed a passion for them. I looked after this one horse, Bombardier . . . When his owner told me he was going to be sold, I decided to buy him.

**What age were you when you decided to buy Bombardier?**
I was fourteen. I had a cleaning job and some other jobs. He cost me £425.

**What did your parents have to say about you wanting to own a horse?**
I didn't tell them until I'd done it. When I got home and announced to my mother that I'd bought this horse she didn't believe me! I said I really had, and she said, 'Well, you can jolly well go and "unbuy" him. I said, 'Right,' but then snuck up to my room. The cleaning job paid me £7.50 a week and that paid for Bombardier's hay and straw. My mother told me a few years later that she and Dad had been secretly very proud of me, but couldn't tell me then.

**In *The Horse Dancer*, there's an extraordinary scene about carriage racing on the dual carriageway above East London. Did you ever witness this yourself?**
Several times, and it happened exactly as I've written it. I moved Bombardier to a funny little stables under the railway arches close to my dad's warehouse. I used to leave home at about half past five in the morning and get the bus there. The first time, someone in the stables was taking some horses to race and asked if I'd like to go along. It was the most exciting thing. The men would do this amazing manouevre to stop the traffic. Of course there was far less of it twenty-five years ago. The money would change hands and it would all be over by 7 a.m. By the time the police arrived all they saw was a pile of droppings.

**Did you travel to Le Cadre Noir in Saumur to research your novel?**
Yes, and it was one of the most enjoyable pieces of research I've ever done. I went first to watch them perform in Paris. It was compelling, with all the men dressed in black, which makes them look quite magnificently French and sexy. It was disciplined perfection. Just lovely and fun and elegant. The following May I went to the home of Le Cadre Noir in Saumur, where I spent some time talking to the riders and going round the stables. To watch a partnership between a man—or a woman, these days—and an animal, which is all about giving and being tuned into each other, is profoundly moving. I really fell in love with it all.

**Have you thought of trying this kind of dressage yourself?**
Since visiting Saumur it has obsessed me, to the point where, if I can afford to I'm going to buy myself a dressage horse for my fortieth birthday. And I'm booked in to do an intensive week in an English equivalent of Le Cadre Noir to celebrate the milestone. I can't wait. I'm going to school myself to ride better!

**You have a horse and ride out near your home in Essex. If you buy a dressage horse and pursue that discipline, would you like to compete on it one day?**
I have this old racehorse, and he's fast but only really good for straight lines. I'd love to compete on a dressage horse. But I'd still be writing every day because that's what I do. I'm a storyteller, and I just want the chance to keep doing it.

# LOOK AGAIN

## LISA SCOTTOLINE

*Where I get my ideas from is probably the most frequently asked question I get—and one that I, too, love to ask other authors.*

*I get them from the strangest things—it can be anything. The truth is that every book I write is from the heart. They may be thrillers, but there is a huge emotional component, and that means the ideas have to come from some place that matters inside me, some place that really connects.*

*In the case of* Look Again, *I was driving home after dropping my child off at college, and thinking, 'I have to let my daughter go. But who really owns a child?'*

# CHAPTER ONE

ELLEN GLEESON WAS UNLOCKING her front door when something in the mail caught her attention. It was a white card with photos of missing children, and one of the little boys looked oddly like her son. She eyed the photo as she twisted her key in the lock, but the mechanism was jammed, probably because of the cold. Snow encrusted SUVs and swing sets, and the night sky was the colour of frozen blueberries.

The card read: HAVE YOU SEEN THIS CHILD? The resemblance between the boy in the photo and her son was uncanny. They had the same wide-set eyes, smallish nose and lopsided grin. Maybe it was the lighting on her porch. She held the photo closer. The boys could have been twins.

*Weird*, Ellen thought. Her son didn't have a twin. She had adopted him as an only child.

She jiggled the key in the lock, suddenly impatient. It had been a long day at work, and she was losing her grip on her handbag, brief-case, the mail and a bag of Chinese takeout.

The lock finally gave way, the door swung open, and she dumped her stuff onto the side table and shed her coat, shivering happily in the warmth of her cosy living room. Lace curtains framed the windows behind a red-and-white-checked couch, and the walls were stencilled with cows and hearts, a cutesy touch she liked more than any reporter should. A plastic toy chest overflowed with plush animals, Spot board books and Happy Meal figurines.

'Mommy, look!' Will called out, running towards her with a piece of paper in his hand. His fringe blew off his face, and Ellen flashed on the missing boy from the white card in the mail. The likeness startled her before it dissolved in a wave of love, powerful as blood.

'Hi, honey!' Ellen opened her arms as Will reached her, and scooped him up, nuzzling him and breathing in the oaty smell of dry Cheerios and the faint almond scent of the Play-Doh sticking to his overalls.

Will squirmed, waving the drawing. 'Look what I made! It's for you!'

'Let's see.' Ellen set him down and looked at his drawing, of a horse grazing under a tree. It was too good to be freehand. Will was no Picasso. 'Wow, this is great! Thank you so much.'

'Hey, Ellen,' said the baby sitter, Connie Mitchell, coming in from the kitchen. Connie was short and sweet, soft as a marshmallow in a white sweatshirt, which she wore with wide-leg jeans and slouchy Uggs. Her brown eyes were bracketed by laughter lines and her chestnut ponytail was shot through with grey. Connie asked, 'How was your day?'

'Crazy busy. How about you?'

'Just fine,' Connie answered, which was only one of the reasons that Ellen counted her as a blessing.

Will was waving his picture, still excited. 'I drew it! All by myself!'

'He traced it from a colouring book,' Connie said under her breath. She crossed to the coat closet and retrieved her parka.

'I *drew* it!' Will's forehead buckled into a frown.

'I know, and you did a great job.' Ellen stroked his silky head. 'How was swimming, Con?

'Fine. Great.' Connie put on her coat. 'He was a little fish.' She got her brown handbag and packed tote bag from the window seat. 'Will, tell Mommy how great you did without the kickboard.'

Will pouted.

Connie zipped up her coat. 'Then we drew pictures, right? You told me Mommy liked horses.'

'I *drew* it,' Will said, cranky.

'I love my picture, sweetie.' Ellen was hoping to stave off a kiddy meltdown. She didn't blame him. He was plainly tired; a lot was asked of three-year-olds these days. She asked Connie, 'Did he nap?'

'I put him down, but he didn't sleep.'

'Too bad.' Ellen hid her disappointment. If Will didn't nap, she wouldn't get any time with him before bed.

Connie said goodbye and left, letting in an icy blast of air. Ellen closed and locked the door.

'I DREW IT!' Will dissolved into tears, and the drawing fluttered to the hardwood floor.

'Aw, baby. Let's have some dinner.'

'All by myself!'

'Come here, sweetie.' Ellen reached for him but her hand hit the bag of Chinese food, knocking it to the floor and scattering the mail. She righted it before the food spilled, and her gaze fell on the white card with the photo of the missing boy. *Uncanny*.

She picked up the bag of food and left the mail on the floor. For the time being.

Ellen put Will to bed, then grabbed a fork and a cardboard container of leftover Chinese. She took a seat at the dining-room table, and the cat sat at the other end, his amber eyes trained on her food and his tail tucked round his chubby body. He was all black except for a white stripe down the centre of his face and white paws like cartoon gloves, and Will had picked him because he looked so much like Figaro from the *Pinocchio* DVD. They couldn't decide whether to name him Figaro or Oreo, so they'd gone with Oreo Figaro.

Ellen opened the container, forked chicken onto her plate, then dumped out the leftover rice. She caught sight of the Coffmans, her neighbours across the shared driveway, doing their homework at their dining-room table. The Coffman boys were tall and strong, both lacrosse players at Lower Merion, and Ellen wondered if Will would play a sport in high school. There had been a time when she couldn't imagine him healthy, much less wielding a lacrosse stick.

She ate a piece of chicken, and pulled over the mail. She was about to daydream her way through the Tiffany catalogue when her gaze fell on the white card. She paused in midbite and picked it up. HAVE YOU SEEN THIS CHILD? At the bottom it read: *American Center for Missing and Abducted Children (ACMAC)*.

Ellen set her fork down and eyed the photo of the missing boy again. There was no blaming the lighting this time. Her dining room had a colonial brass candelabra that hung from the ceiling, and in its bright light, the boy in the photo looked even more like Will. It was a black-and-white photo, so she couldn't tell if they had the same eye colour. She read the caption under the photo:

| | |
|---|---|
| Name: | Timothy Braverman |
| Resides: | Miami, Florida |
| DOB: | 19/01/05 |
| Eyes: | Blue |
| Hair: | Blond |
| Stranger Abduction: | 24/01/06 * |

She blinked. They both had blue eyes and blond hair. They were even about the same age. Will had just turned three on January 30. She examined the photo, parsing the features of the missing boy. The similarity started with his eyes, which were a generous distance apart, and the shape, which was roundish. They both had small noses and shared a grin that was lopsided, turning down on the right. Most of all, there was a likeness in the steady, level way that they looked at the world.

Ellen reread the caption, noticed the asterisk and checked the bottom of the card. It read: **Timothy Braverman, Shown Age-progressed to Three Years Old**. The picture of Timothy Braverman wasn't a current photo, though it looked like one. It was an approximation of how the boy would look right now, a projection done by computer or artist. The thought eased her, and she remembered the day she'd met Will.

She'd been doing a story on nurses in the paediatric cardiac intensive-care unit at Dupont Hospital in Wilmington, and Will was in the CICU being treated for a ventricular septal defect, a hole in his septum. He lay at the end of the sunny unit, a tiny boy in a diaper, in an institutional cot with high white bars. He was undersized, failing to thrive, and it made his head a bobblehead doll's on a bony frame. His large blue eyes were his most prominent feature, and he took in everything around him, except people. He never made or held eye contact with anyone, which Ellen later learned could be a sign of neglect, and his was the only cot with no plush toys or colourful mobiles attached to the bars.

He was between heart operations when she first saw him and he lay silently, never crying, surrounded by monitors. An oxygen tube was taped under his nose, a feeding tube disappeared into a nostril, and a clear tube popped grotesquely from the centre of his naked chest, emptying fluids. His IV snaked to his hand, jury-rigged to make sure he didn't pull it free. Unlike the other babies, Will never tried.

Ellen kept researching the story and found herself visiting Will more frequently than necessary. The story became a series, and the angle changed from the nurses to the babies. But amid the cooing, gurgling and crying babies, it was the silent one who held her attention. She wasn't allowed to approach his cot because of CICU regulations, but she would watch him from a short distance, though he always looked away at the blank white wall. Then one morning, his eyes found her, locking in and latching on, their blue as deep as the sea. They shifted away, but after that stayed on her longer and longer.

Will never had any visitors, and one of the mothers, who had a baby awaiting a heart transplant, told Ellen that his mother was a young girl, unmarried, who hadn't even seen him after his first operation. Ellen followed up with his caseworker, who investigated and told her that adoption was a possibility, and she'd gone home, elated. She'd been elated ever since, and in the past two years had come to realise that even though Will wasn't born to her, she was born to be his mother.

Her gaze fell again on the white card, and she set it aside, feeling sympathy for the Braverman family. She couldn't imagine how she would cope if someone kidnapped Will. A few years ago, she'd done a piece in which a father had kidnapped his children after a custody dispute, and she toyed with the idea of calling the mother, Susan Sulaman, and doing a follow-up. She had to keep the story ideas coming if she wanted to keep her job, and it would give her an excuse to meet with her new editor, Marcelo Cardoso, a sexy Brazilian who'd come to the paper a year ago, having left behind the *Los Angeles Times* and a model girlfriend. Maybe a single mother would make a nice change, and if he'd seen enough of the fast lane, she could show him the checkout lane.

Ellen smiled. She used to think she was too smart to have a crush on her boss, but Marcelo was Antonio Banderas with a journalism degree. And it had been too long since the man in her life was older than three. Her last boyfriend had told her she was a 'handful', but Marcelo could handle a handful. And a handful was the only woman worth handling.

She scraped sauce from a few chicken pieces and slid her plate over to Oreo Figaro, who ate with a purr. She waited for him to finish, then cleaned the table and threw away the junk mail, including the white card. It slid into the plastic kitchen bag, and the picture of Timothy Braverman stared at her with that preternatural gaze.

She closed the cabinet door and put the white card out of her mind. She loaded the dishwasher and counted her blessings again. Butcher-block counters, white cabinets with glass fronts, and a splashback with hand-painted wild flowers, matching walls of pinkish white. It was a girl kitchen, down to the name of the wall colour—Cinderella. Though there was no Prince Charming in sight.

She locked the back door and retrieved the used filter from the coffeemaker. She opened the base cabinet to throw the grinds away, but Timothy Braverman looked back at her, unsettling her all over again.

On impulse, she rescued the white card from the trash and slipped it into her jeans pocket.

The alarm went off at six fifteen, and Ellen got out of bed in the dark and hit the shower. She had to be ready by seven so she could get Will up and dressed before preschool, which started at eight thirty. Connie would arrive at seven thirty to feed and take him.

'Honey?' Ellen switched on the Babar lamp, but Will was sleeping soundly, his mouth partly open. His breathing sounded congested, and when she stroked his forehead, it felt hot.

'Will?' she whispered, already wondering if she should send him to preschool. A crust had formed around his nostrils, and his cheeks looked pale. His nose was a ski slope that was the beginner version of hers, and people often mistook him for her biological child.

She decided not to send Will to school. She switched off the lamp, tiptoed from the bedroom, and went back to her room to use the extra fifteen minutes.

'Don't you look nice!' Connie said with a smile, coming out of the dining room, and Ellen grinned as she tiptoed down the stairs. She had used the extra time to change into a tan corduroy jacket, nipped at the waist, and brown suede boots worn on top of her jeans. She had even done a better than usual job on her make-up, blow-dried her hair, and put her liquid eyeliner back in rotation. She was going to see Marcelo this morning and wasn't sure if she wanted to look hot, employable, or both.

'Will's running a low fever, so I figured he'd stay home today.'

'Good decision.' Connie nodded. 'It's twenty degrees out.'

'Yikes.' Ellen crossed to the closet and grabbed her black down jacket. 'So stay inside, take it easy. Maybe you can read to him?'

'Will do.' Connie set down her tote bag and slid out her newspaper. 'I loved your story today, about the old man who trains pigeons.'

'Thanks.' Ellen tugged her coat on.

'The other sitters all read your articles, you know. I'm like a celebrity.'

Ellen smiled. She knew that the sitters were curious about her, the single reporter with the adopted kid. 'Thanks for everything.' Ellen felt a familiar tug inside her chest. 'I hate when I don't get to say goodbye to him. Give him a kiss for me, will you? Tell him I love him.'

'Gotcha.' Connie opened the door, and Ellen stepped reluctantly out. A frigid wind bit her cheek. She wished she could run back in, send Connie home, and take care of her own child, especially when he was sick. But the door was already closing behind her, leaving her outside.

Ellen entered the building with a street-vendor coffee and flashed her ID at the security guard. She wanted to hit the ground running on the Sulaman follow-up story, but her thoughts kept returning to Timothy Braverman. She made her way through the dim hallways of the old building and finally popped out into the newsroom, a bright rectangle that ran the length of a city block, its ceiling three storeys high.

Sunlight filtered in from tall windows covered with old-fashioned blinds, and banners that read CITY, NATIONAL, BUSINESS, NEWSDESK and COPY DESK hung over the various sections. She started down the aisle to her desk, but everyone was collecting in front of the glass-walled editorial offices that ringed the newsroom, and gathering round Marcelo.

She caught the eye of her friend Courtney Stedt, who detoured to meet her midway up the aisle. Courtney was her usual outdoorsy self in a green fleece with jeans, but her expression looked uncharacteristically grim. The office earth mother, Courtney was the one who got cakes for everybody's birthdays. If she was worried, something was wrong.

'Please tell me this is a surprise party,' Ellen said. They fell into step.

'I can't. I have a journalist's respect for the truth.'

They reached the back of the crowd. Staffers filled the aisles between the desks. Ellen leaned back against one of the desks next to Courtney, and thoughts of Timothy Braverman flew from her head. Unemployment had a way of focusing the brain.

Marcelo motioned for order, and everyone quieted, a sea of heads turning to him. He was tall enough to be seen by everyone, with a lean frame, and his thick, dark hair curled unprofessionally over his collar in a raggedy line. Strain showed in his dark brown eyes, and a forked line creased his forehead. His eyebrows sloped down unhappily, and his pursed lips spoke volumes.

'First, good morning, friends,' Marcelo said, his voice deep and soft, with a pronounced Portuguese inflection. 'I'm sorry, but we have another round of layoffs to make.'

The crowd stiffened. Ellen and Courtney exchanged glances.

'I have to make two cuts today and one more by the end of the month.' Marcelo began rolling up the sleeves of his black shirt, European-cut, which he wore without a tie. 'No newspaper has the readers it used to. We're doing everything we can here, and I know you guys are working very hard. None of this is your fault, or management's. We can't dance any faster than we are. So we have to deal with the reality of more cuts, and it's terrible, because I know you have families. You'll have to find another job. Relocate. Take kids out of schools, spouses from jobs. I know all that.' Marcelo paused, his sombre gaze moving from one stricken face to the next. 'You know, when my mother used to spank me, she would always say, "This hurts me more than it does you." But, *Sabia que não era verdade.* Translated? I knew it was bullshit.'

The staff laughed, and so did Ellen. She loved it when Marcelo spoke Portuguese. If he could fire her in Portuguese, she would be happy.

'So I'm not going to tell you it hurts me more than it hurts you. But I *will* tell you that I know how you feel, and I do.' Marcelo's smile reappeared. 'You all know, I've been laid off by some of the best papers in the world. Even by the *Folha de São Paulo*, my hometown paper.'

'Way to go, boss,' a designer called out, and there was more laughter.

'But still I survived. I'll survive even if this paper lets me go, and I'll never quit the newspaper business, because I love it. I love the smell of a good lead. I love finding out something nobody else knows and telling them. That's what we do, and I know you love it, too.'

'Hear hear!' somebody called out, and even Ellen took heart. She loved the business, too. She'd grown up with the newspaper on the kitchen table, folded into quarters for the crossword, next to her mother's coffee cup, and she still got a charge when she saw her own by-line. She had never felt so right for any job in her life, except motherhood, where the pay was even worse.

'But this business doesn't love us back, all the time, and especially not lately.' Marcelo shook his head. 'After all we do for her, after how much we love her, she's a faithless lover.' He flashed a killer smile. 'She goes home with other men. She's always looking around. She strays.'

Everybody laughed, more relaxed now.

'But we love her still, so we'll stay with her, as long as she'll have us. There will always be a place for the newspaper, and those of us, the crazy-in-love ones, we will put up with her.'

'Speak for yourself!' cracked one of the business reporters, but Marcelo's expression changed, his forehead creasing again, so that he looked older than his forty-odd years.

'So I will make the hard decisions. To those I have to let go, please know I won't hand you off to human resources and forget about you.'

Somebody at the front nodded, because they all had heard that he had helped place one of their laid-off business reporters at the *Seattle Times*.

'I think you're all terrific journalists. I'll do everything in my power to help you find another job. I have friends all over. You have my word.'

'Thank you,' a reporter said, and then another, and there was even a smattering of applause, led by Courtney. Ellen found herself clapping, too, because Marcelo reached her at a level she couldn't explain merely by good looks, though it helped. Maybe it was his openness, his honesty, his emotionality. No other editor would have talked about loving the business, or taken the reporters' side. Marcelo's eyes swept the crowd, meeting hers for a brief moment, and Ellen got so flustered she barely felt the nudge in her side.

'Down, girl,' Courtney whispered, with a sly smile.

**A** ladies' room is a girl headquarters, so it was only natural that Ellen, Courtney and another reporter, Sarah Liu, would end up talking about the layoffs by the sinks. A photographer had been let go after the meeting, so they were waiting for the other shoe to drop. Courtney and Sarah were in News, but Ellen was in Features, traditionally the area with the most dispensable reporters.

'Marcelo won't fire anybody in Sports,' Sarah said. She was slim and petite, with pretty eyes and a small, lipsticked mouth that never stopped moving. 'I think it's going to be a reporter, News or Features.'

'One more to go today,' Courtney said. 'I think it'll be News.'

'No, it can't be. They need us.' Sarah raked a hand through her glossy black hair, layered around her ears. Diamond studs twinkled from her ear lobes. She looked typically chic, in a tailored white shirt with black slacks and a skinny, ribbed black sweater. 'They can't get it all off the Associated Press.'

'That's why God invented Reuters.' Courtney chuckled, mirthlessly.

Ellen caught sight of herself in the mirror. She'd swear she had more crow's-feet than when she got up. Her makeup emphasised the hazel green of her eyes, but she felt like she'd dolled up for her own firing.

'You're wrong, Courtney,' Sarah was saying. It reminded Ellen of why she disliked her. Aggressiveness was an occupational hazard in journalism, and Sarah never knew when to turn it off. 'They need news reporters, with Iraq and the new administration. If it's News, it won't be me.' Sarah folded her arms. 'I'm too well sourced in City Hall.'

'It'll be me,' Courtney said.

'No, Court, it won't be you.' Ellen managed a smile, but she knew the truth. 'It'll be me, and we all know it. Marcelo thinks Features is kitten-up-a-tree, so I'm outta here. At least I'll get canned by somebody hot.'

'There's the upside.' Courtney smiled. 'I heard he made *Philadelphia* magazine's list of the most eligible bachelors.'

Sarah, deep in thought, looked up. 'It's gonna be you, Courtney.'

'Sarah!' Ellen frowned. 'Don't sugar-coat it or anything.'

'She said it herself,' Sarah shot back.

'That's not the point.' Ellen turned away, ashamed of her next thought. Courtney's husband owned three summer camps in Maine, and Sarah's was a surgeon. She was the only one who didn't have a husband, like a salaried safety net. 'Look, let's calm down. We'll know any minute which one of us is getting let go. It doesn't help to obsess.'

Sarah turned to her. 'Oh, get real. You know Marcelo will never let you go. He's hot for you.'

'He is not.' Ellen felt her face flush.

'He looks at you from his office, like you're the one behind glass, like a fish in a bowl.' Sarah's eyes flickered. 'Like a little blonde fishie.'

'That's ridiculous,' Ellen said.

But Courtney placed a hand on her shoulder. 'El, here are my famous last words. You're single, he's single, and life is short. I say, go for it.'

Filling the newsroom were fifty-odd L-shaped desks furnished with computers, multi-line phones and atmospheric clutter, but only a few were occupied. Ellen had been at the paper long enough to remember when all the desks were full and the newsroom had the self-important hustle-bustle depicted on TV and the movies. There had been an electricity in the air then, from working at the epicentre of breaking news. Now the epicentre of breaking news had moved to the Internet, leaving too many of the desks vacant, now one more. Courtney's.

Ellen sat at her computer. She was supposed to be starting her follow-up story and looking for Susan Sulaman's phone number, but she felt shaken. Courtney hadn't shed a tear when she'd packed her desk, which only made it harder, but they'd hugged and promised to stay in touch, even as they both knew they'd get too busy.

Her thoughts circled back to Timothy Braverman, and she reached into her handbag and slid out the white card. The bottom of the card read *ACMAC*, and she Googled it, then clicked through. American Center for Missing and Abducted Children, read the screen.

She found the search box, typed in 'Timothy Braverman' and pressed Enter. The screen changed. And Ellen's jaw dropped.

On it was a colour photo of Timothy Braverman as a baby, and his features were identical to Will's, especially the eyes. Timothy had blue eyes, a shade she had never seen in anyone's eyes but Will's.

The web page said, TIMOTHY BRAVERMAN, and underneath were two photos: on the right, the age-progressed picture from the white card; on the left, the colour photo of Timothy that had made Ellen gasp.

Timothy at one year old, read its caption. The photo had been cropped, a close-up of the baby's face in excellent focus, taken outdoors in front of a lush green hedge. Timothy's blond hair caught the light, his highlights ablaze in the sun, and he grinned broadly, with his mouth turned down on the right, showing only two front teeth. Ellen had seen that very same grin on Will, after he'd finally got healthy.

She studied the screen, wondering what Will looked like when he was that little. She hadn't met him until he was a year and a half old, and the shape of his face then had been more elongated than Timothy's, due to his illness. He had been paler, his skin thin and curiously aged.

Timothy had the exact same face, only healthier, his cheeks a rosy hue under a cheery layer of baby fat.

The page said: For further information, please see www.HelpUs FindTimothyBraverman.com. Ellen clicked on the link. The screen changed, and the top of the page read: Help Us Find Our Beloved Son, Timothy Braverman. It was a homemade website with Thomas the Tank Engine chugging round the perimeter. Her heart fluttered, then she dismissed it. It didn't mean anything that Will loved Thomas the Tank Engine, too.

The web page showed the same baby picture as the ACMAC site, but the photo hadn't been cropped, and she could see the whole picture. Timothy was dressed in a blue Lacoste shirt and jeans, his feet in new white Nikes. His pudgy fingers grasped an oversized set of Fisher-Price plastic keys, and he was sitting very straight in his stroller. Will used to sit that way too, remarkably erect, as if he didn't want to miss anything.

It was so damn eerie, like seeing Will's double. Was it possible that he had a twin somewhere? A brother she hadn't been told about?

Ellen clicked the link for the next page. There were more photos of Timothy; nine in all, a chronological progression from birth to his first birthday. She scanned the photo. As she had never seen Will as an infant, she had no idea how he'd looked, but at about ten months old, Timothy began to look exactly like Will. She read the text:

> We, Carol and Bill Braverman, will be eternally grateful to anyone who can help us find our son, Timothy Alan Braverman. Timothy was kidnapped by a Caucasian male, about thirty years old, approximately five foot ten and 170 pounds. The man stopped the Mercedes driven by Carol, pretending to be a motorist in distress. He pulled a gun on Carol, carjacked the Mercedes, and shot and killed Timothy's nanny when she began screaming. He drove away, with Timothy still in the car seat. The suspect called with a ransom demand, which we paid in full, but Timothy was never returned. For a composite drawing of the suspect, see below.

Ellen looked at the composite drawing, sketched with simple pencil lines and only slight shading. The suspect had a thin face with close-set eyes, a long nose and high cheekbones. She continued reading:

> Carol Braverman says: 'In the year God shared Timothy with us, we came to know him as a loving, happy, joyful little boy who adores Thomas the Tank Engine, his cocker spaniel Pete and lime Jell-O.'

Ellen would have felt exactly the same way, if it happened to her. She never would have given up on finding Will. She returned to the web page:

The kidnapper is currently wanted by federal and state authorities. The Braverman family has posted a reward of $1,000,000, payable to anyone who has information that leads to finding Timothy.

Ellen's heart went out to the Bravermans. A million bucks was a huge amount for a reward, so the family must have been wealthy, but all the money in the world hadn't kept them safe from harm. She clicked back to the first page of the website and looked again at the baby photo of Timothy. She scrolled over the picture and hit the Print button.

'Hey, girlfriend,' said a voice at her shoulder, and Ellen reflexively clicked the mouse, so her screen saver of Will popped back onto the monitor. Standing next to the desk was Sarah Liu. 'How you doing?'

Ellen felt unaccountably nervous. The photo of Timothy edged in noisy increments from her printer. 'I feel bad about Courtney.'

Sarah lifted an eyebrow. 'She was the obvious choice. She wasn't sourced that well, and her writing wasn't as good as yours or mine. What are you working on, anyway?'

'A follow-up on an old abduction story.' Ellen wondered why she lied. She could have just told the truth. *Funny, I just saw a picture of a kid who looks exactly like Will.* But something told her to keep it to herself.

'What abduction story?'

'Sulaman, a family abduction I did a while ago.' The photo of Timothy had almost finished printing, and suddenly she wanted Sarah gone. 'Sorry, but I have to get back to work.'

Sarah's gaze fell on the printer as the photo shot out, and she plucked it from the tray. 'Aha! You're not working.' Sarah scanned the photo of Timothy. 'You took more baby pictures than anybody I know.'

'Guilty.' Ellen didn't know what else to say. Obviously, Sarah had mistaken Timothy for Will.

'See you later.' Sarah handed her the photo and took off.

Ellen slid it into her handbag, then phoned Susan Sulaman.

**F**ifteen minutes later, Ellen had hung up the phone, and Marcelo was motioning to her from his office doorway.

'May I see you for a minute?' he called out, and she nodded, seeing through his glass wall that Sarah was sitting in one of the chairs across from his desk.

'Sure.' She rose and walked to his office.

'Please, take a seat.' He gestured her into a chair, and Sarah smiled quickly at her. He took his seat behind his desk, and sighed. 'First let me say, I know it's hard on you both, losing Courtney. If I could have

avoided it, I would have. Now, Sarah just told me a great story idea.'
Marcelo brightened, nodding at Sarah. 'You wish to explain or shall I?'

'You can.'

'Fine.' Marcelo faced Ellen directly. 'We all know that Philadelphia's homicide rate is among the highest in the country; we cover some angle of it every day. Sarah's idea is that we do a major think piece on the issue, not treat it as episodic news. Sarah, this is where your editor steals your idea.' Marcelo flashed Sarah a grin, and she laughed. He continued, 'We need to explain why this is happening here, as opposed to other big cities in the States. What's more important? It's life or death.'

'Exactly,' Sarah said, and Ellen felt a half step behind, like a middle schooler during a pop quiz.

Marcelo nodded. 'I see this as a cause-and-effects story. A thoughtful, in-depth examination. I will assign Larry and Sal to analyse the causes. Talk to social scientists and historians.'

Ellen blinked. Larry Goodman and Sal Natane were the A-team. All of a sudden, she was playing in the hard-news bigs.

'I'd like to get you two started on the effects, and it has to be good, new work. Sarah, I want you to look at the effects from the perspective of costs. How much does violent crime cost the city in law enforcement, cop and court time, lawyer time? How about in tourism, lost business, and prestige, if you can quantify that.'

'Will do.' Sarah took notes, her glossy head down.

'Ellen.' Marcelo turned to her. 'I want you to put a human face on it. The homicide rate has to be more than a number.'

Sarah interjected, 'I have good stats on the race issue, and that's the part I already wrote. Maybe I should take that angle, too.'

Marcelo dismissed her with a wave. 'No, give your notes to Ellen. As far as deadlines, today is Tuesday. Let's talk on Friday. Can you do that?'

'No problem,' Sarah answered, then rose, papers in hand.

'OK by me.' Ellen may not have studied for the quiz, but she was a fast learner. 'By the way, can I ask you about another story?'

'Sure. Go ahead.' Marcelo leaned back in his chair, and Ellen became aware that Sarah was lingering behind her in the threshold. Marcelo seemed to read her mind because he raised his gaze. 'Thank you very much, Sarah. You don't have to stay around.'

'Thanks,' Sarah said, and left.

'OK, what is it?' Marcelo asked, his voice imperceptibly gentler.

'I did a story once on the Sulaman family, a wife whose kids were taken by her ex-husband. I'd like to do a follow-up.'

'Why? Did she get the children back?'

'No, not yet.'

'Then what happened?'

'I thought it would be interesting to let Susan tell us how it feels.'

Marcelo frowned, with sympathy. 'A mother who grieves the loss of her children still. It's terrible for her, but there's no story there.'

'It's more than that.' Ellen couldn't explain the pull of the story, but then again, she never could with any of her stories. She sensed that the idea was connected to the Braverman baby. 'Why don't I go see Susan, then write it up and see what you think? It might pay off.'

'I don't understand you.' Marcelo shifted forwards on his chair, a smile playing round his lips. 'I just asked you to make our readers feel the tragedy of murder. Isn't that enough to keep you busy, Ellen?'

She laughed. Humour was as strong an aphrodisiac as power, and the man had both. Also that accent, with the soft esses like a whisper in her ear.

Marcelo leaned further forward. 'Sarah told me you were no longer a fan of mine, because I let Courtney go. I made the best decision I could.' Marcelo's expression darkened. 'Please, try to understand that.'

'I do understand.' Ellen didn't get it. Why would Sarah tell him such a thing? 'So what do you say, about the Sulamans? Gimme a chance?'

'No. Sorry.'

'OK.' Ellen rose, hiding disappointment. It wouldn't do to give him a hard time. She had to get out of the office before she got herself fired.

'Good luck with the homicide piece.'

'Thanks,' Ellen said, leaving to talk to Sarah.

# CHAPTER TWO

SARAH'S DESK WAS EMPTY and her coat wasn't on the hook, so Ellen went to the desk nearest hers, where Meredith Snader was on her computer, her short grey hair barely visible above the monitor.

'Meredith, excuse me, have you seen Sarah?'

Meredith looked up over her tortoiseshell glasses. 'She left. So how are you, now that Courtney is no longer?'

'Sad. How about you?'

'Terrible.' Meredith shook her head. 'I heard how upset you are.'

'What do you mean?'

'Sarah said you took it hard.'

Ellen could barely hide her pique, and Meredith leaned over her keyboard, lowering her voice.

'She also mentioned that you blame Arthur. By the way, so do I. It's corporate greed of the highest order.'

Ellen stiffened. Arthur Jaggisoon and his family owned the newspaper, and it was career suicide to badmouth him. In truth, she didn't blame him for the layoffs at all. 'She said that?'

'Yes.' Meredith's phone rang, and she turned away. 'Excuse me, I've been waiting for this call.'

**E**llen sat in a lovely family room that had everything but the family. Susan Sulaman was curled up in a matching chintz couch opposite her, in jeans, a pink crew neck and bare feet; a down-to-earth woman who looked oddly out of place in her own home. An Oriental rug covered a floor of resawn oak, and the couches faced each other in front of a colonial-era fireplace. A cherrywood table held the latest magazines, art books, and a tape recorder, running, now that the small talk was over.

'So you've heard nothing about the children at all?' Ellen asked.

'Nothing,' Susan answered quietly, raking fingers through thick brown hair that curved softly to her chin. Her pretty eyes were brown, but her crow's-feet went deeper than they should for her age. Two lines had been etched in her forehead, over the bridge of a perfect nose. Susan Thoma Sulaman had been Miss Allegheny County when she became the trophy wife of multimillionaire builder Sam Sulaman.

'What have you done to find them?' Ellen asked.

'What haven't I done? I hound the police and the FBI. I hired three private investigators. I posted on the missing kids sites on the web.'

'Like the ACMAC site?' Ellen was thinking of the white card.

'Of course. I offered a fifty-thousand-dollar reward. Real money.'

'Sure is.' Ellen thought of the Bravermans' million-dollar reward.

'I'll never forget the day he took them. It was October, a week before Halloween. Lynnie was going as a fish, Sam Junior as a turtle. My ex picked them up, loaded them in the car, and I never saw them again.'

'I'm so sorry. Does it get easier with time?'

'No, it gets harder. I think about all I'm missing with them. All that time. I think that, even when I get them back, I'll never be able to catch up. I worry they won't remember me. That I'll be a stranger to them.'

'Is it easier because at least you know they're with their father? That they're not abducted by some stranger, who could be doing them harm?' She was thinking of the Bravermans again.

'Honestly, no. Sam was a terrible father. He lost the custody battle and he didn't like the settlement, so this is the way he got me back. At the end of the day, they need me. I'm their mother.'

'So you're hopeful.'

'I have to be. The FBI thinks he took them out of the country. I don't agree, and if I tell you what I think, it'll sound crazy.'

'No, it won't, and honestly, I don't even know if this will run. It depends on my editor.'

Susan frowned. 'Any press at all could help find them.'

'I'll try my best. Please, go on.'

Susan shifted forward. 'I believe my kids are in the country. Near here. I think it because I feel them, inside. I feel my children, close to me. I drive around the neighbourhoods, the schools. I check out the Gymboree for Lynnie and the T-ball leagues for Sammy. In summer, I troll the beaches in Holgate and Rehoboth. Sooner or later, I'll spot one of them, I know it. There's not a minivan goes by I don't look in the back seat, not a ball field I don't look on the bench and the bases. I stop by pet stores because Lynnie liked kittens. If a school bus passes, I look in the windows. I drive around and call the kids' names at night.'

Susan stopped. And Ellen understood first-hand that after the loss of a child, a mother would be haunted for the rest of her life.

**B**ack in her car, Ellen stopped at a traffic light. She'd had a glimpse of Susan Sulaman's world, and it made her want to drive home and hug Will. Her BlackBerry rang, and she rooted in her handbag until she found it, then hit the green button.

'Elly Belly?' said the familiar voice.

'Dad. How are you?'

'Fine. I'm about to have lunch. You free? I'm just back from the doc's.'

'Why'd you go to the doctor?'

'A checkup, is all.'

Ellen glanced at the car's clock. Don Gleeson lived in West Chester, forty-five minutes from the city. Being closer to her parents was the reason she had come here from the *San Jose Mercury*.

'Are you home today?'

'Yeah, doing email and expenses.'

'Why don't I drop by? I'm actually in Ardmore.'

'Great. The door's open. Love you.'

'**H**i, Dad.' Ellen entered her father's kitchen, which overlooked the golf course at Green Manor, which billed itself as a Community for Active Adults. Her father had moved here after her mother died.

'Hi, sweetheart,' he said, standing at the counter, slicing a tomato. His wrinkled forehead knitted over his hazel eyes, set close together and hooded now, and his nose had a telltale bulb at the tip from the drinking he'd given up, years ago. Even at sixty-eight, her father had enough black in his thinning hair to make people wonder if he coloured it.

'Dad, are you gonna die?' she asked, only half-joking.

'No, never.' Her father turned with a broad smile that served him well on the golf course and the road, where he drove a thousand miles a week as a sales rep for an auto-parts company.

'Good.' Ellen slid out of her coat, dumped it on a kitchen chair, and kissed him on the cheek, catching a whiff of strong aftershave. None of her perfumes lasted as long as her father's aftershave.

'You look nice, honey. Dressed up.'

'I'm trying not to get fired.'

'Don't let the bastards get you down. How's my grandson?'

'He has a cold.'

'I miss him. When am I gonna see him?'

'Soon as I can. So, what's up with the doctor? You're scaring me.'

'I waited lunch for you.' Her father eased into a chair with a theatrical groan.

'Dad, tell me.' Ellen sat next to him, worried. Her mother had died from lymphoma, having lived only three months after her diagnosis.

'OK, here it is. I'm getting married.'

'What?' Ellen was dumbfounded. 'To who?' She had no idea.

'Barbara Levin.'

Ellen didn't even know the woman. Her parents had been married forty-five years, and her mother had passed away two years ago. She hid her ambivalence. 'This is kind of a surprise.'

'A good one, right?'

'Well, yes. Sure.' Ellen tried to get a grip, but a hard knot in her chest told her she wasn't doing such a great job.

'I needed a cholesterol check. That's why I went to the doctor's.'

'Oh. Thank God you're not sick.'

'You got that right.' Her father placed the tomato on some bread, pressed the sandwich closed and eyed her. 'You don't look happy, El.'

'I am.' Ellen managed a smile. She loved her father, but he had spent her childhood on the road. The truth was, everyone had a go-to parent, and with him away from home so much, Ellen's had become her mother.

'I guess I knew you'd get upset. You and your mother were two of a kind. Peas in a pod.'

Ellen's mother had been her best friend in the world. She flipped her thinking. 'So when's the wedding? I need to get a dress and all.'

'Uh, it's in Italy.'

'Italy? Why?'

'Barbara likes it there, near Positano.'

'Am I going? Is Will?'

'Sorry, but no. It's not a big deal, not at our age. We're just doing it, no muss, no fuss. We're getting on a plane end of the week.'

'Wow, that soon? So tell me what she looks like. Is she nice? Are you going to move in with her, or is she moving in here?'

'I'm selling the house and moving in with her. She's got a corner unit with a deck.'

'You gold digger, you.'

He smiled again, then leaned back in his chair, regarding her for a moment.

Ellen felt the knot again. Time to change the subject. 'Hold on, let me show you something.' She got up, opened her handbag, and extracted the photo of Timothy Braverman as a baby, then handed it to her father. 'Do you know who this baby is?'

'What am I, stupid? It's Will. He's grown up a lot since then, hasn't he?' her father asked, holding up the photo with unmistakable pride.

'How so? I mean, what differences do you see?'

'His forehead got a lot bigger, and his cheeks, they're full now.' He handed her back the photo. 'He just grew into his face.'

'He sure did.' Ellen lied more easily than she thought, for a bad liar.

**E**llen finally got home. 'How is he?' she asked Connie, voice low.

'Hanging in. I gave him Tylenol at two.' Connie checked her watch. 'He's been asleep since four.'

'Did he eat?' Ellen shed her coat and hung it in the closet as Connie reached for hers, the domestic changing of the guard.

'Chicken soup and crackers. All he wanted to do was go back to bed.'

'Thanks so much.'

'Give him a kiss for me.' Connie got her handbag, and Ellen opened the door, said goodbye, then shut the door and locked it, preoccupied.

Half an hour later, she was sitting crosslegged on her bed. A blown-glass lamp cast an ellipse of light on two photos of Timothy Braverman, the age-progressed picture from the white card and the computer print-out of his baby photo from ACMAC.com. Next to those were a pile of ten photos of Will, chosen because they showed his features the best.

Ellen arranged Will's photos in two rows. The top row was a younger Will, the first year she had him, aged one and a half to two and a half. The bottom row was the second year she'd had him, aged two and a half to present. She looked at them all, examining his face over time, from its thinnest and least healthy to a beaming little boy.

She returned to the top row of photos and picked the youngest one that was the most representative of Will's features. It showed him at about one and a half years old. She held it next to the photo of Timothy, taken at about a year old. When Ellen put the photos side by side, she felt an undeniable jolt.

Their faces looked so alike that they could have been identical twins. Their blue eyes were the same shape, size and hue, their noses carbon copies, and their mouths plastered with the same goofy smile, in which the right corner turned down. Both boys were sitting in the exact same way; oddly upright for such young children.

She went to the second row, of older photos of Will. She picked the most recent, in which Will was wearing a green T-shirt, green shorts and green socks. It was an unfortunate choice for a favourite colour, unless you were a leprechaun.

She picked up the age-progressed photo of Timothy and held it next to the photo of Will. They were dead ringers. Their eyes were the same shape, round and wide set. The smiles were similar.

'Connie!' Will called out from his bedroom.

'Coming, honey!' Ellen called back, leaping from the bed.

'It's Mommy, honey.' Ellen went over to Will's bed.

'I'm hot.'

'I know, baby.' Ellen scooped him up and hugged him, and he flopped onto her, resting his head sideways on her shoulder and clinging to her. His face was damp against her neck, and she rocked him.

'My poor baby, let's get you out of these clothes, OK?' She lowered him back to the bed. He had fallen asleep in his turtleneck and jeans.

'Reach for the moon, partner.' She pulled off his damp shirt as Will raised his arms, and she could barely see the thin white line that divided his little-boy chest down the centre. Once it had been a knotted zipper of flesh, in days she would never forget.

'How about we cuddle up? Scoot over.' Ellen eased herself over the side of the guardrail, and gentled Will up and onto her chest, where she wrapped her arms round him.

'Tell me a story, Mommy.'

'OK. An old or a new one?'

'An old one.'

Ellen knew the one he wanted to hear. She would tell it and try not to think about the photos in her bedroom. 'Once upon a time there was a little boy who was very, very sick. He was in a hospital, all by himself. And one day, a mommy went to the hospital and saw him.'

'What did she say?' Will asked, though he knew.

'She said, "My goodness, this is the cutest little boy I have ever seen. I'm a mommy who needs a baby, and he's a baby who needs a mommy. I wish that little boy could be mine." So the mommy asked the nurse, and she said, "Yes, you can take that little boy home if you really, really love him a lot." So the mommy said to the nurse, "I really love this baby a whole lot and I want to take him home," and they said okay, and the mommy adopted the little boy, and they lived happily ever after.' Ellen hugged him close. 'And I do. I love you very much.'

'I love you, too.'

'That makes it perfect. And oh, yeah, they got a cat.'

'Oreo Figaro's head is on my foot.'

'He's telling you he loves you.'

'He's a good cat.'

'A very good cat,' Ellen said, giving Will another squeeze. He fell silent, and in time she could feel his skin cool and his limbs relax.

She eased Will from her chest and shifted out of bed. She got up, covered him with his thermal blanket, and padded out of the room.

Ellen went into her home office, flicked on the overhead light, and sat down at her fake-wood work station, that held an old computer and monitor. The room was tiny and it barely accommodated the work station and mismatched filing cabinets containing household files, research, appliance manuals and old clippings.

Ellen opened her email, and wrote Courtney an email telling her she loved her, then logged on to Google and typed in Timothy Braverman. The search yielded 129 results. She read the line of links, scanning each piece on the Braverman kidnapping. There was a lot of press, and she contrasted it with Susan Sulaman, who had to go begging to keep the police interested. She learned from the articles that Timothy's father, Bill Braverman, was an investment manager, and his mother had been a teacher until her marriage, when she stopped to devote herself to being a mother and doing good works.

Ellen logged on to Google Images, searched under Carol and Bill Braverman, then clicked the first link. A picture appeared on the screen, showing three couples in elegant formal wear, and her eye went immediately to the woman in the middle of the photo.

*My God*. Ellen checked the caption. The woman was Carol Braverman. Carol looked so much like Will, she could easily have been his mother. Carol had blue eyes the shape and colour of Will's. Her hair was wavy and dark blonde, almost his colour. Ellen scanned Bill Braverman's face; he was conventionally handsome, with brown eyes and a nose that was straight but on the small side, a lot like Will's. His smile was broad, easy and confident, the grin of a successful man.

She went back to Google and clicked the second link, which retrieved another group picture of them all in shorts and T-shirts at a poolside. Carol's hair had been cut round her ears in a boyish style that made her look even more like Will. And Bill's body looked lean but toned, with muscular arms and legs that showed the same wiry build that Will had.

Ellen shoved the computer mouse away, got up from her chair and went to the first filing cabinet. She slid open the top drawer, moved the green Pendaflex files aside until she found the Will file. She slid the file out, removed a manila envelope and, taking them back to her chair, she opened the envelope on her lap.

On top were folded clippings of the series she'd done on the CICU nurses, then the one she did on adopting Will. She leafed through them. Finally she found Will's adoption papers and slid out the packet.

At the top of the final adoption decree, it read, 'The Court of Common Pleas of Montgomery County, Pennsylvania, Orphans' Court Division,' and the order was in bold: **The Court hereby orders and decrees that the request for adoption is hereby approved and that the above-captioned adoptee is hereby adopted by Ellen Gleeson.**

Will's adoption was all sewn up; legal, certified and irrevocable.

It gladdened her to remember that day, holding baby Will in her arms, her first day as a mother. She read the decree again: **The needs and welfare of ADOPTEE will be promoted by approval of this adoption and all requirements of the Adoption Act have been met.** Will's adoption was closed, meaning that she didn't know the identity of the birth mother and father. They had consented to relinquish their parental rights, and their written consent forms had been submitted to the court by Ellen's lawyer, as part of the adoption papers. The lawyer's name and address were at the bottom of the page: Karen Batz.

Ellen remembered Karen well. Her office was in Ardmore, fifteen minutes away, and she had been a competent family lawyer who had guided her through the adoption process without overcharging her.

Karen had told her that the birth mother was thrilled to find someone with the desire and means to care for such a sick child, and that taking a sick baby would be her best chance to adopt as a single mother. Even the judge had commented: *It was a stroke of luck, for all concerned.*

The next morning, Ellen slipped a down coat over her jeans-sweater-clogs ensemble. She felt raw and tired, after a sleepless night.

'You're leaving early?' Connie asked, shedding her coat by the closet.

'Yes, tons of work,' Ellen lied, then wondered why. 'He didn't have a fever this morning but he slept badly. I wouldn't send him to school.'

'We'll take it easy.'

'Good, thanks.' Ellen grabbed her bag and the manila envelope, then went to the door and hustled across the porch and towards the car.

Ten minutes later, she reached the two-storey brick building behind Suburban Square and pulled up at the kerb in front of the sign that read PROFESSIONAL BUILDING. She'd called Karen Batz's office, but no voicemail had picked up, so she'd decided to drop in. It was on the way to the city, and she was hoping Karen would see her.

Ellen grabbed her bag and the envelope and got out of the car. She walked down the walkway and went inside the blue door, which they kept unlocked. There was a colonial-style entrance hall with a hunting-scene umbrella stand, and she opened the door on the right, which read LAW OFFICES, and went inside. She stood, disorientated, for a moment.

Karen's office was completely different. There was a navy carpet and a paisley couch and chairs she didn't remember from before. The huge bulletin boards blanketed with baby photos had been replaced by beach-and-surf scenes and a mirror framed with fake seashells.

'May I help you?' a receptionist asked, coming out of the back room.

'I was looking for Karen Batz,' Ellen answered.

'Her office isn't here any more. We do real estate.'

'Sorry. I called Karen's old number, but they didn't pick up.'

'They should disconnect the line. I keep telling them to.'

'I'm a client of hers. Do you know where she moved to?'

'I'm sorry to have to tell you this, but Ms Batz passed away.'

'Really?' Ellen asked, surprised. 'When? She was only in her forties.'

'About two years ago. That's how long we've been here.'

Ellen frowned. 'That would be right around the time I knew her. What did she die of?'

The receptionist hesitated, then leaned closer. 'It was a suicide.'

Ellen felt stunned. '*She killed herself?*' Memories came back to her.

Karen's desk had photos of her sons. 'But she was married, with kids.'

'I know, such a shame.' The receptionist turned towards a noise from the back room. 'If you'll excuse me . . .'

'I wanted to talk to her about my son's adoption.'

'Maybe her husband can help you. I've directed her other clients to him.' The receptionist went to the computer and hit a few keys. She pulled a pen from a mug, then scribbled on a piece of paper. 'His name's Rick Musko. Here's his office phone.'

'Thanks,' Ellen said, accepting the sheet.

Back in her car, Ellen was on the cellphone to Karen's husband before she pulled away from the office. A man answered the phone.

'Musko here.'

'Mr Musko?' Ellen introduced herself and said, 'I'm sorry to bother you, but I'm, er, was, a client of Karen's. I'm very sorry for your loss.'

'Thank you,' Musko said, his tone cooler.

'She helped me adopt my son, and I have a question or two about—'

'Another lawyer took over her practice. You should have received a letter. I can give you his information.'

'I just wanted my file. Does he have the files, too?'

'How old is the case?'

'It was about two years ago.' Ellen winced at the coincidence of timing, but if Musko noticed it, he didn't miss a beat.

'I have the dead files in my garage, at the house. You can come by and look for your file. That's the best I can do.'

'Wonderful. When could I come by?'

'I'm busy this month, we have a project at work.'

'Please, could it be sooner? This is important. If I could just come over this week? Tonight, even? I know it's short notice but I won't make any trouble for you, I'll just go out to the garage and find it myself.'

'I suppose the housekeeper can let you into the garage. Her name's Wendy. I'll call her.'

'Thanks so much. I'll be there by six.'

'Make it seven, then the kids will have eaten. Look for the U-Haul boxes in the garage. Wendy will show you. You can't miss them.' Musko gave Ellen an address, and she thanked him and hung up.

'**E**llen, come on in!' It was Marcelo, calling from his office.

'Sure.' She waved to him, spotting Sarah sitting inside his office.

'Good morning.' Marcelo stood smiling behind his desk, in dark trousers and a matt black shirt that fitted close to his body, showing broad shoulders tapering to a trim waist.

'Hi.' Sarah nodded at her, and Ellen took a seat, managing to give her a half smile.

Marcelo sat down. 'Sarah was just telling me she spent the afternoon with the new police commissioner. He was willing to talk on the record about the homicide rate. Wait until you see her draft, it's terrific.' Marcelo turned to Sarah. 'Make sure you copy Ellen. I want you two to keep each other up to speed.'

Sarah made a note on her pad; Marcelo was already turning to Ellen.

'How's the story going?' His dark eyes flashed expectantly.

'Nothing significant yet.' Ellen had to think fast. 'I have a lead but nothing to get excited about.'

'Fair enough.' Marcelo nodded, and if he was disappointed, it didn't show. 'Let me know and copy Sarah when you get something drafted.'

Ellen left the office behind Sarah, who slid a sleek BlackBerry from her waist holster and started hitting the buttons. Ellen caught up with Sarah before she started the call. 'Hold on, wait a sec.'

'What?' Sarah turned, her cell to her ear.

'We need to talk, don't you think?'

'Maybe later,' Sarah answered, but Ellen snatched the phone from Sarah's hand and pressed the End button, then turned on her heel.

'Meet me in the ladies' room if you want your toy back.'

'**G**ive me back my phone!' Sarah held out her hand, her dark eyes flashing. 'What's your problem?'

'What's *my* problem? Why are you talking to everyone about me?'

'What do you mean?'

'You told Marcelo I was upset about Courtney, and you told Meredith that I was badmouthing Arthur.'

'I did no such thing and I want my phone back.' Sarah wiggled her hand impatiently, and Ellen slapped the BlackBerry into her palm.

'Meredith told me, and Marcelo mentioned Courtney. *Marcelo*, Sarah. Our *editor*. You can get me fired, talking me down to him.'

'Oh, please.' Sarah scoffed. 'Meredith misunderstood. I didn't say you said anything bad about them, specifically.'

'And what about Marcelo? You said I wasn't a fan of his.'

'He asked me how morale was in the newsroom after Courtney got fired. I told him it was bad and that you felt the same way. That's all.' Sarah put her hands on her hips. 'Are you telling me you didn't feel that way? That you're happy Courtney got fired?'

'Of course not.'

'Then what are you whining about?'

'Don't talk to the boss about me, got it?'

'Whatever I said, it's not gonna hurt you. Marcelo wants you around, and you know why.' Sarah brushed past her for the door.

**N**ight came early to this neighbourhood, the sun fleeing the sky, leaving heaven black and blue, and Ellen circled the block, scribbling notes as she drove. Trash blew in the gutters, stopping when it flattened against older cars. Sooty brick terraced houses lined broken sidewalks; some houses had graffitied plywood where windows used to be, and others had only black holes. Porch roofs sagged, peeling shutters hung crooked, and every home had bars covering its doors.

Ellen's research for the homicide piece had given her a lead. A boy had been shot to death on this block of Eisner Street, only two weeks ago. Lateef Williams, aged eight.

Ellen turned right onto Eisner, where only one streetlight worked; it threw a halo over a pile of trash, rubble and car tyres dumped on the corner. She stopped at number 5252, Lateef's house; his memorial out front was bathed in darkness, the shadows hiding a purple rabbit that sat against Spider-Man figurines, crayoned drawings, a kingsize box of Skittles, sympathy cards, and a mound of spray-painted daisies and roses, still in plastic wrap. A sign written in Magic Marker read: WE LOVE YOU, TEEF, and a few candles sat round it, unlit in the cold wind.

Ellen parked, then gathered her things to meet Lateef's mother.

Laticia Williams was twenty-six, with a slim, pretty face, brown eyes, high cheekbones and a prominent mouth. Earrings with wooden beads dangled from her ear lobes, showing just under chin-length hair coloured reddish. With her jeans, she wore an oversized black T-shirt that bore her son's photo and the caption R.I.P. LATEEF.

'I appreciate you coming,' Laticia said, setting a mug of coffee in front of Ellen as they sat at her round table.

'Not at all, I appreciate your talking to me at a time like this,' Ellen said. 'I'm so sorry for your loss.'

'Thank you.' Laticia sat down with a weary smile, showing the gold rim of her front tooth. 'I want it to be in the paper, so everybody know kids are gettin' killed every day. So it's not just a number.

'But you know what they're never gonna understand? That it's like Hurricane Katrina; we're livin' in a different country. We got two sets of rules, two sets of laws, two things you can get outta life, whether you're white or black, rich or poor.' Laticia pointed at Ellen. 'You live in America, but I don't. You live in Philadelphia, but I don't. Where I live, kids can get shot on the street, and nobody sees nothin'. You wanna blame them, tell people to snitch, I know, but you can't blame people. If they snitch, they're *dead*. Their family's *dead*. Their kids are *dead*. So I could sit here and tell you all about Teef and how cute he was, 'cause he was.' Laticia smiled briefly, light returning to her angry eyes, softening them for an instant. 'But even though Teef was mine, what matters is he isn't the only one killed here. Three other kids were killed in this neighbourhood, all of them shot. Teef was killed in this *room*, thanks to some trigger-happy kid out in the street. Lemme ask you, that happen where you live?'

'No.'

'And that jus' this year. You figure in the year before that and the one before that, we got eight kids killed. We don't have kids walkin' around here, we got *ghosts*. This neighbourhood's full a ghosts.' She paused, then asked abruptly, 'You got a child?'

'Yes,' Ellen answered. 'A boy.'

'That's good.' Laticia smiled. 'You hold that baby close, you hear? Hold him close. You never know when you gonna lose him.'

Ellen nodded, because for a minute, she couldn't speak.

**E**llen surveyed the garage, her breath chalky in the cold. Kids' bicycles stood propped in front of metal shelves that held footballs and black plastic mountains of Rollerblades and kneepads. Fluorescent panels overhead cast light on the left well of the garage, where Rick Musko must park, because there were a few grease spots on the concrete floor. In the other well, where Karen Batz's car would have been, sat cardboard boxes piled like a Rubik's Cube. *Dead files.*

Ellen went over to the boxes. They were piled alphabetically, and she searched for the Gs. Ten minutes later, boxes lay all round the garage floor. She wedged off the lid of a box labelled GA–GO and looked inside. It held manila folders packed tight. Each file had a white label with the client's name, last name first. No Gleeson. Not even misfiled. Puzzled, she looked up at the pile of boxes, then eyed the ones she'd left lying around the floor. There had been other G boxes, and Gleeson could be misfiled anywhere. She took a deep breath and got busy. She was finished two hours later, but still hadn't found her file.

She was putting the Rubik's Cube back together when she heard the rumbling of a car engine, and the garage door slid up, leaving her in the blinding glare of the high beams from an SUV. The driver stepped out, walked towards her, and introduced himself as Rick Musko.

'You're still here?' he asked, stepping into the fluorescent lights. He was tall and bald, in his fifties, older than Karen.

'Sorry, but I can't find my file.'

'Wait a minute.' Musko blinked. 'I know you. Aren't you the reporter who did the story on the baby you adopted?'

'Yes, right.' Ellen introduced herself again.

'Your name didn't register, when we spoke.' Musko extended his hand, and they shook. 'I was pretty rude to you; I wish I had known who you were. That story you wrote made Karen so happy.'

'She was a great lawyer. I'm so sorry about your loss.'

'Thank you.'

'Do you know where my file could be? Could it be with the lawyer who bought her practice? I figured I'd call him tomorrow morning.'

'No, he won't have it.' Musko straightened up a box. 'He took only Karen's active files. I have some of Karen's personal papers inside, from her desk drawers. Maybe your file is in there.'

'Why would it be?'

'Because of the article? She bought thirty copies. Maybe she saved the file. I haven't even looked in those boxes yet.'

Ellen felt a twinge of guilt. 'I hate to put you to this, if it's difficult.'

'No, let's get it done.'

# CHAPTER THREE

MUSKO LEFT ELLEN in a home office that put hers to shame. Built-in bookcases ringed the room, holding technical manuals about structural engineering. The walls were lined with golf scenes and framed photographs of three towheaded boys. There were no photos of Karen.

Ellen turned her attention to the three boxes on the desk. She took off the first lid, which read TOP DRAWER. She found a few legal pads with notes and recognised the neat handwriting, with its detached capitals, as Karen's. She flashed on the lawyer, who had joked that her penmanship was so parochial school.

*Odd.* Ellen was a lapsed Catholic, but even she knew that suicide was one of the bigger no-noes. She wondered what would have driven Karen to such an act, and she moved to the second box, whose lid read SECOND DRAWER. Still no client files. She closed the lid and moved to the last box, which reminded her of a joke her father used to tell: *Why is the thing you're looking for always in the last place you look? Because after you find it, you stop looking.*

She opened the box and started rummaging, then, all of a sudden, spotted a letter from Karen to her, notifying her about Will's adoption hearing. *Bingo!*

She shuffled papers aside until she came across an email from her to Karen, asking about adoption procedures. She rummaged further, spotted some newsprint, and pulled it out excitedly. It was the front page of the Features section, and on the bottom right was Ellen's piece on Will's adoption. The headline read: HAPPY ENDING, and on the right was the photo of Will, looking so sick. She dug back into the box, and at the very bottom lay a manila folder. She read the label: GLEESON, ELLEN.

'Yay!' She tore it open, but it was empty, which was when she realised that the contents of her file folder were mixed up with the other papers.

'Did you get lucky?' asked a voice from the door, and she looked up to see Musko smiling tiredly in the threshold. He entered the study and sat down heavily in the leather chair across from his desk.

'Sort of.' Ellen held up the empty folder. 'This is my file, but the papers are scattered all over the box.'

Musko leaned over and eyed Ellen's article. 'You know, it wasn't long after this article appeared that she was dead.'

'When was it that she died, if I can ask?'

'July thirteenth.' Musko's smile vanished. 'Her secretary found her at her desk when she came in that morning.'

'That was about a month after Will's adoption was final, on June fifteenth. The article ran about two weeks after that.' Ellen paused, puzzled. 'I'm surprised I didn't hear. I paid my final bill, and the office didn't send me a letter that she was dead. I didn't even see an obit.'

'I didn't run one. I kept it quiet, for the kids' sake. The funeral was just family. The neighbours know from the gossip mill, but I never told them. I still haven't told the boys how she really died.'

'Didn't they ask questions?' Ellen asked, surprised.

'Yes, but I just said she was sick and we didn't know it. I know, it was probably wrong, but what do you say—hey, guys, Mommy went to work today and put a gun in her mouth?' He laughed, but it sounded bitter. 'The cops told me it was unusual for a woman to use a gun.' Musko jerked a thumb behind him. 'I got three kids who pray for her every night. What kind of mother abandons her kids like that?'

'We can never really understand why people do the things they do.' Ellen was trying to say something comforting, but knew she sounded like a Hallmark card.

'Oh, I *know* why she did it. She did it because I caught her having an affair.'

'Really?' Ellen said, shocked.

'He called her at the house one night, and I picked up. Then she went out and didn't get back until after midnight. She said she was at the gym, but it was the same night they had an electrical fire.' Musko snorted. 'She was getting her workout from her boyfriend.'

Ellen rose to go, but it didn't stop Musko from continuing.

'I confronted her, and she admitted it. She had to, I knew there was something going on. She'd been acting funny, moody. Anyway, she said she would stop seeing him, but I told her I wanted a divorce, that I'd fight her over the kids, too.' Musko stopped abruptly, as if he'd just heard himself. 'The next morning was, you know, when she did it.' He began rubbing his eyes. 'You found the papers you needed?'

'Well, they're in the box somewhere but I didn't get a chance to go through and see which papers are mine.'

'Then take the whole box. Take all three, for all I care.'

'Thanks,' Ellen said. 'I'll send you back what's not mine.'

The night was starless and black, and the windows dark mirrors that reflected Ellen at her dining-room table, sifting through the contents of the third box, sitting next to an emergency glass of merlot. Oreo Figaro sat at the far end of the table, watching with a disapproving eye.

She pulled out the papers that should have been in her file and put them in chronological order, re-creating Will's adoption file. She unearthed a typed letter to Karen, printed in a large font, on thin paper:

Amy Martin
393 Corinth Street
Stoatesville, PA

Dear Karen,

  Here are the papers you asked me to get signed in our meeting. They are from the baby's father and he says he will give up his rights to the baby. Please make sure the woman who wants to adopt him takes good care of him. He's a good baby, and it's not his fault he's fussy and sick. I love him but I know this is what is the best thing for him and I will remember him always and keep him in my prayers.

  Sincerely,
  Amy

Ellen's heart thundered in her chest. It was from Will's birth mother. So her name was Amy Martin. She sounded sweet, and her pain in putting Will up for adoption came through even her simple lines. It was all Ellen could do not to pick up the phone and call her, but instead, she reached for her wine and raised her glass in a silent toast.

*Thank you, Amy, for the gift of your child.*

She kept digging, finally reaching court papers. *Consent of Birth Parent*, read the heading, and the form showed Amy's name and the Stoatesville address, and her birth date, which was July 7, 1983, and marital status, which read *Single*. The paper was signed by Amy Martin under the sentence, *I hereby voluntarily and unconditionally consent to the adoption of the above-named child*. The paper had also been witnessed by Gerry and Cheryl Martin, from the same address.

Ellen skipped to the next form, which was the consent of the birth father, and she learned his name and address:

*Charles Cartmell*
*71 Grant Avenue*
*Philadelphia, Pennsylvania*

She eyed his signature, a messy scrawl with barely comprehensible loops. She couldn't help but wonder what Charles Cartmell had been like. What he looked like. What he did for a living.

She found nothing else relating to Will. She took a last sip of wine and set the wineglass down next to the box, and a bright pink splotch amid the clutter caught her eye. It was the hot pink of Karen's leather Filofax.

She opened it, idly. It was a standard date book, a week on two opposing pages, and each page bore Karen's neat script, noting her appointments and meetings by client name. Ellen flipped through the Filofax, slowing when she reached the week of July 13, the day on which Karen had committed suicide. That week began on Monday, July 10, and the Filofax showed a neat line-up of appointments.

Ellen scanned the rest of the week, including the day Karen died. The lawyer had had appointments scheduled all day long, which made sense. Karen couldn't have known that the night before, her husband would find out about her affair. Ellen was about to close the book when she noticed that one of the appointments, on Wednesday, didn't have a name, but only an initial: *A*, written next to the time: *7.15 p.m.*

Ellen was intrigued. A night-time meeting? Maybe A was Karen's lover? She skipped back to the week before that, but there was no A, and then the week before that. There, in the middle of the week, on Wednesday, June 28. A, also at 7.15.

She flipped pages to the week before, and then the week before that, which brought her to Wednesday, June 14. A, this time at 9.30 p.m.

She mulled it over. That was the day before Will's adoption was final, on June 15. She flipped back to earlier weeks, checking each one, but there were no other meetings with A. She sat back, thinking, and her gaze shifted to the letter on the table, from Amy Martin. The date on the letter was June 15.

Ellen thought a minute. There had been a meeting with A, and then the next day, a letter from Amy Martin. 'A' could stand for Amy.

She looked again at the letter. It even said 'in our meeting'. So Karen had met with Amy. But Ellen didn't remember seeing Amy's name in the Filofax. She paged through it again, around June, and double-checked. There was no notation of a meeting with Amy Martin or Charles Cartmell, though all the other client meetings had been noted.

Ellen eyed the cars stacked ahead, their red taillights a glowing line, their exhaust trailing white plumes. The day was overcast and cold, and freezing rain had left an icy sleeve on the tree branches and a black veneer on the roads. The traffic stayed bad on the two-lane roads to Stoatesville but, in time, she found Corinth Street among the warren of terraced houses in a working-class neighbourhood around an abandoned steel mill. She travelled down the street. Suddenly her cellphone started ringing in her handbag, and she fumbled for it. The display showed a number she didn't recognise, and she hit Ignore when she realised that the house coming up was number 393. Amy Martin's house.

A woman stood in its driveway, scraping ice off the windshield of an old black Cherokee. Her back was turned, and she wore an Eagles knitted cap, a thick black parka, jeans and black rubber boots. *Amy?*

Ellen pulled up in front of the house, grabbed her bag and file, got out, walked up the driveway. 'Excuse me, Ms Martin?' she asked, her heart thumping like crazy.

The woman turned, startled. She looked to be in her late sixties, and her hooded eyes widened. She said, 'Jeez, you scared me!'

'Sorry.' Ellen introduced herself. 'I'm looking for Amy Martin.'

'Amy's my daughter, and she don't live here any more. I'm Gerry.'

Ellen tried to keep her bearings. Gerry Martin had been one of the witnesses on the consent form. She was looking into the eyes of Will's grandmother. 'She gave this address as hers, two years ago.'

'She always does, but she don't live here. I get all her mail, all those damn bills, I throw 'em all away.'

'Where does Amy live?'

'Hell if I know.' Gerry returned to scraping the windshield. 'Amy's over eighteen. It ain't my business no more.'

'How about where she works?'

'Who said she works?'

'When was the last time you saw her?'

'A while.'

'A year or two?'

'Try five.'

Ellen knew it couldn't be true. Gerry had signed the consent form two years ago. Why was she lying? 'Are you sure?'

Gerry looked over, eyes narrowed. 'She owes you money, right?'

'No.' Ellen paused. 'Actually, I'm the woman who adopted her baby.'

Gerry burst into laughter, showing yellowed teeth. 'You better come in. We got some talkin' to do,' she said, placing her hand on Ellen's shoulder.

Gerry went into the kitchen to make coffee, leaving Ellen in the living room. Beige curtains covered the windows, and the air was thick with stale cigarette smoke. Flowered metal trays served as end tables flanking a worn couch of blue velveteen, and three mismatched chairs clustered round a large-screen TV.

Ellen crossed the room, drawn to photographs that ran the length of the wall. There were oversized school pictures of boys and girls, photomontages, and a wedding photo of a young man and a woman in an elaborate bridal headdress. She shook her head in wonderment. They were Will's blood, but complete strangers.

*Which girl is Amy?* The photos showed girls and boys at all different ages, and Ellen tried to follow each child as he or she grew up, picking blue eyes from brown and matching young smiles to older smiles, age-progressing all of them in her mind's eye, searching for Amy. One of the girls had blondish hair and blue eyes, plus Will's fair skin.

Gerry came into the room with a skinny brown cigarette and two heavy glass mugs of murky coffee, one of which she handed to Ellen.

'Thanks. Can I ask, is this one Amy, with the blue eyes?'

'No, that's Cheryl, her sister. I had three girls, one boy.'

Ellen remembered the name Cheryl Martin as the other signature on the consent form.

'This one's Amy, the baby of the family in more ways than one.' Gerry tapped a smaller photo in the corner, and Ellen walked over.

'So this is Amy, huh?' She leaned close to the photo of a young girl, maybe thirteen years old, leaning on a red Firebird. Her dark blonde hair was in corn rows, and her blue eyes were sly. She had a crooked grin that telegraphed too-cool-for-school, and Ellen scrutinised her features. Amy and Will had the same colouring, but their features weren't alike. 'Which of the other photos are Amy?'

'Uh, lemme see.' Gerry eyed the photos with a short laugh. 'None! I tell you, by the time you get to your fourth, you're a little sick of it, you know what I mean?' Gerry motioned to the couch. 'Come on, sit.'

'Thanks.' Ellen walked over, sank into the couch.

Gerry sat down heavily, diagonally to the couch, pulling an ancient ashtray onto the chair arm. Her expression looked softer, hard lines smoothed by the low light. Her hair was a tinted brown with grey roots, the ends frayed, and she wore it tucked behind her ears. Her nose was stubby on a wide face, but she had a motherly smile.

'Why did you laugh outside?' Ellen asked.

'First, tell me about Amy and this baby.' Gerry took a drag on the brown cigarette.

'He was sick, in the hospital. I did a story on it, a series.' Ellen reached into her handbag, pulled out the clipping from her file and showed it to Gerry, who barely glanced at it. 'Will, the baby I adopted, was in cardiac intensive care when I met him. He had a heart defect.'

'And you think he was Amy's baby?'

'I know so.'

'How?' Gerry sucked on her cigarette, then blew out a cone of smoke from the side of her mouth. 'I mean, where'd you get your information?'

'From a lawyer, who died. My lawyer, mine and Amy's. It was a private adoption, and she brokered the deal between us.'

'Amy brokered it?'

'No, the lawyer. Karen Batz. Does the name mean anything to you?'

Gerry shook her head. 'You *sure* it's Amy? My Amy?'

'Yes.' Ellen set the coffee down on the metal tray, reached into the envelope and rifled through the papers. She found Amy's consent to the adoption and the letter with the Corinth Street return address, and handed them to Gerry, who took them, reading to herself.

'This is nuts,' Gerry said, half to herself, and Ellen's chest tightened.

'Is that Amy's signature, on the consent?'

'It looks like it.'

'How about on the letter?'

'There, too.'

'So it's your Amy.' Ellen reached over and turned the page to the consent form, pointing. 'Is that your signature?'

'No way. I never signed this.' Gerry's lips flattened to a grim line. 'And this other signature, it's not Cheryl's, either.'

'Maybe Amy forged the signatures. Maybe she wanted to put her baby up for adoption and didn't want her family to know.'

'That can't be it.'

'Why not?' Ellen asked, and Gerry shook her head.

'One day, when Amy was seventeen, she woke up in cramps real bad, so I knew she wasn't fakin' to get outta school. We took her to the emergency. They said she had a twisted ovary. They had to take it out right away. They said she had almost no chance of getting pregnant.'

'But not no chance. She still had one ovary left, right?'

'Yeah, but they said it was very unlikely she could have kids. If you take out an ovary, it affects the hormones, at least that's what they said, something like that. Whatever, if she had a kid, it's news to me.'

'She didn't tell you?'

'No, like I said, we haven't talked. She didn't tell me nothin' anyway. I don't even know where she is. I was tellin' you the truth, outside.'

'What about either of her sisters, or her brother? You never heard from any of them about her having a baby?'

'I don't think she talks to anybody but Cheryl, and she lives down in Delaware. I can call her and ask. I will, later.' Gerry snorted, her nostrils emitting puffs of smoke. 'Nice to know if I had another grandchild.'

Ellen tried another tack. 'Or maybe when the baby got really sick, that's the kind of thing you might tell someone.'

'If Amy had a baby that got really sick, she couldn't handle it. She'd be lookin' for an easy out.'

Ellen cringed at the harsh words. 'That's the sort of thing that would overwhelm anyone, especially a young girl.'

'It didn't take much to *overwhelm* Amy. If I asked her to take out the trash, that *overwhelmed* her.'

'Can you just tell me a little more about her? What is she like?'

'She was my wild child. I never could get a handle on that girl. Smart, but lousy grades. Didn't give a shit. Did her share of drink and drugs. I had no control with her. She was outta here after graduation.'

'Hold on a sec.' Ellen rifled through the papers and handed Gerry the father's consent form. 'Look at this. My son's birth father is Charles Cartmell, from Philly. He lives on Grant Avenue in the Northeast.' Ellen had checked online last night but couldn't get a phone number or find a listing of the address. 'Do you know him?'

'I don't know the name.'

'If Amy is twenty-five now and gave birth to Will three years ago, it means she had him when she was twenty-two. So maybe the father was someone from high school, or the area?'

'She didn't go steady in high school.' Gerry shook her head. 'She saw a lot of different guys. I didn't ask no questions, believe me.'

Ellen began thinking out loud. 'She must have stayed in the Philadelphia area, because she chose a lawyer in Ardmore. She even had meetings with the lawyer.'

Gerry shrugged. 'Cheryl might know.'

'Can I have her number?'

Gerry hesitated. 'Why exactly are you tryin' to find Amy?'

'It's a medical thing, about the baby,' Ellen lied.

'Does she have to give it a kidney or something?'

'No, not at all. At most it's a blood test. His heart is acting up again, and I need to know more about her medical history.'

'She didn't have no heart problems. None of us have heart problems.'

'I'm sure, but the blood test will show more than that. Maybe you could give Cheryl my number and ask her to call me?'

'OK, I'll do that.' Gerry reached out and patted her hand. 'Don't worry. I'm sure the baby will be OK.'

'I don't want to lose him,' Ellen added, unaccountably.

Ellen got into the cold car and took off down the street. Her BlackBerry started ringing, and she dug in her handbag with one hand, finding the device by its smooth feel. She pulled it out, and the screen showed the same unknown number as before, so she answered the call.

'Ellen, where are you?' It was Sarah Liu. 'I've been calling you. You missed the projects meeting. Marcelo asked about the think piece.'

'Damn.' The Thursday projects meeting. She'd forgotten about it. 'I wasn't feeling well this morning.' Ellen was fast becoming an accomplished liar. 'Was Marcelo pissed?'

'What do you think? When are you coming in? We should meet about the think piece. I want to see your draft.'

Ellen tensed. She hadn't even transcribed her notes from Laticia Williams. 'We don't need to meet and my draft isn't ready—'

'When will it be? Our deadline's tomorrow.'

'Sarah, we're grown-ups. I don't have time to give you a draft, and I don't need yours. Don't tell Daddy.'

'Have it your way, but make that deadline.' Sarah hung up.

Ellen got hold of Lateef's teacher, Vanessa James, while her class was down the hall at the library. Tall and rail-thin, the teacher moved quickly round the classroom, picking up stray books and crayons, straightening chairs, and restoring a woolly hat to its cubbyhole.

Vanessa asked, 'It's all right with Laticia if we talk, right?'

'Yes, I called her on the way over. Sorry it's such short notice.'

'No problem.' Vanessa wore a long red sweater with black slacks and low heels. She had large eyes, a smile slick with lip gloss, and her hair straightened into a stiff bob, which showed off tiny diamond earrings. 'We have fifteen minutes 'til they get back. What do you want to know?'

'Just a few things.' Ellen slid her notebook from her handbag and flipped over the cover, pen at the ready. 'What kind of kid was Lateef?'

'Teef was like a light. You could say he was a class clown, but that wouldn't do him justice. He was the one who made everybody laugh. But he was a leader. All the kids looked up to him. For Martin Luther King's birthday, Lateef was voted Dr King. He memorised a few lines of "I Have a Dream", and he did a great job. He liked to be in front of the class. He was quick as a whip. We do basic addition and subtraction, but he could have moved on to the third-grade curriculum, fractions and geometry. He was good on sentence structure, too. On our report cards, I have to pick from a lot of categories, like: "Eager to try new things."' Vanessa chuckled softly. 'Lateef was my category buster. He was his own little category.'

Ellen made rapid notes. 'So how did the class deal with his murder?'

Vanessa shook her head, with a sigh. 'These kids, they're used to death. We lost two kids already this school year, and it's only February. But Lateef, everybody knew him. Everybody *felt* him. The District sent us grief counsellors. That child was too full of life not to be missed.'

Vanessa pointed to one of the desks by the window, in the second row. 'That was Teef's seat. It's there, empty, every day. The first week, we made a little memorial and the kids brought flowers. Here, look at this.' Vanessa crossed to the desk with Ellen following, and lifted up the lid. Inside the well sat a pile of cards and dried red roses, their petals shrivelling. 'These are his Valentine's Day cards. Every day somebody comes by with another one.' She paused. 'You know who you should talk to, if you really want to understand the effects of the murders in this city?'

'Who?' Ellen asked her.

'My uncle. He'll see you, if you can handle it.'

Ellen stood in the Glade-scented entrance hall of the funeral home with its proprietor, Ralston Rilkey. He was a slight man with a compact frame, in his early sixties, and wore his hair cut short and natural. He had a short forehead, and his eyes were worried above a wide nose and neatly groomed moustache.

'And what is it you want to know again?' Ralston asked.

'I'd like to know how you've been affected by the murders in the neighbourhood. There've been so many lately, especially of children like Lateef Williams. Your niece told me you might help, and Laticia gave her permission to talk to me.'

'Then follow me.' Ralston left, and Ellen followed him across a red-carpeted hallway, through a panelled door that read: EMPLOYEES ONLY, and downstairs into the basement of the converted terrace house. The carpeting morphed into institutional grey tile, the temperature dipped and the fake-floral scents were eradicated by a medicinal odour.

They reached a set of white double doors, which Ralston opened. The odour grew stronger. On the wall hung white smocks and plastic face shields. Stainless-steel shelves held boxes of cotton and bottles.

Ralston opened another door, and Ellen found herself in a larger room with a glistening white table at its centre, tilted at an angle. He stood behind the table. 'This is our preparation room.'

'Would you fill me in on the procedure, generally?'

'The first step is washing and disinfecting the body. Embalming is simply displacing blood with fluid, usually of formaldehyde preservative. This machine replaces the blood with fluid.' Ralston rested his hand on a pump at the head of the table. 'We apply lotion, to protect against dehydration. After death, the eyes sink into the skull, and we pack cotton into the eye socket, place a plastic eyecap under the eyelid, then pull back the eyelid to apply adhesive and keep the eye closed.'

Ellen's stomach turned over.

'Death also causes the facial muscles to relax; the jaw drops open. We make the eyes and mouth as lifelike as possible. We set the features.'

'Now, how was the procedure in Lateef's case?'

'With Lateef, there was so much damage on one side of his face that we had to use his school photo as a guide and build from that.'

Ellen tried to visualise it. 'Couldn't you use the other side of his face?'

'No. With the wounds he had, there was significant facial swelling, which distorted even the good side of his face.'

'How did you cover the bullet wounds?'

Ralston frowned. 'There was no covering. There was nothing there. So in his case, we reconstructed. We snipped away the excess tissue round the wounds and glued the skin that was left to his cheekbone and eye socket. We poured wax into the bullet holes to fill the gap and used cosmetics to match the shade of the wax to his skin.

'Even for a single gunshot wound, we wouldn't cover it. The putty would simply sink into the wound.' He held up an index finger. 'That's one thing I've had to order more of, wax and putty. We've already used

224 | Lisa Scottoline

four times the amount that we did last year, and the manufacturer can't keep it in stock. I have a friend in Newark, he's in the same bind.'

Suddenly Ellen's cellphone rang. Embarrassed, she reached for her handbag. 'I'm so sorry,' she said, digging. 'I should have turned it off.'

'Feel free to take the call. I should get back to work.'

Ellen found the phone and switched it off, but not before she saw the area code. 302. Delaware. *Cheryl Martin.*

**E**llen tore south towards Wilmington. The sky had turned black and snow flurries had begun to fall. The radio news was predicting a storm.

Cheryl's home was lovely, set among plenty of open space. A white sedan sat in a circular driveway, and the evergreens and hedges landscaping the property were dusted by new snow flurries. Ellen grabbed her bag and file and got out of the car.

They were sitting in a beautiful living room, on an L-shaped couch in an oatmeal fabric that coordinated with a sisal rug. The walls were eggshell white, adorned with horsy landscapes.

Cheryl was saying, 'I have to admit, part of the reason I wanted to meet you is because I read your articles.'

'Thank you.' Ellen remembered the photos of Cheryl Villiers, née Martin, from her mother Gerry's house. In person, she resembled Will.

'It's so strange to think that little baby is Amy's. My new nephew. A cousin for my twin girls.' Cheryl smiled uncomfortably. 'My mother said you showed her some court documents. Could I see them?'

'Yes, of course.' Ellen dug in her handbag and produced the adoption papers. 'I really need to find Amy. To get some medical history.'

Cheryl read the papers, her head inclined at an inquisitive angle.

'Do you think that's Amy's signature?'

'Yes, I do. It's absolutely her signature.'

'How about on the consent form. Is that your signature?'

'No, I never signed this.' Cheryl looked up.

'So what do you think's going on here?'

'Amy didn't want us to know about the baby, obviously.'

*Bingo.* 'What about this twisted ovary business?'

'My mom thinks that Amy couldn't have had a baby, but I don't agree. All the doctor said was that she probably couldn't have a baby.'

'So do you think she had a baby?'

'It's possible. We all stopped seeing her about the same time. If she had a baby three years ago, I have no way of knowing it for sure.'

'So do you have any idea where Amy could be? Your mom thinks she stays in touch with you.'

'Amy does email, but hardly ever. When she needs money.'

'May I have her email address?'

'I should email Amy first and make sure that she wants to hear from you. After all, if she gave up her baby for adoption, she had a choice about whether she wanted to hear from you, didn't she?'

'Would you give Amy my email address and have her contact me?'

'OK.'

'Thanks.' Ellen thought of her earlier request, which she'd made by phone. 'I was wondering if you were able to find any photos of her.'

'Sure, I found two I had scanned on the computer.' Cheryl turned to the end table, picked up two pieces of paper and handed one to Ellen, pointing with a manicured index finger. 'That's Amy, when she was little.'

Ellen looked down at a photo of a cute girl holding an American flag and wearing an Uncle Sam hat. 'How old is she in this picture?'

'She'd just turned five. Does your son look like her?'

'Not that much.' Ellen had to admit it. Amy's nose was wider than Will's and her lips fuller. 'Frankly, he looks more like you.'

'It must run in our family. I look nothing like my twins, either.'

'Will must look more like his father, but I don't know what his father looks like. Does the name Charles Cartmell mean anything to you? According to the adoption papers, he's the father.'

'Never heard of him. Amy dated tons of guys. She was never in a committed relationship.'

'If she got pregnant, would she feel as if she should tell the father?'

Cheryl scoffed. 'Are you kidding? If I know my little sister, she probably didn't know who the father was. She could have made up the name on the form, couldn't she?'

'But why would she make up his name and not her own, or yours?'

'I don't know.' Cheryl shrugged, but Ellen considered it for a minute.

'Wait, I bet I do. She couldn't make up her name because she had to produce ID at the hospital when Will got sick. But if she never married Charles, or Will's father, he never appeared. She could make up his name.' Ellen's thoughts clicked ahead. 'Tell me, did she have a boyfriend back then, three years ago, that you remember?'

'Oh, she had plenty. Is that the same thing?' Cheryl laughed.

'No name you can recall?'

'No. Maybe this photo will help. It has a guy in it, and they look pretty chummy.' Cheryl handed over the second photo. 'This is the most recent picture I have of Amy. She sent it to me, and you can see the date. June the fifth, two thousand and four.'

'That would be shortly before she had Will,' Ellen said. It was a picture of Amy, grinning on the beach, in a black bikini, with a beer bottle in her hand. Her arm was looped round a shirtless man who raised his bottle to the camera. If Will was born on January 30, 2005, she would have been about two months pregnant when the photo was taken, assuming it was taken when it was sent. But she had no baby bump, though maybe she wasn't showing yet, and there was that beer bottle.

'What are you thinking?' Cheryl asked.

'That if Amy was seeing this man then, he could be Will's father.'

'He's so her type. Amy went for bad boys.'

Ellen eyed the man, who wasn't bad-looking for a bad boy, with close-set eyes and long brown ponytail. Something about him looked almost familiar, but maybe it was that he looked a little like Will. He had the smile, a little tilted down, but it looked like a smirk on him. The photo was too blurry to see more detail and it had been taken from a distance. 'When Amy sent it, did she say who he was, or where they were?'

'No.'

Ellen's gaze remained on the photo. Charles Cartmell, if it was him, had a sleeve of multicoloured tattoos she couldn't read and he looked a little drunk, even in the fuzzy resolution.

'The focus is so bad on this.'

'It could be my printer. I'll email you another, if you want.'

'Please, do.' Ellen told Cheryl her email address, said her goodbyes and left, wondering if it was really Charles Cartmell in the photo. She hit the cold air outside and looked up at the sky, dark and starless.

Maybe it wasn't too late to take a drive.

# CHAPTER FOUR

ELLEN SAT IN HER CAR with the engine off, watching the snow fall in the dark, holding the court papers. She was parked outside an elementary school, a three-storey redbrick edifice that had been there since 1979, according to its keystone. The school was at Charles Cartmell's address, but obviously, he didn't live here. He had never lived here. Amy must have pulled the address out of thin air, and made up the name, too.

'Thanks so much for staying, Con.' Ellen closed the front door behind her. It was after eleven o'clock. 'I really do appreciate it.'

'S'OK.' Connie rose from the couch. 'Your meeting OK?'

'Yes, thanks. How's my baby boy?'

'Fine.' Connie slipped into her coat and opened the door, letting in a blast of cold, wet air. 'Snow's already stopping, isn't it?'

'Yes, but drive safe.' Ellen held the door, then closed and locked it behind her. She took off her coat, went into the kitchen and brewed herself a mug of coffee, pushing Amy to the back of her mind. She had a story to write and she was starved. She quickly ate a bowl of Frosted Mini-Wheats over the sink, leaving her leftover milk to Oreo Figaro.

Up in her home office, she began as she did with any story, transcribing her notes. If she needed to quote, she'd go to the tapes. Then, usually, if she'd had enough caffeine, her brain would lurch into action and an angle for the story would suggest itself. She started with Lateef's mother, typing, trying to remember the mood of the interview and how she felt sitting in Laticia's kitchen, but her thoughts strayed back to Cheryl's house and the picture of Amy and the man on the beach.

Ellen kept transcribing, but it was mechanical. She'd learned a lot about Will in one day. She'd met his mother, grandmother and aunt. She might have seen what his father looked like. She tried to keep typing but her fingers slowed and thoughts of the Martin family intruded. She found herself wondering if Cheryl had emailed her a copy of the photo of Amy and the man on the beach.

She opened up Outlook Express. Incoming emails piled onto the screen, and she ignored the one from Sarah with the attachment and subject line: FYI, I EMAILED MARCO MY PIECE. Suddenly an email came on the screen from twinzmom373@gmail.com.

Ellen clicked it open. It was Cheryl's. The message read, 'Nice meeting you', and there was an attachment. She opened the attachment, and the photo of Amy and the man on the beach popped onto the screen.

She squinted at the picture. It was brighter online, but still blurry and the images distant. She knew how to rectify that. She saved the photo to My Pictures and opened Photoshop, then uploaded the photo, drew a box round Amy's face and clicked Zoom. The image exploded into pixels, so she telescoped it down a little, then examined Amy's features. The shape of her eyes didn't look much like Will's, though they were blue, but her nose was longer than Will's and too wide.

*Not everybody looks like their mom.*

Ellen zoomed out to the original photo, outlined the man's face with the mouse, then clicked. The man did look familiar, and his smile was like Will's, with that downturn on the right. She sipped some coffee and clicked Zoom again, enlarging his face to fill the screen. She set down her coffee, almost spilling it on her notes, so she moved the notebook out of the way. Sticking out from underneath was the white card with the photo of Timothy Braverman.

She slid out the white card and looked at the age-progressed version of Timothy, then set the card down, went back into My Pictures and found Will's last school picture. She enlarged it and set it up on the screen next to the photo of the man on the beach. Then she compared the two photos—the most recent of Will, with the man on the beach:

*Will, eyes blue and wide-set; Beach Man, eyes close together and blue*
*Will, nose, little and turned up; Beach Man, long and skinny*
*Will, dark blond hair; Beach Man, light brown hair*
*Will, round face; Beach Man, long, oval face*
*Will, normal chin; Beach Man, pointed chin*
*Similarities—blue eyes, lopsided smile. Hair?*

Ellen wasn't able to reach a conclusion. Beach Man could be Will's father, or maybe he was someone Amy was dating around the same time, or a random guy with a beer.

Ellen went back online. She clicked through to the Braverman family's website, then captured the age-progressed photo of Timothy and saved a copy to My Pictures. She was going to put it on the screen next to Will's and Beach Man's then compare all three of them, when something else on the Braverman family website caught her eye.

The composite drawing of the carjacker.

On impulse, Ellen captured the composite and saved a copy to My Pictures, then uploaded it and placed it next to Beach Man. The photos were different sizes, so she outlined the composite drawing and clicked Zoom to enlarge it to the approximate size of Beach Man, and clicked.

The composite drawing of the carjacker looked like Beach Man.

'Oh my God,' she said aloud.

Ellen looked back at the screen, getting a grip. It was impossible to compare a black-and-white pencil drawing with a colour photo of a flesh-and-blood man. She flashed on Will's tracing of a horse from the other day, and it gave her an idea. She clicked Print, and her printer chugged to life. Then she got up and hurried downstairs, rummaged through the toy box, and ran back up with a roll of tracing paper.

The printer had spat out a copy of the composite drawing, and she took a black pencil and went over the lines of the carjacker's features, blackening them so they'd be darker and thicker. Then she took the piece of tracing paper and placed it on top of the composite drawing, tracing the image onto the crinkly transparent paper. She set the traced composite aside, slid the copy of the Beach Man photo from the printer tray, then moved her computer keyboard to the side and set the printed photo on the desk. Then she took the traced composite of the carjacker and placed it over Beach Man's face.

It was an exact match.

Ellen felt her gorge rising, and she bolted for the bathroom.

**E**llen lingered on the threshold to Will's room, lost in thought. She couldn't work any longer, not after what she thought she'd learned.

*Is Will really Timothy?*

She tasted bile and Colgate on her teeth, and sagged against the doorjamb, trying to work her way through the scenario she feared. If the composite matched the photo of the man on the beach, then Beach Man was the carjacker. He had shot Carol Braverman's nanny. Kidnapped Will. Taken the ransom money but kept the child. He had a girlfriend who pretended to be the baby's mother. Amy Martin.

*Why not kill the baby right after the kidnapping?*

Ellen shuddered, but she could guess at some answers. Amy wanted a baby and couldn't have one. Or they thought they could sell the baby on the black market.

*Why give him up for adoption?*

Because he got sick. Will had a heart problem no one knew about. At least she assumed as much, because the Braverman site didn't mention that Timothy had any heart problems. The doctors at Dupont Hospital had told her that his murmur had gone undetected, which wasn't unusual. Will would have failed to thrive. He wouldn't eat well and he'd have been sickly. That would have overwhelmed Amy, even her mother said so, and it would have made it too risky to keep him. Too many blood tests, forms and questions that could show Amy wasn't the mother and the boyfriend the father.

*So what do they do next?*

They'd take the baby to a hospital far from Miami, back to where Amy had grown up. They'd abandon the baby in the hospital.

'Mommy?' Will asked sleepily, from the bed.

Ellen padded over to the bed, and leaned over Will, brushing his fringe from his forehead. 'Sorry I woke you.'

'Are you home?'

'Yes, it's night and I'm home.' Ellen reached down and stroked his cheek. 'You're the best kid in the world, do you know that?'

'You brushed your teeth.'

'I did and I'm coming in. We're having a slumber party.'

'What's that?' Will scissored his legs.

'It's people having a party when they should be sleeping.' Ellen eased onto the narrow bed, on her side. 'Scoot over.'

'OK.' Will edged backwards, and Ellen reached for him and wrapped him up in her arms.

'How's that feel? Good?'

Will hugged her back. 'Do you have to go to work tomorrow?'

'Yes.' Ellen didn't know what would happen at work tomorrow, with her story unfinished. Right now, she didn't care.

'I hate work.'

'I know, sweetie. I'm sorry I have to work.'

'Why do you?'

'I work so we have all the things we need.'

Will yawned.

'Maybe we should go to sleep. Party's over, slumber is beginning.'

'Good night.'

'I love you, sweetie. Good night.' Ellen cuddled him, and in the next minute, she could feel his body drifting back to sleep. She caught herself beginning to cry and willed herself to stop. *Flip it.*

She really couldn't be sure that Beach Man was the carjacker. A tracing couldn't tell anything with accuracy, and composites were based only on a verbal description. Lots of men had close-set eyes and long noses. If the composite was too unreliable to prove that the carjacker was Beach Man, then there was no link between Will and Timothy.

Ellen felt a tiny bit better. Maybe Amy would email her, tell her the story of Will's birth and explain why she'd put him up for adoption.

Will shifted in his sleep, and she snuggled him to her. She couldn't resolve tonight whether her fears were founded or insane. But behind them lurked an unspoken question, one she couldn't begin to acknowledge, much less articulate to herself. It had been lurking in the back of her mind from the moment she'd seen the white card in the mail.

She hugged Will closer, there in the still, dark room, and the question hung in the air above the bed: *If Will is really Timothy, what will I do?*

Ellen entered the newsroom the next morning, exhausted after only two hours of sleep. She hadn't been able to stop her brain from thinking about Will and Timothy, and she felt raw, achy and preoccupied. She had on the same jeans and shirt she'd worn yesterday, but with a different sweater, and she hadn't had time to shower.

She tried to put the Braverman business behind her, but her head was pounding. The newsroom was mostly empty, and she hustled down the aisle, trying to get her thoughts together for the meeting about the homicide piece. Through the glass wall of his office, she saw Marcelo at his desk and Sarah sitting across from him, laughing.

Ellen figured the laughter would stop when she told them she'd be late with her end of the story. She dropped her handbag on her desk, shed her jacket, and hung it on the coatrack, seeing that Sal and Larry were entering Marcelo's office, holding Styrofoam cups of coffee and looking like the journalists Ellen had grown up idolising. She hated that she was about to crash and burn in front of them. She girded herself and headed to Marcelo's office, where he looked up expectantly from behind his desk.

'Come in, Ellen.' Marcelo smiled, his eyes flashing darkly. 'I didn't get your draft. Did you email it?'

'Marcelo, I don't have the piece done. I'm sorry.'

Sarah looked over. Larry and Sal turned round. Marcelo blinked. 'You don't have it?' he asked, lifting an eyebrow.

'No, sorry. I got a little bogged down and I need a few extra days.'

'Maybe I can help. That's what they pay me for.'

'No, you can't,' Ellen blurted out, but Marcelo was still smiling, his head cocked and his eyes sympathetic.

'Let me see what you have so far. I'm not looking for perfection. I can't be, with these two slackers on the story.' Marcelo gestured at Larry and Sal. 'Their draft needed the usual overhaul.'

'Kiss my ass,' Sal said, and they all laughed except Ellen.

'Marcelo, to be honest, there is no draft. Not yet.' She felt sick. She cleared her throat. 'I interviewed one of the mothers who lost a son, a second-grader who was murdered. I also spoke with the boy's teacher and the funeral director who prepared his body.'

Sal whistled. 'Grieving mothers are a home run.'

Larry nodded. 'I like the funeral angle, too. It's different. Original.'

Marcelo looked relieved. 'OK, Ellen. Good. So you just don't have the draft yet. When can you finish it?'

'Next Friday?'

'She's been working on that Sulaman follow-up,' Sarah interrupted. 'That's the real reason you blew this deadline, isn't it?'

'That's not true!' Ellen shot back.

'Yes, it is,' Sarah continued. 'I know because Susan Sulaman called yesterday. She said she couldn't reach you, so the switchboard sent the call to the newsroom, and I picked up. She said you'd interviewed her and wanted to know if you'd talked your editor into running the story.'

Marcelo's eyes widened, and Ellen's face burned.

'You have no idea what I've been doing, so stay out of my business! Your story is separate from mine!' She couldn't stop herself from shouting even though everyone had fallen into shocked silence. Her head was about to explode. 'It's not your concern whether I make my deadline!'

'Beg to differ.' Sarah sniffed. 'I pitched the piece in the first place and you're screwing it up. We're all ready, why aren't you?'

'Ladies, hold on.' Marcelo stood up behind his desk, raising his hands. 'Everyone, please, give Ellen and me a minute.'

Sal and Larry edged past Ellen, who turned her head away when Sarah brushed by her, trailing perfume and adrenaline. After they had left, Marcelo put his hands firmly on his hips.

'Close the door, please,' he said quietly.

Ellen did, then faced him.

'What's going on? You never miss a deadline.' Marcelo looked mystified, and his tone sounded more disappointed than angry. 'Is she right? Was it the Sulaman follow-up that delayed you?'

'No.'

'Did you interview the mother?'

'Yes. Only once.'

'But I asked you not to.' Marcelo's tone wasn't disappointed but hurt.

'I'm so sorry. I just had to see her again.' Ellen knew it sounded lame, and Marcelo looked grave, his eyebrows sloping down.

'Ellen, let's be honest. Ever since I let Courtney go, you've been distant. You've acted towards me as if we're on different sides.'

'No, we're not, I swear.'

Marcelo finger-raked his hair from his forehead and fell silent a moment, eyeing her. 'I can tell something's wrong. You're not yourself. Is it Will? I know he was sick when he was little. Is he sick again?'

'No.' Ellen couldn't tell him anything. 'I'll have the story to you early next week. I said Friday because I wanted to be realistic.'

'Tell me what's wrong,' Marcelo said again, his voice even softer. 'You look tired.'

'I don't feel that great.' Ellen winced inwardly. *You look tired* was code for *you look ugly*.

'Are you sick?'

'I threw up last night,' Ellen blurted out, then watched Marcelo's eyes flare in brief surprise. Throwing up was definitely not hot, and suddenly she felt like a mess. Doing and saying the wrong things, exhausted and undone. 'I should just go home. I really don't feel well.'

'OK, that's fine, of course.' Marcelo nodded, walking round his desk towards her. 'If you're sick, you must go home. Take care of yourself.'

'Right, thanks.' Ellen moved to the door, feeling dizzy. She broke out into a sweat. Her head was light. She hadn't had time for breakfast.

And in the next second, the office went black.

'**S**urprise, I'm home!' Ellen called out from the doorway, slipping out of her coat. The living room was bright and peaceful, with a winter sun streaming through the windows, and the sight brought her back to reality, after having fainted in Marcelo's office. She'd blamed it on her mystery illness when she regained consciousness in his arms, their faces close enough to kiss. Or maybe she had imagined that part.

'Mommy!' Will zoomed from the dining room.

'Honey!' Ellen let her coat fall to scoop him up and give him a big hug, and Connie came out of the kitchen, looking pleased.

'Hi, El. Is there much ice on the road?'

'No, and thanks for shovelling the walk.'

'That's all right. Will helped.'

'Good for you, sweetie.' Ellen set Will down. 'No school today, huh?'

'No, Mommy. We read four books!' Will held up four fingers.

'I don't know why they closed,' Connie said. 'It's a gyp, for what you pay.'

'It's all right.' Ellen smiled at Will. 'Let's have some fun. How about sledging?'

'YES!' Will shouted, jumping like crazy.

Ellen smiled. 'Will, say goodbye and thank you to Connie.'

'Goodbye, I love you!' Will shouted, throwing his arms round Connie's legs, and Ellen winced.

'See ya later,' Connie said, bending over and hugging Will back.

'Alligator,' he replied, his face buried in her coat. Ellen opened the door, and Connie left, waving happily.

After lunch, Ellen got Will dressed in his snowsuit and retrieved the orange plastic saucer from the basement. She slid into her coat and took him in one hand and the saucer in the other, then went outside.

Ellen scanned the street, which was covered with a soft snow that blanketed the rooftops, filled the gutters and lined the porch steps. The houses, mostly stone or clapboard, sat close together, and many of them shared driveways, like freshly shovelled Ys. Narberth was a stop-time neighbourhood, where everybody looked out for each other.

They were making their way down the porch steps when Ellen realised her neighbours must have got the white card in the mail, showing the photo of Timothy Braverman. They could have noticed how much he looked like Will, and everyone on the street knew that Will was adopted. They had all read her series, and she had even thrown a welcoming party for him when he was well enough. She used to be glad that Narberth was so chummy, but now it terrified her.

Two doors away, Mrs Knox, an older woman, was brushing snow from her sidewalk and, on the far side of the street, stay-at-home moms Elena Goldblum and Barbara Capozzi were talking while their kids played in the snow. Ellen stood frozen on the sidewalk.

'Mommy?' Will asked. 'Are we going?'

'I'm just looking at the street. It's so pretty with the snow, isn't it?'

'Go!' Will tugged her hand, but Ellen's thoughts raced ahead. They always went sledging a few blocks away at Shortridge Park, and the place would be packed with Will's friends, their mothers and the occasional stay-at-home dad. All of them would have got the white card.

'Will, guess what?' Ellen knelt and held him by the shoulder. 'Today, how about we go to a new place to sledge? Valley Forge. I used to sledge there when I was growing up. Let's try it.' Ellen took him by the hand, and walked him over to the car before he could object. She got her keys from her pocket, chirped the back door unlocked, hoisted him into his car seat and locked him in. 'This will be an adventure.'

Will nodded, uncertain.

Ellen closed the car door, stuck the saucer in the trunk, and was going to the driver's side when Mrs Knox appeared from nowhere.

'Why you drivin' to Shortridge?' she said. 'It's only round the corner.'

'See you!' Ellen shut the door, started the engine and backed out of the driveway, giving a disappointed Mrs Knox a last wave.

'Mommy,' Will said from the back, 'Connie doesn't like Mrs Knox.'

'Really?' Ellen said. 'Why not?'

'Connie says Mrs Knox is a busy-busy.'

Ellen steered the car down the street. 'You mean a busybody?'

'Yes!' Will giggled.

Ellen hit the gas, hard.

**E**llen trudged along the top of the hill carrying Will, who was crying and hollering in a full-blown tantrum.

'Mommy! Please! I want to . . . go again!' he sobbed.

'Will, try to calm down, honey.' Ellen's head pounded at his screaming, and teenagers packed the hill, shouting and laughing, adding to the din. She sidestepped to avoid two older boys shoving each other, and she accidentally dropped the rope to the saucer.

'Oh, no!' Ellen yelped, turning round, but before she could catch the saucer, it went spinning down the icy slope. She had no choice but to let it go. She needed to get both of them home and down for naps.

'I can . . . do it myself!' Will wailed.

'Please, honey, settle down. Everything's going to be all right.' She finally reached the car, where she stuffed Will into his car seat, jumped behind the steering wheel, started the engine and pulled out of the parking lot, looking for the route back into the city. Traffic was congested. She slowed through the intersection, trying to read the route signs, which were confusing, and horns honked behind her.

'I want to do it . . . again!' Will cried. 'We only went one time!'

'We'll go home, and I'll make some hot chocolate. How about that?'

'Please . . . Mommy, please, again!'

'When you're older,' Ellen said, but she knew it was the wrong thing to say the moment the words escaped her lips.

'I'M A BIG BOY!' Will howled, and Ellen didn't rebuke him, knowing it was disappointment and fatigue. She took a left turn, looking for the highway entrance, when suddenly she heard the loud blare of a siren.

'Is it a fire truck, Mommy?' Will's sobbing slowed at the prospect, and Ellen checked the rearview mirror.

A state police cruiser was right behind her, flashing its high beams. She hadn't even known he was there. She said, 'Perfect.'

'What, Mommy?'

'It's a police car.' Ellen didn't know what she had done. She waited for traffic to part and pulled over to the shoulder, with the police cruiser following.

'Why, Mom?' Will sniffled.

'I'm not sure, but everything's OK.'

'Why do they make that sound?'

'So you know they're there.'

'Why are they there?'

Ellen sighed inwardly. 'We'll find out in a minute.' She waited as the cruiser door opened and a tall cop emerged and walked along the side of her car, holding a small clipboard. She pressed the button to lower the window, letting in a blast of cold air. 'Yes, Officer?'

'Licence and registration, please.'

'Oh, no.' Ellen realised that she had neither, because she hadn't taken her handbag. She had been going to Shortridge before she changed the plan. 'This isn't my day. I left the house without them.'

The cop frowned. He was young, with light eyes under the wide brim of his brown hat. 'You don't have any ID on you?'

'Sorry, no. It's at home, I swear it. What did I do?'

'You ran a stop.'

'I'm sorry, I didn't see it. I was looking for the sign into Philly.'

'What did you do, Mommy?' Will called out, and the cop bent from the waist and eyed Will through the open window.

Ellen felt a bolt of panic, out of nowhere. What if the state police had a register of kidnapped kids? What if there was an amber alert out for Timothy Braverman? What if the cops got those white cards? What if the cop somehow recognised Will as Timothy?

'Cute kid,' the cop said, unsmiling.

'Thanks.' Ellen gripped the steering wheel, heart thumping.

'He looks unhappy,' the cop said, his breath foggy in the frigid air. His gaze remained on Will, and Ellen told herself to stay calm.

'He's just tired.'

'I'M NOT TIRED, MOMMEEEE!' Will screamed.

'I got a nephew hollers like that.' The cop finally cracked a smile. 'All right, ma'am, this is your lucky day. I'll let you slide on the licence but don't make a habit of it, we clear?'

'Yes, thank you, Officer,' Ellen said, hearing the tremor in her voice.

'Goodbye now, and be careful pulling out.' The cop backed away from the car, and Ellen pressed the button to raise the window. She exhaled with relief as the cop rejoined the line of traffic, then she checked the rearview mirror. Will was falling asleep, his head listing.

She looked for an opening in the traffic, then pulled back onto the highway. Her head hurt, and she wished for the umpteenth time that her mother was still alive. She needed to talk to someone about Timothy Braverman; her mother would have known what to do and think.

Ellen felt like she was losing her grip. Fainting in the office. Blowing her deadline. She could lose her job to Sarah if she didn't get her act together. She needed a saner head to prevail.

The traffic started to move, and she accelerated.

She had a new destination in mind.

'Hey, Dad,' Ellen said, closing the front door behind them.

'Pops!' Will raised his arms to her father, revitalised after his long nap. Given the traffic, it had taken over an hour to get to West Chester.

'My little buddy!' Her father's face lit up, his hooded eyes alive with animation. 'Come here, you!' He reached for Will, who jumped into his arms, wrapping his legs round him like a little monkey.

Her father carried Will into the living room. Ellen took off her hat and coat, set them on a chair, and looked round. The rug was rolled up, and cardboard boxes sat stacked all over. Her father set Will down, then unzipped his coat, tugged it off and tossed it aside.

'Hope this isn't a bad time.' Ellen gestured at the boxes.

'Nah. Barbara did all that. She's finished for today.' He gestured to a small cardboard box. 'That one has some things from your mother, pictures and whatnot. You might want to take it home.'

'Where's my Thomas the Tank Engine?' Will asked, looking round, bewildered. The toy box that had been tucked in the corner was gone.

Her father took Will by the hand, and walked him to a cardboard box, with the top open. 'Look inside, cowpoke. The gang's all here.'

'My truck!' Will dug in the box, pulled out a red truck.

Ellen said, 'Will, I'm going to talk to Pop in the kitchen.'

Her father straightened up, and they went into the kitchen.

'Right. What's on your mind, kiddo?' her father asked.

'This is going to sound strange, so prepare yourself.' Ellen lowered her voice, though Will was out of earshot.

'Dad, what if I told you that Will might really be a boy named Timothy Braverman, who was kidnapped in Florida, two years ago?'

'What?' Her father's eyes widened, and Ellen filled him in quickly.

'So, what do you think?' she asked, when she was finished.

Her father shrugged. 'You dreamed this up. It's crazy. You don't have any facts. You're assuming lots of things that may or may not be true.'

'OK, remember that photo I showed you, last time I was here? You thought it was Will. It wasn't, it was Timothy Braverman. They look that much alike, exactly alike.'

'There's no way you can tell who a composite is by tracing over his face. You adopted that little boy in there legally. You had a lawyer.'

'Who killed herself.'

'So what? What are you saying?'

Ellen didn't even know. 'It just seems strange. Coincidental.'

'Bah! You adopted that boy, and he loves you. He was half-dead. Nobody wanted him but you. Nobody was there for him but you.'

'But what matters now is whether he's Timothy.'

'He is *not* Timothy. He's just a kid who looks like Timothy. He's not the same kid. He's Will. He's *ours*.' Her father paused, then looked at her with a half smile. 'El, listen to me. Barbara's grandkids, Joshie and Jakie, you could swap 'em out and nobody would know the difference.'

'Are they twins?'

'No, but they look alike, and they look like Will, too. They're all little boys, and they all look alike. Didn't anybody ever say to you, "Hey, you look just like somebody I know?" That ever happen to you, Elly Belly?'

'Sure.'

'Of course. It happens to me all the time. I look like people. Handsome men. George Clooney, maybe.' Her father grinned. 'That's all you got goin' on here. Don't worry about it.'

Ellen's heart eased a little. 'You think?'

'I know. They look alike but they're not the same kid. Will is ours, for ever. He's *ours*.' Her father gave her an aromatic, if awkward, hug and Ellen knew he believed he had closed the deal.

'You sold me, Dad.'

'I'm always selling somebody, kiddo.' Her father grinned again. 'But it's easy when you believe what you sell, and I believe this. Relax, honey. You're getting all worked up over nothing. Forget this nonsense.'

Ellen wanted to believe him.

'You seein' anybody?'

'Huh? You mean, like a date?'

'Yes, exactly like a date.' Her father smiled.

'No.'

'Not since what's-his-name?'

'No.'

'Not interested in anybody?'

Ellen thought of Marcelo. 'Not really.'

'Why not? A knockout like you? Why put yourself up on the shelf? You should go out more, you know? Live a little. Go dancing.'

'I have Will.'

'We'll sit for him.' Her father took her hand in his, encircled her with his other hand and started humming. 'Let me lead, you follow.'

'OK, OK.' Ellen laughed, finding the box step of the foxtrot, letting herself be danced round the kitchen to her father's singing 'Steppin' Out with My Baby' as he steered her from the small of her back.

'Will, come see your ol' Pops!' he called over his shoulder and, in the next minute, Will came thundering into the kitchen.

'Ha, Mommy!' He ran to them, and they took his hands and the three of them shuffled round in a ring-around-the-rosy circle, with her father singing and Will looking up from one to the other, blue eyes shining.

Ellen couldn't sing because of the sharp ache she felt inside, a sudden pain so palpable that she almost burst into tears, and she wished that her mother were still alive to take Will's hand and dance with them in a circle, all four of them happy and whole, a family again.

But it was an impossible wish, and Ellen sent it packing. She looked down at her child with tears in her eyes and all the love in her heart.

*He's ours.*

# CHAPTER FIVE

IT WAS LATE by the time Ellen got Will home. She read him a book before bed and tucked him in, then went downstairs to close up the kitchen. The cardboard box of her mother's things sat on the counter.

Ellen opened the lid of the box. Stacked inside was a set of photographs in various frames; the top one was a colour photo of her parents at their wedding. They stood together under a tree, her father wearing a tux and his I-made-my-quota smile. Her mother's smile was sweet and shy, making barely a quarter moon on a delicate face, which was framed by short brown hair stiffened with Aqua Net. She had roundish eyes and a small, thin nose, like the tiny beak of a dime-store finch, and at only five foot one, Mary Gleeson seemed to recede in size, personality and importance next to her larger-than-life husband.

Ellen wiped the dust from the top photo with a tissue, then cleaned all of the frames until she noticed that between two of the photos was a packet of greeting cards. The top one was a fortieth wedding anniversary card. She took out the packet and went through the cards, but the last envelope wasn't a greeting card. It was an envelope of her mother's stationery, the pale blue of the forget-me-nots that grew by their sugar maple in the back yard.

Ellen knew what it was, instantly. She had received a note like that from her mother, too, written right before she died. The front of the envelope read, *To Don*. The envelope was still sealed. Her father had never opened the note.

Ellen didn't get it. Didn't he want to hear the last words of his wife, written after she knew she was going to die? She slid a nail under the envelope flap, tugged the note out and opened it.

*Dear Don,*

*I know that you have always loved me, even if you have forgotten it from time to time. Please know that I understand you, I accept you and I forgive you.*

*Love always, Mary*

Ellen took the note and went to sit in the dining room. The house was still and quiet. The windows were inky mirrors, the dark sky moonless. She closed her eyes, feeling the note's heavy paper beneath her fingers, letting it connect her to her mother through space and time. And at that moment, she knew what her mother would say about Will and Timothy, in that soft voice of hers. It was what she had written to Ellen in her final note: *Follow your heart.*

And so there in the quiet room, Ellen finally let herself listen to her heart, which had been trying to tell her something from the moment she first got the card in the mail. Maybe her father thought it was crazy to worry, but inside, she knew better. She couldn't pretend any longer and she couldn't live the rest of her life looking over her shoulder. She couldn't feel like a criminal when a cop pulled her over. She couldn't hide Will from his friends and neighbours.

So she vowed to follow her heart. Starting now.

**E**llen entered the lawyer's office and took a seat, surrounded by bronze, glass and crystal awards, like so many blunt instruments. She had met Ron Halpren when she did the series on Will's adoption, having interviewed him for his expertise on family law, and she counted herself lucky she could call on him at such short notice.

'Thanks for meeting me on a Saturday,' she said, and Ron walked round his cluttered desk and eased into his creaky chair.

'That's OK, I'm in most Saturday mornings.' Ron had light eyes behind tortoiseshell glasses, a halo of fuzzy grey hair and a shaggy greying beard to match. His frame was short and pudgy, and he looked like Paddington Bear in his yellow fleece pullover and thick jeans. 'Sorry we're out of coffee. I was supposed to bring it in, but I forgot.'

'No problem, and thanks for accommodating Will.' Ellen gestured to the secretary's desk outside, where Will was eating vending-machine Fig Newtons and watching a *Wizard of Oz* DVD on the computer.

'It's great to see him so healthy. What a difference, eh?'

'Really.' Ellen shifted forward on her chair. 'So, as I said on the phone, I'm seeing you in your official capacity, and I want to pay for your time today.'

'Forget it.' Ron smiled. 'You made me look like a hotshot in the paper. I got tons of clients from that press. I owe *you*. Now get to the point.' Ron gestured towards the door. 'I hear the scarecrow singing. We don't have much time.'

'Wait, let me ask you something first. Is what we say still confidential if a crime is involved? I didn't commit it, but I know, or I suspect, that a crime has been committed by someone else. If I tell you about this crime, would you have to report it to the police?'

'I'd be barred from so doing.'

Ellen loved the authoritative note in his voice. 'Here goes. I think that Will could be a kid named Timothy Braverman, who was kidnapped in Florida two years ago.'

Ron lifted an eyebrow. 'So the crime in question is the kidnapping?'

'Yes, it was a carjacking gone wrong, and the kidnapper murdered the boy's nanny. Here's what I need to know. If Will is really Timothy, what are my legal rights? Could the Bravermans, his birth parents, take him from me? Would I have to give him up if they found out? Wouldn't it matter to the court that he lived with me for two years? That I'm the only mother he's ever really known? Would that—'

Ron held up his hands. 'Tell me how you found this out, about Will.'

So Ellen told him the story from the beginning, showing him the adoption file, the composite drawing, and her computer print-outs of Timothy and Will. 'By the way, my father thinks I'm crazy. He's the only other person I've told.'

Ron studied the photographs on his desk. 'You're not crazy, but you are speculating. You can't support your belief that Will is Timothy Braverman by comparing the composite with a photograph. It just isn't reliable enough. I see some similarity, but I can't be sure it's the same person. Any one of my first-year law students can tell you that a composite is merely an aid to the identification and apprehension of a suspect. They're not a positive identification.' Ron shook his head. 'You don't have enough information on which to base any conclusion that Will is the kidnapped child.

'Now, the first question you should have is whether you have an obligation to go to the authorities with your suspicion. Answer? No, the law doesn't impose responsibility on the citizenry to report crimes that are so speculative in nature. That's not to say that you couldn't voluntarily report your suspicion to the authorities, if you wished. I'm sure there are blood tests that could be done, or DNA analysis that would determine if Will is Timothy.' Ron tented his fingers in front of his beard. 'Obviously, you're concerned that if you tell the authorities and you're right, you would lose Will.'

Ellen couldn't even speak, and Ron didn't wait for an answer.

'Let's assume for a moment that you're right. Will is Timothy.'

'Could that even happen?'

'Hypothetically, it's easy. All that's required for a valid adoption is a birth mother to produce a birth certificate, which as we all know is easy enough to fake. It doesn't even have a photo. And she has to supply a signed waiver of her parental rights, from the birth father, too, which is also easy to forge. She could have easily made up the father's name.'

Ellen was remembering the school where Charles Cartmell's house was supposed to have been. The Charles Cartmell that nobody had heard of and who didn't exist.

'The second question is what are your parental rights, if any?'

Ellen couldn't take the suspense. 'Just tell me, would I get to keep Will or would I have to give him back to the Bravermans?'

'The Bravermans, as the child's birth parents, have an undisputed legal right to their child. They're alive, and they didn't give him up for adoption. If he was kidnapped, your adoption is simply invalid. Therefore, as a legal matter, the court would return Will to them.'

'Would I have the right to visit him?'

'No.' Ron shook his head. 'You would have no rights at all. The Bravermans may permit you to, perhaps to wean him from you, so to speak. But no court would order them to permit you to visit.'

'So it doesn't matter that I'm the only mother he's ever known? My house is the only house he's ever known. The school, the classmates, the neighbourhood, the baby sitter. We're his world, and they're strangers.'

'Aw, wait.' Ron's voice softened. 'We were speaking hypothetically. There is no reason in the world to think there was anything wrong with his adoption. You want my advice? Take these papers and put them away, at the bottom of a drawer.' Ron slid the file, the photographs and the composite drawing back across his messy desk. 'Your adoption was valid. Will is your child. Enjoy him, and invite Louisa and me to his wedding.'

Ellen packed up her papers, wishing she could take his advice. 'I can't do that. I want to know what's true.'

'I told you what's true. You've elevated suspicion to fact.'

'But it doesn't feel right. You know what I really feel? I feel that my kid is sick, but the doctors keep telling me he's fine. Not just you, my father, too. But *I'm* his mother. I'm Dr Mom. Call it a mother's instinct, or intuition, but I have it inside, and I know better.'

'But you have to have valid proof to support your certainty.'

Ellen gathered up the photographs and papers, and rose with them. 'If proof is what I need, then proof is what I'll get. Thanks for your help.'

'You're very welcome.' Ron rose, too, his expression darkening. 'But be careful what you wish. If you find proof that Will is Timothy Braverman, you'll feel a lot worse than you do already. You'll have to make a choice I wouldn't wish on my worst enemy.'

'What would you do, if it were your kid?'

'Wild horses couldn't make me give him back.'

'Then let me ask you this, Counsellor. How do you keep something that doesn't belong to you?'

'Och. My.' Ron cringed. 'Excellent question.'

'And how do I explain that to Will, when he grows up? What if he found out? What do I say? That I loved you, so I kept you, even though I knew the truth? Is that love, or just selfishness? This is the thing, Ron. When I adopted him, I felt like he belonged to me because another mother gave him up. But if she didn't, if she had had him taken from her by force, then he doesn't belong to me. Not truly. It'll be in the back of my mind for the rest of my life, if I don't resolve it.'

'Then I feel for you,' Ron said softly, meeting her eye.

Ellen spent the afternoon with Will, building a castle from Lego, stamping Play-Doh with cookie cutters and making burgers for dinner. Will sat at the table, and Ellen felt as if the kitchen was their domestic cocoon, with its soft lighting, warm stove and purring house cat.

'I have a surprise dessert for you,' Ellen said, but Will flashed her his picky-eater frown, as dubious a look as a three-year-old can muster.

'What is it? Don't we have ice cream?'

'It's better than ice cream. Wait right here.' Ellen got up, collected the dinner plates, and took them into the kitchen, where she set them in the sink. She fetched the dessert from the refrigerator, carried it to the dining room and placed it on the table.

'Eeew, Mommy!' Will scrunched up his nose, the only reasonable response to what looked like a bowl of green plastic.

'Give it a chance. It's Jell-O, in your favourite colour.' Ellen had spent last night rereading the Braverman website and had seen the detail that Timothy loved lime Jell-O. Will had never eaten it before, as far as she knew, and she wanted to see if he liked it.

Will wrinkled his nose. 'Is it spinach?'

'No, it's lime.'

'What's lime?'

'Like lemon, but better. Did you ever have lime Jell-O before?'

Will eyed the bowl warily. 'I had red. Can't you make red?'

'Not this time. Today, let's try green Jell-O.' Ellen scooped some Jell-O into his dessert bowl and held her breath as he picked up his teaspoon, dipped the tip into the shiny green mound, then touched the tip of his tongue to the spoon. She said, 'Give it a real taste.'

Will put the Jell-O in his mouth and, for a moment, didn't react.

'Well, do you like it?'

'It's good!' Will answered, his mouth full.

Ellen spent the evening in her home office, figuring out where and how to find the proof that Will was or wasn't Timothy. She took her BlackBerry from the holster and pressed speed dial C.

Connie picked up. 'Hey, El, how are you?'

'Fine, thanks. I have a huge favour to ask you, Connie. Something big came up at work, and I have to leave town for a few days.' Ellen hated lying, but she couldn't risk telling even Connie the truth. 'Is there any way you can cover for me?'

'Sure. Where you goin'?'

'I'm not sure yet. I'll pay you overtime, whatever it takes.'

Connie hushed her. 'Can it wait until Monday?'

'Yes, I really appreciate it.'

'I'll pack my toothbrush. How many days will it be?'

*God knows.* 'Just a few, the situation is fluid. Can you live with that?'

'Yep. See ya then.'

Ellen hung up, with one more thing to do. She logged on to Outlook, skimmed her incoming email and found one sender that surprised her. Marcelo. She clicked Open.

Dear Ellen,
I'm concerned about you. I hope you're feeling better. Please do call a doctor. We lack a human face without you! Best, Marcelo

Ellen felt a little thrill. He was such a great guy. It was worth fainting to get him to hold her. She smiled at the memory of being cradled against his chest, but it faded when she thought of what she had to do next. She hit Reply and started typing:

Marcelo,
Thanks for your nice note but, unfortunately, I need to take this week off. I have plenty of vacation time coming, and I'll take the time out of that. I'm not sure if I'll get my piece finished by deadline, but I'll stay in touch with you about this. I'm sorry, and hope this doesn't cause too much of a problem. Thanks and best, Ellen

She clicked Send and swallowed hard. Taking a vacation with a layoff pending could be career suicide, but she had no choice. The situation with Will and Timothy put everything into perspective, and her job would always be second to her child.

Ellen woke to the ringing of her BlackBerry, which she kept on the night table as an alarm clock. 'Hello?' she asked, muzzy.

'It's Marcelo.' His voice sounded so soft on the phone, his accent more pronounced. Ellen checked the digital clock. Sunday morning, 08:02.

'Oh, jeez, hi.'

'Did I wake you?'

*Yes.* 'No.'

'Sorry to bother you, but I got your vacation request and I wanted to discuss it with you. It's a problem for us, right now.'

'It's just that—'

'I'm going to be in your area tonight. I can stop by, if you like, and we can talk about it.'

*Marcelo, here? I'll have to vacuum. And put on make-up. Not in that order.*

'Ellen? I don't mean to intrude—'

'No, it's fine, a great idea.'

'What time is good?'

'Will goes to bed around seven thirty, so any time after eight o'clock.'

'I'm free at nine. See you then.'

'Great. Thanks.' Ellen pressed End. Marcelo was coming here? Her boss, her crush? Was this a date or a firing? It was exciting and unnerving, both at once. At best, she'd have to lie to his face about where she was going on Monday, which wouldn't be easy. Especially if he wore that aftershave, eau d'eligible bachelor.

'Marcelo, hi, come in,' Ellen said, opening her front door onto a living room that looked as if no one lived there. Will's toys, books and DVDs had been put away, the rugs had been vacuumed. Cat hair had been lint-rolled from the sofa, and paw prints wiped from the coffee table.

'Thanks.' Marcelo stepped inside, and Ellen edged back, awkward.

'Let me take your coat,' she said, but Marcelo was already sliding out of his black leather jacket, and she caught a whiff of his spicy aftershave, a scent that spoke directly to her I'm-Very-Single cortex, bypassing the saner He's-Your-Boss lobe.

'What a lovely house,' he said, looking round. He had on a black ribbed turtleneck with nice brown slacks, and Ellen found herself wondering if he'd been on a date. He asked, 'How long have you lived here?'

'Six years or so.' Ellen brushed a stray hair from her eyes, surprised that even a single strand had escaped her product-heavy blow-dry. She had changed her outfit three times, only to end up in her trademark loose blue sweater, white tank underneath, jeans and Dansko boots. 'Would you like a Diet Coke or something?'

'Sure, great. Let me help you. I'd love a house tour.'

'OK, but it's a short one.' Ellen waved awkwardly at the dining room. 'Speaks for itself, huh? And over here's the teeny tiny kitchen.'

'Very nice.' Marcelo followed her, looking round with his hands linked loosely behind his back. 'It's warm and friendly.'

'And clean.'

Marcelo smiled. 'I was going to say it was clean. Very clean.'

'Thank you.' Ellen went into the cabinet, found a decent tumbler, then went in the fridge and got him ice and a soda. Oreo Figaro sat on the counter, watching the goings-on with interest.

'I like cats. What's his name?'

'Oreo Figaro.'

Marcelo lifted an eyebrow. 'Back home, many people have two names, like my brother, Carlos Alberto. But I didn't think that was so common in the States.'

'It's not. He's Brazilian.'

Marcelo laughed. He popped the soda and poured it. 'I live in town.'

*I know. We all know. You're the hot, single Latin boss, and therefore the most-talked-about person in the newsroom, if not the Western Hemisphere.*

'I think about moving out here, but I wonder how you meet women in the suburbs.' Marcelo paused. 'I was out here on a blind date. Can you imagine that?'

'Yes.' Ellen liked the way his accent made it *e-magine*. 'How was it?'

'Excruciating.'

'Been there. Excruciating conversation, excruciating kiss good night.'

Marcelo laughed again. 'Glad to see you're feeling better.'

*I always make jokes when I'm nervous.*

'It was very strange to have you faint, so suddenly.' Marcelo frowned slightly, and Ellen recognised a flicker of concern behind his eyes.

'Thank you for being so kind about it.'

'Give me no credit. I wanted to leave, but you were lying in my way.'

Ellen laughed, and Marcelo sipped his soda and set it down.

'So, to your email. Let's be honest with each other. You're reliable. You make deadlines. You didn't take a vacation last year, I checked. All of a sudden, you're fainting and you need time off for a mysterious reason.' Marcelo glanced away, then back again. 'If you have some illness, you can be sure I'll keep it confidential.'

'All I can tell you is that I need to take these few days off to settle something personal.' Ellen was so tempted to tell him, but she couldn't.

'Are you going somewhere or staying here?'

'I'd rather not say. I'm taking vacation time, is all.'

'Will you get the homicide piece written on time?'

'Honestly, I don't know.'

'How does your draft look?'

'I haven't started drafting yet.' Ellen felt a wave of guilt at his dismayed expression.

'How am I supposed to give you an extension and no one else? How can I justify treating you specially?'

'If you have to fire me, I understand. But I need this time for myself.'

'Would you rather get fired than tell me what's going on?' Marcelo asked, his eyes disbelieving. 'Can that be what you truly want?'

'Yes,' Ellen answered, though she hadn't thought of it that way.

'It matters *that* much to you, whatever you're doing?'

'It matters more to me than anything in the world.'

Marcelo blinked.

Ellen blinked back. For a moment, they played eye chicken.

Marcelo sighed, and his expression softened. 'OK, you win. Take the time you need this week, but that's it. I'll tell everyone you're not feeling well. It'll make sense, after you fainted dead away.'

'You're saying yes?' Ellen was dumbfounded. 'Why?'

'I'm trying to show you that I'm not a jerk.'

'I never thought you were. What about the homicide piece?'

'It can wait a week. The fire in the Yerkes Building is the new story.'

'What fire?' The Yerkes was one of the biggest buildings in town.

'Three people killed. Police suspect arson.'

'Does that mean you didn't really need my draft, just now?'

'Uh, yes.' Marcelo looked sheepish. 'Oh, well.'

'You rat!'

'You don't think I'm a rat. You like me.'

Ellen was mortified. 'How do you know?'

'I run the newsroom. You think I don't know the news?'

Ellen laughed, embarrassed. 'Oh, yeah, so what else do you know?'

'Is it true?' Marcelo's dark eyes glittered in a teasing way.

'You answer me. Then I'll answer you.'

'I know everybody believes that I'm attracted to you, and that's why you're not getting laid off.'

Ellen flushed.

'And I have to say, they're half-right,' Marcelo answered, his voice suddenly serious. His eyes met hers across the counter, with a very adult honesty. 'I would love to take you out, I admit it.'

Ellen felt a smile spread across her face.

'But that's not the reason you're keeping your job. You're keeping your job because you're a great reporter.'

'Thank you. And what if this crush is mutual?'

'So is it?' Marcelo was grinning.

'Yes.'

'That's very nice to hear, but it's too bad. Nothing will happen between us. It compromises you. It compromises me. This is romance in the time of sexual harassment, and that means nothing good happens, never ever. Except maybe this.' In the next second, Marcelo leaned over and planted the softest, sweetest kiss on her unsuspecting lips, and when it was over, he pulled away. 'Never ever again.'

'Excruciating,' Ellen said, meaning it.

The sky was supersaturated teal, and kelly-green fronds on the palm trees fluttered in the breeze. Lush green hedges lined the kerbs, and thick lawns, edged to perfection, bordered dense reds of climbing bougainvillea, the orange and yellow of tiny lantana flowers, and dark purple jacaranda. And that was just Miami airport.

Ellen slipped on sunglasses, driving a rental car, leaving the window open until the air conditioning kicked in. According to the dashboard, the temperature hovered at ninety-nine degrees.

She dug in her handbag and found the paper with the Bravermans' address, which she'd found online and MapQuested last night.

She left the highway at the exit, and found herself cruising along a smooth concrete causeway over a turquoise bay lined with mansions, many with glistening white boats parked along private slips. She reached the other side, where the traffic was lighter and the cars costlier. She took a right and a left, then saw the street sign. Surfside Lane. She took a right onto the Bravermans' street.

She passed a modern house, its front a huge expanse of glass, then a Spanish mansion with a red-tiled roof, and finally an ornate French chateau. Each house was different from the next, but she noticed that they all had one thing in common. Every home had a yellow ribbon tied out front, whether it was to a palm tree, a front fence or a gate.

She sensed the explanation before she saw it, cruising ahead to 826, then closing in on 830, which confirmed her theory.

HELP US FIND OUR SON read a large sign festooned with yellow ribbons, and it stood planted in an otherwise picture-perfect front lawn. The sign showed the age-progressed photo of Timothy Braverman from the white card, and tiger lilies and sunny marigolds grew round its base, a living memorial to a son the Bravermans prayed wasn't gone for ever.

Ellen looked past the sign. The Bravermans' house was like something out of *Architectural Digest*, a large contemporary with a crushed-shell driveway that held a glistening white Jaguar.

She circled the block, getting the lie of the land. She parked across the street from the entrance to Surfside Lane, but didn't park on the Bravermans' block for fear of being noticed.

She cracked open a bottle of warm water and checked the clock— 1.45 p.m. She watched the traffic to the causeway. By 1.47, her sunglasses were sliding down her nose, and the car had grown impossibly hot. Then she saw the chrome grille of a white Jaguar nose out of Surfside Lane, pause at the stop sign, and pull a left. It had to be the Bravermans' car because theirs was the only Jaguar on the block. In the driver's seat was the outline of a woman, alone. She had to be Carol Braverman.

Ellen turned on the ignition, hit the gas and found a place in the brisk line of traffic to the causeway. Carol was two cars ahead as they picked up speed and soared over the causeway. She kept an eye on the white car as they wound through the streets, which grew increasingly congested, but she stayed on Carol as she turned into a strip mall and pulled into a parking spot.

Ellen parked several rows away and cut the ignition.

The next moment, the driver's door opened.

Ellen couldn't see Carol Braverman's face because she had on large black sunglasses and a hot-pink visor. Carol got out of the car, tall and shapely in a white cotton tank top and an old-school tennis skirt. Pink pompoms wiggled from the backs of her sneakers, and a bouncy dark blonde ponytail popped out of her visor. She slipped a white bag over her shoulder and hurried to the gourmet grocery, where she picked a shopping cart and rolled it inside the tinted glass doors of the store.

Ellen grabbed her keys and handbag, got out of the car and hustled through the parking lot to the grocery, snagging a shopping cart for show. The entrance doors slid aside, and the air conditioning hit like January. She kept an eye on Carol but didn't want to draw attention to herself, especially when she realised how out of place she looked. Nobody else had on a thick white turtleneck, Mom jeans and brown clogs accessorised with Pennsylvania mud.

She didn't know when she'd get another opportunity and she had to see Carol's face, close up. She drifted sideways past a wall of nuts and fake-browsed the almonds. Out of the corner of her eye, she could see Carol looking at the peppers, her back turned.

Ellen spotted Carol moving round the perimeter of the produce department, back still towards her. Ellen crossed nearer to Carol, keeping her head down in the apple aisle. She positioned herself midway down the aisle, so she could get a good look at Carol's face if she turned.

Ellen picked up a Granny Smith and examined it with ersatz absorption, and in the split second she bent over to put it back, Carol spun round with her cart.

Carol's cart crashed squarely into Ellen's hip, startling her so that she backed into the apple pyramid and, before she could stop them, Gala and Fuji apples were rolling towards her in a pesticide-free avalanche.

'Oh, no!' Ellen yelped, punching up her glasses.

'I'm so sorry!' Carol tried to catch the apples, but they hit the polished floor and shot off in all directions, like billiard balls.

'Oh, jeez!' Ellen bent over to hide her face, collecting apples, just as Carol straightened up, cheeks slightly flushed, her hands full of apples.

'I can't believe I did that! I'm so sorry!'

'It's OK,' Ellen said, but she glanced up and almost gasped.

Carol had taken off her sunglasses as she entered the store and, in person, the resemblance between her and Will was obvious. She had Will's sea-blue eyes and creamy colouring. Her lips were on the thin side, like his, and her chin was a similar shape, too. Carol struck her instantly as being *of* Will. Stricken, Ellen put her head down, but Carol knelt next to her, gathering apples in her tennis skirt.

'It was my fault. That's what I get for rushing.'

'No, it was me. I knocked them over.' Ellen collected the escaping apples, flushed with emotion, keeping her face to the floor.

'I always think I can squeeze in one little errand. You ever do that?'

'Sure.'

'Of course that's when things go wrong.'

'Mrs Braverman, let me help you,' a stockboy said, hurrying over in a green smock and checkered trainers. He bent down and corralled some of the apples, his fuzzy dreadlocks falling into his young face.

'Thanks, Henrique.' Carol rose, brushing off a pair of tanned, finely muscled legs. 'I'm such a klutz today. I hit this woman with my cart.'

'Really, I'm fine.' Ellen rose, looking for the exit.

Carol placed a manicured hand on her arm. 'Again, I'm so sorry.'

'It's nothing, thanks.' Ellen shed Carol's hand, turned away as calmly as possible and walked out of the store. She hit the humid air and made a beeline for the rental car. Her eyes welled up behind her sunglasses, and her throat thickened. She fumbled in her handbag for the car keys, let herself inside, then slumped low in the driver's seat.

She sat in the car, staring out of the windshield without really seeing, wiping her eyes and trying to process what she'd seen. Carol Braverman, a grieving mother. She seemed like a nice woman; she seemed like Will.

Ellen thought of Susan Sulaman, and then Laticia Williams, bereft.

She knew how they felt, and she could guess how Carol Braverman felt. A wave of conscience engulfed her, and she felt awful that she might be causing another woman that sort of pain. Another mother.

A swinging white bag drew her attention, and Ellen looked out of the window. Carol was leaving the grocery store and hurrying to her car, carrying a brown paper bag, then she chirped the car unlocked, got in the driver's seat, turned on the engine and reversed neatly out of the space.

# CHAPTER SIX

CAROL DROVE faster than before, and Ellen had to concentrate not to lose her in the heavy traffic. Her subjective sense that Carol was Will's mother wasn't scientific. She still had to get the proof she needed, despite what her heart was telling her.

*Ring!* The sound jarred Ellen from her thoughts. It was her Black-Berry; she kept an eye on Carol as she hunted for the device with her hand, fumbling around in her handbag until she located it and checked the display. She recognised the number. It was Sarah Liu's cell number.

Ellen pressed Ignore and tossed the phone aside. She followed Carol over a causeway, and Ellen spotted a sign painted melon-green which read BRIDGES. Beyond it lay a building with a red-tiled roof. A hedge concealed the building, and two women drove in ahead of her. She stayed behind Carol as they snaked through the tall hedge.

Ellen was last in the line of cars that trailed up the lovely winding drive. A large group of children toting backpacks clustered round several women, obviously teachers, under the shaded entrance to the building. The children couldn't have been more than five years old.

Carol peeled to the left and found a space in the parking lot. Ellen hung back, idling the car and, the next minute, Carol got out with a black Adidas bag and hurried towards the entrance. The teachers waved to her as she jogged up to them, greeting her with smiles and chatter.

Ellen took a quick right and parked at the far end of the lot, reversing into the space so she could have a clear view of the entrance, to see when Carol left. The dashboard clock read 14:55.

By three fifteen, she was sweltering in the car. The thermometer on the dash read 100 degrees. By three thirty, she'd rolled her jeans up to capri length and wrapped her hair in a messy topknot, having found a stray hair-slide in her handbag. By three forty-five, her sunglasses were melting onto the bridge of her nose, and she decided to take a risk.

She grabbed her bag, got out of the car and walked through the parking lot to the entrance. There were no teachers or children out front, and she walked to the front door and tried it, but it was locked. A VISITORS MUST REPORT TO THE OFFICE sign was taped to the glass.

Ellen pressed a buzzer beside the door, and almost immediately a mechanical voice asked, 'Can I help you?'

'I'm new to the area and I'd like to see the school.'

'Come right in. The office is on your right.' A buzz sounded, and she let herself in. A slim, attractive woman with dark, curly hair emerged from the office and strode towards her with a smile, extending a hand.

'Welcome to Bridges, I'm Janice Davis, the assistant director.' She looked pretty in a pink cotton top, white pants and light blue flats.

Ellen shook her hand. 'I'm Karen Volpe.'

'Did you have an appointment?'

'No, I'm sorry. My husband and I haven't moved down yet, and I wanted to see the preschools in the area.'

'I see.' Janice checked her watch, a slim gold one. 'I don't have time now for the meeting we like to give with the tour. Let's make an appointment and you can return.'

'I'm not sure when I can get back. Can you give me the quick version of the tour? We can chat as we walk.'

'Sure, OK.' Janice smiled. 'You must be from New York.'

*Works for me.* 'How did you know?'

'Everything's quicker. I'll show you our classrooms and our media centre.'

Janice stopped at the first door. 'This is our classroom for two-year-olds, the ones who stay later, that is.'

Ellen looked through the window in the door, and inside was a sunny classroom with two teachers, finger-painting with toddlers in smocks. Carol wasn't inside.

'Admissions are very restrictive.'

'My son is very bright.' *He can trace all by himself.*

Janice led her to the next door. 'The three-year-olds,' she said, and inside sat a circle of children shaking tambourines, two teachers standing at the front of the room. Still no Carol. Janice showed her to the next door. 'And this is our classroom of four-year-olds. Learning French.'

'Really?' Ellen peered through the window. But there was no Carol.

'What is it you do, did you say?' Janice asked, but Ellen walked ahead and peeked into the classroom full of five-year-olds in little chairs, books open in their laps. No Carol.

'Which language are they learning?' she asked, to avoid the question.

'Reading skills. We drill and drill.'

'Good.' Ellen straightened up. 'And the media centre?'

'This way.' Janice led her down the hall to a double door. 'This is one of the special enrichment events we have each day . . .'

Ellen tuned her out when she saw what was going on inside. Children sat in a semicircle, laughing while a teacher in a Mother Goose costume read to them. But a telltale pink pompom stuck from beneath the hem of her hoop skirt. It was Carol in the Mother Goose get-up.

Janice said, 'Here, you see, we perform stories for the children.'

'And the teachers do this?'

'She's not a teacher. She's one of our moms, who used to be an actress. She worked at Disney World. She was Snow White.'

*Of course she was.* 'Is her child in the class?'

'No, Carol just comes to read to the children.'

'That's very nice of her, to do that. I guess you pay her very well.'

'Oh, she won't take a dime for it. Carol does it because she loves children. Come with me.' Janice took Ellen by the elbow and led her back up the hall. 'It's actually a terrible tragedy. Carol's little boy, Timothy, was kidnapped a couple of years ago and they never got him back. That first year, she was a mess. Depressed, in hell. But she pulled herself together and decided that it actually helps her to be around children.'

The late-day sun was even hotter, and Ellen was trailing Carol back through the luxurious suburbs when her BlackBerry started ringing again. She plucked it from her handbag and glanced at the display, which showed the newspaper's main telephone number. *Marcelo!*

'Hello?' she said, picking up, but it wasn't him, it was Sarah.

'Marcelo told us you're taking a few days off. Listen, I won't keep you, but I wanted to apologise.'

'That's OK,' Ellen said, surprised. Sarah sounded genuinely contrite.

'I'm sorry I got so hyper. When you fainted, I felt awful.'

'Thanks. It's just this bug, I feel dizzy. Listen, I gotta go back to bed.'

'Feel better. Take care.'

'Thanks. See you.' Ellen hung up and accelerated to make a green light as they wound left and right through traffic and finally travelled over the causeway to Surfside Lane.

Carol turned right onto Surfside, and Ellen drove down the main drag and took a U-turn, coming back to park in her position across the street, so that she could see if Carol went out again.

*Ring ring!* Ellen reached for her BlackBerry again, checking the screen. HOME. It had to be Connie. 'Hey, Con, how's it going?'

'Another day, another macaroni picture. I don't know if this matters, but somebody just called here. Her name was Sarah.'

Ellen tensed. 'When was this?'

'Half an hour ago. Will answered and told her you weren't home.'

'*What?*'

'I'm sorry. He got to the phone before I did. He thought it might be you. He talked to her and hung up. I heard him say Sarah.'

'Will said I wasn't there? Tell me exactly what he said.'

'He told her you went on the airplane for work.'

'Oh, no!' It was what Ellen had told him yesterday. She rubbed her forehead and came away with sweat. 'This isn't good, Connie.'

'Why doesn't she know what you're doing for work, anyway?'

'My editor wanted to keep it on the q.t.' Ellen was trying to figure out what to do. Sarah had caught her in a lie, then called her to confirm it. It was great journalistic technique, and it would get her fired for sure.

'Will wants to talk to you, OK?'

'Of course.' Ellen could hear Will calling for her.

'Mommy, Mommy! When are you coming home?'

'Soon, sweetie. Tell me about your macaroni picture.'

'Come home soon. I have to go.'

'Love you,' Ellen called after him. She hung up and called Marcelo.

'How are you?' Marcelo asked, his voice unusually cool.

'Sarah called my house and Will told her I went away on business.'

'I know. She just left my office. She came in to tell me you lied to me.'

*Oh, no.* Ellen reddened. 'I'm so sorry, Marcelo.'

'So, in theory, you lied to me, and I lied to the staff.'

Ellen had undermined Marcelo's authority. A reporter couldn't lie to an editor without consequences. The entire newsroom would be talking about it, waiting to see what he would do. 'So what did you say?'

'I told her I'd talk to you about it when you got back. I can't show you any favouritism, and I don't want to have to let you go.'

'There's no reason to do that, not yet. I'm still away, and that buys us a few days. I have to get clear of this situation.'

'What situation?' Marcelo asked, a new urgency in his voice, but all of a sudden the white Jaguar was pulling out of the Bravermans' drive.

'Uh, hold on.' Ellen tucked the BlackBerry in her neck, twisted on the car's ignition and launched herself into the rush-hour traffic.

'Ellen? Are you there? Please tell me what's going on. I can help you.'

'Sorry, but this isn't the best time for me and—' Suddenly, Carol took an unexpected right turn before the causeway. Ellen steered her car right but the movement dislodged her BlackBerry, which fell near the gas pedal.

'Bye, Marcelo!' she called out, then she hit the gas.

Ellen followed Carol through the carnation-and-canary-hued buildings of South Beach. They travelled up a narrow backstreet lined with delivery entrances to a cigar store, boutiques and restaurants. Carol pulled up behind a parked convertible, leaving Ellen no choice but to keep going or risk being recognised.

She cruised slowly ahead, and watched Carol in her rearview mirror. The driver-side door opened. Carol emerged in a tight-fitting tomato-red dress, her long dark blonde hair loose to her shoulders. She chirped the car locked and headed for the side street over the road.

Ellen parked illegally, turned off the ignition, grabbed her handbag, jumped out of the car and hustled down the street.

Carol took a left down the side street, Ellen tailing her at a safe distance. Carol paused at a sushi restaurant and talked with a maître d', so Ellen slowed. In the next minute, a tall, dark-haired man slipped from the crowd and stopped beside Carol, kissing her on the cheek and encircling her slim waist in a proprietary way. *Bill Braverman.*

She recognised him from the online photos. He was slim, in a light-grey sports jacket with jeans, too covered up to show the wiriness she'd seen online. She fake-read a menu posted in front of one of the restaurants, waiting to see what the Bravermans would do. She glanced back at them and, hidden by the crowd, edged closer to their table.

They were seated in the centre of the outdoor dining area. She got a good look at Bill's face. He was handsome, with a thick black fringe over dark round eyes and a nose that looked an older version of Will's. From time to time he leaned back in his chair, cigarette smouldering between his fingers, and he spoke animatedly, laughing frequently.

*Time to rock.* Ellen slipped her handbag onto her shoulder, walked towards the maître d' of their restaurant and asked, 'Is there a ladies' room inside?'

'In the back, to the right.'

'Thanks.' Ellen went inside the restaurant, found the ladies' room and went inside. She headed into one of the stalls, closed the door and went into her handbag. At the bottom was a white plastic bag, her DNA kit: directions she'd downloaded from a website; two pairs of new, blue plastic gloves she'd had under the sink; and two of the brown paper bags that she used to pack Will's snack for school.

Ellen slipped a pair of the plastic gloves carefully into her jeans pocket. It was showtime.

Ellen got a table in the outdoor dining area of the restaurant next door to the one with the Bravermans, with a clear view of their table. While the couple ate dinner, she called home, said good night to Will and devoured a delicious sushi meal, finishing with a frothy cappuccino.

She watched the Bravermans finish their coffee and share a tiramisu. Bill smoked a final cigarette, but Carol didn't smoke, so Ellen would have to take her glass to get a DNA sample from her. The couple had laughed and talked throughout the dinner, a happily married couple.

Carol signalled for the bill, so Ellen did the same, catching her waiter's eye. They paid at about the same time, and she rose right after the Bravermans, ready to swoop down on their table.

They left and Ellen made a beeline for their table. Suddenly a group of tourists shoved in front of her, blocking her way, and she didn't reach the table until after the waiter had gathered the glasses.

'Table no is clean,' the waiter said, picking up the plates.

'I'll just sit a minute.' Ellen plopped into Bill Braverman's chair.

'No is clean.' The waiter reached for the ashtray, but Ellen grabbed it.

'Thanks.' It contained three cigarette butts, all Bill's. 'I'll need this.'

The waiter walked away, but the maître d' was peering at the table, along with a foursome of hungry patrons. She slid the gloves from her pocket and shoved her right hand in one. The maître d' was making his way over, with the foursome. She gathered the three cigarette butts from the ashtray, opened one of the paper bags under the table, tossed the butts inside, then closed it up and shoved it back into her handbag.

'Ma'am, do you have a reservation?' the maître d' asked, as Ellen rose.

'Sorry, I was just resting a minute, thanks.' She headed out of the dining area to the sidewalk, and melted into the crowd, exhilarated.

Ellen cruised round the block after Carol had pulled into her driveway, followed by Bill driving a grey Maserati. The sky was a rich blue, and the street silent, the fancy cars cooling for the night.

She had a second wind, and was thinking of the other ways it was possible to get DNA samples. Cans, glasses, licked envelopes.

Ellen rounded the corner onto Surfside and eyed the Bravermans' mailbox. It was at the end of their driveway, but the red flag wasn't up, so there was no letter for sending inside. *Rats.*

She drove slowly past the house and parked. Next minute, the front door opened and Bill emerged, carrying a black trash bag.

She ducked a little and watched in the outside mirror. Bill put the bag in a tall trash can and rolled it to the end of the driveway, then went back towards the house. She stayed low until she heard the front door slam, then eased up in the seat, looking behind her. The house went dark.

*Trash could contain DNA.*

She scanned the street, front and back, but there was no one in sight. She slid off her clogs, opened the car door as quietly as possible and jumped out. She bolted for the trash can, tore off the lid, plucked out the bag at warp speed and dashed back to the car.

She jumped in the car, threw the bag in the passenger seat and hit the gas, speeding to the causeway. Once there, she pulled over and turned on the interior light. Grabbing the trash bag, she undid the drawstring, held the open bag directly under the interior light and peeked inside. On top of the trash sat a heap of grey-blue shrimp shells that stank to high heaven; she pushed them aside, going through wet coffee grounds, the chopped bottom of a head of romaine, and underneath, a mother lode of mail. None of this would yield a DNA sample for Carol. *Bummer.*

She pulled out the mail on the offchance there was a sealed envelope, but no luck. It was all junk mail, plus a copy of *Departures* magazine. Stuck inside the magazine was a pink card from the dentist, a reminder that somebody had to get their teeth cleaned next month. She flipped the card over. The front read, Carol Charbonneau Braverman.

'Charbonneau' sounded familiar. She couldn't place where she'd heard it, or if she was imagining it—her exhaustion finally catching up with her. She took off for the hotel and threw the trash in a Dumpster on the way.

When she finally reached her hotel room, she checked her email.

Amy Martin hadn't written yet, but her sister Cheryl had.

**E**llen sank slowly onto the quilted bedspread, staring at her glowing BlackBerry screen. The email from Cheryl read:

Dear Ellen,

I'm sorry to tell you that yesterday, we found out that Amy passed away. She died of a heroin overdose in her apartment in Brigantine on Saturday. Her wake will be Tuesday night, but there will be a private one for the family before her burial, on Wednesday at ten o'clock in

Stoatesville, at the Cruzane Funeral Home. My mother says you can come to either, and she would like to see you.
Sincerely, Cheryl

The thought overwhelmed her with sadness. Amy was too young to die, and Ellen thought of how Cheryl must be feeling, then Amy's mother, Gerry. Her thoughts came eventually to herself and Will. She had just lost her chance to learn anything from Amy.

She felt undone, again. She had a nagging fear, gnawing at the edges of her mind. *Quite a coincidence.*

It seemed odd that Amy would turn up dead now, just when Ellen had begun asking questions about her. It seemed stranger still, considering the suicide of Karen Batz. Now, both women with knowledge of Will's adoption were dead. The only one left alive was Amy's boyfriend, and he was the one who looked like the kidnapper in the composite.

*Not just a kidnapper. A murderer.*

Ellen started to make connections, but even she knew she was entering the wild-speculation realm: there were innocent explanations for everything. She flopped backwards on the bed, and exhaustion swept over her, muting even her darkest fears.

The next morning, Ellen parked in the same spot, perpendicular to Surfside Lane. It was another hot, tropical day, but she was dressed for it today. She'd stopped at the hotel's gift shop and bought a pink visor, a pair of silver Oakley knockoffs and a chrome yellow T-shirt that read SOUTH BEACH, which she'd paired with white shorts from home. In her pockets were a plastic glove and a folded brown paper bag.

She took a slug from a bottle of orange juice, still cold from the minibar. She felt weighed down by the news of Amy Martin's death and couldn't shake the fear that the overdose wasn't accidental.

She set the bottle in the cup holder and scoped out the scene, which was quiet except for people exercising. Two older women power-walked round the block, carrying water bottles and yammering away, and a younger woman was running in a sports bra with a black bathing-suit bottom. Yet a fourth woman walked her white toy poodle.

Ellen got out of the car and started walking. No one had any red flags up on their mailboxes, and she wondered what time the mail would be picked up. She still hoped Carol would mail a letter, so she could get DNA from the envelope.

She picked up the pace, gaining on the two older women who motored ahead in their sneakers. They wore Bermuda shorts in pastel colours and patterned tank tops, and even at seventy-something, looked in terrific shape. Each had short silver hair, but the woman on the left wore a terry-cloth visor, and the one on the right had on a base-ball cap. Ellen fell into stride with them before the Bravermans'.

'Excuse me, ladies,' she began, and they both turned round. 'Do you know what time the mail pick-up is in this neighbourhood? I'm house-sitting on Brightside Lane for my cousins, and I forgot to ask them before they left this morning.'

'Mail gets picked up around eleven in the morning,' Terry-cloth Visor said. 'I'm Phyllis, and you're welcome to walk with us, if you're alone.'

'Thanks, I appreciate that.'

Phyllis's friend in the baseball cap looked at Ellen with a warm smile. 'I'm Linda DiMarco. And you?'

'Sandy Claus,' Ellen answered, off the top of her head. They approached the Bravermans', where Carol's car was in the driveway, but Bill's was gone. She gestured casually to the memorial on the lawn. 'What's that sign all about, do you know? And all these yellow ribbons?'

'Oh, my, yes,' Phyllis answered. A petite woman, she had bright eyes, a hawkish nose and deep laughter lines that bracketed thin lips. 'Their baby was kidnapped a couple of years ago.'

'Do you know the family?'

'Sure, Carol's a doll, and so is Bill. They were in terrible shape, after it happened. There were reporters camped out on the street, bothering them all the time. Cops and the FBI, always coming and going. Bill was a great father, too. You know, he has his own investment company. He makes a lot of money for people in the neighbourhood, and he doted on his son. Bought him golf bibs and a golf hat, too. Remember that, Lin?'

Linda nodded. 'Carol had a hard time getting pregnant. I'm not telling stories out of school here. She talked about it all the time, right?'

'Yes, she had a very hard time.' Phyllis's lips flattened. 'They tried for a long time. She really wanted that baby, they both did.'

'Poor woman.' Linda wiped her upper lip. 'Isn't that just the worst luck? They finally had their miracle baby, then they never see him again.'

Phyllis and Linda fell silent, their gaze on the door of a wooden con-temporary on the left side of the street, diagonal to the Bravermans'. A pretty redhead was emerging in a crisp black dress, a black bag on her arm. She locked the door, then clacked in stylish black pumps down a concrete path to her driveway and a silver Mercedes.

'Who's that?' Ellen caught the look Phyllis and Linda exchanged.

'She's a big snob.' Phyllis smiled. 'Her name is Kelly Scott and her family has more money than God. She's from Palm Beach. I've met her at least four times, and she acts like she never met me. I hate that.'

'Me, too,' Linda said.

'Me, three,' Ellen said, and they all laughed.

Ellen sat low in the driver's seat of her car with the window open, watching the Braverman house. It was 10.36 a.m., but there'd been no sign of Carol, and the red flag on her mailbox was still down.

She kept an eye on the house and straightened up as a mail truck appeared on the main drag and began stopping at the houses, delivering packets of mail. No sign of Carol with an envelope to be mailed, and now it was too late.

Ellen felt on edge. Hot and testy. She sipped warm juice, then dug in her handbag for the notes from the DNA test, reminding herself of the sample possibilities. Gum, soda can, cigarette butt, blah blah blah. She tossed the list aside and glanced back at the Bravermans' house, where there was finally some activity. Carol was stepping out of the front door.

Ellen's senses sprang to alert. She couldn't keep waiting for something to happen. She had to make something happen. She got out of the car in her sunglasses and visor and went into her I'm-just-a-walker routine, strolling across the main drag and entering Surfside. She walked slowly, staying on the opposite side of the street as Carol walked from the front door and disappeared into the garage.

The next minute, Carol came out of the garage with a green plastic gardener's tote. She had on a cute sundress and another visor, with her dark blonde hair in its ponytail again.

Ellen watched Carol cross the lawn to the memorial to Timothy, then she knelt down, setting the gardener's tote next to her. She slid on a pair of flowery cotton gloves and began to weed in front of the memorial.

Ellen turned the corner and, as soon as she was out of sight, broke into a light jog. She was panting by the time she lapped the block and reached the intersection of Surfside Lane and the main drag, where she knelt next to a tall hedge, pretending to tie her sneaker laces.

Carol pulled the weeds and put them in a neat pile. A bag of peat moss and a large tray of yellow marigolds were sitting on the lawn next to the memorial. Full sun bathed the lawn. Ellen's breathing returned to normal, but she was sweating behind her sunglasses, and Carol must have been feeling the same way, because in the next second, she took off her sunglasses and visor and set them down. Ellen shifted her feet and fake-tied the other sneaker, watching as Carol moved to the marigold tray and twisted off a small packet of flowers. Carol gentled the plant and set it on the ground. She reached into the gardener's tote and pulled out a can of soda, then popped the tab and took a sip.

*Bingo!* Ellen scanned the block. There was no one in sight. She slid the plastic glove from her pocket, put it on her hand and rose slowly. Then she slid her BlackBerry from her other pocket and pressed the number for information in Miami. She asked for the Bravermans' phone number, and while the call connected, she walked towards Carol, who was bent over her flowers, making a hole for the new marigolds with her fingers. The phone rang once in Ellen's ear, then again and, in the next second, Carol looked up at her house.

Ellen slid the paper bag from her pocket and started walking down Surfside Lane, keeping her gloved hand at her side, out of view. In the meantime, Carol was rising, taking off her gardening gloves on the fly, and hurrying towards the house.

Ellen crossed to the Bravermans' side of the street, heart pounding. She moved up the sidewalk. There was nobody exercising or walking dogs. She broke into a light run, the ringing cellphone to her ear. Ten feet away, then five, then right in front of the Braverman house. Carol's soda was a Diet Sprite, sitting next to the tote.

She ran straight up the Bravermans' lawn, swooped down with her gloved hand, grabbed the Diet Sprite and took off like a shot, running down the block. She turned the can upside-down so the soda poured out, and she ran like she'd never run in her life. She tore round the block, bolted all the way to the main drag, then darted across the street.

Ellen tore open her car door, jumped in and dumped the can in the brown paper bag. She twisted on the ignition, floored the gas pedal and headed straight for the causeway. She felt like cheering. Wind off the causeway whipped her hair around, and she hit a red light, taking off the glove and leaving it on the seat, its purpose served. She took off her visor and sunglasses, relieved to finally shed her disguise. She caught a glimpse of a street sign and did a double take. *Charbonneau Drive?*

The traffic light turned green, but instead of going straight over the causeway, she turned right onto the street.

Charbonneau Drive read the street sign, and Ellen flashed on the dentist's reminder from the Bravermans' trash bag. She had known that Charbonneau sounded familiar, though she couldn't remember how. She'd passed the street every time she'd driven to and from the causeway. Charbonneau Drive had to be connected to Carol Braverman.

Curious, she drove along Charbonneau Drive, which was winding and pleasant. The houses had the same variety as on Surfside Lane, but all of them were the same, more recent, vintage. Palm trees lined the road, but they weren't as established as the palms on Surfside, and the vegetation, white oleander and bougainvillea, looked newer.

She followed the street, and at the end of a cul-de-sac stood an immense mansion of pink stucco with a clay tile roof. It was three storeys tall, with at least thirty arched Spanish windows and a covered walkway that sheltered a grand main entrance. A sign on the lawn read CHARBONNEAU HOUSE and, underneath that, OPEN TO THE PUBLIC.

Ellen pulled into a parking lot of crushed shells and turned off the engine. She got out of the car and walked to the house. The stucco had been repainted and the tiles on the roof meticulously maintained, but the mansion was much older than the houses surrounding it on the drive. The lot was at least three acres of lush lawn, the breeze was fragrant, and the place a reminder of a slower, older Florida. She walked up the breezeway, climbed stairs of red Mexican tile and went inside.

The entrance hall had a black-and-white tile floor and was dominated by a huge staircase, covered with an Oriental carpet. There were three large rooms off the hall, furnished as meeting rooms, and she entered the centre room, which overlooked an expanse of green lawn and a small circular fountain.

'May I help you?' a voice asked, and she turned. It was a woman with a brown bob, light eyes and a warm smile.

'I was driving past, and I thought the building was so pretty, I wanted to see it.'

'Why, thank you. We're very proud of Charbonneau House and the work we do here.'

'What is that, may I ask?'

'We promote theatre arts and other cultural events to children in the community.' The woman, professional in a crisp white blouse and a khaki cotton skirt, with red espadrilles, gestured to the hallway. 'In addition to the conference rooms and classrooms, we have a theatre that seats seventy-five people. We stage three productions a year.'

'How nice,' Ellen said. 'And I see there's Charbonneau House and Charbonneau Drive. I assume it's related to the Charbonneau family?'

'Yes. The Charbonneaus are one of the oldest families in the area, and they've donated the house for the community's use.' The woman gestured to an oil portrait in an ornate golden frame, one of two flanking the windows. 'That's our benefactor, Bertrand Charbonneau, who passed away about five years ago, at the age of ninety-one. He was one of the community's first residents and developed much of the real estate here. This house, his childhood home, was his gift to our community.'

Ellen was trying to piece together where, if anywhere, Carol Charbonneau Braverman fitted in. 'I gather Bertrand Charbonneau had an interest in theatre?'

'His wife Rhoda had a brief career as an actress before she retired to raise their children. Even then, she remained active in children's theatre.' The woman strolled over to the other oil portrait, and Ellen followed. The plaque read Richard Charbonneau.

'So this must be Bertrand's son?' Ellen asked, scanning the man's features. He had the same blue eyes she'd seen on Carol, and Will.

'Yes, thankfully Richard and his wife continued his father's efforts. Unfortunately, they both passed away many years ago in a car accident.'

'That's too bad. Do you think the family will carry on the tradition?'

'No worries there.' The woman smiled. 'Richard and his wife had a daughter, Carol, and she works with the children every Wednesday and Friday.'

'Well, that's wonderful.' Ellen's chest tightened, and she looked away from the portrait, hiding her emotion. If Will was really Timothy, then Bertrand Charbonneau would be his great-grandfather and Richard Charbonneau his grandfather. Will would be part of a wonderful family, born to extraordinary wealth.

'Will that be all?' the woman asked, cocking her head.

'Yes, thanks,' Ellen answered, turning away.

It was time to go home.

# CHAPTER SEVEN

THE TICKETING LINE wound back and forth, and Ellen assessed it, worriedly. She didn't want to miss the flight and she'd been lucky to get a seat. She couldn't wait to see Will, and she felt almost herself again, having changed back into her sweater and jeans, which she needed in the air-conditioned terminal.

She checked her watch. She'd eaten quickly a turkey sandwich in the first fifteen minutes of her wait in line, and now she had nothing to do but look at the other travellers who had nothing else to do. The man in front of her talked on a cellphone in rapid Spanish, which reminded her of Marcelo. She'd called him this morning but he hadn't answered, so she'd left a message saying she'd be back to work tomorrow.

Her gaze drifted to the first-class line, only four people deep, where a pretty redhead had just arrived, rolling a Louis Vuitton bag behind her, her head held high. She looked vaguely familiar and when she dug in a black handbag, Ellen remembered where she had seen her before. It was the young woman who lived across the street from Carol Braverman.

*Her name is Kelly Scott and her family has more money than God.*

Ellen watched the redhead fan herself with some papers, looking sexy in black stilettos and a cobalt-blue dress, whose bold colour stood out among the Miami pastels. Passing businessmen gave her more than a second glance, running their eyes over her body and shapely legs.

The line shifted, and Ellen moved up. Another businessman strode past her, carrying a lightweight bag and moving so quickly that his tailored sports jacket blew open. He joined the end of the first-class line, and Ellen looked over. She recognised him instantly, stunned.

The businessman was Bill Braverman, and Ellen marvelled at the odds that he would show up at the airport at the exact same time as his neighbour. She got a closer look at him than before; he was attractive with a tall, wiry build, dark hair, and a nose that looked like Will's, even in profile. He took out his wallet and cleared his throat, and the redhead turned round and glanced behind her. She looked right at Bill, but strangely, she didn't say hello. She turned and faced the ticket counters.

Ellen didn't get it. Kelly Scott had to have seen Bill. He was right behind her, the tallest man in the line, not to mention her neighbour.

Ellen shifted forward, glued to the goings-on. Something fishy was going on between Bill and the redhead. Bill faced the front of the line, showing no sign that he recognised his neighbour, who was standing in front of him, with bright red hair and a killer dress. Men all over the terminal were looking at her, yet Bill was pointedly looking away.

Ellen considered it. These two people had to know each other, and they clearly had seen each other, but they were acting as if they were strangers. There was one possible explanation, but she resisted it.

Ellen kept watching, hoping that she was wrong. Kelly walked to the ticket counter, and the balding ticket agent brightened. The redhead got her ticket, bunny-dipped for her Vuitton bag and rolled it away. Bill seemed not to notice her as she sashayed off, and Ellen lost sight of the woman as she walked towards Security.

The line shifted forwards, and one of the ticket agents walked to the front of the line and called out, 'Anyone for Philly? Philly, come on up!'

'Here!' Ellen ducked the tape to get out of line and hurried to the front, manoeuvring to stand next to Bill. As casually as possible, she said, 'Hard to go back to Philly in the cold.'

'I bet.'

'Where are you headed?'

'Vegas.'

'Wow. I've never been. Have fun.'

'You, too. Safe trip.' Bill flashed her a grin, then went to the desk, got his ticket and walked off towards Security.

Three people later, Ellen got her ticket. She made it through Security, then took a quick look at the departure signs for Las Vegas. The Vegas gate was two down from hers. She hurried towards the gate, scanned the passengers waiting for the flight and spotted them in no time.

Bill sat reading a *Wall Street Journal* in one of the wide grey seats, and directly across from him was Kelly, flipping through a thick copy of *Vogue* and crossing and uncrossing her legs. It was a game they were playing, frequent-flier foreplay.

Ellen lingered behind a round pillar and watched Bill and the red-head until it was time for first class to board. They joined the line, leaving a few travellers between them. Kelly got her boarding pass swiped and, just as she entered the jetway, she turned behind her, ostensibly for her bag, flashing Bill the briefest of smiles.

*He's cheating on Snow White?*

Ellen went ahead to her gate, disgusted and sad. She boarded, and her heart went out to Carol, planting marigolds on Timothy's memorial on the front lawn. Being nice to the grocery stockboy. Playing Mother Goose to toddlers. Teaching children's theatre at Charbonneau House.

'**M**ommy!' Will ran to meet Ellen as she closed the front door.

'Honey!' she called back, hoisting him up and hugging him close.

'I'm making a castle! A big castle!' Will kicked to be let down.

'Good for you.' Ellen set him on the ground.

'Welcome home!' Connie smiled, as she came into the living room.

Ellen felt happier than ever to be home. Oreo Figaro looked up from the back of the sofa, where he lay with his front paws neatly underneath him. The living room smelt deliciously of hot coffee and chicken with rosemary. 'Connie, am I dreaming or is that dinner?'

'It'll be ready in ten minutes.'

Ellen grabbed Connie and gave her a huge hug. 'Will you marry me?'

'Anytime,' Connie answered, releasing herself with a grin, then she went to the closet, got her coat and put it on. 'You got sunburnt, eh?'

'I know.' Ellen's hand went to the tip of her nose. It would be hard to explain at work tomorrow.

Connie picked up her overnight bag and turned to Will. 'See you later, alligator!'

'In a while, crocodile,' Will called over his shoulder, playing happily on the floor.

'See you!' Connie let herself out, and Ellen went over and touched Will's hair. The dark blond filaments felt soft under her fingertips, and she tried not to notice his hair colour was almost the same as Carol's.

Ellen scanned the directions for the DNA sample while Will stood at the kitchen sink and rinsed his mouth with warm water, his small fingers wrapped like a gecko's round the glass tumbler. She was collecting Will's sample by the conventional method, and she had to get it tonight because all the samples had to be sent to the lab together.

'Spit, Mommy?' Will asked, his eyes trustful over the rim of the glass.

'Two more times, pal.'

Will took a second gulp of water and spat it into the sink.

'And we have to do one more thing.'

'OK.' Will took his third gulp, letting the water dribble out of his mouth and down his chin for fun.

Ellen wiped his wet grin with a towel, then took the glass from his hand, set it on the counter and turned to face him, placing a hand on his shoulder. 'Now open up, sweetie, just like you do for the doctor.'

'Is it gonna hurt?'

'No, not at all.' Ellen took the Q-tip in hand. 'I'm going to rub the inside of your cheek with a Q-tip, that's all. Ready to open up?'

Will opened his mouth like a baby bird, and Ellen rolled the swab on the insides of both of his cheeks for about a minute, making sure to cover most of his inner cheek. Then she withdrew the swab and set it on a folded piece of paper to dry, according to the instructions.

Ellen had just stepped out of the shower when her cellphone started ringing. She ran into her bedroom, picked up her BlackBerry and checked the display screen. It was a 215 area code, a Philly phone number she didn't know. She pressed Answer.

'Hello?' It was Marcelo, and Ellen warmed to the sound, sinking onto her bed and drawing her pink chenille robe closer around her.

'Hey, hi.'

'I got your message. Sorry I couldn't get back to you until now. Are you at home?'

'Yes, I'll be back to work tomorrow, like I said. If you're free, we can meet in the morning and talk over this thing with Sarah.'

'I don't think it can wait. I'd like to come over tonight, if I may.'

Ellen checked her watch—9.08 p.m. Will was in bed, fast asleep. 'Sure.'

'It's not a social call,' Marcelo added, and she felt herself flush. 'I'll be there in half an hour.'

'Great,' Ellen said and, as soon as they hung up, she bolted to the closet. She changed her clothes four times, ending up with a light blue V-neck and jeans, but instead of a tank top underneath, she went with a lace-topped ivory camisole.

By the time Marcelo knocked on the door, Ellen's hair had dried loose and curly to her shoulders and she had doused herself with perfume, made up her eyes and patted concealer on her telltale sunburn.

'Hello,' Marcelo said, unsmiling as he came inside.

'Good to see you.' Ellen knew she couldn't kiss him hello, but she didn't want to shake his hand, so she settled for closing the door behind him. 'Can I take your coat?'

'That's OK, I won't be staying long.'

*Ouch.* 'Would you like a drink or something?'

'No, thanks.'

'Do you want to sit down?'

'Thanks.' Marcelo crossed to the couch and sat down stiffly, and Ellen took the chair opposite him. He said, 'I thought it would be better to talk here than in the office, since we're conspiring.'

'I'm really sorry about what happened.'

'I know.' Marcelo looked tense, a new tightness round his mouth. 'I've been struggling with how to handle the situation.' He linked his fingers over his knee. 'To start with, I shouldn't have done what I did . . . started anything romantic with you. It was wrong, and I'm sorry.'

Ellen swallowed, hurt. 'You don't have to say you're sorry, and it wasn't so terrible.'

'It was, especially considering how it turned out.'

'But we can set it right.'

'No, we can't.'

Ellen felt like they were having a lovers' quarrel, and they weren't even lovers.

'I'm your editor, and there's no way we can be together, in the end.'

'Other couples at the paper date.'

'Not editor and staffer. Not a direct report.' Marcelo shook his head, downcast. 'Anyway, to the point. I lied to my staff. I've never lied to my staff, ever. I showed you favouritism I wouldn't have shown anyone else, and I did it because I care for you.' His voice softened, but his gaze remained firm. 'But now I know what to do.'

'I do, too.' Ellen had thought about it on the plane.

Marcelo held up his hand. 'Let me, please. That's why I came here tonight. I don't want you to come in to work tomorrow morning.'

*No.* 'Why not?'

'I'm going to hold a meeting of the staff and I don't think you should be there. I'm going to tell them what happened. Not about my . . . feelings, I'm not that crazy.' Marcelo smiled. 'I'm going to tell them that I lied about your whereabouts because you had a personal matter that you didn't want me or them to know about, and I thought it was the best way to handle the situation.'

'You're going to tell the truth?'

Marcelo chuckled. 'It's not that crazy. We're reporters. We care for truth.'

'But not this way.' Ellen couldn't let him do it. It was career suicide.

'I'm going to apologise and say that I realise, in retrospect, that it was poor judgment on my part.'

'You can't do that. It undermines your credibility. You'll never live it down.' Ellen leaned forward, urgent. 'That's not the way to handle this. One of us has to admit they were lying, and that person can't be you.'

'You have no say,' Marcelo said with a sad smile, and Ellen realised that if he wouldn't do it for him, maybe he'd do it for her.

'They'll think we're sleeping together, and I'll be branded for ever. It's better for me if you suspend me for lying to you.'

'You *want* that?' Marcelo frowned.

'It's the only way. If you suspend me, I look like just another employee who lied to the boss. Everybody lies to the boss.'

'They do?' Marcelo looked horrified.

'If we tell them I lied to you, then I'm just somebody who played hooky. I even have a tan. But, on the other hand, if you tell them you lied for me, it makes it a bigger deal and it never goes away.'

Marcelo pursed his lips, searching her face, and Ellen could see she was making headway.

'You're a journalist, so you should know. Employee lies to boss. That's no story. Boss lies *for* employee? A headline.'

'I don't know.' Marcelo ran his fingers through his hair, muttering.

'Marcelo, if you care about me, you'll suspend me without pay.'

'Is that what you want?'

'Yes. For a week.'

Marcelo's lips flattened to a sour line. 'Three days.'

'Done.'

Marcelo eyed her, his regret plain. 'It's a disciplinary action against you. It jeopardises your job.'

'Look on the bright side. If you fire me, you have to take me out. I could lose a job, but gain a boyfriend.'

'You're killing me.' Marcelo rose, and Ellen stood, too. They were standing about three feet apart, but nobody was touching anybody.

'I'm joking,' she said, but Marcelo turned away and walked to the door, where he stopped and flashed her a final, sad smile.

'Then why aren't we laughing?' he asked.

For that, Ellen had no answer.

Ellen set her DNA instructions on her bedspread and unpacked the two paper bags from her suitcase, the one containing Bill's cigarette butts and the other Carol's soda can. She set them next to the white business envelope that contained the Q-tips with Will's sample.

Ellen picked up the Paternity Testing Form she had downloaded.

The form contained various lines to fill out to identify the sample: Name, Sample date and Relationship; Suspected Mother; Suspected Father; and Other. She filled in Suspected Mother for Carol's sample, Suspected Father for Bill's and Child for Will's. Then she made matching labels that the form requested, cut them out with scissors and taped them on the two brown paper bags and Will's envelope.

She gathered the brown bags, the envelope and the forms, and placed them in a padded FedEx Pak. She filled in the address slip, sealed the FedEx envelope and set it on the nightstand. She would mail it after she dropped Will at school.

She sat on the bed. In three days, she could find out that Will didn't belong to the Bravermans and she could keep him happily for the rest of their life together. Three days seemed for ever to wait, and at the same time not nearly long enough. Because in three days she could also find out that Will did belong to the Bravermans, then . . .

That was where Ellen stopped her thinking.

The next morning was freezing, the sky an opaque grey and the air holding a wet chill in its clenched fist. Ellen was sitting in her car in the parking lot of a local strip mall. She had dropped Will off at school only half an hour ago, but it seemed longer. The FedEx Pak containing the DNA samples sat next to her like an unwanted hitchhiker.

Ellen was stalling. All she had to do was slide down her car window, pull up the metal handle on the FedEx mailbox and toss the package inside. As soon as she did that, it was out of her hands. The deed would be done. The lab would charge her credit card, process the samples and email her the results. Yes or no. Hers or theirs.

Ellen reminded herself that she didn't have to do anything with the test results once she had them. Even if it turned out in the Bravermans' favour, she didn't have to tell a soul. *I can forget the whole thing.*

She turned on the ignition and the car turned over, throatily. She didn't have to mail the samples. She could just drive away and let them decompose. She could stop this insanity right now. The car idled. Still she didn't hit the gas. *I can't forget the whole thing.*

She pressed the button and lowered the car window, struck by the frigid blast, then she yanked the handle on the mailbox and tossed the FedEx Pak inside. The drawer closed with a final *ca-thunk*. *So be it.*

**E**llen pressed thoughts of the DNA samples to the back of her mind as she drove to Amy Martin's funeral. She steered through the run-down neighbourhood outside Stoatesville, finally spotting the funeral home.

She found a space on the street, parked and got out of the car. Cold air blew hard, and she drew her black dress-coat closer as she walked down the street. Her boots clacked against the gritty pavement, and she reached the funeral home, with a fake gold sign beside the door. She yanked on the handle and went inside, warming up momentarily. An entrance hall contained a few oak chairs and a fake-walnut credenza, on which rested a maroon vase of faded silk flowers and an open guest book with a vinyl cover. A burgundy rug covered the floor and there was a long corridor to the left, leading to two louvred doors. The second door was open, and light spilled from the room.

Ellen crossed to the guest book and looked at the open page, scanning the list of names: Gerry Martin, Dr Robert Villiers and Cheryl Martin Villiers, Tiffany Lebov, William Martin, those last two being Amy's other two siblings, Ellen assumed. She picked up the long white pen next to the book and signed her name.

She walked down the hall towards the open door, lingering on the threshold. The room was rectangular and large, but only two rows of brown folding chairs had been set up towards the front, where a group of women huddled together. The casket was closed, and she was almost disappointed. She wouldn't get a chance to see what Amy Martin looked like, even in death, to compare her features to Will's. But it didn't matter now anyway. The DNA samples would solve the mystery that was Amy Martin.

Ellen walked towards the group at the front and saw that Gerry was being comforted by Cheryl, who caught her eye and smiled.

'Ellen, how nice of you to come,' she said softly, and Gerry turned in her embrace and looked up. Grief deepened the folds bracketing her mouth, which tilted down, and she looked like she was sinking in an oversized black trouser-suit.

'I'm so sorry about your loss.' Ellen approached, extending her hand.

'Real nice of you to come.' Gerry's voice sounded hoarse, and she blinked tears from her eyes. 'I know Amy woulda wanted to meet you. Someday maybe you can bring your little boy over to the house.'

Behind her, Cheryl nodded. 'I'd like to meet him, too.'

'I'd be happy to do that,' Ellen said.

Cheryl said, 'Too bad you missed my husband and brother. They were here last night and earlier but they had to go.' She gestured at another mourner, a young woman. 'This is a friend of Amy's.'

'Melanie Rotucci,' the girl said, extending her hand. She looked to be in her twenties and, on another day, would have been pretty, if a little hard-looking. Her grey eyes were red and puffy from crying, and her fair skin pale and wan. She had a cupid's-bow mouth, and long dark hair that spilled over the shoulders of her black leather jacket.

Ellen introduced herself, surprised to meet her. Cheryl and Gerry had told her that Amy didn't have girlfriends.

Cheryl must have been reading her mind. 'Melanie met Amy in rehab, and they were really good friends.'

'Amy was in rehab?' Ellen asked, confused. It was all news to her.

'It turns out Amy was really trying to turn her life around. She went to rehab twice, for heroin. She was almost better, right, Melanie?'

'I really thought she was going to make it.' Melanie's mouth made a resigned line, in dark lipstick. 'She was clean for thirty-five days the second time. At ninety days, she was going to tell everybody, all of you.'

'My poor, poor baby,' Gerry whispered, collapsing into new sobs.

Strain etched Melanie's face. 'I need a cigarette,' she muttered, rising.

'I'll keep you company,' Ellen said, intrigued.

'This must be hard on you,' Ellen said as they stepped outside the funeral home and shared a grimy top step. 'Were you good friends?'

'We didn't know each other that long, but when you meet people in rehab, you get tighter a lot faster.' Melanie dragged on her cigarette, and smoke leaked from her sad smile.

'Can I ask, did Amy ever mention to you having had a child?'

'No way! Amy didn't have a kid.'

'I think she did and she put it up for adoption.' Ellen almost didn't believe it herself, after Miami. 'I guess she didn't mention it to you.'

'It's possible, I guess.'

'It was a very sick baby, with a heart problem.'

'I didn't know *everything* about her.' Melanie's eyes narrowed behind a curtain of cigarette smoke. 'Amy was her own girl, but we went through group together, the seminars, rec activities all day long. We even spent our smoke breaks together. She never mentioned a baby.'

'She ever mention a boyfriend? Someone called Charles Cartmell?'

'No. She used to date a lot, but she was changing that, too. She said in group that she was sick of hooking up with abusive guys.'

'Did any of them visit her at rehab?'

'No. We're allowed visitors on weekends but she never got any.'

'I'm wondering about someone Amy was dating about three or four years ago. He wasn't a bad-looking guy, on the short side, white, with longish brown hair. They might've gone on a trip together, to some-place warm. Did she ever mention a vacation with a guy, at a beach?'

Melanie paused a minute, frowning. 'No, but I know that a while ago, she used to see a guy named Rob. Rob Moore.'

Ellen felt her heartbeat quicken. 'What did she say about him?'

'Just that he was a jerk.'

'How long ago was this, that she saw him?'

'I don't know, but it was old news.'

'Three or four years ago?'

'Yeah. Really in her past.'

'Did she tell you anything else about him?'

'No, just that he was a bad dude. Used to smack her around, and she dumped him. She wouldn't take that, for ever. That was the thing about Amy. She was the one we all thought would make it.'

'What happened to her? How did they find her?'

'I was the one who found her,' Melanie answered flatly.

'That must have been awful for you. Was there a needle in her arm?'

'No. She didn't shoot it, she snorted it. There was junk on the table and the credit card she used. We were supposed to go out that night, but she never met me, so I went over around nine the next morning. She was on the couch, dressed to go out.'

'How did you get in?'

'I have a key. The family thinks she overdosed, but I wonder if it was bad junk.' Melanie faltered, then took a drag.

'Why do you think it was bad junk and not just an overdose?'

'You never know with street junk.'

'She lived by herself?'

'Yeah. She got a room in a nice house and a new job, waitressing. She was going to meetings, too, every day. She never missed.' Melanie shook her head sadly. 'She's the one who told me to carry Subutex.'

'What's that?'

'A pill. If you take it and you do H, you don't get high. Amy always carried two pills with her.'

Ellen had heard of drugs like that. She'd done a story once involving Antabuse, a drug that made alcoholics sick if they drank.

'But that night, she didn't take a pill. The bottle was right on her nightstand with the two still in it.'

'So why did she take heroin instead of Subutex?'

'She musta missed it so much. Heroin's like that. You love it and you hate it, so much.'

'Wouldn't she have mentioned to you that she was thinking of using again? How often did you speak to her, generally?'

Melanie tossed her cigarette butt to the sidewalk. 'We talked on the phone every day, and she was queen of texting. She texted all the time.'

'Did you look at her texts from before she died?'

'Whoa, weird. I didn't. I totally forgot.' Melanie was already reaching into her handbag and extracting a phone, which she flipped open. She pressed several buttons to retrieve the texts, then started scrolling backwards. Ellen edged close to her, and they read the text together:

Scored new 7 jeans on sale. wait till u see them! xoxo

Ellen glanced at the top of the screen, which showed the time the text had come in—9.15 p.m. 'She sounds happy.'

'Yeah, you're right.' Melanie pressed a few more buttons. 'Here's another one, from earlier that day, around five o'clock.'

Ellen and Melanie put their heads together, and read:

$228 in tips, my best day ever! going 2 the mall 2 celebrate! see u soon! xoxo

'That's so random.' Melanie shook her head. 'It doesn't sound like she was thinking about using.'

'It sure doesn't.' Ellen thought about it. 'Recovering addicts get sponsors, right? Did Amy have a sponsor?'

'Sure, but if you want to know more about Amy, you should ask Rose. She was in rehab with me and Amy.'

'Great, can I have her phone number?'

'I have her cell number right here. Give me your cell number, and I'll text it to you.'

Rose Bock turned out to be a middle-aged African-American woman. She wore her hair cut natural and had on a blue-checked Oxford shirt underneath a navy suit, looking every inch the accountant. Ellen had reached her on her cellphone, and she was in Philly, so they'd met at a burger joint full of noisy students near the Penn campus.

'Thanks so much for meeting me.' Ellen took a sip of a Diet Coke. 'My condolences about Amy. Melanie told me that you two were close.'

'We were.' Rose's smile faded quickly. 'So how did you know her?'

'Long story short, I adopted a baby that I think was hers. At least that's what the court papers say.'

'Amy had a baby?' Rose's eyebrows rose.

'Hi, ladies.' The waitress arrived with a cheeseburger, set it down on the table, then went off. Rose picked up the burger and smiled.

'I can't resist the double cheeseburger here. I traded one addiction for another.'

'Enjoy yourself.' Ellen managed a smile. 'If you don't mind my saying so, you don't look like the typical drug addict.'

'Yes, I do,' Rose said without rancour. 'I was addicted to prescription drugs, Vicodin and Percocet, for almost nine years. I started with a back injury and never stopped.'

'I think of Vicodin as in a different category from heroin.'

'You shouldn't. They're both opiates. I might have been in a different income bracket from Amy, but we're both junkies.'

'Melanie told me that Amy still had her Subutex on her, which she didn't take, and we both read her last texts, which were upbeat. Amy didn't mention to Melanie that she was looking to start doing drugs again. Had she mentioned anything like that to you?'

'No, not all.' Rose reached for her coffee and took a sip.

'I wonder why she didn't call you or Melanie.'

'*You* wonder?' Rose winced. 'I'm not her sponsor, but I am, was, her friend. I would think she'd call me if she wanted to use. I'll never get over this. I would have bet a thousand bucks on Amy. She had relapsed twice, but that's part of the process. She was finally able to get clean.'

'So she never called you, to say she was tempted?'

'No, never.' Rose's face fell into pained lines. 'We talked on the phone every couple of days, and all the talk was easy. She got a new job and she was getting ready to reconcile with her family. So that she started using again, two days after we spoke, well, it was a real blow.'

'Melanie told me about a guy named Rob Moore, who Amy dated three or four years ago. He was abusive and she got away from him. You know anything about him?'

'Not really. Amy told me that she had a toxic relationship once. I never knew his name. She talked about him in group.'

'I ask because there's an outside chance he's the father of my son.'

'Last week, she called me. I wasn't there to take the call, but she left a message, saying something about a visit by a blast from the past.'

'What did she say when you called her back?'

'She said she was fine. You think that this guy came back in her life, but she didn't want to let on? Or she thought better of it?'

'I don't know what I think. What day was it that she called you?'

'Friday. I missed the call because I was at my son's piano recital.'

Ellen thought back quickly. She had met Cheryl on Thursday night, after which Cheryl sent Amy the email telling her that Ellen was looking for her. Friday would be the night after Amy got the email, assuming she checked her email with any frequency. Ellen sensed that Amy's death was connected to her visit to Cheryl. That she had set it all in motion. And that Rob Moore had everything to do with Amy's death. She fake-checked her watch, then rose. 'Jeez, I'm late, I should probably get going, thanks so much.' She grabbed her coat and handbag from the seat. 'I'll follow up and let you know if I learn anything new. Thanks again.'

'You think we should call the police?'

'No,' Ellen said, too quickly. 'I'm sure it's speculation, but I'll give it some thought. Have to go now. Thanks again.'

She hurried from the restaurant, head swimming, and broke into a light jog, pulling her coat round her with a shaky hand. She reached her car, fumbled for her keys, jumped in and turned on the engine, then lurched into the lane of traffic.

It was late afternoon and a premature night was falling, frigid as black ice. She drove on autopilot, through a world that had gone topsy-turvy around her. She had thought that Will was hers and would be for ever. She thought that he had a young mother somewhere and a wandering father. She thought that they were gone for good, a young couple who made a mistake. But it had been a fantasy. All of it was fiction. And now Ellen was deathly afraid of what was true.

Her hands gripped the wheel. Her heart thundered. She skidded to a stop at a traffic light. She was too emotional to think straight. She didn't know where to go or what to do. She couldn't go to the police because she'd lose Will. She had been going it alone for so long, she couldn't do it for another minute. She picked up her phone and punched in a number.

'Please be there,' Ellen was saying, when the call connected.

# CHAPTER EIGHT

'COME IN, what's the matter?' Marcelo swung open his front door, and Ellen hurried past the threshold. It had taken her an hour to get to his house in Queens Village, but the ride over hadn't calmed her down. It had been all she could do to hide her panic when she'd called Connie and asked her to stay late.

'There's a problem but . . . I don't know where to begin.' Ellen raked a hand through her hair and found herself pacing back and forth in his neat living room, a blur of exposed-brick walls, glass tables and black leather furniture. Marcelo closed the front door behind her.

'It's all right,' he said softly, his dark eyes steady. 'Try the beginning.'

'No, I . . . can't.' Ellen didn't know why she'd come. She wasn't sure it was the right thing. She knew only that she needed to talk to someone.

'Did you do something illegal?'

'Yes, and no.' Ellen didn't know what to think. Her hands flew to her face, and she felt her fingerpads burrow into the flesh of her cheeks. 'No, but . . . I think I stumbled onto something . . . I wish I never started. It's the worst . . . the worst thing that could happen.'

'What could be so bad?' Marcelo asked, disbelieving, stepping closer to her and taking her by the shoulders. 'What is it?'

'It's too awful, it's just . . .' Ellen heard herself erupt in a sob that came from deep within. The next thing she knew, she was crying and Marcelo had put his arms round her, wrapping her in a strong embrace, and she could feel herself sagging against his soft shirt, hiccupping in the civilised office smells clinging to him, the remnants of her life before.

'Whatever it is, we can figure it out. Everything is going to be all right, you'll see.' Marcelo held her tight, rocking her slightly.

'I made a . . . a mistake, a terrible mistake.' Ellen looked up at him through her tears. He stroked her cheek gently, brushing away her tears, and Ellen felt his other arm behind her back and leaned against it fully, letting him support her. His eyes met hers, so full of feeling that she felt a kind of wonderment, and she couldn't remember anyone ever looking at her that way, and in the next instant he lowered his face and kissed her softly on the lips, once, and then again.

'Everything's going to be all right,' he murmured. 'You're here now, and we'll make it right.'

'Really?' Ellen asked, and when Marcelo leaned down to kiss her again, more deeply and with urgency, she had her answer. She gave herself over to him and her own emotions, kissing him back deeply, drawing from him comfort and strength, escaping into his embrace, just for now, for the few moments before he learned the truth and understood that everything was most decidedly not going to be all right.

And in the next minute Ellen felt her own hands reaching up Marcelo's back, pulling him as close as she could, and he responded, holding her tighter, kissing her with more urgency, his breath quickening as they sank, fumbled, and stumbled together onto the couch.

Ellen felt him press her backwards against the leather, or maybe she pulled him up and onto her, almost embarrassingly eager to lose herself in him and forget about everything else. For a moment she wasn't a mother any more but simply a woman, and the heat of Marcelo's kiss and the weight of his body chased every thought from her head and obliterated every worry. In the soft light, she saw him smile as he helped her out of her coat.

'Allow me,' Marcelo whispered, and Ellen put her arms in the air, letting him pull her sweater over her head, and when her head popped out of the black neckline, she saw the softest expression cross his face.

'*Meu Deus, você é tão linda*,' Marcelo said softly, and though she didn't know the translation, the way he said it communicated so much desire that it slowed her down and stopped her teenaged clawing.

'You are so beautiful,' Marcelo said again and, for a second, they were both suspended in place and time, letting the frank lust of their first kisses cool and ebb away, and they regarded each other as two mature adults, each sensing that they were starting something real by whatever came next. Marcelo looked down at her with a grave smile, then he cocked his head in what could only be a question, silently asked.

'Yes,' Ellen whispered, sliding her arms round him.

Marcelo lowered himself onto her in reply, and they kissed deeply and slowly, wrapping their arms and legs round each other, their tongues flickering and teasing and, in time, their clothes peeled off layer by layer until skin met skin, warmth met warmth, and heart met heart. Until there was nothing between them at all.

Ellen woke up naked, her limbs intertwined with Marcelo's and her head resting on his chest. Disentangling herself, she propped herself up on an elbow and squinted at her watch. Nine o'clock. Her life rushed back at her like a freight train, full of noise, power. And fear. Suddenly she knew what had happened, as if she had seen it in a nightmare.

*Amy was murdered. So was Karen Batz. Rob Moore is killing everyone who could know that Will is really Timothy.*

Ellen sprang from the couch. She wriggled into her skirt, slid into her sweater, jumped into her boots. Marcelo slept on, his breathing soft and regular, and she didn't wake him to explain. She didn't have a minute to lose. She grabbed her coat, found her handbag and fumbled for her car keys, her heart beginning to beat fast. She crossed to the front door, something telling her that she had to hurry home. Right now.

Ellen shut Marcelo's front door behind her, clutched her coat closed and hurried down the stoop into a snowstorm.

She chirped the car door open, jumped inside and turned on the ignition and windshield wipers. She cranked the defrost, backed out of the space, and reached into her handbag for her BlackBerry. She pulled it out and pressed speed dial for Connie as she pounded the gas. The car zoomed down the dark street, and the call connected.

'Connie? You hanging in?' Ellen asked, trying to keep the nervousness from her tone.

'Sure. I'm watching TV. Take your time.'

'How's my boy?'

'He's out like a light.'

'Good.' Ellen waited for the familiar easing in her chest when she heard that everything was fine, but there was no easing tonight.

'Oh, yeah, the cat's throwing up. I had to put him out for a while.'

'OK. I'll be home in less than an hour.'

'Drive safe. It's really coming down here. We already have six inches.'

'I hear you, bye.' Ellen pressed End, tossed the BlackBerry aside and fed the car gas, heading home.

Ellen hurried to her front porch in a fully fledged snowstorm.

She plunged her key into the lock and twisted, opening the door onto a comforting scene that brought her no comfort.

Connie greeted her with a big grin. 'It's Nanook of the North!'

'Cold out there.' Ellen fake-smiled and slid out of her coat. She grabbed Connie's coat and handed it to her, barely able to hide her urgency. 'You'll be safe going home, right? You have four-wheel drive?'

'Sure. It's no problem.' Connie put on her coat, then got her tote and handbag from the window seat.

Ellen opened the door to let Connie out. 'Be careful out there.'

'No worries, I'm invincible.' Connie flashed her a smile and headed outside, and Ellen shut the door, locked it and threw the deadbolt.

Ellen didn't know how or why, but she knew what she felt inside. If Rob Moore was killing people who were linked to Timothy, then she and Will had to get out of there immediately, tonight. She hurried up the stairs, hustled into Will's room and hurried to the bed.

'Will, wake up, honey.' Will slept on his back. Oreo Figaro didn't move, a black-and-white ball at the foot of the bed. She lifted Will up, hoisted him to her shoulder in his thermal pyjamas.

'Mommy?'

'Hi, honey.' Ellen rubbed his back. 'You can just stay asleep, I want to put you into something warmer.'

Will put his arms round her neck, and Ellen moved to the bureau, dipped sideways to yank open the bottom drawer and grabbed one of his snowsuits. She crossed back to the bed, unfolded the snowsuit, and fumbled to stuff Will's feet into the legs. 'Mommy, what?'

'Everything's fine, sweetie. We're just going out for a little bit.' Ellen pulled the snowsuit up and unwrapped his arms from her neck, then stuck on his sneakers. 'Hold on round my neck. We're going for a ride.'

'OK,' Will said sleepily, holding tight as she picked him up again, left the room and hurried downstairs. She reached the bottom, grabbed her handbag, then remembered she needed cash. She kept two hundred bucks in the kitchen drawer for emergencies.

She hurried with Will through the dining room and turned the corner into the dark kitchen.

She went to flick on the light switch, but all of a sudden there was a shadowy blur and the back of her head exploded in pain.

Her arms released their grip. Will slipped through her fingers. Everything went dark, and the last thing she heard was Will's scream.

Ellen regained consciousness, lying on her side on the kitchen floor. Her head thundered and she tried to scream. Tape covered her lips. She tried to move her hands but they were wrenched behind her back, stuck together. Pain arced through her shoulder joints. Her ankles were bound. She was facing the dining room, her back to the kitchen.

Ellen heard a noise behind her, a harsh ripping sound. She rolled herself over on the floor, in horror at the sight.

Will lay on his side facing her, a strip of duct tape over his mouth. He was crying hard, his small body shaking with sobs. A man bent over him, wrapping duct tape round his ankles in his blue snowsuit.

'Good morning,' the man said, looking up with a sly grin.

It was the man from the beach. Rob Moore. He had a droopy brown moustache and he looked older and craggier than he had in the photo with Amy, but it was the same man. Shaggy brown hair curled over the collar of an old black coat he had on with jeans and snowy Timberlands. A red plastic jug with a long spout sat next to him on the floor. Gasoline. The kitchen reeked of it. Ellen screamed in her throat.

'I second that emotion,' Moore said, chuckling again as he tore off the duct tape with the side of a crooked incisor.

Tears poured from Will's eyes, and they widened in fear. Ellen shimmied closer to him, making noises.

Moore straightened, a smile twisting his lips. Suddenly he lifted his foot in the heavy boot and put it down hard on Will's head. 'Move and I'll squash him like a bug.'

Will burst into new tears, his cheeks turning a violent red. Moore leaned forward and stepped harder on his head.

Will squeezed his eyes shut, his small forehead buckling with pain. Dirt and snow from the boot dumped onto his little face.

Ellen screamed and screamed, shaking her head frantically.

'Lady, get back and shut the hell up.'

Ellen scrambled backwards, writhing this way and that. She looked up at Moore, begging him to stop.

'Is that the look of love you're givin' me?' Moore kept his boot on Will's head but eased backwards slightly. The redness ebbed from Will's cheeks. He was choking under the duct tape.

Moore said, 'I woulda thought you got your fill with your boyfriend.'

Ellen struggled to think through her panic. Moore must have been following her. Had he been to the funeral?

'Oh, shut up.' Moore took his foot from Will's head, leaving him crying hysterically, his tears mixing with the mud on his face.

Ellen silenced herself, making eye contact with Will, trying to tell him that everything would be all right.

Moore picked up the plastic jug and twisted off the lid. He tipped the container over on top of Will and gasoline spewed from the spout, splashing onto Will's legs in the snowsuit.

Ellen started screaming behind the duct tape.

*Bing bong!* Suddenly, the doorbell rang in the living room.

Ellen screamed behind the tape, though she knew it was useless.

'Shut up!' Moore stepped hard on Will's head again.

Ellen shook her head back and forth like a madwoman.

*Bing bong!*

Moore grimaced, angry. Will's face turned blue-red before her eyes.

A silent scream contorted his features. Tears poured from his eyes. Snot streamed from his nose over the duct tape.

*Bing bong!*

'Give it up!' Moore whirled round, finally taking his foot off Will.

*Bing bong!*

'Shit!' Moore flew into a rage, his eyes wild and out of control. He plunged his hand into his coat pocket and, when he withdrew it, he was holding a large revolver with a steel barrel. 'You see your kid?' Moore bent down and drilled the barrel of the gun into Will's temple. 'I'll blow his head clean off. I'm gonna cut you loose, only because they're not goin' away. You answer the door and tell whoever's there to go. Do one thing wrong, and I blow this kid's head offa his shoulders.'

Ellen nodded frantically, pumped her head, yesyesyes.

'All right then.' Moore raised the revolver, sprang over to Ellen and reached behind her back. He yanked her into the air by her wrists, hissing into her ear. 'Up to you, bitch. One word and I shoot the kid.'

Ellen shook her head, desperate to reassure him. In the next second, her hands were cut free and she fell to the hardwood floor.

Moore cut loose her ankles, flipped her over and tore the duct tape from her mouth. It stung until he drilled the gun between her eyes.

'No tricks.' Moore's face was six inches from hers, a close-up of bloodshot eyes, greasy moustache and breath foul with beer.

Ellen scrambled to get her feet under her, her knees jelly. 'What if it's my neighbour? What if she won't go?'

'Make her.' Moore shoved her from the kitchen, and she half walked, half stumbled through the dining room. Her heart thundered, and she crossed the living room towards the door.

*Bing bong!*

Ellen couldn't see the face at the door, but a shape stood silhouetted in the yellowish porch light. She opened the door and stood stricken against a blast of frigid wind. At her front door was the last person in the world she ever expected to see.

**I**t was Carol Braverman, standing in a long black coat. Her eyes glittered with emotion. She asked, 'Ellen Gleeson?'

Ellen nodded, stunned as Carol entered the house, looking round.

'I'm Carol Braverman, but you knew that already.' Carol looked at Ellen with determined blue eyes. 'You adopted my son.'

'What? I'm sorry?' Ellen struggled to react.

'I came as soon as I had it verified. He's my son, Timothy. He was kidnapped in Miami right after his first birthday.'

'I don't know what you mean,' Ellen said. Moore could hear every word. She had to get Carol out of here.

'Sorry, but I think you do.' Carol's eyes softened slightly. 'I can only imagine what you must be going through, and I feel sorry for you. But we both know the truth. You have my baby, and I want him back.'

'No, I don't.' Ellen stepped towards her, leaving the front door open, filling the living room with frigid air. 'Please, leave my house.'

'Don't pretend you don't know. You were in Miami two days ago. A reporter who works with you called me and told me everything. Sarah Liu is her name. She caught you on our website, printing out my son's picture. She called your house and verified that you were out of town. She figured you'd come to Miami. Why? Did you want to check us out? Sarah claimed the reward, of course. It's a million dollars, life-changing money. That's why we set it so high. We knew that sooner or later it would bring somebody out of the woodwork, and it did.

'I Googled you online, I found the articles you wrote about him. I know you didn't know he was kidnapped, but that's not my problem. He's mine, and I want him. My husband's on the way. His plane was delayed in the snow, and I didn't want to wait.'

Suddenly a noise came from the stairwell, and they both turned. Oreo Figaro appeared on the stair landing, where he stopped and sat.

'Where is Timothy?' Carol asked. 'I demand to see him.'

'He's not Timothy, he's my son, and he's at a sleepover.'

'A three-year-old, at a sleepover?' Carol moved towards the stairway, but Ellen shifted over and blocked her way.

'Stop right there. You have no right to walk round my house.' She raised her voice. If Carol took one step closer to the stairway, she'd be able to see the kitchen from its other entrance. She'd smell the gasoline, and they'd all end up dead. Ellen put a firm hand on Carol's coat sleeve. 'Get out, right now!'

'I thought we could do this without the police, but maybe not. You have my son, and I won't leave here without him.'

'Get the hell out!' Ellen fought a rising panic.

'We hired a detective, and he confirmed everything Sarah said, including your plane ticket down to Miami and back.'

'Go!' Ellen shoved her, but Carol shoved back, her expression fierce.

'I'm not going!' She braced herself in the threshold. 'I want my *son*!'

'He's not here!' Ellen shouted. 'Go! NOW!'

'Call the police then.' Carol folded her arms. 'But you won't do that, will you? Because you know that you're keeping my child.'

'Get OUT!' Ellen shouted louder, fighting a wild impulse to run to the kitchen, grab Will and go like hell, but Carol's eyes narrowed.

'Your eyes just moved. You just looked somewhere in back, behind you. He's back there, isn't he?' Suddenly, Carol hit Ellen in the face.

Ellen reeled backwards, off-balance, recovering too late. 'No, stop!'

'Timothy!' Carol broke free and bolted for the dining room.

Ellen took a desperate flying leap and caught Carol by the hem of her long coat. The two women fell to the dining-room floor.

'I want my son!' Carol screamed, as the two mothers wrestled on the dining-room floor, bumping the chairs aside.

'NO!' Ellen struggled to pin Carol to the floor, and had almost succeeded when they both heard the sound of raucous laughter.

Rob Moore stood over them, his legs spread like a commando. He aimed his gun down at them. 'Girl-on-girl action,' he said.

'*You!*' Carol said, hushed, and Moore smiled slyly.

'Carol? Long time, no see.' Moore gestured towards the kitchen with the muzzle of his revolver. 'In the kitchen, ladies.'

'I could kill you!' Carol shot back. 'You kidnapped my baby!'

'Boohoo, princess.' Moore snorted.

'I got you the money, and you were supposed to give the baby back! That was the deal. You were never supposed to keep the baby. Never!'

'The deal changed.'

Ellen looked from Moore to Carol, dumbfounded.

'Why did you do it, why?' Carol cried. 'You got your money.'

'My girlfriend wanted him. She was always sayin' she couldn't have a baby, and when I tol' her no, she split with him.'

Ellen needed to stall, to give herself time to think. 'Was that Amy? Was Amy Martin your girlfriend?'

'Yeah. The dumb bitch.'

'You killed Amy?'

'Duh,' Moore answered.

'And the lawyer, too? Karen Batz?'

'Sure.'

'But why? Did she know?'

'I wasn't leavin' a loose end. If she figured it out, she woulda squawked. Carol woulda had the best lawyers money could buy, and I woulda gone to the joint.'

'You bastard!' Carol's gaze bored into him. 'You ruined my life!'

'You ruined your own life. You went through your money like water.'

'Do you know what you did?' Carol scrambled to stand up, and Oreo Figaro walked into the dining room. 'You almost killed my husband. You *ruined* my marriage.'

'You shoulda told your husband the truth, then. You shoulda said to him, "Honey, wifey-poo isn't the good girl you think. I used our kid to pay for my little hobby."'

'She used her kid?' Ellen said, stalling. '*She* did it?'

'Yeah, it was all her idea.' Moore sneered. 'Little Miss Goody-Goody here, she gambled up all her money, so she needed to tap her kid's.'

'Shut up!' Carol shouted, but Moore ignored her.

'She knew me from the casino, Miccosukee. I was parkin' cars for rich bitches, and she hired me to kidnap her kid. She got the ransom from the kid's trust fund. She told me the nanny would be there and—'

'Stop it, stop it!' Carol shouted louder, startling Oreo Figaro, who ran under the dining-room table. 'You weren't supposed to kill her.'

'Enough!' Moore gestured towards the kitchen. 'Your son's in there.'

'He is?' Carol's face flooded with happiness. She rushed to the kitchen, and the sudden movement sent Oreo Figaro scooting to Ellen.

Just then a lethal glimmer flickered through Moore's eyes. Ellen didn't have time to think, only to act.

And everything happened at once.

Carol reached the kitchen threshold and saw Will, lying on the floor.

'My baby!' she cried.

Moore raised the gun and aimed it at the back of Carol's head.

Ellen scooped Oreo Figaro off the floor and threw him right at Moore's face.

'Reowwh!' The fat cat screeched in protest, his thick body twisting this way and that, and the surprise knocked Moore off-balance. He raised his hands and fell backwards. The gun fired into the ceiling.

Ellen launched herself like a missile, aiming for Moore's gun. She barrelled into him, and he staggered backwards into the kitchen. She grabbed the gun with all her might and struggled to wrest it from him.

Moore whipped Ellen round and slammed her into the doorway. Her head banged against the wood but she hung on to his wrist, fighting for the gun even as he pointed its muzzle at Carol, who had picked up Will and was taking him out of the other doorway.

'RUN!' Ellen screamed.

'Shut up!' Moore threw her against the stove, shaking her hand loose and training the gun on Carol.

Carol looked over her shoulder and, in one motion, put Will on the landing behind her, blocked him with her body and raised her arms protectively, facing Moore.

Moore squeezed the trigger, firing point-blank, and Ellen screamed.

Carol's chest exploded in wool tatters. Her mouth dropped open. Her head snapped forward. She dropped onto the kitchen floor, crumpling at the knees, her legs grotesquely askew.

'NO!' Ellen hurled herself at Moore but, this time, in her hand was the cast-iron burner from her stovetop. She swung the burner as hard as she could into Moore's face. The spiked end speared his forehead and a gaping hole appeared. The next second, it spurted blood. Moore's eyes flew open, and he slumped against the wall, then slid down, insensate. He landed in a sitting position, a crooked grin crossing his face before his gaze fixed.

Ellen hurried over to Carol, feeling under her chin for a pulse. There was none. Blood soaked her coat from the hole in her chest.

Ellen bent over Carol and listened for breath. No sound. She opened Carol's mouth and began to breathe air into her, but it was no use. Carol's head fell back, too loose on her neck, mouth hanging open, and Ellen heard herself moan, stricken. She set her down on the floor carefully, saying a silent prayer.

*Will.*

Ellen stumbled to the landing, where Will lay bundled, sobbing. His terrified eyes met hers, so much like Carol's that it gave her a start. She picked him up and hurried out of the kitchen, shielding him from the grisly scene and telling him everything was going to be all right. She hurried him into the living room and sat with him on the couch, putting him on her lap and comforting him as she unpeeled the duct tape from his mouth

He erupted in a full-blown wail. 'Mommy! Mommy! It hurts!'

Ellen tried to comfort him as she untaped his hands and feet, the stench of gasoline filling her nostrils. She was sliding him out of his wet snowsuit when she glimpsed blood behind his right ear.

She pulled a Kleenex from the box on the coffee table, held it to the wound and flashed on Moore's big boot crushing Will's face. She didn't know if Will was bleeding internally. He needed an ambulance. She pressed the tissue to his wound, hurried with him to the phone and called 911.

'What is your emergency?' the dispatcher asked, and Ellen collected herself, composing a lead paragraph on the spot.

'An armed intruder broke into my house. He tried to kill me and my son, and I killed him in self-defence. He killed a woman named Carol Braverman. He also injured my son, who's three, and he's bleeding from behind his ear. I need an ambulance, and the police.'

'Keep him awake, and the ambulance will be there right away.'

Ellen hung up, hugged Will close and rocked him until his tears finally slowed.

'Let's get your coat,' she said as she walked to the closet, took his corduroy hoodie from a hook and sat back down on the couch with him, slipping his arms into the puffy sleeves, getting him ready. His sneakers reeked of gasoline, so she took them off.

'Stinky shoes, huh?' Ellen asked, and Will nodded, his small chest shuddering from his final sobs. She touched lightly behind his ear, and in the lamplight she could see a large cut on his scalp. She prayed there wasn't a skull fracture and reached for another tissue.

'Mommy, what?'

'You have a boo-boo behind your ear. We're going to take a ride to the doctor. We have to get you looked at.'

'Who was that man?'

'In the kitchen? A very bad man. A terrible man, but he's not going to hurt you any more.'

'Did he hurt you, Mommy?'

'No, I'm OK. So are you. You're going to be fine after we see the doctor.' Ellen cuddled him, and Will rubbed his eye with a fist.

'Stay awake, OK, honey?' Ellen jiggled him a little and talked to him about nothing, even as the bright red blood from his cut soaked Kleenex after Kleenex. Oreo Figaro wandered in, sat down in front of the couch and tucked his legs underneath him.

Will sniffled. 'You hurt Oreo Figaro, Mommy.'

'No, I didn't. I knew he'd be OK.'

'You throwed him. That wasn't nice.'

'You're right.' Ellen turned to Oreo Figaro. 'I'm sorry, Oreo Figaro.'

The cat signified his forgiveness by looking up and blinking, and he kept watch over them both until the police cruisers arrived, their red lights slashing the cosy living room with blood-red splotches.

'What is that, Mommy?' Will asked, twisting to see.

'It's the police, here to help us, buddy.' Ellen rose and looked out of the window to the street. Police cruisers were parking out front, their exhausts billowing into the snowy air and their high beams slicing the dotted darkness. Uniformed cops sprang from the cars, black figures against the whiteness, running up her front walk to the porch.

'Here they come, Mommy.'

'Right, here they come.' Ellen crossed to the door as the cops hustled onto the porch, shoes heavy as soldiers as they reached the front door.

They were coming to save Will.

And to destroy the only life he knew.

**E**llen opened the door, and police filled the living room and began looking round, hurrying into the dining room and towards the stairs. Will quieted in her arms, gazing wide-eyed at an older cop with wire-rimmed glasses who took her aside, his hand on her elbow.

'I'm Officer Patrick Halbert,' he said. Snowflakes dusted the shoulders of his nylon jacket. 'You're the homeowner who called nine-one-one?'

'Yes.' Ellen introduced herself. 'Where is the ambulance?'

'On its way. Are you injured, ma'am?' Officer Halbert looked at her coat, and she realised that there was blood all over her.

'No, this isn't my blood. It's my son who's hurt. When will the ambulance get here?'

'Five minutes, tops.' Officer Halbert's tone sounded official, but under the bill of his cap, his eyes looked concerned and they scanned Will. 'Now, you told our dispatcher it was a home invasion?' He plucked a Bic from his jacket, slid a notepad from his back pocket and flipped open the pad. 'Why don't you fill me in on what happened?'

'There was an intruder in my house. He had a gun. He broke in and tried to kill me and my son. He poured gasoline on him. Then a woman named Carol Braverman came in and interrupted him, and he shot her.' Ellen caught a glimpse of bright red lights in the street. It was the ambulance pulling up. 'They're here.'

'Let's go.' Officer Halbert quickly put away his pen and pad. 'We'll escort you to the hospital.'

Ellen was already out of the door, cuddling Will against the storm, and he held her tight as Halbert and some other cops fell in beside them, and they descended the porch stairs into the snowy night. A paramedic jumped out of the cab and flung open the ambulance's back doors.

Ellen hurried down the walk with Will. Officer Halbert steadied Ellen by the arm as the paramedic rushed to meet them.

'This the boy?' the paramedic shouted over the idling engines. He held out his arms for Will, and Ellen handed him over.

'Yes, he's three, bleeding from behind his ear. His head was . . . pressed from the side.'

'You ride in the back, Mom.' The paramedic hustled Will to the back of the ambulance and climbed inside, and Ellen followed.

'Wait, wait!' came a shout, and they all looked back. A black sedan had pulled up behind the police cruisers, and a man was running towards them in the snowstorm, waving his arms, his sports jacket flapping in the whirling snow. Cops surged towards him, blocking him, but in the light from the open ambulance, Ellen recognised Bill Braverman.

'Stop, wait!' He fought the cops to get to the ambulance. 'Let me see!'

'Mister, get outta here! We gotta go!' the paramedic shouted back, pushing him away, but Bill took one look at Will and his expression filled with joy.

'Timothy, it's *you*! Thank God, it's you!' Bill held out his arms, and Will burst into terrified tears.

'Mommy!' he screamed, and Ellen jumped up, blocking the way.

'Bill, we'll sort this out later. I have to get him to the hospital. He has a head injury.'

'*You!*' Bill went wild. '*You're* the one! You're the woman who adopted our son!' He started to climb into the ambulance, but the cops pulled him back. He shouted, 'That's *my boy*! That's Timothy! Where's my wife? What did you do to my wife?' He turned angrily to the cops flanking him. 'I'm Bill Braverman! Is my wife here? Is she all right?'

Halbert put a hand on Bill's arm. 'Sir, is your wife Carol Braverman?'

'Yes, where is she? Is she all right?'

'Please come with me,' Halbert said. 'I need to speak with you.'

'But that's my son! Is he hurt? Where's my wife? That's our *son*!'

'We gotta go!' the paramedic shouted, buckling Will onto the gurney, then he shifted over to shut the back doors and twisted the handles closed. He climbed round Ellen and leaned towards the driver in the cab. 'Locked and loaded, Jimmy!'

Through the back window, the cops became stick figures against the whirling white, and Ellen felt a wrench of deep sadness. For Bill, for Carol, and for herself. And especially, for Will.

# CHAPTER NINE

ELLEN SLUMPED in the cloth-covered chairs of the waiting room of the emergency department. The place was empty except for two young cops, who watched TV on low volume. The doctor had sent her out to the waiting room while Will was taken up to MRI and X-ray.

The doors of the emergency room whooshed open, and through the glass she could see Bill Braverman, sports jacket bloodied, entering with Officer Halbert and another cop. She felt a sinking feeling in the pit of her stomach as they spotted her, then came into the waiting room.

'Ms Gleeson?' Officer Halbert's smile was wearier than earlier. 'How's your son?'

'Not sure yet.'

Officer Halbert pulled up a chair opposite her, while the other cop took a seat to the side. Bill Braverman sat with them, glaring at her. His eyes flashed with hostility, and his mouth became a straight line.

Ellen couldn't help meeting his eye. 'I'm so sorry about your wife.'

'Thank you,' Bill answered, hoarsely, but his dark eyes, puffy and red, didn't soften. 'I'd like an explanation from you.'

Officer Halbert raised a hand. 'Mr Braverman, we'll get her statement later, as I told you.'

'I'd like to know now,' Bill shot back. 'She's sitting here, my son is in the hospital and my wife is dead. I want to know what happened.'

Ellen raised a hand. 'It's OK,' she said. 'He has a right to know and there's no reason to stand on formality.'

Halbert pursed his lips. 'We'll still need your statement. Later.'

'Fine.' Ellen took a deep breath and shifted in her chair to face Bill. 'It all started with a white card I got in the mail, about a kidnapped boy.' She filled them in on what she'd figured out about Amy Martin and Rob Moore while Officer Halbert took notes, and she brought them up to date. 'I was worried that Moore might come after Will and me, and I was trying to get us out when he showed up.'

Officer Halbert broke in, 'We were wondering, how did Rob Moore get into your house? There was no sign of forced entry.'

'I think the back door was left open. The cat goes in and out a lot, and we leave it unlocked sometimes. It's Narberth, after all.'

Halbert checked his pad. 'Now, can you tell us what happened when Carol Braverman came over?'

Ellen nodded, suddenly shaky. She hated Bill to find out this way, but it couldn't be helped. 'Well, evidently, they had planned to kidnap the baby together. Carol paid Moore to do it.'

Bill reddened. '*What?*'

'Carol said Moore was supposed to give the baby back but he didn't. That she had gambling debts and had to use her son's trust fund to pay them off.'

'That's not possible!' Bill shot back. 'How would she even know Moore? There's no way she knew such trash.'

'She said they met at a casino. Miccosukee, I think they said.'

'What is Miccosukee?' Halbert interjected.

'It's a casino, on an Indian reservation outside Miami,' Bill answered.

Ellen breathed a relieved sigh. 'Moore said he was a parking valet there.' She told them every detail of what had happened, from Carol's entering the house to when Moore pulled the gun on them in the dining room. 'He said Carol had used up her trust fund money to pay her gambling debts and she wanted to use Will's, er, Timothy's money.'

Bill's eyes narrowed. 'Who said that?'

'Moore did, and Carol didn't deny it. How else would I have known it? She said you didn't know anything about the plan. She said you were so upset when he kept the baby that it almost killed you, that it ruined your marriage.'

Bill scoffed. 'We have a wonderful marriage.'

'I saw you catch a plane a few days ago, from Miami to Vegas.'

Bill raked a hand through his hair. 'OK, well, we did have problems. We tried so hard to have Timothy and, after we did, it was like Carol didn't want anything to do with him. She had postpartum depression. She'd always gambled, poker on the computer, but then it got worse. I confronted her and she told me she was going to casinos. She told me she would stop. I thought she had.' Bill hung his head. 'I told her if she kept gambling, I'd leave her and take Timothy.'

'Maybe that's why she kept it from you.'

'I'm sure,' Bill said, subdued, and Ellen saw a change in him, as if together, they were solving a puzzle, each providing some of the pieces.

She asked, 'I'm curious, how would she pay the debts off with the ransom? How did that work?'

Bill rubbed his face. 'Lemme think. The kidnapper, when he phoned—this Moore—said that no FBI or police could be involved. He said the mother had to deliver the money. I said no, I was worried about her safety. But Carol said she wanted to do it by herself. She said she felt responsible because she didn't get Timothy out of the car in time.' Bill shook his head. 'Before Carol made the delivery, she must have taken some cash off the top. That must be what she used to pay off her debts. If Moore had given Timothy back, the plan would have worked. But he kept Timothy. God knows why.'

Ellen told him that Amy wanted the baby because she couldn't have one herself, and Bill's eyes widened in disbelief. 'So why not keep him then?'

'He got sick.'

'I'm sorry,' Bill said after a moment. Ellen nodded, trying not to cry.

'Me, too. But I want to tell you how Carol died, because she gave her life, for Will. For Timothy. She saved his life.'

'What happened?' Bill's lip trembled, and Ellen told him the story, after which he heaved a great sob, then collapsed into hoarse, choking sounds that hunched his broad shoulders, collapsing his frame and driving his face into his hands, in his own private hell.

There was a soft knock at the doorway, and the emergency-room nurse appeared. 'Ellen, your son is back from X-ray.'

'How is he?' Ellen asked, rising.

'The doctor will give you a full report,' the nurse answered.

'Bill, I'll ask someone to come out and tell you how he is,' Ellen said, following the nurse, who led her to the emergency unit.

They reached Will's examining room. Will lay under the covers, wearing a print hospital gown, looking tiny in the adult-size hospital bed. His head was bandaged with gauze, and he lay on the pillow with his eyes closed. A nurse was putting up the guardrails of his bed, next to the ER doctor, a young man with rumpled hair.

The doctor flashed Ellen a reassuring grin. 'Don't worry, he's fine. There's no fracture. The cut behind his ear is all stitched up.'

'Thank God. How about his heart?'

'All good.' The doctor looked sympathetic. 'He's fine. I'd like to admit him and keep an eye on him overnight.'

'Sure, better to be on the safe side. I can stay, right?'

'Yes. We'll get him a room and put in a bed for you.'

'Great.' Ellen looked down at Will. 'He's sleeping so soundly.'

'I gave him a light sedative, and he'll rest until morning.'

'Good, thanks.' Ellen pulled up a chair. 'You know, he saw terrible things tonight, people getting shot in front of him, and in the next few weeks, there'll be a major disruption in his life. Can you give me the names of some counsellors that can help him with the transition?'

'I'll have the social worker make some recommendations.'

'Thanks.' Ellen turned to the nurses. 'Would you tell the man in the waiting room that he's OK?'

Ellen woke up slowly, cuddling Will, and lay in bed, listening to the hospital come slowly to life, with the nurses talking in low tones about the snowstorm, and the mom with the kidnapped baby in Room 302.

'Mommy, when we get home, can we make a snowman?' Will asked, after the doctor had cleared them for discharge.

'We sure can.' Ellen zipped his hoodie, and he was dressed to go, except for being shoeless. All he had on was a pair of blue cotton socks.

Just then the nurse came in. 'Just to give you a heads-up, there are reporters out front.'

'Great.' Ellen managed a smile for Will's sake, then turned to him. 'Hear that, pal? You know what a reporter is, don't you?'

'*You're* a reporter!' Will pointed at her, smiling, and Ellen grabbed his finger and gave it a quick kiss.

'Right, and there'll be lots of people like me out front, only they might shout your name and take your picture. You ready for that?'

'Ready!'

'Good. Let's go home.'

The nurse asked Ellen, 'Do you have a ride home?'

'I called a cab. I used my cellphone, so please don't throw me in hospital jail.'

'Don't worry.' The nurse waved her off. 'If I were you, I'd call the cab back and tell him to go to the emergency exit, not the main entrance. The security guard can give you the nod. His name is Mel.'

'Good idea,' Ellen said, grateful. 'I'll stall in the gift shop. Thanks.'

Ellen carted Will out of the room and down the hall, where he waved and thanked the nurses, all of whom waved back with warm smiles.

'Bye, Will!' the last one said, sitting at the desk nearest the elevator.

Ellen hit the button to go down. 'Let's go to the gift shop.'

'Yay!' Will said, and the elevator came, the doors opening. 'I want to push the button!'

Ellen stepped inside, and Will twisted himself to lean down towards the button panel. The doors slid closed. When they opened again, Ellen stepped out of the elevator and looked for a sign to the gift shop.

'There she is!' a man said, and she looked over, startled. People were rushing towards her, and she raised a hand.

'I have no comment, boys. Not now, not ever.'

'We're not the press, Ms Gleeson,' the man said. 'I'm Special Agent Manning from the FBI and this is Special Agent Orr.'

'Oh,' Ellen said, surprised. She noticed that a few uniformed cops stood behind them. Something was wrong. Her mouth went dry.

'Mommy, where's the gift shop?'

'In a minute, sweetie.' Ellen asked the first FBI agent, 'What are you doing here?'

'Is this boy Will Gleeson?'

'Yes.'

'We're here to take him into protective custody.'

'What? Why? He doesn't need protecting. He's with me.'

'As you know, he's Timothy Braverman, a child of Carol and William Braverman, kidnapped in Miami, and we're here to facilitate his return.'

'What? Here? *Now?*' Ellen's arms tightened on Will. She hadn't expected this, not yet. 'He has no shoes. We have to go home.'

'Ms Gleeson, we are authorised to take the child. Here are the papers, you can take a look.' Special Agent Manning extended a packet of blue-backed paper folded in thirds, and Ellen glanced at the caption. The words WARRANT and SEIZURE swam before her eyes.

'Wait, listen, I know Bill Braverman. I was going to get his number from the police and set up a timetable that's best for Will.'

'Ma'am, we're here at the request of Mr Braverman. I'm sorry but, by law, you can't keep the child. We have to make certain that you don't abscond with him.'

'We're going to the gift shop, Mommy!' Will said loudly, his voice trembling with new anxiety.

'I won't abscond with him, I promise. I know I have to make a transfer, but just not yet. Not this way. I wanted to explain it to him, and—'

'Ms Gleeson, we have to take him now. Please don't make this harder on the child than it already is.' Special Agent Manning held out his hands, but Ellen stepped back with Will.

'I'm not giving him up this way. I'm still his mother.'

'I told you we'd have a problem,' said a voice from behind the FBI agents, and Bill Braverman emerged from the back of the group, flanked by an older man in a suit. 'I told you she'd try to run.'

'I'm not trying to run!' Ellen shouted. 'I just didn't think we'd be doing it this morning, right now. I need to talk to him, to prepare him—'

'Mommy, who are they?' Will asked, clutching her shoulder.

Bill pushed next to the FBI agents, his dark eyes cool, his expression hardened. 'I'm his father, and I have a legal right to him. Right now.'

'We have to talk about it. The timing, I mean.'

'No, we don't.'

'Mommy, what?' Will started to cry.

'Bill, look at him, think of *him*,' Ellen said, desperate. 'This is the craziest way to do this. This is the worst possible thing for him.'

'You mean for you,' Bill shot back, and Ellen's heart pounded.

'He doesn't know what's going on. I have to explain it to him. I was going to call a therapist when we got home.'

'I'll call a therapist. We have them in Miami, too. I'll take good care of him. He's mine.' Bill advanced a step, but the man in the suit restrained him and turned to Ellen.

'Ms Gleeson, I'm Mike Cusack and I'm representing Bill. You have no right to the child by law, and we have reason to believe you will leave the jurisdiction with him.'

'I won't, I swear. I wasn't going anywhere but home.'

'My client wants his child back, and the police are here to enforce his legal right. Please, don't be selfish. Do the right thing.'

'Mommy?' Will sobbed. 'Mommy!'

'Honey, it's all right.' Ellen patted his leg, frantic inside. She turned to the FBI agents. 'I'll turn him over, I promise, just not this minute. Come to my house. Follow me home. You'll see, I'm not going anywhere.'

'We can't do that, Ms Gleeson. We're here to take him, whether you cooperate or not. If you have a complaint, you can call—'

'I don't need to call!' Ellen exploded, losing control. 'I'm going to give him up, later! I just want to make this orderly! He's a boy, a little boy!'

'Mommy, no!'

'I'm sorry, Ms Gleeson.' Special Agent Manning reached for Will, and the cops advanced behind the agents as if on cue.

Ellen shouted, 'We're not doing it this way! Not this way!'

'Ms Gleeson, please.' Special Agent Manning grabbed Will by the shoulders and he screamed.

'Mommeeee!'

'Don't touch him!' Ellen stepped back with him, but the elevator door was closed behind her. Will cried louder, and she whirled round holding him tight, looking for the emergency exit, but one of the FBI agents grabbed her elbow, and Special Agent Manning wrenched Will from her arms. 'He's my son!' she screamed, suddenly empty-handed.

Will wailed louder. 'MOMMEE!'

'We're moving, people!' Special Agent Manning called out, carrying a hysterical Will out towards the exit.

'No!' Ellen screamed, trying to grab Will's foot but coming away with his blue sock. 'Will! It's all right!'

'MOMMEEEE!' Will's eyes widened with fright, and he reached for her over the FBI agent's shoulder, his bandaged head bobbing as they swept him through the entrance hall in a moving phalanx.

'WILL!' Ellen lunged after them, but two cops held her back, and she fought them while Officer Halbert tried to get her attention.

'Ms Gleeson, please stay here. Please, stop. Don't make us arrest you.'

'MOMMEE, COME!' Will screamed, before the hospital doors slid closed behind him and a thousand light bulbs went off.

'Let me go, you bastards!' Ellen screamed, out of control. She couldn't stop screaming. She couldn't breathe. The room spun round, a blur of polished floors, shocked faces, camera flashes. She felt as if she were going crazy. She flailed out with the court papers, then her open hand.

'Ellen, no!' a man called out, and the next thing she knew, Marcelo appeared next to the cops, and she reached for him.

'Marcelo! They took Will! Call Ron Halpren! Call Ron!'

'Let her go!' Marcelo shoved the cops aside. 'Are you guys insane? You're hurting her! I have her, I've got her now.'

'She has to let the kid go!' one of the cops shouted.

'She did! What, are you trying to kill her?' Marcelo circled an arm round Ellen and, in one sure motion, ran her away from the cops and the entrance. She half stumbled and half sagged against him, her brain finally giving up and her heart taking over.

'WILL!' She heard herself howl at the top of her lungs.

Ellen screamed again but Marcelo kept her from falling, and suddenly security guards in dark blue uniforms were running beside them and Marcelo said something to them, and they all ran down a shiny hallway until they hit doors and freezing air and a parking lot and a red-lighted sign that read EMERGENCY, and there was a maroon car with the engine running and another security guard in the driver's seat.

Marcelo shoved her into the back seat and she landed screaming with her wet face and snotty nose against the cold leather seat and Marcelo threw himself in after her, holding her from behind as she fought and howled and choked and cried, and the car lurched finally off.

**W**hen Ellen woke, she was lying in her clothes in a bedroom she didn't recognise, and Marcelo was sitting at the end of the bed, holding her hand. Her head felt fuzzy and strange. The room was dark. The wood blinds were closed, the walls covered with black-and-white photographs.

Marcelo focused on her, a tiny frown creasing his forehead. His expression looked strained, the corners of his lips turned down. He had on an open white shirt. 'You awake?' he asked softly.

'What time is it?'

Marcelo's gaze shifted left, then back again, presumably to check a bedside clock. 'Seven thirty at night. You've been asleep since this morning.'

Ellen tried to understand. 'I slept the whole day?'

'You needed to.'

'Where am I? I feel funny.'

'You're at my house, and you took a Valium. You were so . . . upset. I offered one to you, and you said yes.'

'Why do you have Valium?'

'An old girlfriend. The relationship expired, but the pills didn't.' Marcelo smiled. Ellen sensed from under her pharmaceutical cloud that he was trying to cheer her up. She didn't dare rewind the day's events to remember why she was here. She knew, but didn't want to know.

'Why did you bring me here and not home?'

'Your house was a crime scene. Though it's since been released. Also, there was press out front.'

'Who did we send?'

'Sal.'

Ellen lifted an eyebrow. 'Just so it's not Sarah. She's the one who called the Bravermans, you know, for the reward.'

'I heard from the police.' Marcelo's smile vanished. 'Which would probably explain why she quit the other day. No notice, nothing.'

'Did she say she didn't need to work, because she's rich now?'

'No, she said I was the worst editor in the country and I was just'— Marcelo paused a minute, smiling—'a pretty boy.'

'She said that?'

'It's not that funny. I am pretty.' Marcelo stroked Ellen's cheek.

'Do you have another pill?'

'Yes, but I don't think you should take it yet. Your lawyer's here. Ron. You asked me to call him, and he came over at the end of the day.'

'He's here?' Ellen started to get up, but Marcelo gentled her down.

'Stay put. I'll have him come up.' He rose and left the room and, in the next minute, footsteps scuffed on the stair and Marcelo came back into the room, followed by Ron Halpren, in a dark suit and tie.

'Hi, Ron,' Ellen said. 'Please don't say anything nice or I'll lose it.'

'Fair enough.' Ron sat down on the bed, his crinkly eyes soft.

'Also don't look at me like that.'

Ron chuckled, sadly. 'OK, I'll be the lawyer, not the friend. I heard what happened, I read the court papers they gave you at the hospital.'

Ellen thought back. 'So is there anything I can do?'

Ron hesitated. 'Nothing.'

Ellen tried to stay in control. 'I mean, just about the timing.'

'It doesn't work that way, at least not with Braverman. I spoke with Mike Cusack, a big gun at Morgan, Lewis. As a legal matter, you can make a transition only if they agree, and they're not agreeing. They don't trust you or the situation.'

'It's not about me.'

'I know that, and you should hold on to that thought. It's not personal.' Ron patted her hand. 'Braverman has to go home and bury his wife, and his lawyer says that he wants to start over. Pick up the pieces.'

Ellen's heart sank. 'I can see that, but what if that's not what's best for Will? Sending Will into a funeral, his father a grieving widower.'

'You're talking best interests again, and remember, that's not the law. It's a power notion. Braverman has absolute power and he's wielding it.' Ron's gaze rested on hers. 'I think you need to pick up the pieces, too. You need to understand that Will will be loved and very well cared for. They already contacted a paediatrician and a therapist.'

Ellen felt tears fighting to surface, but held them back.

'We have no choice, and he will be fine, in the end.' Ron patted her hand, then squeezed it, as Marcelo left the bedroom for a minute, then came back with a glass of water.

'Have another pill,' he said, offering her the tablet in his open palm, and Ellen raised herself, popped the Valium and drank the water.

'Ron, can I call Will? Can I talk to him at least?'

'No.' Ron shook his head. 'They think a clean break is best.'

Ellen hoped the pill worked fast. 'Where is he now, do you think?'

'Will? In the city, still. They'll be in town until the coroner releases Carol Braverman's body.'

Ellen felt a pang. 'When will that be?'

'A couple of days.'

'So, knowing Bill, they're at the Ritz or Four Seasons. I say the Ritz.'

'I say the Four Seasons,' Marcelo said, but Ron frowned.

'Don't even think about it, either of you. Cusack told me if you try to see Will, they'll take out a restraining order.'

Ellen tried to process it. 'I really can't call Will?'

'No. Their child therapist said it would be confusing for him and prevent his bonding with his father again.'

'An expert said that?'

'You can find an expert to say anything.'

'Then we should find our own expert.'

Ron shook his head. 'No, there's no trial here, and no judge. They won. On the good-news front, I asked if they'd give you an update on his condition, physical and emotional, next week, and they agreed.'

'Big of them.' Ellen felt anger flare up, muted by the drug.

'We'll take what we can get and go from there.' Ron rose. 'Call me if you have any questions. Hang in there. I'll be thinking of you.'

'Thanks.' Ellen watched Ron go to the door, followed by Marcelo. They walked down the steps and, in time, Marcelo came back upstairs.

'Thank you for being so nice.'

'Ron's right, you have to pick up the pieces. I'll help.'

'You don't have to.'

'I want to. I'm privileged to.' Marcelo stroked her arm.

Ellen felt her body relax. 'Am I staying here tonight?'

'Yes.'

'Where are you sleeping?'

'You tell me. I have a spare room, but I'd like to stay here with you.'

Ellen's head started to fog. 'Is this a date?'

'We're beyond dates.'

Ellen closed her eyes. She liked Marcelo's voice, nice and deep, and the accent that made his words sibilant, his speech more like a purr than words. 'But what about work? I mean, you're my editor.'

'We'll figure it out.'

'You were so worried about that, before.'

'Let's just say that since then, I've got a better perspective.'

And whether Marcelo kissed Ellen on the cheek or she just dreamed it, she couldn't tell.

Ellen woke up, and the bedroom was still dark. She was lying on top of the bedspread in her clothes, and Marcelo was spooning her, fully clothed, his arm hooked over her waist. The bedside clock glowed 03:46, and she waited for sleep to return, but it was as if a switch had been thrown in her brain. A light seared through the dark room of her mind, illuminating every corner, flooding every crack in the plaster, filling the grain in the floorboards, setting even the dust motes ablaze.

*Will is gone.*

Ellen imagined him in a hotel. He'd be wondering where she was, what had happened, why he wasn't home. Bill would be calling him Timothy and smiling in his face, and there would be lawyers and paediatricians and shrinks, but there would be no mother. His world had been turned upside-down and stood on its head. He'd gone from life with a mother and no father, to a life with a father and no mother.

*He's just a little boy.*

Ellen knew what she had to do next, or tears would engulf her. She plucked Marcelo's hand from her hip, edged towards the side of the bed and rolled out as quietly as she could. She padded downstairs in the dark, running her fingertips along the rough brick wall to guide her. Her feet hit the floor, and she crossed the room to the glass coffee table, where she knew Marcelo's laptop permanently sat, lid open. She hit a key. The screen saver appeared.

She opened Microsoft Word and pressed a key, so that a bright white page popped onto the screen, then slid the laptop round and sat down on the couch, pausing a second before she began. The title came easily.

## Losing Will

She swallowed hard, then set her feelings aside. She had to do this for her job. And for Marcelo. And mostly, for herself. Writing had always helped her, before. It clarified her feelings and thoughts, and she never felt as if she could understand something fully until she'd written about it. In fact, it was writing that began her relationship to Will, and she found herself coming full circle again, so she began:

Last week, I was asked to write a story about what it feels like to lose a child. We were concerned that, among all the statistics attending an article about the city's escalating homicide rate, the value of a child's life would be lost. So I set out to interview women who had lost children.

I spoke to Laticia Williams, whose eight-year-old son Lateef was killed by stray bullets, a victim of violence between two gangs. I also spoke to Susan Sulaman, whose two children were abducted by their father several years ago. And, as you may know, I lost my son this week when I learned that my adoption of him was illegal. My son is, in fact, a child by the name of Timothy Braverman, who was kidnapped from a Florida couple two years ago.

I know that my child is alive, unlike Laticia Williams. But forgive me if I suggest that how you lose a child doesn't alter the fact that he is lost to you. Whether you lose him by murder, abduction or a simple twist of fate, you end up in the same place.

Your child is gone.

What does it feel like?

To Laticia Williams, it feels like anger. A rage like a fire that consumes everything in its path. She feels angry every minute she spends without her child. Angry every night she doesn't put him to bed. Angry every morning that she doesn't pack him his favourite peanut-butter-and-banana sandwich and walk him to school. In her neighbourhood, all the mothers walk their kids to school, to make sure they get there alive.

Of course, that the children remain alive after they get home is not guaranteed. Her son was shot in his own living room by bullets that flew through a window to find their lethal mark. The funeral director who prepared Lateef's body for burial took all night to restore the child's face. His teacher said Teef was the class clown, a leader among the classmates who stuffed his desk with posthumous Valentines.

To Susan Sulaman, losing a child feels like emptiness. A profound vacancy in her heart and her life. Because her children are alive with their father, or so she assumes, she looks for them everywhere she goes. At night, she drives round neighbourhoods where they might live, hoping for a chance sighting. In the daytime, she scans the small faces on school buses that speed past. Susan Sulaman is haunted by her loss.

I asked her if she felt better knowing that at least the children were in their father's hands. Her answer? 'No. I'm their mother. They need me.'

I know just how she feels, and Laticia, too. I'm angry, I feel haunted, and it's still fresh. It's so new, a wound still bleeding, the flesh torn apart, the gash swollen and puffy, yet to be sewn together or grafted; years from scar tissue, bumpy and hard.

Losing Will feels like a death. My mother died recently, and it feels a lot like that. Suddenly, someone who was at the centre of your life is gone, excised as quickly as an apple is cored, a sharp spike driven down the centre of your world, then a cruel flick of the wrist and the almost surgical extraction of your very heart.

And like a death, it does not end the relationship.

I am still the daughter of my mother, though she is gone. And I am still the mother of Will Gleeson, though he is gone, too.

I have learned that the love a mother has for her child is unique among human emotions. And it remains true, whether the child is adopted or not. Just as it doesn't matter how you lose your child, it doesn't matter how you find him, either.

I didn't give birth to Will, but I am tied to him as surely as if we shared blood. I am his real mother. It's the love, that binds.

And though, as his mother, I certainly felt tired at times, I never tired of looking at him. I never tired of watching him eat. I never tired of hearing the sound of his voice or the words he made up, like the name of our cat. I never tired of seeing him play with Lego.

It's hard to compare loves, and it may be silly to try, but I have learned something from my experience in losing Will. Because I have loved before, certainly. I have loved men before, and I might even be falling in love with a man now.

Here is how a mother's love is different:

You may fall out of love with a man.

But you will never fall out of love with your child.

Even after he is gone.

Ellen sat back and read the last line again, but it began to blur, and she knew why.

'Ellen?' Marcelo asked softly, coming down the stairs.

'I finished my piece.' She wiped her eyes with her hand, and Marcelo crossed to her through the darkness, his mouth a concerned shadow in the glow of the screen. He reached for her hand.

'Come and lie down,' he whispered, pulling her gently to her feet.

# CHAPTER TEN

THE NEXT MORNING dawned clear, and Ellen rode in the passenger seat of Marcelo's car, squinting against the brightness of the sun on the new-fallen snow.

Last night after she'd finished her piece, she'd fallen back into a restless sleep and felt raw and nervous. A morning shower had helped, and she'd changed her top, slipping into an old grey sweater of Marcelo's. Her hair was still wet, falling loose to her shoulders, and she didn't bother with make-up. She took it as a measure of confidence in her new relationship, and she didn't want to see her face in the mirror, anyway.

'I should call my father,' Ellen said, mentally switching topics.

'Your phone's in your handbag. I charged it for you.'

'Thanks. I feel bad that I didn't call Connie, either.'

'She called you, and I spoke to her. She's meeting us at your house. I hope that's OK with you. She thought it would be.'

'It is, sure.' Ellen felt her heart gladden. 'How is she? Is she OK?'

'She's very upset, but I think it will do you good to see her.' Marcelo swung the car onto her street, and Ellen swallowed hard. Newsvans parked in every available space, with microwave towers that pierced the blue sky. Reporters with video cameras mobbed her sidewalk.

Ellen said, 'I hate the press.'

'Me, too. Looks like national, too, and TV.' Marcelo craned his neck as they neared the house. 'I'll let you read Sal's piece before we file.'

'You filing this afternoon, by two?'

'It can wait. I'll email it to you.'

'Thanks. Come in and meet Connie, then I think I'll be OK.' They approached the house. Her neighbour Mrs Knox was out front, shovelling her walk for her. Maybe she wasn't such a busybody, after all.

'Here we go.' Marcelo pulled up, double-parked, and hit the emergency lights. 'We'll have to do this fast.'

'OK.' Ellen grabbed her handbag, and they both opened their doors and jumped out. Ellen hustled round the front of the car, almost slipping on the snow, and Marcelo took her arm and they hurried together to her front walk. The reporters surged towards them almost as one, brandishing microphones, aiming video cameras and shouting questions.

'Ellen, when did you know he was Timothy Braverman?' 'Ellen, were you gonna give him back?' 'Hey, El, how did the FBI find out who your son was?' 'Marcelo, give us a break! You're one of us!'

Ellen hurried up her walk with Marcelo right behind her, keeping the press at bay. She ran up the porch steps, spraying snow, and crossed to the front door, which Connie opened for her.

'Connie!' she cried, more in anguish than in greeting, and the women fell into each other's arms.

After Marcelo had gone home, Ellen sat with Connie in the living room, telling her everything while they shared a box of tissues, and they cried all over again when they came to the same awful conclusion, that Will was gone from both their lives.

Ellen stroked Oreo Figaro, who sat on her lap. 'You were the best baby sitter I could have ever asked for. You can't imagine how grateful I am. I could never have done my job without you, and I needed to do my job. For Will and for me. You know, I used to be a little jealous of your time with Will. Of how close you were. It threatened me.

'I'm sorry about that, because now I know better. The more people who loved that boy, the better. We loved him up, really, between the two of us. I used to think that kids were like a glass or something, that they'd break if you poured too much love into them. But they're like the ocean. You can fill them up with love, and just when you think you've reached the brim, you can keep on pouring.'

Connie sniffled. 'I agree, but here's the thing. Will may have loved me, but he always knew who his mother was. He knew the difference between you and me, and he never forgot it.'

'Thanks.' Ellen set the cat aside on the couch and rose slowly. 'Well, I guess I have to go see what the kitchen looks like.'

'No, you don't.' Connie wiped her eyes with finality. 'I went in there. It made me sick to see it, and it'll make you even sicker.'

'I have to live here. I thought about moving, but no way.' Ellen walked into the dining room, which was still in disarray. She picked up a chair from the floor and slid it noisily into place under the table, feeling the beginning of an odd sort of satisfaction. Maybe this was what everybody meant by picking up the pieces. She took a deep breath, braced herself and headed for the kitchen. 'Let's see how bad it is.'

'Right behind you,' Connie said.

*My God.* Ellen supported herself against the doorjamb, scanning the scene. A large, shiny pool of black-red blood had dried into the floorboards. It must have been where Carol had died. Across the room lay another island of blood, smaller but just as nauseating, where Moore must have fallen. The stink of gasoline hung in the air, and a dozen yellow spots stained the floor where the solvent had splattered.

Ellen bit her lip, thinking. 'Do you think I can scrub the blood out?'

'No, and I swear I smell it.'

'There's only one solution.' Ellen crossed to the window and opened it, then fumbled round for the metal slides and threw open the storm windows, letting in a blast of fresh, snowy air that somehow felt cleansing. 'I'm going to rip up the whole damn floor.'

'You mean do it yourself?' Connie smiled, surprised.

'Sure. How hard can it be? It's just destruction. Any idiot can destroy something.' Ellen went to the base cabinet, found her toolbox and took out her hammer. 'If I start now, I can get it done by tonight.'

'You want to do it *now*?'

'Why not? One way or the other, this floor is getting thrown away. I don't want it in my house another minute.' Ellen took a gulp of fresh air, raised the hammer high over her head and brought its claw end down with all her might.

*Crack!* The edge of the hammer splintered the wood, but unfortunately embedded itself there.

'Oops.' Ellen yanked on the handle of the hammer and its head came free, splintering the wood. 'Looks like it works, but at this rate, I'll only be finished by next year.'

Connie opened the door to the basement and went downstairs. By the time she returned, Ellen had destroyed only part of a single floorboard. She looked up to see Connie hoisting a crowbar.

'Way to go!' Ellen said. 'I didn't even know I had one of those. Thanks.' She reached for the crowbar, but Connie held it tight.

'I'll use this. You use the hammer. We'll get this done together. It'll go twice as fast, and besides, I wanna destroy something, too.' Connie got down on her hands and knees, then wedged the end of the crowbar underneath the splintered floor.

The two women worked together for the next several hours, grimly destroying the evidence of a nightmare, with the only tools they had on hand. A hammer, a crowbar and the human heart.

After Connie had gone home, Ellen piled the last of the broken floorboards on her back porch because reporters were still camped out front. She stepped back inside the kitchen. The gasoline smell was gone, but the subfloor was a mess.

She checked the clock on the wall—2.25 p.m. Odd that Marcelo hadn't called, and she had yet to call her father. She went into the living room, found her handbag and dug inside for her BlackBerry, but it wasn't there. She must have dropped it in Marcelo's car.

She looked up, aggravated, and through the windows she could see a commotion on the sidewalk. Reporters and photographers clustered round a taxi pulling up in front of the house and, in the next second, emerging from the crowd was her father.

Ellen ran to the door as he waved off the press, taking the arm of an attractive woman in a chic white wool coat, presumably his new wife.

'Honey, what the hell?' her father asked, stepping inside, his hazel eyes round with disbelief. 'This is crazy!'

'I know, it's awful.' Ellen introduced herself and extended her hand to his wife. 'Barbara, right?'

'Hello, Ellen.' Barbara smiled with genuine warmth, her lipstick fresh and her teeth white and even. She was petite with smallish features, tasteful make-up and highlighted hair coiffed to her chin. 'I'm so sorry we have to meet in these circumstances.'

'Why didn't you call?' her father interrupted. 'Thank God for the Internet, or we wouldn't have known a damn thing. We're in the hotel, and I went online to check the scores, and there's my daughter's picture and my grandson's gone! We got on the next plane.'

'Why don't you go sit down, and I'll explain everything.' Ellen gestured them towards the couch, but her father waved her off, agitated.

'I remember when you came to see me, you thought that kid in the picture was Will. So I got it wrong. Ya happy now?'

'What?' Ellen asked, stricken.

'Don!' Barbara shouted, so loudly that he stood stunned for a moment. 'Shut up. Right now.' She faced him head-on, despite her tiny frame. 'I can't believe what I'm seeing. I can't believe this is the man I just married. I know you're a better man than this.'

'Wha—?' her father said, but accusation had left his tone.

'This isn't about you, or even Will.' Barbara raised a manicured hand. 'This is about your daughter, your only daughter. Start focusing on the child you have, instead of the one you don't.'

'But she shouldn'ta said anything. She shoulda just shut up!'

Ellen felt slapped, and Barbara's mouth dropped open.

'Don, she did what any good mother would do. She did what was right for her child, even though it cost her.'

Her father's gaze shifted from Barbara to Ellen, suddenly very sad. He raked his thin hair with trembling fingers. 'Sorry, El. I didn't mean it.'

'I know, Dad.'

'It's just that Will was my . . . chance.'

'What do you mean?' Ellen asked, mystified, and tears came to her father's eyes. The only other time she'd seen him cry was at her mother's funeral, and the sight caught her by the throat.

'He was my chance, El. My second chance.'

Ellen touched his arm, sensing what he'd say before he said it. She gave him a big hug, and he eased into her arms, with a little moan.

'Everything I did wrong with you, I was gonna do right with him. I wanted to make it up to you. To your mother.'

Ellen thought her heart would break, and in the next minute, her eyes brimmed with tears, and she found herself crying like a baby in her father's arms.

'I'm so sorry, honey,' he whispered as Ellen sobbed and breathed in his expensive aftershave, and she drew real comfort from his embrace in a way she never had before. The deepest pain in her heart eased just a little, and she let herself feel how very powerful is something so simple, yet so profound, as a father's love.

And she thanked God he was alive.

**I**t wasn't until they had gone and Ellen was rinsing their coffee mugs that the phone rang in the kitchen. She crossed the room and checked caller ID, which showed the newspaper's main number. She picked up. 'Hello?'

'Ellen?' Marcelo asked. 'Are you OK? I've been calling your cell.'

'I think I left it in your car. I was going to call you, but my father and my new stepmother just left.'

'How are you?'

'Good, OK. You probably want me to look at that story, huh?'

'Only if you feel up to it.'

'I'm not sure.'

'Then let it go. I loved what you wrote for the homicide piece.'

'Good, thanks.' Ellen felt a warmth she couldn't deny.

'I'll be done here around nine. Happily, there's news besides you.'

'You'd never know it from the crowd outside.'

'Would you like company tonight? You shouldn't be alone.'

'I'd like that.'

'I'll be there. Take care of yourself, 'til then.'

'See you.' Ellen hung up, left the kitchen and climbed the stairs. She reached the top of the stairs, which ended in front of Will's room, and faced his closed door. She opened the door, and the Cheerios-and-Play-

Doh smell caught her by the throat. She didn't know how long she stood there, but long enough for the daylight to leak away, so stuffed animals dematerialised into shadowy blobs and the spines of books thinned to straight black lines. Stars glowed faintly from the ceiling, and took her back to the countless nights she'd held him before bed, reading to him, talking or just listening to his adorable up-and-down cadence, the music of his stories from school or swimming, told in his little-boy register, like the sweetest of piccolos.

She watched almost numbly as Oreo Figaro leapt noiselessly onto the foot of Will's bed, where he always slept, curled next to a floppy stuffed bunny whose ears were silhouetted in the soft light from the window. Will had got that bunny at a party that Courtney had thrown for her at work, when she adopted him. Sarah Liu had given it to him.

Anger flickered in Ellen's chest. Sarah, who was supposed to be her colleague. Sarah, who would later sell both of them out, for money. Sarah, who stole from her the choice about when or whether to give Will up. He could be here right now, home where he belonged, cuddled up with his cat, instead of in a strange hotel room, lost and confused, in all kinds of pain, going home to a house without a mother.

'You bitch!' Ellen heard herself shout. In one movement, she lunged into the room, grabbed the stuffed bunny and hurled it into the bookshelves, where it hit a toy car. Oreo Figaro leapt from the bed, startled.

Anger flamed in Ellen's chest, and she hurried from the room.

Ellen stood on a snowy brick doorstep and knocked on the front door of the gorgeous Dutch Colonial. The ride to Radnor hadn't dissipated her anger, even with newsvans trailing her, and she knocked again on the door, drenched in the calcium white light of the cameras' klieg lights. Reporters recorded her every movement, but she didn't care. They were doing their job, and she was doing hers.

'Hello?' Sarah opened the front door, and her dark eyes flared in alarm. She shielded her eyes from the lights with a raised hand. 'What are you doing here?'

'Let me in. We're on TV, girlfriend.'

'You have no right to come here!' Sarah tried to shut the front door, but Ellen straight-armed it open.

'Thanks, don't mind if I do.' She powered over the threshold into a warm, well-appointed living room, where two young boys were sitting on the floor, playing a noisy video game on a wide-screen TV.

'Boys, go to your room,' Sarah said, staccato, and they set down the game controllers and rose instantly, astounding Ellen. She couldn't get that kind of obedience from her hair, much less her son. They left the room, and Sarah switched off the TV.

'Sarah, how could you do it?' Ellen kept her temper in check. 'Not just to me, but to Will? How could you do that to Will?'

'I didn't do anything to him, nothing wrong anyway.' Sarah edged backwards, tugging at the hem of her skinny black sweater. 'Your son is where he belongs, with his real parents.' Sarah didn't look regretful in the least, her mouth tight. 'I did the right thing.'

'You didn't do it because it was the right thing. You did it for the money.' Ellen took a step closer, fighting the impulse to hit Sarah in the face. 'You couldn't wait to quit your job, now that you're rich.'

'It doesn't matter why I did it, what matters is that he wasn't legally yours. He was Timothy Braverman.'

'I might have told them, but you took it out of my hands.'

'No, you wouldn't have. No mother would.'

'Maybe you wouldn't, but I might have and, because of you, Will was taken in the worst possible way.' Ellen's anger bubbled to the surface. 'No explanation, no phasing in, just *taken*. It's the kind of thing that can mess him up for life.'

'He wasn't your son. He was their son.'

'He was *my* son until I said different.' Ellen felt angry tears, and at some level, even she knew she was yelling at the wrong person. She wasn't angry at Sarah, she was angry at everyone and everything. 'I would never do anything to hurt your children, no matter what.'

'You're not worried about Will. You're worried about yourself.'

'You know what, you're right. I love my son and I want him home and I'm never going to have him again. But most of all, I want him to be happy. If he's happy, I'm happy, and thanks to you, he's in pain and—'

There was a noise behind them, from the other end of the living room, and Ellen turned round, shocked at the sight. It was Myron Krims, Sarah's husband, but he was in a wheelchair. She had met him only once, years ago, and he had been walking fine. Then he was one of the top thoracic surgeons in the city, but now he was clearly ill. His black sweater and khakis were swimming on him, and his hair had gone completely grey. Circles ringed his eyes, and his aspect looked vague.

'Dear?' Myron asked, his voice shaky. 'I've been calling you.'

'Excuse me.' Sarah hurried to her husband, and Ellen watched as she bent over him, whispered in his ear, then wheeled him out of the room. Sarah returned, her face a tight mask. 'So. Now you see.'

For a moment, Ellen didn't know what to say. 'I had no idea.'

'We don't advertise.'

'What happened?'

'He has MS.' Sarah straightened a suede cushion that didn't require it.

'For how long?'

'For the rest of his life.'

Ellen reddened. 'I mean, how long has this been going on?'

All this time Ellen had thought she was the only one on a single income, but she'd been wrong.

'I was doing what was right for my family.' Sarah's voice remained controlled, and her gaze unwavering. 'I was doing what I had to do.'

'You could have told me. You could have warned me.'

'What would you have said? Don't take the money? It was my family or your family. I chose my family. You would have done the same.'

Ellen couldn't tell what she would have done in Sarah's position. She knew only that Will was gone, and there was a deep rent in her chest where her heart had been. Her shoulders sagged, and she felt herself sinking onto the couch. Her face dropped into her hands, and in the next second, the seat cushion dipped down as Sarah sat beside her.

'I tell you this,' Sarah whispered. 'I am sorry.'

And at that, Ellen let slip the few tears she had left.

Ellen got home, hollow and spent, raw and aching. She tossed her handbag and keys on the window seat, took off her coat and hung it up, and went upstairs to read Sal's piece.

She went into her office, flicked on a light and crossed to the computer. She sat down and moved the mouse, and her computer monitor woke up with a screen saver of Will posing with Oreo Figaro.

*Please, no.*

She opened up Outlook and watched the names pile into the In-box. She waited for Marcelo's email to load and braced herself to read the article. But Marcelo's wasn't the email that caught her eye. She moved the mouse, clicked on another email and opened it, reading quickly. And then she screamed.

And when she stopped screaming, she reached for the phone.

Ellen hurried from the waiting room behind Special Agent Orr, passing the thick gold seal of the FBI, the framed picture of the president and the attorney general, and the Ten Most Wanted posters. She followed Special Agent Orr down the glistening hallway and reached a wooden door with a plaque that read CONFERENCE ROOM.

Special Agent Orr twisted the knob. 'Here you go, Ms Gleeson,' he said, admitting her, then leaving.

Ellen stepped inside, getting her bearings. She had driven the far-thest to get here, so they were all already in place. Special Agent Manning stood up at the head of the table, and on the nearside, Ron Halpren stood up, too, with an uncertain smile. He was dressed in a tux from a benefit dinner, and Ellen shook his hand.

'Sorry to disrupt your night, gentlemen,' she said, sitting down next to Ron. She nodded at Special Agent Manning, who retook his seat at the head of the table. 'Thank you, too, Special Agent.'

'It's my job.' His smile was only polite and he was dressed casually, with a blue FBI windbreaker over a light Oxford shirt. Behind him was a large smoked-glass window that overlooked the snowy city at night. 'I just hope this isn't a wild-goose chase.'

'It isn't.' Ellen looked at the other side of the table, where Bill Braverman sat glaring in a sports jacket and polo shirt, next to his lawyer, Mike Cusack, who dressed like him.

'So why are we all here?' Bill demanded, his eyes flashing with anger.

Ellen composed herself, folding her hands on the conference table, and took a deep breath. She was about to drop a bomb, and she met Bill's eye with sympathy. 'The fact is, you're not Will's father.'

'That's a lie!' Bill shot back. 'You're insulting me *and* my wife!'

Cusack placed a restraining hand on Bill's arm. 'Please, allow me.'

'Why should I?' Bill tore his arm away, glaring at Ellen. 'You don't fool me for one minute! What kind of scam is this?'

'Ms Gleeson,' Cusack broke in, looking askance. 'You should be aware that intentional infliction of emotional distress is civilly action-able, and we won't hesitate to file suit against you.'

Ron frowned. 'I won't let you threaten her, Mike.'

Special Agent Manning cleared his throat. 'Let's settle down and let Ms Gleeson tell us what this is all about.'

'Thank you.' Ellen gathered her thoughts. 'To make a long story short, when I was in Miami, I got DNA samples from both Carol and Bill Braverman. I followed them to a restaurant, and I collected some cigarette butts that Bill left in an ashtray—'

'You did *what*?' Bill interjected.

'—I also got a Diet Sprite can that Carol drank from, and I sent them both to a lab that I found on the Internet.'

'This is ridiculous!' Bill slammed the table with a heavy hand.

'I got the results emailed to me, and Ron has forwarded the email with the results to you. Honestly, I'd forgotten about the tests, and I had no doubt that Will was really Timothy, after that night in my kitchen. Rob Moore said that his girlfriend was Amy Martin, and I knew that

Amy was the one who put Will, or Timothy, up for adoption. The results of the test came back, and they show that Carol was Will's biological mother. But Will has none of Bill's DNA. Bill is not Will's father.'

'You're saying that Carol cheated on me?' Bill's eyes flew open.

'I'm sorry, she must have.' Ellen felt terrible for him, but still. 'You said your marriage wasn't the best.'

'She wouldn't!' Bill flushed red. 'She didn't, and she certainly wouldn't fool me into thinking another man's child was mine!'

'I'm sorry, I really am.' Ellen took a second to compose herself, then said the words she'd been rehearsing all the way here. 'Will is not your son, so you have no legal right to him. My adoption remains legal, and I want my son back.'

Ron added, 'My research showed the law would be the same in almost all jurisdictions, including Florida. As Carol has no living parents, Ellen is entitled to keep Will.'

'This is a trick!' Bill shouted, jumping to his feet.

'Based on an *Internet* DNA test?' Cusack remained in his chair, his expression only slightly less hostile. 'What do you take us for?'

Manning waved Bill into his seat, and he complied, albeit angrily.

'It's a legitimate lab,' Ellen said, willing herself to remain calm. She had discussed the way this meeting would go with Ron, who had been her first phone call after she read the email. 'But if you want to run another test to confirm the results, you're welcome to.'

'I'm *welcome to*?' Bill repeated, incredulous.

'I will agree to a lab of the FBI's choosing, with the test to be administered under their supervision.'

'I won't take any damn DNA test!' Bill's jaw set with determination. 'Timothy's *my* son, and I'm keeping him!'

Ron raised a finger. 'As a legal matter, we could require you to take a DNA test. If we take this matter to court, any judge would order you to do so. In fact, bear with me.' Ron reached into a briefcase sitting on the floor, extracted some papers and handed them to Special Agent Manning, Bill and Cusack. 'These papers are ready to file. I have an emergency judge standing by. It's your choice, Mr Braverman. If you and Will don't voluntarily take the DNA test, the court will order you to do so. I'll also ask the court to place Will in protective custody in the interim, so that you don't leave the jurisdiction with him.'

'You *have* to be kidding!' Bill grabbed the papers and skimmed the front page, his eyes darting rapidly, his mouth pursed in fury.

But Ellen could see Cusack, sitting next to him and reading the papers, lifting his eyebrow.

Ron added, 'Mike, if you'd like a minute alone with your client, Ellen and I would be happy to step outside.'

Cusack looked up after a minute, deep in thought. 'Yes, thank you. I'd like to confer with my client.'

Ellen and Ron rose from the table, left the conference room and went into the hallway, where they closed the door behind them.

Fifteen endless minutes later, the door to the conference room opened and Special Agent Manning stuck out his head. 'We're ready for you,' he said simply.

**E**llen filed back into the conference room with Ron behind her and took her seat at the table across from Cusack. Bill had deserted his chair but was standing by the window, his arms folded and his expression grim. Ellen saw the strain round his eyes and knew that he was more anguished than angry, and her heart went out to him.

Cusack began, 'We've decided, in a spirit of cooperation, to undertake a DNA test. The FBI has recommended a lab that it uses all the time, and we'll be taking the samples of Bill and Timothy tonight.'

'We'll fast-track it,' Special Agent Manning interjected. 'We should have the results by Monday.'

Cusack continued, 'However, we don't believe it's necessary to place Timothy in protective custody with the Bureau, pending the results. Timothy is at the Four Seasons with a baby sitter who comes highly recommended. Bill would like to keep the boy with him at the hotel and he won't leave the jurisdiction. We trust you'll agree.'

'What do you want to do, Ellen?' Ron asked. 'You can leave him with Bill, or the FBI can make him comfortable in a hotel.'

Ellen's eyes met Bill's from across the room, and she felt their shared bond. 'I trust that Bill will take care of him, and right now, that's what's best for him. I don't want to disrupt him again if the test is wrong.'

'Thanks,' Cusack said, and Ron nodded.

But Bill didn't reply, just turned away and gazed out of the window into the cold, dark night. He was facing the prospect of losing his son.

And Ellen knew exactly how he felt.

**A** new snow had fallen, covering the minivans, swing sets and lawn furniture in pristine white. The afternoon sky was sunny and bright blue, and the wind frigid and fresh. Ellen breathed it in, standing on her porch with no coat like a crazy lady, folding her arms against her chest.

'Ellen, we could wait inside,' Marcelo said, standing on her right.

'Nah, let's stay here,' her father said, on her left.

'I agree,' Barbara said, next to her father in her lovely white coat.

Behind them, Connie stood with her husband, Chuck. She said, 'Wild horses couldn't drag me off this porch.'

They all smiled, Ellen most of all, despite the reporters, TV anchorpersons and photographers who mobbed the sidewalk in front of her house and spilled into the street, shouting questions, taking videos and pictures, and requiring five uniformed cops to keep traffic moving.

Marcelo smiled, puzzled. 'Let me get this straight. It's freezing outside, but we're on the porch?'

'Right,' Ellen and her father answered in unison.

Marcelo threw an arm round her shoulder. 'You know what? I like it.'

'Good,' she said, snuggling against him.

Suddenly a black sedan turned onto the street, and Ellen felt her heart start to thunder. She stepped forward for a closer look, and the sedan slowed when it reached the photographers, who started hoisting video cameras to their shoulders. The sedan's emergency lights went on, flashing yellow as it braked in front of the house.

'My God,' Ellen said under her breath, already in motion, and the press surged forward, pointing their cameras and microphones to the sedan. The doors were opening, and Bill emerged from the driver's side and Cusack from the passenger's. Reporters swarmed round them with cameras and microphones, and Ellen ran down the front walk towards the crowd, and in the next instant she heard a little voice from its centre.

'Mommy! MOMMY!'

'WILL!' Ellen shouted, tears blurring her eyes as she hit the crowd and elbowed her way through, reaching the sedan just as Bill unlatched Will from the car seat and carried him through the reporters to her.

'MOMMY!' Will screamed, his arms reaching for her, and Ellen took him in her arms and hugged him so tightly she almost squished him.

'It's all right, it's all right now,' she said, as Will burst into tears and wrapped his arms round her neck. Reporters shouted questions and stuck cameras in their faces, but Ellen caught Bill's eye, and his expression was pained. She called to him, 'Want to come in, have a soda?'

'No, thanks,' he called back, then gestured at Will. 'I got him new shoes.'

'Thanks.' Ellen felt a stab of sympathy. 'Another time, then?'

'See you,' Bill said, his eyes on Will's back. Grief flickered through his expression, then he turned away amid the clicking cameras, and so did Ellen, with a guilt that swiftly vanished with happiness when Marcelo, her father and Chuck arrived at her side and ran interference as she held Will close and hurried back up her front walk, hustled across the porch to the open front door and swept inside the warm, snug house.

Will didn't touch the ground until half an hour later, after being passed from mother to grandfather to mother to new stepgrandmother to mother to Marcelo to Connie and Chuck then back again to Ellen, until he had stopped crying and everybody held him tight, kissed him too much, and reassured themselves by feeling his weight in their arms that he was, really, safely, and finally back home.

Ellen felt her heart truly at peace for the first time since she'd first seen that white card, so long ago. She set Will down in the living room, but, oddly, he frowned, even as he stood at the centre of an adoring circle. His glistening eyes scanned the room, ignoring the twisted streamers of green crepe, the green helium balloons on the ceiling and even the pile of wrapped gifts from a love-crazed family.

'What's the matter, sweetie?' Ellen asked, puzzled.

'Where's Oreo Figaro, Mommy?'

'Oh. He was here a minute ago,' Ellen answered, looking round and, in the next second, they both spotted the cat under the dining-room table, running from all the commotion.

'There he goes!' Will hollered, taking off after the cat, who bounded into the kitchen.

'Uh-oh.' Ellen went after Will, and everyone watched him, collectively holding their breaths. They had all discussed how he would react to seeing the kitchen again.

'Mommy!' Will hollered, surprised. 'Look in here!'

'I know, it's a surprise for you.' Ellen came up behind him and rested a hand on his head. She and Marcelo had worked in the kitchen all weekend, installing laminated wood over the subfloor and painting the walls to cover the bloodstains. The wall colour had been the easiest choice, although when sunlight flooded in through the back window, the room looked as if it was growing. She doubted she'd ever get used to a bright green kitchen, nor should she.

'It's my favourite!' Will exclaimed. 'Can I open my presents now?'

'Yes, but gimme a kiss first.' Ellen bent over, and Will threw his arms round her neck. If she was expecting a big reunion kiss, she wasn't getting one, not when there were gifts waiting to be unwrapped.

Ellen went to the cabinet and got a trash bag for the gift wrap, then straightened up, remembering that the last time she had stood here, she had killed a man. She turned to the wall where Moore had slid down.

A sudden flashback shot out of nowhere. Before her eyes, Moore slumped against the wall. Bright red blood spurted from a deep hole in his forehead. A crooked grin crossed his face.

Ellen froze, remembering. That smile was crooked because it turned down on the right. Like Will's.

She put it together, stunned. She hadn't noticed it then, because she was sure that Bill Braverman was Will's father. But now that she knew that he wasn't, the crooked grin assumed a new significance. Then she remembered what Moore had said that night to Carol.

'You shoulda said to him, "Honey, wifey-poo isn't the good girl you think."'

If Bill wasn't Will's father, she had at least a guess who was.

# EPILOGUE

ABOUT A YEAR LATER, there was another winter snow and another party with wrapped presents, balloons, and crepe streamers crisscrossing the living room, which this time was packed with noisy, sugar-fuelled classmates of Will's. They ran back and forth, played with new toys, ate cake, and generally wreaked havoc for his fourth birthday.

'Watch out!' Will shrieked, running with a new laser sword.

Ellen grabbed it. 'Don't run with this. You'll hurt somebody.'

'Aw, Mom!' Will took off after his friend Brett, and Ellen's father came over, his eyes glittering with mischief.

'I'll take that weapon, my lady.'

'What for?' Ellen handed it over.

'You'll see. This will do nicely.' Her father examined the laser sword, and Barbara joined him in her elegant white trouser-suit, a multi-coloured party hat perched atop her head.

'Ellen, don't let him have that. He'll embarrass us all.'

'Too late for that,' Ellen said with a smile. She had come to love Barbara, who wisely hadn't tried to replace her mother, because no one could. But somewhere along the line, she had opened her mind to the possibility that if you could love a child no matter how he came to you, then you could also love a mother, no matter how she came to you.

'I need this for my golf lesson.' Her father gestured across the crowded room to where Bill Braverman and his pretty date were talking with Connie and Chuck. Her father called to him, 'Bill, come here. I need your expertise.'

'Coming.' Bill strode over in his out-of-place linen jacket, trousers and tassel loafers, making his way through the kids and ruffling Will's hair.

'Look how fast I go, Bill!' Will called after him.

'Good for you!' Bill entered the dining room, grinning.

But her father was all business. 'Show me what you were saying before, about my grip.' Her father flipped the sword round so that the point faced the floor, then wrapped his fingers round the hilt, swinging it like a golf club. 'You said it was my elbow? Not tucked in enough?'

'Not exactly, let me show you.' Bill focused on his task.

Barbara moaned. 'Please, guys, anything but golf.'

'There is nothing but golf,' Bill said, smiling, then turned to Ellen. 'By the way, I have those papers for you to sign, for Will's trust. When he's of age, he can decide how much he wants to set aside for Charbonneau House.'

'Great, thanks.' Ellen smiled, and in the next second she felt an arm encircle her waist and tug her into the kitchen. Before she knew it, Marcelo had taken her into his arms, hugged her gently, and given her one of his best kisses.

'This is a wonderful party,' he purred into her ear. 'Very romantic.'

Ellen put her arms round him, stretching out her left hand over his shoulder. Her engagement ring sparkled prettily in the sunlight, and she never would have guessed that green would make such a nice backdrop for a diamond. Suddenly Will burst into the kitchen and stopped himself before he ran into them.

'Marcelo,' he said, looking up, 'are you gonna kiss Mommy?'

'If you say it's OK, Will.'

'Do it! She likes it!' Will hugged Marcelo round the leg, then ran out of the kitchen, and Ellen smiled.

'Good move, asking permission.'

'I know who the boss is.' Marcelo kissed her softly and sweetly, then whispered, '*Eu te amo.*'

And for that, Ellen didn't need a translation.

# Lisa Scottoline

Born and bred in Philadelphia, Lisa Scottoline went to the University of Pennsylvania to read English, specialising in contemporary American novels. She then went on to attend the University's Law School and, after graduation, landed a coveted clerkship with a state judge, before eventually joining a prestigious law firm as a litigator.

Although her career was on the right path, Lisa's home life was not. She had married, but the relationship fell apart shortly after the birth of her baby. Determined to raise her new daughter herself, she gave up the law to stay at home with her child, but she needed to find a way to pay the bills.

As she'd always been interested in writing and a big fan of the hot new writers, John Grisham and Scott Turow, Lisa realised that no women lawyers were writing legal thrillers and decided that there might be a gap in the market. Living a life financed solely by five Visa cards, she allowed herself three years or $35,000 worth of credit (whichever ran out first) to write and sell her first book. 'When I decided to try to become a writer, I did so to stay home with my baby daughter, Francesca, but I had always wanted to write a novel, and the more I thought about it, the more I wanted to give it a shot. So finally I did, and there followed years of rejection. My favourite rejection letter came from a New York agent who wrote: "We don't have time to take on any more clients, and if we did, we wouldn't take you." Ouch.' When the three years were up, Lisa Scottoline had one finished novel, a daughter starting school, and five maxed-out credit cards. Debt-ridden, she took a part-time job as clerk to a federal judge. Just a week later, her first book, *Everywhere That Mary Went*, was bought by a publisher. Critically acclaimed, it also went on to be nominated by the Mystery Writers of America for an Edgar Award, suspense fiction's premier honour. The very next year, Lisa's second novel, *Final Appeal*, was also nominated for the Edgar—and won.

Lisa, who is a true believer that you should write about what you know, sets all of her books in Philadelphia, and most that came before *Look Again* feature the all-female law firm of Rosato & Associates. Through her novels, she has created an array of unforgettable female characters; ordinary women who have extra-ordinary qualities, much like the women Lisa knows, and much like many of those who read her books. Lisa's stories are about women who are strong, smart, resilient, loving and sexy, with a touch of humour. Her characters work hard at their jobs, but dedicate themselves to life's most important things—family, friends, love, truth and justice. In *Look Again*, Ellen Gleeson has to courageously face the painful possibility of letting go of her child. 'I've written before about how parenting is watching your child take a series of baby steps, all of them away from you, which is as it should be. It's both the happiest and saddest moment in the life of any mother and father. But for Ellen it is so much worse because she runs the risk of losing her child altogether.'

Her research has led Lisa down some very interesting paths, from mining her own and her family's experiences, to less close-to-home pursuits. She has taken boxing lessons, visited a convent, driven up the front steps of the Art Museum in Philadelphia (the famous 'Rocky' stairs) just to make sure it could be done, stood on the roof of her car in a parking garage to figure out a real-life escape route for one of her characters, visited junkyards, and participated in weekly poker games. But her very favourite reseach by far would have to be the shoe-shopping expeditions she had to undertake for *Courting Trouble*!

Apart from being a prolific novelist, Lisa also writes 'Chick Wit', a fun weekly newspaper column for the *Philadelphia Inquirer* and teaches a Justice and Freedom course at the University of Pennsylvania. She also contributes regularly to her website at www.scottoline.com. She admits to being a workaholic but when she does get some free time, Lisa just loves to hang out at home on her farm and enjoys cooking—she describes her tomato sauce as her 'best per-sonal quality'. She also enjoys reading, watching television and playing with her many animals. Nothing can turn Lisa from professional author into to a mushy, ball-throwing woman like her beloved dogs—she has two Golden Retrievers, a Corgi and a Cavalier King Charles Spaniel.

# A Spring Affair

## Milly Johnson

*A Spring Affair is the most autobiographical of my books, so far. The idea came to me quite suddenly as I was clearing out my garage when my marriage was breaking down. I enjoyed chucking things out so much that I became totally obsessed with the decluttering experience. It was almost magical how energised and alive all that physical activity and clean space made me feel. The skip I hired really was the start of a total life change for me and I thought: What would happen if a woman started clearing up her house and then moved on to clearing out her life? A woman like me, who (then) didn't have a lot of confidence, was locked in a loveless marriage and had a head full of unlived dreams. Now I'm thrilled to bits that readers are enjoying Lou's journey back to her former glory via the medium of skips!*

Milly x

*Spring-clean Your Life!*

*Life feel too heavy and cluttered sometimes? Feel like you're going nowhere? Did it ever cross your mind that all those little unwanted items in your cupboards are controlling you, draining your energies and anchoring you to the past? If you think all this sounds far-fetched, check out Mavis Calloway's report on page 14 and see just how simple acts of clearing out some rubbish can put you on a path to your whole life moving forwards.*

*Women by Women*, Contents page, March edition

# CHAPTER 1

SOMETIMES THE COSMOS goes to a lot of trouble to help shift a life from its rut. On this occasion, for instance, it held up the dental technician at the M1 roadworks, gave the practice secretary some tricky double bookings to cope with, and lumbered the dentist, Mr Swiftly, with a particularly awkward extraction that made his appointments run over by more than half an hour. All this so that the anteroom would be extra packed with bored people whiling away the time with the magazines in the rack, leaving just one tatty copy of *Women by Women* for Mrs Elouise Winter—*the* mag for women whose once-young and carnal energies were now ploughed into studying variations on hotpot and various crafts that were a bit too fuddy-duddy for Lou, despite the fact that, at thirty-five, she was starting to edge dangerously close to the chasm of middle age. Still, it was better than reading posters about plaque.

Lou turned to the recipes first: *Five delicious ways to serve a leg of lamb.* She shuddered. Not even a naked Marco Pierre White carrying a sheep limb in on a platter with a red rose between his teeth could make *that* sound attractive to her. She could never think of lamb without picturing rubbery seams of fat and mint sauce and being six years old, sitting alone in the school dining room, pushing it round her plate, willing it to get smaller and disappear so she could go out to play and join the others.

Lamb was her husband Phil's favourite, although she had hardly ever cooked it for him before things went wrong between them, before his affair. Since those dark days, three and a half years ago, it had appeared quite a lot on her menu, as it would this very evening, as a direct result of that little comment he had made last night about her putting some weight on. Lou had tried to shut it out of her mind, but it had continued to rotate in there like a red sock in a whites boil wash—destructive and unstoppable.

Lou carried on flicking through the mag, desperate to find something to divert her thoughts. There was a pattern for a crocheted lampshade that had a certain kitsch charm—except that Lou's crocheting foray had begun and ended aged eleven. She never could work out how to make the intricate tea cosies or granny-square blankets that her sister Victorianna (or 'Torah' as she referred to herself these days) could so effortlessly make. Then again, Victorianna could always turn her hand to anything, as their mother boasted to unfortunate visitors when showing off her younger daughter's accomplishments. '*Except to ringing home when she doesn't want something or to asking you to visit,*' Lou had wanted to snipe. But didn't. It wouldn't have made any difference anyway. Victorianna had been on her pedestal for so long, not even a nuclear explosion would nudge her off it.

*Top ten dressing gowns. Write your own will. Spring-clean your life!* Jeez, is this what is waiting for me round the age corner? thought Lou. It was looking more and more as if, one day, her interest in shoes and handbags would suddenly be diverted to mastering the art of laughing safely without causing a Niagara Falls in the knicker area. Nevertheless, there were three people in front of her to see Mr Swiftly, so there was nothing for it but to try to be interested in having a good clear-out.

The article explained how *unburdening your cupboards of those unwanted and unused knick-knacks will lighten your spirit to a degree you would not think possible. How liberated you will feel, throwing away those garments in the wardrobe which are four sizes too small—the clothes you hoped you'd slim into and never did.*

That struck a chord with Lou. How long had those grey check, size eight trousers been waiting for her super-slim bum to rematerialise?

She did a quick tally and was horrified to discover they had clocked up twelve years on both premarital and postmarital coat hangers. In fact, she had gone up nearly two stone since deciding once and for all that she was going to slim down into them and, if Phil was to be believed last night, she was getting even bigger.

She had lain awake in the wee small hours, thinking how she needed to throttle back on the calories—she didn't even dare to imagine what would happen if Phil's eyes started wandering again. To thin women.

*Clear your house and clear your mind. Don't let life's clutter dictate to you. Throw it away and take back the control!* the article cried, and some blind, lost part within Lou Winter lifted its head as if sensing light. She couldn't remember the last time she had thrown anything out that wasn't everyday wheelie-bin rubbish, and yet her cupboards were full to bursting. At worst it would give her something to do that might divert her thoughts from where they had started to go.

Wearing her best 'nothing to declare' face, she slipped the magazine into her bag when it was her time to be called. It wouldn't be missed, she decided and, to compensate, she had a huge pile of magazines at home that she would bring over and donate in its place, when she began her so-called 'miraculous' clear-out. If only she could start by clearing out her husband's comment from her head . . .

**A**t eight thirty that evening, Philip Michael Winter, thirty-eight years old, owner of P. M. Autos as well as the first sign of a paunch and a bald patch that was becoming harder to hide with every passing day, sat back in his chair and let rip with a long fruity burp of approval.

'Fantastic that, love.'

Lou smiled and he basked in the fact that he had made that smile happen. Never let it be said that he was one of those blokes who didn't compliment his wife. She deserved to know when he had enjoyed his dinner. Lou was a good wife—the best. He never had to hunt around for a fresh shirt, the house was always clean, she cooked like an angel and she never turned him down in the bedroom. She was the perfect 'surrendered wife'—well, she was now, after a bit of training. Although, let's face it, Lou was pretty lucky to be married to *him*. He had put a nice four-bedroomed roof over her head and, thanks to the success of his used-car lot, they had all the latest mod cons, decking in the garden and plasma TVs in three rooms.

Lou had been with him from the beginning, when all he had were dreams of running his own car lot. P. M. Autos was a family business, and as such he liked Lou to do all the accounts for him because no one was more trustworthy than his wife and she was bloody good at number-crunching. There was plenty of money in the bank so she could pay all the bills. He even encouraged her to have a little part-time job so she could have some independence and extra money for shoes and things. Only part-time—he didn't want anything that might tire her too much, or interfere with his coming home every evening to a meal made by his own personal chef. He saved a fortune on restaurants. What was the point in going out? No one could cook like Lou. He'd had the dining room and kitchen made into one huge cooking area for her and built a beautiful conservatory onto the side of the house in which to feed-up and seduce potential business contacts with his wife's superior fare. And she was more than happy to do that for him. He knew this, although he hadn't actually asked her. But to be fair to him, had she ever said, 'Let's go out for a change'? Well, not since his diversion from the straight and narrow she hadn't, anyway.

Tonight's offering was melt-in-the-mouth lamb cutlets, mangetout, sweet potatoes, apple and caramelised carrots (that Phil would desecrate with half a pint of homemade mint sauce)—and it was his absolute favourite. There were no sharers either, for he knew Lou and lamb went together like Dracula and garlic cloves. She had a small, bland egg salad herself, he noted with a little twisted smile. It was amazing how many ripples he could cause just by slapping his wife's backside as she climbed into bed and saying oh-so-innocently, *Putting a bit of weight on again, aren't you, old girl?* The merest hint that she might be letting herself go and Lou was thrown back to that place of insecurity that he considered it healthy for her to visit occasionally—just to keep her on her toes and make her appreciate what she had.

To an outsider that might have sounded hard—sadistic even—but Phil Winter would have argued how wrong they were. He cared about his marriage—and needed to be reassured that his wife felt the same and was prepared to put her share of the effort in as well. He didn't want Lou falling down the slippery slope of not caring what she looked like and ending up like his business colleague Fat Jack's wife, Maureen, who hadn't just gone downhill, she'd travelled there on a bobsleigh.

And now, while Lou had a Müller Light, he shovelled down a toffee-apple crumble with Calvados cream and Lou poured him out a whopping great brandy to follow. If he wasn't too tired, he thought he might even initiate some hanky-panky this evening, knowing that Lou would be more than grateful for a bit of sexual security. A woman on the edge tried so much harder in bed, as he had found. For Phil Winter, life couldn't have been better.

**B**ut it could have been better for Lou Winter, even though she did have what her mother would have said was a very good thing going on, what with her nice house, healthy bank account, holidays abroad and a husband who worked hard. One of Phil's most attractive features in his wife's eyes was how much he enjoyed his food. She could never have married a man who was picky.

In saying that, her unmarried fantasies had been more about staring into the eyes of Marco Pierre White, the candlelight between them emphasising his saturnine glower as he savagely ripped up hunks of garlic-heavy ciabatta to feed to her, his lips glistening with traces of oil, balsamic vinegar and a blood-red Shiraz. He was the only man she and her old friend Deb would ever have fought over. Lou didn't really go for tall men like Deb did, but he ticked so many other boxes on her list that she would have overlooked that aspect—if she'd been given the opportunity. A passionate, food-adoring Yorkshireman-cum-Italian . . . oh, especially the Italian part . . .

The thought of Deb brought a smile to her lips and an unexpected lump to her throat. She coughed it away and cleared up the plates, slotting them into the dishwasher, slamming the door on the sickly, minty smell. No one could ever guess how much she hated lamb.

**L**ou dropped her bag at the side of her desk, eased out of her overcoat and prepared to fortify herself with a coffee from the swanky new machine in the staff canteen. It was very strong, very black, and had what looked like spit floating on top of it.

'Who goffed in your coffee?' said Karen, her work partner-in-crime currently sticking her chin over Lou's shoulder. 'Yuk! What *is* that?'

Lou smiled. Their relationship wasn't the deep alliance that she had shared with her once-best-friend, Deb, but Karen was a true comrade in the office. She worked, as Lou did, job-share Monday, Thursday and Friday. Karen made Lou laugh with her irreverence, her warmth, her gorgeously plummy accent and her big snorty chuckles. Plus their banter coloured the days that their common enemy, Nicola 'Jaws' Pawson, did her best to reduce to monochrome.

Nicola was a weird one, that was for sure. Pretty and slim, she looked quite benign until she opened her mouth to reveal a gobful of metal that would have made her an indispensable tool to a plumber. There had been a lot of crude jokes about what she was supposed to have done to the chief accountant, Roger Knutsford, in the lift at the Christmas party with that mouth, especially when he lost his voice in the New Year and started talking like a eunuch.

In stark contrast, Karen was a dark-haired farmer's daughter, built like an Amazonian warrior but with the most beautiful posh husky voice, thanks to good genes, old money and a grandmother who had been a private elocution teacher. Karen wore the brightest colours in the spectrum and the reddest lipsticks in House of Fraser, and decorated her largeness with no attempt to hide anything she had. In fact, the combined ingredients of Karen Harwood-Court cooked up to make one hell of a sexy woman.

'You seem in an extra-relaxed mood today,' Lou said.

'Nicola's off. Can't you tell? The room temperature's up twenty centigrade and there aren't any thunderclouds above us.' Karen's eyes floated round the room as if feasting on a tangible lightness.

Stan Mirfield, the oldest office administrator, bounded in and threw his briefcase on the desk as if it were an Olympic finishing line and every nano-second counted, which with Nicola in charge, it did. He lived out in some country place and didn't drive. That hadn't been a problem until the last few months when the council had farted around with the timetables and the first bus of the morning got him into the town centre at ten to nine, leaving him with a paltry ten minutes to get to the office by nine. Huffing like an old asthmatic steam engine, Stan wiped frantically at the sweat on his face.

'Chill, Stanley, she's not in,' called Karen.

She leaned into Lou. 'Is it worth getting himself in a state like that? He'll have a heart attack before he gets to his pension,' she said, with some anger on Stan's behalf. They both watched him go through his normal routine before settling down to work where he would graft quietly and efficiently at his desk like a well-oiled machine all day.

'If I ran a department with people like him in it, I wouldn't give a bugger if they were a few minutes late,' Karen went on.

'Has he had a word with HR to give him some leeway?' asked Lou.

'*She* has, apparently,' said Karen. 'Stan said she told him that Bowman said it wasn't an option.' She pulled back her top lip, exposing the maximum of teeth for her to do a Nicola impression: '"*By not starting at nine you are in breach of your contract.*" Or words to that effect.'

'Poor old Stan,' tutted Lou. 'I bet she never told them that the guy hardly ever takes his full lunch-hour.'

'No. Instead, she told him that he should take part-time hours, but that would affect his pension so he can't—although she knows that, of course. Right, must get on,' said Karen, rubbing her hands together.

'Hmm, that looks exciting,' Lou said with sarcasm as she pointed to an enormous bound set of computer print-outs.

'I have an anomaly to find. Rogering Roger has lost twenty thousand pounds somewhere in here and he gave it to lucky me to find it for him.'

'So much for being the big cheese. You should ask him for some of his salary,' said Lou, adding slyly, 'of course, you could always aim to be a senior accountant yourself . . .'

Karen sighed. 'Shut up, Lou, and lend me your ruler.'

Lou opened her drawer, which was a veritable Aladdin's cave of disorganised stationery, and handed over her rather grubby ruler.

*Clear that clutter.*

The thought came to her as surely as if someone had whispered it softly and seductively in her ear.

'**W**hat on earth are you doing?' Karen asked five minutes later as Lou heaved the drawer out from the body of the cabinet under her desk, turned it over and emptied the contents onto the carpet, dropping to her knees by the small mountain of detritus.

'Well, seeing as Jaws is not in,' Lou panted, 'I'm going to clear out some rubbish. I'm having a spring-clean.'

'You've timed it perfectly. It's March the 21st—the first day of spring today, but you're NOT going to burn that burgundy suit at long last, are you?' asked Karen, laughing hard at her own wit.

'There's nothing wrong with my suit.' Lou put her hands mock-indignantly on her hips. The suit cladding them was functional, if a little old-fashioned, but she felt nicely inconspicuous in it.

'It messes about with your shape. Makes you look dumpy.'

'I am dumpy,' said Lou. 'Plus, at thirty-five, I don't think anyone is looking to me to be a fashion icon.'

'Lou Winter, you have great hair, great tits, and eyes that make you look about sixteen. You just don't appreciate what you've got.' She stared down wistfully at her own A cups. 'You are such an attractive woman. Why the hell do you insist on hiding yourself away?'

'I'm not hiding myself away. But at thirty-five—'

'Listen to yourself! Thirty-five isn't old.'

'You're twenty-five—you're supposed to say I'm ancient.'

'You have an outstanding talent for not making the best of yourself, you know. You push everyone onwards but yourself.'

'Keep your hair on,' said Lou, but Karen was on a roll and had no intention of stopping now.

'You could have had Jaws's job if you'd applied for it. So really it's your fault we're all so bloody miserable, if you think about it. It makes me so cross to see ability go to waste.'

'Oh, is that so?' countered Lou. 'Well, while we're on the subject of "making the best of ourselves" . . .' She walked on her knees over to her handbag, humming, 'Hi ho, hi ho . . .' then got out a leaflet and rustled it at Karen. 'Here. I got you this.'

'What is it?' Karen took it tentatively.

'Accountancy courses. I picked it up for you at the college.'

'Oh, I haven't got time for all that education stuff.' Karen dismissed it immediately.

'One day a week, that's all.'

'And what about the children?'

'They're at school, as you well know.'

'And what do I do in the school holidays?'

'Well, the college will have the same holidays, won't it, twerp? And your mum and dad would have the children at the farm.'

'What about the cost?'

'You could go down to Human Resources. They're always harping on about courses so they must have a decent budget for them. If not, beg, steal, borrow it—you'd recoup your costs when you qualify.'

'*If. If* I qualify.'

'Come on, Karen! Roger Knutsford is sending stuff down to you that he won't give to his own team. You won't have the slightest problem.'

'You're better than I am with numbers. Why don't you do it yourself?'

'Because I have no interest in carving out a career in accountancy like you do,' Lou volleyed. 'My heart belongs to pastry.'

Karen stamped down on the smile that was forcing itself out of her. 'You've got all this worked out, haven't you?' Lou was so comical sometimes. Really nice and funny and such a warm person. She would have made some kid a fantastic mum.

'Seriously, you would walk this course,' said Lou with conviction. She tickled Karen's Achilles' heel. 'And think of what you could do with a qualified accountant's wage. You could give your two boys a private education, buy them elocution lessons so they could drive their own office managers insane with jealousy one day. You could work from home, get an au pair in . . .'

'You really are a dreadful, manipulative old bag, Lou Winter!'

'Or you could be running this place, making Stan's life less of a misery, getting Zoe through a day where she wasn't in tears.'

'OK, OK, I'll read it. *If* you burn that suit.'

Lou laughed. 'You enrol on that course and I'll burn all my suits and replace them with crop-tops and miniskirts.'

'Now, I'm interested,' said Karen, opening up the college leaflet.

The magazine article had promised that clearing out unwanted items would dramatically improve her mood and energy levels. By four o'clock, Lou wasn't quite convinced that clearing out a couple of drawers had been wholly responsible for her having had such a good day. It could have been because Nicola wasn't there, or because it was a Friday—and one preceding a week where she had booked the Monday off to use up some holiday. But she had to admit it had made a weird contribution to her happy mood and sense of real achievement.

There had been a healthy satisfaction in seeing all her paperclips and staples in their organised compartments, the files in the drawer now emptied of all outdated paperwork, and all the information scribbled down on scrappy notes transferred into her desk diary. And when she came to do some actual accounts work in the afternoon, the tidiness of her workspace somehow made her feel extra efficient.

At the end of the day, she put everything she usually left out on her desk inside her drawer. It looked so fresh it almost made her want to sit at it and start working again.

'Good God,' said Karen, poking her head round Lou's section. 'I need my sunglasses on to look at your desk.'

Lou smiled. 'Clean as a flute, if I say so myself.'

'*Whistle*, Lou—*clean as a whistle*.' Karen smiled. Lou should never have been given unsupervised charge of the English language. 'Have a lovely long weekend and I'll see you—without your burgundy suit, I hope—next Thursday.'

Phil liked a curry on Friday nights after he had been for his usual workout at the gym, so the kitchen had a warm and exotic air as Lou stirred a selection of her own mixed spices into the pot of chicken.

Her text alarm went off. It was from her friend Michelle. Off out to snare Dave. Wish me luck. That came as a bit of a surprise to Lou, as the last conversation they had had was that he was a complete dickhead. Lou texted back Good luck! She knew in her heart of hearts though, that Michelle was heading for disappointment and would probably be on the phone tomorrow in tears.

Michelle had fancied rugged builder Dave for ages and had got lucky one night, two months ago, when he was exceedingly drunk. However, since then, he had made polite but hurried exits from her company. Michelle pursued him at every turn possible. He was apparently the most gorgeous man she had ever met, although she had said the same about Colin—and Liam and John and Gaz and Jez, two Ians and a Daz. Lou's advice to her that maybe she should be less keen had been interpreted in Michelle's own special way, and now, whenever she had managed to seek poor Dave out, she proceeded to ignore him—laughing loudly and flirting outrageously with anyone nearby.

The opening notes to *Coronation Street* played out on the portable TV in the corner, signifying the time that Lou called 'wine o'clock'. She always had a glass of red while she was cooking, but when she went to get the corkscrew, it was as if she was looking at the cutlery drawer for the first time. Lordy, this could do with a clear out, she thought, staring down at the strange gadgets she had bought to experiment with and never used. She opened the drawer beneath it too—the one she used for scraps, string, Sellotape, nail clippers and all the familiar bits and pieces which didn't belong anywhere else. She picked out an old green scrunchie stained with ink from a leaky pen, a rusted-up padlock and a pamphlet for the Indian takeaway in town that had closed down last Christmas. She dropped them in the bin and wondered why on earth she hadn't done such a simple and easy thing as that before.

She pulled open the bottom drawer. It needed an extra tug because it was so crammed with cloths made from cut-up tea towels. Did she really need so many? The timer buzzer went then, demanding her attention, and Lou closed all the drawers. 'Tomorrow,' she decided.

At the car lot, Phil shook his head in disgust and prepared to be in pain.
*Sharon Higgins, the sum of two hundred and fifty pounds.*

Whenever he wrote out the wording on these cheques his mind always whirred with calculations. Ten years of £200 per month was £24,000, plus another eight years of £250 per month brought the total to £48,000. Not counting the fact that the bitch might ask for another increase at some point. It was lukewarm comfort that he'd received no surprise letter from the Child Support Agency, who would demand a hell of a lot more money from him.

He had only laid eyes on the leech children once, when he and Lou were shopping one Christmas at Meadowhall five years ago. They had literally bumped into Sharon and her mother and the kids outside the Father Christmas grotto. No words had been exchanged. Sharon had whipped the kids away with a sort of panic that suggested he might immediately bond with them, although nothing could have been further from the truth. To him, they were just two small, ordinary, dark-eyed, blonde-haired kids who he hadn't felt a thing for then, or since.

Two nights he had spent with Sharon. One of which he couldn't remember at all, he was so drunk. But apparently they'd done *it* three times, *which would work out at £16,000 per shag!*

Phil had first met Sharon on a night-out in Chesterfield a couple of years before Lou came on the scene. She was the clichéd twenty-year-old bimbo barmaid with long legs, massive tits, blonde hair and eyes like big blue sapphires. He hypnotised her easily by flashing a bit of cash and, two bottles of champagne later, she was in his bed. She had said that the champagne was too dry (why didn't the silly cow tell him that in the first place and save him fifty quid then?), and had a Diet Coke instead, so he was lumbered with it, and he wasn't going to waste it at those prices despite the fact that it didn't sit happily with the lager and the vodkas already sloshing round his system. She had assured him he had been fantastic though.

The second time, he had made sure he was stone-cold sober but the sex had been a bit of a let-down, to say the least. He was, quite frankly, bored by the morning and decided, over their post-coital Little Chef breakfast, that she had to go. He had a feeling she might have turned out to be too clingy and expensive if he didn't sever it, although he didn't realise just how expensive until she turned up unannounced at the car lot that he managed five months later, waddling like a fat duck, not only pregnant with one sprog, but two. They were his apparently, without a doubt. There was a history of twins in the Winter family which added immediate credibility to her claim.

She said she didn't want him in the twins' life but she expected him to contribute £200 per calendar month. Payment on the dot and she would keep the CSA out of it. It was at that point that he asked her if she was sure he was the father.

She had turned on him like a Tasmanian Devil. 'What do you think I am!' she screamed. 'You seduced me with lines like, "You've got the most beautiful blue eyes I've ever seen,"' (which he remembered saying), 'and, "We don't need to bother with condoms because I've had the snip!"' (which he couldn't remember saying at all).

'You used me,' she had spat, 'then when you got what you wanted, you didn't want to know me. I believed you so much about the snip, it never crossed my mind I could be pregnant—and when I found out that I was, it was too bloody late to abort. So this is all your fault.'

Phil did actually have a stab of guilt at that point, especially when she started crying, although it didn't stop her ranting. He pacified her with a coffee and a Kit-Kat and the promise of a taxi home, and made a mental note never to have casual, unprotected sex again.

He had got a birth announcement seven and a half months after the shag-he-couldn't-remember. It was a perfunctory note with her bank details at the bottom. The babies were premature but doing well, she said. The unsaid message was: *Start the payments*. He didn't hear any-thing from her again until the children were ten, when she asked for fifty pounds more per month. He complied because it wasn't worth rocking the boat over. In fact, until he and Lou had bumped into Sharon that Christmas, he didn't even know that she'd had one of each. He remembered no details about the kids except for their eyes, which were round and brown like a pair of fledgling owls, or should that be cuckoos. Bloody evil cuckoos nesting in his bank account.

The Sharon-and-kids episode had been a great shake-up for Phil. He'd had a charmed life until then. When Phil and Celia, his sister, were small, their parents had split up and compensated by spoiling their children rotten with the best things money could buy. The Winter children had grown up with an inflated sense of their own worth, a habit of getting all their own way and an obsession with hard cash. They entered adulthood feeling that they were invincible, which was reinforced when business success and money gravitated towards them.

Their confidence helped them attract the attentions of the opposite sex, but Sharon's outsmarting of Phil had knocked his self-belief. Since then he had striven for bigger deals than anyone else, to prove to him-self that he was once again top dog. Nor did he ever again get out of his depth when flirting with a woman. Everything that happened to Phil Winter, Sharon Higgins excepted, had to be on Phil Winter's terms. That included pulling the rug from under his wife's feet every so often. That she never failed to climb back on it for him was the biggest indi-cation he had that he was back on the right track.

Just as he had sealed the envelope and thumped a second-class stamp on it, Bradley, his second-in-command, popped his head round the door and grinned, waving a log book. 'Got it!'

'The MG?'

'Yep. Daft old cow took the twelve hundred cash, and young Colin's taking it over to Fat Jack's in the morning.'

'You bloody star!' Twelve hundred in cash, for a vehicle that would be worth four times that by the time it came back from Fat Jack's body shop. And that wasn't counting the best bit—the personalised number-plate that was worth at least ten grand. Maybe there was a God. A good old capitalist God Who helped those who helped themselves.

As Lou snapped on her Marigolds on Saturday morning, the phone rang.

'Hello, how are you?' said an over-chirpy voice. It was Michelle.

'I'm OK. You're up early. You all right?'

'Yes, I'm fine,'—although the crescendo of sniffs told otherwise.

'Sure?'

'Nooo . . .'

Michelle was never all right. Well, that wasn't quite true, for she had been quite all right three years ago when they had first met at the Advanced Indian Cuisine course, on which Lou had enrolled to make herself more indispensable in Phil's eyes.

Lou and Michelle had swapped phone numbers and met outside class a couple of times, and the increasingly frequent calls between their houses were as light and frothy as a six-egg sponge cake. There was a big fat space waiting in Lou's heart for a friend after Deb had gone from her life, and Michelle filled it perfectly. Well, in the beginning, anyway.

Sometimes Lou was ashamed that she felt so drained by Michelle's constant depressions, especially when she thought back to the giggles they'd had in their cookery class, before their friendship had been tested by any outside traumas. Then she remembered her own neediness in those awful months when Deb was there to listen to her, often in the middle of the night when she couldn't bear the thought of going to sleep and dreaming distorted dreams. When she felt half-insane, unable to see past her own pain. She had clung to Deb like a vine, as Michelle now clung to her. True friends stuck around when the going got tough, so how could Lou even think of turning her back on Michelle in her hour (well, many hours) of need?

'Well, I got to the pub,' snuffled Michelle. 'And Dave was there. And he turned round in front of everyone,'—more tears and sniffs—'and he said . . . he said, "Stop stalking me, get a life and piss off, you bitch!"'

Lou cringed. What on earth would be the right thing to say to that? She decided, unwisely, to respond with: 'Oh, well, that's that then.'

'Is that all you can say?' Michelle half screamed at her.

'I . . . I didn't mean . . .' Lou stuttered. 'I just meant that now you're in no doubt that . . .' *He's not interested.* ' . . . he's not the man for you.'

'But what if this morning he's thinking, God, I was a bit hard on her last night—and now he feels guilty and really sorry for me?'

'Do you really want a man who feels sorry for you?'

'I don't care, I just want him.'

'Michelle, let him go,' Lou said, as warmly and supportively as she could. 'Maybe you should stay away from men until you have given yourself some time to get strong. You're giving out signals that say, "Hello, idiots of the world! Come and get me—I'm vulnerable!" And you don't want just any man, do you?'

'Nobody loves me though, Lou. I'm so lonely,' said Michelle.

Oh, how Lou wished she had the courage to say, 'Please grow up, Michelle,' after twelve exasperating loops of the same conversation.

'Isn't loneliness a little better than being tormented like this?' said Lou eventually.

'How do you know what loneliness is? You're married!' Michelle cried. Which was so funny, Lou almost cried herself.

'Look, Lou,' said Michelle, after another ten minutes, 'why don't you come round for a bit and I'll cook lunch?'

'I can't this morning,' said Lou. 'I've got stuff to do.'

'Like what?' Michelle replied with a little huff.

'Well, domestic things, then I'll be making Phil's lunch,' Lou said, wondering why she was explaining but still doing it all the same.

'Phil, Phil, Phil—all you think about is Phil,' Michelle snapped. 'See you when you're not so busy.' The phone went down hard at Michelle's end. *Ouch*, thought Lou, although she didn't have time to wallow in guilt, as the phone rang again in a breath.

'I had you on ringback—you've been ages,' huffed her mother.

'I was talking to Michelle.'

'Oh, *her*,' said Renee Casserly disapprovingly. 'When are you going to the supermarket?'

'Well, not this morning anyway, I've got things to do.'

'Victorianna wants to know if your email's broken. She's written to you but she's not had a reply so she's told me what she wants instead.'

Lou crossed her fingers and lied. 'No, I don't think anything's arrived.'

She had heard from her sister and it was another Victorianna classic. Her email had said:

> Hi there, weather fab here as usual. I'm now a size zero, can you believe, and it feels just great. How's your diet going? Can you help Mum to send a couple of things over?

(Diet? Little bitch!) There followed a shopping list longer than a giraffe's leg, and no please or thank you, as usual. Most of the stuff on the list she could get in the States anyway. She just wanted the kudos of getting a 'home parcel'.

This was the umpteenth 'hamper' she'd sent for. Lou had once received a T-shirt by way of thanks. The words 'thank you' weren't actually said. Her mum got a framed photo of Victorianna posing formally with live-in lover Edward J. R. Winkelstein the Third and his expensive hairweave. Victorianna looked like a younger, more glamorous version of Renee. He looked the way Lou would expect an Edward J. R. Winkelstein the Third to look.

'Well, just let me know when you're going and I'll come with you. She's got a dinner party soon and wants some of the stuff for then.'

'OK, Mum. How about Tuesday?'

'Yes, but no later otherwise she won't get the stuff in time. And you want to check your email. Your sister said she wrote two days ago.'

'Well, I do have other things to do besides jump when Victorianna asks, Mum. And a please and thank you and a cheque for you wouldn't go amiss. Doesn't she realise how much you spend on these flaming hampers?' asked Lou. 'You could have taken the stuff over yourself for how much it's cost you in postage and packing.' *If your beloved daughter ever had the decency to invite you over there.*

'I *am* her mother. I don't expect anything in return.'

'Yes, but it's not as if she's poor. She's always bragging about how loaded she and Baron Frankenstein are.'

'Jealousy won't get you anywhere,' said Renee, totally missing the point.

Lou surrendered. 'Tuesday then, Mum, definitely,' she said with a sigh. She put the phone down and vowed she wouldn't answer it again. 'Right, to business,' she said to herself with a big smile and a clap of the hands, and shook open a large black binliner in preparation.

*Be ruthless*, the article had said. *Ask yourself, 'Have I used it in the last six months (seasonal goods—allow one year)? Am I likely to ever use it in the future?' If the answer is no, can it go in a recycling bin, or to charity, or to a car-boot sale? No? Then throw it away without a second glance.*

Some things she questioned, such as the ancient tin-opener that looked more like a medieval instrument of torture. It had a handy bottle-opener at the top, but as she couldn't remember the last time she had opened a bottle with it, she launched it at the binliner.

When the cutlery drawer was completely emptied, she scrubbed it down, washed the utensils she was keeping and slotted the whole thing back. It was crazy how something as simple as throwing out some old rubbish gave her such a sense of accomplishment.

Next, she tipped out the odds and sods drawer. A broken mirror, five combs (none of which had a complete set of teeth), an incomplete set of playing cards . . . into the bin went everything but the scissors and a pair of tweezers that she thought she'd lost months ago. She collected all the loose paperclips into an empty matchbox, which she also found in the drawer, and took them to the desk in the small study next door. *Clear and redeploy as you go*, the article dictated. And the newest disciple to the religion of clutter-clearing obeyed.

Then she tackled the cloth drawer, throwing out all the tatty floor-cloths because she had found three new packets of J-cloths that had been hidden under everything. She had just got on her knees to do the under-sink cupboard, when the doorbell rang.

She hoped it wasn't Michelle, then felt immediately mean and treacherous. She stole over to the window and sneaked a look. It was a lot worse than Michelle and her mother combined. It was Mr Halloween himself—her brother-in-law, Des.

'Oh, knickers,' Lou said, and quickly stepped back against the wall, confident that she hadn't been seen. Luckily for her, there was no detectable sign that she was in. She waited in the silence until she was pretty sure he must have gone—then, to her anger and amazement, she heard a key in the lock, the door opening and footsteps in the hall. She really would kill Phil when he got home. He'd obviously done what she told him never to do again, and lent Des his key. There was nothing for it now, no place to hide. And, even worse, she'd got the old white T-shirt on that made her boobs look massive.

Lou braced herself and burst into the hallway. Hands going to her chest, she feigned shock. 'Des, it's you! You scared the life out of me.'

'I rang the bell,' said her brother-in-law in his nasal monotone drawl, thumbing back to the door, 'but I didn't think you were in. I called in to see Phil at the garage. He lent me a key.'

'Oh, right then,' said Lou, who really wanted to say other things that weren't so polite. 'So, what is it that you want?' she urged after waiting in vain for Des to explain.

'I just came to borrow Phil's golf clubs.'

'OK,' said Lou. 'Did he say where they were?'

'No,' said Des helpfully. Not.

Lou was forced to go from room to room with Des following behind her in that way of his that had no respect for personal space. Phil said he was just stupidly insensitive, but Lou sometimes wondered if he got kicks from being such an unsettling presence.

Des Winter-Brown arriving at your door could make you think it was trick-or-treat night. Tall, skinny and corpse-pale, his shoulders were rounded from stooping and his hair was lank and black from over-zealous dyeing. There was something about his strange quietness and the way he would turn up close beside Lou, without a clue of his approach, that made her dread the merest hint of a visit from him.

When Phil had lent him a key to get something from the house on a previous occasion, he had failed to see Lou's problem.

'You shouldn't be giving him a key to our house!' said Lou crossly.

'Well, excuse me, but I think you'll find it says *my* name on the deeds,' said Phil then, with a dangerous degree of impatience.

'I think *you'll* find that since we're married, it's *ours*,' said Lou, her voice firming as much as Lou's voice could.

'I think *you'll* find, if you want to push it, we can carry on with our original plans to split up and find out exactly what the law says!'

She hadn't argued any more.

Lou flicked on the cellar light. God, it's a mess down here, she said to herself. Her new rubbish-alert radar had already spotted twelve things that they would never use again and which should be thrown out.

'Nope. They're not down there,' said Lou, returning as quickly as she could upstairs.

There was only the garage left to check, and the loft—but Lou wasn't going up there. She pressed the electronic opener for the garage door, which slid up and over. Relief washed over her as she saw the clubs poking out from under some dustsheets, next to some cracked plastic garden chairs and a grimy table that would never see sunshine again.

Des left her to heave the clubs out by herself because his mobile was ringing. 'Hello, baby,' he said to the caller.

*Yeuch*, thought Lou.

'I'm at Phil's . . . Yes, he is but I'm with Lou.' He winked at her, and Lou shuddered. 'Golf clubs . . . I'm going to have a cup of tea here then I'll be off . . . Oh, you are? See you in about quarter of an hour then.'

Lou really hoped she hadn't filled in the missing gaps correctly.

'Celia thought she'd pop in,' said Des, as he heaved the clubs into his car. 'She's just coming from Meadowhall with the children, so I might as well have a cup of tea and wait here for her.'

*No, get lost, I want to clean my cupboards out. I don't want your wife looking down her nose at me and showing off her new Prada handbag. I don't want your kids prying into my cupboards!*

But while Lou screamed this in her head, aloud she said. 'Oh, right. Well, I'll put the kettle on then.'

She ripped off her rubber gloves, angry at herself for letting everyone walk over her with their unthinking, unfeeling hobnailed boots. She wished she'd gone supermarket shopping with her mother now.

She stood over the kettle as it boiled, only to find that Des had appeared at her back, staring out of the window with some lame comment about the lawn looking good. Ludicrously, in a kitchen as big as hers, she found herself in the position of having to squeeze past him to get the milk and the cups. She half wished he would grope her, just the once, then she could have the excuse to belt him across the chops and ban him from the house.

There was a knock on the back door. 'Come in!' shouted Des.

Cheeky swine, thought Lou.

In spilled the twins. Well, Hero spilled in, pretending to be a plane, and Scheherazade waddled in behind with a puppy-fatted belly poking out of a Bratz crop-top. Celia huffed behind them, laden with posh carriers, which she could have left in her boot, and gabbling to Des about some shirt she had bought for him that cost more than Lou's car. She had just got it out to show him when Phil put in an early appearance.

He ignored the withering look his wife gave him because he had had a very profitable morning. 'You are looking at one successful mother,' he beamed. 'What's for lunch then?'

'I'm hungry, too,' said Hero.

'Lou, sort us out, love!' said Phil.

And Lou, silently from her niche in the background, abandoned her own plans for the day in order to make lunch for a room full of people.

# CHAPTER 2

THE NEXT MORNING, Phil stood in front of the mirror and put on his standard work uniform: a crisp white shirt, a heavy splash of a very expensive aftershave lotion, a blue tie that complemented the shade of his still sparkly, bright blue eyes, and a perfectly cut navy suit jacket with a subtle P. M. Autos tiepin. He was wearing well and he knew it (well, except for that monk-hole in his hair). He smiled at himself and £18,000-worth of cosmetic dentistry work smiled back at him. It was *simply the best* investment. Women customers, especially, were very judgmental about bad teeth, Phil had learned. They knew bugger-all about cars and looked for other indicators that they weren't about to be sold a duff. Women *so* wanted to trust you.

He had a quick read of the *Sunday World* newspaper while he was fortifying himself for the day ahead with one of his wife's extra super-dooper Sunday grills, which he would burn off with some serious gym work later. Then he fired up his Audi TT and set off for the car lot.

After Phil had left, Lou had a banana and a yogurt in the conservatory-cum-dining room. The smell of Phil's bacon in the kitchen was making her stomach growl in jealous protest. He had gone off to work, whistling because of some exciting find in an old widow's garage and his plans to start up another new business with Fat Jack selling exclusive classic cars. She had been eaves-dropping yesterday while he was showing off to Des about it—anything but listen to Celia's boring commentary about her latest Karen Millen acquisitions, although she hadn't heard the whole story because she'd had to go and locate the children who were poking worryingly around the house, as usual. She was pretty sure Celia would have something to say if Lou went into *her* bedroom and started rooting nosily through *her* drawers.

Lou cleared away the breakfast things then locked all the doors. The phone rang as she was snapping open some binliners. The caller display announced that it was Michelle. Lou's hand twitched dutifully towards the receiver, but she was strict with herself. Today was her day.

The under-sink cupboard was disappointingly full of currently useful bottles and tins, but the remainder of Lou's kitchen cupboards more than made up for it. She hadn't realised just how many forgotten cans and packets lurked there. There were never-to-be-used bulk supplies of Trimslim milk shakes, which had tasted like melted-down Play-Doh. There were glasses that Phil had got free with his petrol years ago, a fondue set, an egg scrambler, an unused yogurt-maker and a never-opened doughnut-maker, which Phil had bought for her last birthday. She couldn't throw away something he had bought her, could she? She referred to the article for guidance. It said that cowardy custards who had misgivings about items could put them in a bag, date it and label it. If nothing inside the bag had been used within six months, then the bag should be removed from the house.

Lou decided to be a hard-liner. Getting out a huge green garden-refuse bag, she wrote *Heart Foundation* on it and put the electrical contraptions in there. After her dad died, all of her charity donations had gone to them. Well, them and the Barnsley Dogs Home.

The kitchen, including the under-stair cupboard, yielded a startling eight full rubbish bags, plus the big green bag for the charity shop.

She rang Phil at work. 'Where's the nearest dump?' she asked. 'I'm clearing out the cupboards.'

'How much stuff is there, for crying out loud?'

'Too much for the wheelie-bin to cope with.'

'Go down Sheffield Hill, past the Miner's Arms and as you get near the bottom, look out for a sign on your left,' he said.

Lou heaved five big bags of rubbish into her car boot and set off. The last time she had been to a dump, admittedly years ago, had been straightforward—drive in, dump, drive off. It appeared times had changed, though, for facing her now were different containers with large signs: HOUSEHOLD, GARDEN, PLASTIC, GLASS and ELECTRICAL.

'Bugger!' she said. She had been planning to just throw everything in one place but there was a fierce-looking commandant on duty. It was quite a faff, but eventually Lou's rubbish was distributed to the relevant places and so she set off back home for the second load. She got back to the dump just in time to see the gates close in front of her.

Oh, *gr-eat*, said Lou to herself. What do I do now?

The answer to that question was literally just round the corner for, as she was waiting for the traffic lights to turn green at the junction, there to her right was a bright yellow skip. There was a name and number stencilled on the side, which she quickly jotted down on her hand. *Tom Broom*. It had a nice purging sound to it.

Tuesday had all the promise of being a day-to-get-to-the-end-of-as-quickly-as-possible. Not only did Lou have the prospect of trailing after her mother in the supermarket, but someone from HR at work had asked if she could spare them an extra afternoon.

Her first job of the day, though, would be to order a skip. Something about the name 'Tom Broom' made her smile; there was a solid, honest quality to it. Then again, with her track record for judging personalities, Tom Broom was most likely a cross-dressing serial killer with a particular hatred of short, auburn-haired women with Yorkshire accents. Nevertheless, she rang his number and a deep-voiced man took down her details. She ordered a mini-skip to be delivered the following Tuesday. Payment on delivery—£70. Blimey!

She suspected her mother might need something the same size to box up all the things she bought for Victorianna's 'hamper from home'.

'I thought American supermarkets were teeming with goods,' said Lou, as Renee picked up a tin of anchovies.

'Oh, Elouise,' was all her mother said, in a very fatigued tone, and added some special offer basic toilet rolls to her trolley.

'She'll not want those, surely,' said Lou. 'She'll want super-dooper-softy-wofty-six-ply-woodland-scented—'

'They're for me,' Renee interrupted.

Her mother's shopping items were nearly all 'super-value' items. She could quite easily afford the branded goods for herself but chose not to. Renee was terrified of running out of money—although she never quibbled about what she paid for those stupid hampers that her youngest daughter asked for, Lou noted.

As they were wheeling their trolleys out of the supermarket door, Lou stopped herself just in time from suggesting they go and grab a pot of tea and a big cream cake in the café. She had long since been aware that the world was divided into those who saw food only as necessary fuel and those who relished it with passion and pleasure. Renee and Victorianna were of the former group. How sad. So, instead of cake-scoffing, she dropped her mother off at her house and went off for a thrilling afternoon in the accounts department at work. Not.

Nicola Pawson was in a foul mood. She was out of her depth running the department and she knew it, and so her defence mechanisms were permanently set to projecting her inadequacies onto other people—one thing she *could* manage with great skill.

She had acquired, through a mixture of flattery and flirting, friends in high places in the company, and basked luxuriously in her association with Rogering Roger Knutsford. She was a master in the art of 'impression management'. Anyone with the slightest potential to be useful to her found her to be a smart, fresh-faced young woman with a prettily symmetrical ready smile (closed-lipped, obviously). They could never have guessed at the hollowness that lay behind her pale eyes.

People were either wary of her or sucked up to her—both of which inflated the sense of her own power. From her school days, all that had mattered to her was playing the game of controlling others. By the time she had reached adult life, her manipulative skills had reached a near-genius level of sophistication and her greatest pleasure was creating fear and discord. She was, in psychiatric terminology, a borderline psychopathic bully. And in conversational parlance, a right nasty little cow.

But two people stopped Nicola from reigning supreme. The first was Karen, who was more amused by her than anything. Karen un-ashamedly relished the fact that Nicola envied her private education and her double-barrelled surname. The second—Lou Winter—would have been gobsmacked to learn that she got to Nicola so much.

Lou and Karen were true professionals: always punctual, always smart, and they knew their financial onions. They were warm, well liked and respected, and people in the company affectionately labelled them 'Little and Large in Accounts'. Neither woman gave Nicola a crack to seep her poison into: one thing Lou had learned from Phil was how empowering a show of indifference—real, or assumed—could be.

But simpler, gentler people like Zoe and Stan were ready meals for sharks like Nicola. She knew they would never report her for her treatment of them, and would bring them to Roger Knutsford's attention in the worst kind of way. Plus Nicola saw to it that anything they might have to report would sound very petty and totally unreasonable. She had a clever way of putting her own warp on things so that her story and the opposing one were almost alike, but her version was infinitely more articulate and believable.

And boy, was Nicola in the mood for taking her frustrations out on someone that day! Rogering Roger was taking one of the newly appointed designers out for a 'business lunch'. Her name was Jo MacLean and she was a serious contender for position of Teacher's Pet. Tall and willowy, her flawless complexion and long, swishy brown hair poked annoyingly at those dark insecure places within Nicola. It was no coincidence that Zoe, with her own flawless complexion and long dark hair, was first in line for Nicola's vented spleen.

Nicola leaned over Zoe's desk. 'May I have a word?'

'Yeah, course,' said Zoe, already nervous at Nicola's tone.

'Roger isn't happy,' said Nicola. Three words only, yet she managed to imbue them with a menace that threw Zoe into a state of distress.

'What do you mean?' Zoe'd just bought a car and was saving up for a house with her boyfriend. She couldn't afford to lose her job. 'With me? Why? What have I done?'

'I haven't got time to talk now. Later,' said Nicola.

'Nicola, please, you can't just say that and then leave it.'

'I said not now,' said Nicola, and swept off leaving Zoe close to tears. She might have been young, but she knew that big companies could get rid of anyone if they felt like it. And how good would that look on her CV, that she'd been sacked from her last position?

Stan saw Nicola edge close to his desk and the hairs on the back of his neck sprang up. Nicola effectively held his life in her hands and he knew she knew that. He couldn't afford to leave this job before his sixty-fifth birthday because it would affect his pension and, ergo, his future security. It never crossed Stan's mind that this was a bullying campaign. He thought bullying ended at the school gates.

'May I have a look at what you're doing, Stan?' she said.

'Here you go.'

She made him feel like a five-year-old in front of the headmistress.

'Ooh, I don't think that's quite right. How can an eight and a six make sixteen? Roger's concerned . . .' she said, trailing dramatically off.

'What about? Me?'

Nicola leaned in conspiratorially. 'I know you're just killing time until your retirement . . .'

'Excuse me, but I'm not—'

'Don't raise your voice, Stan. I'm trying to help.'

'Sorry.' *Was* I raising my voice? he asked himself.

'As I was saying, Roger's been picking up on all the mistakes.' She said 'all' as if he were churning out one every thirty seconds. 'He's concerned. I'd be careful.' She drifted off back to her desk leaving him with an increased heart rate. The effect made her feel good, in control. It was fun and it distracted her from thinking about what crap Roger Knutsford was spouting to Miss Jo 'Long Legs' MacLean.

Neither Zoe nor Stan looked up when Lou came in. Their heads were down, concentrating hard on work. Lou felt so sorry for them. She would have bet the contents of her purse that Nicola had been on their backs again. It wasn't fair and she wished she could do something. But standing up for her colleagues might only make things worse. Of course, if this had been school, Lou would have had Nicola by the scruff of the neck as she'd had her then nemesis—Shirley Hamster—on numerous occasions for bullying the younger kids. But that Lou was long gone. This Lou sat at her desk and got on with her work quietly and efficiently, and didn't rail against the social order. She couldn't have known that some primitive sense in Nicola was alert to the dormant strength that still lay within her. The irony was that Lou felt the weakest of them all, especially at the moment. Never had her name been so apt. Inside, she felt as cold and dead as winter itself.

**T**he night before the skip arrived, Lou totted up ten binliners-full of throwaways. Her initial plan might have been merely to clear out a few drawers and cupboards, but once she had started, she couldn't stop. How could she have lived for so long with so much rubbish and not seen it? Plus she hadn't had as much enjoyment from getting her teeth into something since she and Deb had planned Casa Nostra, despite the fact that all her nails were broken.

'Well, if that's how you want to spend your leisure time, Lou, you go right ahead,' said Phil, watching her heave binliners downstairs. 'But all I want to do when I get home from a hard day's work is sit down, have my tea and read the paper.' He omitted to mention that he had spent most of that day sitting down, drinking tea and reading the paper.

The skip wagon reversed down her drive at nine o'clock the next morning and out of the cabin jumped a man and a shire horse. Well, the dog was certainly as big as a shire horse, anyway, and he stole Lou's heart instantly. He bounced over to her and dropped into the play position, his great furry head on his paws, his huge dark eyes looking up pleadingly at her for attention.

'Clooney, you big tart, come back here!' said the skip man gruffly.

Lou bent and ruffled the huge German Shepherd's head. 'Clooney, what a great name,' she said, taking in the skip man for the first time. He was a wardrobe in overalls, with dark hair that flopped at the front over a pair of very smiley, bright grey eyes. He wasn't her type, though. Lou had never really gone for big men. It was too impractical for a five-foot-one woman. Marco Pierre White excepted, Lou's tastes had always been for the smoother, average-heighted blokes. That said, Lou's inner checklists, for some unknown reason, were telling her that this was a man who was making her pupils dilate.

'He gets all the women. I wish I had his knack,' said the man, unloosening the giant hooks on the skip.

'Shall I pay you by cheque or cash?' asked Lou.

'Either's fine,' said Skipman. 'But, let's say cash is slightly better.'

'No worries,' said Lou, who had the money ready. 'Although these days with all the fake fivers about, I wonder!' she laughed.

They both instinctively looked down at the money she was holding out towards him.

'Not that these are fake,' she said quickly. 'I didn't mean . . .'

Skipman let loose a deep, gravelly laugh. 'I'd set the dog on you if they were, but I don't think he'd be much of a threat.'

Clooney was trying to scratch an itch on his nose and not hitting the spot. He overbalanced with the effort, looking clumsily adorable.

'Give us a call when you've filled it,' he said.

'Saturday would be great,' said Lou without hesitation.

'Sure?' asked Skipman, helping Clooney out with a good old scratch.

'I'll have it filled by then,' said Lou decisively. 'And can you deliver another one as soon as you can after that, please?'

'I can deliver it Sunday, if you want. I'm a seven-day-a-week man.'

'Perfect.'

'You're going to be a busy lady, I see, filling my skips in between printing out some more fake fivers to pay me with.'

*My skips.* So this must be Tom Broom himself then. He had a very curvy smile. Nice teeth. Natural.

Lou laughed. 'Precisely. Not enough hours in the day for us forgers.'

'Well, see you Saturday then.' He hoisted Clooney into the cab and held up his hand in a masculine wave.

**T**wo days later, the small accounts department surprised Lou the day before her birthday with a big fresh cream cake bearing the number '100' in wax candle figures, accompanied by a rousing rendition of the 'Happy Birthday to you, you were born in a zoo' version of the song.

'Very funny,' laughed Lou and divided the cake between them. Nicola wasn't there. She had taken an extended lunch break to go shopping for Sheffield's best designer gear.

Karen gave her an envelope and ordered Lou to open it up there and then. 'This is to say Happy Birthday from us all and to thank you for your support in our continuing fight against evil,' she said. It was a voucher for a colour and restyle at the trendiest hair salon in Barnsley.

'We've fixed it for ten o'clock tomorrow. If you can't make it, ring them now and say so, but it's with Carlo,' said Karen. 'He's an Italian. A drop-dead gorgeous Italian, as well. I couldn't resist booking him.' Karen knew all about Lou's penchant for things Italian.

'I'll be there; I'm not doing anything else,' said Lou. 'And can I just say, that's a fantastic present. Thanks, guys. I'm touched.'

Lou looked at the smiling crescent of people surrounding her and suddenly felt very emotional, which led to Zoe having to give Lou one of her tissues, and to Karen having to put her arm round her and give her a big sisterly squeeze. She thought that Lou was worth a lot more than a hairdo and, if ever her numbers came up on the lottery, she would force her friend on a grand tour of Italy so she could visit all those wonderful things and places she dreamed of. Karen had the impression that something was very wrong in Lou's world, despite her jolly exterior.

'I'm having my hair done tomorrow,' said Lou to Phil that night over their customary Friday curry. He grinned.

'That's good, because I've got a little birthday surprise for you myself. Be ready for half past seven in your glad rags and don't have anything to eat before.'

Lou gave a small gasp. 'Are we going out?'

'Might be,' said Phil. Lou's face lit up like Bonfire Night.

It takes so little to please her, thought Phil. Half of him smiled at that; half of him thought that sometimes it was like being married to a puppet. Therein lay the irony of having a surrendered wife.

The next morning, Phil gave her a big sloppy card and a big sloppy kiss and tapped his nose on the way out of the door. 'Remember what I told you. Seven thirty!' he said.

Lou had a birthday call from her mother, who reminded her of the arranged Sunday lunch as the usual birthday treat.

'I've sent your card—have you got it?' she said. 'I didn't post your present; it's here waiting for you.'

There were quite a few cards to open from work colleagues and her old friend Anna and her old Auntie Peggy in Cork who had put ten euros in it. Victorianna sent an ecard, on time for once. There was a beautiful 'best friend' card from Michelle with a flowing verse and a *Sorry I've been such a miserable cow, I really will make it up to you* hand-written message. Lou smiled. If Lou could have had one birthday wish granted it would be that Mish would sort herself out and once again be that nice, smiley, considerate person she had met in the cookery class.

There was nothing from Deb, although Lou didn't really think there would be. Really.

Lou got dressed and walked into town. It was a dry day, devoid of April showers and full of the promise of bright sunshine, both outside in the sky and inside in her spirit.

The hair salon was very white and very chrome. The receptionist smiled and led her to a chair which was pumped up so her legs dangled, and then the Angel Gabriel appeared behind her and started weaving his hands into her hair.

'Hi, I'm Carlo,' said a voice rich in bolognese sauce.

He was front-cover magazine-stunning with dark colouring, a pencil-line of black beard and spiky, platinum hair that shouldn't have worked, but did to great effect. He was far too young to fancy, but she could easily appreciate his gorgeousness. For a split second she imagined that she was his mother. What would that feel like? To look at a boy as beautiful as this and know he was your son? It threw her a little because she hadn't had thoughts like that for a long time.

'So, what are we doing for you today?'

'I don't know, to be honest. What do you think?'

Carlo stared at her reflection in the mirror and then, obviously inspired, he reached for a colour chart. After a lot of page-turning his eyes locked on a loop of dyed hair. 'What do you think?' he said.

Lou gulped.

'Trust me,' said the Italian Angel Gabriel.

Two hours later, Lou was watching wide-eyed with horror as Carlo snipped at her hair in much the same wildly extravagant way that she used to when playing hairdressers with her dolls.

'Relax!' said Carlo. 'You will look fan-tas-tico!' He spun her round so she couldn't see the finishing touches he was making. He fluffed, he sprayed, and when he turned her back to face the mirror, Lou's eyes widened like a startled owl's. Then her lips curved into a smile.

'I can't believe it. You've made my hair actually look longer!'

'It was too heavy before—you really needed those layers and a good cut. And it's much lighter up top so you can achieve some volume. What do you think of the colour? Not so frightening now?'

Lou examined the effect of the chilli-pepper orange heavily highlighting the front of her auburn waves, with just delicate touches of it at the sides. She felt trendier and looked younger than she had done in years. Why on earth had she ever stopped having her hair done?

'I absolutely love it!' said Lou.

'It brings out the colour of your eyes,' drawled Carlo sexily. 'My, they're so green. *Mamma mia!*'

Sod being his mother, now she wanted to snog him. That voice!

Her hair was heavily sliced at the front and flicked round onto her face, with choppy layers at the back. He'd even managed to sex up her blunt fringe. It made her want to go out and buy a new outfit. Bugger it, it was her birthday—she *would* go out and buy a new outfit.

Lou had a pleasant mosey round town and bought a very brave orange top and some bronzy copper jewellery, and a thrilling glossy lipstick that was guaranteed to stay on through dinner, drinks and a world war. She felt a buzz of excitement vibrate down her veins at the thought of the evening to come. *Please make him take me to an Italian*, she dared to ask the cosmos.

The skip was still there when she got home, but by the time the kettle had boiled there was the *beep-beep-beep* of something large reversing into the drive.

'Hi there,' called Lou, emerging from the front door as Tom Broom jumped down from the cab and started unrolling a huge net. She looked round the truck. 'No dog?'

'He's in the cabin. Not everyone likes seeing a hulking great beast bounding towards them. Or the dog either,' he joked.

'Oh.' She couldn't hide her disappointment.

'What? You want him out?'

'Well, if it's no trouble,' said Lou.

'No trouble to me,' said Tom and seconds later, Clooney was bounding towards Lou with his tail wagging a force-twelve draught.

'Shall we see if we can get you a biscuit?' said Lou.

Clooney woofed and turned excited circles.

'He can understand "biscuit", just to warn you,' said Tom with a lazy grin and, as he hooked up the skip, Lou went into the kitchen, closely followed by Clooney, where she gave him some of the dog biscuits she had just bought for him that morning in the pet shop.

She so missed having a dog. They'd had a German Shepherd-cross called Murphy at home. Her dad had been dead only weeks when Murphy's back legs collapsed. The vet put him to sleep, and she had scattered his ashes in the same place where they'd scattered her dad's. She dreamed of them together a lot. Phil was dreadfully allergic to all animals with fur, so a 'proper' pet was out of the question.

'Still want another skip tomorrow?' Tom Broom enquired, helping Clooney back up into the truck.

'Yes, please,' said Lou. She noticed the wrinkles round his eyes, then quickly reprimanded herself. She was a married woman, and her husband was taking her out tonight. Was this new hair-do of hers turning her into a sex maniac, eyeing up two different men in the space of a couple of hours? Both sharing that sexy Mediterranean look.

'Nice colour, by the way.'

'Sorry?'

'Hair. You've have it done since last time. Looks nice. It suits you.'

Then Tom Broom climbed up into the driver's seat and was gone before Lou could register that, before today, she couldn't remember the last time a man had complimented her appearance.

**A** long soak in a deep bath would have been a nice birthday treat. Lou gave her quarter-finished building site of a luxury bathroom a hard, frustrated look and went into the ensuite for a shower. Bloody Keith Featherstone! Phil refused to get involved in Lou's dispute with the builder. She'd wanted the fancy bathroom so she could sort it out. He reckoned she should cut loose from the man and organise another firm—it wasn't as if she'd paid Featherstone in advance or anything stupid like that. He told Lou to use her feminine charms. Builders always responded to a nice cleavage and a bit of eye-fluttering. Well, lazy, useless, unreliable Keith Featherstone hadn't.

Lou had a blissful half-hour after her shower reading a romance and nibbling on a couple of the Godiva truffles that had been put through the letterbox, courtesy of Des and Celia Winter-Brown. No ordinary 'Brown' surname for Celia—she had insisted they both adopt a double-barrelled one after their wedding vows. How Lou and Deb had laughed. God, she so wanted to pick up that phone now and dial Deb's number.

When Phil arrived home at half past six, he had a strange sneezing fit in the kitchen. 'Have there been any animals in here, Lou?' he said.

'Don't be silly,' said Lou. *Whoops.*

He had two presents for Lou, one in a carrier and the other in a gold gift bag. 'Here you go, babe. You know I'm no good at wrapping.'

Well, blokes weren't, were they, Lou agreed silently. She opened the white bag to find another of his amazing electrical appliance purchases. 'Oh, an omelette-maker! Great—thanks, love,' she said, overdoing the enthusiasm a tad to override the guilt she felt because she had already earmarked it for the charity bag. Phil seemed very keen for her to open the other present. Smiling, Lou reached in and pulled out something on a plastic hanger. It was a minuscule nightie in something scratchy with holes in strategic places.

'I thought we could have some fun with it when we get home later.'

'We'll see.' Lou smiled a paper-thin smile. Why couldn't it have been something sweet and sexy, not this tacky thing? Then again, this meant that he still fancied her, didn't it? Surely that was a good sign?

Phil slapped her bottom. 'What colour's that supposed to be on your head?' he laughed, before heading off to the ensuite for his shower.

**A**t half past seven that evening, the taxi pipped its arrival outside.

Lou slipped on her jacket and followed Phil outside into the spring-chilly night. She felt great in her new outfit and make-up, and Phil looked extra-handsome in his dark green suit. She was going to have a wonderful evening, she just knew she was.

There were people already in the car so Lou turned back.

'False alarm, Phil, it's not ours,' she said. 'It's got people inside.'

'Little birthday surprise. I asked Fat Jack and Maureen to join us.'

'You. Are. Joking,' said Lou.

'I thought it would feel more like a party with another couple. This is all for you, Lou, please don't spoil it for me.'

'Don't give me that. You're going to talk business, aren't you, and leave me with Boring Maureen all night? It'll be just like last flaming Christmas all over again,' said Lou, gritting her teeth.

**F**at Jack and Phil moved into the restaurant, their identical smiles flashing superiority at the Chinese waiter, one an older, brasher version of the other. The ladies followed an almost dutiful five paces behind.

Jack seemed more colourful and dynamic than ever but Maureen seemed to have aged a few years in the few months since Christmas. Her customary 'teak sideboard' hair shade hadn't been touched up and she looked as thin as a baby bird, hollow-cheeked and pale—almost as if she was fading away to ultimate transparency.

As Lou had predicted, Jack and Phil talked cars, with the occasional foray into what Barnsley Football Club should do, and then on to the fascinating subject of Jack's new koi carp fishpond. Halfway through her crispy duck, Lou gave up trying to catch Phil's attention, she gave up trying to start up a conversation with monosyllabic Maureen and she gave up believing that this evening had anything to do with her birthday, or her. Stupid Lou.

Lou ate her food and drank her wine and watched the hands of the wall clock circle lazily. Maureen had eaten hardly anything, but had been drinking wine at a surprising rate. It was a wonder she wasn't on her back by the time the bill arrived.

'We thought we'd just nip to the club down the road for a couple,' said Phil as he helped her on with her coat. 'Birthday drink?' he added.

'Oh, so you remember it's my birthday, do you?' said Lou quietly.

The club was slightly more depressing on the inside than the rough brick exterior suggested, which was a feat in itself, but it did serve the best pint in the area, apparently. It had a very long bar, to accommodate 'leaners', and the comfortable women's seats were deliberately positioned a small taxi ride away from it. Phil brought Lou and Maureen two double vodkas and Cokes each, then he rejoined Jack at the bar.

Lou sipped her drink, her eyes flitting round the flaked paintwork. The pressure to engage with Maureen all night had tired her brain out, so she was startled when Maureen suddenly started to talk.

'I'm a grandmother, did you know?' she said with a slurring pride.

'Congratulations,' said Lou. She knew their only son, Peter, lived out in Australia. 'When did that happen then?'

'Five years ago today,' said Maureen.

'Well, slightly belated congratulations then,' said Lou. 'Boy or girl?'

'Girl,' Maureen sniffed. She opened the locket round her neck with trembling fingers to show Lou two blurry pictures. 'This is my Charlotte,' she announced, gulping on the name.

'Aw, she's bonny,' said Lou truthfully. 'You must be feeling as if you want to just hop on a plane and go out there. Have you any plans to?'

Maureen shook her head. Then Lou realised she couldn't speak because there were great big fat tears dropping down her face.

'Maureen, are you OK?' asked Lou. She fished in her bag for a tissue, which Maureen utilised completely.

'Jack wouldn't ever go and see Peter now, so I've never seen my granddaughter,' Maureen said at last. She took a long swig from her drink. 'Our Pete always wanted to travel but Jack was all on for forcing him into the business. He said if Pete didn't stop his fancy ideas then that would be it, he could sod off and not come back. Pete told him he was quite happy to do that and went out of the door with just a bag on his shoulder. That was the last time I saw my son.'

Lou watched the older woman blow her nose and take a long, shuddering breath. Phil had told her that Maureen had once been Miss South Yorkshire, something Lou had scoffed at until now, looking side-on at the remnants of a much-faded beauty.

'Pete was never interested in cars,' Maureen sniffed. 'He used to draw. That's what he's doing now—graphic art in Sydney—and he's done really well for himself, despite his father telling him over the years that he'd "come to nothing, painting all the bloody time."' Maureen laughed a little manically. 'All those years I stuck with Jack to keep the family together, turning a blind eye to his women—and for what?'

'Jack had other women?' said Lou. As if on cue, Fat Jack laughed loud and crudely at the bar, his great blubbery belly years past the effort of being sucked in, and Lou wondered what Maureen had ever seen in him—never mind what anyone else had seen in him.

'He could always get women, love,' said Maureen, looking at him also but seeing a younger, slimmer Jack. 'It nearly killed me the first time I found out about it, but I didn't want him to leave me so I just let him get on with it. There was Peter to think of, you see.' Maureen gave a bitter laugh. ''Course, his flings always ended. His tarts weren't exactly the type to have his tea on the table for him every night.'

Lou felt quite sick and very guilty. To her shame she'd presumed Maureen had always been a limp lettuce. But then *this* Maureen at the side of her, crying softly into a glass of vodka, would never have attracted someone as strong and forceful as the young Jack. Once upon a time, it seemed, there had been a sparky beauty queen and a dynamic go-getter who had butted together perfectly, but then the power balance had somehow tipped and kept on tipping until they had evolved into little more than parasite and host. Jack the lad and Miss South Yorkshire were long gone, leaving two strangers behind.

'Pete told me when he got settled he'd send for me and I'd go over there.' Maureen dabbed at the tears that flowed down her cheeks.

'And did he ever send for you?' asked Lou softly.

Maureen nodded. 'Aye, he sent for me, lass. Jack said I'd to make a choice. Him or Peter. I couldn't have both.'

'No!' said Lou incredulously, although she didn't know why that surprised her. There was meanness behind Jack's eyes.

'There were always choices with Jack—him or my sister, him or Peter, him or my friend Bren, and, fool that I am, I picked Jack every time because I couldn't bear to lose him. He doesn't know I've got this picture of Charlotte. Don't tell him, Lou, will you? He won't let me contact our Pete again and it's the only thing I've got of her.'

*Let?* Lou's body stiffened. How on earth did a woman get into the position of 'letting' a man make her choose between those she loved?

Maureen's thin hand fell onto Lou's. 'It wasn't all his fault. I didn't stop it happening.'

'*Why* didn't you?' Lou asked. She wanted to go much further and ask: *Why didn't you stand up and fight your corner? Why didn't you leave him? Why did you let go of all you had been?*

Maureen looked up at Lou with eyes that had nothing behind them but tears and alcohol. 'I just left it too late,' she said.

'Come on, you drunken old mare!' said Jack, bursting into their conversation, laughing and pulling Maureen to her feet a little too roughly.

Lou followed them to the taxi, a thought flickering in her drink-fuzzy brain, but it was just a little too out of reach to be caught and examined.

Back at home, Phil was waiting for Lou with two glasses and a bottle of fake champagne when she came out of the cloakroom toilet. She was annoyed, he could tell, but Lou was so easy to play. She was incapable of staying pissed off with him for any longer than five minutes. 'Fancy trying out your birthday present?' he said, swivelling his hips.

'You want an omelette at this time of night?' Lou answered glibly.

Phil swaggered over to her and pressed his groin against her, crooning seductively, 'Don't be silly, babe, you know exactly what I mean.'

But Lou surprised him by stepping out of the closing cage of his arms. 'Not tonight, thank you, Phil,' she said wearily.

**F**or as long as he could remember in his marriage, the smell of bacon wafting up the stairs had been Phil's gentle Sunday-morning alarm. Ironically, it was his senses in shock from the defiance of custom that now sparked him awake. He padded downstairs to the kitchen to find out what was going on. There he found Lou, sitting on the floor like a desert island in a sea of books. There was evidence that she had intended his breakfast at least—the pans were on the hob and the eggs and bacon out on the work surface, but her present absorption had assumed importance over tending to his needs.

'What are you doing?' he asked.

His voice jolted her momentarily from her concentration. 'Clearing the bookshelves,' she said, returning to some file she was reading.

'Never!'

When she didn't engage, the effect on him was tantamount to a smack. He knew only too well the power of indifference. It was his own personal favourite weapon. Not that he was worried she wouldn't be back to her old Lou self in no time. OK, she was still annoyed about last night, but he and Jack had got a lot of important talking done.

'Er, I thought instead of the usual that we might try out your birthday present? The other one?' He was careful to say 'we'.

'Yes, I'll sort it in a minute. I've run out of black pudding, though.'

It occurred to him that she wasn't listening.

'It's OK, I'll have peas instead,' he tested.

'No worries,' she replied.

Lou hadn't planned to clear out the books. She had gone down, automaton-style, to cook Phil's Sunday breakfast, but what she saw when she first opened the door was the last remaining vestige of disorder in the kitchen—the bookshelves. On the bottom shelf there was a stack of holiday brochures. She thumbed through them, and pictures of Venetian canals and pretty hotels taunted her from the pages. The next shelf up was full of her Midnight Moon romance collection, and a box full of instruction manuals and guarantees for appliances, most of which she no longer had. On the other shelves were all her cookery books and the files of recipes she had collected over many years. She had quite forgotten the Casa Nostra file was among the recipe files.

Casa Nostra. The name set off a flare in her head and she glimpsed all the associated memories. The premises they'd found, the furnishings they had planned, the excitement when the bank manager agreed to the loan, and how they'd jumped up and down hugging each other (and the bank manager). Casa Nostra was a working title, but whatever it was going to be finally called, it would be a coffee-house like no other. It was going to bring a little Italy to their corner of Yorkshire, with proper fortifying coffee to wash down the most extravagant, indulgent cakes in the world. It was to be the start of their empire that couldn't fail because they knew that, together, they were an indomitable force.

Deb's big, rounded handwriting was scribbled everywhere: *Lou— what do you think of this for a pud of the week? Lou—let's make it our aim to de-naff Black Forest Gâteau. Lou—let's make the biggest pudding in the world and call it a Brando. What should it be, I wonder?*

They had been touching the dream, until the day when she had found Deb on the doorstep in a dreadful state and, five minutes later, Lou's world had fallen apart. Her agony had been unbearable, but Deb's had been too. *Lou, I've got something awful to tell you . . . Phil's having an affair. I've seen them together.*

Yet Deb had nursed her through the heartbreak with patience and selflessness. Then Phil came back and made her choose. And Lou had chosen him.

Lou made Phil a smaller than usual fried breakfast and she hadn't used her new omelette-maker, he noted. 'One egg?' he questioned.

'We'll be at my mother's eating lunch in two and a half hours.'

Phil groaned. 'Oh, flaming Norah—can't I give it a miss?'

'You can if you want, but you'll have to make your own lunch.'

'OK, I'll go.' Phil loved his food. 'Er, I've been thinking about holidays,' he said. 'Fancy going somewhere different this year?'

Lou looked up. 'What, like Italy?' she said with a gulp.

'No, I don't fancy Italy,' said Phil. 'It's full of Italians.'

'Precisely,' said Lou. 'And fantastic Italian architecture—'

'Boring churches, you mean.'

'The Colosseum isn't a church,' said Lou. 'Neither is the Circus Maximus or the Forum or Pompeii.' *Places she so wanted to see.*

'I hated Latin at school,' said Phil. 'And I've seen Hadrian's Wall.'

'OK, then,' said Lou, trying a tack tailored to his likes, 'what about the wonderful food and the beautiful wines?'

'I hate pizza and I'm not that bothered about wine.'

'Sunshine, Phil, Italy is bursting with sunshine!' Lou half screamed. She knew she had him here. Phil worshipped at the altar of Apollo.

'Yeah, but it's Italian sun, it's different. I was thinking about Torremolinos. I've seen a five-star that you'd love, Lou.'

Phil's voice faded to white noise in the background as he blah-blahed on about a holiday he had probably already booked. They always holidayed where and how Phil wanted. Lou slid the brochures into a carrier bag to take out to the skip. There was no point in keeping them.

At a quarter to ten, while Phil was engrossed in the *Sunday World,* the skip wagon reversed into their drive. Lou went out to meet it.

'Good morning,' said Lou breezily. It was such a crisp day, refreshingly chilly, and as bright and beautiful as the hymn. There were still snowdrops lingering in the borders, but purple crocuses and daffodils with their trumpets as orange as fresh egg yolks had pushed through for their turn in the limelight. 'And good morning to you, Clooney.'

Clooney started play-biting at Lou's hand, until Tom shouted at him to stop.

'He's not hurting me,' said Lou, getting a dog biscuit out.

'You're spoiling him,' said Tom. 'He'll not want to come home.'

'I'd have him like a shot . . .'

Tom coughed. 'I was just wondering if you'd like to go . . .' He was talking at the same time as Lou added, '. . . but my husband is allergic to pet hair. Oh, I'm sorry, you were saying?'

'No, it's fine,' said Tom quickly, giving the back of his neck a rub and muttering: 'Oh, well, that's that then. What a shame.'

'Oh, don't feel too sorry for him—he doesn't like dogs anyway.'

Tom looked confused by what she had just said, but before Lou could retrack on the conversation, Clooney barked and distracted them. He'd found a rubber ball under the hedge.

Lou played fetch with him on the lawn while Tom lowered the skip off his wagon. 'You're keen, I'll give you that,' he said, looking at the bags of rubbish piled by the wheelie-bin awaiting his arrival. 'Maybe you should have got one of the bigger-sized skips.'

'The mini-skip will be fine. I can't have that much more stuff,' said Lou. 'I'll have this filled today so you could pick it up tomorrow. Do you know,' she went on, 'I would never have imagined that clearing out could make me feel so . . .' She hunted for the word but couldn't find it, so gestured joy with enthusiastic hands instead.

'You're not the first to tell me that,' said Tom, nodding with understanding. 'Some say it's better than therapy. I might change my name to "Tom Broom, Waste Therapist", and charge double. Not that that would matter too much to someone who prints her own money.'

Lou smiled a smile that mirrored his.

'I bet that was a nice little cracket in its time,' Tom commented, pointing to a small crude rectangular stool amongst the pile of stuff. 'A really handy piece to have around.'

'It was, and just the right size for sitting on or standing on to reach things, as I invariably have to,' said Lou with a little tut. 'I must confess I still feel a bit guilty throwing it away, but it's so battered now.'

'It still looks pretty solid to me, despite the knocks. It must feel like you are giving up an old friend,' said Tom. 'It's harder than it looks sometimes to let things go, even if they are old and useless. Things gather emotions to them so that people often feel they are throwing so much more away than an old vase that their granny gave them.' He smiled and Lou gulped. This big man standing in front of her in his overalls sounded almost as if he was reciting poetry. 'It's amazing how attached some people can get to old rubbish. They've lived with it for so long that throwing it away is scary and doesn't feature as an option.'

A picture of Maureen drifted into her mind and Lou nodded.

'That's very true, Tom.'

He had stubble this morning. She wondered fleetingly what it might feel like rubbing against her chin, or elsewhere. Enough of that, Lou Winter, she reprimanded herself. Still, it was an interesting thought that left behind quite a quivery sensation in its wake. She quickly got out the money from her back pocket. It was embarrassingly warm.

'Hot off the press, is it?' Tom said to her horror. She felt her cheeks heating up too, but attempted to laugh it off. 'Yes. Be careful, the ink's not quite dry yet.'

He grinned. Stubble and grins. Lou went even hotter.

'Anyway, thanks. Just give us a ring when you want it picked up. Come on, Clooney, we've got kids to take to the park.'

A bucket of water hit Lou's heart and extinguished the smiley feelings that were hopping about in there. Of course someone like him would be married with children, she said to herself. Anyway, what difference did it make? Why was she suddenly upset to learn that he was married with children? Her head was all over the place this morning.

When Tom's wagon drove off Lou rolled up her sleeves to start, but the sight of that faithful old stool on the heap of rubbish brought a sudden rush of tears to her eyes.

'You've had your hair done,' said Renee.

'Birthday treat from the people at work. Do you like it?' said Lou.

'It's a bit orange,' Renee replied.

Renee had bought Lou a jumper for her birthday. It was a very nice plain black top, slash necked with three-quarter sleeves and four pearl buttons off centre.

'Mum, that is really lovely,' said Lou. 'Thank you.'

'It's very slimming, is black,' said Renee. 'I didn't know whether to get you a size smaller to give you some encouragement.'

Lou gulped her sherry. Her mother meant well, she told herself.

Renee Casserly served up a very nice pork lunch. Lou noticed her portion was considerably smaller than Phil's but she didn't comment.

Just after the washing-up had been done, the phone rang.

'Oh, hello, lovey.' Sunshine flooded Renee's voice. Lou could name that caller in one. 'How many degrees? Ooh, that is warm, isn't it? . . . Smashing . . . Yes, I've packed it. I just have to get it to the post office.'

Aha, thought Lou. *When's my hamper coming, Mummy dahling?*

'. . . Tuesday, I hope. Elouise is here if you want to have a quick word . . . Oh, I see. Well, never mind . . . She sends her love.'

No, I bloody well don't, Lou thought loudly.

'Bye-bye, dear . . . Yes, I love you, too.' Renee put the phone down looking as if she'd just had a private audience with Daniel O'Donnell. 'That was Victorianna. She sends her love.'

No, she bloody well doesn't, thought Lou again.

'Will you give me a lift to the post office with that parcel for her on

Tuesday? Everything's all wrapped up now,' said Renee, pointing to an enormous box in the corner.

''Course I—flaming heck, Mum. That'll cost you a fortune. I don't know, she really is a . . . making you do this.' Lou omitted the word.

'She didn't make me, she asked. I could have said no. Oh, Lou, why are you always so aggressive where Victorianna is concerned?' snapped Renee. 'What on earth did she ever do to deserve all that sniping?'

*Mum, you really don't want to know the answer to that one.*

'Anyway, are you going to do it for her or do I have to get a taxi?'

'Yes, of course I will,' sighed Lou.

'**H**ello, Keith Featherstone here,' announced a voice thick with the smoke of twenty years of filterless fags.

'At last, Mr Featherstone! It's Mrs Winter,' said Lou, with half-shock, half-relief at finding herself speaking to his actual voice and not the gravelly answering machine message. 'Mr Featherstone, I really need you to finish this bathroom. It's been over six weeks now since you left it.' Lou dropped her voice so Phil wouldn't hear the next bit, as he would have gone totally bonkers. 'And I did pay you cash in advance so you'd treat this as a priority. As you promised you would.'

Lou felt sick saying it. Sometimes she was like a puppy that trusted everyone and invariably got booted, although no one could have kicked her more over this bathroom business than she had kicked herself.

'You are totally right, Mrs Winter. I feel awful about it.'

'I must have this finished. It's not very fair of you.' Crikey, she'd stamp her foot in a moment and that would really show him.

'I can't leave what I'm on at the moment, that's the problem. Old lady, you see, got broken into. I couldn't forgive myself if I didn't sort her out. I'll be there as soon as this is finished, Mrs Winter. I promise.'

'OK, Mr Featherstone. As soon as you can then. Thank you.'

She could have sworn she heard sniggering before the line went dead.

**H**er phone bleeped the arrival of a text message as Lou pulled into the office car park. It was from Michelle: Let's go out Friday to celebrate your birthday. Sorry haven't rung. Met gr8 bloke. Need to talk soon xxx

Lou shook her head. She thought back to the one and only time she had agreed to go out with Michelle on a Friday night. Her whole evening consisted of being dragged from pub to pub while Michelle trailed after various fanciable men and then, when she got an audience with one of her quarries, Lou was pushed off to entertain 'the mate'. At the end of the evening, just when she thought her feet might drop off from shoe-pain, Lou was forced to stand for three-quarters of an hour at a freezing taxi rank and then take an extremely drunk and sobbing Michelle home and make sure she was safely tucked up in bed. Then, and only then, could she jump back into the waiting taxi to head across town to her own house. It was worth every penny of the exorbitant fare just to take off her shoes. Going round town at seventeen in skyscraper stilettos with mates like Deb was brill, but doing it in her thirties with someone like Michelle had been excruciating.

When Michelle rang her the next weekend to ask if she was up for another 'fun night out', Lou used Phil (who hadn't been at all pleased about the last one) as a convenient excuse, saying that he wasn't keen on her going out at nights. That exchange marked the start of the first big crack in their friendship as Michelle made a couple of snide comments about Lou being under the thumb. Maybe, once upon a time, Lou might have been under the illusion that Michelle's birthday invite was borne of selfless motives. But not now. She texted back: Glad about the man. Talk later. Can't do nights, sorry. Lunch would be good though xxx

If we must, text-sulked Michelle, although Lou knew it wouldn't happen. There weren't that many desirable men to stalk at noon in the Edwardian Tea Rooms over giant scones.

Lou walked into the office and her heart sank immediately on seeing that Karen's space was unoccupied. Stan wasn't in either. 'Where is everyone? It's like the *Marie Celeste* in here,' said Lou to Zoe after Nicola had marched off with a very important walk and a folder.

'Stan's wife phoned him in sick—migraine, apparently—and Karen's little boy is poorly so she's taken a day off,' said Zoe, in a voice more cracked than Keith Featherstone's smoke-ravaged voice.

'Hell, girl, you should be at home with that throat,' said Lou.

'I rang in this morning but *she* said that if I didn't get in here then I'd be in trouble, what with everyone else being off.'

'She can't do this sort of thing.'

'She can, because she's doing it, isn't she, Lou?' croaked Zoe.

The skip was just being lifted by the truck when Lou arrived home. The skip man acknowledged her with a nod but, to her disappointment, it wasn't Tom. She had been looking forward to seeing Clooney, too.

'No dog today?' she said lightly, despite the sensation of a cannonball in the pit of her stomach. 'The German Shepherd,' she clarified.

'Clooney, you mean? He's the boss's dog. Only ever goes with him.'

'Oh, what a shame. That's the bloke who usually comes, is it? He's the boss?' Lou said with breezy innocence. 'I didn't realise he had anyone else working for him.'

'There's a few of us,' said the skip man. 'There's me, Steve and "Part-time Eddie", except those two are off at the mo' and Tom's not been working the last couple of days, which is why we're short-handed and I'm having to do this so late on.'

'He's not ill, is he?' said Lou, poking a little further.

'No, he's not ill, but someone in his family is.'

'Not one of his children, I hope?' said Lou, slightly ashamed that she was being so nosy, but unable to stop herself all the same.

'Tom ain't got any kids. I think it's his sister who's poorly.'

*Tom ain't got any kids.*

That little cloud nudged in her chest although she was then cross with herself for not having had the forethought to say, *Not his wife or his children, I hope?* He hadn't been wearing a wedding ring, but then she didn't half the time. Then again, what difference did it make if he was married with forty-five children or single, gay or celibate, for God's sake? She was married, and Tom Broom was a bloke who was nice and chatty because he had a business to run. Anyway, even if he was straight and unattached, he wasn't exactly going to be interested in a dumpy little married woman coming up to the back end of her thirties with a bum so big it could be seen from orbit. Considering she wasn't interested, she was spending a lot of headspace on not being interested, she realised. What the hell was up with her?

# CHAPTER 3

SPRING HAD TO BE Lou's favourite season for flowers. It was so pretty when the sun shone and woke up the buds. Her stocky hyacinths on the windowsill were releasing their pungent scent into the kitchen. Outside, the cherry blossom was thick on the tree branches and banks of daffs nodded to each other in the breeze. But according to the weather forecast, Sunday was going to be the last day of good weather for a week at least, and so Lou was up early to make the most of it. She had decided that the garden was next in line for an overhaul.

She had rung for one of the larger skips midweek, dictating her order to an answering machine, and it hadn't been Tom who had delivered it either. By nine o'clock today, it was already half-full of the bonfire pile that had been waiting for a match for a year and a half. It was only since she had started this clutter-clearing that the sight of it had begun to annoy her, and it was far too sodden to burn now.

She set to, sawing all the tree branches into smaller pieces, then wheelbarrowed them over to the skip. She wrestled a plastic garden chair, entrapped by a clingy weed behind a row of conifers, with a force that suggested she was battling something else. But triumphing over a bulky bit of plastic could not quite take away her frustration and disappointment. Well, she might not be able to control who delivered her skips, but at least she could have the upper hand over the chair.

Phil teased back the curtain to see Lou pulling at something white from behind the line of firs. His stomach growled like a caged bear. Where was his wife? Out wrestling rubbish like a small Big Daddy—again. He went downstairs, opened the back door and called out to Lou. His shout coincided with her last heave and Lou dropped the chair on the grass before strolling back across the lawn to the house. Her arms and clothes were filthy. She was panting like an animal.

It must have been his imagination, but she looked leaner. Actually, he thought, she looked quite sexy. 'I'm awake,' he announced.

'Yes, I see you,' Lou replied breathlessly. It was backbreaking work but exhilarating. The harder she worked, the more energised she felt, and it had the unexpected side effect of revving up a libido she thought had been waiting for its last rites.

'Break for breakfast?' queried Phil, who really meant: *Leave the sodding trees alone and get out the Big George grill.*

'Yes, OK,' said Lou, stripping off her gloves.

Her lips are blood red, thought Phil. He steered Lou into the house. No sooner had they made it through the door when Lou turned round, they collided and then he couldn't believe what sparked between them. He struggled her bra off and started rolling her nipples round in his hands, a quick grope before he moved in for the main event . . . but Lou, it seemed, had other ideas. She grabbed his hand and made it do her bidding. He barely had to do anything before she was gasping out her orgasm. Then, before Phil had a chance to protest, Lou pushed him onto a kitchen chair and pleasured him in his absolute favourite way.

'Wow,' said Phil breathlessly, popping his spent equipment back under cover as Lou stood up and started dressing. If the truth be told, he had been getting rather annoyed with all this skip and cleaning business and had decided not to let her carry on with it any more, but if this morning was anything to go by, maybe he should, because advantages were starting to manifest themselves. And he had really noticed changes in the house. It sounded daft, but every time a skip left, he could have sworn the house felt lighter.

'I think we could definitely do with some breakfast now,' Phil grinned. 'I'm starving.'

He gave her breast a squeeze, not noticing how Lou suddenly shrank from his touch. With her body now satiated, her brain was busy trying to analyse what had just happened. Lou Winter had just shamelessly used her husband to satisfy a basic need, and it didn't make her feel very good about herself to admit that, for a few minutes back there, she had been imagining someone else's hands all over her. It was thinking about *him* that had brought her to that wild point of no return.

She was thirty-six and this was her only experience of sex that had everything to do with selfish gratification and nothing to do with affection. Was it this detachment that let men cheat on their wives and then jump back into bed with them before the top note of the other woman's scent had faded on their shirts?

Adventurous sex had never been a priority in her marriage. She and Phil hadn't even made a dent in the index of the *Kama Sutra*. 'Mr Missionary' got bored doing foreplay but then again, he had rather been led to believe that he did the business superbly well because of his wife's kind but misguided attempts to fake her pleasure. Lou found herself trapped in a web of her own making and, as such, had to put up with it. Actually, she could take or leave sex but Phil took a pleasure from her, usually on Sunday mornings, which she was happy to give. Her own sex-drive was so low, her libido was barely breathing. At least, she had thought so, until the injection of freak hormones that morning. There was nothing written about that in the clutter-clearing article!

While Phil was happily reading his usual spread of Sunday newspapers, Lou's phone announced the arrival of a text message: Can u talk? It was from Michelle. Now was as good a time as any for a chat. She couldn't put anything more in the skip now, it was filled to the max.

'Hiya.' Michelle answered the phone sounding breathless but bright. 'Oh, Lou, it's official, I've got a boyfriend,' she squeaked excitedly.

'Come on, then, tell me the details.'

'His name's Craig, he's thirty-three . . .'

'Ooh, toy boy . . .'

'Only two years! Anyway, he's a mechanic, comes from Leeds, six foot, blond hair, blue eyes, nice smile, unattached, no kids . . .'

Well, so far he sounded promising—suspiciously so.

'He's in-between jobs at the moment. It's killing him being on the dole. Anyway, he was married but he's separated. They're at that sorting-out-the-financial-stuff stage at the moment. He's sleeping on the couch.'

Ah, here we go, thought Lou. She knew it was too good to be true.

'Met him in the White Hart last weekend, then we went clubbing and I invited him back for a coffee. We started snogging on the sofa like teenagers and then we just seemed to float up to bed—it was weird. My clothes just seemed to fall off like they do in films. We spent the whole weekend at it, apart from him watching the match on Saturday afternoon and the sports highlights at night. I tell you he's got some stamina, it was fantastic. He even got up to make my breakfast. Well, tea and toast. God, Lou, he is the most gorgeous man I've ever met.'

'Have you heard from him since?' said Lou, trying hard to sound frothy and positive and not like the angel of doom.

''Course I have. I said to him, "Ring me when you get home and let me know the taxi arrived safely", and he did. Well, he phoned from his mate's house—he hasn't got a mobile.'

A bloke without a mobile? 'Taxi to Leeds? Crikey, that will have taken care of his week's dole money, won't it?' Lou said.

'It was my fault he missed the taxi home with his mates, so I gave him the money for it. And I know what you're going to say about that, but listen to this, he's coming over next Friday night, and he's making me a meal here, as a thank you, so it's a good job you can't do *evenings*, because I would have had to cancel anyway,' Michelle added pointedly.

'That's nice,' said Lou. It wasn't her place to turn into her mother and start fire-extinguishing Michelle's happiness. 'So, are you looking forward to him turning up on Friday then?'

'Of course,' said Michelle tightly. 'Why did you say it like that?'

'Like what?' said Lou. Heck, how had she said it?

'Sarcastic. That little phrase about him "turning up". You don't think he'll turn up, do you?'

'I hope he does,' said Lou.

'Hope? You *hope*?'

Lou obviously wasn't equipped for this conversation with Michelle. She wasn't in full military anti-landmine gear. 'Oh, Mish, I really *really* want you to find someone nice, and what I'm trying to say is that I hope he does turn up and you have a great time.'

'He *will* turn up!' Michelle was cross now. 'You know, Lou, I was dying to tell you, my *friend*, all about him but I just knew you'd have to try and spoil it *as usual*. Speak to you later. Maybe.'

With that, Michelle slammed the phone down, leaving Lou wondering once again why she always seemed to be on a different footing to the rest of the universe.

The skip was lifted the next day while Lou was having a horrible Monday at work: Karen had been sent off on a course, leaving Lou alone with Jaws. Still, it made the Tuesday that followed it all the sweeter, not only to be away from the place but to be up early waiting for the next skip to arrive. Lou got all her old garb on then twisted off her wedding ring, leaving it in its usual 'waiting place' in the spoon rest. She and Phil had chosen their rings together. His was a huge, heavy rose-gold hoop, and he had chosen a similar one for her over her choice of a delicate plain band. It was far too wide for her little hand and totally impractical to wear and, since she had put on extra weight over the last year or so, it felt tight and uncomfortable when her fingers were warm. Not that she would admit that to Phil—for with the way he and her mother harped on about her bum, she sometimes felt she should pack in her job in Accounts and go and enroll on a sumo wrestling course. It would be OK when she lost a bit more weight, she knew, but for now she sneaked the ring off when Phil wasn't around.

The air was nippy and damp, but that didn't stop her tackling the five-foot nettles, the last leg of the garden clearance. Then what—the cellar or the loft? The cellar, she decided. She was in no way ready to clear out what lay in wait for her up there.

Phil pulled off his wedding ring and rubbed at his finger to try and reduce the slight indentation it made. Women customers always flashed a glance towards that third finger, left hand. To some that ring was a symbol of a solid, trustworthy soul, but he could also instinctively spot the others who preferred to see that finger naked because it gave them a guilt-free opportunity to flirt down the final figure. And he always left enough margins in his prices for them to be able to do that.

Reading people was all part of the game and Phil was an expert at it. That sunkissed little blonde number in the scarlet suit, for instance, eyeing up the quality end of his car market, was definitely the rings-off, full-throttle flirtation type. Popping his wedding band into his pocket, Phil prepared his smile.

Lou barely registered the arrival of the skip lorry, her head was so full of its own debris as she heaved on the devil foliage. She had been thinking about work and what an increasing nightmare it was for everyone who worked in the department, and that Sunday sex episode with Phil was still circling her head like a deranged vulture. Also she didn't know whether to ring Michelle and apologise for coming across as St Elouise of Doom.

It made her revisit those easy friendship days with Deb for the zillionth time. They'd only ever argued about one thing—the ratio of flour to egg in a Yorkshire Pudding.

'Hello.'

Lou snapped her head up and immediately swallowed. It was *him*, complete with dog, which he was holding by the collar as Clooney whined and pawed to get to the nice lady who gave him biscuits.

'Oh, hello,' she squeaked. He really did have a lovely, lovely grin— STOP! She quickly bent down to beckon Clooney, who broke free from Tom and bounced towards Lou with such enthusiasm that he knocked her backwards into the wet grass.

'Clooney, down!' boomed Tom. 'Are you all right? He's bloody barmy that dog, sometimes,' he said, striding over to her.

'Yes, I'm fine,' said Lou, shrugging bravely. Fine apart from feeling a total twerp, that was. Suddenly he was standing over her, bending, and his hands were under her armpits. *Oh no. Oh no no no no no!*

Most women have a fantasy about being lifted effortlessly up into a man's arms as if they were light as a size zero feather. However, Lou was all too aware that Prince Charming would probably buckle over with the surprise weight of her and completely knacker his back. Tom Broom, however, was a strong bloke and Lou found herself lifted easily to her feet without any snapping of spines.

'Thank you,' said Lou, not really knowing where to look, and simultaneously displaying every nervous gesture that was possible: blinking; neck rubbing; hair fiddling; turning into a living, breathing beetroot.

'I'll leave him in the van in future,' said Tom.

'No, no, it's not his fault. Please, don't, I love to see him,' she pleaded.

They both looked at Clooney who was lying, nose down on the ground, great dark eyes flicking from one to the other in desperate appeal for forgiveness, although for what he hadn't a clue.

Lou's head was a blender full of mixed-up ingredients. She was feeling sorry for the dog, feeling embarrassed for herself, feeling God-knows-what at being airlifted up from the ground by this man with hands the size of spades and a face that said *Made in Italy*.

'Have the other skip lads been looking after you then?'

'Oh, y . . . yes,' stuttered Lou.

'And did you palm them off with some more counterfeit money?'

'Absolutely. Fifteen-pound notes this time.'

'Ha! I shall make sure I check the tills when I get back.'

Good—they were suddenly back on a normal footing. Lou took a deep breath. 'They . . . er . . . said someone was ill in your family. I hope he . . . or she . . . is better now.'

'Well, she's not exactly ill. It's my sister—she's pregnant with her fourth kid.' Tom tutted fondly. 'She's been having a bit of a rough time, though. My brother-in-law is working away at the moment. I sometimes take the kids off her hands to give her a break.'

'No children of your own then?' *Wow, big brave Lou!*

'No.' Tom shook his head. 'Not that I know of, anyway. Me and the wife were never really that bothered.'

'Ah, I see.' So he was married then.

'Then we split up just as I was starting to get interested. Being close to my sister's kids made me see just how great it would be to have my own. Ah well. *C'est la vie*—or *Così va il mondo*, as the Italians say.'

Lou tried to rope in the smile that threatened to spread right across her face and meet full circle at the back of her head.

'You got any kids?' Tom asked.

'No,' said Lou. 'I can't, I'm afraid.'

'Oh, bloody hell, I'm sorry,' said Tom. His hand twitched as if he might have wanted to give her a comforting touch. 'Sorry for saying "bloody hell" then, by the way. Shouldn't swear in front of ladies.'

*He* needed rescuing now, Lou realised. People never knew what to say when an inability to conceive was admitted to. 'It's OK, I'm fine with it,' Lou said, switching on her totally-at-ease-with-the-subject face, which would have fooled all but the most discerning eye.

Clooney gave a low *woof* to remind them of his presence.

'Can I give h-i-m a biscuit?' Lou whispered, in all innocence.

Clooney barked joyfully. He was forgiven. Otherwise, why would she have said 'biscuit'?

Tom Broom laughed. 'Y-e-s, you can give him a *biscuit.*'

The joke passed two feet over Lou's head as she took Clooney off to the biscuit cupboard. There was still a ghost of laughter playing round Tom's mouth when she returned the dog to him, then he gave her a cheery wave and a 'See you soon, no doubt' and drove off. Lou tried not to notice that her insides felt as if they were full of warm olive oil.

**R**enee twisted the three gold bands round her finger. One a thin, old gold wedding ring; one studded with a full range of precious gems that Shaun had bought her to say he would love her for ever; the third an

engagement ring with three emeralds and five diamonds. They had cost
him a fortune at the time, but they were exquisite. He couldn't have
known what an investment he'd made when he bought those rings.
He had placed them on Renee's finger when his heart was full of the
ambitions that charmed her down the aisle with him. Shaun's enlarged
heart was always going to be the undoing of him.

When Elouise came along, Shaun decided he didn't want to be a
man who worked all hours and never saw his wife nor his child, so he
found the plateau job that enabled him to provide well for his family
but be home every evening to eat with them and enjoy them. No one
could say that Shaun Casserly didn't provide for his family; they
wanted for nothing. Well, none of the basics anyway. Renee had been
shocked to find out the true extent of his provisions for her, just in case
they didn't make it to his pension together. The insurance policy he had
in place would see her in good stead for the rest of her days, but it had
all been much too late for Renee.

Elouise's birth had marked the death of all Renee's greater plans for
their early married years: the monstrously huge house and three-acre
garden, the flash car, the holidays cruising the Mediterranean . . . She
wanted so much more than this three-bedroomed bungalow. Love was,
she found, a cheap firework that blinded with its flare before dying and
leaving nothing of its original promise.

Renee treasured her rings, though, even more so since they went
missing a few years ago. She had taken them off to get a manicure and
couldn't find them afterwards. She and Victorianna had looked everywhere but they'd vanished. She couldn't have imagined how much they
meant to her until then, which somehow managed to assuage some of
the guilt she felt at never missing Shaun as much as she should.

It was a big relief when Lou managed to find them, but oddly enough
they had turned up in a place that Renee was sure she had searched
quite thoroughly herself. It had been a very strange business.

Lou had promised Phil she would make the car showroom accounts her
priority the next morning, but instead she found herself in her old jog-
ging bottoms and T-shirt, heading down the cellar steps with a roll of
black binliners. She intended to clear out the cellar in the morning and
then spend all afternoon doing the books. The showroom accounts were
a nightmare. Phil had so many little tax fiddles going on, most accountants would have gone insane with it all, but at least they would have got
paid while they were going doolally, which is more than Lou did.

There were three big dry cellars under the house. Most of the junk was concentrated in the first, where the many shelves were full of 'useful' items: bags of screws and nails, light fittings, paintbrushes with bald patches resembling Phil's, a selection of torches that needed batteries and bulbs, rusty hammers, and lots of plugs that Phil had cut from defunct electrical appliances 'just in case'. There was a big box of his old videos covered with dust and mildew. She carried them back upstairs in a binliner and threw them in the skip before breaking for a sandwich. Now that she had got stuck in, there was no way she was going to do any accounts before the space was totally clear.

She swept up shovelfuls of dust and cobwebs, trying to avoid the spiders. A thought of her dad visited her, telling her what an important job they did in killing the big noisy germ-ridden flies who filled up their clogs on dung-heaps then went tap-dancing on cakes. Her dad had been full of little stories like that to make her laugh. She'd hoped one day to tell them to her own children. Ah, well.

Under the shelves she discovered with glee the antique airer she had bought the previous summer and totally forgotten about. She had been unable to find any pulleys to lower and raise it. The spring-cleaning article had said that if she was to mend any such broken items which had potential for use then she should strike while the iron was hot. *Utilise or bin it.* With that in mind, Lou made a mental note to go pulley-hunting at her earliest convenience.

Stored underneath the airer was a shirtbox full of photographs and, as she had just about finished and was ready for a cuppa, she took it upstairs. Seating herself on the floor in the conservatory with a mug of coffee, she tipped the box out onto the rug to look at the stills of her past. Among the boring landscapes was a family shot of her wedding. Her mother was in dark blue, colour coordinating (by prior arrange-ment) with Phil's mum, also in navy. Lou had never really got to know Sheila Winter much, beyond the fact that she had indulged her offspring to nutter proportions. She had retired to Devon and died suddenly three months after the wedding.

Phil had been subdued at the funeral, but was back at work the next day, with a 'life goes on' comment. Celia mourned openly, but was soon out shopping 'to take her mind off things'. It was all so different to when her dad died. Lou hadn't stopped crying for months.

Feeling tears building now, Lou turned resolutely back to her wed-ding pictures. Phil looked so lean and handsome, with thick fair hair. He wasn't smiling like everyone else in the photograph; in fact, he looked rather surprised. At one side of him was Victorianna, a younger, more glamorous version of Renee, and the minx was wearing a white dress. It had caused a bit of an incident on the day, as the organist had started playing 'Here Comes the Bride' when she walked to her seat. The angle of Victorianna's arm disappearing behind Phil's back made it obvious that she had just nipped his bottom. And *that,* Lou remembered, was why this photograph was in the reject bag.

In the line-up, Lou was smiling, looking exceedingly pretty in a long, plain, ivory dress that pushed her in and out in all the right places. She had always had a shape—Phil hadn't complained then about her not being like a beanpole. In fact, if her memory served her right, he'd rather savoured her curves. Then there was Deb, her one and only bridesmaid, in scarlet, looking slim and blonde and gorgeous and more like a blood relative of Victorianna's than Lou did. That similarity had come in exceedingly handy during Operation Great Ring Rescue.

There were some holiday shots: a pinprick in the sea, which she remembered as being a dolphin she'd spotted on their honeymoon in Benidorm; the façade of the Hotel Artemis in Corfu. They had gone there to celebrate their sixth wedding anniversary. Lou had wanted to go to Rome but Phil had 'surprised' her and booked Greece instead. He had gone missing after their celebratory meal. She found him emerging from an olive grove with a woman called Wanda from Wakefield. She was a brassy piece in her fifties who was residing in the same hotel. He said he'd been helping her look for her husband and, of course, Lou had believed him. It was only later, when Phil left her for Susan Peach, that Lou had wondered if he had, after all, indulged his passion for mutton that night among the fruit trees of Greece.

There was an old school photograph in the pile, taken when she was sixteen. Two faces stood out from the rest. The pixie-faced Gaynor Froggatt, who was to die in an alcohol-and-heroin haze six years later, and Shirley Hamster who was so jealous of Lou's long hair that she had once snipped some off during Latin. She had been little-prepared for Lou swinging round and giving her a right hook that sent her flying backwards over the chair and into the bookshelf behind. Elouise Angeline Casserly. In those days she was scared of nothing and primed to take on the world. She was a demon on the hockey pitch and was still dancing in the college disco long after the die-hards had dropped with exhaustion. She was indestructible, spirited, marvellous. So what had turned her into this little woman who was terrified that the wrong word or an extra inch on her waist would spell the end of her marriage? Where had Lou Casserly gone with her passionate, determined spirit? The woman who was going to open up the best coffee-house in the world with the best friend anyone could ever have in the world?

Before thought, sense or reason could get in the way, Lou reached for the telephone. She could still remember the number. Wasn't it a bit stupid, ringing during working hours? But she dialled the number all the same and it connected and burred five times before a dear, familiar voice answered. 'Hello.'

'It's me—Lou . . . Casserly . . . Winter,' Lou said with a cracked voice. 'Deb, is it possible? Can we meet?'

'**D**ebra Devine,' was how Deb had introduced herself to Lou on their first day at college. 'I know, I know, I sound like a crap nightclub singer or at best a porn star. Let's go and get a coffee and have a natter.'

Lou had laughed, following her to the college cafeteria where their friendship was born over cappuccino. She had missed that friendship so much these past three years. The ache of loss had never faded.

The two women arranged to meet at the weekend in Café Joseph just behind Barnsley Park. The phone conversation had been short and polite; there would be plenty of time for talking when they met.

Needing a distraction, Lou reached for Phil's accounts. It was midnight by the time she had completed them, heaving a huge sigh of relief. Even at the best of times, they were like unravelling a ball of wool that a barmy cat had tried to destroy.

Thursday and Friday were just ordinary days at work. She had long since abandoned any hope of getting job satisfaction there, but finding the old Casa Nostra file again had made Lou realise that she wanted more for herself than a part-time job in an accounts office.

She desperately tried to keep a cap on being excited about the imminent prospect of meeting Deb again, but various thoughts tortured her. What if they had nothing to say to each other? What if Deb didn't turn up? It wasn't unlike the anticipation that preceded a blind date.

**L**ou arrived at Café Joseph ten minutes before time. She had just sat down at a table next to a giant paper-flower display when Deb arrived. She stood up again and waved tentatively with a nervous but excited smile. Deb came over and they both missed the moment when an embrace would have been natural. They sat down opposite each other.

'Hello, Deb,' said Lou. 'It's really nice to see you.'

'Hello, Lou. How have you been?'

Lou opened her mouth to reply, 'Fine,' but nothing came out. She suddenly felt ashamed, unable to put this right. It was such a terrible, terrible thing that she had done. How the hell had she ever let it happen? Against all her best intentions, she started to cry.

Deb came round to her side of the table immediately and hugged her. 'Give up, you daft tart. Now look what you've made me do! Everyone will think we're lesbians.'

Lou snorted with involuntary laughter, still crying even though she desperately wanted to stop. She couldn't bear it that she was drawing attention to herself, but Deb's perfume was the same as she always used to wear and it hurt her heart to smell it.

A young, fresh-faced waiter arrived to take their order.

'Two coffees, please, and two of your biggest pieces of cheesecake if you have any,' said Deb, in her poshest voice.

'I'm sorry,' Lou said, as Deb handed her a serviette. 'I wasn't prepared for this. I don't even know where to start saying what I feel.'

'Elouise Winter, if I had any negative feelings about us meeting again, I wouldn't have turned up. You don't know how many times I've wanted to pick up the phone and see what we could do to sort this out.'

'I bet I look gorgeous now, don't I?' said Lou.

'Absolutely gorgeous. Besides, I've always liked pandas,' said Deb.

Lou smiled a red-eyed smile as she did a quick repair job on her face.

'How's your mum these days?' asked Deb, moving back round to her side of the table and sitting down again.

'Oh, still playing one-upmanship with her mate Vera.'

'And Victorianna?'

On the sound of her name, they instinctively both held up their fingers in the sign of the cross and chuckled together.

'She is most definitely still the same. She's shacked up with this bloke who's stinking rich and looks older than God's dog. Any man on the scene for you?' asked Lou.

'I'm having a rest from the unfairer sex, and jolly nice it is too.'

'How's your mum then?'

'Oh, we lost her last year, Lou. I had my sister there but I wished I'd had you to talk to.'

They clutched hands over the table, just as the waiter arrived with their coffees. He had never actually seen any real-life lesbians before, and the image of these two good-looking, mature women 'at it' would feature in a few of his future fantasies.

'He definitely thinks we're a couple,' said Deb, pointing at his back. 'I think we've turned him on. Pervy little bugger.'

Lou laughed. She realised then why she liked Karen so much. There were so many echoes of Deb in her.

'How's Phil?' asked Deb. 'More to the point, how are *you* and Phil?'

'Oh, we're fine,' said Lou, aware that they had temporarily strayed into Polite Land again. 'We're still together. He's still obsessed by cars.'

She didn't say she was happy, Deb noted.

'You ever . . . managed . . . did you have any . . .?'

'No, no children,' said Lou, saying 'the word'. 'Wasn't to be.'

'You never went for IVF or anything?' Deb was amazed. She knew how much Lou had wanted a child of her own.

'It's pretty gruelling, is IVF, and I'm certain that Phil wouldn't do all the stuff it entails. We're sure he's OK, of course, because of his twins, so it's obviously me who has the problem. Anyway, I know he doesn't really want children. I've come to terms with it. I'm fine, really,' said Lou.

Yeah, right, thought Deb, changing to a lighter subject about their jobs. It was so good to see Lou. She noted her friend's curvy pink smile, but she wasn't as contented-looking as Deb would have expected. Not after all she went through to get that piece of crap back anyway.

'Are you still working in Sheffield?' Deb asked.

'Yes, I'm still stuck in Accounts. Great bunch of people, except for the office manageress who is a total witch, but it's a job. You?'

'Yes, still living just outside Maltstone, still running Mrs Serafinska's bakery. And yes, I'm still dreaming of opening up working-title-Casa-Nostra and ruling the world.'

'Cheesecake,' interrupted the waiter, slightly disappointed that they just looked like two old friends having coffee now.

'Thank you,' said Deb, poking the hardened exterior of a dessert that was as fresh as one of her Uncle Brian's jokes. When the waiter had gone to another table she whispered over to Lou, 'We would never have served stuff like this in our establishment.'

'Why didn't you go it alone and open up a coffee shop?' Lou asked.

'Didn't want to,' said Deb. 'Plus I don't think *I* could have. It was always a joint thing.' She melted into a soft couch of nostalgia. 'We had fun planning it all, didn't we? I've never yet been in a coffee shop where I didn't think we could do better.'

'I know how you feel. It didn't die for me either.'

'Really?' said Deb, tilting her head. 'Because I'll tell you this, Lou babe, it certainly hasn't died for me.'

Their eyes locked. Lou felt a glimmer of excitement. She looked at Deb who was feeling it too, she just knew it. *This is crazy! We've only just met again.* 'So,' she said, 'are we going to see each other again or have I turned into a hideous old bag and you're sorry you came?'

'Yes, of course you have, darling,' said Deb. 'But let's meet up anyway.' She dropped her eyes and inspected her nails. 'Will you tell Phil? I presume he doesn't know you're here.'

'I'll pick my moment then tell him we bumped into each other in town. I'll take it from there. He can't stop me having friends.'

But he can and he did, thought Deb. However, she stayed silent.

Lou hugged her tightly before they got into their respective cars, then watched her friend drive off with a thrill akin to having a secret affair. That was how Phil would definitely see it, anyway—a threat to his marriage, an illegal union. But there was no way Lou was going to stop seeing Deb now. She realised, as she climbed into the driver's seat, that she really hadn't thought this through at all.

Sometimes, when Lou did a crossword and couldn't get the solution, she'd put it to the back of her mind and later, when she was least expecting it, the answer would deliver itself unbidden to the front, just like that. She employed the same strategy now with the problem of how to bring her renewed friendship with Deb into the open. So, after saying goodbye, she concentrated on getting those pulleys sorted out for her wooden airer and drove to a small timber yard. They wouldn't have them but they might know a man who did.

'You want to try the Ironmonger's Tub,' said the ruddy-faced owner.

'Where's that?'

'Townend. St William's Yard, side of the old tin factory. They'll fix you up. No bother.'

Nothing much went on in the Townend, except for graffiti. Once it had been a lively quarter but the major commercial emphasis had shifted to the other end of town. The shop rents were cheap, which attracted transient businesses that held little shopping appeal, and the lack of passing trade soon spelled their demise. Lou hadn't ever noticed an ironmonger anywhere around there, but then again, she had never had any cause to go to the back of the derelict tin factory.

She was surprised to find a large car park full of trucks, vans and cars there. A very old row of buildings faced her, suggesting, by the number of their doors, four shopfronts. The two on the right were unoccupied; the third, a decent-sized transport café with a sign above the door reading Ma's Café, looked healthily occupied inside, and the end shopfront was the ironmonger's—very Dickensian, with scrubbed small-paned windows and a swinging sign that read Ironmongers T.U.B.

Lou pushed the door open and a bell tinkled. She walked into an Aladdin's cave of floor-to-ceiling wooden shelves, drawers and huge apothecaries' cabinets that gave her the feeling she'd just broken through a time barrier into the past.

'Two ticks,' said a man's deep voice from the back.

A movement to her right caught her eye. The paws of a big dog on the floor there twitching in sleep. It looked like . . .

'Can I help you?' The man who had called out to Lou came into the front of the shop. He was out of his skip-wagon context, which confused her for a brief moment.

'It's you!' exclaimed Lou with a surprised grin. He didn't look as bulky in jeans and a denim shirt as he did in his skip overalls, but the small shop only served to emphasise his height and bigness. 'I didn't recognise you with your clothes on,' she joked.

'I think you're thinking of my twin, Tom,' the man said. 'Big handsome bloke, black hair? Runs the skips?'

'Oh, I'm sorry,' said Lou, feeling herself go warm on the inside, a sure indicator she was going red on the outside. This man was the spitting image of Tom. 'You're so alike.' Best to get down to business quickly. Then she could go home and drown herself. 'I'm looking for a couple of pulleys for a wooden airer,' she said, adopting a business-like tone. 'I've been told you can knock me up with some.'

Tom's brother turned quickly away to look through some boxes. He appeared to be biting his lip. Did they all do that in their family—laugh at people, she wondered.

'Here we are,' said the brother, reaching up to take down a box. 'You'll need a single pulley and a double one, if you want a workable system.'

Lou nodded and Tom's twin brother got some rope out from a drawer and fed it through the pulley wheel to show her how to set it up.

'I'll need a cleat as well,' said Lou.

'Call it three pounds fifty, please,' said the nameless brother.

She handed over a five-pound note which he held up to the light to inspect. Cheeky so-and-so, Lou bristled. She and Tom might have shared the jokes about counterfeit money, but she didn't know this bloke from Adam for him to take such a liberty. It crossed Lou's mind for a moment that this was actually Tom himself. But that would be taking a joke a bit far, wouldn't it?

'Is that Clooney?' asked Lou, receiving her change with a cool and collected 'Thank you'.

'No, it's his brother from the same litter,' said rude-man.

He even has the same twinkle in his eye as Tom, thought Lou, although he was too familiar with strangers for her liking, and so when he disappeared to his back office to get a receipt book, she sneaked out. She'd had enough of people thinking she was a joke.

When she got home, there were two calls waiting for her. One from Michelle saying Craig was there and they were having a fantastic time.

The other was from her mother saying that Victorianna was going to some dinner with Edward Wankystein and that the vice-president of the United States was going to be there as well (big wow—*not*). Keith Featherstone still hadn't rung. She got on with preparing Phil's evening meal: pea soup, lamb fillet and treacle sponge with homemade custard. She needed him in a good mood for what she was about to tell him.

'Hello there!' said Phil, flashing his perfectly white teeth at Miss Scarlet Suit. This was the second time she had been in this week. He never forgot a face. Or a pair of tits, especially not ones as perky as those. She reminded him of someone he couldn't quite place.

'You told me to keep popping in, if you remember,' the rather lovely punter said. 'Stock changes daily?'

'Indeed it does,' said Phil. 'Have you any idea what you are looking for in particular? You weren't quite sure last time, as I remember.'

'Something older perhaps,' she said, looking up at him from under a sexy little fringe. 'Classy, though. I don't mind a few miles on the clock if I know it's going to be reliable.'

Cheeky little minx, he thought. As if he didn't know what she meant!

'Have you seen this one?' said Phil, leading the way over to a Jag.

'Too big,' she said. 'I want something sporty. I want something *me*. I want something—'

'Singular?' suggested Phil.

'Yes,' she said, obviously flattered he'd applied such a word to her.

Phil mulled this over, and then suddenly snapped his fingers. 'I've got just the thing for you, although it's not in the showroom yet. A nineteen sixties MG Roadster, British racing green, absolutely beautiful—and, less than forty thousand on the clock. It's a fantastic car. It's even got the original green log book, and a full service history, of course.'

'Is it a hard top or soft?'

'Hard. You don't want a soft top in this climate.'

'Oh, yeah, and what do you drive then?' she tested.

'Audi TT,' said Phil, adding, 'Hardtop!' accompanied by his best grin.

'Nice. Not exactly a family car, though?'

Ooh, she really was pressing for info, he thought. Clever.

'No family,' he said, with the tiniest regretful sigh.

'So where's the MG now?'

'It's getting the full treatment, once-overed, valeted, polished, one hundred and thirty point check. It really is absolutely stunning.'

'How much are you looking at for it?'

'Not one hundred per cent sure, but it will be in the region of nine . . .'

She didn't flinch.

'. . . nine and a half maybe. Thousand,' he clarified.

'Obviously. When will you have it in for me to look at?' she asked.

'Couple of weeks, maybe three. Tell you what, you leave me your number and the moment I have it in, you will be the first to know.'

'I'll give you my mobile number and my name is Miss Susan Shoesmith.'

She definitely emphasised the 'Miss', he was sure of it. Sexy, sassy, spirited Susan Shoesmith, he said to himself, trying to trigger a memory that he knew was there. Who was she like?

'Don't forget me,' she winked. She had British-racing-green eyes.

'Forget you? Not a chance,' said Phil.

As if the day at work wasn't good enough, Phil opened the door to his favourite smell of all time: lamb fillet in a rosemary and honey sauce. Lou was having a plain chicken fillet.

'What have I done to deserve this?' asked Phil, starting conversation after he had got to the end of the interesting bits in his newspaper.

'Nothing,' said Lou, shaking her head in a fine semblance of innocence. 'I fancied chicken and I know you aren't really keen, so I just picked up some lamb in the butcher's while I was there.'

'Accounts all up-to-date are they, love?' he enquired.

'Yes, of course. Treacle sponge?'

Phil rubbed his stomach. 'Oh, go on then. Just a bit.' He had a little portion then followed it up with a big one; after all, she had gone to all this trouble. More trouble than usual . . . now the big question was *why*.

Lou poured him a brandy and delivered it to him with a cigar and the matchbox. He watched her with suspicious eyes. He knew how much Lou hated lamb; he wasn't stupid. Whether she realised it or not, she served it up when she felt desperate for his approval.

'So,' he said, as he puffed on the cigar. 'What's all this about then, Lou? Lamb? Treacle sponge? What are you building up to tell me?'

'Well, actually, there is something.' Lou started clearing up the plates.

'What?' he asked again, impatiently.

Lou took a deep breath and tried to begin. 'Phil . . .' This was stupid. Just say it. Why was it so difficult to say she'd met up with Deb again? She opened her mouth to speak. 'Phil, I want to throw away the arm-chair in the conservatory.'

He tutted. 'Is that it?'

'Yes. I . . . I just wanted to make sure you were OK with that.'

'You can throw it out, if you want. It's hell to sit on anyway.'

'Right, well, that's that then,' she said, carrying on clearing.

Phil took a big swallow of brandy and studied her as she moved round the table. That wasn't it, though, was it, Lou? he thought. No, it was something much bigger. What was really going on in that little brain of hers?

Lou started her Sunday morning as she meant to go on: leaping out of bed and getting right down to the business of ridding the house of yet more rubbish. The anger Lou felt at her own weakness ironically generated enough adrenaline-driven strength for her to drag the ugly old conservatory chair out of the back door and heave it into the skip.

Talking of ugly old things . . . Lou snapped off a binliner from the roll. In her present mood, there were some things she wasn't going to shy away from any more. Phil's mother had bought them a ceramic vase as a wedding present. It was so hideous that it was an offence even to blind people, and thoughts of taking it to the charity shop didn't even feature. She just wanted to blast it to smithereens so some other poor sod wouldn't have to be tortured by the sight of it. *Throw out everything ugly and broken*, the article went on. *Your space should only be full of things pleasing to your eye with pleasant emotional vibes giving out positive energy.*

'Right,' said Lou, geeing herself up. Grabbing the hideous vase from the small spare room, she dropped it into the binliner. The carriage clock with the dodgy movement joined it seconds later and shattered in the bag, as did a grotesque warped glass ornament. In the larger spare room there was a collection of brass ornaments that Celia had palmed off on her and which Lou had always felt obliged to display. She wiped them from the shelves into the bag. Next were lucky pixies, castanets, maracas, some coloured glass-ball things encased in knitted string that Renee had bought her. She knotted up the bag, only to unknot it again to put in another couple of pictures of lamenting women taken down from the landing wall. They had a sad energy about them in their scenes of pain and loneliness and Lou needed no pictorial reminders of what those feelings were all about.

She heaved the sack downstairs and swung it onto the skip. Her neck spasmed after that final exertion and she was forced to take a moment to rub some warmth into it. She needed to sink her whole body up to the nostrils in a warm bath, big-time. *Bloody Keith Featherstone*. His name brought a surge of frustration. What was she going to do? Threatening him with legal action wouldn't get her anywhere: there was no proof she had paid him any cash up-front, and he could simply deny everything. She had left another message on his answering machine and was still waiting for him to return the call.

She settled for a steamy shower. Afterwards, wrapped up in the towel, she found more things to be cleared in the mirrored bathroom cabinet, including loads of free sample sachets she had been storing.

She didn't wear pink eye-shadows or lipsticks any more and yet she had a cache of them in her make-up basket. The article had said that old make-up collected bacteria and should be thrown away after six months. Whoops, thought Lou, as she spotted the lovely dark wine-red lipstick she had worn at her wedding. It had been a nice wedding day, although her dad hadn't been there to give her away. The sun had shone, the wedding breakfast had been superb, and her groom was the most charming, loving, caring bloke in the world. Just like her dad. A Winter family future stretched before her. They would have a lovely house, a son, a daughter, a puppy, a summer villa on a Tuscan hillside, a car lot, a restaurant, and they were all going to live happily ever after.

Lou put the lipstick in the bin bag.

She rang Tom's number to tell him that the skip was ready for collection and Part-time Eddie told her that they could lift it that afternoon.

Lou's hair wasn't even dry from the shower when she heard the wagon reversing and went out to greet it.

'Hi there,' called Tom, while Clooney came straight over to Lou for a fuss and, obviously, a biscuit.

Looking for a point of conversation she asked: 'Where does it all go?' indicating the rubbish.

'Well, it gets loaded into a massive ejector trailer and then goes off to a landfill site on the other side of Leeds. We recycle what we can. For instance, we get the occasional piece of old but good furniture and there are places that will redistribute it to people who need it. Sometimes we find old medicine and pills and take them back to pharmacies in case they fall into the wrong hands.'

'I did wonder what happened to it all,' said Lou. She hadn't really; she just wanted to chat to him.

'You can wake up now,' said Tom.

'No, really. I wanted to know.'

Tom narrowed his eyes at her in mock-suspicion and said, 'I shall ask you some questions the next time I see you and test you.'

*The next time I see you!*

God, she was turning into Michelle, analysing everything he said.

'You must be nearly at the end though, surely?' said Tom.

Lou laughed. 'I thought I was,' she said, 'but it's never-ending once you start clearing stuff out.'

'Did you get your airer fixed up?' he then enquired.

'Not yet, that's this afternoon's job. I got some pulleys from your shop. I didn't realise it was your place until your brother served me,' said Lou, her lips tightening as she thought of Tom's darker half. 'I made a bit of a twerp of myself actually. I thought he was you.'

Tom stopped dead, trying to loop the last hook onto the skip. 'He *was* me,' he said with a disbelieving little laugh. 'I haven't got a brother. That's why I held your money up to check it—to see if it wasn't one of your counterfeits.' He grinned.

Lou sifted through her recollection of buying the pulleys. It seemed so obvious in retrospect that he had been having her on. How would he know about the airer if he hadn't served her? She felt her brain blushing and the heat radiate out to the surface of her skin.

'I'm sorry,' said Tom. 'I thought you guessed. I wondered why you ran off when I went to get you a receipt.' He laughed heartily. 'Didn't you hear me say, "You must be thinking of my big, handsome brother" or something like that?'

*Is that Clooney?* she had asked as well. *No, it's his brother.* God, she deserved to be laughed at. A stupid, silly woman who was having stupid, silly daydreams about a man who took her rubbish away. He had probably had a good laugh about her to all the skip lads. Lou felt sick. *When will you ever learn, Lou?* said a weary inner voice. *When are you ever going to realise that you are just one of life's stooges?* Jaws, Phil, Renee, Victorianna, Michelle, bloody Keith Featherstone—they all thought she was a bit of a joke. And now him—(drum roll)—Mr Funny Skipman and his amazing performing brother. Tom Broom laughing at her felt worse than the rest of them put together.

Some little part of her that used to be Elouise Angeline Casserly flared up inside her and forced herself to make a semblance of joining in with the hilarity and say, 'Silly me, yes, I see my mistake now.'

It made her give Clooney a final pat on his great soft head and say a courteous goodbye to Tom Broom. Then it gave her the strength to walk calmly back to the sanctuary of her kitchen without giving into an all-escaping run. There, it decided for her that there would be no more skips or contact with Mr Tom 'Mick-Taker-Extraordinaire' Broom again. She didn't need anyone else around who made her feel inadequate; she didn't need rubbish like him in her life.

**P**hil walked in at four o'clock to find Lou putting the finishing touches to the airer, which she had just screwed into the kitchen ceiling beams. Lou knew her way round a toolbox, thanks to years of trailing after her DIY-mad dad and learning from him.

Phil watched her screwing some metal thing into the wall. She still hadn't told him what all that buttering-up meal business was about yesterday, but he knew he wouldn't have to wait long to find out. Lou couldn't keep secrets. She would have been hopeless having an affair, not that Lou would ever do that to him. Lou was a lovely person, even if she did have a bit of an arse on her these days, unlike the trim Miss British-racing-green-eyes. He really would have to watch that. Phil was going places these days and he needed Lou to look good on his arm. He didn't want people laughing at him, as they laughed at Fat Jack when he brought Maureen out of her coffin to socialise.

As Fat Jack said, 'When women start neglecting themselves, they deserve everything they get.' When a bloke's eye wanders, his missus should get the wake-up call to go and sort herself out. Jack himself had been unlucky on that front because Maureen had only got worse. At least his Lou had cared about their marriage enough to fight for her man, and he'd had some very attentive sex and fantastic meals as a welcome-home-from-your-affair present.

The telephone rang as Phil was in the shower. Lou let the answering machine take it while she listened: *Mrs Winter, it's me, Tom Broom. I wasn't sure if you said you wanted me to bring another skip or not earlier on when we were talking. If you do, can you call me? Thanks. Hope you had a nice weekend. Bye now.*

*Hope you have a nice weekend*, Lou mocked. He was obviously crawling now because he was scared he wouldn't get her business any more. And with good reason. Lou went to the cupboard and got out the dog biscuits, which she thrust down to the bottom of the kitchen bin. No, Lou wouldn't call him back. She wasn't going to pay him for the privilege of being an object of ridicule.

Lou had found an alternative skip-hire company, Harrison's Waste Disposals, after searching through the *Yellow Pages*. They turned up the following Saturday. Seeing Tom's name in the book had given her a nip of sadness. His absence had cheated her of a secret fantasy that had brought a harmless thrill to a life that she was increasingly recognising as joyless, empty and boring. She hated that Tom Broom's brief cameo appearance had caused so much disruption. She had been content with her lot before he came on the scene. Hadn't she?

In the week that had passed, Lou's subconscious still hadn't presented her with the solution to the letting-Phil-know-about-Deb problem. The only thing it had come up with was the thought that maybe she should talk to someone about it. But who was there. Karen?

Too young. Her mother? Do me a favour! That left Michelle. Michelle hadn't been in touch since the text message saying that she was loved-up. Lou supposed she had been forgiven now and rang.

Michelle answered after three rings and sounded really glad to hear from her, apologising as usual for not being in touch: busy, busy, gym, gym, sex with Craig, sex with Craig . . . 'He is gorgeous! He can't keep his hands off me!'

'That's great, Michelle. Look, the reason I rang you—'

'Hang on, I must tell you this—we were going to pick up fish and chips last night and he said he thought he was falling for me. Can you believe it? I just melted.'

'I want to ask you—'

'Mind you, he hardly got any when he was married, so he's just making up for lost time with a decent woman.'

'Michelle, can you help me on something—'

'You should hear some of the tricks his wife's done on him . . .'

Lou gave up trying to interrupt and there followed a half-hour character assassination of Craig's wife. Lou heard it but didn't listen, because five minutes into the monologue, Michelle's voice became white noise.

The Deb and Phil thing was something Lou would have to sort out.

# CHAPTER 4

FOR THREE CONSECUTIVE Saturdays now, Lou had been slipping out to meet Deb. It felt as if they had never been apart, except for one big difference. In the old days, there was nothing they couldn't talk about; now there were a couple of taboo subjects. Phil being the biggest. And as much as Lou would have liked to have exorcised the ghost of Tom Broom through a good gossip, it seemed a bit of a cheek to talk about a bloke she fancied—*had* fancied—with a friend she had once given up to save her marriage. There, she had finally admitted it to herself: she had fancied him. Not that it mattered any more.

She and Deb had talked on the phone a few times during the week, on her mobile because she didn't want the number showing up on the house phone bill. She had the distinct feeling that Phil knew she was *up to something*. Some sixth sense within her was waving a bright red warning flag. Phil was as wily as a fox and nothing got past him. And she *was* deceiving him. She had fibbed twice, saying she was shopping in Meadowhall when all the time she was drinking coffee and eating cake with Deb. That couldn't be right, could it?

In the Maltstone Garden Centre café, Lou and Deb were devouring two slices of chocolate fudge cake. Talk flowed easily enough between them, but Deb seemed a little distracted.

'You OK?' Lou asked.

'No, I'm not actually.' Deb stared hard at Lou. 'I've got something to ask you.' She was biting her bottom lip. She used to do that when she was nervous, Lou recalled.

'God, it sounds like you're going to propose. If you are, I have to tell you I'm married already.'

'Yes, to a total prick though,' said Deb without thinking. She took a sharp intake of breath. 'Sorry. I didn't mean for that to come out.'

Lou let loose a bark of laughter. 'It's actually a big relief,' she said. 'I know you can't stand him and you really don't have to pretend.'

'Anyway, this isn't about *him*,' Deb carried on. Not dignifying *him* with a name. 'This is about you and me.'

'Go on.' Lou was all ears.

'Working-title-Casa-Nostra,' blurted Deb. 'I don't suppose you fancy giving it another go?'

'Yes,' said Lou immediately.

'Take your time, I know it's a big decision. I so want to do this but—' Deb's brain suddenly caught up with her ears. 'You're joking!'

'I've never been more serious in my whole life.'

They stared at each other, hardly daring to breathe. Then they valved out to a childish bout of giggles.

'I could scream I'm so excited,' Deb said with a full-capacity smile.

'So where do we start?' asked Lou.

'Well, you're going to have to start by telling Phil about me,' said Deb. 'And I'll start by borrowing the Casa Nostra file from you and refreshing my memory.'

'I won't let you down this time, Deb. Whatever happens.'

Lou opened her wardrobe doors and looked through the banks of clothes for her black skirt and red top. She was taking her mother out for her birthday lunch to a lovely Italian restaurant just outside Wakefield, but what should have been a simple clothes-choosing exercise turned out to have complications. The realisation struck her like a slap: she really did have some awful clothes. Her eyes were tugged towards the burgundy suit she wore so often for work. Looking at it, she could see why Karen took the mick out of it. It looked short and thick and squat—was she really that shape? There was no way that it was going back in the wardrobe. Sliding it from the hanger, she dropped it quickly onto the floor before she could change her mind.

She checked the clock; she had a spare half-hour to make a start, if she wanted to do what had suddenly landed in her mind. She could no longer tolerate *any* potential rubbish that she spotted, and she had spotted a lot in her wardrobe. *Do you wear twenty per cent of your wardrobe, eighty per cent of the time?* the article had asked and she concluded that she probably did, looking at this junk hanging up.

She pulled out a loose black dress in which the whole Billy Smart family and some Bengal tigers could adequately have performed. *But it's comfortable and OK for lounging about the house in*, said a weak little inner voice. *Tough*, returned Lou, and replaced the empty hanger on the rail. 'And there's another for the rubbish pile,' she said to herself, seizing a faded pair of red track-suit bottoms that were big enough for Santa.

The blue suit was a bland necessity for work. The black one had been a 'to slim into' purchase, and she never had. It was very classy though, she thought. She tried it on again for old times' sake and found with some surprise that it slipped over the hips it usually snagged on. The jacket, which she had never been able to close across the bust, buttoned up beautifully now. Looking at herself in the mirror, she was pleasantly taken aback. *I've lost weight! When did that happen?*

Within twenty minutes seventy-five per cent of Lou's wardrobe was crammed into four binliners, including the old black skirt that Lou was originally going to wear for lunch, along with the gathered red top.

It would be quite fun to replenish her wardrobe, she thought. But from now on there were to be no big fat comfortable clothes that made her feel like an old frump, or impossibly small clothes that made her feel bovine. She put her black suit back on and looked forward, for once, to her mother's verdict.

**M**other and daughter strolled into the Italian restaurant and were led to their table by a round-faced waiter with a pronounced accent.

'Have you lost weight?' asked Renee, who had been studying Lou.

'Yes, I think I have,' Lou confirmed. 'It must be all that exertion filling my skips.'

'Well, you want to keep it up and before you know where you are, you'll look nice again.'

'Thanks, Mum,' said Lou tightly.

Once seated, they studied the oversized menus over slimline tonics, ice and lime.

'Thank you for the flowers, they were beautiful,' said Renee.

'Good, glad you liked them,' said Lou, aware that her mother had shifted her scrutiny from the menu to her face.

'Your skin's looking nice,' she said at last. 'Have you been doing anything to it?'

'Just drinking a lot of water,' said Lou. 'Filling skips is thirsty business.' Wow! Two compliments on the trot. She curled her fingers away before her mother noticed them. The life-improving qualities of intensive clutter-clearing didn't extend to cuticle care and nail preservation.

'What are you going to have?' said Renee.

'I think I'll start off with garlic mushrooms.'

'Oh, you're not, are you?' Renee screwed up her face, disapproving. 'You'll undo all that good work if you eat a big plateful of butter.'

Lou snarled inwardly. 'Then I'll have the tiger-prawn salad.'

'What about for main?' asked Renee.

'Lard pie and chips,' Lou answered with flat petulance.

'Don't be ridiculous, Elouise,' said her mother, as if she were nine.

Lou decided on chicken in a mushroom and wine sauce. 'Have you heard from Victorianna?' she asked after the waiter had taken their order.

'Yes, she rang early this morning and her card is on its way, apparently. Their post takes ages,' said Renee, waving away the whole American postal system with one sweep of her thin hand. 'Vera's going to visit her son in Germany for her birthday, did I say? Her son's paying for her to go out there.' Renee couldn't help the almost indiscernible sigh that came out with it and, despite all her criticisms and pettiness, Lou felt a sudden all-engulfing wave of sympathy and love for her mother. Victorianna must know how much their mother wanted to go out there and how it hurt her that she had not once been asked.

'You should tell Victorianna to invite you over,' she said.

'I can't *tell* her to invite me, Elouise,' Renee snapped.

No, thought Lou, with a plan sparking to life in her head. But I can.

Later that evening, Lou was snuggled up in bed as the wind howled outside and rain lashed against the window. Phil had tried to initiate sex, but she had said she was too tired. He punished her with his back, which didn't bother her half as much as it was intended to.

She had just drifted off to sleep when she was woken by a shake.

'Lou, Lou, what's that noise?' Phil was hissing. 'Listen.'

Lou did as instructed. Her ears caught a scratching noise.

'There's someone trying to get in the back door,' whispered Phil. 'Did you put the alarm on?'

'Yes, of course I did. Go and see who it is,' Lou whispered back.

'There's no way I'm going downstairs,' said Phil gallantly.

Threaded among the whistles of the wind was a whimpering. Whatever it was, it was animal not human, and sounded in pain. She hopped out of bed. There it was again, a clear yelp.

'That's not a burglar, it's a dog,' said Lou, slipping on her dressing gown and heading for the stairs. Phil followed her tentatively down to the kitchen as Lou turned off the alarm and unlocked the door as far as the chain would allow. There on the doorstep was a very soggy and bedraggled German Shepherd.

'Chuck this at the bloody thing,' said Phil, handing her a pan. 'SHOO!'

Lou huffed loudly and slipped the chain off.

'Don't let it in!' Phil yelled as she flung open the door and Clooney shivered into the kitchen.

'It's the skip man's dog,' said Lou, grabbing a towel. Clooney was shaking, trembling, his ears flat against his head.

'Well, what's he doing here?' Phil watched incredulously as she made soothing noises and attempted to rub the dog dry.

'How do I know, Phil? He's obviously remembered the house.'

Clooney sneezed and then Phil sneezed.

Lou couldn't resist. 'You're allergic to each other,' she smiled wryly.

'It's not funny. Get it out of here,' said Phil crossly.

'You *are* joking,' said Lou. 'You can't let him back out in this weather, poor thing. Pass me the phone. I'll ring the skip man. He'll be frantic.'

'He's not going to be at work now, is he? It's'—Phil looked at the clock on the oven—'half past one!'

'Well, I don't know where he lives, Phil, so leaving a message is the only thing I can do!'

As expected, an answering machine clicked on. 'Hello, Mr Broom,' began Lou efficiently after the announcement and the long beep. 'It's Mrs Winter, number One, The Faringdales, Hoodley. It's one thirty on Wednesday morning and I've got your dog here. He's OK but very wet. I'm going to bed him down here for the night . . .'

'Oh, no, you're not, Lou!' screamed Phil in the background, then he sneezed again dramatically.

Lou ignored him and carried on, '. . . so there's no need to worry. He seems fine. Oh, and here's my number . . .' She put down the phone and turned to defuse Phil. 'He can sleep in here,' she said calmly. 'I'll disinfect the place tomorrow. You won't know he's ever been here.'

Phil's brain recalled that he'd sneezed like this before in the kitchen. *Have there been any animals in here? And she had answered, 'Don't be silly!'*

'He's been here before, hasn't he?'

'I brought him in for a biscuit once, that's all,' said Lou.

'Where are you going now?' asked Phil as Lou marched out of the kitchen, leaving him alone with the Hound of the Baskervilles. The vicious-looking thing was enormous. Phil did a quick exit and trailed behind Lou as she went upstairs and pulled down the loft ladder.

'There's a sleeping-bag up here,' said Lou, climbing into the loft.

Lou switched on the light and saw that the sleeping-bag was right by her feet. She hadn't been up to the loft for over two years now, into this final resting-place for things she didn't want to think about. As soon as she saw the shadowy shapes up there again, she knew that there were ghosts here she must exorcise. And she needed a hell of a lot of binbags and yet another empty skip. For now, though, there was a dog to sort out.

'**Y**ou're cooking chicken at this time of night?' shrieked Phil, watching in disbelief as Lou cut up fillets and poured some rice to boil in a saucepan. 'Want me to toss it up a side salad, as well?'

'Phil, just go to bed,' said Lou wearily, resisting the urge to point out that he was already being a big enough tosser as it was.

But Phil had another aggressive sneezing fit which made up his mind for him. This was his house, after all.

'No, no, I'm sorry, it's not staying here. It can go in the garage.'

'No, he can't,' said Lou quietly but firmly.

'Yes, it can, Lou!'

'No, he can't!'

She matched him for intensity if not volume, but she was aware that she had now strayed into the sort of argument that she always lost, the type where strength of will was involved.

His voice spiralled to a scream. 'I'm not letting you keep that animal in my house and that's that!'

*Let?* It was that word again. Lou's mind wagged her own words back at her. *'How on earth did a woman get into a state where a man was "letting" her do things?'* LET?

Like a long-dormant volcano stirring into life, Lou's inner magma suddenly started to rise and spit. 'Oh, by the way, I meant to tell you, I bumped into Deb,' she said with calm defiance. 'We've had a few coffees together. And I may be going into business with her. Our coffee-house, do you remember?'

'What? Well, I'd give up any plans of seeing *her* again or—'

'Or what, Phil?' Lou snapped. She was looking at him in a way that reminded him of when they were courting; in those days, she had a fire that he had loved to poke into even more flames. It was only when he realised that the blaze was getting away from his control that he'd put it out. Phil suddenly realised who Miss British-racing-green-eyes reminded him of.

He chain-sneezed.

'Oh, I'm going back to bed,' he said grumpily. He'd give her a fight any night of the week and win it, because he knew exactly what to say to make his wife start sobbing into a hankie and saying her sorries, but presently he was debilitated by itching eyes and a nose full of snot. He thudded back upstairs, his head bursting.

Lou wrapped up her loudly ticking travel alarm clock in a tea towel and put it under the sleeping-bag for Clooney. Her dad had done that for Murphy on his first few puppy nights at home, to give him the comfort of a simulated fellow heartbeat. How had she ever once thought that Phil was like her dad, Lou wondered?

Upstairs, Phil was thinking. So that's what she's been up to—meeting that bitch Deb again. Not only that, but she had been *lying* about having dogs in their house—*his* house, actually—and she had started refusing him sex. Lou Winter, he decided, needed bringing back into line. And Phil Winter knew the best way to make that happen.

**P**hil went down to the kitchen for a quick pre-work coffee, totally forgetting about the presence of Scooby Doo. On seeing the dog, he spasmed backwards, sending himself careering into the table and chairs. Scruffy, smelly hound asleep on his best sleeping-bag!

'Get rid of this dog quick, Lou!' Phil shouted up to Lou.

Clooney opened one eye, viewed him briefly and closed it again. This totally infuriated Phil. He grabbed his jacket and shouted again, 'I'll get my breakfast at work,' then stamped out, swearing to himself.

Lou hadn't got to bed until nearly three o'clock and it was only seven o'clock now. Thank goodness it was Wednesday and she wasn't at work today. When she came downstairs, having put make-up on the black circles under her eyes, Clooney was up on his feet, tail wagging and pleased to see her. Rain was still lashing down outside and she dreaded to think what state he would have been in, left outside all night—and he would have been, if she hadn't stood up to Phil. Thanks to her not backing down for once, Clooney was warm and dry and breakfasting happily on more chicken and rice.

Lou was washing-up when there was a firm knock at the door. Clooney started whining and howling and getting very excited—and that was all the evidence Lou needed to know that it wasn't the postman. She went to open the door, her heart thumping.

Clooney barged past her to get to Tom, who bent down and scrubbed him with his hand. 'Hello, lad, how ya doing?'

'Come in out of the rain,' Lou said.

He walked in and tried to wipe his boots on the mat, while Clooney fussed round him.

Tom had circles round his eyes that matched her own. 'Thanks so much for taking him in,' he said to Lou. 'I didn't get your message till I arrived in the office. I was out all night looking for him. A mastiff went for him on a job down in Ketherwood last night and chased him off.'

'Ketherwood? That must be at least two miles away!' said Lou.

'How he got here I'll never know,' said Tom, giving his adoring friend an extra-hard scratch.

'Would you like a coffee?' asked Lou graciously.

'Am I holding you up? You off to work?'

It would be unforgiveable, really, to pretend that all this had caused her a lot of trouble, but this guy needed bringing down a peg or two.

'No, I took a day off,' she said stoically, lying through her teeth.

'Because of this? Oh, I'm so sorry!'

'It's perfectly all right. I couldn't have left him now, could I?' she smiled so sweetly that the sugar almost crystallised on her lips. 'Please sit down, have a coffee.'

He sat down meekly at the table, Clooney at his side, head resting on his master's knee. Lou got two cups and filled them from the hissing, spitting percolator.

'White or black?' she asked.

'White, please. No sugar.'

'Ah, me too,' she said with a nice-lady-hostess laugh.

'Thanks, I needed that,' he said after a big glug. His jacket was so saturated that Lou just couldn't stop herself from asking, 'Look, why don't you take your clothes off for a minute and get dry. Uh, outer clothes, I mean. Your coat! Obviously not all of your clothes. That would be ridiculous . . . being naked . . . in my kitchen,' Lou struggled.

'Thanks,' he said. He was doing that grin thing again as he slid off his coat and hung it over the radiator. Even her rescuing his dog didn't stop him from thinking she was a living, breathing joke.

'I hope it didn't cause any problems for you last night,' said Tom. 'I remember you saying your husband was allergic to dogs.'

'No, he was fine about it,' said Lou with a fixed smile.

Tom didn't say that he had heard Phil's voice-over on her message, nor did he reveal that, as he was driving up The Faringdales estate, he was just in time to see a man slamming the door to Number One and stomping over to his car issuing expletives. It was obvious that Clooney's arrival at Lou's house *had* caused her hassle.

'I think I owe you an apology,' said Tom.

'Really, Clooney was absolutely no trouble at all. Don't even think—'

'I didn't mean about that,' said Tom, putting his cup down. 'Because you've got a full Harrison's skip parked on your drive.'

*Oh, nuts!* She had forgotten about that.

'I wasn't sure if I'd upset you with all that twin business. When I saw you'd defected to the enemy, it was obvious that I had. I *knew* there was something wrong when you walked out of the shop without waiting for that receipt,' he said. 'And then, when I didn't hear from you about any more skips . . . I'm really sorry if you thought my joke went too far.'

'Forget about it,' said Lou, suddenly feeling a little silly.

'I take up more than my fair share of the world as it is—it wouldn't be environmentally friendly of me to have a twin! There's just me and my sister Sammy. Well, my half-sister. The shop is all mine as well as the skips. That's what the T.U.B. stands for—Tom Broom, although everyone's called the place the Ironmonger's Tub since I put the sign up.' He looked genuinely contrite.

'So . . . what's the "U" initial stand for then?'

'It's one of those embarrassing names you don't want to admit to,' Tom smiled. 'If you promise not to laugh, I might just tell you.'

Lou crossed her heart.

He took a deep breath and then said, 'Umberto.'

It wasn't that funny but Lou laughed anyway because promising not to laugh automatically made her want to laugh, and her insides had felt like a pressure cooker that had wanted to burst open since he walked in with his big soggy coat on and tired eyes.

'See, I told you that you'd laugh,' said Tom with mock-indignation.

'I'm sorry, I'm only laughing because I'm not supposed to. It's a nice name. Where does it come from?'

He leaned in conspiratorially. He has such a nice face, she thought.

'My grandmother was Italian,' he began. 'She came over here when she met my grandfather.'

Gulp, you're a quarter Italian! thought Lou.

'And when she was sixteen, my mum went across to Italy to stay with the family for a holiday and met a guy called . . .'

'Umberto?'

'Precisely. Need I say more? Signor Umberto Baci.'

*More than half Italian!* 'So.' Lou gulped. 'Do you speak the language?'

'Indeed I do,' said Tom. 'Do you?'

'I did a year at college, but that was way back,' said Lou, thinking, *Another thing I let go of when I shouldn't have.* 'It's a beautiful language—so expressive.' *Il mio tesoro, ti amo.* Lou had a flash of being in bed with a big sweating man whispering passionate Roman endearments in her ear. She hoped her head wasn't transparent.

'Mum was never on the scene much so our grandparents brought us up and *Nonna* used to speak only Italian to us. Sammy speaks it to the kids and we've been over to visit the relatives a few times in Puglia.'

'Lucky you. I've never been to Italy,' said Lou with a heavy sigh.

'You should go,' said Tom, 'it's beautiful.'

'My husband is more of a Spain man.' She shook him out of her head. 'Your mum never married Umberto then?' she asked.

'Ah, well, it seems that naughty Umberto was already married. A couple of years later, Mum played out exactly the same scene on a trip to Norway with a guy called Sigi, which is why my sister is all blonde. We were brought up between my grandparents and my Uncle Tommy and Auntie Bella—they couldn't have kids of their own. Am I going on too much?' Tom asked suddenly.

'No, not at all,' said Lou, who was thinking that it wouldn't matter if he was expounding on the history of plastic injection moulding, it was just nice to be near him.

'Uncle Tommy built up the ironmongery business and ran a skip and cement sideline and, when he died, he left it all to my sister Sammy and me. I bought her shares so now it's all mine. She's happy to help me out part-time, we work it around the kids.' He smiled fondly. 'She's a good girl, is Sammy, she's just finding that carrying this one is harder than all the others put together. They were so easy.' He stopped, remembering again what she had told him about her inability to have children and silently cursed himself for his insensitivity. He drank some coffee.

'Do you get much trade in the shop?' enquired Lou, guessing why he had closed up that line of conversation.

'Loads,' said Tom, happy for the change of subject. 'You wouldn't believe how far people will travel to have a poke around. Whatever anyone wants, I guarantee to get it for them. I love that whole detective part of it. I have a store on the Internet too, which my sister runs from her home. I sold off the cement side, but I like getting out in the skip wagon and meeting nice people . . .' Tom coughed, embarrassed. 'Anyway, this is all about me. What do you do for a living?'

'I'm a part-time accounts clerk,' said Lou, 'but I'm in the process of setting up a business with my friend Debra. We're both qualified chefs and we wanted to set up a business a few years ago but plans got altered, so . . . better late than never, we've started looking for premises with a view to launching ourselves upon an unsuspecting public.'

Tom was leaning forward with wide-eyed interest. 'A restaurant business? Wow! What sort of food?'

'By a startling coincidence, an Italian coffee-house, specialising in proper coffee and incredible cakes.'

'I love cakes. Can you tell?' said Tom, jiggling his tum, which looked pretty firm to Lou. A small silence hung between them before Tom broke it with a loud tut. 'Harrison's Waste, eh?' he said, shaking his head accusingly. 'I don't know. You give someone superior service and look what they do to you.'

'Defecate to the enemy, like you said,' said Lou.

At Lou's unconscious misuse of her native language, Tom's grin appeared again, but she saw it for what it was, gentle and totally devoid of any malice. She had misread him over the twin business.

'More coffee?' she asked, guiltily avoiding his gaze.

'Thanks, but no. I'll be running to the loo all day if I have any more.' Disappointingly he got slowly to his feet and turned to get his still-damp and steaming coat off the radiator.

'Look, thanks again for taking care of Clooney. May I . . . I don't know . . . buy you lunch or something to say thanks?'

Lou smiled regretfully. *Damn.* 'Thank you, um, but I don't think that would really be appropriate.'

He blushed, saying, 'Yes, of course, I understand. You don't have to explain. It was just lunch. I shouldn't have . . . I wouldn't . . .'

'Oh, of course! I didn't think that you meant anything else,' Lou interrupted, over-anxious to make sure he didn't think that she thought that he might fancy her, which he didn't anyway, clearly.

Tom stood in the doorway and looked down at her. 'Well, I'd like to say thanks, other than just saying "thanks" if you know what I mean. What can I do for you?'

Don't answer that, Lou Winter, she said to herself with a bit of a sneaky giggle. Her jerked hard on her imagination's rein. She thought for a moment, sensibly though. There *was* one thing she needed.

'Tell you what,' she said tentatively. 'If it's not too much of a cheek after my betrayal . . . That skip outside will be getting picked up any time now, so . . . I'd like one of your mini-skips, please.'

'I'll get Eddie to drop one off for you this afternoon, no charge.'

'No! I didn't mean for free!' Lou protested.

'You don't think I'd take any money off you after what you did for Clooney, do you? Oh, no,' he insisted, quelling her argument with a big arresting palm. 'Just ring and tell me when you want me to pick it up.'

'As near to four o'clock on Saturday as you can, please,' she said.

'OK, then,' said Tom, wondering about the precision. 'And look, I'm sorry if I went too far with the twin joke. I really am.'

'You must have thought I was a real bimbo,' admitted Lou quietly.

'God, no, Lou. I think you're—' He stopped and started again. 'You're not someone I'd feel happy about upsetting, that's all. Thanks again.'

He went, he turned back, he waved. Lou waved back, she came inside, closed the door and slid down it. *Lou.* He had called her Lou.

'Can I ask you a question?' said Lou at work the next day.

'Ask away,' replied Karen, wolfing down a piece of lemon pie.

'When you were still married to your husband, in the early days, when you were happy, did you ever look at anyone else?'

Karen, who had been expecting a frivolous conversation, put down her fork. 'As in other men, you mean?' she asked. 'Why, Lou, have you got a *friend* that this has happened to?'

'No, I've got my reasons for asking and they aren't anything like you think. So, did you?'

The tone of Lou's voice made Karen suspend the teasing. It was pretty obvious why she was asking, whatever she might have said.

Karen leaned on the table and looked back at her life with Chris, the father of her babies, who had run off with her best friend's mother. So *had* she ever looked at anyone else when they were in that love-you-for-ever place before the carnage his affair had caused?

'Well,' Karen began slowly, 'Chris had a friend—James. I used to think he was nice, really good-looking and so funny.'

'But did he make your heart go faster when you were in the same room together?'

'No, not really,' said Karen, thinking back to how it was. 'He was a lovely man—your typical tall, dark and handsome catch. I could *appreciate* him, but I didn't want anyone else but Chris in those days.'

There. That was Lou's answer. It wasn't normal behaviour, looking at other men when she was in love with the one she had. She needed to get a grip.

'Hello, is that Sue?' asked Phil, knowing full well it was.

'Yes, it is. Who is this, please?' she said efficiently.

'This is Phil Winter about the green MG.'

'Well, hello,' she said, like a female Leslie Phillips.

'The car's coming in on Saturday morning. Would you like to see it?'

'Saturday morning? Let me just look at my diary.' Of course she will, thought Phil. 'Yes, what time do you open?'

'Well, to the public, nine a.m., but I could give you a private showing at eight,' said Phil. 'It won't be on my shop floor long, I warn you.'

'OK, I'll be there,' she chirped.

'Look forward to it, Sue,' smiled Phil, deliberately using her name. Women liked that.

Later that afternoon, Lou found Zoe in the toilets reapplying her eye make-up. 'You OK?' she asked.

'Sort of,' said Zoe with a very wobbly voice. 'No, I'm not, actually. I hate that bitch, Lou. I'm going to smack her right in the gob soon.'

'You do realise she feeds off you getting upset?' Lou said. 'The best way to deal with her is not to let her have any inkling that you are bothered by her petty behaviour. Rise above it, lovey. Think of it as the more she tries to bring you down, the more important a threat you are to her.'

'I am going to have her,' snarled Zoe, curling up her fist.

'Promise me you won't do that. It would get you sacked instantly.'

'But it would feel good, wouldn't it, for those few seconds?' grinned Zoe, savouring the thought of her fist crunching into all that metal.

'No, because then she would have won. Trust me, in real life you wouldn't feel half as good after doing it as you might think.' Lou wished someone had given her this advice, before she'd lamped Phil's other woman in the middle of a crowded Boots in Barnsley town centre.

Tom was as good as his word—Eddie had delivered the skip as promised. Wouldn't it be nice if she could put Nicola Pawson in it and save everyone in the office from her sadism, Lou mused. Then creepy Des and Celia could join her, and Victorianna, and big Shirley Hamster with her scissors. And Susan Peach . . . *and Michelle and Renee and Phil!* her mind screamed. The shock of those last three additions brought her daydreams to an abrupt end.

That lunchtime, and after work, Lou had gone clothes shopping and was surprised to find that she had dropped a whole dress size. She'd gone slightly mad in celebrating her new size and bought far more clothes than she intended to. Now, hot and exhausted, Lou opened the front door to One, The Faringdales and dumped the bags on the table.

She got a coffee and went into the study where she kept her big Filofax. She turned to the address pages, which were a mass of scribbles, Tipp-Ex and alterations, and ripped them all out. Then she took some blank paper and started to copy some, but not all, the names back in. Her doctor, dentist and electrician, and Carlo the hairdresser.

Next, only the people who were relevant to the Lou she was now and would be part of her life from here on—people who meant something to her and to whom she meant something—were written down. Lou knew that the time had definitely come to fill the last skip.

Phil hadn't really taken all that nonsense seriously about Lou starting up the coffee-house business. Where would she get the money for it? However, he found himself on the horns of a dilemma. He needed her on side because he'd invited Des and Celia plus brats round for Sunday dinner. He'd got a lovely Audi in and Des was interested but wavering like a total old woman. A nice piece of lamb cooked Lou's way could just tip the balance in his favour. Still, for the lying and wet-dog episode and meeting-that-Deb-again business, his wife needed to know he wasn't happy by a long chalk.

He made sure that Lou knew he'd got up an hour earlier than normal that Saturday morning and that she saw him putting on a shirt for work that he only ever wore for best. He made a point of humming merrily because he never hummed and that was bound to raise her suspicions.

'Just in case you try to get hold of me later, I'd better warn you that my mobile might be off for a while,' he threw behind him as he headed out. Phil could hear the cogs cranking up in her brain already.

Lou parked at the supermarket but her head was back at the house, watching Phil go through his morning routine. Of course she had noticed the best shirt, as she was meant to. And he never turned off his mobile. Did he want her to think he was up to mischief? To throw her off-balance for seeing Deb again? Or was he really up to something?

Sue Shoesmith was there waiting when Phil got to the showroom. Slipping off his wedding ring, he stuck it in the glovebox before getting out of his Audi. 'Oh, no—am I late for you?'

'No, I'm just keen,' said British-racing-green-eyed Sue with a glossy red smile.

'Come on in before you get cold,' he said, even though it was a May-mild morning.

He had to admit, the MG did look bonny. Sue gasped open-mouthed and Phil knew he had sold it. 'It's absolutely gorgeous,' she breathed.

'Told you,' he said. He opened the door and she climbed in elegantly. Nice legs. Very nice, in fact.

'Can I take it for a test run?' she asked.

'I'd have to come with you,' he replied almost apologetically. 'Quick coffee before we head off?'

'That would be lovely.' She didn't get out of the car as gracefully as she got in. He got a lovely flash of her thighs and some stocking lace. They both knew that was deliberate.

After Lou had unloaded the food shopping from her Saturday-morning supermarket trip she changed into her scruffy clothes. Despite telling herself to keep Phil's little game in perspective, she had spent the last two hours ripping apart that little domestic scene this morning like Quincy did with a corpse. Finally she had managed to convince herself that Phil wouldn't be playing Happy Families with Des and Celia on Sunday if his head was being turned by another woman. He was just trying to unsettle her for talking to Deb again and letting Clooney into the house. He would be far more secretive if he was having a flirtation.

Sue put her foot on the accelerator and the car zipped forward. 'Wow! Powerful, isn't she?'

'Oh, yes. Quick as a cat, but the control is all yours—we're both in your hands,' said Phil graciously.

Sue gave a throaty laugh. 'In that case, I may be ready to slip it up a gear and see what happens,' she said, with obvious double meaning.

Phil responded with a shy cough. Not too much, too quick, he thought. Slowly slowly catchee monkey.

Armed with her binliners, Lou pulled down the loft ladder and, with a fortifying deep breath, climbed up the steps. It was so quiet and still up there; it was as if the stored items wanted to be left alone in peace. But the things up here didn't rest in peace, did they?

After the paperwork was completed and the monies transferred, Phil presented Sue with a P. M. Autos fob bearing her new keys and a bottle of Moët. 'There's a full tank of fuel for you and a set of new car mats,' he winked in a 'You are so special' kind of way.

'And if I have any problems with anything, can I call you . . . personally?' she asked, her eyes not blinking as they locked with his.

'I would expect you to,' he said, smiling and softly stroking the bonnet of the car as if it were a woman's skin. He could sense her brain purring. 'What a very special lady. And the car's not bad either.'

'Aw!' she said, taken aback with delight at his compliment.

'You take good care of yourself,' he said, feigning bashfulness, as if he had just gone too far and was knocking down to first gear again. 'Drive carefully, but enjoy her. Life's too short not to have any thrills.'

'You're a man after my own heart,' she said.

Sue British-racing-green-eyes climbed into the driver's seat and waved goodbye to him out of the window with a long elegant arm. She'd call, of course, on some pretext or other. He gave it three days.

Lou looked around in dismay at the amount of Phil's rubbish: it was hard work carrying it all downstairs and she was soon looking like a Dickensian chimney-sweep child, stiff with grime. The thought of a good long soak brought with it the far more unpleasant one of Keith Featherstone. The issue consigned itself back to the 'to do' tray in her head. Again.

She had a small break for lunch—mineral water and a sandwich. Her stomach had obviously shrunk recently because the sandwich filled her adequately, but her hand reached automatically for the biscuit barrel anyway. The chocolate digestive had just touched her lips when she realised she didn't really want it—it was just habit. She was clearing out the house but still filling herself up with rubbish. Lou threw it away and headed, once again, up the stairs.

Back up in the loft, Lou found a box full of souvenirs from school: exercise books and paintings and her school diary from when she was eight. She flicked through it and found the story of when Dad took her to the zoo and she heard a bear trump, which made Lou laugh out loud to read again. She remembered it so well, still. For a moment it felt as if that young Lou was a separate entity from herself, one blissfully unaware that her father's heart would start to fail in a few years and that he would be taken away from her for ever, that she wouldn't have his love to lean on when she would most need it, when she discovered that all men didn't come up to the benchmark he had provided.

There was a broken cuckoo clock that her dad had bought her from Germany. Lou put the clock into the binbag, then immediately brought it out again. She couldn't let it go—it would be like saying goodbye to her dad all over again—yet hadn't she kept it unlooked-at for years? Lou smiled tearfully. She thought it through until a clear voice of reason, made both from the words of the article and her own common sense, directed her what to do. She didn't need the corpse of a broken clock when she had the living memory of walking into her bedroom and seeing it hanging there on her wall for her. She wasn't letting *him* go by letting *it* go. Lou bravely put it back in the binbag.

Next came a suitcase containing old summer holiday clothes from their Corfu trip. It was the last time she could remember feeling truly content with Phil—getting off the plane into the hot Greek sunshine, discovering the little bay where they snorkelled, eating meze. Lou didn't need the clutter-clearing article to tell her she had kept this case in order to hold on to a fortnight of time, a time when she was lovable. She couldn't go back to those days, however many reminders she had kept of what life had been like before she and Phil had started drifting apart, before Phil had his affair with Susan Peach. She took the bulky case straight out to the skip.

Lou knew only too well what lay in the hoard of boxes and carrier bags in the binliners that were coated with years of dust. Handbags and shoes that she had bought when Phil had left her, purchases made in the hope of stemming the crater-sized hole in her heart. There were hundreds of pounds' worth of goods there—never used or worn.

The article sat in her pocket but it had been long absorbed into her psyche. She knew her struggle to let these purchases go was all to do with feeling obliged to make use of them. *You can't get rid of us, we cost too much.* Things had controlled her, she now realised. Well, she didn't want them. The Heart Foundation women were going to have a field day, but it gave her some comfort to know that people would re-buy the items in happier circumstances and the charity would profit. She put them straight into her car boot for drop-off first thing on Monday.

Downstairs the phone rang, but Lou ignored it. There was just the one corner left in the loft to clear. Steeling herself, she pulled off the dustsheet that covered the pieces of cot, never constructed, the carrier bags of soft baby clothes, sheets and blankets, a mobile of cotton-woolly lambs that would never hang above a sleeping baby. It was the bag of tiny white socks that sent her crumpling to the floor. And yet people said you couldn't grieve for what you never had.

Just after they married, Phil suddenly announced that he didn't want children. Then two years later, he just as suddenly announced that if she still wanted to try for that baby, then they would. Lou threw her pills away with a happy flourish, but the longed-for baby never arrived. She had started fantasising about Phil and his twins reconciling and visiting, but that dream had died the day they met them in Meadowhall.

'Chuffing hell, it's Sharon and the kids,' Phil had said with horror.

A passing glance at the blonde woman told Lou she was indeed every bit as pretty as Phil's sighing recollections of her (whenever he wanted to stir up Lou's insecurities) made her out to be. It was the children, however, who stole her attention. They were beautiful: honey-haired with huge chocolate-brown eyes and thick dark lashes. How could any father not have wanted them? But Phil's extreme reaction made it perfectly clear that Lou would even be denied a stepmother-ship.

Then, not long after Phil returned home from his affair with Susan Peach, Lou's periods had stopped. Not only that but she felt decidedly queasy. Lou didn't need to do a pregnancy test—it was obvious she had caught on. Of course it would have been wise to wait and not buy stuff yet, but stocking up on a few odd things wouldn't hurt, surely? She had a true taste of happiness arriving at the hospital for her first scan.

The doctor at the hospital had been kind. Her scan, and the follow-up urine sample, said there was no baby. He explained that in rare cases, the body can cruelly mimic the signs of pregnancy to this degree.

'Pull yourself together, love,' Phil had said, when she told him that night through tears. 'You can't miss what you never had.'

But Lou knew that you could.

And saving these things had not helped to keep her dreams of being a mother alive; they had done the opposite. As she piled them all into the skip she knew she was saying that final goodbye. It felt as if she had ripped part of her heart out and put that into the skip too. Back upstairs, she sank to her knees, howling from some primal place within her that held the mother lode of her agony.

At four o'clock exactly, Tom reversed the skip wagon up the drive. As soon as he saw what was in the skip, he understood completely why she wanted it cleared away that day, and he could only guess what it must have been like for her to let those things go. He felt her sadness acutely on this day—the same day when his sister Sammy had brought her new little daughter into the world.

He rapped hard on Lou's door. He had the weirdest feeling she was in, and, inappropriate as it might have been, he so much wanted to see that she was all right. No, more than that, he wanted to put his arms round her and hold her.

When Lou was little, she used to have terrible migraines, but the day after, she would awake with a sense of inner peace that was almost worth the previous night's pain. Not at all dissimilar to how she felt that morning after the final skip had gone.

Lou was up and dressed before Phil woke up to the smoky aroma of his breakfast. He gave off a sullen air which hinted that things were most definitely not back to normal between them. His toxic seed had obviously started to germinate, it seemed, because yesterday, when he came in from work, she looked as if she had been crying for hours.

Of course, Lou *had* heard Tom knock the previous day, when he came to take the skip away. There was no way she would have let him see her in that state—scruffy and swollen and ugly from crying. The merest hint of sympathy would have opened up the floodgates in a dam of grief, and goodness knows what she would have said or done.

It had drained her to lose so many emotional possessions at once. They had anchored her firmly to places in the past where she was comfortable—with the devil she knew. Taking them away cut her adrift, to a place where the waters were dark, scary and unknown.

At first she panicked when Tom's wagon started up to transport them to where she would never be able to see them again, and she almost ran after him to tell him that she was taking them back. Nonetheless she took a deep breath and finally let them go. They were just things. The facts were clear: there was no loving father waiting in the wings to make everything better; she couldn't wipe away Phil's infidelity; she would never hold her own baby in her arms. *Deal with it, Lou, and move on. Time to start looking forwards instead of back.*

She had slept the solid, dreamless sleep of the exhausted and now, in the morning, life felt fresher. Life was suddenly before her as a whole new space to fill with Casa Nostra and Deb and a new, stronger phase in her marriage, free from the long shadow of Phil's affair dulling everything. She had to put that fact to the forefront of her mind: their marriage *had* survived Susan Peach. Phil was a controlling man—true—and he had made a mistake once, but there were much worse husbands out there. He was generous and hard-working, and *her husband*, after all; the man she'd been pledged to *till death do us part*.

The aroma of meat wafted towards Phil's receptive nostrils as Lou opened the oven door to baste it. Then it hit him that it wasn't the smell he was expecting.

'That's beef! I told you to get lamb! I'm trying to butter up Des to buy a twenty-seven-grand car, for God's sake!'

'Phil, I don't like lamb and I presume I'm going to be eating, too. Besides, I don't know whether Celia likes lamb but I *do* know she likes beef. It'll be every bit as nice. Better even,' said Lou. 'Trust me.'

'This is gorgeous beef,' said Des, swirling it round the onion gravy.

'I like my beef more pink,' commented Celia.

'Me, too,' said Phil in agreement. 'I think Lou's overcooked it slightly.'

'No, Lou hasn't,' clipped Lou sweetly. 'Lou just hasn't *under*cooked it. I don't like the idea of giving children pink meat.'

'More wine?' said Phil, slightly taken aback by her verbal parry. Was this the start of The Change? he wondered. It would go some way to explaining all this clearing-up bollocks and that impromptu sex they'd had in the kitchen.

Celia initially refused a slice of the chocolate tarte when Lou put it on the table. She patted her concave stomach and said something about already being half a micro ounce overweight.

'Oh, I don't know, it would be nice to have something to get hold of,' said Des, his eyes darting involuntarily to Lou. It was only a flicker, but one noted by both Lou and Celia.

'Yes, but you can have too much to get hold of,' said Phil, also flicking his eyes at Lou and making sure she caught his meaning.

'I think Lou has lost a little weight, am I right?' said Des. 'On a diet?'

'Lou's on the rotation diet,' said Phil. 'Every time I turn my back, she eats something.' He howled at his own joke.

Lou experienced a pang of humiliation that quickly changed to anger. 'Hark at Twiggy!' she said, and watched Phil's lips contract. She had never come back at him with a spiky riposte.

'Well, maybe I'll have just a little pudding,' said Celia, popping the bubble of tension. 'It does look delicious.'

Scheherazade stuck her finger into the remaining cake, scooped out a digitful and transferred it lasciviously to her mouth. Lou waited in vain for either parent or Phil to reprimand her because she had never felt it was her place to say anything when the children were bouncing on the furniture or nosing around in her drawers and cupboards upstairs. But Lou Winter was indeed going through a change (just not The Change) and she was thinking at that moment that Scheherazade and Hero might not be her children, but this was her house, and that beautiful chocolate tarte was her creation and she wasn't going to stand by and see it wrecked. Scheherazade's finger came out again and Lou whisked the tarte away before it made contact. 'Now would anyone like me to cut them an extra piece? Scheherazade?' asked Lou.

'Yes,' said Scheherazade.

'Yes, what?'

Celia's eyes snapped up.

'Er . . . yes, please,' said Scheherazade.

'Right,' said Lou with a knife in her hand and a knife in her smile. 'I'll give you this piece that you've just stuck your finger into, shall I?'

Scheherazade took the plate, which Lou didn't relinquish until she got a stunned 'thank you'. The withering effect rippled through everyone at the table. They continued to eat in silence.

'Gorgeous, that tarte,' said Des, spraying crumbs as he spoke.

'If you like it, darling, I'll get the recipe,' said Celia.

'Sorry,' said Lou, tapping the side of her nose. 'Trade secret.'

'For God's sake, Lou, it's only a bit of cake,' said Phil. She'd better not cock up this sale for him. What the hell was up with her?

'I'm sure Colonel Sanders had plenty of people saying, "For God's sake, Harland, it's only a chicken!" Good job for him that he didn't give his recipe out to everyone who asked, wasn't it?'

'Hardly the same, is it?' said Phil with a crooked little smile. 'A multi-million-pound industry versus one woman and a few buns.'

'Everyone has to start somewhere. Who knows, I might have overtaken him in profits if I'd started my business when I was originally going to,' returned Lou.

'What's this?' said Des, jumping in with interest.

'I'm opening up a coffee-house,' said Lou. 'With my friend Debra.'

'Debra?' said Celia with a sniff. 'Isn't that the person who nearly broke up your marriage?'

'No,' Lou said flatly. 'That was Phil.'

Phil went beetroot. Even Lou was a bit taken aback by her audacity. The room temperature dropped like the track on a white-knuckle ride.

'Go and play, children,' said Celia.

'Can we go upstairs?' asked Hero.

'Yes, of course,' said Celia, at exactly the moment when Lou said, 'No, you can't.'

'Jesus Christ!' Phil snarled quietly between his teeth.

Ignoring him, Lou got up from the table, holding out her hands to the children. 'Come on, there are lots of DVDs in the lounge you can watch, kids, but please, don't go poking around upstairs. It isn't polite.'

Des, Celia and Phil crossfired glances at each other while the children grumpily found a DVD they were vaguely interested in. This wasn't Lou. This was a Doppelgänger from Planet Crank.

Phil was about to whisk Lou aside and ask her what the hell she was up to when he realised that, now the kids were out of the way, they could get down to business. He'd deal with her later.

Lou went into the kitchen and filled up the dishwasher with what she had carried through. As she straightened up, she turned to find herself face-to-chest with Des and his dirty plate. He was so close to her that they could have auditioned for *Dirty Dancing*. Lou's hand came out and she pushed him back. 'Steady on there, Des,' she said as frothily as a soufflé. 'Don't they have personal space on your planet?'

Celia snarled loudly from the conservatory. 'Des! Here—now!' and he slunk back to the dining table like a kicked dog.

Interesting, thought Lou. So Celia was aware of his quirk. Maybe that's why she bought all those designer shoes and handbags. Perhaps she too was clinging on to something she felt was slipping away and was trying to comfort herself.

Tension hung over the table like a hydrogen-filled Zeppelin flying low on Bonfire Night. Phil annoyed with Lou, Celia annoyed with Des.

'So,' said Phil, attempting to divert the conversation back where he needed it to go. 'Has he told you about the car, Ceel?'

'Yes, he has,' she said, attempting to smile and look normal.

Lou poured four coffees and dispensed homemade truffles.

'Fantastic machine.' Phil passed the box of cigars over to Des before choosing one himself. 'Two years old and less than six thousand on the clock. You name it and that baby's got it.'

'I'll get you an ashtray,' said Lou, scurrying off meekly—like her old subservient self, they were all relieved to note.

'So—are you going for it then, Des? I'll cut you a deal.'

'Oh, I don't know,' said Des with a regretful shake of the head. 'I've seen a gorgeous silver BMW in Buckley's.'

'It's a lot easier to keep clean than black,' said Celia, who had set her heart on a car with the blue and white BMW button.

Phil knew instinctively that they'd already made up their minds before they came today and had taken advantage of his hospitality. Even worse, they were buying from Mr 'New-Kid-on-the-Block' Jack Buckley, his sworn business rival. Well, if they weren't buying then they might as well piss off until December, he thought. Oh! He must remember to tell Lou that he'd invited them for Christmas dinner. His classic car business would be nearly up and running by then, and he and Fat Jack could apply pressure on Des to invest, greased further by copious amounts of brandy and Lou's turkey and trimmings. Oh, yes, and he must tell her Fat Jack and Maureen were coming as well.

'I've got a surprise for Christmas dinner this year,' said Phil, five minutes after waving off Des and Celia.

'Christmas? But that's half a year away yet!'

'It'll be on us before we know it. I want to get plans in place.'

'Well, if you're already thinking about it, how about going out for the big meal this year? Apparently Queens Hotel do a fantastic one.'

'Er, even better than that, I thought a traditional family Christmas at home. I thought we could have the kids round at Christmas. I know that would be nice for you, Lou—kids and Christmas and all that.'

Manipulating git, thought Lou, but listened on.

'And obviously Des and Ceel.'

'Obviously,' said Lou. She knew what was coming next.

'And your mother. We can't leave her out.'

'No. Absolutely.'

'And . . . Fat Jack and Maureen. I noticed you got on like a house on fire with her last time. Chatting away together for ages, you were.'

He made a move to hug her, but she put up a hand to stop him. 'So let me get this straight. Instead of a six-course meal made by someone else in a lovely hotel, with no washing-up to do afterwards, I get to make dinner for nine with no one to help me cook it or clean up?'

'I promise, I'll help you. It's important to me, Lou. This new joint venture with Fat Jack is my . . . our future.'

'What about what's important to *me*? What's in it for *me*, Phil?'

'Why are you suddenly so "me, me, me", Lou?' he barked.

'Maybe I've suddenly remembered there is a "me" worth considering. Everyone else seems to have forgotten!' said Lou, sweeping past him, grabbing the first coat to hand and striding out into the afternoon.

Let her have her tantrum, Phil thought. By Christmas she would be nice and compliant again. His game was well underway now and pretty soon he knew that she would be agreeing to anything he suggested.

**A**s soon as Lou had got to the lip of the estate, the heavens opened; although she hardly noticed because her brain was too busy churning over the events of that hideous afternoon.

She was automatically heading in the direction of Michelle's end-of terrace house half an hour's walk away. She just wanted to talk. And, more importantly, she wanted for once to be listened to.

Lou was saturated by the time she got there. She knocked on the mustardy painted door and it opened immediately.

'You were quick—oh!' said Michelle, holding a thin baby-pink satin dressing gown shut across her obviously naked body. 'Sorry, I thought you were Craig. He's just nipped out for some fags,' she said, smiling a little awkwardly. 'He'll be back in a minute.'

'I was just wondering if you were free, but obviously not,' said Lou.

'No, sorry, I'm not really,' said Michelle.

'Oh, it's OK, please don't worry.' Lou smiled. Her escapee tears were camouflaged by the rain.

'Look, I'll ring you as soon as he's gone,' Michelle said. The door was already closing.

Lou turned back down the street, passing a tall, hollow-eyed, scruffy-looking bloke with facial piercings and some weird blue tattooed writing on his neck. He was opening up a packet of Embassy and dropping the wrapping on the ground. Surely that was never him—*the most gorgeous man she'd ever seen.*

The rain was relentless and she didn't even have her purse to get a taxi. She faced a long, hard and wet walk home.

For once, Phil was wrong. Sue Shoesmith left it a full seven days before she contacted him with a text: Hi Mr Audi TT. Car is grrreat. Slight problem though. Can I bring it in and show you?

He texted back. When? You name the time.

The response was immediate. Can do this afternoon. 5?

5 OK. I won't turn the coffee off he responded.

Strong, black, 1 sugar x came the quick reply. Christ, she must have had a texting speed of 300 wpm. A fast bird, in all senses of the word.

'Salad?' said Deb, recoiling with horror.

'Yep, salad and a sparkling mineral water, please,' reiterated Lou to the Maltstone Garden Centre café waitress.

'Don't tell me you're going all healthy on me,' said Deb. 'Especially as we're planning to open up the artery-clogging-capital of the world!'

Lou laughed. 'Don't be daft, I just feel like a nice crisp leafy salad.'

'Seriously, though, Lou, you have lost weight since we met up again,' said Deb. 'I did mean to say it before, but I know your mother is always on about your figure and I didn't want you to think I'd joined the "Let's monitor Lou's weight" club. Have you been dieting?'

'I've lost this just by clearing out some rubbish from the house and getting physical filling skips and drinking lots of water. Ironic, isn't it, that I lose it when I'm not even thinking about losing it?'

'Well, you look lovely,' said Deb, 'not that you didn't before.'

'I am much more energised. I'm enjoying the feeling so much, I'm not going to go back to my old ways of comfort eating.'

'Well, good for you,' said Deb steadily, and meaning it, but not asking why she would need to comfort eat at all if things were OK.

'But, don't you worry,' said Lou. 'The day I stop enjoying desserts will be the day I ask you to shoot me. I'm not turning into Victorianna.'

'On that horrible thought, down to business,' said Deb. 'The biggest problem we have is premises. I've totally drawn a blank with the estate agents, apart from the kebab shop on Pitterly Lane.'

'Hardly central, unless you're a druggie,' said Lou. 'No, we can wait.'

'For a miracle.'

'Either that or a fairy godmother.'

And funnily enough the fairy godmother appeared that very afternoon in the form of a six-foot-six skip man.

**A**s Deb was paying the bill, Lou rang home on her mobile to listen to any answering machine messages: *Hello, this is Tom Broom. I hope you're OK. I just wondered . . . I know you said you were looking for some premises for your coffee shop . . . well, I might be able to help. Can you ring me?*

Lou stabbed in the number without delay. 'Oh, hi, it's Lou.'

An embarrassing silence—he'd obviously forgotten her already.

'Er, Lou Winter,' she clarified. 'Number One, the Faringdales.'

'Yes, sorry, I know who you are. The line just went a bit fuzzy then,' he explained. 'Look, I'll be back at the Tub in about twenty minutes—can you meet me there?'

**W**ould you like to tell me why *your* skip man is looking for premises for us, why you refer to him as *your* skip man and who your mysterious skip man *is*?' Deb was grinning.

So Lou began at the beginning and, as she drove, told her friend everything about the article and clearing out the house and spotting Tom Broom's name on a skip.

'What's he look like?' said Deb.

'You'd love him,' said Lou. 'He's just your type.'

'Ooh,' said Deb, whose type was tall, wide men. She was almost six foot herself so the bigger the better. 'Hair?' she enquired.

'Black with grey flecks.'

'Eyes?'

'Grey.'

'Aha—that was a test question. How come you know what colour his eyes are?' said Deb, amusedly pointing an accusing finger at Lou.

'It's the first thing you notice about him,' said Lou matter-of-factly.

'Something you're not telling me, Lou Winter?' asked Deb.

'Nope,' said Lou. 'I don't look at other men in that way.'

Having parked the car, Lou led Deb into the ironmongery and there she watched her best friend's eyes round in approval as they took in Tom Broom. She also watched how warmly Tom looked at Deb. They were two single, lovely, tall, good-looking people, so of course they were going to be attracted to each other.

'Come on,' said Tom. 'I'll take you both for a coffee.' He led them next door to the grotty transport café where Lou and Deb sat on a bench while he went to the counter to get the coffee.

'How come it's so busy?' murmured Deb. 'It's a total dump.'

They were surrounded by big burly men eating belt-buster all-day breakfasts. The air was full of the smell of cheap bacon. The crockery was jumble-sale oddments in all shapes and colours, the ceiling purple and the walls a shade of yellow that was reminiscent of a bad cold.

Tom returned with a tray. He was obviously a valued customer since he managed to get three unchipped mugs.

'So?' said Deb. 'Apparently you have something exciting to tell us.'

'Well,' began Tom, looking at Lou, 'the reason I didn't say anything before was that I didn't want to insult you, so please hear me out.'

Lou and Deb nodded.

'The premises I was talking about?' said Tom. 'You're in them now. May's Café. Although the "Y" fell off the sign so people know it as . . . er . . . "Ma's".' He watched their faces drop, as he knew they would.

'It's not really . . .' began Deb diplomatically.

'Let me finish, please,' said Tom. 'May is giving up the lease. This place is full from first thing in the morning to last thing at night—see, there's loads of parking space for lorries. The factory is getting knocked down and will be made into a shopping area with luxury flats to the side. I've seen the plans and it looks pretty good. Obviously, until it's finished you'd be taking a risk on the sort of establishment you want to open until you build up some clientele because this area, at the moment, isn't exactly renowned for passing street trade. The upside of that is the lease is nice and cheap. And you could take over the business as it is for now and convert it as and when. It does a cracking trade.'

'What's the landlord like then?' Lou asked.

'He's a great bloke. Fantastic. He owns my lease, too,' said Tom fondly. 'Really fair, very trustworthy—big, good-looking kid.'

'Where can we find him?' said Lou.

Tom leaned over the table and whispered conspiratorially, 'He's sitting opposite you with a mug of the world's most disgusting tea in his hand.' He tutted at Lou. 'Haven't you learned anything yet?'

'You!' said Lou. 'I should have guessed.'

'Big, good-looking kid! In your dreams,' said Deb, with a smile. Turning to Lou she said, 'We need to talk.'

'I'm going to have to leave you ladies, anyway. I've got skips coming out of my ears today,' said Tom. 'Think about it. The development will bring a lot of business back to this end of town. I'm not trying to off-load the lease onto you. It's such a well-established business, I know I wouldn't have a problem letting it.'

'We'll let you know as soon as we can,' said Lou.

'Right,' said Tom. 'I won't advertise the lease until I hear from you. Bye, Debra, it was nice to meet you.'

'Bye,' said Deb sweetly. 'It was nice to meet you too, Tom.'

He winked at Lou. 'See you again, too.'

Deb left it a respectable three seconds after Tom had left before gossiping about him.

'So that was your Tom Broom then.'

'He's not *my* Tom Broom,' said Lou. 'What do you think of him?'

'Very nice,' said Deb with emphasis. 'However, we'll dissect the lovely Mr Broom later. For now, Lou, let's talk shop. Literally.'

'**I** can't understand it,' said Sue Shoesmith. 'There was a clanking noise I wanted to talk to you about and now it's gone.'

Amazing that, thought Phil, handing her a cup of coffee. 'Black, one sugar, just as the lady ordered. Please sit down.' He pulled out a chair.

'Don't let me hold you back from going home, though,' said Sue. 'It is Saturday night, after all.'

Phil dropped an almost inaudible sigh. 'Nothing for me to rush home for,' he said, casting his eyes down. 'Anyway, how's the car been?'

'Fantastic. I've seen a lot of heads turn my way recently.'

'I'm sure you'd see that whatever you drive,' said Phil, smiling widely.

'Aw, thank you, that's so sweet. Anyway, an Audi TT is far more impressive. You were saying you drive an Audi because you don't have any children to consider?' she continued.

'No, no kids. My wife was never really interested. We talked about it before we were married but she changed her mind afterwards.'

'Oh, no!' said Sue with a 'what-a-total-bitch' expression.

'You married with kids?' asked Phil softly.

'No. Never met Mr Right,' said Sue. 'Met a few Mr Wrongs and a Mr Complete Tosspot, but not Mr Right. Are you still married then?'

Phil nodded slowly. 'Yes, sort of. What I mean is that we're joined by name, but we lead separate lives these days. She . . . sorry, I shouldn't be saying this, but you know men, we don't talk things over like you girls do and stuff gets stored up inside us.'

Sue leaned forward supportively. 'No, go on. I'm a great listener.'

Phil took a deep, dramatic breath. 'She—my wife—had an affair a few years ago. It nearly killed me, to be honest. Of course I don't entirely blame her. I work too hard and thought I could make my absences all right with a few nice bits of jewellery.' A man who could admit his faults to a woman was irresistible and, as negatives went, these came across as pretty positive ones. 'Anyway, she came back but now she lives at one end of the house and I live at the other.'

Expert touch, implying separate bedrooms *and* a massive house.

'She's a lovely person, but I feel'—pat of heart—'nothing.' Never diss the ex. Those women's magazines of Lou's always pointed that out as a sign to look for in a total bastard.

'Oh, that's so sad,' said Sue with great feeling.

'By Christmas we'll have the house sold and be well on the way to divorcing. A New Year and a fresh start.'

Sue's hand fell on top of his and she squeezed it. 'Look, I'm a legal secretary. If you need any help with that side of things, I would be only too glad to point you in the right direction.'

'Thank you,' said Phil, looking very vulnerable. 'You're just great and I'm glad our paths crossed. Can I . . .' He shook his head.

'Yes?' Sue's pupils were like open black caves.

'I was going to say, can I take you out for a drink some time? But I'm aware I'm still married and I don't want you to feel awkward,' said Phil.

'I'd love to meet up with you again,' said Sue keenly.

Phil made his eyes light up. 'Really? Oh, wow, that would be great!'

She stood to go. 'You have my number.'

'I do indeed.'

He led her to the door and there he placed a kiss on her cheek.

'Goodbye, Phil Winter, you nice man, you,' she said.

'Goodbye, Miss British-racing-green-eyes.'

'Wow! What a lovely thing to say!' she said.

He watched her float to the car. What simple machines women were. They could run for miles on a mere promise.

**D**eb threw herself, as heavily as someone so slim could, onto the chair opposite Lou in Café Joseph on the following Tuesday. 'God, I'm glad to be here!' she exclaimed.

'Tough morning?'

'No, just glad to be here. With you. Talking about you-know-what.'

The waiter, Mr Teenage Hormones himself, flashed her a glance. What was 'you-know-what'? he wondered. Perhaps they were going to have one of those marriage ceremonies.

'So, what do you say?' asked Deb.

Lou took a deep breath. 'I think we should go for it.'

'Me too.'

They both clapped their hands in glee.

'I've been thinking about the decor,' said Lou. 'There's no reason why we can't go with the theme we picked last time. If we strip it out totally but put in those American diner kind of benches, it would work for phase one—the continuation of the transport café—and we wouldn't have to alter it when the coffee-shop takes over as the main business.'

Deb tried to visualise it. She had always really liked that whole 'milk bar' retro concept. 'So we need to see Tom, get some measurements, costs for the lease and builders' quotes.'

'Then we see the bank,' said Lou. 'I'll present our case to them exactly like last time. They seemed to think we'd done a pretty good job. I think we could get away with local joiners rather than anything specialist, so we'll need to get them in to look at the place a.s.a.p.'

'Then we find a name for it,' said Deb. Ma's Café wasn't fair on Lou.

The sandwiches arrived. The service was quick here.

'Have you told Phil?' asked Deb tentatively.

'I've told him I'm going into business with you,' said Lou.

'What was his reaction?'

Lou's shrug was her answer. 'Not that I'm bothered,' she went on. 'It's not going to stop me that he thinks I'm making a mistake.'

'Things OK between you two?' asked Deb tactfully.

'Yes, of course,' said Lou, with a smile that didn't quite do the job. 'He's still a bit annoyed about the weekend before last. I think he blames me for Des not buying that car. I stirred up trouble between him and Celia when I pushed Des away from me in the kitchen. Any closer and we would have fused.'

'Phil should have *done* something about Des a long time ago. It's a shame you aren't married to someone who would have sorted him out.'

Lou melted into a little private fantasy where Tom pulled Des off her.

'Like Tom,' said Deb, as if Lou's skull was projecting images. 'He's a strong lad, isn't he? Looks the protective type.'

'Yes, I suppose he does,' said Lou, avoiding Deb's eyes.

'We'd better ring him and arrange a meeting. Can I leave you with that?' said Deb. 'It will be lovely to see him again. He's really nice.'

Lou sipped her coffee. She was sure Deb fancied Tom.

'Er, is that Tom?' asked Lou, knowing that it was.

'Hello, Lou, how are you?'

How silly was it to feel as if her stomach had just been hit by a big glass of vodka, just to hear him say her name. 'Tom, the reason I rang was, we are really interested in the lease, so if it's OK by you, can we meet you again and talk over some facts and figures?'

'Yes, of course,' said Tom. 'Maybe it would be best if you were to come to my house. I've got all the paperwork there and the plans. Oh, by the way, there's a small flat above the caff. It's not occupied.'

*Come to my house?*

'Well, I'm sure it would come in handy for storage,' said Lou.

'How about Friday at, say, six?' said Tom.

'OK, then. Bye!' Lou flipped shut her mobile thinking she had handled that in a business-like fashion without any major gaffes. Just as she put it in her bag, it rang and the screen said that it was Tom.

'Hello, again,' he said. He was grinning, she could tell. What on earth had she done now to make him laugh? 'Don't you want my address?'

Whoops, thought Lou.

Lou quickly scribbled the dictated address—*The Eaves, Oxworth*—it sounded very grand. She suddenly felt like Anne in *The Famous Five*. This was all starting to feel like an adventure.

Phil came in at seven o'clock. He called, 'Hi,' peering over her shoulder to see what he had to look forward to gastronomically, and went upstairs to change out of his suit. It was his normal routine—with one notable exception. This was the third night in a row that he had kept his mobile with him and not put it on charge in the kitchen.

Now why would he not leave it lying around? a voice in her head questioned. Lou tried to ignore it. She didn't want to go down that analytical road to Nightmare Land again. After Phil's affair she had found herself in that mad place where women sniffed shirts and checked cars for unfamiliar-looking hairs. She couldn't eat, couldn't sleep, couldn't think straight. Her mind tore her to shreds with questions. No, she would never go back to those days of obsessive suspicion. Phil was not having an affair. End of.

But the question of the phone kept poking at her, long after Phil had eaten his meal and gone to bed. And swept up in that thought-path was his strange behaviour of late—the constant humming, the change of aftershave. She needed to think straight. It was Phil's way of punishing her about the Des and Celia afternoon, not forgetting her friendship with Deb. He was trying to drag her attention back to him and away from the coffee shop. Despite his little jabs at her insecurities in the past three years he hadn't been with anyone else, she was as sure as she could be of that. But she didn't wholly trust him. Maybe another Susan

Peach was just round the corner, waiting to seduce her husband away.

Sitting there with a coffee at the dining table, Lou gave herself a slap. She was being ridiculous, torturing herself with thoughts like these. She should go about her daily business and allow Phil to think he was teaching her his 'lesson'. She would let his game run its course. There was no other woman. Even Phil wouldn't be that cruel.

**P**hil's phone buzzed in his pocket, just as Lou had waved goodbye to him on Friday morning. It made him tingle as he read the sauce that appeared on the screen. The texts had started off very friendly and benign, but soon innuendo had started to creep in. Isnt it cold 2day? he had sent. And the reply came: I am pretty hot myself.

Yes, a good soup was all the better for a simmer, as Lou would say; and didn't he know it. Bring it to the boil straight away and you spoil it.

**T**here was a small bag waiting for Lou on her desk when she walked into work. She opened it to find a box of matches. She didn't understand, then she saw Karen smirking—and then she *did* understand.

Lou bounded over and hugged her.

'Well, I didn't want to say anything before in case it didn't work out,' said Karen. 'But, yes, I'm on the course and, Lou, I have to say I'm really enjoying it. Thank you for forcing me to join. Now take those home and burn that bloody burgundy suit!'

Lou's face was all smiles. 'Did you ask HR about funding you?'

'No, Mum and Dad've chipped in for the course fees. It's manageable. So . . .' she rattled the bag. 'Do as you agreed, Skinny.'

'I think "Skinny" is pushing it a bit,' Lou smiled, but enjoyed the novelty of being called it all the same. 'Anyway, I already put my burgundy suit in a skip,' she told Karen, 'so I can't set fire to it.'

By then everyone was clustering round Karen's desk to see what the fuss was all about. Stan gave her a big kiss and Zoe gave her a hug and said she wished she'd known.

As they stood around, Nicola came in with a, 'What's this? What's going on?'

'Just a private meeting,' sniffed Karen.

'Roger will be thrilled to know he's paying wages to people so they can hold private meetings in work time,' said Nicola with malevolence. 'Lou, have you finished the return I left with you yesterday?' There was no way she could have. Not unless she was Superwoman.

But with accounts, Lou *was* Superwoman and so could reply with all honesty, 'Yes, it's on your desk.'

After work, Lou picked up Deb from the bakery and they headed into the lovely countryside on the outskirts of Oxworth, where Tom lived.

'That is nice,' said Deb, when they had turned onto a leafy lane.

In front of them was an old, double-fronted Victorian villa with gables, set like a neat diamond in a very lovely garden.

Tom came to the door and led them inside with a large shepherding hand that touched Deb's back slightly, Lou noticed with a pang of envy.

A wide hallway greeted them: black and white tiles on the floor, fresh white walls and a beautiful chunky staircase in dark wood. There was a huge, stained-glass window where the stairs turned, which was flooding the hallway with lovely late-spring evening light.

'This is beautiful,' said Deb, rotating to take it all in.

'It's been a bit of a labour of love,' said Tom, 'but at least I've done all the knocking-down bits and am now at the putting-up stage.'

They followed him into a large echoey room, where the walls were bare and replastered in patches. Tom brought a pot of pre-prepared coffee through and a big tin of biscuits. Being a bloke he didn't put them on a plate, which made Lou smile a little. There was no false ceremony with this guy—but he was all man. Unlike Phil, she couldn't imagine him sneezing because an animal had looked in his direction. Which reminded her. 'Where's Clooney?' she asked.

'He's with my sister. He's too distracting, so he's playing with the kids. I'm going to pick him up after we've finished.'

'So to business . . .' said Deb, starting their meeting by using a pink wafer as a gavel.

An hour later, after Tom had shown them the plans, discussed terms and payment and presented May's neat set of accounts for Lou to cast her expert eye over, Lou and Deb were even more happy with their lot. He advised them to go and have a formal word with May if they wanted to check out his suitability as a landlord. Deb would, of course, and told Tom so. There were very few people she trusted on face value, however nice a profile they presented.

They were getting ready to leave when they heard Tom's outside door open and slam shut and a jolly female voice shouted out an echoey, 'Hello!' Tom leaped up but he was too late to stop the owner of the voice coming into the dining room, carrying a car seat, with Clooney bounding behind her. 'Sorry, am I interrupting?' said a petite lady with short white-blonde loose curls.

'No, we were just going,' said Deb, curious as to who this was.

Right on cue Tom said, 'This is my sister, Samantha. Sam, this is Debra and Lou, who are going to take over May's lease.'

Sam said hello. 'Sorry, I didn't realise you had company. I had to pop out for some nappies and I thought I'd bring Clooney back so you wouldn't have to come and fetch him. Plus I thought Lucy might like to see her Uncle Tom.' She twisted the car seat round and there, nestled inside a cosy pink blanket, was a baby with a golden quiff of hair. Tom looked helplessly at Lou, Deb looked helplessly at Lou, while Sammy looked at the three stiff statues that now faced her in utter confusion.

Realising that she was the only one of them that could rescue this, Lou gulped hard and came forward, bending to let the baby's hand grip her finger. 'She's absolutely beautiful,' she said breathlessly.

'Want to hold her?' said Sam proudly, wondering why her brother was doing all those gurning faces at her behind the woman's back.

'Yes, please,' replied Lou softly. Sam unstrapped her new daughter and handed her over to Lou. She had butter-soft skin and smelled of baby powder. Lou had never held a newborn before. She could not have imagined how delicate they were; their hands, their nails, the thin legs, the tiny socks. Again the socks triggered the passage of tears to her eyes and she had to work hard to get them to sink back. Lou knew, though, that she could no longer go through life getting upset if she was within cuddling distance of a baby. She jollied herself up and handed back the armful of pink softness to Tom's sister.

'We must be getting back,' said Deb, grabbing Lou by the elbow and steering her towards the door. 'Goodbye, Sam, it was nice to meet you. Bye, Tom, I'll go to see May tomorrow.'

Once outside, Lou sucked in two big lungfuls of fresh air.

'You OK?' Deb asked.

''Course I am,' said Lou, over-brightly.

**P**hil couldn't remember the last time he'd had to turn off the burglar alarm and switch on the lights when he came home. Where was Lou?

A text message buzzed again in his pocket. He would have to slow down on those. Then again, if Lou couldn't be a proper wife, who could blame him? Hope you are doing something nice this weekend x it read.

You 2 typed Phil in return. Then he erased it and stabbed in something far less harmless. Free for lunch on Sunday? xx Sod it, he thought. The time had come to slam his foot right down on the accelerator.

**L**ou woke up at 3 a.m. after Phil shouted out something in a dream. She could have sworn he said, 'Sue'. It didn't help in getting back to sleep.

She decided to get up. It would be just after ten o'clock at night in Florida. She could ring Victorianna and get her little 'mum-visiting' plan working. But in the present emotional climate that didn't necessarily seem like a good idea. Instead, she went downstairs for a hot chocolate.

Upstairs, Phil cocked open an eye and allowed himself a moment of smugness before snuggling his head back down in the pillow.

Saturday was uneventful. Lou took Renee food shopping and then out for lunch. Renee wasn't herself at all. Her friend Vera was in Germany at the moment with her son and Renee seemed to be missing her very much. Plus it hammered home the fact that she wasn't afforded the same courtesy by her own so-called nearest and dearest. Lou wished she had just phoned Victorianna in the night and got it over with, but she wasn't ready for that one just yet. Her sister was a dirty fighter.

Phil seemed distracted that evening. He kept disappearing to the loo.

'You want to get your prostrate checked out. That's the eighth time you've gone in the last hour,' Lou said with an attempt at a light laugh.

'I think you'll find it's *prostate*,' said Phil coolly on the way out again, 'but there's nothing wrong with mine.'

It was in fact a blatant act of 'Look at me, I'm up to something'. And every time Phil came back to the sofa, he tried to appear as though he was covering up a smile, which funnily enough he was. Sue was pretty prolific on the text front and she was most definitely hot for him.

Lou expected her husband to initiate sex the next morning. She felt him shift in bed and braced herself, but to her surprise he swung his legs outwards. 'Where are you going?' she asked.

'I often work on Sundays, as you well know,' said Phil.

'Yes, but you never said you were working today.' She was aware that that sounded a bit wheedling and reeled herself in. 'Will you be back for lunch or shall I cook a later dinner instead?' she said more steadily.

'Late dinner,' he said. He put on a good shirt and his expensive going-out aftershave again. 'Don't get up, I'll send out for a bacon butty.'

Lou lay in bed, thoughts tumbling round her head like jigsaw pieces that wouldn't fit together. Phil was not playing his normal sulking game; it had gone beyond that. *What if there is another Susan?*

Sue Peach had been a rough-looking tart, but all Lou could focus on was how cocktail-stick thin she'd been. It had to be the absence of flesh on her bones that had attracted her husband because she wasn't beautiful, or classy, or Brain of Britain. But Lou had never once asked him for a definitive answer. She had been so grateful to find him there on the mat, days before what was looking to be the worst Christmas of her life, that she had just dragged him over the threshold and taken him to bed. The gaping wound to her heart, though, had never been stitched up and treated. She had just stuck a quick plaster on it. So was it any wonder it had never healed, and continued to bleed?

She picked up the phone and rang Michelle.

'Oh, hi, Lou. How's things?' asked Michelle, but then before Lou could answer she jumped in with, 'You just can't believe how great Craig is—*at everything*. He is simply the best. I was telling Ali about him and she thinks he sounds great too.'

'Ali?' asked Lou, aware that the name had been dropped into the conversation like a little pebble to see how far the ripples went.

'Oh, haven't I told you about Ali? She's fab. She's new at work. I've been given the job of "baby-sitting" her. She's been round here to the house a few times—you know how it is.'

*Ali* must be another of Michelle's temporary friends. Each 'friend' took an intense but brief starring role in her life, only for a period of obsessive bitching to ensue and eventually a consignment to oblivion.

'Ali and I have had a great laugh since the first moment we sat together. Anyway, Craig won't be here this weekend, so Ali and I are going around town on Friday. I'd ask you to come with us but I know you don't do nights,' and with that she sniffed, making the point.

Lou suddenly wanted to giggle. An old picture flared up in her head of Shirley Hamster at school parading 'prize friend' Julie Ogden past her one day in a misguided effort to make her jealous.

'Well, I hope you have a good time,' said Lou, trying to sound serious.

'We will, don't you worry,' said Michelle with conviction. 'Anyway, I'll have to go soon because Ali said she might pop round so we can go shopping for something to wear next week. We're going to get a bottle of wine in before we go out and have a girly trying-on session.'

Lou and Deb used to get a bottle of wine in before going out when they were at college. She had never questioned whether what she shared with Deb was friendship, as she did so often these days with Michelle. She wasn't sure if she understood what relationships meant any more.

**P**hil pulled into the pub car park in the vacant space next to the natty green Roadster. As he got out of his car, Sue got out of hers.

'Busy morning?' asked Sue, daring to link her arm through his as they walked into the part of the pub signposted Maltstone Arms Bistro.

'Yes, very productive. I sold a beautiful Mercedes sports.'

They walked past a long table laid for thirteen with *Goodbye, we'll miss you* balloons, and Phil made a joke about the Last Supper which made Sue giggle. Her eyes had that misted, happy look that told him she was wriggling on his line like a doomed worm. He felt a prick of guilt, but then told himself that, after all, she was safe. He had no intention of having an affair with her and, if she misread the signs, he wasn't to blame.

They had starters and a main course. Sue had a coffee, while he had a syrup sponge and custard.

'I am really enjoying your company,' said Sue, with the sort of sigh Snow White did at the wishing well. She put her hand on his.

The Last Supper party started to file in. They looked old enough to have been at the original event, he thought, apart from the . . . he couldn't believe it! Judas 'Debra' Iscariot herself! Even after all this time he would recognise her anywhere, although for one fleeting moment he thought it was Lou's sister. He shifted his stare to the hand placed on his, momentarily freezing with panic. He knew he had been seen—in flagrante delicto. Hang on, said his brain, this couldn't have been better if you'd planned it. It was history repeating itself—*another pub, another Sue*. And what had the outcome been? Pretty damn satisfactory, actually. Debra had scuttled off to tell Lou, thereby unwittingly saving his marriage and ending their friendship. And he bet it was all going to happen just exactly the same way again.

Aware that Deb's eyes were burning holes in his cheek, he lifted Sue's hand to his lips, making it obvious to his observer that this was no innocent contact. He kissed the top of it and then gave the space between her fingers a suggestive lick, and when Sue pulled her hand away, shrieking with outraged delight, he made a move to gather up his coat and Sue followed. Still not letting Deb know that he had seen her, he guided Sue out, his hand hovering near her bottom, pushing the point of intimacy home, as if it hadn't been already.

**P**hil was very chirpy when he got home that night. He read the Sunday papers and ate Lou's pork Sunday dinner with approving lip-smacks. 'Fantastic, love,' he said. 'You have to be the best cook in the world.'

Lou smiled, not realising he was setting her up for a fall.

'You'll never guess what happened today. A woman came into the showroom and she was the spitting image of you when you were younger. It was uncanny. Lovely, she was. Just like you used to be before you put on all that . . . well, like you were, shall we say?'

He watched the gulp in her throat and then she disappeared quickly into the kitchen and did something noisy with the dishwasher. *Bullseye!*

# CHAPTER 5

WHEN DEB GOT HOME from Mrs Serafinska's lunch party at the pub, she opened up a bottle of Merlot, poured herself a big glass and sat at her kitchen table, where she dropped her head into her hands and tried to work out what to do for the best. Exactly as she did three years ago? she asked herself—when she had seen Phil snogging that cheap barmaid over a grotty pub dining-table. Back then, she had decided instantly. Lou needed to be told. What woman wouldn't want to know that her husband was making a total fool of her? Thoughts of how it might alter the plans for their business venture had been way at the bottom of Deb's list. Lou's welfare was her only concern.

Back then, it had taken Lou less than a minute to change from the smiling woman who answered the door of One, The Faringdales, into a wounded animal fighting for her life. One minute she was ushering Deb inside, the next she was tearing through Phil's wardrobe, scavenging for any clue that could help her understand *why*.

Deb had still been at the house with Lou when Phil came in from work—cocky as a dog with two dicks. But he had known that the game was up as soon as he saw the devastation. He'd grabbed a case and run.

Deb had moved in and stayed with Lou, hearing her crying in the night, watching her get thinner and more hollow-eyed with every day, until Deb wasn't so sure she had done the right thing any more.

Then, just before Christmas, three years ago, Deb had turned up at Lou's house to find her totally revitalised. Phil had suddenly arrived back home, with his suitcase.

'What did he say for you to let him back?' Deb had asked.

'I don't want to even talk about it,' Lou had replied.

'So you've let him off totally?' asked Deb with hard disbelief. She knew that Phil was listening from upstairs and she wanted him to hear this. 'Lou, please think! He will cheat again—you'll never be able to trust him. I never did like the balding, greasy git.'

Balding, she knew, would really piss him off. Phil did hear, and he made Lou choose because of it. The deal was simple: if she stayed friends with Deb then he was off—permanently. Their marriage couldn't repair itself with Deb insulting him. So Lou chose him, because Phil Bastard Winter had spent years chipping away at her self-worth with his rasping little comments about her looks and her weight and her abilities, until she had only weak scraps of herself left.

Yes, Deb had been upset, but it was Lou's life, not hers. Deb loved her friend so much she hated the idea of her being in pain. So what on earth was she going to do this time?

'**A**re you all right? You look absolutely pants,' said Karen, when Lou got into work the next day.

'I didn't sleep very well,' she explained.

'I'll get you a coffee from the super-dooper machine,' said Karen.

'Lovely,' said Lou, sticking on a smile.

Nicola kept a low profile that day and everyone else seemed in a good mood. Karen was telling them all that she had hooked up with a single dad on her accountancy course—Charlie—who was 'awfully kind'. She said it wasn't serious, but her eyes were too dreamy to carry off that lie. That weekend, Stan had five numbers up on the lottery and won enough to finance a nice sunshiney holiday for him and his wife for their ruby wedding anniversary. And Zoe's man was making her extra twinkly at the moment, and not even Nicola could dampen her spirits.

But thunderstorms often follow the brightest sunshine, and so it was, later that same day, the dark cloud that was Nicola started to announce itself. Stan had accidentally deleted something from his computer, and where had Zoe put those promotional gift vouchers?

'If you've taken them, you know they're all traceable, so don't even think about spending them,' said Nicola with affected concern.

At the implication of theft, Lou saw Zoe's hand start to rise and she moved in like a cheetah, grabbed Zoe's arm and marshalled her out of the office, saying, 'We're going for a coffee.' Let Jaws report her to HR for that if she dared.

Down in the canteen, Zoe's anger had softened into tearful frustrated rage. 'She accused me of stealing! I would have hit her, Lou.' Zoe tore open a sugar sachet and sprinkled it into her coffee. Her hands were shaking so much, the table top got most of it.

'I'm going to tell you something,' said Lou, 'about a friend of mine. It's private, so I'd rather you didn't spread it around. But I think . . . I *hope* it might help you. Just over three years ago, my friend's husband had an affair. He went back to her but my friend's hatred for the other woman just wouldn't go away. She was totally convinced that the only way she was going to get any sense of relief was to find the other woman and smack her in the mouth. Anyway, one day, my friend saw this other woman in Boots, buying condoms of all things.' Lou gave a dry little laugh. 'She knew it was definitely *her* because she had once called into the pub where the woman worked just to see what she looked like. When she turned round, my friend slapped her as hard as she could. Suddenly there were people swarming everywhere giving my friend the filthiest looks, calling for the security man. My friend ran out of the shop in a blind panic, leaving the woman wailing and crying with a big crowd cooing over her, thinking this poor innocent soul had just been attacked by a nutter. In that moment, my friend knew that she had just thrown away her biggest advantage—her dignity.'

Lou gulped. Telling this story had been harder than she'd anticipated. 'My friend couldn't sleep for days, wondering whether the police were going to appear at her door, or if she would open up a newspaper to see her name plastered over the front page. She said it was one of the worst experiences of her life, and she hasn't been back to Boots since.'

Lou squeezed Zoe's hand. 'Zoe, sweetheart, get another job, walk away, bash a wall, but take it from me, hang on to your dignity. Nicola would love it if you slapped her. She would have the perfect excuse then to sack you. You wouldn't feel victorious—all you would feel is shame and anger that in the end she *did* have the power to make you snap, after all. Trust me on this. I know.'

Zoe looked at Lou's lovely face with her kind green eyes and gave her a big hug. She knew perfectly who Lou's 'friend' was.

'Hang on in there, Zoe, please,' said Lou as they went back up the stairs to their office. 'This situation can't go on for much longer; someone will come along and change things. I'm sure of it.'

**L**ou pulled into the car park and looked at the grotty exterior of Ma's Café and she smiled because she could feel her dream stepping out of her imagination and becoming reality. This was so long overdue. She had never allowed herself to picture what would have happened if she and Deb had not abandoned their plans, because back then she couldn't have had both the café and Phil.

He had seemed normal enough the previous day, though he was still hiding away his phone and smiling too much for Lou's liking, which was actually starting to annoy her more than it upset her. How long had he been this pathetic? When did he become someone who had to torture, to control, to hurt? Or had he always been like that, and she was just wising up to it?

So far though, Lou was coping. The obvious timing of Phil's behaviour only galvanised her sheer bloody-mindedness. She would show him that, this time, he wasn't going to manipulate her into dumping her dream. She was, however, worried that the time for ultimatums was looming and she wasn't sure what she would do if he tried to pin her down to 'Debra Devine or me'. One thing was for sure: whatever happened, she would not let Deb down again. So, didn't that indirectly answer it for her?

**D**eb was taking that week off work and her Mini was already parked when Lou got to the café. They were going to have a look at the flat above the business and she saw that Deb was waiting at the top of the stairs for her, smiling broadly. 'Welcome to our empire HQ,' she said with a flourish, leading Lou into a small, dingy room furnished with a dining-table, already covered with Deb's homework, and two chairs.

Give or take a layer of dust and a neglected musty smell, the flat was clean. However, the lime-green walls and purple ceilings were a bit violent on the eye, especially when complemented by a burgundy alcove where the carcass of a double bed stood snugly between wall and window. A tiny bathroom leading off had a seventies chocolate suite and the galley kitchen with its ancient appliances was navy-blue.

'Where the hell did this paint come from?' said Lou. 'I thought May used this place for storage?'

'Apparently her nephew had the flat for a while at Easter so she emptied it for him. I think painting it was his way of paying rent.'

'Dear God, I hope he's not at art school,' said Lou. She had brought a basket with tea and coffee and cups and set it down on the table.

Deb thought her friend looked weary. She wondered if she knew about Phil already. Perversely, she both hoped she did and hoped she didn't, for obvious reasons.

'You all right today?' Lou asked her. 'You look a little tired.'

Deb wanted to laugh: Lou asking if *she* was all right. 'Start of a headache, that's all,' she said.

'I have tablets,' said Lou, fishing in her handbag.

'Thanks,' said Deb, who doubted that Semtex, never mind Ibuprofen, would shift what was making her brain throb.

**A** cup of coffee and a shared Twix later, Deb was showing Lou the list of builders she had rung for quotes. 'I'm seeing three lots this afternoon and taking them round the café. I told them it's urgent and that I want the figures back as soon as. I reckon we'd need to shut the café for maybe four to six weeks. But what do you think about this . . .' She leaned forward. 'We offer a free belt-buster breakfast to the regulars when we reopen.'

Lou nodded enthusiastically. 'I was thinking the same myself.'

'So, want to hang around and see some big hunky builders with me?' asked Deb. 'I've got this man coming at one,' she said, handing Lou a letter of introduction from a builder. 'They were keen, I'll give them that. And they guarantee to deliver on time.'

Lou studied the letter. 'I'd love to be here to meet this guy with you, Deb, I just need to nip home and change. Would you do me a very great favour when I come back?'

And as Lou told her what that favour was, Deb's first genuine smile in the last forty-eight hours spread over her face.

**D**eb led the builder round the café, which was busy with drivers. 'As you can see,' she said, 'we picked this place because of its popular location. You are familiar with our chain of coffee-houses in America?'

The builder nodded and mumbled, 'Oh, yes, certainly.'

'It's quite a phenomenon, how quickly it's grown,' said Deb, trying to rein in the giggle.

The builder had taken all his notes and measurements and now she was leading him upstairs to the flat. Deb gestured, inviting him to sit at the table. 'I apologise for the surroundings. It's a little different to our base in New York.' She gave a tinkly laugh. 'Five million square metres of office space. In the eighteen months since our chain was established in the States, the number of outlets has increased twenty-seven per cent more than McDonald's, Pizza Hut and KFC did in their first five years.'

The builder hadn't a clue how huge that was but made a series of impressed wheezes and accordion-like grunts.

'This may seem like an odd place to base our first UK opening, but our chairman has ancestral connections with this part of the country. Plus, as you may or may not know, an American conglomerate, which has integral business dealings with our chain back home, is buying up the land round here. Phase one involves two hundred new refurbs and we are looking for a team of builders who we can *one thousand per cent* rely on.'

The builder's eyes were dilating. 'We have a very good reputation for h'our work,' he said, with a misplaced aitch. 'No job too big h'or too small for us, and reliability and satisfaction always guaranteed.'

'Perfect!' said Deb. 'Of course our newly appointed head of ops is the one who will ultimately decide, which is why I am going to introduce you to her now. She has absolute authority in this matter. I asked her if she would mind meeting us here at quarter to.'

Right on cue, Lou teetered into the room in her beautiful black suit, seamed stockings and her tallest going-out heels.

'Ah, Mrs Winter, I think we've found our man. Mrs Winter, meet Mr Keith Featherstone. Mr Featherstone, meet Mrs Elouise Winter, head of global operations for Casa Nostra International PLC.'

**F**ifteen minutes later, down in Ma's Café, Lou wiped away her tears with a serviette. Deb's head was in her hands and she was sobbing. That was the scene that met Tom as he pushed open the door.

'What's the matter?' he asked softly. 'Are you both OK?'

Deb tried to tell him but dissolved into hysterics. Lou attempted to take over and did the same. 'I'll get a round in,' said Tom with a grin.

By the time he had returned with a tray, Lou and Deb had calmed down just enough to relate the story to him.

'What did he do when he saw you, Lou?' said Tom.

'He did this,' and Deb made a strange gurgling sound. 'I thought he was going to choke! Oh, you should have seen my friend here, Tom. She glared at him with her big green eyes and said, "I know Mr Featherstone's work *very* well, Miss Devine. We'll be in touch with our decision." Then she said, "Thank you," which sounded like "You are dismissed," and he scuttled out like a crab with his rear end on fire.'

The girls crumbled into laughter again, both glad for it. Both with so much on their minds where laughter had no place.

Deb checked her watch. 'Anyway, in fifteen minutes I've got another builder coming in, so I'd better sort out my face.'

They all stood to go. Oh, hell, Lou thought, now Tom would see her walking on those impossible heels, which were like stilts.

'Want a lift to your car?' grinned Deb, nodding towards her shoes.

'I can give you a piggyback?' said Tom.

'No, get lost the pair of you,' said Lou, shooing them away.

'We won't watch you walk across the car park—promise,' chuckled Deb, and waved before she followed Tom into the ironmongery.

**W**hen Lou reached the Townend roundabout, she realised she had left her notebook in the psychedelic flat. Doing a full circle, she came back into the car park, braking in a spot just opposite Tom's shop. The door was ajar, and through the aperture she allowed herself the luxury of watching him, unseen, his big powerful profile, his large gentle face, his wild, wavy black hair through which her fingers itched to weave themselves. Then Lou saw Deb move into his arms and she froze.

She watched her best friend bury her head into Tom's shoulder. They looked so good together—*so right*. Now he was holding her at arm's length and talking to her, then Tom cupped Deb's face in his hands. Tenderly, lovingly. Was he kissing her? She couldn't tell.

Lou started up the car. Her sight was blurred. Her whole body seemed to be one big heartbeat. She should be happy for them, she liked Tom and Deb so much, but it still hurt. Lou hadn't known how deeply her feelings for Tom had taken root until she saw him holding her best friend the way she wanted to be held by him.

**W**hen Lou got home there was a message on the answering machine. It was Keith Featherstone in his poshest voice: *Erm, this is Keith Featherstone. Would it be convenient for us to call tomorrow morning at eight o'clock to start work h'on your bathroom? I really must h'apologise for the h'inconvenience to you. Could you ring me back . . .*

Lou dialled.

'Oh, Mrs Winter, h'I am so glad you returned my call.'

'I got your message, Mr Featherstone. Yes, it is convenient for you to call tomorrow at eight,' said Lou with icy politeness. 'And I want this work done quickly after all the "inconvenience". Is that understood?'

'Yes, certainly, Mrs Winter. My lads will be there at eight prompt.'

'Thank you and goodbye, Mr Featherstone.'

Lou put the phone down first. Those with the power always made the break first. *Result.* Lou was shaking—but smiling too. She felt absolutely empowered, so much so that she could have tackled Victorianna. She needed to keep this feeling on a simmer—and only bring it to the boil at 3 a.m. when her sister would be home from work.

**P**hil misinterpreted his wife's distraction that evening. He concluded that she was in psychological hell—wondering why he was hiding his phone and behaving slightly oddly. He gave it another two weeks, then it would be a feast of lamb dinners, and life would settle down to being blissful again. Marriage was all about keeping an even power balance. There was only room for one partner with the upper hand in a relationship. He had a good marriage—it was worth his efforts to save it.

**A**t three o'clock exactly, her heart thumping, Lou picked up the phone and dialled the dreaded number. There was an echoey foreign dialling tone and then that voice—that affected, jolly-hockey-sticks public-school accent of a woman who had graduated from a Barnsley comp with one GCSE in French.

'It's me,' said Lou.

There was a telling pause before Victorianna said with tight politeness, 'Oh, hello, Lou, how are you? What do you want?'

Victorianna had already worked out what time it was in England. She knew her sister wasn't ringing her for a 'how are you?' chat.

Lou took a big gulp of air. 'I think you should invite Mum to visit.'

Victorianna did one of those incredulous laughs that would shatter crystal. 'Lou, I'll invite my mother out when *I* see fit. Not when *you* tell me to. Who the hell are you to tell me what to do?' Victorianna's posh accent was losing its grip on the Klosters slopes.

'How long is it since you've seen Mum? How long have you been having her racing round buying parcel stuff for you? Do you ever think about paying her for it all? Do you ever ring her when you don't want something? Have you any idea how much she's missing you—?' The line went dead.

Lou growled and stabbed in last-number redial. The dialling tone changed to a chirpy American answering machine message: *Hi, this is Edward and Torah; we're not at home right now . . .'*

'If you don't pick up this phone, you little cow,' said Lou with all the control of Ben Hur over his chariot horses, 'I will tell the good old British police and your precious Edward exactly how you financed your trip to the US of fecking A.'

When fighting Victorianna, it was best to dredge up a few Anglo-Saxon-cum-Irish roots, thought Lou. It worked, for the phone was snatched up at the other end.

'What are you talking about?' Victorianna demanded waspishly.

'I know all about it, Vic. Now, get two tickets over to the States for Mum and her friend Vera. They're spending a couple of weeks in your chuffing big house with you and your amazing hospitality.'

'I haven't a clue what you're on about,' said Victorianna through her clenched new dentalwork. The posh accent had now left Klosters and was heading on public transport for Cleethorpes.

'Oh, I think you do,' said Lou, sensing the panic behind the aggression. For the second time today she was actually enjoying the feeling of power over someone. 'Allow me to explain. I opened a letter that arrived for you after you'd flown off. First-class ticket, was it? You could have afforded it, for what you got pawning your own mother's rings.'

'What?' said Victorianna, but a tremor had appeared in her voice.

'I. Opened. The. Letter. From. The. Pawn. Shop,' said Lou slowly. 'Let me refresh your memory, shall I? After you left to go and live over there, a letter arrived from the pawn shop wanting to know if you had any intentions of buying back your goods, because otherwise they would be sent on for polishing and re-sale. I rang the shop but they wouldn't deal with anyone but the ticket-holder. Of course, I always wondered if you had anything to do with Mum's missing rings. All those manicure treatments you did for her, taking off her rings while you painted her nails for her. Weren't you the perfect daughter?'

'You're barmy, you,' spat Victorianna.

'I rang them back, you know, pretended to be you and said I'd lost my ticket and what was I to do? They told me I had to pick up a form from them, take it to a solicitors with some ID and swear an affidavit that I was who I said I was, then they would release the goods.'

Lou let this sink in. What Victorianna didn't know was that luck was on Lou's side because she'd found a passport that Victorianna had claimed she'd lost (because the photograph wasn't flattering), which had since been replaced, so she had the form of ID that the pawnbrokers and solicitors required. The problem was, Lou didn't look enough like Victorianna to pass for her. Deb did, though. It was Deb who'd stood in a solicitor's office for her and risked prosecution as she swore that she was Victorianna Casserly in order that Lou could go into the pawn shop and pay a small fortune for her mother's rings. Then Lou had to hide them at Renee's and stage a grand search through the house, for them to turn up miraculously under the dresser in the dining room.

'You pretended to be me?' Victorianna said, not quite believing that any firm of solicitors could mistake a little, plump, dark-haired blimp for tall, willowy, beach-blonde her. Who had she got as lawyers—Stevie, Wonder & Wonder?

Lou didn't see the need to put her right and drop Deb in the mess, so she simply said, 'Yep!' Thinking anyone could mix up the two of them in the looks department would probably make Victorianna spontaneously combust, she thought with an inner snigger.

'I know what all this is about,' Victorianna spat. 'You're pissed because of what happened between me and Phil, aren't you?'

Lou steeled herself. This was the part of the conversation she had been dreading. She had to stand firm. 'Nothing happened between you and Phil, Victorianna,' she said, hoping it was true.

Her sister laughed. 'No, you're right, it didn't. I'm not a total bitch.' She had flirted with Phil shamelessly, but she hadn't wanted him. She'd just enjoyed the effect her teasing had on him.

Lou breathed a sigh of relief. For so long now, she had wondered . . . Victorianna had been an extraordinarily pretty teenager when she and Phil had started courting. Putting a teenage brain in a body like hers was like putting a child in charge of a Ferrari.

'He would have been off with me at the first opportunity if I'd wanted him,' said Victorianna. 'I drove him crazy.'

Lou laughed. 'I think you'll find he was flattered, that's all,' she said, hanging on to her bravado for grim death. 'It doesn't take much to do that to a man.'

'Yeah, right. Well, you keep telling yourself that's the way it was if it makes you happy. You should be delighted I moved over here. Out of your way. Out of Phil's way.'

'On stolen money.' Lou dragged the conversation back to the point. 'Money you got from taking the rings that our father gave to Mum.'

'But hang on, *big sister*, you've just told me you're guilty of fraud! Swearing on oath that you were me in front of a solicitor? Tut tut!'

'Very true,' said Lou, glad Victorianna couldn't hear her knees knocking. 'But I'm willing to take the risk if you are, *little sister*. You do your worst, Victorianna, and I. Will. Do. Mine. Let's see who comes off better in the newspaper articles, shall we? Will you still go hobnobbing with family-value-loving vice-presidents when it comes out that you stole off your own mam?' Lou sounded chilling even to herself.

Victorianna articulated her defeat succinctly. 'Fuck off!' she said, and the phone at the Florida mansion end slammed down.

Lou didn't need to ring back this time. She breathed in a long, slow breath and put the receiver back on the cradle. Sister or no sister, she knew they would never speak again. Victorianna was as good as in one of Tom's skips, as far as Lou was concerned. She went to bed, and slept the sleep of the victorious.

Lou let in the builders as the clock in the hallway struck eight and then went to work in the small study downstairs. At nine thirty she called the bank to make an appointment to see the business manager the following week and sent Deb a text message to say she had done so.

Deb replied with: Fantastic. Are you OK?

Of course Lou was OK. Never better. She just didn't want to meet or talk to her best friend for a few days because she was scared Deb was going to tell her that she'd just had fantastic sex with Tom.

In the afternoon, Lou called in at her mother's. Renee had the grin of a Cheshire cat with a coat hanger stuck in its mouth. 'You'll never guess who I had on the phone this morning,' she said, putting the kettle on. 'Victorianna. And do you know why she rang?'

'Mum, I can't guess, just tell me,' said Lou.

'She has invited me and Vera over for the whole of September!' Her smile was fixed on with Superglue.

'Well, I'm stunned,' said Lou—and she was. Boy, Victorianna must have been really shaken up to act that fast.

'I knew she would invite me in her own time,' beamed Renee.

'I've got some good news too,' said Lou, thinking there was no more ideal moment than this to introduce her forthcoming business venture. 'I'm opening up a coffee-shop with my friend Deb.'

The glue on Renee's smile gave out. 'Deb? Not *that* Deb, surely? When did she come back on the scene?'

'A few weeks now,' said Lou with a sigh.

Renee shuddered. 'And what's Phil said about all this?'

'What do you mean?' said Lou, wishing she had never brought it up.

'Well,' said Renee, 'Deb almost wrecked your marriage.'

Lou shook her head in disbelief. 'Why on earth does everyone think Deb, "wrecked my marriage"? Didn't the fact that Phil was having an affair have anything to do with it at all?'

'You've just said yourself that everyone thought she'd wrecked your marriage. We can't all be wrong, can we?' said Renee with a sniff.

'Well, anyway, we've got premises and we're going ahead with it,' said Lou, finishing off her story, even though her enthusiasm to tell it had totally withered.

'And what about your job?' said Renee.

'I shall leave it, of course.'

'But it's a good steady job! Honestly, Elouise—have some sense.'

Lou felt like a punctured balloon, but Renee didn't notice.

'**D**on't suppose you know any good butchers, country girl?' Lou asked Karen in the office the next day.

'My dad's got a farm shop and my brother's the butcher there,' said Karen. 'Why?'

'Come for a coffee to the canteen,' said Lou. Nicola was out doing something in the Manchester office. And so, over a *delicissimo*, Lou told Karen all about the coffee shop that was presently a transport café and how they needed to find a supplier of good bacon, fresh eggs and fab sausages for some nice big breakfasts until that side of the business died out gracefully, to be replaced by coffees and puddings.

'God, Lou, I'll miss you like hell,' Karen said.

'I shall miss you too,' said Lou with genuine feeling.

'I tell you what, I'll ring Dad and get him to drop off some sausages and bacon for you to test. Then he can give me a lift home. Ha!'

That night, Lou and Phil sat down to a dinner of breakfast, which threw him slightly, although it was lovely stuff and he commented favourably on the sausages especially, before earmarking the rest of the bacon for his breakfast the next morning. Then he announced they were going to Torremolinos for a fortnight at the end of June. Lou couldn't muster up so much as a 'Wow'.

Lou had booked the next day off work because she needed to see Deb with café plans. She let the builders in and then she set off for Ma's Café.

Deb was already there, her car parked cosily next to Tom's, which seemed pretty symbolic. Lou sighed. *Best get this over with.* She just wanted to hear it from Deb's lips that she and Tom had become an item and then everything would be out in the open.

'Oh, hi,' said Deb. 'You're early.'

'Hi,' said Lou. 'Well, the house is full of builders.'

'Lou . . . I've got something to tell you,' said Deb hesitantly. 'I really hope you don't mind. Tom and I—'

Then the door behind Lou opened and Tom himself walked in. 'Hi there, Lou,' he said stiffly, 'I've just seen your car. Thought I'd come over.' But he didn't bend to kiss her hello. 'Er . . . have you told her?' he said to Deb, clearing his throat.

Deb sighed. 'Lou, come upstairs a minute will you, please?'

Lou followed them silently up the stairs. It was like being led to a place of slaughter. Still, it would all be over in five minutes.

Tom opened the door and the light hit Lou immediately. The flat was totally whitewashed.

'Lou—Tom and I . . . we painted the flat. I just went ahead and made the decision. I know you'd have said yes, but I'm sorry I didn't ask.'

'Is that it? That's what you have to tell me?' Lou felt like laughing hysterically and was really having to stop herself from doing so.

'Yes,' said Deb cautiously. 'What did you think I was going to say?' She hoped Lou hadn't found out about her knowing about Phil. But, how could she? Unless Phil had told her, and he was hardly likely to do that, was he? Or was he? This subterfuge was doing Deb's head in.

'It looks great, Deb, and course I don't mind, you daft bat.'

'Well, I have to go on official skip business,' said Tom. 'Bye. I'm so glad I'm not in your bad books, Lou, for aiding and abetting Deb.'

'Don't be silly, it looks great,' said Lou.

'Bye,' he said again, and appeared to look at Lou for far longer than the simple word demanded.

'He's looking at me funnily,' said Lou, when his heavy tread had reached the bottom of the staircase.

'You're imagining things,' said Deb, deciding to mention to Tom later to stop staring at Lou in such an over-concerned way. Did he want her to smell a rat?

'So, Tom helped you do all this then?' said Lou, determined to get to the bottom of all that cuddly stuff between them and bring it into the open. Deb still hadn't said anything and Tom hadn't given her friend more than a friendly wave on his way out. It was all very odd.

'When he had some spare time,' said Deb. 'By the way, the builder's quote came in. I'll get it out. How's Thingy doing with your bathroom?'

'Very well,' said Lou. 'Shame, really—he's a good worker, just unreliable. But I won't tell him that until he's finished. I don't want him to know he hasn't won the multi-billion-pound contract just yet.'

'Good girl,' said Deb.

Oh, sod it, thought Lou. It was time to stop pussyfooting. 'So, tell me about you and Tom,' she said. 'Are you together?'

Deb whirled round. 'Whatever gave you that idea?'

'I saw you cosying up in his ironmongery,' said Lou. 'The day Keith Featherstone came round. I'd forgotten something and came back.'

Deb hooted with laughter. 'Lou, you've got that so totally wrong. I was . . .' *crying on his shoulder over what to do about you and that cheating-louse husband of yours.* Deb had to think fast on her feet now: '. . . panicking, I suppose. It hit me that we were actually going to do this at last, and I came over a little emotional. Tom's a great bloke. But I don't fancy him a bit. He's fitted into my life very quickly as a friend. That's all.'

'There's more, isn't there? I think I know what you're scared to say.'

'What?' said Deb, her heart starting to thump faster.

'It was at this stage that I backed out last time. It's bound to be on your mind. But whatever happens, I swear to you, Deb, I won't back out. I promise. Not this time.'

Phew, thought Deb. She had only to nod an admission that Lou had hit the nail on the head and that would be the end of the matter.

'I know,' said Deb. That stupid idiot Phil—did he know what he had in Lou? She hoped he didn't and that he drove her away to find someone who deserved her. Someone, Deb thought, like Tom Broom.

Lou was in bed by the time Phil came home that night. His curry was cremated and his rice dried to desiccated coconut in the pan on the hob. Not that he was hungry. He stank of the garlic-heavy meal he'd already had and Sue's smoky perfume. It was getting harder and harder to stop at the kissing stage with her.

He was more than a bit pissed off that Lou wasn't sitting on the stairs worrying and awaiting his return. He checked his mobile. There was a missed call from her over two hours ago, but she hadn't left a message.

He didn't shower, just crawled into bed, hoping Lou would sniff out her rival bitch on his skin in the morning.

Lou woke early to an overwhelming aroma of second-hand garlic that hadn't come from the curry she had made for Phil. But questions on the subject of his mysterious movements were stemmed by the excitement of a catalogue of flavoured coffees arriving in the post.

She had just settled down to read it when the phone rang.

'Hiya, Lou,' said Michelle. She sounded cross and huffy.

'You're up early,' said Lou.

'Well, I got to bed early, didn't I?' said Michelle grumpily.

'Wasn't it your big night out with *Ali*?' Lou gave the name an amused emphasis. She had a good idea from Michelle's tone that Ali might have toppled off her pedestal already.

'Huh, don't talk to me about Ali,' said Michelle.

'OK, I won't,' said Lou.

'What a bitch,' said Michelle. 'As soon as we were out she hardly spoke to me. I tell you, I'd had enough by nine. By half past ten she was so pissed I had to half carry her to the taxi place and you know what the queues are like at that time. It was freezing and my feet were killing me. I had to go home with her and pay for the taxi. I stuck her in bed in the recovery position and then I had to wait there for another hour until I could get another taxi. I was so angry. I tell you, never again.'

Lou bit down hard on her lip. She tried to make sympathetic noises but, as usual, Michelle wasn't listening. 'I'll have to go, Lou, someone's at the door,' she said mid-sentence, and put down the phone.

Phil came downstairs rubbing his eyes. 'Thanks for leaving me out a dried curry last night,' he said.

'I can reconstitute it for breakfast, if you wish,' she said coldly.

'No, it's all right, thanks. Anyway I ate out.' He waited for her reaction. She twitched slightly, but his radar still picked it up.

'Bacon and eggs then?' said Lou.

'Yes, that would be wonderful, love,' said Phil. Switch to being nice now—keep the ground like quicksand under her feet.

As Phil chewed on the last of his toast he said, 'Isn't that your daft mate coming up my path? She's got a sore eye, by the look of it.'

'What did you say?' said Lou, coming out of the kitchen to see.

The front doorbell rang and Phil grabbed his jacket, sensing a heavy female session with tears and tissues and 'all men are bastards' philosophies. He escaped out of the back door to the car.

Lou opened the front door to see Michelle sobbing and looking as if she'd done ten rounds with Mike Tyson.

'What the heck happened to you?' said Lou.

'Craig . . .' she managed in between big snorty tears.

'Craig did this to you?' Lou was horrified.

'Nooo, Craig's . . .'—more snot, more tears—'. . . wife!'

Lou was even less surprised.

'Remember when we were talking this morning and I had to go because there was someone at the door?'

'Yes, I remember,' said Lou, guiding Michelle's hand to some tissues.

'Well, I opened it and there was this woman—really hard-faced, ugly, fat, horrible thing. She says, "I believe you're seeing my husband?" and I say, "Craig?" and she says, "Yes" and then she just punches me right in the face. "Keep away from my husband, you cow, or I'll kill you next time." Then she gets back into this old car and drives off. There were two little kids in the back, Lou. He never said he had kids!'

'It *must* have crossed your mind, surely, that something wasn't right.'

'Why should it? I trusted him!'

'Well, you didn't have any phone numbers for him and he was still living at home with his wife. Didn't you think that was a bit odd?'

Michelle dissolved into a fresh cascade of tears. She wanted more sympathy than this. 'How could he do this to me?'

'How could he do that to *her*?' said Lou fiercely.

'I don't give a shit about her!' spat Michelle. 'I'm going down to the police station in a minute to report her for assault.'

'Don't you think she's had enough crap?' snapped Lou. 'She's got two kids and a husband who is playing about, no wonder she's in a state.'

'Whose side are you on, Lou?' said Michelle.

Lou looked hard at Michelle. 'Well, if I'm honest, anybody's but Craig's,' she said. 'His wife shouldn't have hit you, no, but I can understand where she was coming from.'

Maybe one of Susan Peach's friends had told Susan the same thing after Lou had decked her in Boots. Maybe that's why she had never heard any more about it.

'How can you say that?'

'She doesn't deserve to be arrested.'

'Why not? Because your husband had an affair and you ended up hitting the other woman?' snarled Michelle, before Lou cut her off.

'This isn't about me, Michelle. I'm trying to help you here. Draw a line under Craig now and move on. Learn the lesson!'

'But I love him!' More sobs.

'How can you love someone who treats people so badly? You're well out of it, surely you can see that now?'

Michelle pulled a mobile phone out of her pocket. 'No, I can't. I'm ringing the police and I'm ringing them now.'

Lou grabbed the phone from Michelle's hand. 'Oh, no, not in my house you're not!' Her words hung in the air.

Michelle was trapped in shock for a few seconds, then she stepped forward and grabbed the phone back. 'Well, I see where your priorities are,' she said. 'Just because your man pissed about, Lou Winter, it doesn't make you patron saint of married women. And I suppose the fact he had plenty of money and a big house had nothing to do with you taking him back. Well, you can stick your friendship, if you can call it that.' And with that, Michelle flounced to the door and slammed it behind her.

Lou replayed Michelle's parting speech to herself—a strangely objective operation for someone as emotional as she. When she had fully processed it, she concluded that these weren't the words of someone upset by a few home truths, they were the tip of a surprisingly deep resentment and jealousy that had no place in friendship. Whatever she'd had with Michelle was not friendship in the Deb sense of the word, but it didn't matter now. When Michelle had slammed that door, it had locked behind her. The relief, for Lou, was almost tangible.

# CHAPTER 6

To LOU'S HORROR and delight it was Mr Clarke who received them into his inner sanctum on the following Tuesday; the same business manager who had interviewed them for their first attempt at Casa Nostra. Lou took as much care now as she did then in presenting their financial case to him. This time, they had some capital so didn't need to borrow as much as before. Deb had savings and Lou, unbeknown to Phil, had a nest egg tucked away too. She'd started squirrelling funds away for the Casa Nostra project years ago and, though it fell through, she'd never stopped adding to the account.

Mr Clarke gave a nervous laugh as he recalled Lou leaping over the desk to kiss him when he had agreed to the bank lending them the money to finance their project three years ago. 'I hope you're going to stay in control this time when I deliver the good news,' Mr Clarke said.

'*When*—not *if*?' said Lou, hardly daring to breathe.

'You're giving us the money?' asked Deb.

As he nodded, Lou reined in the desire to let history repeat itself and settled for a vigorous handshake instead. Mr Clarke had to admit to himself to being somewhat disappointed.

The next stop was the solicitors to sign the lease and then Deb ran off to work, leaving Lou to pay Tom a cheque and start the fun activity of ordering equipment. Debra Devine and Lou Winter were in business.

'Tom, I can't pay you the rent,' said Lou.

Tom came round to her side of the table, already loosening his belt. 'Then I'll have to exact what you owe in other ways. Get on the bed, Elouise, and take all your clothes off . . .'

There was a loud knock on the flat door which shook Lou out of her daydream. Tom walked in to find her quite red-faced.

'I've just seen you come up. Wow, you look hot!' he said.

Had he really said that or was she still dreaming?

'Are you all right? Shall I open a window for you?' he went on. *Oh, that sort of hot. Stupid woman.*

Lou put her hands over her cheeks. 'Oh, er, just excited,' she said. 'We got the finance!'

'Fantastic!' Tom beamed. 'We'll have to celebrate.'

'I just came back to write you a cheque for the rent.'

'Lord, there's no rush for that,' said Tom.

He seemed to have substituted his grinning thing for that intense caring look that a parent gives to a small child on his first day at school. His grey eyes were soft and trained intently on her face.

'What's the matter?' said Lou. Had she smudged her make-up?

'No, there's nothing,' said Tom, giving himself a mental kick up the backside. 'I was, er, just thinking that maybe you could both pop round to the house and we'll crack open a bottle of champagne.'

'That sounds nice,' said Lou.

'Good. Right, well, I'm a boring bloke with no social life, so you pick any evening and come round and I'll cook something. Italian?'

'Wow, super nice,' said Lou. 'We're pretty boring too, so I think any night will be good for us as well.'

'Tomorrow, then?' said Tom.

'Fine. I'm sure it's clear for Deb, too.' She knew it was because they had arranged to go to the cinema, but this seemed an unmissable event.

**P**hil was virtually beating Sue Shoesmith off with a stick. He didn't really want to have an affair again—and affairs, to him, were anything more than snogging. He hadn't been found out the first two times he'd done the dirty behind his wife's back, but the last time had been a big mistake. Susan Peach was a sleazy barmaid who had paid him some attention when Lou was neglecting him for her stupid café idea. It was just bad luck that in the place he had picked to take Susan for a meal and a grope, there was Lou's friend Deb with a group of her cronies.

He had expected Deb to call in to the office and rant and rave at him. What he hadn't expected in a million years was for her to go marching round to Lou to tell her everything. When he'd arrived home from work, Lou had looked as though she'd had all her stuffing taken out. The easiest thing had been to pack a bag and run away.

He'd gone to live at Susan's place and she'd taken all the immediate guilt away from him with some very energetic sex, but after a few weeks, her tiny, dank flat, a constant stream of Australian soaps on the TV and a diet of takeaways, were driving him stark staring mental.

In the end, Phil had gritted his teeth and turned up at the house, hoping that Lou would be so upset at the prospect of spending Christmas alone that she would let him in. And Lou had just pulled him into the house and never mentioned it. If he'd known how easy it was going to be, he'd have been back a fortnight sooner.

Now he just wanted life to return to how it was before all that stupid skip business started kicking off. No Deb on the scene, no talk about stupid cafés and businesses and less of Lou's lip—then they could get back to being happy again.

**L**ou was very much on Deb's mind too. She had never got over the feeling that she could have tackled it so differently last time. She could have confronted *him* rather than lay everything on her friend. So what about this time? Despite promising Tom that she wouldn't interfere, she waved goodbye to Lou outside the solicitor's office and set off to P. M. Autos. She took a deep breath and barged into Phil's office.

'How can I help you, Debra? Coffee?' said Phil.

'I don't want a coffee and I think you know why I'm here,' snarled Deb. 'Maltstone Arms, weekend before last, you and a bimbo—*that's* why I'm here. I know you saw me, so let's cut the crap. Didn't you learn anything from last time? How much more shit are you going to put your wife through, eh?'

'What has my life got to do with you, Debra?'

He's calm, thought Deb. Too calm. 'Finish it, Phil, or . . .'

Phil's eyes rounded. 'Or?' he urged.

He wasn't smiling, was he? Deb looked at his twinkling blue eyes. Her brain did a few quick calculations and came up with a ridiculous explanation. *It couldn't be possible. He wasn't that sick, was he?* 'My God, you *want* me to tell her you're having a fling, don't you?'

Phil affected shock. 'That's ridiculous. I think you'd better go,' he said. 'But I will tell you that I'm not finishing my "friendship" with *Sue.*'

'You evil bastard!' said Deb. 'You even picked someone with the same name. Was that stage-managed?'

She didn't resist as he ushered her out of his office.

Could that have gone any better? Phil gloated. He knew Deb wasn't physically capable of keeping this sort of information to herself.

Deb walked to her car in total astonishment. There was nothing she could do to stop Lou getting hurt—really hurt. She couldn't tell Lou—then again, she couldn't *not* tell her. She would just have to carry on as if everything was normal and hope that this time, their business venture was Lou's salvation when the big crash came.

Lou spent an exciting Wednesday ordering more equipment and distributing the fliers that she had designed to some of May's regulars. They were invitations to the grand opening in eight weeks—August 1.

May was closing at the end of that week and the builders were coming at seven on Monday morning. And at number One, The Faringdales, Keith Featherstone would have finished the bathroom by the time she got home. Lou felt slightly guilty that they still thought they were in the running for the café business, but she overcame it.

And since her dramatic exit from Lou's house, Michelle had bombarded Lou with text messages and phone calls. Lou deleted them without reading them or listening to them and Tipp-Exed her out of her diary. Michelle was out of her life.

Lou picked up Deb from the bakery to go to Tom's house. 'You look nice,' she said. Deb had on a navy-blue dress and a matching long jacket, and was wearing impossibly high stilettos.

'You don't look so bad yourself,' said Deb, giving her a longer than usual hello hug. 'And you're getting even thinner. I'm going to make you a Brando, that'll fatten you up,' she said.

'Oh, so you've created it!'

'Nearly. I think I know where I'm going with it.'

'What's it going to be made out of?' asked Lou excitedly.

'Wait and see . . .'.

**A**s they pulled into Tom's drive, Deb said, 'We should have got a taxi,' suddenly realising that Lou couldn't drink much because she'd insisted on driving.

'It's OK,' said Lou. 'Remember, I'm supposed to be at the cinema. Turning up home drunk in a taxi might blow my cover story slightly.'

Tom greeted them at the door. His hair was tousled and he looked harassed. 'I can't believe I'm doing this,' he said. 'I've invited two professional cooks for dinner and I can barely boil an egg. How stupid am I? Let me take your coats.'

Clooney was trying to get to Lou, wrestling his canine excitement at seeing the biscuit woman against his recent training that forbade him to jump up. He settled for lots of tail-wagging and happy whining instead.

Deb and Lou followed Tom into a very nice farmhouse kitchen with a big chunky wooden table in the middle. It had a recipe book open on it. 'You aren't supposed to be in here,' he said. 'I'm nervous enough as it is. Go and open some wine. The bottle and corkscrew are in there.'

Lou and Deb went into the dining room. There was a CD playing soft rock music and wall lights gave the room a gentle and friendly glow.

'OK, ladies,' Tom said, coming into the room soon after with a huge bowl of pasta and a large plate of garlic and tomato pizza bread. 'Please be seated. I never asked if you were vegetarian or liked seafood or anything, so I hope this is going to be all right.'

'I don't think there's anything I don't like,' said Deb.

'What about you, Lou?' said Tom, breaking off some bread.

'Lamb,' said Lou, not needing to even think about that. 'I hate lamb.'

'Ugh, me too,' said Tom, shaking his head. 'Never have liked it. School-dinner lamb—I could retch thinking about it . . .' He shuddered at the memory. 'Let's talk about you two making loads of money instead, although you can do that quite happily by yourself,' and he turned to Lou with his smiley grey eyes.

'What's this then?' asked Deb with sudden interest.

'Tom's got this idea that I make counterfeit money,' Lou told her.

'Well, feel free to print me a few fifties, Lou. Ooh—and talking of making money,' said Deb, reaching for her bag. 'Before I forget—here, this is for you,' and she handed Lou a telephone number on a Post-it note. 'Mrs Serafinska's number,' she explained. 'We were talking about you and your clutter-clearing. She'd like you to help her.'

'Help? In what way?'

'Clearing some clutter, perhaps?' Tom suggested with gentle sarcasm.

Deb punished him with a good-humoured glare. 'I'm being serious. Lou, she's been widowed for over three years now and never cleared out Bernie's stuff. She happened to say she wished she had professional help. *I* happened to say that I knew a professional who could help.'

Lou nearly spat out her wine. 'I'm not a professional!'

'Four days at one hundred and fifty quid a day says you are.'

Tom nearly spat out *his* wine.

'Come on, Lou,' Deb said. 'These professional clutter-clearers charge over a grand and a half just for a consultation. She's a lovely woman. She's determined to get some help and she's prepared to pay. If you don't want the job, she'll go to someone who probably hasn't got half the experience you have for twice the price. *Pleeease!*'

Lou considered it. What harm would it do? And if Mrs Serafinska wasn't happy, then Lou wouldn't charge her. 'OK, I'll give her a ring.'

'Hey, you can use my skips,' said Tom. 'But I'll take a cheque this time. That last batch of notes, the Queen had a pierced nose.'

And they laughed and ate pasta, sweetcorn and asparagus and washed it down with Chablis, and grape juice for Lou. Then Tom opened the champagne and they raised a glass to their culinary venture.

'That was lovely, Tom,' said Lou, as she helped him clear the plates. Her eyes were sparkling like the champagne in the glasses. She stared at Tom's big, wide back as he bent down at the dishwasher. No man had ever cooked her a meal before. Her head was full of ridiculous, wonderful feelings that were zapping and fizzing round inside her. She'd never had them before. Yes, she had fallen in love with Phil, in a comfortable, coupley way, but her heart had never sparked like a night full of fireworks just because she was near him.

Tom straightened up. God, he was so big. God, he was so close.

'Here, let me have those,' he said, his large square hands reaching out for the plates. She passed them over carefully, taking great care not to accidentally touch him nor daring to look up at him, because if she did, he would have seen everything in her eyes she wished she were free to say. She turned away, noticing as she did so the time on the kitchen clock. It was later than she expected. 'Oh, damn, we'd better go.'

Deb retrieved their coats. Tom helped Deb on with hers. Lou got into hers before he could offer.

'Tom, it was wonderful, thank you.' Deb threw her arms round him.

'Thanks, Tom,' said Lou quietly but with a warm smile. 'It was nice.'

He bent and kissed her cheek, but this time, as his lips left her, his arms enfolded her in an unexpected and tight squeeze. His scent filled her nostrils . . . She staggered when he let her go. Her brain was mush. God knows what state she'd be in if he ever bonked her. Not that she'd ever find out.

Deb hugged her good night as the car pulled up at her flat. 'You smell of Tom,' said Deb.

'Are you sure you two don't fancy each other?' said Lou.

'Lou, I love you to death but you can be so thick at times,' said Deb.

**P**hil was tucking into beef chow mein, fried rice and prawn won tons. 'I had to send out for this,' he said. 'I didn't expect you to be so late.'

'Phil, it's half past nine. Even Cinderella got two and a half hours more parole than this.' The magical night out was over.

**K**aren put two pre-work cappuccinos down on the canteen table and pulled an envelope out of her bag. 'Guess what this is?'

'An envelope,' said Lou after considerable scrutiny. 'I have been wrong in the past about these things, though, so please feel free to correct me. Stationery was never my strong subject at school.'

'It's my notice,' said Karen. 'I know you're going to hand in yours soon—and I can't work without you.'

'But—'

'Listen to the rest,' said Karen, holding up a shushing hand. 'I love this accounts course, so, I'm moving back in with Mum and Dad on the farm so I've got twenty-four-seven child cover, and I'm going to college full time, starting as soon as they'll let me go.'

'Crikey, you have been busy! I am absolutely thrilled you're going for this all the way.' Lou gave the tall young woman a big squashy hug.

'You look very sparkly today, by the way,' said Karen, scrutinising Lou. *Were you with your mystery man last night?*

'Do I?' said Lou. She had felt quite sparkly during the night after a very nice dream about her very nice evening.

'I'm pretty sparkly, too,' said Karen. 'Charlie and I aren't "just friends" any more. He's taking me to Paris when I finish here. I wish you could find someone nice, Lou. Someone who made you feel like I do at this moment in time.' She looked at Lou with real tenderness.

'What on earth makes you think I'm not happy?' Lou asked.

'Oh, Lou,' was all Karen said by way of a reply.

**Z**oe was waiting for them just outside the office door. She was all dressed up in a trendy blue top and a black skirt. 'I've got an interview at lunchtime,' she whispered. 'It's with a firm of solicitors.'

'Good for you, darling,' said Lou. 'You look lovely.'

'Hope so. This outfit cost loads. I just hope I can keep it clean.'

The clock said that it was one minute to nine. Nicola gave them all a satanic glare for cutting it so fine. She stamped on Zoe's buoyant mood by telling her to add some toner to all the machines on the floor. Just about the messiest job she could saddle her with.

'But that's not my job!' cried Zoe. 'And I've got my new top on.'

'Isn't your appraisal happening soon?' said Nicola.

Zoe slumped off to the stationery cupboard just as Stan bounded in at nine minutes past nine. Nicola stalked towards him.

'Can I have a word, Stanley, please? In the bubble.'

Stan followed her to the said meeting room where the walls were Perspex. Lou noticed how stooped his shoulders were. He had always been so smart and straight-backed until Nicola's regime began. It wasn't right that she could strip away a man's dignity like that.

'I've got toner on my jumper,' said a quietly horrified Zoe, with tears flooding down her face—and, at that moment, something within Lou boiled up and over like milk in a pan.

*When did I become the sort of person who doesn't make a stand?* said Lou suddenly to herself. *When did I start watching the little guys get hurt and turn the other way? And when did I stop protecting myself?* Shirley Hamster would have wiped the floor with Lou Winter. She wasn't her father's daughter any more. Maybe it was time to be Shaun Casserly's girl again.

'I've had enough of this,' Lou said, striding out with purpose.

'Lou, where are you going?' called Karen.

'Somewhere I should have gone ages ago,' she said over her shoulder.

**A**s luck would have it, the head of human resources, Bob Bowman, was by the executive floor's coffee-machine.

'Mr Bowman, can I have a word,' said Lou confidently.

'Official or unofficial?' he said, recognising her immediately as 'Little' from Accounts.

'Both,' she returned.

He checked his watch. 'I've got ten minutes now if you have.'

Lou followed him into his office.

'So what can I do for you . . . Lou, isn't it?'

'Lou Winter, yes,' she said. 'Well . . .' She took a big breath and blurted out: 'It's about the accounts department. Something needs to be done about the management there. I'm a bit too old to stand by and watch people I like and admire being bullied on a daily basis without taking some sort of stand.'

Bob Bowman pricked up his ears at the use of the word 'bully'. 'Go on,' he said. 'Start from the beginning. What's the problem?'

'It's Jaws—er—Nicola Pawson—*that's* the problem. Our office junior is half-terrified to come into work. She's presently filling machines with toner and has just ruined her clothes.'

'That's the technician's job, not hers, surely?' said Bob Bowman.

'Yes, you're right, but when you're threatened with a bad appraisal for not doing it, you do it. Or that's how it works in our department. Did you know that my fellow accounts clerk, Karen Harwood-Court, will today be handing in her notice because no one here's done anything to advance her career? Roger Knutsford sends work down to her because she's far more competent than members of his own team who are on twice the salary, so she is going somewhere that *has* recognised her abilities and *will* capitalise on them.'

Bob Bowman stiffened at the name Roger Knutsford. It wouldn't be the first time he had had to sort out one of Knutsford's messes.

'Then I come to Stan Mirfield. You know what a good worker he is, Mr Bowman.' Lou took a deep breath. She had to get this part right for Stan.

'He'll be retiring soon, won't he?'

'Less than a year,' said Lou. 'If he makes it.'

'Why on earth shouldn't he? He's not unwell, is he?'

'He lives in the country, he doesn't drive and his bus timetable was changed—so to get in at nine o'clock on the dot he has to run like a maniac. If he doesn't die of a heart attack then Nicola will kill him with stress. It's bordering on sadistic, the way she treats him.'

'What time does he get in?' said Bob Bowman.

'I don't think he's ever been later than quarter past.'

'But every department has a flexi-time option. He could come in any time from eight until ten. Why isn't it exercised?'

'Nicola said she had a word with you and you denied him the right to flexi-time.'

'I certainly did not!' Bob Bowman was outraged.

'Stan puts more time in than any of us. He works through his lunch-hour, he stays late and yet that doesn't count, apparently.' Lou could feel her temper rising inside her. 'These are good people being tyrannised by a woman who has created a climate of misery and fear.'

Bob Bowman flicked on his intercom and spoke to his PA. 'Fiona, ask Stan Mirfield to come to my office at ten thirty, please. Then get Nicola Pawson here at eleven.'

Lou had a momentary panic. 'Please, Mr Bowman, Stan won't want to stir up any trouble. Jaws will make life hell for him.'

'No, she won't,' said Bob Bowman firmly. Stan Mirfield had slipped under his radar for some early-retirement packages he had created recently. He was going to make that up to him and more in the next hour.

'I know I risk being labelled an insurgent,' Lou said. 'I also know there isn't such a thing as an "off-the-record" chat with HR, so I'm putting all my cards on the table to you, and then I'm leaving too. Now. Today. I've had enough.' It was an impulsive decision but it felt right.

'There won't be any need for that,' said Bob Bowman softly.

'I don't want to work here any more, Mr Bowman,' Lou said. 'Thank you for the wages you've paid me over the years but I don't want to be in a company that promotes bullies and tyrants.'

Bob Bowman nodded. 'I'll make sure there are changes. But I won't accept this as your notice. Please take some time to think . . .'

'No, I've made up my mind,' said Lou adamantly.

Bob Bowman considered her determined face. Blasted Roger Knutsford again! He'd be the first to dance on that man's professional grave when his reign ended. And he'd do his own investigations on this Jaws . . . er, Nicola Pawson . . . woman—discreetly, of course.

'I'll make sure you aren't penalised for leaving without notice,' Bob Bowman said. He held out his hand to her and she shook it.

**A**ll eyes were on her as she strode into the office. Nicola slid straight over, smiling like a crocodile with a mantrap hidden in its mouth. 'A word in the bubble with you now, please, if you don't mind.'

'No,' said Lou, and walked past her to Zoe. She gave her a tight hug and said quietly in her ear, 'Make a joke about the jumper in your interview and they will love you. Good luck, love.' Then Lou gave Stan a big hug and said, 'Have a wonderful holiday and a wonderful retirement.' She gave an astounded Karen the biggest cuddle of all and said, 'It's been totally rubbish working with you. Go knock 'em dead, kid.'

Then Lou Winter grabbed her coat and her bag and faced Nicola with eyes that glittered like chips of green ice. Nicola squared up to parry verbally whatever Lou might say on her exit. Something beautifully bitchy, no doubt. Something that would bring them to confrontation point at long last. But Lou Winter said nothing. She merely walked out of the office with her head held at a dignified angle, uncrushed, un-defeated—mistress of the unspoken word.

People in the building talked about it for months, long after Stan Mirfield left with a fantastically generous retirement package. What could 'Little' in Accounts have done to have such a weird effect on Rogering Roger's bit on the side? Office legend had it that Nicola turned into a sort of rabid combine-harvester and had to be tranquillised with WD40. And why was she moved so quickly over to Manchester?

**F**illet steak with all the trimmings, thought Phil with suspicion as Lou delivered his tea to the table. He didn't have to wait long to learn why a king's supper had been served up to him.

'I packed in my job today,' Lou said. 'With immediate effect.'

'Now why would you do that?' asked Phil with calm annoyance.

'Because I hated working there, that's why,' she said.

Phil needed this like a hole in the head, especially today. There had been a letter delivered in that morning's post from Sharon. The twins were going to be thirteen in a couple of weeks. They were getting expensive, she said, so she thought an extra payment of £500 on their birthdays and at Christmas wouldn't be unreasonable. Phil spent ten minutes on the calculator working out how much extra that added to the overall bill. Then he came home to find that Lou wanted to parasite off him as well.

'The café will be up and running in eight weeks anyway, so I'm sure I'll have lots to do.'

Phil stopped chewing his meat, dropped his cutlery and rotated his finger in the air. 'Whoa, rewind—*café*? What do you mean, *café*?'

'What do you mean, "what do you mean, *café*?" *My* café!' said Lou, totally bemused. 'I told you I was going into business with Deb.'

'Talk sense, Lou,' said Phil, laughing mirthlessly. 'You haven't got any money, you haven't got anywhere to put it—'

'We've got finance and property and we open in August.'

Phil couldn't believe his ears. 'You've done it all behind my back?'

'I have not!' said Lou indignantly. 'I did tell you.'

'I don't believe I'm hearing this.' Phil got up slowly. 'You're nuts, you are, Lou. You need to see a doctor.' He tapped his temple with his finger. 'Loop the fucking loop.' He pushed away his plate and stood up.

'Where are you going?' said Lou. If Phil had left a steak, he was seriously annoyed.

He didn't answer her. Just grabbed his car keys and his jacket and slammed the door behind him on the way out.

**A**fter she had tidied up the table, Lou took herself off to her new bath to try and relax her nerves. She took a glass of wine with her and the cordless phone and checked the messages that were flashing up on the handset. Firstly she heard Keith Featherstone's humble-pie voice asking her if she was happy with the work, and if she had made up her mind about the Casa Nostra quotation.

The second message was from Michelle. She told Lou that she was a heartless bitch and this was the last message she would ever leave. The third message was Michelle who said that Lou was never to call her again and this was the last message she would ever leave. Lou deleted all three messages without a second thought, and then she called Deb.

'Hi,' said Deb. 'What sort of a day have you had then?'

'Ooh, you know, ordinary. Packed in my job, stalked by crazed ex-friend, Phil's stormed out somewhere, Keith Featherstone's hounding me about the first phase of Casa Nostra Europe Inc . . .'

'Ho, so nothing to chat about then,' laughed Deb. 'Tell me about the job. How come you're not working your notice?'

Lou told her.

'Well, you know what you need to do now,' said Deb. 'Ring Mrs Serafinska. Get on to it straight away.'

'OK, I will,' said Lou. 'I promise,' and as soon as she put down the phone to Deb, she did indeed call Gladys Serafinska and made arrangements to see her the very next day.

Phil wasn't speaking to her next morning. Lou wasn't surprised by that, but what did shock the living daylights out of her was that he had slept in the spare bedroom. He had never slept in there before.

Lou arrived at the bakery, gurned at Deb through the window and knocked on the adjacent cottage door. She had always imagined Mrs Serafinska would be a tiny little wisp with a foreign accent, not the great battleship that came to the door and said in a gravelly South Yorkshire accent, 'Come in, lass.'

It was a typical cottage: low ceilings, beams, shiny brasses and wall-to-wall chintz and ornaments. Lou sat on a big plump sofa while Mrs Serafinska wheeled in a little trolley set with china cups, a teapot and biscuits made in the bakery.

'Debra said you'd help me,' said Mrs Serafinska.

'Mrs Serafinska—'

'Call me Gladys, please. For years I've told Debra to call me that, but she never does.'

She seems nervous, thought Lou, watching her hand pour out the tea none too steadily.

'Gladys,' Lou smiled. 'I'll help you all I can but I do warn you, it might be harder than you think to let stuff go, so rather than me tell you what to do, how about we do it together?'

'Oh, could we?' said Gladys with a gasp. 'You know, it's the silliest thing, but I think I'm scared.'

'You'll be fine,' said Lou, who knew exactly what she meant.

After their tea, Lou followed Gladys to a big room upstairs, off the main bedroom, decorated in darker, gentleman's colours. The wardrobes were walnut and the furniture masculine.

'This is Bernie's dressing room. I made a start . . .' Gladys pointed to some suits laid out on the floor. 'Sorry,' and her eyes started to gush.

'Come on,' said Lou, leading her out of the room. 'Let's start with a drawer in the kitchen.'

Two drawers and an under-stairs cupboard later, it was clear that they would need to order a skip. Gladys Serafinska was thoroughly enjoying herself, warming up to the project by clearing out the kitchen detritus. Lou rang Tom's mobile.

'Hello there, Trouble,' said Tom merrily.

If he'd called her 'Cowface' she thought his voice would have had the same effect on her knees. 'I need a skip at the back of Serafinska's Bakery in Maltstone,' said Lou. 'I think a mini will do, please.'

'I haven't got anything until tomorrow morning. Is that OK?'

'Harrison's have got them,' said Lou naughtily.

'I shall come round there and spank you in a minute, young lady.'

Lou gasped, not sure if she was horrified or thrilled and then deciding she was both—in a highwayman/bodice-ripping way.

'That's OK then, bye,' she said quickly. Her head was sparking with pictures that wouldn't have been out of place in a porn film.

The next morning Lou got stuck in traffic and missed the skip arriving.

'What a beautiful dog that man had,' said Gladys Serafinska. Damn, thought Lou. Tom had delivered it himself. Although maybe it was better that she didn't see him for a couple of days. Her imagination had nearly blown the top of her head clean off last night. Then again, she had plenty of time to think, what with Phil not coming home from work until ten. He'd slept in the spare room again, which unsettled her.

'What are these?' Lou asked, pulling a bag out of a cupboard.

'Oh, er, just things I keep,' said Gladys quietly.

Lou spilled them out onto the floor to find children's books, pencils and crayons—all unused. 'Grandchildren?'

'Not yet,' said Gladys sadly. 'I bought them just in case, you know.'

Lou gave her hand a squeeze. 'You do realise that every time you open this cupboard and see these, it reminds you of what you don't have?' she said, then: 'Let's put them in the charity pile. Then when you do get grandchildren, you can enjoy going out and buying some more.'

Gladys was about to protest, but she pulled it back. Lou was right, of course. Why hadn't she given them away before?

Gladys disliked ornaments, but she had an excuse why each one couldn't be given away. This one was a present from a friend, this one cost a lot of money . . . Lou cut her off, holding up a particularly revolting porcelain hound. 'Gladys, do you like this dog?'

'Not really.'

'Then which pile do we put it on, because we are not putting it back on that shelf.'

'OK, the car-boot one.'

The room looked so much lighter by the end of the third day and Gladys felt the same way. Lou was the best tonic she'd had in years. She'd told everyone she knew about her and hoped the young woman wouldn't mind that she'd passed her telephone number round.

**P**hil did something he rarely did that Sunday morning, namely check the messages on the home answering machine. It seemed it was the only way to find out what his so-called wife was up to these days. *'Hello, this is Mrs Alice Wilkinson. Would you please give me a ring back on this number as I am interested in a consultation?'*

What the hell else was Lou doing now? Not only had he to make his own Sunday breakfast but there wasn't anything resembling a joint or a fowl in the fridge. Where had Lou said she was going? 'Out' was all she said on her way—*out!* Then again, she was probably annoyed that he was sleeping in the spare bedroom, but it hadn't had the effect on her that he had hoped for. She should have been falling over herself to seduce his attentions back to her, but—bold as brass—she appeared to be playing him at his own game. There wasn't even any evidence that she'd made him a meal last night to come in to.

He didn't want to sleep with Sue Shoesmith, but it was looking like he might have to go that far to prove his point. And Lou would have only herself to blame if he did.

**'S**o, Gladys, are you ready for the next round of clutter-clearing?' Lou smiled at the old lady.

'As I'll ever be.'

They went upstairs into Gladys's dressing room—the penultimate step before the big one. The gown she wore as a bridesmaid for her best friend's wedding over fifty years ago was the first to go on the charity-shop pile and was quickly joined by more outdated separates and a Norma Desmond turban. Gladys started to panic.

'But look how much more room there is in your wardrobe now,' said Lou. 'Every single item in here now is something you use.'

Gladys had two drawers full of loose photographs that she had been meaning to put in an album for years, but never had. 'I think I can get rid of a lot of these,' she said. She lifted one up and beamed at it. 'Not this one though. This is my Bernie. Wasn't he lovely?'

Bernie was tall and straight with a big nose and a big smile. He wasn't classically handsome but the appeal was obvious in his cheery face.

'This is him and me at Blackpool, on our honeymoon.'

Bernie had his arm circled round a young, rounded, big-busted Gladys and they were both grinning at the camera. Gladys lifted another.

'And this is him and me just before our Golden Wedding on a cruise.'

The couple in the photo were standing just as closely together as on the previous picture and they were wearing those same smiles.

'You look happy,' said Lou quietly.

'Happy doesn't even touch it,' said Gladys. 'I loved him from the first moment I saw him. We had such fun. Of course, like any married couple, we had our moments. But the making up was always very nice. Look at him there,' said Gladys, handing Lou a picture of a much older man, drawn and pale in a dark suit. 'That was at our son's wedding—the last do he went to. Do you know, he made my heart beat just as fast on that day as it did when we were first courting. As we were posing for that picture he said to me, "Gladys, my love, I've never met a woman that was as bonny as you in my whole life." He was such a gentleman; never treated me like anything less than a queen.' She laughed. A big tear landed on the photo, but it didn't come from Gladys's eye.

'Sorry,' mumbled Lou. Sometimes other people's possessions held more answers for you than your own, she thought.

**P**hil had made himself a cheese sandwich and was eating it in the lounge. He was pleased to see that Lou was very quiet when she came in. Good—his cold-shoulder treatment was working. He might not have to sleep with Sue Shoesmith, after all.

'I'll make some pasta,' said Lou, going into the kitchen.

He had placed his phone quite specifically on the worktop after erasing all Sue's saucy messages, but had left a couple of tame ones there to set Lou thinking—if, as he imagined, he had driven her to take a sneaky peek at his Inbox.

Just as she was supposed to, Lou spotted the phone immediately. She knew he had left it there deliberately, just to make her believe there was another woman sniffing around him. So she left it. She poured some pasta in a pan and chopped vegetables for the sauce, her eyes drawn to that phone, however much she tried to resist its lure. *What if he hadn't left it there deliberately?* she started to think. *What if it was just a happy accident? Maybe this was a golden opportunity to stop the annoying questions in her head. Just one quick peep . . . go on!*

With a pounding heart, she picked up his phone and pressed the message Inbox button. There were four messages from Sue BRGE. *A pet name. Another Sue.* She knew instinctively it must be the woman who came into the showroom looking like a younger Lou with her green eyes. Is that what the last two letters stood for—*Green Eyes?* Lou felt her stomach muscles clench. She checked behind her again; Phil was still reading the paper. Actually he wasn't, he was just holding it up in front of his face, his ear picking out the pronounced silence in the kitchen as a clear indication that Lou was looking at his messages.

Hello there, you said the first message.

Thx 4 everything said the second.

Have a gr8 day said the third.

But Phil had not considered that Sue might send him a new message. The phone rumbled in Lou's hand, causing her almost to drop it in shock. She opened the new mail quickly before the tinkly alert went off and, when she read it, it told her everything she needed to know.

Lou waited for the anaesthetic of shock to clear and then for her to be plunged back into that dark hellish place. She waited for her eyes to be flooded with a damburst of tears; she waited for her legs to carry her at a pace into the lounge; she waited for her voice to demand answers as to why some woman was writing porn to her husband . . . But none of those things happened.

As she read the text, she realised her head had just caught up with a fact that her heart had apparently known for some time now: her marriage was dead. Yes, it had survived the affair with Susan Peach, but it had been mortally wounded and somewhere along the line, though she couldn't quite pinpoint the moment, it had taken its last breath. And still she had clung faithfully, devotedly, hopefully, on to it.

Lou deleted the message and put the phone down in the place she had found it. She was at the sink when Phil came in. She saw him in the reflection of the window. He was looking out into the garden.

'I think I might get some koi carp for the pond,' he said, and Lou knew when the crippled heart of her marriage had stopped beating: the night of her birthday. She had seen it then, but not recognised it. She and Phil were Fat Jack and Maureen waiting to happen. Two strangers.

There were no tears as Lou lay alone in bed that night. Maybe she had cried so much in advance of this moment that she did not need the comfort of fresh tears now. She slept soundlessly and dreamlessly.

The next morning, she answered Phil's cheery, 'Bye!' with an equally cheery one of her own. She set off for Gladys Serafinska's quite calmly and was totally in control as they shared tea and thickly buttered toast. Then they finally went up to Bernie's dressing room.

There were quite a few tears in store that day for Gladys, but none for Lou, who felt as if her emotions had gone into hibernation. The two women bagged up Bernie's suits ready to be taken to the charity shop. When it was all done and the empty space had been washed down and Gladys Serafinska had cried her last, she hugged Lou and pressed a thick wad of bank notes into her hand. 'You've earned every penny of this, Lou,' said Gladys. 'It's been a fantastic cleansing experience. I feel stronger than I have done for a long time, and so *light*. Me, light— imagine!' Her chins wobbled as she laughed. 'Thank you, lass.'

Lou knocked on the bakery door and Deb waved her over. 'Hiya,' she said. 'Have you finished sorting out our Gladys then?'

'I have,' said Lou. 'Got time for a quick drink?'

'Thought you'd never ask. Come on.'

They went across the road to the Bonny Bunch of Bluebells.

'I'll get these,' said Lou, turning to the barman. 'A brandy, no ice thanks, and a—'

'Diet Coke,' said Deb, looking wide-eyed at Lou. 'I didn't know you drank brandy.'

'I don't.'

Deb noticed Lou's hand was shaking as she carried the brandy balloon to a darkened booth in the corner.

'Lou, what's up?'

'Phil's having an affair,' Lou said without emotion.

Deb sucked in her breath. In part she felt relief that the grubby little secret was out before she could be linked to it in any way this time. 'How do you know?' she asked softly.

'I've had my suspicions for a while, but yesterday Phil left his mobile out—deliberately, of course. There was nothing on it, just a few tame messages from some woman called Sue. But another message came up while I was holding it. I don't think he'd allowed for that to happen.'

'What did it say?' asked Deb tentatively.

Lou told her.

'The bastard!' was Deb's only comment. The message had left no room for misinterpretation. 'Come and stay with me for a bit,' she said.

'You've got one bedroom, Deb.' Lou looked at her friend's kind, worried face and knew what she was thinking. 'Don't worry, Deb, this time it's different. I know our marriage is over. There are things I need to do and I need to do them alone. It's the only way I'll get through this. And I have our lovely café to look forward to. Last time I ran away from it instead of running towards it. I won't make that mistake again.'

'OK,' said Deb. 'I'm here if you want me.'

Sue Shoesmith was crying. 'Phil, don't finish this. I love you.'

Oh, that's all I need, thought Phil. 'Sue,' he said tenderly. 'I can't do this any more. I am a married man and it just doesn't feel right.'

'But you don't love her and you're going to get a divorce.'

*In your dreams, sister. This time next week I'll be stuffed full of lamb and loving.* 'I'm not sure I can give you my best, and you deserve the best.'

'I don't care.'

For fuck's sake! Her nails were digging into his skin. She'd draw blood in a minute. 'I'm sorry, Sue. You will thank me for this one day. I'm doing this for you more than me.' He stood to go but she held firm. He kissed the top of her head. 'Please don't cry, love. Goodbye, and thank you for bringing some sweetness and light into my life.'

He extricated himself with a sharp tug and she collapsed onto the pub table like a puppet with its strings severed. Phil made a hasty exit while her head was in her hands. The blast of cold Monday-night air as he opened the door hit him like a fresh morning shower. He was free.

Lou looked round her house and made a mental list. Clothes, make-up, treasure box, shoes, handbags, laptop, the recipe books, umbrella, radio alarm, couple of toilet rolls, some blankets. She streamlined it to basic essentials and the barest of emotional possessions.

She made Phil venison for dinner. Beautiful dark red slices with herby shallots and sweet potatoes and green beans sautéed with walnuts. It was even better than her lamb. She made chocolate and hazelnut sponge pudding with Chantilly cream that dribbled down Phil's chin as he devoured it with the greed of an all-conquering hero. She served him brandy and coffee and then, while she was clearing up, he went to sleep in the spare room for the very last time. Tomorrow, Phil thought happily, he would smile at her and open his arms and she would run into them and everything would be back to wonderful normality. The war was over—and he had won.

Lou clicked the dial on the dishwasher for the last time. Then, taking a coffee into the study, she logged on to the computer. Lou did what she had to do. It was two o'clock in the morning when she logged off and went up to bed.

# CHAPTER 7

THIS WAS SURELY PHIL'S lucky day. Titanic Tuesday. Four brand-new cars all on finance, a text message from Sue to say she wouldn't be bothering him again, and Des was asking pertinent questions about the Classic Car business and would call round to the house later for five minutes. Yeah, well, Phil would only give him five minutes before chucking him out. He wasn't going to have his plans for him and Lou that night upset for anything.

He had some P. M. Autos champers already on chill to take home with him, and rang up to order a huge bouquet from Donny Badger's Floristry, which he sent Bradley out to collect.

'Honey, I'm home!' he boomed comically that evening, as he came through the door brandishing the bottle and assorted blooms, but there was no answer. The lights were on but no one appeared to be in. He went into the kitchen to plug in his mobile phone, and there he found the letter propped up against the charger. He opened it and read the words on the lined paper. *Phil, I've left you. I think you know why. Lou.*

It didn't cross his mind that it could be true. Full of disbelief, he went into their bedroom and paused for a moment before he opened their wardrobe doors. There followed a slight shift in his thinking when he discovered that her clothes were gone, and that her jewellery box and her make-up bag were no longer on the dressing table, but that appeared to be all that was missing. He nodded and smiled. When wives left, they took half the house and the roof with them. *Touché.*

Lou wouldn't—*couldn't* leave this house and all these things she'd so carefully chosen over the years—and there was no way she would leave her new bathroom. Not after the battle she'd had to get it done. She was playing her own little game, showing him she wasn't going to lie down without putting up a fight.

Phil defrosted one of Lou's superb chillis in the microwave and read the letter again. He'd had far too good a day for any silliness to spoil it, he thought, rubbing his hands together. My, there was going to be some red-hot loving tonight when she turned up!

Lou carried the last of the boxes up into May's old flat. She clicked on the electric fire, hoping the small room would heat up quickly as she felt chilled, both inside and out. She set down the old cracket she had retrieved from the skip and rested her radio alarm clock on it. Switching on the radio for the comfort of some background noise, she unpacked some sheets and made up the bed.

She was just about to put the kettle on when someone pounded on the flat door. 'Who is it?' she asked, grabbing the bread knife.

'Lou, is that you?' said Tom's voice.

She unlocked the door and he came in, followed by his faithful hound. 'I saw the light on and thought someone had broken in,' he said, looking round. 'What are you doing?'

'I'm, er, moving in. I've left my husband,' Lou explained. Said out loud, the words made everything seem suddenly very real, very scary. She felt a bit wobbly and reached for the diversion of the kettle. 'Tea?'

'Yes, I will, please,' said Tom slowly. 'So, hang on, you've left home and you're moving in here? Why here?'

'I've nowhere else to go,' said Lou with a shrug.

'Deb's, surely?'

'Deb's only got a tiny place and I need to think.'

'But, Lou, it's cold and grotty. It's a storeroom, for Christ's sake.'

'Honestly, I'll be fine.'

'There isn't even a wardrobe or a sofa.'

'There are a couple of chairs, a table and a bed. It'll do until I get myself sorted out.'

Tom scratched his head in thought and then he grabbed one of her suitcases. 'Right, you're coming home with me.'

'No, Tom,' said Lou decisively. 'It's really sweet of you, but no, I'm staying here. I want to be on my own.'

He put down the case and dropped heavily onto a chair, which creaked in shock. Lou passed a cup of tea to him. He was all work-dirty, he needed a shave, his hair was full of dust, he was gorgeous. Then her head went into reverse thrust and suddenly she wanted to go home to the familiarity of Phil and all her nice things and her big warm house. She felt as if she had jumped off the edge of the world.

'The workmen have started, you know. They'll be here at seven. They're ripping out stuff, you won't sleep past then.'

'I'll be OK. My eyes usually snap open at half past six anyway.'

'Lou, please, let me help you.'

'I'm all right, Tom, really. I just need to be alone.'

He took the hint, drained his cup and reluctantly stood. 'OK, but I'm leaving Clooney. He knows where to do what in the morning, when you let him out. I'll just whip him out now for you.'

'Very well.' She allowed herself to be defeated on that point.

Tom returned ten minutes later with Clooney, a box of dog biscuits, a water bowl and the bean-bag bed that Tom kept for him in the iron-mongery. 'Can't I change your mind?'

'No, you can't, Tom,' said Lou. 'And don't tell Deb, not tonight. Please, promise me. I need space and she'd be round here like a flash.'

'You shouldn't be alone,' he said.

'I'm not alone.' She stroked Clooney's head fondly. 'You're leaving me this big bad burglar detergent.'

*Detergent?* He felt himself smiling inside at her Lou-ism, despite his concern. He wanted to pick her up and put her in his pocket. She looked so little, so cold, so vulnerable, but he didn't try to touch her in any way. Her body was missiling out vibes that he was not to do so.

Clooney and Lou slept soundly, and, yes, she had to admit, having him there was a big comfort. It helped to have a living presence in the room, especially one that she didn't have to put on a brave face for.

She couldn't sleep past six o'clock so she got up, had a coffee and dressed. The builders were there at seven, singing loudly to their radio.

Half an hour later, just as Lou had delivered four cups of tea to the builders, female shoes clattered up the stairs.

'How crap a friend do you think it makes me feel, that you can't ask me for a bed for the night?' said Deb crossly.

Oh, that old chestnut, the guilt tactic, thought Lou wryly. 'Coffee?'

'Damn right I want a coffee,' said Deb.

'When did Tom phone you?' said Lou.

'Seven this morning. He's worried about you,' said Deb.

'Well, he shouldn't be. What did he say?'

'He said, "I'm worried about Lou." The bloke's in love with you—of course he's worried about you, you daft cow.'

Lou spilled her coffee all over herself and yelped.

'God, are you OK?' said Deb.

'No, I'm not!' said Lou, hopping about in pain. 'What did you say that for?'

Deb threw a tea towel at Lou and went to make her another coffee. 'I'm not blind or thick. You two might be, but I'm not. Lou, the guy's eyes light up like a kid that's been told he's going to be locked in a Toys "R" Us overnight whenever he sees you.'

'No, that's rubbish,' said Lou. 'He wouldn't anyway . . .'

'He wouldn't what? Fancy someone like you?' said Deb with a laugh. 'Well, here's news for you, Lou Winter: he does, and that is because you are gorgeous and you're sweet and you're funny and you've got great knockers and beautiful eyes, and any bloke who got you should get on his knees and worship you like the goddess you are.'

Lou stared at her open-mouthed.

'Don't you dare cry, Lou Winter!' cried Deb fiercely.

'Then stop saying nice things,' said Lou, as her eyes started to fill up.

'I can't tell you that I'm not over the moon about seeing you and that baldy knobhead split up, Lou, but I don't want you to go through any of this on your own. Come and stay with me,' Deb pleaded.

Lou said, quietly but firmly, 'Please, Deb, I need to be on my own. I know what I'm doing. Go on, go to work.'

**B**y nine o'clock, Lou was on the telephone working her way through the listings for solicitors. She wanted an appointment that day. Number five on the list said that if she could get there for ten, there was a window with Beverley Brookes. Lou said she could and she did. First, she dropped Clooney off at the ironmonger's with Eddie. Tom, apparently, was on his way in.

At the solicitors, she cited 'unreasonable behaviour' as just cause. It seemed easier to prove than adultery. As she gave Beverley Brookes some cold examples of Phil's treatment of her over the past few years, she wondered how she had put up with so much for so long.

Phil would get the divorce papers within twenty-one days, Beverley Brookes said as she shook Lou's hand on the way out.

The realisation that she had started divorce proceedings chilled Lou more than the drizzly weather did. And talking of chill, it was now time to tell her mother.

**P**hil had slept soundly. He knew Lou hadn't left permanently. Late last night, just in case, he had gone online and checked their joint bank account: it hadn't been touched. But, just in case, he had transferred the funds over to his personal account. He wondered what she would have on the table for his tea tonight when she came out of her woman-sulk.

**I**t was early afternoon when Lou got to her mother's house.

'Mum,' said Lou, standing on her mother's sheepskin rug. She had decided on the way there to lead into it gently. 'I've left my job and I've left Phil as well.' Then again, the best-made plans . . .

'Left your job? What on earth have you done that for? Have you taken leave of your senses? And what do you mean, you've left Phil?'

'I left him yesterday afternoon.'

'But what for?'

'Because I don't love him any more. And he's having an affair.'

'Elouise, what are you playing at? Do you need a doctor?'

Even Lou was astounded by her mother's lack of sympathy. 'Mum, I'm not looking for your approval. I'm only telling you because you need to know I'm not at the old address any more and I figured you would want to know why. I've instigated divorce proceedings.'

'But you were happy!'

'No, *he* was happy, *I* was miserable!' Lou's voice crescendoed.

'I can't believe it,' said Renee, dropping onto the sofa.

'Which bit? That Phil's having another affair?'

'No, that you're not thinking straight!' cried Renee. 'Was it that Deb again, stirring things up? Has it crossed your mind that she's jealous of what you've got?'

'What have I got, Mum?' demanded Lou. 'I've got a pig of a man who can't keep it in his trousers, that's the sum of it.'

'You've got security, a lovely home, money in the bank, a husband with a growing business. Aren't you going on holiday soon as well?'

Lou laughed bitterly. 'I thought for once you'd be on my side.'

'I *am* on your side, Lou. That's why I don't want you to throw your life away,' said Renee, with something akin to panic.

'What am I throwing away that's so great, Mum?'

'Elouise,' said Renee, almost distraught, 'marriage is about riding the bad times. Have you looked at yourself to find out why he did it?'

'Why on earth would I do that?' asked Lou.

'Because . . .'

'Because what?'

'No, forget it,' said Renee.

'No, I won't forget it,' said Lou angrily. Let her have her say and get it over with. 'Because what, Mum, because WHAT?'

'Because that's what I had to do when your father did it to me!'

Lou didn't move. A pin-drop silence fell on the room.

Renee took a linen handkerchief from her sleeve and blew her nose with it.

'What do you mean?' said Lou eventually, in the faintest of breaths.

'I shouldn't have said anything. Forget it.'

'No, no, you have to tell me now.' *Please don't tell me.*

Renee licked her dry lips. 'Your father had . . . an . . . We picked up the pieces. It was hard but we did it. We didn't throw it all away for a couple of rough years. It took time but it was worth it. That's why I know your troubles will pass.'

'Dad did this to you?' Lou couldn't take it in. Her beautiful, wonderful, kind, smiling father put her mum through this pain?

Renee didn't move, didn't look up, didn't make eye contact.

Lou's stomach spasmed, not that there was anything in there to throw up. Her head went swimmy. *Her dad and another woman?*

Lou had to get out. The air in that room was thick and sucked dry of oxygen. 'I have to go,' she said.

She drove blindly to the town park, got out of the car and followed the path up the hill. Lou and her father and Murphy walked here a lot. She felt close to her dad here. She could see him: big-shouldered with large hands that were so gentle with plants and kind to animals. That was the dad she wanted to remember—not a dad who hurt hearts that loved him. She felt as if someone had scooped out all her innards. Futures were taken away from people all the time, but Renee's disclosure had taken away her past—a past that should have been set in stone, unchangeable, a solid foundation. And now it was gone, crushed, and the rubble blown away.

It was quite dark when she realised she should go home, wherever that was. Her big comfortable house called. She could have a nice, warm Keith Featherstone bath and crawl into bed beside Phil. Maybe it *would* be all right in time, as her mother said. They *had* been happy once, her mum was right. Well, content—was it the same thing?

She called in at the White Rose corner shop on the way back to the flat and bought a box of After Eights and a bottle of brandy. The silence was hard on her ears in the flat, so she clicked on the radio. Then she twisted the top off the brandy and tossed some into her mouth. It burned the back of her throat. It gave her an excuse to sob.

It was late when Tom let himself into May's flat. Lou was so locked in her grief, head in her hands, sobbing like a child, that she wasn't conscious of another presence until Tom was a step away from her. He sat beside her on the bed and placed his arm round her shoulder, pulling her to him. He noticed the brandy bottle, but there weren't enough of the contents gone to have caused any major damage.

'Can I get you anything?' he said softly.

'No,' she said. 'Not unless you can get me a new dad.'

'A new dad?' he asked. 'Why a new dad?'

The story spilled out of her. Lou told him what a wonderful man her dad had been, and then she told him what Renee had said, and Tom used his thumbs to wipe away the tears she didn't think would ever stop. They were like giant facial windscreen wipers.

'Lou,' Tom said softly, 'your dad obviously loved you very much. You have to hang on to that.'

'Every time I've tried to visualise his face this afternoon, I can't. All I see is Phil.' Dad. Phil. They were the same man, a generation apart.

'Let me make you a cup of tea,' said Tom.

'I want another brandy. I want to get so drunk I pass out.' And Lou reached for the full mug on the table, but Tom snatched it away.

'All that's going to do is give you a blinding headache,' he said. 'Besides, I need that mug, so give it here.'

The radio was playing ballads. Some Country and Western woman with a smoky mountain voice sang, *Dance with me tonight. Make everything all right . . .*

'Dance with me,' said Tom instinctively, while he was waiting for the kettle to boil. 'Come on.'

'Don't be ridiculous,' said Lou, giving vent to a reflex laugh.

'Come on, I mean it.' Tom pulled her to her resisting feet and took her hand in his. Lou tugged it back, but he held on. He circled her waist with his arm and placed his cheek on the top of her head. They rocked gently, barely moving, his hand gripping hers.

She shouldn't be letting him hold her like this. But her body needed his warmth, his unthreatening affection, those lips in her hair.

*Dance with me tonight . . . And make everything all right.*

He pulled slowly away from her when the song ended and took her face in his big hands. 'Lou,' he said, but the tone of his voice said much more. His lips brushed against her salty cheek. He shouldn't be doing this, he knew, but when she didn't resist, he kissed her lightly. He felt her lips part in response as his touched the corner of her mouth, and then his lips fell full on hers, tentatively, before they made firmer contact. His arms came round her, hers were round him.

'Lou, I shouldn't say this, I know, but I can't help it. I've liked you—*really* liked you—for so long.'

'Tom . . .' Hearing his name said in that way was enough for him to know he wasn't about to make the world's biggest plonker of himself.

She felt so wonderful in his arms, so warm, so right—but she was vulnerable and he didn't want to take advantage. But Lou was driving this and her need for what was happening between them was as great, if not greater, than his own.

A small chemical factory had exploded in Lou's brain and, when they began to undress each other, feeling Tom's skin next to hers made her shudder with delight. He was gentle with her, tentative, giving her a chance to back out at every step of the way, but she didn't—nor did she want to, because for once, Lou Winter was taking everything on offer.

Waves of pleasure started washing over her as Tom entered her. She had never, *never* experienced anything as raw and powerful as this before. And when it was over, he wrapped his great arms round her and pulled her into the warmth of his chest, his heart beating against her back—and together, in the lumpy, bumpy bed, they went to sleep.

**O**f course he was gone the next morning. Last night had been a beautiful escape, but it couldn't take away the smashed dreams and ugly truths that were waiting for her in the daylight. And now she had another problem—how to recover her precious friendship with Tom, who was no doubt too embarrassed to face her. Was it possible to go back to how things were? How did you undo falling in love?

Just then, she heard the door open and in he walked.

'Oh, it's you,' said Lou. Her initial joy at seeing him slumped when she saw how difficult it was for him to make eye contact with her.

'I bought you a bacon sandwich, although it's probably a bit cold now because I had to drive miles to get it,' he said. 'I thought you might be a bit . . . hung over.'

'I wasn't drunk,' she said, a little defensively.

'Well, I didn't know if you'd have regrets about waking up with a strange person then,' said Tom, in a pseudo-jolly voice.

'Why, do you?' asked Lou cautiously.

'I asked first.'

They both laughed gently.

'OK, then, I'll answer first. No, I don't,' said Tom. 'Not one bit. And you're not strange, you're lovely.' He took her cheek in his hand and stroked it with his thumb and she leaned into it. Then, when he realised she wasn't going to say that it was all a huge mistake, he felt at liberty to kiss her gently on the mouth and whisper, ''Morning.'

''Morning,' she replied.

'I was awake for a while this morning just lying next to you,' said Tom. 'Watching you.'

Lou was horrified. 'Was I snoring?' she gasped. *Or worse, dribbling?*

'Don't be silly,' said Tom. 'But you were dreaming. I thought you'd got two butterflies caught under your eyelids. You started me thinking,' said Tom. 'Please don't bite my head off, but from what you were saying about your dad . . . and your mum . . . She couldn't be not telling you the truth, could she?'

'Why would she do that?' said Lou.

'Well, maybe she's worried you're making a mistake?'

'She *is* worried I'm making a mistake.'

Tom shook his head. 'I'm sorry, I shouldn't interfere. Strike it from the record. I don't know either your mum or your dad.'

But Lou knew them both very well and the seed of Tom's thought quickly took root in her subconscious.

'I'd get back in there with you, but I . . .'

'Don't want to?' Lou suggested.

'No, I don't want to actually,' said Tom decisively. 'But not in the way you think. Lou, last night was fantastic. It was wonderful. And I've imagined it since the first time I saw you.'

'Rubbish! Have you?' said Lou, gobsmacked.

'OK, male chauvinist pig that I am, I thought, This woman hires and fills her own skips so she can't have a bloke around. And then I saw you didn't have a wedding ring on. I was about that far,' he held up a minuscule space between his thumb and forefinger, 'from asking you out for a meal and then you started talking about your husband being allergic to animals. I thought, That's that, then. She's married. End of.'

Lou was staring at him the way a baby owl looks at its first moon.

'What I'm trying to say, in a really clumsy way, is that I want to court you, Lou. I want to snog on the sofa in front of a film and walk round the park and go to the cinema and then say good night to you on the doorstep and go home counting the minutes till I see you again.'

Lou looked into his shiny grey eyes. It could be a line. Phil had always been very good at staring you in the face and telling you lies, but she didn't think this was applicable in Tom Broom's case. She liked him so much—and this was exactly what she wanted to hear, because she needed space to do all the tasks that lay ahead of her. Plus, she was still married. Legally, if nothing else.

'Thank you,' she said. 'I appreciate that.'

He sighed with deep relief, and kissed her. He asked her if she would be OK. Did she want him to go with her anywhere? Could he do anything for her? Lou smiled and said she was fine and, after he left her, his caring stayed with her, like a big, snuggly, invisible coat that she would wear all day.

The seed that Tom had planted regarding her parents had grown to beanstalk proportions by the time Lou arrived at her mother's house. She didn't knock. She marched in to find her mother getting ready to go out.

Timidly Renee asked, 'Hello, love. Are you feeling better?'

Lou had decided on a strong opening gambit. It had worked with Victorianna. 'It was all lies, wasn't it? About Dad?' she bluffed. 'He didn't play around, did he? You just said that to make me change my mind about Phil, didn't you?'

Even Lou wasn't prepared for her mother to cave in so quickly. Renee covered her face with her hands. 'Elouise, I'm sorry. I don't know what came over me. I thought if I said it you might not leave Phil. You're so well set up with him. You don't know what you're throwing away.'

'What are you saying, Mum?'

Renee grabbed Lou's hands. 'Elouise, I'm sorry. I knew your dad wouldn't mind me saying it if it meant you would be happy in the end.'

Lou struggled to take in what Renee was saying. Surely she hadn't been so sick as to lie like that and insult her dad's memory? A horrible thought popped into her head. 'You weren't going to tell me, were you? If I hadn't come round now and confronted you, you were just going to let me keep on believing he was a bastard, like Phil.'

'I *was* going to tell you. Really I was. I was going to ring you when I came back from the hairdresser's.'

'The hairdresser's!' repeated Lou, incensed. 'I've been going out of my mind all night, and you were planning to let me know *after you came back from the hairdresser's!*' Hot tears of rage came unwanted and she flicked them away. 'How could you, Mum? How could you denigrate Dad's name like this?'

'You don't understand! I was doing it for the best,' cried Renee. 'I don't want you to be alone and poor. I want you to have nice things and holidays abroad and to make something of yourself.'

'You never loved Dad, did you? You couldn't have, if his memory is that cheap to you.' In one clear, crystallised moment she saw how much her parents' matrimonial template was echoed in her own. Had she copied this? One partner taking all the other had to give, one partner jumping through hoops of fire to make the other one happy? 'Dad did everything for you that was important, Mum. He loved us with all his heart. He did everything, except buy you a big fancy house so you could show off to your friends. You'd have loved him then, wouldn't you?'

'You're wrong,' said Renee, with so weak a protest that Lou knew she was right.

'And I was just like him, wasn't I? Such a great disappointment because my priority was being happy. I was "wasting my time" on the cookery course that I loved but, wow, it was OK when I got a well-paid job in something respectable like accounting, even though I hated it.'

'Accounting was a far better career choice for you, you must see that,' tried Renee. 'Where's the money in catering?'

'Money, money, money!' Lou clenched her fists and growled. 'Do you know, I wonder now if the big attraction of Phil was that I'd actually found someone you approved of. I'd pleased you for once, because I'd met a bloke who was going places; someone who could give me all the fancy stuff my dad didn't give you. That was what mattered, wasn't it?'

'Phil's not a bad man,' sniffled Renee.

'You're so lucky that you never had anyone who treated you badly, Mum,' said Lou. 'Dad treated you like a queen and you couldn't possibly have appreciated it because you are so shallow. What a total waste of a good man's love.'

'I did love him,' Renee protested. 'In my own way.'

'You don't know what love is!' Lou cried. 'Love isn't a double garage and three P and O holidays a year. No wonder you prefer Victorianna, with her manor house and her rich boring partner.'

'I always loved you both the same,' Renee protested weepily.

Lou was spent. She would never have her mother's full approval, but she didn't need it. She was a big girl now—Shaun Casserly's big girl.

Drying her eyes, Renee dredged up a limping line of defence. 'When did you ever take the time to show me you loved me?' she accused. 'When did you go clothes shopping with me or . . . or . . . do my nails for me or anything, like Victorianna did? You talk about *you* feeling unloved—well, what about *me*? You never loved me as much as you loved your dad.'

Lou opened her mouth. She would have liked to have told her mother all about one very special manicure—the one when her rings mysteriously went missing. But, tempting as it was, that would be doing what her mother had tried to do to her—take away her past, tarnish the shining image of her darling baby, and Lou, despite everything, didn't want to hurt her like that.

'Oh, but I do love you, Mum. You don't understand how much,' said Lou, and she left her mother to her self-pity and her forthcoming cut and blow-dry.

There were no signs of life at One, The Faringdales as Phil keyed in the burglar alarm code: no evidence that Lou had even been back to collect some stuff, which was encouraging. She wouldn't be able to stay away from the luxury of his financial support and a house with all mod cons for long. A weekend in Deb's poky flat sleeping on a couch would soon have her crawling back. He had no doubt that was where she was holed up—she couldn't stay at her mother's as Renee would nag too much. Lou would be back all right, and probably in the next couple of hours. She didn't have the guts to leave, and he'd seen to it that she didn't have access to any money in their joint account. That would smoke her out, if nothing else.

Sighing, he switched on the sports channel, poured himself a stiff one and picked up the Indian takeaway menu.

Lou arrived at Deb's with a carrier bag and rang the bell.

'Ah, our Chinese banquet. Welcome!' said Deb. 'How are you?'

'I'll tell you when I've unpacked.'

'You're staying?' gasped Deb with glee.

'Unpacked the fried rice, I mean. No, I'm staying put at May's flat.'

'You're mad, Lou.'

'After all that's happened to me in the last few days, I'd be mad if I wasn't mad. Mum told me Dad was unfaithful. I found out she was lying. Oh, and I slept with Tom.'

Deb grabbed the carrier bag. 'You get the plates, I'll open the plonk.'

Lou told her everything.

'Bloody Norah, you and Tom Broom,' said Deb, shaking her head in thrilled amazement. 'Is he in proportion?'

'Deb!'

'I'm your best friend and, as such, there are no sacred details about your boyfriend.'

*Boyfriend.* That word made the smile slide from her face.

'What's the matter?' said Deb, watching the smile wither.

'I'm married. I'm having an affair. It's so wrong.'

'Well, you're not really having an affair, are you?' Deb said reasonably. 'You're not cheating on Phil because you've left him. You're free. You just have to deal with the technicalities now and get unmarried.'

'Yes,' said Lou, not sounding totally convinced. She wasn't even sure if Phil realised his marriage was at an end.

'Talking of Phil, have you heard from him?'

'No, but I think I might soon,' said Lou. 'After what I did.'

'What have you done?' asked Deb, stuffing in a piece of prawn toast.

Lou told her that bit too, and Deb listened with fascinated shock.

Lou slept so soundly in the lumpy, bumpy bed above Ma's Café that the noise from the builders didn't wake her until an hour after they had started work. They were blowing wolf whistles and taking the mick out of someone. She realised who and why a minute later when there was a knock on the door and she opened it to find Tom, standing there with a bouquet of pink and white flowers.

'Good morning, gorgeous,' he said, sweeping her to him with his free arm. They kissed, and it was rather lovely, give or take the angle her neck had to bend in order to enjoy it.

'Can I take you out to dinner?' Tom asked.

Lou smiled but she was shaking her head too. 'This is awkward,' she said. 'I wouldn't want to be . . . seen . . . out.'

'It's OK, I understand,' said Tom. 'You wouldn't enjoy yourself out on the town with another man just after you've filed for divorce.'

Lou stared open-mouthed at him. It wasn't a myth then—there really were blokes who understood the female mentality. 'Yes,' she said slowly. 'I wouldn't want to rub Phil's nose in it, if he found out.'

'Didn't stop him doing it to you, though,' said Tom.

'In what way?' said Lou.

'Flaunting another woman when you could have—' He realised his mistake immediately.

'What woman?' asked Lou, stiffening.

Tom's mouth opened and shut like a distressed goldfish.

'Tom?'

Tom Broom was a man of straight lines and for that reason he felt he could do nothing other than come clean. 'Deb saw him with someone. She was worried sick about you. She didn't know what to do for the best. I didn't either.'

'So that's what all those concerned little looks you were giving me were about then,' said Lou crossly. 'You both knew and neither of you thought to tell me I was being cuckooed in public.'

Any other time and Tom would have smiled at that, but Lou was hurting and it made him want to wrap her up his arms and hug her tightly. 'Lou. Think about what happened last time when Deb told you. I found her breaking her heart because trying to stick a brave face on in front of you just got too much. I made her tell me what the matter was. She was terrified of smashing up your life all over again. Please don't tell her I told you. I don't want you to fall out with her about this.' He rubbed his forehead. 'God, I'm so crap at covering stuff up.'

Lou took a long, hard look at him and a great warm feeling washed over her because she was so highly regarded by two people like this. Two lovely, dear people, who hated lies and deceit and had tried their best to protect her from them. She reached up and kissed him.

'Can I come round tonight? I'll cook for you,' she said.

'Oh, yes, please,' he said, pulling her into his arms.

# CHAPTER 8

'LEAVE IT WITH ME, Jack. I'll get the monies transferred now,' said Phil. He hung up and Tannoyed his secretary, telling her to go out and get him a bacon and sausage sandwich from the shop round the corner. *Where the fuck was Lou?* The washing was piling up and the freezer stocks were fast diminishing. All plans of a cosy reconciliation were now gone.

He hit the speed-dial button for the bank and went through the security questions that confirmed his identity. Then he gave instructions for monies to be transferred over to Fat Jack's account. The woman at the bank kept him on hold for an eternity. And when she eventually came back to him, he listened in frustrated disbelief to what she had to say.

'You must have that wrong, love,' he argued. 'There's plenty of money in that account to cover this transfer. More than enough.'

He was put on hold once again and, just when he was about to slam down the phone, she came back to him with her information. Phil listened in jaw-dropped horror.

'When? Who? *How* much?' Phil put down the phone before his shaking hand dropped it. It appeared that lamb roasts were not going to be on the agenda for the foreseeable future.

He hadn't wanted to ring first, but she had left him no choice.

Lou saw Phil's name flash up on the mobile. She took a deep breath and pressed connect.

'Lou?' he said, as calmly as his adrenaline levels would allow.

'Phil,' she said, as calmly as her adrenaline levels would allow.

'Where are you? What's going on?'

'I've left you. Didn't you get my note?'

OK, thought Phil, working through a process of logic. Deb had probably told her about seeing him with Sue after all, and she was really, *really* pissed off. He needed to stay calm and pitch this correctly.

'Yes, I got your note, Lou.' He used her name, women liked that, so he used it again. 'Lou, I know you're angry, love, but don't do anything hasty. Please, I know you want space to think . . .'

'I've done all the thinking I want to,' said Lou, wondering when he was going to mention the business account money. She knew that was the only thing that would have caused him to ring her.

'Lou, I'm not going to harass you but please, promise me you will take some more time to mull things over—*please*.'

The word sounded very genuine and it threw her. Maybe he needed a little time too, she thought—to come to terms with the fact that she wasn't coming back. So kindly she said, 'OK.'

'That's all I wanted to say. Bye, love.'

'Bye.'

Phil knew by the soft way she said that single word that she still wanted him. She just felt the need to stamp her foot a bit. He gave her a fortnight max. Then he'd review his tactics.

That evening, after a delicious pork and mustard casserole, Lou stood up to leave. Tom tried to pull her back down onto the sofa where they had spent three solid hours talking.

'I have to go, Tom.' She smiled.

'Lou, can we just pretend I never said I wanted to do all this courting stuff. I can't stand it. I want you to stay.' He caught her arm and despite her giggling protest, he rolled her underneath him. 'Please, Lou, stay or I'll squash you flat. No pressure, of course.'

The combination of her wriggling and giggling beneath him was turning him on so much he had to let her go before he exploded.

'Don't go. Move in. *Per favore, non andartene, bella signora . . .*'

'That's not fair, using Italian! Below the belt, Tom Broom.'

'I know, I know,' he conceded. He knew Lou had her values, and despite his frustration, Tom loved her all the more for them. Yes, he loved her. Thank God Phil Winter was such a total fool.

As if he had transmitted that name psychically to her she said, 'Phil phoned me today.'

Tom bristled. 'What for?'

'He wanted to give me some time to think about what I was doing,' said Lou indifferently, although her tone did nothing to stop Tom's smile drying up faster than a raindrop on the sun.

'And do you need time?' he asked softly.

Lou gave him a reassuring hug. 'Do you think I'd be here with you if I needed time? Phil's reason for phoning was purely financial. He doesn't fool me. Right, I'm going home.'

Deb had said Phil was a manipulative cunning fox, thought Tom as he waved Lou off, and it very much appeared as if he had started mounting his offensive to win her back. Tom was worried.

**P**hil finished the call to the travel agent in a foul mood. He had left it to the very last minute before cancelling the holiday they should have been taking tomorrow. How ironic it was that this non-affair could spell the end of his marriage, when the others hadn't. They'd survived the Susan Peach thing beautifully, but Lou had known nothing about the one-night stand at a sales conference early in their marriage. He had felt so guilty that he had tried to make it up to Lou by telling her they could start trying for a family if she wanted. Thank goodness nothing had come of that. Then there was a near-miss with that old bird in Corfu. He'd had the luck of the devil that night. It would have been a tragedy to lose his marriage for a drunken bonk against an olive tree.

He had, out of respect for Lou, worn a condom every time though. Plus he didn't want to get one up the duff and relive the whole Sharon nightmare. Talking of which, he had better write out that cheque for her and have done with it. Now, what sort of flowers did Lou like again?

**J**ust before lunch, Bradley said there was a pretty woman who'd asked to see him privately in his office. Phil smiled, but his smile soon dropped when he saw that the 'pretty woman' was loony Michelle. He led her into the office out of staff earshot and politely offered her a coffee, which he hoped she'd refuse. She didn't.

'Is it true Lou's left you?' Michelle asked.

*Pretty?* He needed to get Bradley an emergency eye-test.

'No, of course it's not true,' said Phil indignantly. 'We're just giving each other some space for a while. Lou has a few problems.'

'She's got a shop in the Townend, hasn't she?' said Michelle. 'A café. One of the builders who is working at the café has a sister who goes to my therapy group. He said she was living up above it.'

Oh, that was where she was staying, was it? Well, the novelty of slumming it in a hovel must be nearly at an end, thank goodness.

'Therapy, eh?' said Phil absently.

'Women in Crisis,' said Michelle.

What a surprise.

'I just came to see if you were OK,' said Michelle, attempting a bright smile. She wasn't bad-looking when her face cracked, thought Phil.

'I'm fine,' said Phil, who had been considerably better since the new cleaner started a few days ago.

'I think she's mad, for the record,' said Michelle. 'If you want to talk, you know, I'm a good listener.'

'Thanks, but I don't have anything to talk about,' said Phil. 'She hasn't left me. She'll be back soon.'

'We could go out for a meal if you wanted some . . . company.'

'I'm so busy here, I've hardly time,' said Phil, 'but thanks.'

'Phil. If you're free, I am. We could stay in and I can comfort you.'

Phil scrunched up his face in thought. Was she saying what he thought she was saying? 'Come again?' he asked.

'If you like,' said Michelle seductively. She was behind him now, kneading her fingers into his stiff shoulders.

'Whoa fucking whoa!' said Phil, standing up and shrugging her off.

'Well, it might just make her change her mind if she sees someone else has moved in on her man,' said Michelle.

'No way, lady!' said Phil, feeling as if he had been transported into a bad dream. 'Aren't you supposed to be one of Lou's mates? That's just sick, trying to make her jealous. I think you'd better piss off.'

Michelle swung her bag onto her shoulder and stormed out of the office with chilli-hot tears stinging her eyes. The feeling of rejection never failed to reduce her to rubble, especially when she had just been rejected by someone who had as few sexual morals as Phil Winter. At least this new therapy group was helping her to work through things. She had made a new special friend there too, who was coming round for tea that night. They'd have a good natter about this later on. Her name was Sue—she looked a bit like Lou with her green, green eyes. Sue was having a really tough time, too. She had just been dumped by this married bloke who didn't want to hurt her. An infinitely more decent bloke than Phil Winter.

**A**cross town, a massive Italian coffee-machine was spurting into action, and soon the aroma of raspberries reached Lou's receptive nostrils. Now that *is* a winner, she thought, and one that definitely wouldn't be joining the coconut-meringue-flavoured coffee on the reject list. She had found that she could only test a few at a time as her taste buds got confused. She turned round to hear a gentle knock on the front door. A small well-wrapped figure was peering through the glass. Her mother. Lou felt her adrenaline start to pump. She tried to stay calm as she unlocked the door and Renee walked in tentatively.

'Hello,' Renee said, with a watery, nervous smile.

'Hello, Mum,' said Lou. 'How are you?'

'Not too bad, not too bad,' said Renee, looking round her at the stark black and white décor. 'It looks very nice in here.'

'Well, we had a good set of lads working for us. They've done wonders. We've still got the kitchen part to finish off, though.'

'Are you going to put some pictures up on the wall as well?'

'Yes—big black and white photographs. They're on order.'

'Oh, that'll be nice,' said Renee.

Blimey! thought Lou. That was edging dangerously close to a positive comment. 'Would you like a coffee?' she offered. 'I'm just testing out some raspberry-truffle flavour. That's what you can probably smell.'

'That sounds nice,' said Renee. She sat down stiffly on one of the black-cushioned benches and Lou brought over a full cup for her.

Renee took a sip. Then: 'This is very nice.'

They sat in silence for a little while as Lou tried to think of something to say that didn't have the word 'nice' in it.

'Where have you been staying then?' said Renee.

'Upstairs here.'

'Here?' said Renee, with some incredulity.

She opened her mouth to say something else and closed it again so Lou spoke it for her. 'Yes, Mum, I do know what I'm doing.'

'I was just going to say you could have come home to me,' said Renee quietly. 'Your bedroom will always be your bedroom if you need it.'

'Thank you, Mum,' said Lou, a little shamefacedly. Her mother looked so dreadfully uncomfortable that Lou was forced to appreciate how much courage it must have taken for her to come to the café. As Lou looked at the hands holding the cup, with their thin, one-ply skin, she noticed just how old her mother was getting. She didn't want to fight with her, whatever had passed between them. They were just two very different people, and they always would be, but Renee was—as imperfect as she was, as annoying as she was—her mother.

'I've just been trying out a lemon cheesecake recipe. Incredibly low-fat, but retaining most of the taste, or so I hope,' said Lou. She stood up and went to the counter, where she cut two small slices. 'I'd appreciate your opinion.'

'Oh!' said Renee.

I've surprised her, thought Lou. Maybe she was right, too, about some things. Maybe I don't make her feel special.

Lou sat down at the bench again, with two plates of cheesecake.

'It's very nice,' said Renee, licking her spoon. 'Very creamy.'

'Does it taste lemony enough to you?' said Lou.

'You could afford to add a bit more lemon. It's a bit . . . tame.'

'Yes, I think you're right,' said Lou, sampling her cake again.

Renee took another dainty forkful. 'If you want my opinion . . .' she said, looking at Lou carefully to see if she really did, and Lou affirmed this with an eager nod. '. . . I think your base could do with a touch of ginger as well. No wait—maybe cardamom or walnut.'

Lou took a forkful and tried to imagine the taste of that. Renee did the same. 'I think you're right, Mum,' said Lou. 'Thank you.'

Renee looked at her daughter and smiled. Shaun's leaf-green eyes looked back at her. 'I do love you, you know,' said Renee, coughing back a throatful of tears. 'And I am proud of you.'

'I love you too, Mum.'

'Lou, my love, I've got to move. I've got the most awful cramp,' said Tom, gently shifting a sleeping Lou.

'Sorry,' said Lou, stretching, and then she noticed the time and bounced to her feet. 'I'd better go, otherwise I'll never get up tomorrow.'

Letting Lou go back to the flat intact after the thoughts Tom was having about her almost did his head in. He knew she had her reasons for keeping him at arm's length, but was it a cover for her cooling off? In the last couple of weeks she had seemed to yawn an awful lot, which hadn't exactly put him at ease. She'd blamed it on the physical tiredness of not only assisting the workmen to clean up, but also helping some little old lady to clear out her house.

'One last cuddle,' said Tom, and pulled her down to the sofa again. He held her face in his hands and smiled. 'Lou, you have eyes like emeralds, has anyone ever told you?'

Lou gave a little laugh. 'Phil used to say that Sharon—you know, the one he had the twins with—had eyes like sapphires. What a strange parallel.' Then she realised what she had said and slapped her hand over her mouth. 'What am I saying? I'm sorry, Tom, that was insensitive.'

'It's OK,' said Tom, who was thinking that Phil was still very much on her mind. 'Did you ever see Sharon?' he asked.

'Once, at Christmas, when we were in Meadowhall.'

'And was she as gorgeous as he made out?'

'She was pretty, with Nordic colouring—and the children were like her too, except they had beautiful brown eyes. Don't know who they got those from, though, because Phil's are blue, too. Anyway, he just looked straight through them, as if they didn't exist. It was horrible.'

'I can't imagine how anyone could do that to their own children,' said Tom, pulling Lou even nearer to him. She felt so good, he couldn't bear it if she went back to Phil.

The next morning Phil was feeling positive. That was until the jolly, whistling postman delivered a long stiff envelope. *Cripwell, Oliver & Clapham—Solicitors* it said on the corner. He ripped it open to find that Lou had filed for divorce. He couldn't believe it. *Why?* He was still convinced the situation wasn't beyond hope. On the day she came home, he'd fill the bedroom with flowers. He'd book a table in a restaurant. He'd cancel Fat Jack and Maureen and everyone coming round at Christmas. They were OK, he and Lou. Really—he could recover this.

**A**t the other end of town, Tom and Lou were sitting in the café with their hands over their eyes, awaiting the arrival of the Brando.

'Ta da!' announced Deb. 'Now you can look!'

Tom and Lou opened their eyes to see two huge ciabatta rolls stuffed with ham, egg, slices of sausage, mushrooms, and a basil-smelling tomato dressing that sent their salivary glands into overdrive.

'Wow!' said Lou.

'I thought it was going to be a pudding, not that I'm in the slightest bit put out,' said Tom, who didn't wait for an invitation to tuck in.

'Well,' hummed Deb, 'it just seemed like too good a name to pass up. A bit classier than a "belt-buster", don't you think?' She noticed that Lou was being reticent. 'Come on, Lou, get that Brando down you!'

Lou picked up her knife and fork and stared at the plate, then dropped them and ran upstairs, holding her mouth.

'Hmm. I thought she was looking a bit pale,' said Deb.

'I'll go after her,' said Tom, but Deb pushed him down into his seat.

'Romantic as your intentions are, Tom, when a woman's vomiting, she likes a little privacy.'

'Has she said anything to you—you know, about *him*? I'm terrified she'll go back to him, Deb. I'm scared I'm too boring for her.'

'What on earth makes you think that?'

'She keeps dropping off to sleep on me for a start.'

'Don't talk wet. We're knackered, the pair of us. Cut her some slack, Tom. She's besotted with you but she's been through a lot recently.'

Five minutes later, Lou came back downstairs to two sympathetic faces.

'Sorry about that—I've ruined your grand launch.'

'It's fine,' said Deb. 'You've been overdoing things. You need to get back to bed for a rest.'

'No chance,' said Lou. 'We've got stacks of things to do and the sooner we finish them, the sooner we open. Plus I've promised another one of Mrs Serafinska's friends that I'll pop in and see her about some clutter-clearing.'

Lou's mobile went off just as they were clearing up the plates. The look on her face told Tom and Deb who it was.

'Hello, Phil,' said Lou quietly. 'Yes, I think a meeting would be a good idea now . . . Yes, ten o'clock—at our house. See you tomorrow morning, then. Bye.'

Our house, Tom thought.

Lou threw the phone down and immediately ran upstairs again with her hand across her mouth. Tom knew how she felt.

**L**ou hadn't stopped scrubbing and cleaning since Tom had left, and Deb was worried about her. She was looking more and more ghost-like.

'Don't worry, I'll be better when my meeting with Phil is over and done with,' Lou answered her concerns.

'Tom thinks you're going to cave in,' said Deb.

'What? Go back to Phil? Not a chance!' said Lou, scratching her breast.

'Why do you keep doing that?' said Deb.

'My bra's killing me,' said Lou. 'It's rubbing me like hell.'

'Have you changed your washing powder?'

'Nope.'

'When was your last period?'

'Don't be ridiculous,' said Lou.

'Have you missed?'

'Yes, but who could blame me with all that's been going on?'

'OK,' said Deb. She nipped out a little later, saying she was going to get some tea bags. Lou put on the kettle and had an instant coffee. It tasted unpleasant. That was all she needed—to have gone off coffee.

**P**hil took the afternoon off and called in at the supermarket for a cake mix. It looked far too professional so he plumped for a Bettermix Instant Victoria Sponge in a nice cheap packet. It turned out a bit too well when he made it, but he cocked it up nicely on the icing. It looked quite pathetic, really, when he had added the little sweetie decorations—just the thing to pull at a woman's heartstrings. As he put on the last chocolate button, his phone beeped. It was from Sue British-racing-green-eyes. YOU EVIL LYING BASTARD it said. Now what was that all about?

**D**eb came back in to find Lou taking a breather on a chair. 'Here, this might help,' she said, and tossed Lou the paper bag.

Lou tipped out the contents and gave Deb a quizzical look. 'Of course, you're joking! I've got a virus, that's all,' she said.

Deb nodded towards it. 'I think you should take the test, Lou. Call it a hunch. Being sick, late periods, being constantly tired and having sore boobs, well . . . Find out for sure, though, will you?'

Lou disappeared with her box. Deb waited outside for what seemed ages before Lou emerged looking like Frosty the Snowman with anaemia. The tears were rolling down her face and she reached for Deb.

'Oh, hell,' said Deb, coming forwards. 'Lou, I'm sorry. I hate myself now. I just thought, with all your symptoms and—'

'Deb, it's positive,' said Lou. 'I did both tests and they both came up positive.' She showed Deb the blue lines in the confirmation boxes on the tests. 'How can I be pregnant, Deb? I can't be!'

'According to those tests you bloody well are! Could it be Phil's baby?' asked Deb, cringing as she said it.

'I haven't slept with Phil in ages,' said Lou. 'It has to be Tom's.'

'Thank God for that,' said Deb, crossing herself internally.

Oh God, Tom! What on earth would he say? thought Lou. After one incident of love-making with him, she had fallen pregnant. *Would he feel that she had trapped him? Like Sharon had with Phil?* She clung onto Deb for comfort. She didn't know whether to laugh or cry so she plumped for both. 'Deb, I'm pregnant!'

'Lou, you're pregnant!'

They both screamed and hugged each other and started dancing and bouncing around. That was how Tom found them five minutes later.

That evening, Tom lay back on the sofa grinning. 'A baby next spring. Season of new birth—could that be any more perfect?'

'I didn't know how you'd take it,' said Lou, 'seeing as we've only slept together once.'

'Don't remind me,' said Tom with amused sarcasm. 'Move in tonight, then you can sleep in my bed and let me be all gentle with you.'

That sounded awfully tempting, thought Lou. But not yet. 'Please, Tom, I need to finish off my business with Phil first, totally and completely. Give me one more day. Just one.'

Tom nodded. Was she playing for time? Giving Phil the chance to win her back? Her hormones were all over the place. She was ripe for being manipulated. What if Phil played on that and convinced her that the best place was with him? Tom knew this wasn't logical—after all, Lou was carrying his child—but feeling something and knowing something were totally different things. He put his hand on her tummy. 'I still can't believe it,' he said.

'*You* can't believe it!' said Lou. 'Not that I want to bring Phil into this, but the amount of accidents we had—and nothing—and only once with you and then "bingo".'

*Phil again.*

'What sex would you like?' asked Lou.

'Any sort of sex; I'm busting for it.'

'No—what flavour baby would you like, you nut?' said Lou, hitting him with a cushion.

'Honestly, Lou, I know it's a cliché, but as long as it's OK, I really don't mind.' *What if she went back to Phil and he never saw his child?*

'I've decided that if Phil wants to put up a fight tomorrow, I'll just get the divorce when I can. He isn't going to settle for a quickie and I'm not going to let myself get worked up about it.'

'I'd settle for a quickie,' said Tom, and dodged the cushion again.

'What if we had twins? One of each,' said Lou. 'Phil's twins were really beautiful.'

*Phil, Phil, Phil.* 'I don't think we'll be having blonde, brown-eyed kids, though—do you?' said Tom, shaking his black hair at her.

'No, I don't think so,' laughed Lou gently.

As they sat, each with their thoughts, Tom suddenly started muttering to himself. 'No, we can't, can we?' he murmured. 'No way. I'm sure that's right. Lou, I think you might get your quickie divorce after all,' he said. Taking a pad out of the dresser drawer, he started to draw little coloured circles on it.

All this stopping at the petting stage had obviously sent him a bit loopy, Lou thought. She realised she would have to make love to him very soon in order to save his mental health.

**N**umber One, The Faringdales looked different somehow. She felt no emotional attachment to the house she had moved into as a bride. She knocked and Phil opened the door and brought her in effusively.

How long was it since he had seen her? She looked like Lou, but different. She looked like an older version of the young, spirited Lou he had fallen in love with.

'I've made tea,' he said, in the manner of a small child who was showing off a pasta picture to his mam. Lou let him pour. 'I've left the milk and the sugar out,' he said, pointing to a bowl and a jug.

'Thanks, but I don't take either in tea,' said Lou.

Bollocks, thought Phil. They'd been together ten years—how come he didn't know that? He got out the cake. It couldn't have been more obvious that he'd made it if he'd iced *Made by Phil* on it.

She wasn't fooled by his trying-so-hard gesture. Did he think she was that easy to manipulate? Probably—because she *had* been that easy to manipulate in the past, hadn't she?

'Would you like a slice?'

'Thanks, but not for me. I appreciate you making it, though.'

*Good, she's noticed.*

'So, to business,' she said.

'Lou, you can't be serious. Come on, love, this has gone far enough,' said Phil, flashing his best smile. 'Come home, Lou, I miss you.'

'Phil. You miss your clothes washed, you miss your meals cooked, you miss . . . having your basic needs met. You don't miss *me*.'

'Yes, I do, Lou. Honest, I do.' Phil clicked his fingers. 'This is about that Sue, isn't it?' he said.

'Yes,' said Lou. She wondered which Sue he was referring to.

'But, love, that was all sorted years ago!'

Ah, he meant the first Sue. 'You never even said sorry, Phil.'

'I'm sorry, then. I'm sorry I put you through all that. It was the biggest mistake of my life.'

Lou drew in a big breath. Hearing that he was sorry changed nothing. It was all too late. 'Phil, I want you to sign the papers and for us both to get on with our lives.'

'Lou, I can't do that.'

Lou stayed calm. 'You'll be wondering, of course, why I took the money from the business account.'

'Well, er, yes, I was, a bit.'

'I took the approximate value of *your* house as it stands now. I subtracted the amount that you paid for it before we were married,' Lou went on, ignoring him. 'I added on a fair figure, I think, for the value of the fixtures and fittings and divided by two, and that's what I took out of the business account.'

'That's very cold for you, Lou,' said Phil, affecting bewilderment now.

Lou went on, 'If you don't agree with the figures, we can always let the courts decide. I think they'll find that I'm also entitled to half your business and a substantial proportion of your pension, but I don't intend to claim that. You can guarantee that because we'll sign for a full and final settlement. I've been a lot fairer than any judge would be.'

'You, lady, are guilty of fraud,' said Phil, trying to tie down his anger.

That was the second time she'd been accused of fraud recently, Lou thought with an inner giggle—first Victorianna, now Phil. 'Let's face it, Phil, you would have stopped my access to the joint account and denied me anything at all, had I not taken it first. This way at least I save you having to spend half of your savings on solicitors' fees. As it stands, we're sorted financially. The rest is just paperwork.'

He picked up his mobile menacingly. The whites of his eyes were startling against his red face. 'I could ring the Fraud Squad right now.'

'Go right ahead. But remember, you gave me authority to transfer monies. I only took my fair share. I could say you gave me the money and then changed your mind. And if you want to talk about fraud . . .' Lou pulled out two computer disks from her handbag and threw them on the table. 'This one has your up-to-date accounts for the last ten years. This one has your *real* up-to-date accounts. I could send the taxman both. I'm sure they'd find enough discrepancies to keep them in a permanent job. Obviously these aren't the only copies. You'll get those when the divorce is final.'

Phil's face suffused with even more blood. But he still had one trump card left. There was one thing over which he still had control.

'Well, you can wait for your divorce for bloody ever,' he snarled.

But Lou didn't even blink. 'I'll make you a deal,' she said. 'Sign the papers now and let me take them in, and I'll refund you over thirty thousand pounds with immediate effect.' She got her chequebook out of her bag and clicked out her pen.

'How much over thirty thousand pounds?' said Phil with a grumbling interest.

'You'll have to gamble and find out.' She held out the pen to him.

Thirty thousand quid was a lot of money and, even now, he knew Lou would be as good as her word. He hated to admit it, but he wasn't going to win this one so damage limitation was his only option. He didn't know this supremely confident and sexy woman in his kitchen. She was a very desirable stranger, though.

'I wasn't unfaithful to you after that Peach woman, you know.'

'It doesn't matter,' said Lou. 'It was never just about another woman.'

He opened his mouth to ask what the hell else it was all about then, but some wiser part within made him shut it. He had been a total bastard to Lou, if he faced it. His life with her flashed past him in a few lousy seconds and it hit him then. Lou was leaving him, his marriage was ending, and he felt a seismic panic rumble through him.

'Lou, come on,' he said, a tremble in his voice. 'Let's renew our vows. You always wanted to go to Italy, didn't you? We could get married in Rome. How about that?' He laughed with an edge of desperation.

'No, Phil,' she said slowly, but decisively. 'Please, sign the papers.'

'I just wanted it to be like it was between us, Lou. I thought I was a good husband. I've never hit you, have I? I'm not mean—'

But Lou was shaking her head and he *knew* he'd slipped from her heart. He'd gone too far. Their clock couldn't be turned back. He sighed, took the pen, got the divorce papers out of the envelope and signed them quickly. Lou checked them over and tucked them into her bag, then she rested her chequebook on her knee and scribbled. Finally she stood to go, and handed him a folded cheque.

'Thanks for the tea,' she said. Phil seemed such a stranger, part of an old life which was now ended—a life that could have been so much better for them both if only they had tried harder. Oh, yes, *both* of them—for she had played her own part in the downfall of her marriage. Like Maureen, she'd *let* her husband do those things to her.

As Phil's hand came out for the cheque he said quietly, 'I love you, Lou Winter. Please don't throw us away.'

Lou's breath caught in her throat. He sounded so desperate, so pitiable. 'You wouldn't have treated me like you did if you'd really loved me,' she said, surprising herself with the strength in her voice.

'I do love you. In my own way, I love you so much.'

*In my own way*. There was nothing more to be said. It was so over.

'Goodbye, Phil.'

**P**hil watched her go. There was something big blocking his windpipe that wouldn't be coughed away. He'd been so caught up in the moment that he had forgotten all about the cheque, which he now picked up—to find that it was totally blank on the cheque side. Then he noticed the writing on the back of the cheque. *Blue eyes + blue eyes = brown eyes. Not very likely.*

He stared at it for a full minute, wondering whether to get into his car and chase Lou. Then his brain began to work. He remembered something he'd seen on the television—some medical thing. Family secrets coming to light when a father offered a kidney to save the life of his son. There was a connection with the colour of eyes that he couldn't quite remember. Then it started to come to him as through a fog. *The bitch. The bloody duplicitous sneaky bitch!!*

His soon-to-be ex-wife was forgotten as he made a frenzied leap for the telephone and stabbed in the speed-dial to the bank.

'Which department, please?' asked the switchboard lady.

'I want to stop a cheque—NOW!' said Phil.

**I** wish you'd sit down, you're doing my head in,' said Deb, putting the newly washed crockery in the cupboards.

'She's later than I thought she'd be,' said Tom.

'She's got a lot to discuss with him,' said Deb calmly.

'What if he tries to talk her round?' Tom fretted, sitting at last.

'He probably will. But Lou isn't a fool, Tom.' *Not any more.*

'He's a used-car salesman. He'll have highly honed manipulation skills,' said Tom, getting up again. He caught sight of his reflection in the glass of a picture and felt suddenly outclassed. What was he? A big, rough bloke in an overall who had a job moving other people's rubbish. OK, he had a solid business and property, but Phil outranked him on all fronts with his posh suit, killer smile, fleets of polished cars and pots of ready money. How could a glorified scrap-man compete?

Lou opened the door and he saw that she had been crying. 'You OK?' he said. He'd barely got the second word out before she moved into his arms to savour the wonderful smell and feel of him. He tried not to squeeze her too hard as relief washed over him.

'How are things?' asked Deb, mouthing, *Told you so* at Tom.

'OK, I think,' said Lou. 'I just need to go upstairs for a bit.'

'To think?' said Tom, tentatively.

'To change into something nice and elasticky round my stomach.'

'Oh,' said Tom. 'Can I get you anything, love?'

'A cup of orange juice and four cardboard boxes would be good.'

'God, her funny cravings have started already,' said Deb, turning to switch on the kettle. 'Would you like them with or without jam?'

'Whatever Tom would like, seeing as they're going to be sitting in his house,' Lou announced. 'I'm moving in with him today, you see.'

Tom said nothing but stood there with his mouth wide open.

'You wanton hussy,' said Deb.

'I'm glad you approve,' said Lou.

# EPILOGUE

'HAPPY ANNIVERSARY, partner!' Deb raised her mug of tea and clinked it against Lou's. 'I can't believe it's been a year.'

'Congratulations to you, Miss Devine. And may it be the first of many,' smiled Lou. 'Biscotti?'

'Don't mind if I do. I'm in the mood for a good dunk.'

'Aren't you always?'

They laughed together as business colleagues and best friends. Both were dressed in black uniforms with their company logo above the breast. They hadn't used the name Casa Nostra—they'd agreed on

Mamma's. Ma's Café was so well known, they had merely Italianised it.

'You need a bigger uniform,' Deb said. 'Your boobs are getting even more massive. We'll need an extension to the building at this rate.'

'It's my milk,' said Lou. 'Franco must be nearby.'

Right on cue, Tom Broom with a papoose carrying his black-haired baby son came shivering from the early chill of the morning into the bright, warm café. At his heels was his faithful dog who was as good as glued to the baby. 'By heck, it was warmer than this on Christmas morning,' he said. Franco was asleep, though, snuggled against his dad's thumping heartbeat.

'Here, have a cuppa,' said Deb, adding cheekily, 'no, please, don't offer me any money, it's on the house.'

Tom tutted and sat down carefully, as did Clooney. It might not have been health-and-safety-regulations-friendly to have dogs in the place, but a few of the truckers travelled with them and the dogs were as welcome as their masters in a special section of the cafe.

'A year,' mused Lou again.

The same thought passed through both women's minds. A year ago today they'd been standing in exactly the same place, shaking with excitement and fear, too. What if no one turned up? What if the scruffy old caravan on the dual carriageway that doled out greasy bacon butties had absorbed all their clientele in the weeks Ma's Café was closed, and refused to hand it back? Their fridges had been bursting with breakfast foods, most of it delivered by Karen's dad; and the cakes were on display in a beautiful rotating cabinet ready for the afternoon clientele. Huge fresh gâteaux—ranging from the 'Marco' (tiramisu with white icing), to the light lemon and cardamom 'Torta Renee'; and in jars on the shelves sat twenty different sorts of coffee ranging from 'Butter Toffee' to 'Summer Pudding'.

They'd opened the red, green and white Italian flag blinds at 6 a.m. precisely, to find no one waiting. Lou's heart had sunk into her boots, and even big hard Debra Devine looked close to tears.

Then, from nowhere, like the zombies in *Dawn of the Dead*, only pinker and infinitely more benign, lumberjack shirts and denim jackets began to head across the car park towards them, and lorries and vans and cars started to turn onto their land. And the only thing both of them could think of to say was, '*Mamma* bloody *mia!*'

And now it was a year on, and Deb was having the flirtatious time of her life behind that counter, and her best friend had been on an Italian honeymoon, acquired a husband and given birth to a son—in that order. Lou's eyes were still full of Venetian sunshine.

The planned phasing-out of the breakfast side of the business hadn't happened. It was too popular, and though it shouldn't have worked that the afternoon-tea set sat comfortably among big hairy lorry drivers, both worlds met and colluded in fabulous harmony. Little old ladies, business folk, students and men built like barn doors all tucked into Brando breakfasts in the mornings and then, in the afternoons, devoured the most wonderful cakes.

Mamma's, it was reported in the local, then national, press, had to be seen and experienced. They'd even had the *Morning Coffee* TV team down. Drusilla Durham, the presenter, had sat with Lou for two hours after the cameras had stopped rolling. She'd been fascinated by Lou's clutter-clearing and had left with a roll of binliners and the hope in her heart that she'd find the same fire that blazed in Lou Broom's eyes.

Tom suddenly clicked his fingers. 'I meant to tell you. I saw Phil.'

'Oh, where was he?' said Lou.

'Driving. He looked very intense.'

'Doesn't he always?' said Deb.

Deb would never forgive him, but Lou wasn't his enemy. He had given her the quickie divorce she'd asked for, and he'd thanked her for alerting him to the fact that Sharon's children probably weren't his. The eye formula wasn't as simple as Tom remembered it from his biology lessons at school—that two blue-eyed people couldn't have brown-eyed children—but it was a strong enough basis for Phil to demand a DNA test. This had revealed that he was not the twins' father, after all.

'He'll be happy enough with his lot,' said Lou. 'He has his car business and that's all he really needs. Now me—I feel as if I own the whole world because of what I've got.'

'And let's look at what you *have* got, Lou: a nocturnal greedy little son, a big ugly skip man and a daft dog named after George Clooney.'

'And what have *you* got, Mr Broom? A plump little midget who bakes buns.' The eyes of Shaun Casserly's daughter glittered Irish-green and mischievously at him.

'You're all I could ever want, Mrs Broom. *Angelo mio, ti amo passionatamente,*' said Tom Broom—who later hijacked his wife at their front door, lifted her effortlessly, Prince-Charming-style in his arms, and carried her upstairs.

*Milly Johnson*

### Can you tell us a little about yourself?

I'm half-Glaswegian and half-Sassenach and I live bang in the centre of Barnsley, South Yorkshire, across the road from my mam and dad. I have two fast-growing sons, Terence and George, a goldfish called Gene Hunt, a bear of a dog called Teddy (who, by the way, is more famous than me in Barnsley after a long search for him on St Patrick's Day, but that's another story) and four cats—two Siamese and two old moggies with no teeth and only three eyes between them. My hobbies include eating Star Bars, singing in the car—I'm word perfect at 'Mr Boombastic'—and, in the name of book research, hanging around with big wrestlers!

### And you believe in the power of decluttering?

Oh, yes. The idea for this novel came from my own life. Like my heroine, Lou, I was in the dentist's reading an old copy of *Woman's Weekly*—but unlike Lou I didn't steal the magazine! I love to read whatever headline grabs my eye. My favourite one ever was: '*I took off my leggings and my guts fell out.*' Enough said, but that definitely spurred me on to the Cambridge Diet! Anyway, back to your question—you do realise that you will never get a short answer from me, don't you? Decluttering . . . Oh, yes. I am a total disciple of the declutter/clearing experience. It's magical, energising and you really do feel lifted and light after shifting rubbish from your house. I found it so cathartic. My whole being went through a metamorphosis. I even managed to throw out my ex-husband as well! Now I'm a decluttering disciple—well, I have to be as I'm always totally seduced by adverts and buy things I really don't want and will never use. Have now become a two-skips-a-year girl, me.

**Some of the characters in your novel are bullies, or their victims. Is this something you planned to write about?**

It's my way of dealing with an event that happened to me. Three years ago I was caught up in workplace bullying and it was one of the worst experiences of my life. I'm rather a toughie and was never bullied at school and could hardly believe that it was happening to me. The bullies are so clever—they chip away at your self-confidence and make you doubt yourself. I became a wreck with the stress and was on antidepressants, and even nearly crashed my car. The crunch came when I turned up at my solicitor's office on a cold day, wearing flip-flops, no make-up, with cold sores, sniffling, coughing—a total shadow of my real self. But bullying is incredibly hard to prove and my case never went to court. When my writing career took off, I decided that I would highlight bullying in my novels. A recent review on Amazon said: 'Ever been bullied—read this book.' That means more to me than the most glowing praise. I set up a website at www.bullyoffblog@blogspot.com, which I recommend to anyone who finds themselves in a similar situation.

**Using single sentences from now on, please, as we are running out of space, how would you describe perfect happiness?**

Being well, having good friends, and enough money in the bank to pay even the surprise bills and a cleaner!

**If you could be anywhere in the world this minute, where would you choose to be?**

On a gondola in Venice with George Clooney and two Cornettos.

**What do you regret most?**

That I didn't go and live in Italy when I was in my early twenties.

**What's your best quality?**

I've got a good heart.

**If you could eat only one thing for the rest of your days, what would it be?**

Egg-fried rice.

**What's your greatest indulgence?**

Just had the most gorgeous handmade four-poster bed delivered—yummy.

**Is there a book you love to reread?**

Jane Austen's *Persuasion*—I'm word perfect.

**Do you have one sentence of advice for new writers?**

Write a little every day and read a little of your chosen genre every day—you'll be honing your craft without realising. Oh, and . . . see! It's so difficult to answer questions in one sentence. I'm just not that kind of a girl.

PICTURE CREDITS: COVER: © PhotoAlto Agency. Jojo Moyes's jacket photograph © Andrew Buurman and page 182 © Mark Molloy Photography. Lisa Scottoline's photograph and page 316 © Carrie Keagy. Milly Johnson's photograph and page 478 © Chris Sedgewick. THE HORSE DANCER: pages 6 & 7: Kate Baxter@velvet tamarind. LOOK AGAIN: pages 184 & 185: Amy Eccleston@velvet tamarind; images: Iconica. A SPRING AFFAIR: pages 318 & 319: Julie Pla@The Organisation.

Printed and bound by GGP Media GmbH, Pössneck, Germany

601-052 UP0000-1